PRAISE FOR THE IMAGINARIUM SERIES

"Crammed with short stories, poetry and longer stories that range from fantasy, horror, supernatural and science fiction, [*Imaginarium 2012*] is the sort of book you would have on your keeper shelf."

—*SF Site*

"The strength of speculative fiction is often that it's so delightfully self-aware, testing the boundaries of tradition and re-imagining old tropes. *Imaginarium 4* really shines when its stories get a little weird and question their own nature. These are the stories that are offered up shaken, not stirred, from some bottom-of-the-ocean sleep: they are having out-of-body experiences and living not just as stories but as answers to the question "What if?""

—*Strange Horizons*

PREVIOUS IMAGINARIUM EDITIONS

Imaginarium 2012: Edited by Sandra Kasturi & Halli Villegas
Imaginarium 2013: Edited by Samantha Beiko & Sandra Kasturi
Imaginarium 3: Edited by Sandra Kasturi & Helen Marshall

IMAGINARIUM 4

THE BEST CANADIAN SPECULATIVE WRITING

ChiZine Publications

Shelfie

A **free** eBook edition is available
with the purchase of this print book.

CLEARLY PRINT YOUR NAME ABOVE IN UPPER CASE

Instructions to claim your free eBook edition:
1. Download the Shelfie app for Android or iOS
2. Write your name in **UPPER CASE** above
3. Use the Shelfie app to submit a photo
4. Download your eBook to any device

FIRST EDITION

Imaginarium 4: The Best Canadian Speculative Writing © 2016 ChiZine Publications
Introduction © 2016 by Margaret Atwood
Cover artwork © 2016 by Kailey Lang
Cover design © 2016 by Samantha Beiko
Interior design © 2016 Jared Shapiro & Samantha Beiko

Distributed in Canada by
Publishers Group Canada
76 Stafford Street, Unit 300
Toronto, Ontario, M6J 2S1
Toll Free: 800-747-8147
e-mail: info@pgcbooks.ca

Distributed in the U.S. by
Consortium Book Sales & Distribution
34 Thirteenth Avenue, NE, Suite 101
Minneapolis, MN 55413
Phone: (612) 746-2600
e-mail: sales.orders@cbsd.com

CHIZINE PUBLICATIONS
Toronto, Canada
www.chizinepub.com
info@chizinepub.com

Edited by Sandra Kasturi & Jerome Stueart
Proofread by Megan Kearns

Canada Council   Conseil des arts
for the Arts   du Canada

We acknowledge the support of the Canada Council for the Arts which last year invested $20.1 million in writing and publishing throughout Canada.

ONTARIO ARTS COUNCIL
CONSEIL DES ARTS DE L'ONTARIO

an Ontario government agency
un organisme du gouvernement de l'Ontario

Published with the generous assistance of the Ontario Arts Council.

Printed in Canada

IMAGINARIUM

EDITED BY SANDRA KASTURI
& JEROME STUEART

4

INTRODUCTION BY MARGARET ATWOOD

THE BEST CANADIAN SPECULATIVE WRITING

Table of Contents

Introduction: Don't Be Alarmed
MARGARET ATWOOD

It's my very great pleasure to be your Imaginarium Introducer. Thank you for inviting me. I will now take off my ordinary head and replace it with the other one. Don't be alarmed.

Since we're told the development of software that enables the automatic generation of texts that sound more or less human is well underway—many corporate reports and political speeches are already generated by robotic thinking, one way or another—I may well be the last of your meatbrain introducers. On the other hand, those who write the kinds of stories you will find herein are a quirky bunch, and might possibly prefer to retain the shambling, uneven services of protein-and-starch-enabled troglodytes such as I, rather than switch over to the more modern and efficient digital model of introducer. A robot, for instance, would probably not use a word such as "herein." Or even a word such as "troglodyte." Nor would it have an extra head. But we shall see.

The overall label chosen by the *Imaginarium* editors as a designation for the wordwares set forth herein is "Speculative Fiction," a term that has been much disputed. I myself have used it to designate the kind of dystopia/utopia that takes place on Planet Earth, somewhere near now, with technology and conditions that are not only plausible but possible, as opposed to fantasy—not possible, may include magic and dragons—and science fiction (spaceships, planets far, far away and in another time, may contain talking squid or other such intelligent life forms). I got my knuckles rapped by Ursula K. Le Guin for the talking squid reference, as she thought it was just me being a disrespectful smarty-pants about scifi. But I protest! I grew up with talking squid, and am very fond of them, and see nothing inherently ridiculous about them, and would be loath to see them banished from Outer Space. (Though maybe it was the talking cabbages she objected to. But surely there is nothing wrong with that. Such a being would only look like a cabbage anyway; as witness the concretely imagined space fictions of China Miéville.)

Point being that terminology such as "speculative fiction" can snarl us up, especially in the *Imaginarium* playing field, which is extensive. Inside these pages you may find some "speculative fiction" in my terms—something along the lines of Jules Verne's submarine epic, *Twenty Thousand Leagues Under the Sea,* or Orwell's *1984,* or Huxley's *Brave New World*—but you will find many other sorts of things as well: stories that might be called "science fiction," stories that might be called "horror," stories that mix and match their memes and forms, stories that don't fit any easy definition. Bruce Sterling invented the term "slipstream" for fiction that didn't fit neatly onto labelled bookstore shelves, but was very odd and gave you an uncanny feeling, uncanny being derived from canny, and thus from "ken," to know. We do get very creeped out by things and especially by people that resemble things and people we know, but that are not really them—like the false mother with button eyes in Neil Gaiman's classic kids' novel, *Coraline.*

The most frightening thing in the old stories about people who were stolen away by fairies was not the fairyland they were taken to. It was their return to our world, and their discovery that they'd been away not for days but for decades, and that their former home was dark and vacant, and that all those they had known and loved were long since dead. Though to be really uncanny, the strange home would need to contain some people that were almost dead ringers for their relatives, but not quite; which is why Ray Bradbury's story about the Martians who create an illusion of the American hometown of the astronauts they intend to kill is so effective. We have dreams like that, from which we wake up shaking.

I grew up reading everything, and everything included pulp scifi and horror magazines and comic books, and Ray Bradbury and John Wyndham, and otherworld stories like Conan Doyle's *The Lost World*, and slipstream fictions like *Dr. Jekyll and Mr. Hyde* and *The Island of Dr. Moreau*, and horror classics like *Dracula* and *Frankenstein* and Sheridan LeFanu's *Carmilla*, and the hair-raising fables of M.R. James, and ghost classics like Henry James' *The Turn of the Screw* and "The Jolly Corner" and Charles Dickens' A Christmas Carol, and, yes, *Wuthering Heights*, which is a ghost story among other things; and more, much more. This kind of reading in no way diminished my appreciation for *Pride and Prejudice* and Thomas Hardy and Hemingway and Katherine Mansfield. It is a fallacy that most readers confine themselves to limited corners of the world of stories—they "only read" detective stories, they "only read" realism. It's another fallacy that "highbrow" readers read only "highbrow" fiction, and so forth. There may be some readers who are like that; we must pity them, and light candles for them, and slip copies of *Imaginarium* into their mailboxes. But young readers in particular, if left untethered, are likely to explore hither and thither in the world of books, as, indeed, they explore hither and thither in life.

What you're holding in your hand is "speculative," then, whatever may be meant by that term. Let's call these stories and poems "wonder tales." They contain wonders, and they cause you to wonder. You wonder many things. Could it happen? What would things be like if it did? Or, for the more visceral kind of tale: what's under the bed?

Now for the Canadian part.

Many years ago, in 1977—long before there was an *Imaginarium*, or much "genre" fiction of any sort written by Canadians, or even an internet—I wrote a piece called "Canadian Monsters: Some Aspects of the Supernatural in Canadian Fiction." It was for a volume titled *The Canadian Imagination*, and it was published in the United States. I was making a case for the Canadian Imagination not being as bland and lacking in lurid layers of weirdness as the literary commentators of that time would have us believe. I managed to come up with a wendigo, and a mystical coyote-god, and a mythical yellow-haired Indian who disappears into the earth, and a magician or two, and some wabenos, and assorted ghostly odds and ends, not to mention a woman who has an affair with a bear, thus doing Goldilocks one better.

In these pursuits, I was following up not only on some of my own earlier preferences, but also on a hint dropped by Robertson Davies, who said, "I know the dark folkways of my people," and who pointed out that Canada was led for many years by Mackenzie King, a man considered featureless to the point of nullity, but who all the time, as his diaries later revealed, was taking political advice from the spirit of his dead mother as incarnated in his dog. "Mackenzie King rules Canada because he is himself the embodiment of Canada," says a Davies character in *The Manticore*. "Cold and cautious on the outside . . . But inside a mass of intuition and dark intimations." How pleased Davies would have been to see *Imaginarium*!

He loved to tell ghost stories at Christmas (which is a good time for them, as the solstice door opens on the 21st of December, allowing entities to pass from the unseen world to the seen).

We now have a proliferation of "speculative fiction" writers of many different kinds in Canada. Boundaries dissolve, memes are exchanged, literary genetic material turns up in curious hybrids. And writing "genre" is no longer accepted as an excuse for not writing well.

Still, lingering doubts remain in the minds of some. Can writing that is transparently so much fun possibly be good for you, let alone good literature? Reading such tales is an undeniable pleasure, but must it always be a guilty one? Put simply: why is it that human beings like stories about the strange, the macabre, the unknown, the uncanny, the impossible? Because they obviously do.

Wayne Grady's charming anthology, *Night: A Literary Companion*, contains a selection by A. Roger Ekirch entitled "Navigating the Nightscape," taken from his book, *At Day's Close*, a history of nighttime. In this chapter, Ekirch first describes the universal fear of darkness that arises in children around the age of two. He continues: "In early modern times, youthful fears, in parents' eyes, often served a salutary purpose. Rather than soothe children's anxieties, adults routinely reinforced them through tales of the supernatural. . . ." This reinforcing has two functions. First, there were places and situations that were genuinely dangerous, and children needed to be warned against them. But second, through such tales, children could learn to face their own exaggerated terrors, and overcome them.

Is that why we like these stories of the dark, and of the dark side of the universe, and of the dark sides of ourselves? So we can face down the darkness—all kinds of darkness—at least in our imaginations? Or perhaps such tales bear witness to a very simple truth, though it's one we seldom consider: most of the universe is unknown.

But read on. And enjoy. As you will.

Now I will resume my ordinary head. Don't be alarmed.

The Exorcist: A Love Story
DAVID NICKLE

McGill smoked in the yard. They wouldn't let him smoke inside. There was a baby there after all. McGill said he understood, but he seemed pissed off about it. He stood by the barbecue, squinting at the tree line, calculating the hour, tapping ashes through the grill top. They were pissed off about *that*. The next round of burgers would have a subtle flavour of McGill and probably the round after those too.

But they would put up with it. Oh yes.

They would bloody well put up with it.

One of them had gone to high school with McGill. But she didn't know him then. He had a bit of acne trouble, did McGill—quite a bit. A Biblical plague of pimples, one might say. Horrific, seeping boils from his forehead down to his neck. One over his lip, round and gleaming and red, like a billiard ball.

An outgoing personality, some athletic talent, a fancy car—any one of these might have saved him. But McGill had none of that. So there he was.

She had no idea that McGill went to the same school. She got his name through another chain of acquaintances. When she contacted him, he did not offer up any hint of their own acquaintance with one another. He did not let the recognition creep into his voice.

It would be generous to say that McGill handled the interview professionally. Because McGill has never been much of a professional.

I wish I could have heard his side of it. But I could guess—McGill and I go way back.

"We're not Catholic," she'd said, and paused, and laughed nervously. "You're not either." Pause. "Yes, Mr. McGill, I guess that is something we have in common." Another pause. "He's six months old. Born February 12." Pause. "Yes. Aquarius." *What's your sign, baby*? Really? "So explain to me how this non-demon—erm, non-denominational business works." And a long silence, as McGill went through the litany:

First, he must come by and meet the child. What if it's not a child? *It's always a child, dear.* Of course, if it happens to be Gran or Uncle Terry who's afflicted . . . well, McGill would try and adapt. But one way or another, in the course of a conversation, he would try and draw it out. McGill explains this part of his process as very simple—non-invasive—but he's not being completely honest.

He spends a lot of time staring, so intensely that sometimes he brings about tears. He mumbles nonsense words in a made-up language. He takes a photograph using a specially treated lens. And finally, under the parents' supervision, he lays a hand on the child's skull—leaving the impression with their parents that he is reading the aura. He is not. He is looking for a soft spot, a tiny hole in the skull—often no bigger than a baby's thumb. That is really the only thing that he's looking for in that first visit. Because if it's there . . . well, that's how we get in, isn't it?

And that is also how he can tell. If he jams his finger into it—with just the right force—well, even if we're reticent to start it up again with old McGill, we have no choice. It starts the real conversation.

And once that gets going, things become, shall we say, fluid.

McGill really needed three cigarettes, given everything—but well-brought-up lad that he is, he cut himself off at just one.

"You finally ready?" Her man was a testy one. He had never met McGill, had attended a different high school, had no earthly reason to suspect. And yet.

"Sure," said McGill. He started to meet his eyes, but didn't get far. McGill looking her man in the eye would have been a challenge. And McGill hadn't the balls for that.

She smiled uneasily, and shared a glance with her man. *Don't fuck this up, darling*, that glance said. He was not easy about bringing McGill, or anyone outside the family physician's circle, in on what he called "the postpartum thing." He didn't entirely buy in to what was going on. And in one sense, he couldn't be blamed. When the door in the basement slammed again and again, seemingly of its own accord, he was already on his way to an early meeting. He had been asleep the whole night, when the business with the hall mirror had transpired. He was at work the day the seven crows got into the nursery, and pecked one another to death as baby laughed.

He was always away, out of earshot, when baby spoke.

"My wife tells me that you're going to go have a conversation now," he said. McGill nodded.

"That's the first part."

He huffed. "Well, good luck. Little Simon's not too verbal. Except around Shelly here. That right, babe?"

"I understand," said McGill. "Maybe I'll have better luck."

"Right. Do they all talk to you?"

"Often they do, that's right." McGill stepped toward the nursery. Her man stepped into his way, but didn't stop him either.

"You're for real," he said.

"He's for real," she said. "Please, Dave, just let him do his work."

McGill wanted to say something reassuring—he knew that he should. Couldn't quite muster it, though; he just hunched his shoulders in half a shrug, smiled in what amounted to an ambiguous shrug, and made another try for the nursery. The man put his hand on McGill's shoulder.

"Hang on there, buddy. This is my boy in there. You won't touch him, will you?"

"I'll put my hand on his head," said McGill. "No more than that."

(McGill stammered when he said that. But it's mean to mimic a stammer.)

"No more than that." The man put his hand on McGill's arm—around McGill's arm, really. "You're gonna wash that hand, then, brother."

"Dave!"

"Shelly." He kept hold of McGill. His tone was one that he thought was reasonable, but that she had told him more than once was a tone that was "goddamn scary." Which was all right, she said; it made her feel safe, she said. Protected.

His grip tightened on McGill's arm. "This is bullshit."

McGill drew in a breath. His arm was hurting, and he was doing his best not to show it. But he wasn't doing it very well, because she pointed out that he was hurting McGill and shamed him into letting go.

"It's all right," McGill lied. "Your husband—Dave's right. That is his boy in there, and it's your boy too. If parents are okay with it, it's better if it's just me and the baby. But we can do this with one or both of you in there too. Or I could come back—"

"No!" she said, too loudly, and then, too softly: "Don't go, Mr. McGill."

Did McGill's heart melt then? Did more than a decade of hope, of prayer, of dirty, dirty moments alone in his bed at the break of dawn . . . did all that draw together now, at the broken, pleading tone of her voice? Oh, how could it not? Was this not his dream, here before him, made flesh?

If it didn't melt—might it not soon shatter?

"I'll go in with you," she said. "Dave will wait here in the kitchen. Right, Dave?"

"I don't—"

"Dave. You promised."

And he had, and he knew it, and so that was that.

When I arrived, the nursery was a cheery space. She had painted the walls little-boy blue, and dangled a mobile of friendly looking farm animals. The changing table was an antique in a tawdry way; it had been a little sheet-metal desk, just the size for a typewriter, an "In" box and a sheaf of paper. This she had painted a bright yellow, covered in terrycloth and stacked diapers and baby powder and a box of wipes. There was a toy box, filled with bric-a-brac from the baby shower, and a chest of drawers, stuffed with more shower swag: jumpers and bonnets and a little denim jacket for baby to wear, eventually. Adorable.

McGill saw none of that.

They had stripped the place bare, but for the bassinet. Nothing sharp, nothing heavy. Nothing that could suffocate, and nothing flammable.

"That's him," he said, peering in.

"That's my baby." She said it jauntily enough but she finished on the edge of bitter laughter.

All business for the moment, McGill took no notice of it.

He reached into his coat, and pulled out his Pentax, with its smeary lens and etched-in F-stops. He snapped two pictures through that vile instrument, and set it down on the floor. "Don't touch it," he said as she leaned to get it. "Please."

"All right," she said.

He leaned farther over the edge and stared at me. I didn't look away. He shifted down to his knees and calmed his breathing. He blinked when I blinked. He breathed when I breathed. This went on for a while. How long? I can't honestly say; this part of things, it's easy to lose track of time, looking into the pale infinity of McGill's baby-blues. . . .

A girl could lose herself in there, don't you think?

"Aka Manah," he said finally.

"What?" She had been hovering by the door, and now she came closer. He just shook his head and continued—"Vassago . . . Furtur . . . Focalor . . ."— shaking his head again after each name.

"Simon," she said.

"I know," said McGill. "That's the boy's name. Looking for the . . . other one's name."

"Do you just guess?"

"Something like that," said McGill. "Vepar. Mammon . . . Räum?"

"Okay."

"Not that," said McGill, "not him. Are you?"

No, McGill, I'm not Räum.

"Ah," he said, and leaned away from the bassinet. He rubbed his hands together, and blew air out through his cheeks. Just what he was afraid of.

"Gremory."

Aha!

"He snapped his fingers!"

"Did he?" said McGill. He was looking away.

"He did," she said. "Like a little Dean Martin." She thought about that for a second. "Is it Gremory? Is that the right name?"

"Think so."

A long breath. "How'd you guess it so fast?"

"Lucky." McGill came back and looked at me. His lips were drawn thin. His eyelids were too. He reached out with his right hand, fingers spread. They trembled as they rested on the baby's skull.

"What're you going to do?" she asked, and he brought his left forefinger to his lips. "Okay, I'll hush," she said, and his right hand tightened, at the little finger and thumb, like forceps behind the ears. His middle finger danced over the back of the skull, until it stopped, and dithered. It didn't last long, though; like a wedding ring spinning round a sink drain, it soon disappeared inside.

I had him to the second knuckle.

What does McGill see? What I wouldn't give to know. I know what I see; his eyelids, flickering like a hummingbird's wings, his mouth hanging open as he mumbles commands, sweat running down the side of his nose, staining his collar. But him? When he looks on me, does he see an obsidian woman, naked and shining, breasts suckling six crows, wormy cunny dripping amarone-scented menses into the deathly loam of Golgotha? Does he cower at my magnificent obscenity?

Does he wish for his mummy?

I cannot tell. All the times we have met, he has never said.

"You need to leave the baby."

No, McGill. I don't.

He said the baby's name.

That means shit to me, McGill.

"It is the owner of that form."

No. It's nothing. Unbaptized. Belongs to me.

"You got no claim. You are Gremory. You trespass here. Go on back to where you dwell."

I am who I am. I dwell where I am and I am here. You go back.

"I cast you out. I cast you out." He said some of those words that his mummy taught him. I let him go on for a dozen of them before I said anything.

Your heart's not in it, McGill. What's the matter now?

"You got to leave." He uttered another stanza.

You have to want it. You don't want it, do you?

"Git. Go on." He paused. His hand gripped the baby's skull tighter. If it were a baseball, he'd have been making ready to throw a curve. "Fuck out of here, you."

You're in such a hurry, McGill. You're missing steps; really, you're far from your usual professional self. Your mother would never have stood for that kind of thing. Never mind the language.

Oh, that got him. McGill's mother . . . what of her, hey? I hear she has been out of the game for some eight years now. She taught him everything he knows, and now everything she knows rests in McGill's unlovely skull. And she and her knowledge were formidable. Truly. None of us could best her like the Alzheimer's did. Now . . . she wouldn't know herself reflected in a mirror, would she?

He told me to fuck right off and called me hell-spawn. He told me I had "no fucking right." Me? I squirted moist feces into my diaper and chortled.

Mothers get them every time.

Eventually he ran himself down. I waited to make sure before continuing.

You haven't asked me what I want.

"You want to leave."

You haven't asked me why I chose this one.

He paused. "Why did you choose this one?"

The answer to both is the same. McGill, I want you to be happy.

His pause stretched into a silence. I let it sit. I didn't wish to insult McGill's intelligence.

She was so lovely, still; it had been less than a decade since he'd first seen her in Grade 10's History of Europe class. She was a mother now, a wife—but did her skin still not glow with the light of youth? She was a freckle-faced girl then, and those freckles had faded over the years, as they do sometimes. But wasn't her mouth just as thick with girlish eroticism now, as it was as he watched her laugh by her locker in the G-section downstairs—the locker that McGill made a point of passing by, even when his next class was at the far end of the school. . . .

"You knew," he said finally.

I knew. You wear it on your sleeve, McGill.

And of course, that was when he gathered the last of his strength. "You can't tempt me," he said. "Begone!"

Oh, McGill. I know I can't tempt you. That's why I think I'll stay here for now. You begone, for a little while. Think about what I said.

He staggered back, ectoplasm dribbling from his middle finger to make a stain down his pant leg, that had she not been standing there, watching, staring, working it out herself, he would never have been able to explain.

The baby started to cry. *I did nothing to calm it.*

Its mother looked at it in wonder. Did she think she could tell—that her child was returned to her, that the miraculous laying-on-of-hands by McGill had done the trick? Oh, why even ask the question. Of course she did. A mother can tell when her child is wailing, and when something else—some otherworldly thing, perhaps—is manipulating its tiny larynx, making it gargle out blasphemes that only she can hear. . . .

She scooped the child up in her arms, and held it close. Its tears subsided, and it began to coo. McGill, meanwhile, steadied himself against the doorjamb. He wasn't in a position to do much else; I'd cast him out, good and proper. A man doesn't just walk away from something like that.

She looked at McGill, and he looked back at her. There was something different in her look, and McGill picked up on it. A hint of recognition, perhaps? Gratitude, certainly. Yes, certainly that—McGill could see it in her eye.

After all, I had put it there.

He drew a shaking breath, and nodded, and might have summoned the will to say something. He scarcely had a chance to, though, because as he straightened, her husband was in the doorway with him. He stood staring at her, hands in unconscious fists—a question in his eye too.

"He's back," she said, wonderingly. "Simon's back, Dave. Whatever he did—worked."

Her husband looked at McGill, at that trouser-stain, at McGill's face, pale and drawn.

"That so, mister?" he asked.

McGill had not yet recovered his words. He gulped air and nodded. Her husband clapped him on the shoulder, and strode into the nursery. He leaned over me—over the baby—and reached out with a tentative finger, to touch its chin. She let him take the baby. It clung to him, as I cooed in his ear.

"It's . . . too soon," said McGill finally, and gasped again, "to say . . . for sure."

Eventually, even a specimen like McGill gets his wind back.

When he did, she saw him to the door, while her husband put the baby down. They paused in the kitchen. She put a hand on his arm. This time, McGill didn't try to worm away. She said something softly to him. A question, yes. *Do I know you, from elsewhere? I feel . . . I don't know, it's silly.*

That's the question. I can tell by the way he shuffled, and looked away before looking back.

She glanced away too—to the nursery, where she saw that her husband was properly distracted. Then she looked back, and leaned closer, and whispered something else.

McGill nodded, and looked to the nursery himself where he saw the baby, head at its father's shoulder, looking right back at him.

"Keep in touch, Mrs. Reesor," he said, finally loud enough for all to hear. "In case . . . you know."

She looked at him with such intensity then—turning away only as her husband turned.

"So he's fine?" he said.

McGill nodded, and chin down, headed for the door.

"I gave him the cheque," she said when McGill had left, and her husband tried to look her in the eye.

"As long as you're okay now," he said.

Oh, she was fine. Better than the day that I arrived in that house, that's for certain. She had been such a melancholic one, that day that I crawled from the dishwater, and slithered on my belly across the kitchen and up and around her leg, to the breast where the infant fussed and suckled. He would not sleep. He kicked and squalled. She was chained to him, that's how she felt. And when I entered him, through the pinhole door in his skull, and had him bite down—he made her shriek. Might she've killed him? Mothers do, sometimes. Their hearts harden. They see the lay of the barren years ahead, serving hand and foot to their child, and its father now grown cold to the touch.

How many times have I been called up by a neglected husband who'd found my name in a grimoire, and begged me on the strength of my reputation, to irrigate the drying slits of their fading brides?

Ah, it would have been the easiest thing for me, to turn her pearl as she looked on her husband—to whisper and suggest—to indicate and to remind her, of what joys the old hunger brings.

But that wasn't why I came to that house. So I held my peace, until McGill came. His aching hunger was nothing I had to tweak.

All I had to do was lay her before him, and reaching into her as McGill reached into me, tweak her heart so, and set her on her course.

Her husband made her dinner.

It involved shrimp and couscous and dried fruit, some curry flakes and fish stock to round it out. He understood it to be a favourite of hers. She did nothing to correct the misapprehension. She washed up, and saw to the baby, and joined him in bed. When he asked if everything was all right, she said yes. When he touched her, she made a noise that he understood to mean no.

In the deep night, I awoke to find her over my crib.

The next morning, after he left for work, she took me out for the second outdoor excursion since I arrived. As she had that first time, she installed me in a great blue stroller, with thick rubber tires, multiple straps to hold me tight and a pouch behind my head filled with the mysterious tools of the mothering trade. It was warmer out of doors than that first time. She wore a red-and-white cotton dress; I, a tiny blue terrycloth jumper.

We made it quite a way—well past the bank building at the corner of the street where things had gone so badly that last time—along past a filling station—and across another street, to a park with a playground and some benches in the shade of thick, blossoming maple trees. She stopped in front of one of these benches, and looked at me and it, and finally she did sit, and turned the stroller around so that I faced her, and she looked at me again—and it dawned on me that she wasn't looking at me . . . she was searching *for* me, in the empty stare of her little son's eye.

Searching for some pretext, perhaps, to call?

Six days she searched in vain. On the morning of the seventh, she picked up the phone.

I could tell it was not McGill she called by her bright and easy tone. "Hey, you!" she said, and after a pause, "Yeah, things are better now." And another pause, as the phone chirped brightly in her ear. "I know!" And more chirping. "Yeah! Right?" She nodded, her smile brighter than I believe I'd ever seen it. "So it's okay if I come? You sure?"

And finally: "Great!"

She switched off her phone and leaned over the bassinet.

"Guess where we're going, Simon?" she cooed. "Can you say 'Brannigan's'?"

The infant blew a snot bubble out its nose and giggled. I kept my peace.

Brannigan's was a little pub a few blocks past the park. Nice and murky inside, it suited my tastes. But we didn't stay there long. She manoeuvred the stroller around the bar to a door to a back patio. There, in the combined shelter of a maple tree and a great red umbrella, gathered two more strollers, and the mothers who pushed them.

"Hey, Shell!" shouted one of the mothers, standing up with her own baby in one arm and extending the other for a hug. The baby—a big bruiser, flabby and blond like its mother—regarded me with dull hostility from its perch. The other infant—a little girl, judging by the pink—stayed in her stroller seat for the second hug and would not meet my eye. Her mother was a wiry one, with enormous white teeth. She smelled of lawn cuttings.

"How you been?" that one asked, and without leaving time for an answer, turned to me. "Look at him! He's so big!"

"Keep feeding 'em, bound to happen."

The two mothers laughed and laughed, and the flabby one pointed to an empty chair. *She* sat there, after tucking my stroller in between her and the blond baby's stroller. Its mother set the infant back into its seat, and launched into a description of how big it was, and then a long talk about nutrition. I stopped paying attention.

Her baby wouldn't look away.

It sat high in its seat, fidgeting with a little blue pacifier in its hands. It stared at me, an expression that might have been indignation on its face. I looked away, and when I looked back, it hadn't moved.

Did it see what *she* could not? That hidden in the soft skull of this one, was a being older than any here? That McGill's exorcism had failed, and the thing inside was waiting like a barely irradiated tumour to re-emerge?

Did it think there was something it could do about that?

The waitress arrived, and it disappeared for a moment behind her muscular legs and tartan skirt as she took lunch orders. It took longer than it needed to, of course.

"Hey," she said when the waitress finally stepped away, "you remember a kid called McGill?"

"Who?" said the skinny one, but the other waved a hand over the table: "McGill. From high school?" and the skinny one said, "Oh, with the . . ." and waved her hand over her face.

She nodded, reaching down to ruffle my hair. "With the acne," she said, "that's him."

"Weird kid."

"Yeah, wasn't he always wearing black—"

"—kind of goth—"

"—but without the style."

"Right."

"I thought he was going to shoot the school up."

"Columbine our asses."

"Would have served us right."

"Shell!"

"Well, we were total bitches."

"Speak for yourself, Shelly."

"Yeah. Speak for yourself. So what about McGill?"

"He—came back into my life," she said. In spite of myself, I grinned and bounced in my seat. She withdrew her hand, brought it into her lap.

"Ooo," said the flabby one, "that's creepy."

"Not really. We hired him. To help with Simon."

"What, as a babysitter?"

She shook her head. "He's . . . a therapist now. Really, you wouldn't recognize him. From before. His skin's cleared up. He dresses better. And it's like . . . he's found purpose."

"A therapist? For Simon? Shell, is he okay?"

"He's fine now. McGill fixed him right up."

"Wow. McGill. A therapist."

She laughed, a little too lightly. "A behavioural therapist, yeah. Little Simon here . . . he was a handful."

I cooed. Under the table, she crossed her ankles, and uncrossed them. She was fidgeting—the way they do as the feelings take hold. She took a sip from a glass of spring water.

"I gotta say, I'm surprised to hear that about McGill. He was such a mess back then."

"Teenage boys are a mess. They grow out of it."

"He had a lot to grow out of. Did you ever see his mom?"

"I don't remember."

"Yeah, you wouldn't have seen her much. You never went on that trip to Ottawa."

"I had the flu. Did McGill's mother go on that?"

"Not exactly. McGill was going to go. He made it all the way to the bus. He had this suit jacket, and this crazy old trunk with him that was way too big. He got it into the luggage compartment somehow—I think Mr. Evans had to help him with it. And just before we were going to leave, she pulls up."

"His mother?"

"His mother. Bat-shit crazy. She was driving this old Lincoln or something like it. Pulled it up right in front of the bus, so it was blocked in. She got out—huge woman. Not fat—but big like a linebacker. Her hair was white—she wore a big black fake-fur coat like it was winter. She climbed onto the bus, and pointed at McGill, and she yelled: 'I Revoke my Permission! Return my Son to me!'"

"Jesus."

"Poor McGill."

"Yeah, well he knew what was good for him. He got up and said he couldn't go to Ottawa any more, and got off the bus. Into his mom's car. Didn't even stop to get his trunk out of the luggage area. Had to collect it when we got back."

"That sucks."

"Yeah. But you know something, Shell?" The flabby blonde leaned across the table. "I think he was kind of relieved."

"How's that?"

"You weren't there," she said. "And it was pretty easy to tell . . . McGill was more interested in you than he was in the Houses of Parliament."

Quiet for just a moment, before the three of them broke into a braying round of laughter. The waitress returned with some salads, drinks, and a plate of fried yams. Trickier job this time; she had to sneak in between strollers and the two rattan chairs that'd been displaced to make room for us. She didn't quite pull it off, and several pieces of cutlery slid off her tray. She promised to get more, bent to grab the ones she could find, and hurried off back into the bar.

"I barely knew he was alive," she said.

"Well, he sure knew you were alive."

"Stop fucking—messing with Shelly's head. Stop messing with her head."

"One for the swear jar?"

"No, really. He was a sweet, quiet kid. With, you know, unfortunate skin. If he had a crush on Shelly—well, everybody had a crush on Shelly. Look—" the skinny one with the teeth pointed at her with her fork "—you're making her blush."

She laughed. "Well, he's turned out all right now."

"It's nice to know that boys turn into men, eh?"

"To boys turning into men!" The blonde one raised a glass of spring water, and the others joined the toast. I let myself giggle and clap, and looked right at her as she glanced down. Things were going well, I thought. And at first, I had no idea why her face fell the way it did.

She nearly dropped her glass as she bent and lunged over me, filling my face for a moment with her sweet-smelling tit. To my side, there was a scream—and I looked over just in time to see her pluck a gleaming blade from the big baby's little hand.

He had gotten out of his stroller. He had crawled around beneath the table unseen—by any of us—and he had located a steak-knife the waitress had dropped. And then, the little worm . . . he found his legs.

He had carried the knife three glorious steps, from his mother's feet to the edge of my stroller. It appeared as though the fat little tyke had been about to plunge the knife deep into my left eye.

This kind of event is rare; usually, it happens with a family pet . . . dogs, to be sure, but more perilously, cats. They've a fine sense of smell, they do. And that's why, when I arrive in a new vessel, that's the first thing I do.

I make sure the cat is dead.

But you know all about that.

The first time McGill and I met after all was over the carcass of a cat.

Remember that place? Squalid little rooms near the very top of a crumbling old apartment building filled with whores and addicts and murderers. Cheap wallpaper peeling off the entry hall. No doors on the kitchen cabinets. No father either. What was it that McGill's mother had said when she first visited the little girl and her overwhelmed, demon-beset mother?

Slattern?

It hadn't gone over well with the mother. I watched from the back of the sofa, where I made the brat I inhabited squat and growl. What, she wanted to know, did McGill's mother have over her, to pass judgement? Could McGill's mother keep a man any better, who didn't want to stay? By the empty divot in her ring finger, she guessed not. That hit a nerve, it did. And so it was that she turned on her heel and strode out of there, and left the poor woman to me.

McGill was the one who finally faced me. His mother had no idea. He came up the next day, on his own, in uniform: a tatty old Nirvana T-shirt, too-loose black jeans and that pustule of a face. He wasn't ready. That was obvious. But for whatever reason, he didn't feel right about disturbing his mother with the contrite phone message, begging her to return because *My God, it's killed the cat!*

I'd done more than that. I'd smashed windows in the bedroom, caved in the ceiling over the door to the balcony, overturned the sofa and caused the television tube to implode. I caused the slattern's neighbour, a man who carried a gun in his trouser-band and dabbled in the narcotics trade to, if not love, then lust for her in an overly solicitous way.

I was, I admit, not pleased when McGill's mother left in such a rage. I wanted her back. To finish things.

McGill found me in the bathtub. The cat, who had been the child's dearest friend, was there too—laid out in the doorframe, its head turned hard back, so it looked at its own tail. I saw to it that it wasn't moved. I wanted McGill's mother to see it. So she'd know who she was dealing with.

It had a different effect on McGill. He didn't know me, then. His mother had left him at home when she met me at the schoolhouse. He'd waited in the car when we danced at the shopping plaza, and she vanquished me again. She obviously didn't tell him about me—about the things I could do, to the world . . . to the hearts and heads of men and women. How formidable I was.

He saw that cat, and he saw me, in the tub smeared with feces and vomit and blood, and there was no fear. All that came up was anger.

"Let that little girl go, you fuckin' cocksucker," he said, and made fists. The camera he'd brought fell to the floor. His eyes filled with tears. And like a stupid, tantruming child, he stepped up to the fight.

That was the first time we met, and the only time I came close to besting McGill. I don't know how his mother taught him . . . what talent he might have simply inherited . . . But even new to the game, blinded by stupid rage . . .

He was a chip off the block.

She was giddy when we got home. She set my stroller in the living room, in front of the TV, and I sat there alone for a time, watching some colourful cartoon show about dinosaurs and science, while she scoured the basement.

She returned with a stack of slim, hard-covered books. Four of them. She settled on the floor in front of the sofa. Opened one of them. The inside flaps were covered in scribbles, notes like a greeting card. She pored over those for a few minutes, then flipped through the pages. It was filled with photographs.

"This is a yearbook, baby," she said, as she noticed me looking over her shoulder. She scudded nearer me, and flipped through it. "This is Mummy when she was a lot younger," she said, stopping at a page filled with faces. Hers grinned out at me. She flipped a few more pages, and there she was, among a crowd of other girls wearing shorts and tank-tops. "This was the girl's track and field team. That's Mummy." And finally, she flipped back, to another of those face-filled pages. There, stuck in the middle like a dried piece of chewing gum, was McGill's grinning face.

"And this is the man who brought you back, baby."

I grinned and waved my hands, and she laughed.

"He's our hero," she said, and when I giggled in what I was sure then to be my triumph, she said, "Yes he is. I wish he was here too."

One more day—an awful, interminable day, filled with tears and silences after questions and accusations—and we were in the car.

She had been fiddling around on her computer, looking things up, putting it together in the morning, after he left, silent and stiff-backed. Oh, how it must have stung him, those words: *You didn't do anything to help! McGill saved our baby, and the best you could do was sulk!*

He hadn't said anything to her, but he came to see me in the night, clutching the waistband of his pajama bottoms, damp-eyed and snuffling, declaring his love for me. "I hope you'll remember that, no matter what happens," he said, and touched my cheek.

She strapped me into the child seat behind her. It offered a terrible view, and that made me fussy. After all these years, I must admit that I was acutely curious as to where precisely McGill bedded down at night. In all of our transactions, the McGill family only ever came to me. Never had I had occasion or opportunity to play the visitor.

We sped along blacktop. She braked three times—the last time hard enough to leave skid-marks—before the surface under the wheels grew rougher, and gravel popped up against the underside. The brilliant blue sky above me disappeared behind a canopy of leaves, and soon after that, the car slowed and lurched to one side as she negotiated a narrow turn, onto an even rougher surface. And then we came to a stop and she climbed out.

"Wish me luck," she said, and kissed my forehead before unbuckling me and lifting me out of the seat, and the car.

We were in a small clearing in the middle of the woods. In the middle of that, was a house that I could only guess belonged to McGill.

It was made of wood, its walls shingled in rough, dark cedar, and happily, it had but a single storey to it. The shadow of the trees all around kept grass from growing, but there had been some attempt at a little garden underneath the living room window. The nose of an old Lincoln poked out from underneath a carport. There was a metal shed behind that.

Although it was the middle of summer, the space here had a chill to it. I fussed, and she held me close, and she fussed too, in her way. She took a step toward the house, and another one—then stepped back. She looked back at the car, and shook her head, and said, "damn" in almost a sob. She might have gotten into it, too, if she'd been left to her devices.

But—lucky her—she was rescued.

"Mrs. Reesor?"

McGill stood at the door. He was wearing an old bathrobe. A cigarette dangled between thumb and forefinger, and he flicked ash away onto the steps. His hair stood up on one side—no doubt where he'd slept.

She turned to him, holding me close. "Hey, you," she said.

"How—" he frowned. "How did you find me here?"

"Online," she said. "I looked up your address online."

"It's not under my name."

"It's not. But it is under your mother's."

He didn't say anything to that.

"Look," she said finally. "I'm sorry for coming here like this. I . . . I hoped it would be okay, but maybe it's not."

"It's okay." He dropped the cigarette to the steps, and put it out with the heel of one bare foot. "Is Simon all right?"

She nodded. "He's fine." And she held me up, jiggling me like a carnival prize. I giggled appropriately. "See?"

"He looks good." McGill set his head forward and squinted at her. "Really good. So you're here . . . why?"

She giggled, inappropriately. She let her bangs fall over her eyes. She smiled at him through them. "I remember now," she said softly.

McGill's mouth hung open stupidly for a second. "Mrs. Reesor?"

"Shelly," she said, and with that, found her courage. She strode across the stony yard, and up the steps, and holding me in one arm, wrapped an arm around his neck, and drew him into a kiss.

It wouldn't be as simple as that soon enough. But for the moment, it was.

McGill's house stank of old smoke and urine. The living room was a shadowy place. Dishes from a recent meal spread across a coffee table. Random-seeming pieces of clothing, yellowing paperbacks and empty bottles and cans clotted its shadowed corners. A large box of adult diapers sat near the doorway to the kitchen. She noticed none of it, of course—love sees, or smells, only what it wishes—but McGill was still ashamed.

"I . . . apologize for the state of things," he said.

"It's okay," she said. "You probably can't afford a housekeeper. You don't charge enough for what you do."

"It's not right."

"You saved my baby. It's right to charge fairly for that."

Of course, that was not what McGill meant. He meant that this wasn't right, that there was no natural way that she would arrive at his door, and kiss him so . . .

How was it for him these past days? I can only guess. When he watched her sashay past his locker those years ago, didn't he dream of this day? When he could grow into and harness the talents of his mother, and use them to rescue that pale princess—to possess her, even as he drove the demons from her? Then, might he not have slipped his finger into the moist caverns of her mind, and communed with her as does my kind? And in so doing, truly possess her?

Shameful thoughts, for men of McGill's avocation. Shameful, but once entertained, so difficult to dismiss.

"Don't worry," she said, standing near him now. Her heart was pounding—I could feel it as she held me to her breast. "I'm not going to try and give you more *money*. Come on with me."

And she led us all, down a hallway, past a shut door—where the stink of piss seemed strongest—and through an open door.

McGill whispered an apology for the state of his bedroom. She told him she didn't care—that she remembered now . . . that she wished she could undo the years and that she should apologize for not being able to.

There was an ache, she said, a hollowness in her that she had dismissed as ennui, until she saw him again. McGill might have said: that is how it feels, when a demon tweaks a heart, and turns it to another direction. He might have made fists, and turned to me, and said, "Let that woman go, you fuckin' cocksucker."

But our McGill . . . in spite of his vow, in spite of his avocation . . . in spite of his other responsibilities . . . he said nothing.

She took the pillows stacked at one end of his sagging bed, and made a small nest for me on the floor beside the bed.

Then she whispered an apology to me, and set me in it. "Mummy's right here," she said, and turned away.

And McGill . . . precious McGill . . . *your* McGill, he took her in his arms, and ran his hands over the soft skin of her waist, the curve of her buttock. For that moment, he forgot everything . . . transformed forever, by his awful dream made flesh.

And so, I crawled.

It was a strain—the infant wasn't really ready for crawling. But such as we know nothing so well as the bending of sinew, the diversion of will. And off I went—out the door, back to the hallway, past the lavatory, and to your door. It opened for me without protest: any wards McGill had ever bothered to place on it had long ago faded.

You smell of piss. I wonder if you know that? I wonder how much you know, locked in that skull of yours? I can see you now, in your old hospital bed.

I can see the leather straps that McGill uses to keep you still . . . to keep you from harming yourself, or burning the place down, or harming him. You could still do a lot of harm—you were always a big girl. I remember how you held down that boy I took, down south, as you slid your thick thumb into his skull and sent me back to hell.

Even then you *stank*.

Are you in hell now? Trapped in that confused swamp of shit that fills your skull these days? Is there any hope you have left?

I'm on your bed now. You can feel me clambering over your fat leg. It's not easy—I'm pushing this little one to its limits to make my way up your torso, over your sagging, spent teats, to your face—your rheumy, drooping eyes.

I want to make sure that you know. McGill is lost. You have no son. Really, as I've proven, you never fully did.

Now, my dear old friend, all the world is only you, and I.

Túshūguǎn

Eric Choi

Fénshū carefully studied the boy with the book.

The youth looked to be in his early teens, but it was difficult to tell. Contemporary Běiměizhōu children always looked much older than their years. This one resembled a skeleton, more bone than flesh, with grimy bug-bitten skin, laddered ribs, twig-thin arms and legs, and bloodied, swollen feet. His face was gaunt, topped by a tangled, greasy mess of long black hair. He also stank, reeking like an oily, salty fish.

Fénshū looked into the boy's green eyes, and while it was impossible to get a sense of the boy's soul, she could discern a certain fire—perhaps of intelligence, certainly of strength.

"Nǐ jiào shén ma míng zì?" she asked. The boy was silent.

"Nǐ míngbái ma?"

Still no response.

"What is your name?" she said at last in English.

"Wu," the boy said. His yellowish-brown teeth were chipped and twisted.

"Hello Wu, I am Dr. Fénshū Zhèng," she continued. "I am . . . an historical archaeologist. Do you know what that is?"

The boy fell silent again.

"How are you, Wu?"

The boy did not answer, looking instead at his inquisitor and returning the question. "How are *you*?"

Definitely intelligence. The boy's verbal language skills, at least in English, were excellent. Fénshū was quite impressed.

"I am sixty years old!" Fénshū cackled in a high-pitched voice, trying to smile.

Wu simply stared.

"Do you have something for me?"

Wu nodded, his calloused hands reverently handing over the book.

"Thank you, Wu." Fénshū gestured to the floor of the tent. "Please, sit down. My colleague will be back for you shortly."

Wu hesitated for a moment, then sat on the ground as instructed.

Fénshū pushed her spectacles up the bridge of her nose and examined the book. It was a brownish-black hardcover, about sixteen by twenty-four centimetres and perhaps three centimetres thick, enclosed within a clear sealable plastic bag of the type that had once been a common means of storing food in pre-Fall Běiměizhōu civilization. The book was in fairly good condition, except for a serrated gash that penetrated the pages from cover to cover. Also inside the plastic bag, collected mostly along the spine, were clumps of a white powdery residue. She held the book up to her nose and sniffed. Through the punctured plastic, it smelled faintly of camphor and another odd odour she could not immediately identify.

"Where did this come from?" Fénshū asked. "Where did you find this?"

The boy looked up.

"Where did you find this?" she repeated.

"In the old shit and piss!"

Over and over again, Wu's mother would ask him the same thing.

"What do you do if you see a Jiangshi?"

"Run," Wu would answer.

"Why?"

Sometimes Wu would hesitate, and his mother would insist.

"Come on. Why?" she would repeat.

"Because a Jiangshi will hurt you, kill you, eat you."

The road upon which Wu walked was wrinkled and cracked like the skin of an old man. Weeds and wild flowers sprouted from every fissure, heaving apart the decaying asphalt. With slow certainty over the long years since the Fall, the pavement was being reduced to the constituent stone, gravel and bitumen from which it had been formed.

For much of this day, Wu had been fortunate in his solitude. It was not to last.

Wu stopped in his tracks and squinted. In the far distance, a Jiangshi came into view. He recognized the brainfrizzed monster immediately, a stained and filthy figure slowly shambling in his direction with that distinctive jerky, unsteady gait.

He didn't think he had been spotted, but he wasn't about to stick around to find out.

Wu ran off the road, through the tall grasses, into the trees. Twigs and branches lashed his body and stones cut his bare feet, but neither slowed his flight. Deeper and deeper into the woods he ran, until his lungs heaved and his heart felt like it would burst from his chest.

Finally, he stopped . . . and stared.

Before him was a ruin of the old world. A house had once stood here, but it had long ago collapsed and been assimilated by the living woods. Only the chimney remained standing, but Wu could see that its bricks were dropping and breaking, little by little, as the mortar crumbled and powdered. Some kind of vine grew everywhere, climbing through the broken windows and up the bars and grillwork.

Wu circled about the stone tower, fascinated.

There was a shallow hill across from the remnants of the foundation. He walked to the hill and climbed. Suddenly, he stopped and looked down.

He had run over something.

Tracing back a few steps, he spotted a patch of dead leaves and twigs collected within a rough square. Resting on his knees, Wu swept away the detritus with his hands. A grey slab with a square metal handle imbedded on top appeared before him.

Wu stared in wonder, uncertain of what to do next. Finally, he reached down and grasped the handle with his small, bony hands.

Nothing happened.

He extended his legs and dug in his feet for leverage, pulling harder with all his strength, but still it did not budge. Exhausted, he released the handle and fell backwards, his legs splayed.

Something moved in the bushes.

Wu turned in the direction of the rustling noise, his eyes wide. He pulled a slingshot out of his pouch, his other hand frantically sweeping the ground for a suitable projectile. Grasping a stone, he loaded the pocket and pulled back the bands with trembling hands.

The leaves rustled again.

Wu drew back the bands a little further, then released.

The happiest times were when his mother told him stories about the things from before, the old world prior to the Fall.

"People flew?"

"Yes. In flying machines. Anywhere in the world, without fear."

And she would tell him about the music that came from a box smaller than your hand, and the heat and light and clean water that came with a touch, and the pictures that moved, and the buildings as high as mountains, and the places with piles of fresh food, and the artificial stars that let people talk to one another across the world, and most wonderful of all, the bound volumes upon whose pages were recorded the knowledge and beauty of Běiměizhōu civilization at its height.

"Books."

"Books," Wu repeated.

The boy emerged from the bushes a split second after Wu launched the projectile. Eyes wide, he instinctively ducked. The stone whizzed over his head, striking the trunk of a tree just behind him.

"What are you doing?" shouted the boy indignantly.

Wu grabbed another stone and reloaded his slingshot, drawing back the band and keeping it trained on the stranger.

The pale, skinny boy looked to be about Wu's age. With the exception of his short curly brown hair, Wu could have been looking at a reflection.

"What are *you* doing?" Wu challenged. He studied the stranger. The boy, though as emaciated as he was, did not slur his words, and he stood firm without the jerky twitches that were the stigmata of those who consumed the flesh of others.

"Are you a Jiangshi?" Wu asked rhetorically.

"Are *you* a Jiangshi?" the boy echoed in retort.

Slowly, Wu lowered his slingshot. "I am Wu."

"I'm Vancott," the boy said. He pointed at the crumbling chimney. "What's that ruin?"

Vancott walked up the shallow hill to join Wu, and the boys found themselves looking at the slab and handle in the ground. They took hold of the handle together and managed to lift the grey slab. Putting the lid aside, they went to the opening and peered down into the darkness.

Wu squinted. "Something's in there!"

A very faint odour wafted out of the opening. Vancott sniffed.

Recognition came to both of them at the same time.

"Stupid!" Vancott shoved Wu, sending him sprawling to the ground. "This is—"

"Old shit and piss," Wu said. He remembered his mother's words. "Skeptic tank."

The two boys sat silently, pondering their next move.

Suddenly, a flock of dark birds took flight from the trees, swirling noisily into the sky. Wu and Vancott turned.

There was a rustling in the bushes.

Vancott grabbed Wu's arm. "I saw a Jiangshi today!"

Wu shot Vancott a fearful glance. "I saw a Jiangshi too," he hissed. "On the road."

The boys looked about, knowing they were badly exposed atop the shallow hill. At once, the same desperate idea occurred to both. They got up quickly.

Vancott slid the concrete lid partially over the opening, while Wu gathered up some dead leaves and twigs and piled them on top. It wasn't much in the way of camouflage, but it was better than nothing. Vancott squeezed inside first, followed by Wu. With great effort, they managed to get the lid almost closed except for a thin sliver.

Wu peered through the narrow slit, and before long saw the monster stumble out of the woods. The gangly, twitching figure, no longer really human, was the same one Wu had seen on the road.

Quietly, the boys drew the lid fully closed, and darkness enveloped them.

Wu and Vancott waited silently in the musty dark, for a sound, a voice, a sign . . . something.

They were sitting on a pile of flat rectangular objects. Wu felt around with his hands. The objects were all roughly the same shape but in different sizes. He remembered seeing something when they first opened the lid, but without light he could do nothing to identify the objects even whilst sitting amongst them.

Breathing was difficult, and the boys were getting sleepy. The stale air would not sustain them much longer.

Cautiously, they pushed the lid and opened up a small crack to look around. The brief inrush of fresh air hit their lungs with an almost icy sharpness, and it took all of Wu's willpower to not dash out right away.

Finally, they pushed the lid all the way open and climbed out. Wu moved to follow, but on sudden impulse grabbed one of the rectangular objects on his way up. Outside, the boys collapsed onto the sweet long grass of the shallow hill, lying on their backs, lungs heaving as they gulped fresh air, their mouths open and trembling like those of fish out of water.

After a long moment of rest, Wu rolled onto his side and saw the flat rectangular object lying on the grass. He sat up and took it with both hands, bringing it up to his eyes.

Wu stared at the object for a moment before recognizing it. "A book!"

"What?" Vancott asked.

Wu turned the book about, examining it from all sides.

It was brownish-black in colour and sealed in a transparent pouch, probably made of the material that Wu's mother had called plastic. A hard seam ran along one side. Wu examined the seam and eventually figured out how to pull the pouch open. There was a faint medicinal smell, and clumps of a white powder fell out.

With deliberate care, Wu reverently extracted the book from the plastic pouch. There were symbols on the cover that he recognized as words, but like all contemporary teenagers he didn't read. He slowly flipped through the yellowish pages, each dense with indecipherable text.

"What is it?" Vancott asked again.

"A book," Wu repeated. "From the old world, before the Fall."

Vancott's eyes widened.

Wu was illiterate, not stupid. He had the sense to know, on an instinctive level, the importance of what he and Vancott had found. Somebody had done this on purpose, creating an improvised library—a túshūguǎn—either before or shortly after the Fall, in the hope that someone like Wu might find the treasure.

Wu put the book back into the pouch and resealed it. The boys covered up the hatch again with leaves and twigs before setting off. They would need to find a person who could read.

Wu and Vancott wandered aimlessly for days. Sometimes, they would walk for hours in one direction when Vancott would suddenly change his mind, and then they would turn about and retrace their steps. On other occasions, they seemed to be walking in circles. Wu began to doubt whether Vancott had any idea where they were going.

Beside him, Wu heard Vancott's stomach growl. His companion always seemed to be hungry. For such a thin little guy, he ate an awful lot. Not for the first time, Wu wondered how Vancott had managed to survive on his own for this long.

A feral rakunk bounded out of some shrubbery a short distance ahead. Vancott had seen the black masked fluffy tailed animal first, putting out his hand to stop Wu and signaling for silence. If nothing else, Wu was grateful for Vancott's sharp eyes. His companion may eat too much food, but at least he was good at spotting it.

Wu slowly knelt to pick up a rock, quietly pulling out his slingshot at the same time. He steadied himself, drew back the band, took aim, and fired.

Killing the game turned out to be the easy part. Starting the fire to cook it proved much more difficult. It had rained earlier in the day, and the boys had trouble finding dry grass and leaves for tinder. More than once, Wu saw Vancott eyeing the book. He pulled it closer.

Night had fallen by the time they got the fire going and cooked the rakunk. In the chilly dark, Wu and Vancott managed to find some comfort in the warming flames and meat. When they had finished eating, they lay on their backs and gazed up at the twinkling tapestry of stars above. Wu thought about his mother's stories of people in flying machines, soaring amongst the clouds and even out to the dark heavens beyond.

Wu closed his eyes, and as sleep came, the book slipped quietly from his arms and fell to the ground.

He dreamed.

It was a strange dream, the kind Wu knew was only a dream even while he was dreaming it, because he was seeing things that he could not possibly have known or remembered. He was in a vast cavern, within which were rows upon rows of shelves, each packed end-to-end with books. The volumes were all of different sizes, thicknesses and colours, with incomprehensible words along the spines. There must have been hundreds, if not thousands of books, stretching further into the depths of the cavern than Wu could see.

He reached out to a book at random and tried to take it off the shelf. The book came out about two-thirds of the way and then abruptly jammed.

Wu pulled harder, to no effect. He grabbed the book with both hands and yanked with all his strength.

The entire bookshelf began to fall towards him.

Wu let go of the book and stepped back. The bookshelf was still falling.

Walking backwards, he tried to quicken his pace. He looked up, and saw that the bookshelf appeared to be of infinite height, stretching upwards without end. There was nothing he could do to avoid getting crushed.

The bookshelf came down.

There was a scream.

Wu woke with a start. The scream had not been his.

Beside the smoldering remnants of the fire, Vancott was locked in a desperate struggle with a monster. His attacker had pinned him to the ground. Vancott squirmed, kicked, and punched, frantically trying to free himself. The Jiangshi was as emaciated as the boys, but he was taller and armed with two lethal weapons—madness and a knife.

Wu was frozen in momentary fear. He tried to yell, but no words came.

The Jiangshi brought the knife down—once, twice . . .

Before there was a third stroke, Wu sprang forth and launched himself at the monster. He ran into the Jiangshi's back and pounded the smelly, sore-ridden flesh with both fists. The Jiangshi grunted and took a swing, sending Wu sprawling to the ground.

Lying on his back, Wu looked up at the looming monster's gnarled, weathered face with its long, filthy tangled hair, twitching unfocused eyes and rotting yellow-brown teeth. Wu backed away on his elbows like a crab.

He hit something on the ground.

The Jiangshi raised his knife to strike.

Wu grabbed the rectangular object and brought it up with both hands. The knife plunged into the book, piercing it from cover to cover, its point protruding out the back.

Grunting, the Jiangshi twisted and pulled on the knife, finally extracting it from the book but stumbling backwards a few steps.

Wu threw the damaged book at the Jiangshi, hitting the monster on the side of the head. Already off balance, the Jiangshi fell onto his haunches. It didn't take long for the monster to get up again, but the delay gave Wu just enough time to load his slingshot and fire.

The mote scored a direct hit into the Jiangshi's left eye.

Screaming and clutching the bleeding eye with both hands, the Jiangshi dropped to the ground. The monster rolled side to side, shrieking and twitching uncontrollably as blood and vitreous fluid oozed between his fingers.

Wu got up and walked over to where Vancott's lifeless body lay in a pool of his own blood. Vancott was on his back, mouth and eyes still wide open. In silence, Wu simply stared at his dead companion with a lack of emotion that would have shocked his pre-Fall ancestors. He left Vancott where he lay, picked up the book, and simply walked away.

Behind him, the Jiangshi's screams went on and on, the cries of a wounded animal. Wu kept walking, book in hand, until he could not hear the inhuman noises anymore.

"I am sorry about your friend," Fénshū said when Wu finished his story.

Wu said nothing more.

"You are a brave young man," she continued, "and extremely lucky as well. We are the first expedition to work in the Vancouver ruins for years, and it is only possible because we were able afford the armed guards to protect us from the Jiangshis." She put the book on the ground. "Did you see anything else down in that . . . um, 'skeptic' tank?"

The boy fell unhelpfully silent, once again.

A young woman entered the tent, carrying a small bundle of clothes.

Fénshū pointed. "Wu, please go with my colleague. She will give you some food. You need to rest, and when you are better, we will need you to take us back to this place you found. Do you understand?"

Wu nodded.

"Gēn wǒ lái," the young woman said, taking Wu's hand and leading him out of the tent.

Fénshū waited a moment, then picked up the book and took it outside. Near the centre of the expedition encampment, a small fire burned. She walked towards the campfire, and without a second thought, casually tossed the book into the flames.

The plastic wrap melted quickly, evaporating like water on a hot plate. Then the flames attacked the book itself, consuming it from the outside edges in. The words on the cover—A Novel, *Oryx and Crake*, Margaret Atwood—were legible for a few moments until the dust jacket blackened and crumbled away. Acrid smoke billowed briefly when the white residue ignited, causing Fénshū to cough and blink. The spine was the last to endure, but eventually it too yielded to the flames.

When the book had been reduced to ash, Fénshū returned to the tent and settled back in her chair. Pre-Fall Běiměizhōu texts were of academic interest and had some nominal value on the antiquities market, but her backers in Běijīng and Clavius had little interest in them. Excavating the Vancouver II site was a costly and very risky venture. Her expedition would need to find something of much greater value, and soon. The boy would take them back to the other site. For her sake—and to some degree, the boy's—she truly hoped that artifacts of real value were still out there, somewhere in the ruins of the old shit and piss.

The Lark, The Peat, The Star, and Our Time

NEILE GRAHAM

And a lark flashed a needle across the west
And we spread a thousand peats
Between one summer star
And the black chaos of fire at the earth's centre.
                                    —*George Mackay Brown*

It was the year of no summer,
when it hid under banks of rain, ducked
behind fog, dashed across the road
in front of us, rolled under a car and out
the other side, its face a flash in a side mirror,
flirting for our notice, as though a test
of our worthiness. We weren't. Worthy that is.
We gave up on it, threw ourselves on autumn's
mercies, deciding the metallic hint of frost was best.
And a lark flashed a needle across the west.

We froze in place. It was the sign we needed:
a sunrise bird, sewing the sky, sowing winter
like a seed in our hearts where it might sprout
and flourish, thicken and keep us chilled
through all the long and glorious nights.
We weren't heroes, we were cheats:
we thought we were big enough to revel in it.
We thought we were brave and brazen.
We weren't. We huddled in our solstice retreats
And we spread a thousand peats

to warm our hearts. And they did. We admitted it.
So spring took pity on us. Raised its head above
our bleak horizon. Thawed playgrounds into blossoming.
Warmed us into fields worth plowing, planting,
all the works of hope, made us truly brave.
Rained and shone into us. Our courages are
more humble now, but no less than the first leaf
tenderly unfurling, spreading its fingers to reach
the first glinting bar of summer sun, just that far
Between one summer star

and the next, the next, and the next, how we
learned to flourish, to abound, to be unbound,
to stop counting each minute and to hold our hands
out to the sun, letting it dry and freckle our skins.
Allowing ourselves touch the minutes like ball bearings
we could let fall one by one, so we could enter
each day and leave it tasted, noted, changed
by our passage. Enjoy that our explorations were
no longer those of children, time was our mentor
And the black chaos of fire at the earth's centre.

Bamboozled

KELLEY ARMSTRONG

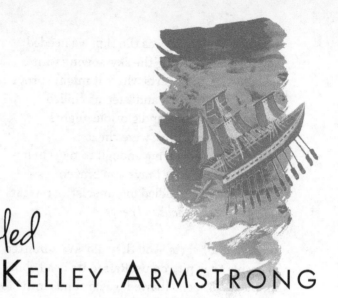

Dakota Territory, 1877

"Are you sure she can do it?" the boy asked Nate as he watered their trio of horses.

Lily could have pointed out that she was standing right beside him and had both a name and ears. But she knew the boy—Will—wasn't trying to be rude; he was simply like most of the young men they recruited: rarely set foot off his family homestead, rarely seen womenfolk other than his momma and sisters. And frontier mommas and sisters did not look like Lily.

Even now, as Will talked about her, he couldn't look her way—as if merely to glimpse her might damn his mortal soul. Lily could point out that his soul ought to be a lot more worried about the thieving that was coming, but to a boy like Will, that was part of life. Pretty girls with painted faces were not.

Lily's face was, of course, not painted right now. She was dressed in breeches, boots, and an overcoat, with her hair pushed up under her hat. It didn't matter. Will still wouldn't look.

"Can she do it?" he asked again. "I mean no offense—"

"Then stop giving it," Nate growled.

Lily noticed a cloud of dust cresting the rise beside them. "I do believe my wardrobe has arrived."

Emmett and Levi rode up, their horses run hard, flanks heaving. They had arranged to meet at midday and the sun had passed its zenith a while back.

"Had some difficulties," Emmett said as he nudged his horse to water.

"That it?" Nate pointed at the wrapped parcel behind Levi's saddle. When Levi nodded, Nate took it and said to Lily, "Come on."

Lily let Nate lead her behind an outcropping of rock. Emmett and Levi knew better than to sneak a look while she was dressing, and Lily was quite certain Will wouldn't dare, but Nate believed in coppering his bets. Otherwise, things would get messy. Nate didn't take kindly to trespass of any sort.

"We cutting the boy loose after the job?" he asked as they walked.

She nodded. "That's best. It's not working out. You promised Wilcox you'd try him. You did."

Nate grunted and handed her the parcel. As she untied it, she snuck a peek at him. Six feet tall. Well built. Rough featured, but not in a way that was displeasing, at least not to her. What she noticed most, though, was what she'd noticed about Nate from the start: the uncanny way he carried himself. When he moved, he was like a catamount on the prowl. Yet most of the time he wasn't moving at all, standing so still he seemed a statue, his gaze scanning the landscape.

It wasn't natural, that complete stillness, that constant alertness. She wondered why others never thought it peculiar. She had right from that first time, seeing him across the saloon. He'd noticed her, too, but not in the way men usually did. He'd only stared, no expression, no reaction. Yet his gaze hadn't left her as she'd taken a table with the rest of her acting troupe.

The trouble had begun later that evening, when a gambler made the mistake of equating actresses with whores. It was a common misconception. Lily couldn't even properly blame the man, considering that her two companions had already accepted paid invitations. The acting life required a second income; Lily made hers with light fingers.

She'd told the gambler she wasn't for sale, but he'd thought she was only haggling. That was when Nate had come over. He'd asked the gambler to let Lily be. When the man laughed, Nate fixed him with a stare as cold as a Nebraska winter. It hadn't taken long for the gambler's nerve to crack. He'd gone for his Colt; Nate broke his arm. Just like that. Lily saw the gambler reach for his piece and then he was screaming like a banshee, his arm snapped, bone sticking out, blood gushing. That's when she realized Nate wasn't quite human.

Now Nate turned his gaze on Lily as she undressed. Lily was used to men staring at her. They'd been doing it since she was fourteen, which was when she discovered it was so much easier to pick a man's pocket if he was gaping at her bosom. Nate wasn't like that. He gazed at her with what seemed like his usual expressionless stare, but Lily had learned to read deeper, and what she saw there now was hunger. He didn't move, though, not until she adjusted the dress and twirled around.

"How do I look?" she asked.

Nate growled an answer and, before she could blink, he was on her, one hand behind her head, the other at her rear as he pulled her into a deep kiss.

"I really ought not to have bothered putting on the dress," she said as she broke for air.

Nate chuckled and hoisted her onto the nearby rocks.

They rode into town after sundown. That was best. There were many variations on their game, but in each they'd learned the value of a late approach. By morning, the town would be buzzing with rumours of the party that arrived under the cover of night. A slip of a girl, bundled in an overcoat but riding a fine horse and wearing a fine dress. A proper young lady, escorted by a surly uncle and three young gunmen.

As the day passed, the story grew. The girl's uncle kept her under close watch at the inn, but they'd had to venture out, as she was in need of a new dress. And what a pretty thing she was, with yellow hair, green eyes, and the sweetest French accent.

The girl was shy, the uncle taciturn, and no one in town learned much from either, but the young fellows with them were far more talkative, especially after a drink or two. They said the girl came from New Orleans. Her parents were in California, expanding their empire. Shipping or railroad, no one was quite sure which, but they were powerfully flush. A suitor waited in California, too. A rich man. Very old, nearing sixty. The uncle was taking the girl to her parents and her fiancé and her new life. They'd been diverted here by news of Indian trouble and were waiting until the army had it in hand. Until then, the party would pass the time in their little town.

Lily's mark came at dinner. It was earlier than they'd expected—most men didn't like to seem eager. But it was said that John Anderson was keen to wed. Or wed again, having recently lost his young wife in a tragic accident. It was also said that "accident" might not have been quite the proper word to use. Anderson hadn't been as pleased with his bride as he'd hoped. Her daguerreotype had sorely misrepresented her and she had not cared for ranch life. She'd also objected to her husband's ongoing association with the town's whores and his penchant for bringing them home. Women could be quite unreasonable about such things. So Mrs. Anderson had perished and her grieving husband was impatient for a new bride.

Lily and Nate were dining at the inn. They'd barely taken their seats when Nate made a noise deep in his throat, too low for others to hear. He kept his attention on the wall-posted menu while Lily glanced over to watch their mark stroll through the door. They said John Anderson was a handsome man, but she couldn't see it. Or perhaps it was simply everything else she'd heard about him that tarnished her opinion. She did, however, watch him until he looked squarely in her direction. Then her gaze darted away as she clutched her napkin and cast nervous glances at her "uncle."

Anderson stopped at their table, took off his hat with a flourish and introduced himself. Gaze lowered, Lily waited for her uncle to reciprocate. He didn't.

"I see that you have not yet begun to dine," Anderson said after an awkward silence. "May I invite you both to join me at my table?"

"No," Nate said.

"Does that mean I may not ask or you will not join me?"

Anderson's lips curved in the kind of smile that would warn another man off. Nate only stared at him.

"No."

"All right then. May I ask—?"

"No."

Lily simpered and shot looks at Anderson, her eyes pleading with him to excuse her uncle's behaviour.

"I see," Anderson said. "Well, then, perhaps I'll have the pleasure of seeing you both around town."

Nate's answering snort said, "The hell you will." Anderson nodded stiffly and retreated to his table.

They had been in town for nearly a fortnight. During the course of it, Lily found increasingly more opportunities to see John Anderson. It was a difficult wooing with her uncle so determined to keep the rancher away, but they met in furtive assignations that grew ever more daring until Anderson finally extended the required invitation to visit him at home. Not that he was quite so forward. He simply said he had a hound dog with pups that would surely delight Lily and he wished for her to see them. Naturally, it would have to be at night—*late* at night, after her uncle was abed. But Anderson would send his foreman to accompany her so she would be safe. At least until she arrived.

And so the foreman—a man named Stewart—arrived at the appointed hour of midnight. Lily informed him that her uncle was deeply asleep, having been aided by a draught of laudanum. They set off into the night.

Nate and the boys followed.

Lily slowed outside the big ranch house and looked about nervously.

"It is dreadfully dark, monsieur," she said.

"Mr. Anderson is right there, miss." Stewart pointed at the lit front window. "Waiting in the parlour."

She gave a sheepish smile. "I am sorry to be such a child. I have not visited a man's home without an escort." She dipped her gaze. "And I have *never* visited at night."

"There's nothing to worry about, miss. Mr. Anderson is a proper gentleman. You have my word on that."

Lily continued to stall. Nate insisted on scouting before she ventured inside. Finally, she caught sight of Nate's distant figure, poised in the side yard, gazing about, face lifting slightly to sniff the breeze. He motioned to say that he'd circled the homestead and all was well.

"I am ready to go in, monsieur," she murmured to Stewart, and he took her up to the front door.

An hour later, Anderson lay passed out on the parlour settee. He looked very peaceful, Lily thought as she knelt beside him. He would not be nearly so happy when he woke, but even without his odious reputation, Lily would not have regretted bamboozling him. Men like Anderson were no better than bunko artists themselves—seducing young women in the expectation the ruined girl would be rejected by her suitor and then she, and her inheritance, would be handed to him by parents hoping to make the best of a bad situation. It proved such men were not as worldly as they believed or they would know it was a ruse unlikely to succeed. This was not English society where one eager bride could easily be exchanged for another. Out on the frontier, a good woman was like a fine horse or pair of boots: you hoped they'd be pleasing and well-formed, but you expected they'd been used a time or two, which only saved the fuss of breaking them in.

Anderson hadn't even won a flash of bared ankle. Lily was adept at the art of the tease, a skill she'd learned as an actress. In cities, she was expected to perform in actual plays, but out in the Territories, men just came to see pretty girls in pretty dresses teasing and dancing and warbling on stage.

Other women who worked this game would be required to lie with the mark, even if she had a beau in the gang. Out here, a girl was lucky if her lover didn't toss her garter onto the poker table and give her away for a night when his luck soured. With Nate, Lily didn't need to worry about that.

Once she'd confirmed that Anderson was out cold, she dashed through the house to be sure it was empty. When she'd arrived, she had Anderson take her on a tour of his "lovely home." He'd dismissed the help, as men usually did. She still checked, in case a maid or hired hand had snuck in the back. The house was clear.

Lily brought Nate and the boys in and gave them quick instructions on where to find the best goods. Emmett and Levi needed little guidance and Will would simply follow them. The five worked together on the parlour and adjoining rooms. Then Nate told the boys he was taking Lily outside to "scout for trouble." Will looked confused. Levi smiled and shook his head. Emmett winked and told Nate to have fun. Nate grabbed a parcel he'd left by the door and off they went.

Naturally, Nate and Lily were not heading outside to scout. This, too, was part of the routine, and Emmett and Levi seemed to think it was quite reasonable that the boss would whisk his girl off mid-job for a roll in the hay barn. After all, they'd been forced to sleep apart for a fortnight now. Could anyone blame him? Well, yes, they could, but the boys never seemed to realize it was the least peculiar. With Nate, they were accustomed to peculiar.

"Did it go all right?" he asked as they slipped around the house.

Obviously it had, if Anderson was asleep and the boys were emptying the home, but Lily knew that wasn't what Nate meant. "He didn't lay a finger on me."

"Good."

As Lily walked, she unfastened her dress, keeping to the shadows of the house. That took a while, and she didn't stop moving until she had to wriggle out of it. She glanced over to see Nate watching her.

"No," she said, waggling her finger.

He growled deep in his throat. She laughed and took the parcel from his arm.

"Don't grumble," she said. "You know it's better if we wait."

Another soft growl, this one less complaint than agreement. She laughed again and tugged on her breeches, shirt, and boots. Her pistol was there, too—a little derringer that tucked neatly under a shirt or a dress.

"Did you find him?" she asked when she'd finished.

"Out back. Farthest building from the house."

She smiled. "That ought to make it easy."

Lily peered through the open window. Stewart was at his kitchen table, playing solitaire while drinking whiskey straight from the bottle.

Growing up in New Orleans, Lily had been subjected to more church-going than any child ought to be, which had much to do with her running off at fourteen. Too many gospel mill lessons pounded in with a strap. From what she'd learned there, the nature of demons was quite clear. They were hideous beasts with wings and scales and horns. They did not, in short, look like Theodore Stewart. But as she'd come to understand, most church lessons were less than useful in the real world.

Stewart was a demon. Or a half-demon, fathered by one of those unholy beasts whom, Lily was quite sure, hadn't borne scales and horns when he seduced Stewart's momma. Stewart had, however, inherited his father's predilection for hell-raising, which was why they were there.

While their thieving provided a handsome income, it was merely a front. The real prize sat at that table, drinking himself to sleep. This was the world Nate had introduced her to, one filled with creatures that the church deemed "monstrous aberrations." Half-demons, witches, sorcerers, vampires, werewolves, and others. Monsters? Perhaps. Monstrous? She glanced at Nate, peering through the window, sharp gaze assessing his prey. No, not always. But they did cause trouble with somewhat more regularity than average folk, which meant there were plenty with a price on their heads, like Stewart.

Nate leaned over and whispered into her ear, so Stewart couldn't hear through the open window.

"I'll go in here. Can you take the front?"

She nodded.

"Be careful," he murmured.

She nodded again, but there was rarely any need for her to be overly cautious. While she had starred in the opening acts of this performance, Nate took that part now. Like the understudy for an actor who never took sick, Lily's new role was rather dull. In all their jobs together, only once had a mark even noticed Nate, and that was only due to an unfortunately placed looking glass. Even then, Nate had taken their mark down before he reached the door.

Lily still undertook her role with caution, derringer in hand as she crept around the tiny house to the front door. There she found a suitably shadowy place to wait.

When she heard a faint noise to her left, she wheeled and swung her pistol up, her eyes narrowing as she strained to see—

Cold metal touched the back of her neck. "Don't move."

She calmly assessed the voice. Did it sound firm? Confident? Or did it waver slightly, suggesting a man uncomfortable with pointing a gun at a girl of twenty? And perhaps even less comfortable with the prospect of pulling the trigger.

"Lower the gun," he said.

She recognized the voice now, though the tone was not one she'd ever heard him use. She cursed herself—and Nate—under her breath.

"Will?" she said.

"I told you to lower—"

"Please don't hurt me, Will." She raised her voice a little, knowing Nate's ace hearing would pick it up. "If you want a bigger share, I'm sure we can manage it. P-please don't—"

He kicked her legs out from under her. She tried to twist as she fell, but he'd caught her by surprise. Will grabbed her gun arm. Before she could throw him off, his fingers burned so hot she gasped as agony ripped through her forearm and Will plucked the derringer from her grasp.

So Will was a fire demon, like Stewart. They'd been euchred.

"William!" a voice called from the cabin. "Bring her in."

Will grabbed Lily by the hair and dragged her to the cabin door. He pulled it open and shoved her through, his gun at her neck.

Nate and Stewart faced off inside. Nate glanced at Lily. Then he looked away.

"Seems we have your girl," Stewart said.

Nate grunted.

"William here tells me you're fond of her," Stewart continued. "That you would, I presume, not wish to see any harm befall her."

Another grunt.

"I'll take that as a yes. Now, as I'm sure you know, there's many a man who'd pay handsomely to mount Nathaniel Cooper's head on his wall. But I have a buyer who'd prefer you alive. He's quite interested in your special skills. There aren't nearly enough of your kind out here. So here's what I'll do. You come with me and we'll take the girl, too. None of my men will harm her. And, yes, I have men. Or half-men, half-demon." Stewart raised his voice. "Bob? Jesse?"

Two answering shouts came from outside. Nate took advantage of the pause to glance at Lily again. She held his gaze before he turned away.

Stewart continued, "As you see, there is little sense in running, although I'm quite certain you won't attempt it, so long as we have your pretty mate—"

Nate spun and fired . . . right at Lily's chest. She managed only a strangled gasp of shock before slumping to the floor.

Theodore Stewart stared down at the girl's body, her shirt bloody, limbs akimbo, sightless eyes staring up.

In the world of supernaturals, it was generally accepted that Nathaniel Cooper was a bastard. That was true of most of his breed—violent, unsociable loners. But even among them, Cooper was renowned as a heartless son of a whore. Still, William had said he was fond of the girl. *Very* fond of her.

Apparently, William had been mistaken.

Stewart crouched to close the girl's eyes. He ought to have foreseen this. William was but a boy and didn't understand the ways of men. And yet Stewart had still been caught unaware by Cooper's move, which was exactly what the bastard intended. He'd killed the girl and then fired off a second round at Stewart as he bolted out the door.

As Stewart rose, the door banged open and William strode in.

"You get him?" Stewart asked.

"Not yet. Jesse and Bob are tracking him. I reckoned I ought to make sure he didn't circle back and try to collect on his bounty." William walked to the girl. "Damnation. She was a pretty painted cat. I was really hoping to get a poke." He nudged the girl's arm with his boot. Then he bent and touched it. "She's still warm." His gaze traveled over the body. "You think it'd be all right if I—"

"No. Get outside and scout."

Stewart waited until William left. Then he looked down at the girl. The boy was right. She was finer than anything he'd seen in a while.

He fingered the bottom of her shirt. He wouldn't do *that*, of course. That was disgusting. But there was nothing wrong with taking a look.

Stewart unfastened her bottom button and then the next one, slowly peeling back her shirt. Out of the corner of his eyes, he caught a movement, but before he could lift his head, a hand grabbed him by the throat and threw him across the room.

Lily reflected that this was perhaps not the most opportune moment to end her performance. Yet she wasn't about to play dead while he disrobed her.

Her side blazed as she sprang to her feet. Bullets hurt, no matter how good a shot Nate was and how careful he'd been to hit her where there wasn't risk of serious injury. Her eyes stung, too, from staring at the ceiling until Stewart had done the Christian thing and closed her eyelids. She supposed she ought to have shut them herself, but she knew that open eyes would be the most damning proof of her death, and she was a fine enough actress to manage it.

Stewart was still lying on the floor, dazed, trying to figure out how he'd arrived there, clear across the room. When he saw Lily coming at him, he only gaped.

Lily yanked Stewart's gun from his holster and tossed it aside. Only then did Stewart snap out of it. He caught her by the arm, his fingers flaring red-hot, fresh pain scorching through her already-burned arm. She ignored it and grabbed him by the neck. His eyes bulged as she squeezed. They bulged even more as her hand began to change, palm roughening, nails turning into thick claws.

"You didn't expect this?" she said as she lifted him from the floor. "You *did* call me his mate."

"No. You can't be—"

"Do you smell that?" Lily turned her face, nose lifting. "I do believe we're about to have company."

The door flew open and Will stumbled in.

"Cooper," he said, panting. "It's Cooper. He's . . ."

He saw them, her hand around Stewart's throat. His mouth worked. He had one hand still on the door. Then it crashed open, sending Will scrambling out of the way as a massive wolf charged in. The beast's nostrils flared. Its gaze swung to Lily. Then, with a grunt, the beast tore after Will as he dashed for Stewart's gun, his own obviously lost.

Will made it halfway across the room before the wolf leaped on him. He hit the floor and rolled onto his back. His hands shot up, fingers blazing. The wolf's jaws swung down and ripped out his throat.

"*No*," Stewart whispered as Will's life's blood spurted onto the floorboards. His gaze shifted to Lily. "I have money."

"And so will we, when we collect the bounty on you."

"Whatever they said I did, it isn't true. I have enemies. Lying sons of whores—"

"A Kansas wagon train two years back," she said. "A train full of settlers massacred and left for the buzzards, after your gang had some sport with the womenfolk."

"I . . . Wagon train? No. That wasn't . . ." He trailed off. "I have money. More than any bounty—"

"I'll take the bounty," she said and snapped his neck.

"Stop grumbling," Lily said as Nate daubed her bullet wound with a wet cloth. "I told you to shoot me."

Which she had, mouthing it when he'd glanced at her during the standoff. That did not, she understood, make him feel any better about the situation.

"It passed clean through," she said. "We heal quickly. I won't want to shift for a few days, but I'll be fine otherwise."

He still grumbled. She leaned forward and brushed her lips across his forehead.

"I need to be more careful," he said.

"We both will be."

"That boy . . ." A growl as he glanced at Will's body. "I ought not to have been duped."

"We both were. We'll have a talk with Wilcox about this. He was the one who asked us to take the boy. And he was the one who set us on Stewart."

Another growl.

"We'll have satisfaction," Lily murmured. "In the meantime, presuming those half-demons were from Stewart's old gang, we ought to be able to collect bounties on them, too."

Nate grunted. The prospect, she knew, did not cheer him immediately, but it would, after she'd recovered and he'd finished chastising himself for letting them be bamboozled.

"You did well," he said as he dressed her wound.

"I've not forgotten how to act," she said with a smile. "And you gave me all the other skills I required."

It had taken work to convince him to share his curse with her. Eventually, he'd come to realize that the only way a werewolf's mate could be safe was if she was truly his mate. The process, as he'd warned, had not been easy. The life, too, was not easy. But she would never regret it. Lily knew what she wanted—the man, the life, the person she wanted to be. And she had it. All of it.

"We ought to hurry," she said. "The boys will be waiting back at the inn by now." She paused. "Do you think they heard anything before they left?"

Nate snorted.

Lily laughed. "Yes, they're not the cleverest of lads. Which is the way we like them." She got to her feet. "Let me find a clean shirt."

She looked at him, still naked after shifting back from wolf form. "And we'd best find your clothing. Although . . ." Her gaze traveled down his body. "The boys *are* very patient. I suppose they wouldn't mind waiting a mite longer."

From Stone and Bone, From Earth and Sky
A.C. WISE

I. The Magician

"What do you think?" the Old Man asks, turning my question back at me. He taps the tarot card with one finger, nail tobacco-yellow and tipped in a crescent moon of dirt. "Sacred or profane? Sinner or Saint?"

He pushes the card closer as if I haven't already looked my fill. The photograph pasted to the board shows the woman whose story I've come to gather—Erzebetta, no last name—the Carnival Queen. Feathers ring her collar and rise from her hair. There are shadows around her head, what could be smudges on the photograph, but distinctly in the shape of feathers, beaks, and the blur of wings.

The photograph is worn, edges made velvet-soft from handling, lightning-struck with pale creases. Even faded, Erzebetta's expression is defiant, head held high. Yes. A queen. A goddess even.

I look up to catch the Old Man grinning. Light slides through his eyes, winking without lowering a lid. It's as if he's read my mind and seen it made up before I even talk to the list of people he's given me. My neck prickles, and I try not to blush.

"I'm just here to write a book, sir," I say.

"But you must have an opinion, hey? It's been nearly a month since the conflagration. Plenty of time for rumour to spread, especially with tongues wagging right from the start."

I shake my head, but it's answer enough for him. He leans back, lanky frame barely contained by the whole of his smoke-stained trailer, crowded with the ghosts of cigarettes past.

"So, you have your list," he says, expectant weight in the words.

"Sorry. I almost forgot. The smokes you asked for." I hold out four cigarettes fished from my shirt pocket. "Are you sure you wouldn't rather have the whole pack?"

"Four will do." He plucks them from my hand one by one, pushes Erzebetta's picture out of the way, and lays them out in a row. He takes a penknife from his pocket and a packet of rolling papers.

"What about the girls?" I ask. "I don't see any of their names on the list."

"Most of them ran off after the troubles. Can't blame them, me. Besides, a man like you doesn't want the chatter of a bunch of silly birds cluttering up his book."

I open my mouth to answer, but the movement of his hands catches my attention, though I swear I never took my eyes off them for more than a second as he slit each of my four cigarettes down the middle and re-rolled their contents in his own papers. The battered table is lined with sixteen cigarettes, sixteen dead soldiers, shroud-wrapped and waiting their burial day.

"Good trick, hey?" He looks up. For a brief moment, his eyes are gold. It must be the light, or all the smoke—curing the Old Man in his trailer, like dried meat and old leather.

At the thought, I can't help another glance at the Old Man's handiwork, mounted on the walls, all the other eyes watching me—The Fiji Mermaid, the Jackalope, the two-headed calf, the werewolf pup, and even a demon or two. The Old Man swears his are the originals, he gave Barnum the idea.

"Smoke?" he offers. I shake my head.

He shrugs, sticks the cigarette in the corner of his mouth and produces a strike box of matches seemingly from thin air. There's a lewd picture of a woman on the top that looks stuck there by hand. The Old Man breathes out, adding more smoke ghosts to the wall. The smell is cloves and cinnamon, nothing that was in the cigarettes I gave him. He smiles slow this time, gaze half-lidded, which only makes him seem more watchful.

"So," he says, and taps the picture again. "I suppose you want to hear about the day Erzebetta fell from the sky?"

II. The High Priestess

Say what you want, but I'm no fool, me. Except when I am, but that's another tale and nothing you need worry yourself with just yet.

I know when trouble's coming. I can feel it like a wind up my tail. That night, it came in a storm, all done up in lightning and thunder. So I set myself up with a smoke, poured a little whiskey in my tea, and stood right in my trailer door to see what the howling night would bring.

That's how I was the first to see her when she fell out of the sky.

She was a sight, right enough, tumbling ass over teakettle into the mess of mud outside my trailer. If I hadn't seen her fall, I would have sworn on my own mother's grave she was nothing but a pile of old rags being picked over by birds. I even heard those birds shriek just before she stood up to show she was a woman, not a bundle of cloth and wings.

Even with her boot-heels sunk deep in the dirt, and mud spattered all up her legs, even wearing scarce more than silk panties, with her skirt bunched behind her, a froth of black fabric just as pretty as a peacock's tail, dragging down in the muck, she lifted her chin and glared right at me like I was the one trespassing. Feathers peeked out from her corset, and only a fool would think they grew right out of her skin, despite the tricks the lightning played. There were feathers in her hair, too, all draggled by the rain. Crow, they were, black as her eyes, which wept more black where her make-up ran. Only thing about her not black or mud spattered were her teeth. They were white as milk and sharp as anything when she showed them to speak.

"Old Man. Aren't you going to invite me in?"

What does a body say to a thing like that? I did the charitable thing, me. No sense giving trouble anger for fuel on top of everything else. I let her track mud all over my floors, let her trail her fingers over my things, like she was marking me by what I owned. I poured her whiskey, which she took without tea. I let her pace round and round my trailer, and never said a word aloud as to how she smelled of life and death, sex and blood.

"Do you know who I am?" she said at last.

Her eyes were fierce, all black lightning and wicked as the storm. I could see by their look she wanted me whipped, tail tucked between my legs and all. She wanted my belly, rolled for her wicked-sharp teeth, or failing that, my throat.

But I'm in no hurry to see my own demise, me, and"I think I got a fair idea," says I to her, stalling for time.

I gave her a look like maybe I was trying to place where I'd seen her before. I knew exactly who she was, but I figured there was no sense in showing my hand too soon. By the look she gave me right back, I wasn't fooling her. Erzebetta wasn't like me. She was in a rush to put her cards on the table and see if I'd fold from the blow.

"Well then, *Dad*," she says. "Since we got a lot of catching up to do and I'm going to be around for a while, why don't you start by offering me a job?"

III. The Empress

Snips, they call me. Ain't my real name, but I reckon you guessed that already, what with your book smarts and all. And I don't guess you want to hear about me or what name my mama gave me. It's no account, like me, which is what Daddy always said about me, so much I almost thought *that* might be my name for a while. No Account. But there I go rambling when you're here to hear about Miss Erzebetta, our Carnival Queen.

She was real pretty. But I guess you know that already, too. She wasn't pretty like the dancing girls, mind you. They were a soft kind of pretty, one you could touch. Miss Erzebetta was different. Like the kind of pretty what scares you, you know? Like a shiny bug, and you don't know if it's poison 'til it bites you.

The Old Man, that's what we call him, he gave her the girlie show to run. She popped right up one day and asked for a job, and he gave it to her, no questions asked. It's funny, though. The Old Man ain't really in charge. Charlie's the boss. Leastwise it's his trailer we line up outside of on payday, but even Charlie knows the real score.

So when the Old Man said Miss Erzebetta was going to run the girlie show, well, that's just what happened. I think he did it to needle her. She was real proud-like, Miss Erzebetta. Like I said, a Queen. The Old Man probably thought it'd be funny to give her girlie show, but if he was looking for her to turn her nose up, she never did give him the satisfaction.

I'll tell you, she flipped the show 'round right quick, and got all the girls eating right out of her hand like birds to seed. One of the first things she did was bring me on her crew.

When she asked "Is there anyone here I can count on to do whatever I say, with no questions or back-talk?" I said right away, "Yes'm, that's me."

The other boys, Rib, and Toad-Licker, and even Geech teased me about being in love with her. I'll allow as maybe they were right. I only knew I wanted to do things to make her happy, you know? Or maybe it was just that I never wanted to find out whether her bite was poisonous. I 'spect Rib and Geech and Toad-Licker felt the same way, though they never said as much, and it never stopped their teasing.

Anyway, she brought me on her crew to work the lights. Geech ran the curtain, Toad-Licker cleaned up the stage, and Rib guarded the door just in case there was any trouble.

I don't know when Miss Erzebetta got all the girls together to rehearse her new show. She never let us see beforehand. I guess she trusted us to get everything right on the first try without any practice, and I'll tell you what—we did.

Thinking on it now, maybe it was some kind of magic, you know? Like maybe there was a spell cast on the whole room the night Miss Erzebetta put on her first show. Otherwise I can't explain it.

Miss Erzebetta's show weren't like no girlie show I ever saw before. It was almost like going to church, and you can say I'm a sinner for saying so, but it's the truth. That's just what it felt like, with all the men sitting on the wooden benches like pews, and a hush over everything while they waited for the curtain to rise.

There was a kind of 'lectricity in the air, like a storm about to break, and I swear the hair stood right up on the back of my neck. I felt like laughing and dancing and crying all at once, and even now I can't say why.

The Old Man even showed up, like he wanted to see what Miss Erzebetta would do, same as the rest of us. He didn't sit in the seats, of course. He just leaned in the doorway with his arms crossed, like he didn't care one way or the other about being there, except he did care. I could tell.

I guess at some point Miss Erzebetta decided the waiting had gone on long enough. I don't remember how I knew the right moment, but I did. Smooth as butter, I flipped the first light on—a spot as full and bright as the moon, right in the centre of the stage—right as the curtains glided back like water. There was a gasp, a kind of rippling thing that spread across the room like wind over tall grass. There weren't no girls on the stage yet, just a pile of rags and a bunch of birds settling their wings.

Before anyone got angry so that Rib had to throw them out, the rags unfolded. I don't know how to say it any better, or how Miss Erzebetta pulled it off. It was like a magic trick. I swear when the curtain went up it was just rags and birds on the stage. Then suddenly Miss Erzebetta was there, stretching herself up to her full height. The birds circled her once, then they just kind of disappeared into her so everyone could see they must have imagined them after all.

After that, Miss Erzebetta started talking. She was wearing a skimpy costume and all, the same thing she always wore, and it showed plenty of skin, but she never took any of her clothes off. She just stood there and told a story. Funny thing is, all those men who'd paid to see girls flash their titties, not one of them got mad or tried to leave. They all sat with their feet rooted in the floor like they'd grown there.

The story Miss Erzebetta told, well, I'll remember it word for word 'til I die. The first thing she said was: "In the beginning, in the dark before the world, there were the People, and the Spirits, and Coyote was among them."

When she said that, it was just like someone dropped a handful of ice right down my back. I don't know what made me do it, but I looked over at the Old Man right as she said those words. He nodded, like he knew what she was going to say, and could tell the story word for word along with her if anyone asked. There was kind of a faraway look about him, too, like he was sad and wicked, mad and bad and crazy all at once. It put a picture in my head of a mangy dog chasing its tail and trying to get rid of fleas, but grinning wild the whole time, with a red tongue hanging out between its teeth as it spun.

I can tell you, it scared me more than anything and I had to look away quick-like. The other funny thing, when I looked away I saw my hands had been working the lights the whole time, like they knew what to do and didn't need me at all.

The stage was lit up all pink and orange like the sun coming up at the beginning of the world. Miss Erzebetta raised her arms, and the dancing girls came onto the stage. They weren't dressed in their spangles and beads, mind you. They were dressed like regular folk, only some were dressed like women, and some like men.

The next thing Miss Erzebetta said was: "The men and women lived in harmony with each other, and with the Spirits, except for Coyote, who grew bored. So Coyote thought of a good joke to play. He pissed a river to separate the women from the men, and he laughed while he did it like it was the funniest thing he'd ever seen."

Pardon my language, but that's just how she said it, and I want to tell it right. She used an awful lot of words most folks don't say in polite company, let alone a lady sayin' 'em. But that's how she was, Miss Erzebetta.

A shadow flickered on the wall behind her. My hands were playing tricks with the light again, making a monster with bristled fur and jaws stretched wide. The light on the stage changed, too, pooling yellow between her feet, like there really was a river of piss there.

Then Miss Erzebetta said: "At first the men and women made a game of the river. They put words and gifts and toys into clay pots and boats woven out of twigs, and tried to float them to the other side. They called to each other, and danced and laughed. But after a time, the women sang, not with words, but with sweet, dark sounds from their throats. And they changed the way they danced so it wasn't playful anymore. The dancing and the song made the men feel their pulsing blood, and it put thoughts of everything they couldn't have into their heads. And you can bet that was Coyote's doing, too."

When she said that last bit, her tone changed, and she looked right at the Old Man. Her eyes were black-black, just like ink, and it scared me almost as bad as looking at the Old Man and seeing that mangy dog.

While Miss Erzebetta stared at the Old Man, the girls dressed like men hung their tongues out and panted, and the girls dressed like women danced. And I don't mind telling you how the dancing put thoughts in my head, just like Miss Erzebetta said in the story.

I'd rolled with a few of the girls from time to time. Lots of us had. If they were in the mood, the girls would give us a good price, and sometimes, if they were in a really good mood, they would roll for free. But even the ones I knew, well, when they danced up there on the stage, they were like nothing I'd ever seen before. They were wild and strange and I don't know what. If I didn't know better, I'd almost say they weren't human.

"And even that wasn't enough for Coyote," Miss Erzebetta said. "So he put thoughts of fucking into the women's heads, too. And because they couldn't reach the men, the women gathered branches and stones, smooth-polished bones and horns from the ground. They stripped off their clothes, and laid down right there on the riverbank and pleasured themselves where the men could see, but not touch."

You'll pardon my language again, but that's just what she said, word for word. Anyway, the girls up on stage acted out what Miss Erzebetta said. They took their clothes off, but it weren't like no normal girlie show. Like I said, it was like being in church, only with naked girls doing all kinds of ungodly things.

Sometimes, when Miss Erzebetta spoke, it sounded like birdsong. Sometimes it sounded like thunder. All the while my hands were doing things with the lights. The girls on stage gleamed blue; they turned into starlight and moonlight.

As Miss Erzebetta spoke, the girls gathered stones and bones, smooth wood and horn and feathers from the stage. I don't know where they came from, they were just there for the girls to pick up. When they stroked them slick and wet between their legs, moaning and crying out just like they were lying with a man, I had to look away. I swear I heard someone in the benches cryin', and someone else being sick.

I didn't look to see for sure, but I'll bet out of everyone there, the Old Man was the only one who never looked away, never blinked either, cuz he'd seen it all before.

Then Miss Erzebetta said: "In their desire, the men built creatures out of mud, things they could fuck while the women pleasured themselves."

I almost couldn't bear to look, but it was like I had to, you know? The girls dressed as men, they were doing just what Miss Erzebetta said, too. They had buckets and they poured mud onto the stage and built it into shapes that looked almost like women, but like monsters, too. I can't say for sure, but I swear some of the girls had man-parts between their legs when they took their clothes off.

The last thing Miss Erzebetta said, while the women writhed around with the bones and the wood, and the girl-men fucked the things made of mud was: "And, because they copulated with bones and horn, branches and feathers and stone, the women became pregnant. And because the men fucked the mud, the riverbank became pregnant, too. And because it was the time before the beginning of the world, the river dried up when the sun rose, and the men and the women, together again, had to live with what they'd done. And the women and the riverbank gave birth to monsters—girls with feathers in their skin, and boys with mud in their bones—by the next fullness of the moon."

Then, just like that, the lights went out. Bam! Without me even touching 'em. I expected folks to yell in the sudden dark, but it was so still you could hear a pin drop. The men just sat there, breathing quiet, and even I felt like I was half asleep. When I finally shook myself up to turn the lights on, I felt all heavy, like pins and needles going up and down my legs.

Well, I got the lights on, and the men were all still sitting right where they were when Miss Erzebetta said the last word. They were staring up at the stage, only it was empty now, like they were waiting for her to come back. If me and Rib and Geech hadn't finally thought to shoo them away, they might be sitting there still.

I don't know what Miss Erzebetta did, but her telling that story was like a magician with a pocket watch. From that night on, Miss Erzebetta was our Queen, without anyone saying so, and we were all under her spell.

IV. The Emperor

I'm going to tell you a story. It'll sound like two stories, but it's really only one story, see? This story is just for you. Oh, you can put it in your fancy book if you want, but really, this story is for you and me.

After the time of the river, the men and women got to being afraid of the things they'd made by fucking mud and bone. So they made offerings of smoke and food to anyone who would listen. A bunch of us got together and came down to see what all the fuss was about, and everyone got to arguing about whether the monsters should live or die.

Those creatures had been born through no fault of their own, but that didn't seem to matter much to anyone. No one likes having their wickedness shoved back in their face, I suppose. Everyone was too busy being ashamed of what they'd done that I guess no one remembered the whole mess was my fault. And since I can yell louder than most, me, everyone listened when I told them I had a plan.

There's a thing about monsters most people don't understand. What really makes a monster is wanting, always wanting to be something you're not, and fighting against what's down deep in your bones. Too many folks spend too much time trying to make their bones match their skin, but a bone's never going to be but what it is. You fight bone-nature, and that's when you become monstrous.

While everyone was arguing and worrying, I'd looked over all those so-called monsters. I knew which ones wanted and which ones knew their bones and skin. I know a thing or two about what kind of monsters the world needs, just to keep things interesting, see? A good joke gets spoiled if you don't tell it all the way to the end.

So I said we'd draw lots for the monsters, a stick that was either cut with a mark or not for each one. If there was a mark on the stick, then the monster would be drowned, and if there wasn't, they'd live in exile, far away from the folks that fucked them into being. The men and women all agreed, because even though they didn't want their get around, no one wanted death on their hands, either. They figured it wouldn't be wicked if they left it up to fate.

I like games, me, but I like the ones where I win the best. So I rigged the draw. And in the end, I decided each and every time which of the monsters would live, and which would die. So I birthed them twice, the ones who lived. I pissed a river so they got born in the first place, and I didn't cut a stick for some, so they'd be born again. Some of them never forgave me for that.

You might think I'm wicked, me. But I am what I am in my skin and my bones. Trying to be otherwise, that would make me a monster.

Now here's the other part of the story, which is the same story, see?

In the Starving Time, there were hard winters, and dry summers. Men didn't have enough food to put on their tables, and cattle were scarce more than skin and bone. There was no grass to feed them, but men went right on breeding, making more mouths they couldn't fill. And I was hungry, too.

There's belly hunger, and there's hunger that goes deeper and wider and all the way through. I was both kinds of hungry, me, so I set to singing under the moon and calling all my brothers and sisters, all my husbands and wives and children together. I told them about all the good things the men had to eat in their camps and behind their fences, and I sent them down from of the hills, all hungry jaws and wide smiles.

Course, when they got there, they found nothing but the bones of cattle, because whatever men had in those days, they'd already picked clean and still their bellies sang for more. My kin, they sang right back to that belly-hunger, howling their frustration in the shadows, just outside the circle of men's hearth fires and campfires.

And didn't that just put fear up the spines of the men, thinking about their loved ones falling to white teeth and wide jaws? So they loaded up their guns. They shot my brother first, and nailed his skin right up a barn door so the rest of us would know to stay away.

With my brother shot, there was more food for the rest of us. Just a mouthful, mind, but it was still one mouthful more than we'd had before. The thing about one mouthful is, it ain't powerful enough to kill a hunger. One mouthful feeds a hunger, gives it teeth, makes it howl.

It wasn't difficult to convince my kin to keep harrying those farms and those campfires, despite my brother's skin up on the wall. Even his sons and daughters went right under their daddy's eyes, all dripping buzzy fly tears, pissing and scratching and trying to mark the farmer's land for their own. They even managed to snatch a babe right out of its cradle, under its mam's sleeping nose, and didn't that make a feast between them, tearing all that lovely red meat from those delicate bones?

If our singing put shivers up men's spines, the death of a babe put rage in their bellies, enough so they almost thought they were full for a while. Those men howled almost as good as me and mine that night, calling for blood.

And while they were all het up, I walked right into the men's circle of firelight, me, going on two legs, growl traded for grin. I told them where to find the dens; I told them where to put their snares; I left the fire and laid down musk and piss as lures, and led my kin right into the muzzles of those death-screaming guns.

Without all my brothers and sisters, husbands and wives, daughters and sons gobbling up what scarceness there was, just imagine how many mouthfuls were left for me.

And with all my kin gone, the men put their guns away. After a while, they felt so safe, they even started leaving their windows open again. And you can just imagine what a feast I had then.

When it was all said and done, my belly was full to bursting. It was a good joke I played, me, but I had no one to share it with. So I lay down among the corpses of my sons and daughters, my brothers and sisters, my husbands and wives. I let the flies tickle my ears and dance on my snout. And I wept a flood to cleanse the earth of every sin. Or enough to end the drought and bring the crops back, leastwise.

V. The Hierophant

I guess Snips already told all about the show, so there's no sense in telling that part again. I can tell you what came after though, cuz Miss Erzebetta kept me on to guard the door, even when she changed everything, on account of I'm big, so people think I'm mean, too.

After that first night, there weren't no more girlie shows. Instead, Miss Erzebetta taught the girls to tell fortunes. She made her own set of cards, Miss Erzebetta, I mean. She used pictures of people in the carnival. She even used one of me. Ain't nobody ever thought I was worth putting on a card before, let alone to tell the future, but she did and that was fine by me.

She said something to me once that I don't full understand, but it stuck with me, I guess. She said: "Rib, if you let the world tell your tale, nothing will ever be like you want it. You have to make your own story. It's the only way to get the world to fall in line. They're powerful things, stories. They can shape just about anything, if you tell them right. You remember that, Rib."

I did just that, I guess, even though I don't know what it means. Except that now I think back on it, maybe that's what Miss Erzebetta was doing with the cards, telling a story. It's like her girlie show told the way the world used to be, and the cards told the way she wanted it to be. I guess that sounds crazy, don't it?

Anyway, even though there weren't no more girlie shows, men still lined up at Miss Erzebetta's to get their fortunes told. Some of the girls got pretty good at reading those cards, too. Some of them even were cards, like me, part of Miss Erzebetta's story.

Well, there's another part, which I probably shouldn't say, but I guess it's all over now so it don't matter much. Even though they weren't dancing no more, you could still pay some of the girls for their time, after they told your fortune and all. I guess that must be how some of them got pregnant.

Anyway, I just wanted to add that bit in case it's important, for your book and all.

Shuffle

"Hey," the Old Man says. "Let me give you a piece of advice for free."

He taps the table, startling me. Then in one smooth motion he sweeps up the cards laid between us, Erzebetta's photographs, and shuffles them in his yellow-nailed hands.

"Stories got their own rhythm and flow," he says. "You got to let them take their own shape, tell the bits they need you to know in their own order and time. That way you get to skip all the boring parts, hey?"

He spreads the cards out on the table in a new order. His hands are quick, just like they were rolling cigarettes that became sixteen from four.

"There," he says, and taps the first card in the new pattern. "That's a good one. Start here."

He lights another cigarette, breathes out a picture in smoke, and grins.

XII. The Hanged Man

That's right, Elb, with an El and a Bee, Constable. You got that down? Right then.

The whole thing was an awful business, I can tell you that much. Right from the get go, the missus got after me about rousting them up and sending them on down the road, going on about the 'sorts' the carnival attracted. Tell you the truth, I didn't like having the carnival right on our doorstep either, but I told her let it be—carnival usually only stays a week at most.

Least that's how it was every other year. They blew into town and right back out again, leaving pockets a few dollars lighter, but folks happier for all that. 'Cept this time, they stayed. Planted themselves down and never got back up again. The missus was right, not that I'd tell her so.

She kept at me, though. Especially after the tent city grew up with all the folks who styled that woman who joined up with them some kind of prophet. I don't rightly know what that was about. I heard tell of some kind of show, and talk that she could tell the future. Most of the time, I just kept my head down and let it wash over me. Weren't none of my business, way I figured it.

Sure, every now and then we'd get a call about a fight getting out of hand, and I'd gather some of the boys to go see. More often than not, all it took was us showing up in uniform for everyone to settle down and go their separate ways. It was a nuisance, but no real trouble. I wasn't fussed much, but the missus, well . . . I guess you're wishing you could talk to her, too. I'm sure she'd give you an earful, but to tell you the truth, she don't even talk to me much these days. She's staying up with her sister now, so I guess you'll have to take my word for her side of the story.

Anyway, she wasn't the only one worked up about matters. There was a whole group that met up at the church pretty regular, the committee for moral decency or some such.

I don't know what all is truth since I never did see anything too bad with my own eyes. But I can tell you what the committee for moral decency thought was going on up there. They said all the folks from the carnival and the folks from the tent city would gather up in the field and dance around without their clothes on, rutting like animals, and worshipping the devil.

Like I said, I don't know what's true and what's not. All I can say is the business with Bessie's little girl was a tragedy, and what happened after with that carnival gal wasn't right neither. A thing like that isn't justice, it's . . . well, I'll just say sometimes even good, decent people can get to feeding off their own bile until they're no better than a pack of starving dogs.

The carnival gal, she was a real looker. She used to be the star of, ahem, the *show*, before that odd bird came in and changed it all. Well, I guess maybe she was still the star, but in a different way. Like I said, I don't pretend to know what went on up there. I never did go and get my fortune told. Truth is, the idea kinda scared me. Though I guess if the cards had told me the missus was gonna up and stay with her sister, maybe I could have done something about it. Maybe not.

What I can say is what set everything to unraveling was Bessie Williams' little girl going missing. She was a pretty thing, blonde curls and sweet little apple cheeks and the bluest eyes you ever saw. She had her daddy and her momma both wrapped around her little finger, and she was barely even talking yet.

Anyway, as soon as she went missing, the committee for moral decency pointed their fingers straight at the carnival. I tried to talk some sense into them, the missus mostly, but she would have none of it. Let's not be hasty, is all I said, and I'll have my boys look into it. And we did, but I don't mind telling you she gave me the cold shoulder just the same.

We did find Bessie's little girl, two days later, but there wasn't much left of her. Nasty business. She'd been tore up, like some animal got at her. My money's on a rabid dog, or maybe a coyote. The committee for moral decency wouldn't hear any of it. They said it was a blood sacrifice, and maybe they fed that little girl to wild dogs after she was dead, but sure as anything, it was the carnival folks who were to blame.

Now, I'll admit, maybe my blood got up a little bit, too, seeing that poor little girl torn apart and Bessie so heartbroken. I like to think I couldn't have done more to stop what happened next, but some days I just don't know.

My boys and me, we did our jobs, I can promise you that. We're not the type of lawmen who look the other way when one of our own is involved, no sir. But there was only so much we could do. A whole mob descended on the carnival, so I can't even say any one person was to blame.

Still, it is a shame. She was real pretty, that carnival gal. Etoile was her name, or at least that's what she called herself on stage. She used to get up all in silver and crystal beads, hanging everywhere in ropes on her so you couldn't quite tell whether she was wearing anything under them. Ahem. Well, maybe it's best you don't put that bit in your book right there. For decency's sake, you know.

Anyway, like I said, it wasn't right what happened to her. It wasn't justice, stringing her up like that by her ankle, her throat slashed, leaving her to bleed dry. They cut her belly, too. There was a baby. Of sorts. At least that's what I heard. I mean, folks said it wasn't natural, but I don't know.

I do have a picture here somewhere, though, if you want to see. A word of fair warning: It's not for the faint of heart.

XV. The Devil

Who was it you think put the idea of the hanging into those people's minds in the first place? Sometimes the old tricks are the best ones. And sometimes what looks like two stories or three, is really all the same story. And every story needs a villain. You either have to be one or the other, hero or villain, to get written into the fabric of the world.

I am what I am, me. In my skin and in my bones.

XVI. The Tower

The Old Man leans back, blowing smoke at the ceiling. Sixteen cigarettes have become four again, but this time by the normal means.

"One spark is all it takes to set a pyre to blaze so long as it's built right," the Old Man says. "Me and Erzebetta, we built that pyre right and high all summer long. She thought she was raising up an army against me with her girls, showing she could birth monsters every bit as good as me, but she had no idea."

He seems proud, like he knows my mind was made up the moment I saw the pictures of the girl with her belly cut and the thing they cut out of her. The way he grins, with all his grisly creations framing him on the wall, it's like he's just waiting for me to ask.

"How did you do it?" I say, not because I want to give him the satisfaction, but because I want him to see how quick I caught on to him.

"Some of my best work, if I do say." The Old Man chuckles. "Turtle skin and squirrel bones, painted with tar. I'm wicked-clever, me. The demon infant cut out of the dead girl's belly—proof the Devil's work was being done. A glimpse here and there, and that's your spark."

I open my mouth, but the Old Man goes right on talking, with only the barest glance to make sure I'm writing everything down. There isn't a bit of shame in him, like he can't wait to boast to the whole world about what he's done.

"Not that it mattered much. Folks had made up their minds already, hey? All they needed was a little shove in the right direction.

"They came with torches in hand, a mob to bring the demon down, to smoke the devil from her hole. Of course the men and women in the tent city fought back. They were ready to lay their lives down for Erzebetta at that point. All the fate and destiny she shaped in her cards did her some good, I suppose."

The Old Man taps the cards piled neat on the table. He picks them and shuffles them slow.

"Course, I doubt she ever promised a conflagration, hey? I doubt many folks would be so eager to sign up if she'd showed them that."

The Old Man deals the cards, face down. They make dry, snapping sounds against the table, like old bones.

"The tents caught first, all that canvas going up in a rush and the smoke pouring over everything and the wind catching and blowing it all around. What the wind didn't carry, the men brought with their torches, marching toward Erzebetta's temple to burn it to the ground. Oh, it was a sight, all that bloody-red gold, and sparks swirling up to kiss the stars."

The Old Man pushes the remaining cigarettes aside to make more room for the cards. I read up on tarot when I first heard about Erzebetta's deck, but this pattern I don't recognize. It loops and swirls, taking up almost the entire table.

"It was a night of miracles," the Old Man says. "Or of black sorcery, depending who's doing the telling." He looks at me, flashing a grin, like he's going to ask my opinion again: sacred or profane? But he says nothing, waiting for me to speak first.

"So what happened?" I ask.

My notebook is full of different versions of what happened that night: Erzebetta walked untouched through the flames and vanished; a flock of dark birds dropped out of the sky and stole her away; she sprouted wings of her own and flew up into the stars. But I want to hear what the Old Man has to say, his side of the tale.

Instead of the glint in his eye and another boast, he surprises me and merely shrugs. "I don't know. She would have said I'm not the kind of daddy that looks back after the birthing is done. Maybe she's right, at that."

"That's it?" I say. I can't help myself, I gape at him.

"That's all," the Old Man says. "Everything you need is right there." He taps the edge of my notebook with one yellow-nailed finger. If I didn't know better, I could swear the nail has grown.

I glance at the pattern of cards spread before him. There's one left in his hand, but he doesn't put it down. He holds onto it and looks up at me.

"Now, if you don't mind, I'm an old man, and old men need their rest, hey?"

That's when the glint comes back into his eye, wicked and bright. He shows his teeth, just a fraction, and this time it isn't a smile. Knowing everything he's done, and proudly claimed, I can't help myself. I gather up my papers and run.

Null. The Fool

I'm going to tell you a story, and it's the same story. It's about a girl and her daddy, and how the girl hated her daddy and blamed him for every wrong thing that had ever happened in her life. It's about how the girl set out to take away everything her daddy had built over long years, on account of hating him so. And it's about how the girl failed, being as how her daddy was wicked old and had been telling tales since before the world had even thought to be born.

Thing is, she saw the carnival and thought it was all of my tale. But the carnival is only one story, which is the same story, and I'm wicked-good at tales, me. I've been telling this one so long hardly anyone sees the head or tail of it. Cut one part out, and the rest just keeps on going.

Now this part here, this is just for you, see? Not that boy and his book. Poor holy Fool, clutching his notes to his chest, full of fire and knowing just what kind of tale he's going to write. Gone running to proclaim my wickedness to the world.

He'd already made up his mind when came to my door with that picture of Erzebetta clutched in his hand, see? He had his hero. All he needed was a villain. I sent him off with the best there is, tucked in his back pocket.

Never let it be said I'm a poor host, me.

I'll tell you a secret, and you can have this one for free. Tell someone they can't have something, they'll go to wanting it so bad it cracks the marrow from their bones. Tell them something's no good for them, and it's all they'll be able to think on for days. Give them a devil, and it'll set thrill up their spines, thinking on all that wickedness. They'll tell its story to their children and their children's children again and again, whispering its name in the dark, so as to keep feeling that thrill. And won't that name just live on and on.

Oh I'm wicked, me.

Here's another secret, and you can have this one for free, too. Misdirection is an easy thing. Put something smack in the middle of the frame, and most people won't bother to look to the edges, the background. When most people look at the Fool card, what do they see? They see the bright, motley jester, dancing his way to the cliff's edge. What they rarely notice is the little dog, snapping his bright sharp jaws at the Fool's heels, driving him closer to the edge.

That's my story, me.

Coyote, blurring out from the edge of the picture frame. Coyote grinning, and driving the tale.

Left Foot, Right
Nalo Hopkinson

"All you have this in a size 9?" Jenna puts the shiny red patent shoe down on the counter. Well, it used to be shiny. She's been wearing it everywhere, and now it's dulled by dust. It's the left side of a high-heeled pump, pointy-toed, with large shiny fake rhinestones decorating the toe box. Each stone is a different size and colour, in a different cheap plastic setting. The red veneer has stripped off the heel of the shoe. It curls up off the white plastic heel base in strips. Jenna's heart clenches. It's exactly the kind of tacky, blinged-out accessory that Zuleika loves—loved—to wear.

The girl behind the counter is wearing a straw baseball cap, its peak pulled down low over her face. The girl asks, in a puzzled voice, "But don't you bought exactly the same shoes last week?"

And the week before that, thinks Jenna. *And the one before that*. "I lost them," she replies. "At least, I lost the right side"—she nearly chokes on the half truth—"so I want to replace them." All around her, other salespeople help other customers. The people in the store zip past Jenna, half-seen, half-heard. This year's soca road march roars through the store's sound system. Last month, Jenna loved it. Now, any happy music makes her vexed.

"Jeez, what's the matter with you *now*?" the girl says. Jenna startles, guiltily. She risks a look at the shoe store girl's face. She hadn't really done so before. She has been avoiding eye contact with people lately, afraid that if anyone's two eyes make four with hers, the fury in hers will burn the heart out of the core of them.

But the girl isn't looking at Jenna. With one hand, she is curling the peak of her cap to protect her eyes against the sun's glare through the store windows. Only her small, round mouth shows. She seems to be peering into the display on the cash register. She slaps the side of the cash register. "Damned thing. It's like every time I touch it, the network goes down."

"Oh," says Jenna. "Is not me you were talking to, then?"

The girl laughs, a childlike sound, like small dinner bells tinkling. "No. Unless it have something the matter with you too. Is there?"

Jenna turns away, pretends to be checking out the rows of men's running shoes, each one more aerodynamically fantastical than the last, like race cars. "No, not me. About the shoes?"

"Sure." The girl takes the pump from Jenna. Her fingertips are cool when they brush Jenna's hand. "What a shame you can't replace just one side. Though you really wore this one down in just a week. You need both sides, left and right." The girl inspects the inside of the shoe, in that mysterious way that people who sell shoes do. "You say you want a size nine? But you take more like an eight, right?"

"How you know that?"

"I remember from last time you were in the store. Feet are so important, you don't find?"

Jenna doesn't remember seeing the girl in the store before. But the details of her life have been a little hazy the past few weeks. Everything seems dusted with unreality. Her, standing in a shoe shop, doing something as ordinary as buying a pair of shoes. Her standing at all, instead of floundering.

The shoe shop girl's body sinks lower and lower. Jenna is confused until the girl comes out from behind the counter. She's really short. She has been standing on something in order to reach the cash register. Her arms and legs are plump, foreshortened. The hems of her jeans are rolled up. Her body is pleasantly rotund.

The girl glances at Jenna's feet. At least, that's where Jenna thinks she's looking. Jenna's seeing the girl from above, so it's hard to tell. In addition to the straw cap, the girl's twisty black hair is in thousands of tiny plaits that keep falling over her face. She must have been looking at Jenna's feet, because she says, "Yup. Size eight. Don't it?"

Jenna stares down at the top of the girl's head. She says, "Yes, but the pumps run small." The girl is wearing cute yellow moccasins that look hand-sewn. She didn't get those at this discount shoe outlet. Her feet are tiny; the toe boxes of her moccasins sag a little. Her toes don't quite fill them up. Jenna curls her own toes under. Her feet feel unfamiliar in her plain white washekongs, the tennis shoes she used to wear so often, before her world fell in. Now she only wears two sides of shoes when she needs to fake normal. Or when she needs to take the red pump off to show the people in the shoe store. The blisters on the sole of her right foot are uncomfortable cushions against the canvas-lined foam inside the shoe. Although she'd scrubbed the right foot bottom before putting the washekong on, she hadn't been able to get all of the weeks of ground-in dirt out. The heel of her left foot, imprisoned most of the time in the red high heel, has become a stranger to the ground. Going completely flat-footed like this makes the shortened tendons in her left ankle stretch and twang.

The girl hands the shoe back to her and says, "I going in the back to see if we have any more of these." She disappears amongst the high rows of shoe shelves. She walks jerkily, with a strange rise and fall motion.

Jenna sits on one of the benches in the middle of the store. She slips off her left-side tennis shoe and slides her left foot back into the destroyed pump. The height of it makes her instep ache, and her foot slides around a little in the too-big shoe. When she'd borrowed Zuleika's pumps without asking, she'd only planned to wear them out to the club that one night. The discomfort of the red shoe feels needful and good. It will be even more so when she can remove the right side washekong, feel dirt and hot asphalt and rocks with her bare right foot. She waits for the girl to bring the replacement pumps. The girl returns, hop-drop, hop-drop, carrying a shoe box.

Jenna doesn't want to be in the shop, fully shod, a second longer. She takes the box from the girl, almost grabbing it. "These are fine," she says, and stumps, hop-drop, hop-drop, to the cash register. She starts taking money out of her purse.

Behind her, the girl calls, "You don't want to try them on first?"

"Don't need to," Jenna replies. "I know how they fit."

The girl gets back behind the counter and clambers up onto whatever she'd been standing on. She sighs. "This job," she says to Jenna, "so much standing on your feet all the time. I not used to it."

Jenna isn't paying the girl a lot of attention. Instead, she's texting her father to come and get her. She doesn't drive at the moment. May never drive again.

The girl rings up the purchase. Her plaits have fallen into her eyes once more. When she leans forward to give Jenna her change, her breath smells like pepper shrimp. Jenna's tummy rumbles. But she knows she won't eat.

Maybe some ginger tea. The smell of almost any food makes her stomach knot these past few weeks.

The girl pats Jenna's hand and says something to her. Jenna can't hear it clearly over the sound of her grumbling stomach. Embarrassed, she mumbles an impatient "thank you" at the girl, grabs the shopping bag with the shoes in it, and quickly leaves the store. After the air-conditioned chill of the store, the tropical blast of the outdoors heat is like surfacing from the river depths to sweet, scorching air. She kicks off the single tennis shoe. She stuffs it into the shopping bag with the new pair of pumps.

What the girl said, it had sounded like "Is Eowyn Sinead."

Jenna doesn't know anybody with those names.

Daddy texts back that he'll meet her at the Savannah, by the ice cream man. He means the ice cream truck that has been at the same side of the Savannah since Jenna and Zuleika were young. Jenna likes soursop ice cream. Zuleika liked rum and raisin. One Sunday when they were both still little, their parents had brought Jenna and Zuleika to the Savannah. Jenna had nagged Zuleika for a taste of her ice cream until Mummy ordered Zuleika to let her try it. A sulking Zuleika gave Jenna her cone. Jenna tasted it, spat it out, and dropped the cone. So Daddy made Jenna give Zuleika her ice cream, which made Jenna bawl. But Zuleika wanted her rum and raisin. She pouted and threw Jenna's ice cream as far as she could. It landed in a lady's hair that was walking in front of them. Jenna was unhappy, Mummy and Daddy were unhappy, the lady was unhappy, and Zuleika was unhappy.

Jenna remembers the odd satisfaction she had felt through her misery. Except that then Zuleika wouldn't talk to her or play with her for the rest of the day. Jenna smiles. It probably hadn't helped that she had followed Zuleika around the whole rest of that day, nagging her for her attention.

Jenna turns off her phone so no one else can call her. Her boyfriend Clarence tried for a while, came to visit her a couple of times after the accident, but Jenna wouldn't talk to him. She didn't dare open her mouth, for fear of drowning him in screams that would start and never, ever stop. Clarence eventually gave up. The doctors say that Jenna is well enough to return to school. She doesn't know what she will say to Clarence when she sees him there.

As Jenna is crossing the street, she walks with her bare right foot on tiptoe. That almost matches the height of the high heel on her left foot, so it isn't so obvious that one foot is bare. But she can't keep that up for long, not any more. After more than a fortnight of walking with her right foot on tiptoe, the foot has rebelled. Her toes cramp painfully, so she lowers her bare heel to the ground. She steps in a patch of sun-melted tar, but she barely feels the burn. Her foot bottom has developed too much callous for it to bother her much. People in the street make wide berths around her in her tattered one-side shoe. They figure she is homeless, or mad, or both. She doesn't care. She makes her way to the 300-acre Savannah. Not too many people walking or jogging the footpath yet, not in the daytime heat. But the food trucks are in full swing, vending oyster cocktail, roast corn, pholourie, doubles. Jenna ducks past the ice cream man, hoping he won't see her and ask how she's doing. He knows—knew—Jenna and Zuleika well. He had watched them grow up.

The poui trees are in full bloom. They carpet the grass with yellow and pink blossoms. Jenna steps over a cricket wicket discarded on the ground, and goes around a bunch of navy-uniformed school girls liming on the grass under the trees. A couple of them are eating rotis. They all stop their chatting long enough to stare at her. Once she passes them, they whoop with laughter.

Jenna doesn't know how she will manage school next week.

She finds a bench not too far from the ice cream man, where she can see Daddy when he comes. She sits and puts the shoe bag on her lap. She clutches the folded top of it tightly. She doesn't put the new shoes on. She never has. They aren't for her. She was wearing the left side of Zuleika's shoes when she surfaced. She has to give Zuleika a good pair of the shoes in return for the ones she took without permission.

For a few minutes, Jenna rests her aching feet. Then she realizes that the air is beginning to cool. The sun will be going down soon. Jenna texts her father again, tells him never mind, that she will come home on her own later. He tries to insist. She refuses. Then she turns the phone off. Is better like this, anyway. Her parents are doing their best. Looking after Jenna, asking after her. Doing their grieving in private. Some days, Jenna can't bear the burden of their forgiveness.

She can't take neither bus nor taxi half-shod the way she is. She gets up off the bench, wincing at the separate pains in her feet. She starts walking. Clop, thump. Clop, thump. One shoe off, and one shoe on.

It's dark when she gets to the right place on the highway. The sight of the torn-apart metal guard rail sets her blood boiling hot so 'til she nearly feels warm enough for the first time in almost a month. Anger is the only thing hotting her up nowadays. When are they going to fix it?

She lets herself through the space between the twisted pieces of metal and starts clambering down the embankment. Below her, the river whispers and chuckles. A few times, she loses her footing in the pebbles and sparse scrub grass of the dry red earth of the embankment, and slides a little way down. She could hold onto clumps of grass to try to stop her skid, but why? Instead, she digs in the heel of Zuleika's remaining pump. Above her, cars whoosh by along the highway. But the closer she gets to the tiny patch of wild between the highway and the river, the more the traffic sounds feel muffled, less important. The moonlight helps her to see her way, but she doesn't need it. She knows the route, every rock, every hillock of grass. She has been here every night for a few weeks now, as soon as the bleeding stopped and the hospital discharged her.

Tiny glowing dots of fireflies prick the darkness open here and there all around her. Jenna's skin pimples in the cool evening breeze. The sobbing river flows past, just ahead of her.

At the shore line, Jenna gets to her knees. "Zuleika!" she yells. She sits back on her heels in the chilly riverbank mud, clutching the shoe bag in her lap, and waits. The heel of the red shoe pokes into her backside, but the mud feels good on the blistered sole of the other, bare foot.

"Zuleika!"

Nothing.

"I sorry about your fucking shoes, all right?"

Nothing.

She gets the new shoes out of their box. She tosses them into the water. They sink. She waits. She is waiting for the frogs in the reeds to stop chirping. For the sucking pit of grief in her chest to fill in.

For Zuleika to forgive her.

When none of that happens—just like it hasn't happened every other time she's come down here—she sighs and stands up. The heel of the left shoe sinks down into the mud. She pulls it out with a sucking sound.

The river isn't the only thing weeping. Someone is crying, over there in the dark, where the mangroves cluster thicker together. Jenna heads, hop-drop, towards the sound. There are tiny footprints in the muddy soil. They lead away from the crying, towards the direction of the embankment. In the dark, Jenna can't make out how far they go. But she can tell where they came from, so she follows the footprints backwards.

There's a child sitting on a big rock by the waterside. The child is the one crying. It is wearing a huge panama hat. To keep from burning in the moonshine? Jenna doesn't laugh at her own joke. The child is wearing jeans rolled up at the ankles, a too-big t-shirt. It has its legs tucked up and its chin on its knees, propping sorrow. In the moonlight, Jenna can see the yellow moccasins on its tiny feet. It's the girl from the shoe store.

When she gets near enough, Jenna says, "What you doing out here? Something wrong?"

"I was trying to catch crabs," the girl replies. "I like them too bad."

Jenna remembers the seafood smell on the girl's breath. "Trying to catch them how?"

"With my hands, nuh?"

"You went wading in this water at night, with nobody around? This water not good," says Jenna. It takes people, she doesn't say. Sure enough, now that she's closer, she can see that the girl is sopping wet. Water is running off her clothes and streaming down the sides of the rock.

"Mummy don't have time for me," the girl replies. "I been trying to catch my dinner myself, but . . ." the girl starts sobbing again. "My feet hurt so much! All that standing in the shoe store, all day. Every time I put my feet down, is like I walking on nails. I keep flinching when I step, and frightening off the crabs-them."

Poor thing. Something small releases inside Jenna, like the easing of a stitch. She squishes through the mud and sits on the rock beside the girl. She puts the bag with the empty shoe box in it down on the rock. "I know how it feel when your feet paining you," she says.

Whimpering, the girl leans closer to Jenna. The smell of seafood makes Jenna's tummy grumble again. Jenna thinks she could comfort the girl with a hug. She doesn't do it, though. Since last month, she doesn't have any business with comfort. But the girl won't stop crying, her shoulders jerking with the force of her sorrow. Unwillingly, Jenna asks, "You want me help you catch the crabs?"

The girl doesn't lift her panama-hatted head, but her crying noise stops. "You would do that for me?" she asks, sounding so young. She's only a child!

"You would have to show me how," Jenna replies. "And how old you are, anyway?"

The girl says, "You have to put your feet in the water, slow-slow and quiet, so the crabs don't know you're there. You have to stay crouched over, ready to grab them when they come up."

Jenna doesn't want to put her feet back into the river that had swallowed her and Zuleika not too long ago. She still has nightmares of escaping through the open driver's side window, of her head feeling light from holding her breath in. Only in her dreams, Zuleika doesn't let go when she grabs Jenna's right foot.

Jenna whispers so the child won't hear her talking to Zuleika. "I told you to undo your seatbelt, don't it? When we started sinking, I told you. You should have come with me. But all you did was scream."

In Jenna's dreams, she isn't able to kick her leg free of Zuleika's panicked hold. In Jenna's dreams, river weed comes pouring out of Zuleika's hand and wraps itself around Jenna's right ankle, and doesn't let go. In Jenna's dreams, she drowns with her sister. Every night, she drowns.

But she's promised the shoe shop child. "Okay," says Jenna. "Just until your mummy comes." She briefly wonders why a little girl is working in a shoe store, why she's hunting for crabs alone down by the river at night, but she doesn't wonder for too long. The world has become strange, and she is no longer part of it.

Jenna takes off the mashed-up left-side shoe and puts it on the rock. She wiggles her toes. Night air slips through the spaces between them. It feels odd. She had put that shoe back on after Zuleika's funeral.

She eases herself down off the rock. Now she's standing, both feet bare, on the riverbank. Her feet are squishing up mud. The left foot sinks a little farther into the mud than the right one. In front of her, black as oil, the roiling river giggles.

She can't do this. Jenna turns to walk back to solid land, to leave the child to wait there alone for its mother.

"Don't be frightened," says the child.

"I not frightened," Jenna replies. She is, but not of the water. Truth to tell, she wants nothing more than to sink down into the river, to join Zuleika. She wants it so badly, but she knows she can't. Can't make her parents lose two daughters to the river in less than a month. And she loves the sweet air. Heaven help her, but she loves it more than she loves her sister.

The child says, "You have to walk slow, keep your eyes peeled on the river bottom. When you see a crab, you reach down and grab it with your two hands."

"And what if it pinch me?"

"They small. They can't pinch hard."

Jenna tries it. She slides her feet along in the shallows. The moonlight lends its glow to the water there. After a minute or two of squinting, she can make out the river bottom. At first, Jenna's feet hurt every time she takes a step, but pretty soon the chilly river water numbs them. A crab scuttles sideways in front of her. Jenna pounces. Splashes. Misses. She falls into the shallow water. She's wet to the waist. The child laughs, and Jenna finds herself smiling, just a little. Jenna picks herself up. "Lemme try again."

She misses the second time, too. At the third fall, she laughs at herself. And at the fourth. By the fifth missed, crab, she and the child are shrieking with merriment.

The child points. "There! Look another one!"

Jenna leaps for the splayed, scuttling crab. She catches it. She's holding it by its hard-shelled body. Its claws wave around and scrabble at her hand, but the crab is too small to do any damage. Jenna rises with it, triumphant, from the river bed. She whoops in glee, and the child applauds. Jenna realises that she's stopped thinking of the child as a girl. Really, she doesn't know whether it's a girl or a boy. She wades closer to the bank with her catch. "What I do with it now?" she asks.

The child hesitates. Then slowly, it removes the large panama hat that's been obscuring its face. It turns the hat over, bowl-like, and holds it out. "I put them in here," it says.

It has no face. Just a small bump where a nose should be, and that perfectly bowed mouth. Jenna is startled for a second, but she recovers. Not polite to stare. Anyway, in a world gone strange, why make a fuss about a missing pair of eyes and a nose with no holes? Jenna drops the crab into the hat the child holds out. Immediately, the child grabs the live crab up and rips into it with tiny, sharp teeth. It spits out a mouthful of broken shell. "You could catch more, please? I so hungry."

Jenna splashes about some more. She catches crabs, and she laughs giddily. Before this, the river has been making fun of her. Now, it is chortling with her. Jenna catches crabs and drops them into the child's hat. Jenna is shivering, belly deep. Maybe from being cold and wet, maybe from giggling so hard. The child smiles and eats and pats its full belly. Jenna pats her empty one. She goes closer to the shore. "Let me have one," she says to the child. She holds her hand out.

The child turns its blank face towards the sound of her voice. "You eat salt, or you eat fresh?" it asks.

"You have salt?" Jenna asks. "I would prefer that over eating it fresh."

"I don't have any."

Why does the child sound so happy about that? Jenna doesn't have patience with gladness nowadays. She has stopped hanging out with her friends and them from since. They would probably just want to go to the club, to dress up nice, to lime. Jenna doesn't want to do any of that any more. Dressing up leads to borrowing your sister's shoes without permission. It leads to quarreling over the shoes in the car on the way to the club. It leads to your sister losing control of the steering wheel and driving the car off the road into the river.

Jenna's eyes overflow. She has become used to the quick spurt of tears, as though someone has squeezed lime juice into her eyes.

Gently, the child says, "And look the salt right there so." It nods approvingly and hands over a particularly big crab. Jenna snatches it. She pulls off a gundy claw. With her teeth, she cracks it open. Crab juice and moist meat fall into her mouth. She sucks the rest of the meat out of the claw. She's so hungry that she barely chews before swallowing. As she eats, she cries salt tears onto the food, seasoning it. She fills her belly.

Jenna stops eating when she notices that the child is trying to reach for its own moccasined feet. Its arms are too short. The child says, softly, "I wish I could take these shoes off." It turns its smooth face in Jenna's direction, and smiles. "She had them with her in the car that night. She was going to give them to you, Mummy. As a present for me."

Jenna's mind goes still, like the space between one breath and the next. Somehow, she is out of the water and sitting on the rock beside the child. Gently, she touches one of the child's infant-fat legs. The child doesn't protest. Just leans back on its hands, its face upturned towards hers. Jenna lifts the child's small, lumpy foot. She loosens the lace on the moccasin and eases it off. The tiny yellow shoe sits in her palm, an empty shell. The child's foot is cold. Jenna cups the foot to warm it, and removes the other shoe. She looks at the two baby feet that fit easily in her hand. The child's strange gait makes sense now. Its feet are turned backwards.

Jenna gasps and pulls the child onto her lap. She curls her arms around it and holds its cold body close to hers. The other life she'd lost that night. The one only she and her older sister had known about.

The child snuggles against her. It puts one hand to its mouth and contentedly sucks its thumb. Jenna rocks it. She says, "I didn't even self tell Clarence yet, you know." The child grunts and keeps sucking its thumb. Jenna continues, "I sixteen. He fifteen. I was trying to think whether I was ready to grow up so fast."

The child sucks its thumb.

Jenna takes a breath that fills her lungs so deeply that it hurts. "Part of me was relieved to lose you." Her breath catches. "Zuleika *drowned*. And part of me was glad!" Jenna rocks the child and bawls. "I sorry," she says. "I so sorry." After a while, she is quiet. Time passes, a peaceful space of forever.

The child takes its thumb out of its mouth. It says, "Is her own she need."

Jenna is puzzled. "What?"

"Is that I was trying to tell you in the store. She don't want new shoes. She have the right side shoe already. You have to give her back the left side one. The one you been wearing."

Jenna surprises herself with a low yip of laughter. All this laughing tonight, like a language she'd forgotten. "I didn't even self think of that."

The child replies, "I have to go now."

Jenna sighs. "Yes, I know." She takes the child's blank, unwritten face in her hands and kisses it.

The child stands and pulls off its t-shirt and jeans. Its body is as featureless as its face. Jenna puts its hat back on. The child says, "You could keep my shoes instead, if you want." It eases itself down off the rock and toddles towards the water, away from life. But in the mud, the imprints of its feet are turned towards Jenna. The child enters the river. Knee deep, it stops and looks back at her. It calls out, "Auntie say she will look after me!"

Jenna waves. "Tell her thanks!"

Her child nods and waves back. It dives into the water, panama hat and all.

Jenna is still holding the tiny, wet moccasins. Gently, she squeezes the water from them. She slips them into the front pocket of her jeans. She goes and picks up the destroyed left pump from the rock. She kisses it. She yells, "Zuleika! Look your shoe here!" She raises her arm, meaning to fling the shoe into the river.

But there. In the very middle of the water; a rising, rolling semicircle, like a half-submerged truck tyre. Blacker than the blackness around. Swallowing light. The back of Jenna's neck prickles. Muscles in her calves jump; her running muscles. She makes herself remain still, though.

The fat, rolling pipe of blackness extends into a snakelike tail that wriggles over to the shore. The tail is un-bifurcated, its tip as big around as her wrist. The tip is coiled around a red patent pump, the matching right side to the shoe that Jenna is holding. In a whisper, Jenna asks, "Zuleika?" The tail tip slaps up onto the bank, splashing Jenna with mud.

Zuleika rises godlike from the river. Jenna whimpers and runs behind the rock.

Zuleika's upper half is still wearing the red sequined minidress, now in shreds, that she'd worn to go dancing the night of the accident. Moonlight makes the sequins twinkle, where they aren't hidden by river weed that has become tangled in them. The weed dangles and drips. Zuleika's lower half has become that snakelike tail. At her middle, the tail is as thick around as her waist. She floats upright. Her tail waves on the surface of the water. It extends as far upriver as Jenna can see in the moonlight.

Jenna's douen child clambers from where she'd been hidden behind Zuleika's back. The child climbs to sit on Zuleika's shoulders. It knots its fingers into the snares of Zuleika's hair. The water hasn't damaged its hat. Is the child smiling, or baring its teeth? Jenna can't tell.

Zuleika raises the whole length of her tail, and Jenna quails at the sheer mass of it, blacker than black against the night sky. Zuleika smashes her tail against the water's surface. The vast wave of sound, echoing up the river, hurts Jenna's ears. Jenna hears cars screeching to a halt on the highway, horns bleating. Jenna puts her hands against her ears and cowers. Not another crash. Please.

But there is no sound of collision. A couple of car doors slam. A couple of voices ask each other what the rass that sound was. Mama d'lo Zuleika hovers calmly in the water. The few trees must be hiding her from view, because soon, car doors slam again. Cars start up and drive off. Zuleika, Jenna, and the douen child are alone again.

Jenna finds that she's still holding the left-side shoe. She gathers her courage. She comes out from behind the rock. She says to her sister, "This is yours." She holds the shoe out to Zuleika.

Zuleika's tail-tip comes flying out of the darkness and grabs the shoe from Jenna. She hugs both once-shiny red shoes—the dusty one and the waterlogged one—to her breast.

The wetness in Jenna's own eyes makes the moon break up and shimmer like its own reflection on the water. "I miss you," she says.

Zuleika smiles gently. Carrying her niece or nephew, Zuleika sinks back beneath the water.

Jenna's hands are cold. She slides them into the front pockets of her jeans. One hand touches the child's shoes. The other touches her cell phone. She brings it out. It's wet, but for a wonder, it's still working. She texts her mother, says she will be home soon. She calls another number. "Clarence, you busy? You could come and give me a lift home? I by the river. You know where. No, I'm all right. I love you, too. Have something I need to tell you. Don't worry, I said!"

She still has her washekongs. She rinses her feet in the river and puts them on. She collects the empty shoe box and the plastic shopping bag. She climbs up the embankment to the roadside to wait for her boyfriend.

Self-Portrait as Bilbo Baggins
ADA HOFFMANN

I am barefoot, eight, and buried in ten thousand teddy bears
while you read to me. I pick them up in twos and threes,
match them to the nonsense names of dwarves.
I march them all around your room
in our little hole in the ground.

I pile the pillows up to make a mountain. Inside
hides a white bear half my size.
I can't cram in all the dwarves
for their dashing around, the theft,
the secret doors. I arrange
and rearrange, undaunted.
You tell my mother later,
"I don't know if she was listening,
but she had a good time."
Over casserole you explain
that hobbits are three feet tall, like me.
I want to stay this size forever.

Later, your *Lord of the Rings* waits on onionskin,
marked by a ribbon. I am nine now, and practical.
You are the hairy-toed audiobook playing,
entertainment while I clean my room,
until it bores me. You have the patience of meadows
but this is an awfully long book,
and there are things to do.
Pictures to draw.

Maybe you already see it,
how thirteen will break me, how even eleven
will grind. Maybe you are a wizard. You're too wise
to call me ungrateful, but maybe you see
how I'm growing too slow and too fast, both at once,
like a lopsided spider. And you are growing
sick.

There will be screaming between these walls
when the poison in your veins and mine
finds its voice. There will be creatures,
veiled in shadow, who ride in through the cracks,
whispering,
Shire.

I know none of this. I have not longed to be invisible.
I have not yet known the hates and needs
that make men wraiths. I am eleventy-one and three feet tall,
and not even I understand
what I have got in my pocket.

The Inn of the Seven Blessings
MATTHEW HUGHES

The thief Raffalon was sleeping away the noon-day heat behind some bracken a short distance from the forest road when the noise of the struggle awakened him. He rolled over onto his stomach, quietly drawing his knife in case of need. Then he lay still and tried to see through the interlayered branches.

Figures scuffled, voices spoke indistinctly, the syllables both sibilant and guttural. A muffled cry, as of a man with a hand over his mouth, was followed by the sharp *crack* of hard wood meeting a human cranium.

Raffalon had no intention of offering assistance. The voices he had heard were those of the Vandaayo, whose border was not far away. Vandaayo warriors left their land only for ritual purposes, and then always in groups of six, and never without their hooks and nets and cudgels. Their seasonal festivals centred on the consumption of manflesh, and if Raffalon had attempted to intervene in the harvesting now taking place on the other side of the thicket, the only result would have been to add a bonus to the part-men's larder.

He waited until the poor captive had been trussed, slung, and carried away, then waited a little longer—the Vandaayo might assume that where they found one fool in a forest they might find another. Only when he heard birds and small beasts resuming their interrupted business did he rise and creep toward the road.

He found it empty, except for the possessions of the unfortunate traveler who was now being marched east into Vandaayoland. He examined the scattered goods: a scuffed leather satchel, a water bottle, a staff whose wood was palm-polished smooth at its upper end. With small expectation, he squatted and sorted through the satchel's contents, finding only a shirt of indifferent quality, a fire-starting kit inferior to his own, and a carved oblong of wood about the size of his hand.

He studied the carvings. They formed a frieze of human and animal figures, connecting to each other in manners that some would have called obscene, but which to Raffalon's sophisticated eye were merely anatomically unlikely. In a lozenge at the centre of the display was a deeply incised ideogram that the thief found it difficult to keep in focus.

That difficulty caused Raffalon's mouth to widen in pleasure. The object had magical properties. It would surely command some value in the bazaar at Port Thayes, less than a day's march in the direction he was headed. Thaumaturges came thick on the ground there. He turned the item over, to see what if anything was on the other side. As he did so, something faintly shifted inside.

A box, he thought. *Better*. He rotated the thing and examined it from several angles, but found no seams or hinges and apparent means of opening it. *Even better, a puzzle box.*

The day was improving. For Raffalon, it had begun with a flight into the forest in the cold dawn, with only two copper coins in his wallet and a half-loaf of stale bread in his tucker bag. There had been a disagreement with a farmer as to the ultimate fate of a chicken the thief had found in a flimsy barnyard coop. Now it was mid-afternoon and, though the chicken had remained in its pen, the bread had been eaten as he marched. He still had the coins and had acquired a box that was valuable in its own right, and might contain who knew what?

The satchel could also be useful. He slung its strap over his shoulder after throwing away the shirt, which was too large and smelled of unwashed body. He uncorked the bottle and sniffed its contents, hoping for wine or arrack but being disappointed to find only water. Still, he tucked it into the leather bag and, after a moment, decided not to take the staff as well, even though there were steep slopes ahead, the land rising before the road descended into the river valley of Thayes—he was better with a knife if he had time to draw it.

As he walked on, he studied the box, and noticed a worn spot on one corner. He pushed it. Nothing happened. He rubbed it, again without result. He tried sliding it, this way and that. He heard a tiny click from within. A sliver of wood moved aside, revealing a pin-sized hole beneath.

Raffalon had no pin, but he had the knife and a whole forest made of wood. He whittled a twig down to the right size, inserted it into the hole, and pushed. A plug of wood on the opposite side of the box popped out. When the thief applied pressure here and there, suddenly the carved side of the box slid sideways a small distance and revealed itself to be the top of the container that moved on a hidden hinge.

Inside was a lining of plush purple cloth, with a hollowed space in the middle in which rested a carved wooden figurine the size of his thumb. It had the likeness of a small, rotund personage, bald and probably male, with head inclined indulgently and mouth formed into a forebearing grin. Raffalon took the carving out, the better to examine it.

When his fingertips touched the smooth wood, a faint tingling passed along the digits, into his palm and through his arm, growing stronger as it progressed. Alarmed, he instinctively sought to fling the thing away from him but found that his fingers and arm refused to obey him. Meanwhile, the tingling sensation, now grown into a full-body tremor, reached its crescendo. For several moments, the thief stood, vibrating, in the middle of the forest road. His eyes rolled up into his head and his breathing stopped, his knees locked, and it seemed as if a strong wind passed through his skull from left to right.

Abruptly, the sensations ended and he had control of his body again—except when he tried once more to throw the carving from him. His arm obeyed him, but his hand did not. The treacherous extremity closed tightly around the smooth wood and all of Raffalon's considerable will would not cause it to open.

Meanwhile, he heard a voice: *We had better move. When the Vandaayo are ahunting, it does not do to lollygag.*

Without much hope, the thief spun around. But there was no one there. The words had formed in his mind, without the involvement of his ears. His hand now opened and he addressed the object nestled comfortably in his palm. "What are you?"

It is a long story, said the voice that spoke in a place where he was accustomed to hear only his own. *And I lack the energy to tell it.*

Raffalon agreed with the sentiments about lollygagging. He set off again in the direction of Port Thayes, his gaze sweeping left and right as far up the forest track as he could see. But he had taken only two or three steps when his legs stopped, and he found himself turning around and returning the way he'd come.

The other way, said the voice. *We have to rescue Fulferin.* In Raffalon's mind, an image appeared: a tall, lanky man in leather clothing, with a long-jawed face and eyes that seemed fixed on some far-away vista. The thief shook his head to drive the unwanted image away—rescuing mooncalves was not on his itinerary—but he struggled without success to regain control of his lower limbs.

The voice in his head said, *You waste energy that you will need when we catch up to the Vandaayo.* Another image blossomed on his inner screen: of half a dozen hunch-shouldered Vandaayo warriors, their heads bald, their ears and teeth equally pointed, their skins mottled in light and dark green. They jogged along a forest trail, two of them carrying a long, netted bundle slung between them on a pole.

He did not try to dispel the vision, but examined it with some interest. He knew no one who had ever had an unobscured view of the Vandaayo; invariably, those who saw them clearly and up close—as opposed to a brief glimpse at a distance before the perceiver wisely turned tail and sped away— saw very little thereafter, except presumably the butcher's slab set up next to the communal cauldron.

Raffalon knew what everyone knew: that they were a species created by Olverion the Epitome, an overweening thaumaturge of a bygone age who had meant the part-men to be a torment to his enemies. Unfortunately, the sorcerer had misjudged some element of the formative process, and his had been the first human flesh his creations had tasted.

Strenuous and repeated efforts by the surrounding communities had managed to confine the anthropophagi to the wild valley that had been Olverion's domain. But all attempts to enter the deep-chasmed vale and eliminate the monsters once and forever had ended in bloody tatters: the thaumaturge had not stinted in instilling his creatures with a talent for warfare and an unalloyed genius for ambush.

Eventually, an undeclared truce established itself, the terms of which were that the local barons would not lead their levies into the valley, so long as the Vandaayo left their towns and villages unmolested. The part-men could snatch their festive meat only from the road that passed through the forest on the west of the valley, and the trail that led over the mountains to the northeast. The locals knew the times of the year when the Vandaayo were on the prowl, and avoided the thoroughfares in those seasons. Wanderers and drifters of the likes of Raffalon the thief and Fulferin the god's man were welcome to take their chances.

The image of the anthropophagi faded from Raffalon's mind as his legs marched him to the spot where the victim had been taken. Without pause, he turned away from the forest road and plunged through some bushes, almost immediately finding himself on a game trail. He saw deer scat but also the splay-footed tracks of the Vandaayo, instantly recognizable by the webbing and the pointed impression made in the soft earth by the down-curved talon on the great toe.

The tracks led toward Vandaayoland. Raffalon also saw droplets of blood on a bush beside the trail. No sooner had he registered these details than he was striding along in pursuit.

Within the confines of his skull, he said, "Wait! We must find a quiet place and discuss this business!"

His pace did not slacken, but the voice in his mind said, *What is there to discuss?*

"Whether it will succeed if you fail to gain my cooperation!"

The man had the sense that the deity was thinking about it. *Fairly said. It would drain my energy less. Let us find a spot out of view.*

The trail led them through a quiet glade bisected by a meandering stream. The thief saw a thick-strand willow and said, "Here will do." He ducked beneath the willow withes and sat on one of the gnarled roots, peered through the green screen until he was sure he was the clearing's only occupant. Then he addressed the little piece of carved wood in his hand and repeated his original question: "What are you?"

Less than I was, less than I shall be.

Raffalon groaned. In his experience, entities that spoke in such a high-toned manner tended to have an acute regard for themselves that was inversely matched by a lack of concern for the comfort of those who minioned for them—indeed, even for their continued existence.

On the other hand, his captor's determination to rescue the unfortunate Fulferin betokened some capacity for consideration of others' needs. Perhaps terms could be negotiated. He put the proposition to the piece of wood.

I see no need for terms, said the voice, its tone maddeningly calm. *Fulferin is in need of rescue. You are between engagements. One is a high imperative, the other mere vacancy.*

"Who says I am between engagements?"

I have access, said the voice, *to the vaults of your memory, not to mention the contents of your character.* It took on a distant tone. *Which scarcely bear mentioning. Fulferin stands in a better category.*

"Fulferin," said the thief, "hangs in a Vandaayo net, and soon will be simmering in a pot—not a category aspired to by men of stature."

His legs straightened and he found himself stepping outside of the willow. "Wait!" he said. "You've already lost one beast of burden to the Vandaayo. If you lose me, do you think you can seize one of the man-eaters to—"

Fulferin, said the voice, *is no beast of burden. He is a devotee, a disciple. He knows the rite that will restore my name.*

"And yet he is on his way to dine with the Vandaayo. Which tells me that at least one of you was in too great a hurry."

His legs stopped moving. *You have a point*, said the voice. *Speak on.*

"Is Fulferin necessary?" said the thief. "If it is only transport you require . . ."

Fulferin is indispensable. Only he is versed in the ritual.

"So I must rescue him from the Vandaayo?"

I have said that it is an imperative.

"Why? For what do I risk my life?"

For matters beyond your ken. Issues sublime and surpassing.

"God business," Raffalon guessed. "You're some kind of worn-out deity, probably reduced to a single devotee. And you're not even able to keep him out of the stew pot."

Fulferin must not stew.

"What can you do to prevent it?"

Send you.

"But I am unwilling."

A problem I must work around.

"Which brings us back to the question of terms."

Raffalon sensed from the silence in his head that the entity was considering the matter. Then he heard, *Speak on, but hurry.*

He said, "You want your devotee rescued. I want to live."

Fair enough. I will endeavour to keep you alive.

The thief's legs started moving again. "Wait!" he said. "Mere survival is not enough!"

You do not value your own existence?

"I already had it before I met you. If I am to risk it on your behalf, that is surely worth some compensation."

Again he had the sense that the other was weighing the matter. Then he heard, *What had you in mind?*

"Wealth—great wealth—is always welcome."

I have no command over gross physicality, said the voice, *only over certain attributes of individuals as they relate to the flow of phenomenality.*

"You mean you can't deliver heaps of precious goods?"

Not even small quantities.

The thief thought, then said, "What 'attributes of individuals' can you alter? Strength of ten men, ability to fly, impermeability to pointed weapons? All of those would be useful."

Alas, none are within my ambit.

Raffalon realized it might be better to come at the question from the supply side. "What exactly can you offer?"

My powers, said the deity, *are in the realm of probabilities.*

"You mean you make the unlikely likely?"

Say rather that I can adjust the odds, as they affect a selected person.

Raffalon brightened. "So you could fix it so that I could win the Zagothian communal lottery?"

I will be honest, said the voice. *In my present condition, I could at best reduce the odds from millions-to-one against to thousands-to-one.*

"But still against?"

Yes.

"So, essentially, you're a god of luck but only in small things?"

At present, my potency is reduced. Fulferin is going to assist me in restoring my powers.

"If he survives," said the thief. Then a thought occurred. "You weren't very lucky for him."

He had not invoked my help. He acted from . . . I suppose I must call it enthusiasm. Besides, I must conserve my strength. The box assists, by acting as an insulator.

Raffalon thought briefly, then said, "I will summarize. You wish me to risk my life, in circumstances in which a bad outcome would be particularly grisly and painful. In return, you will make sure that, along the way, I do not stub my toe or lose my comb."

In a close-run contest, I can tip the balance in your favour.

"Me against a half-dozen hungry Vandaayo does not meet my definition of close-run."

These are, said the deity, *the only terms I can offer.*

"You control my body. Can you not at least alter it?" Raffalon touched his prominent nose. "Perhaps make some part smaller?" He clutched another organ. "Or make this more prodigious?"

I control only certain interstices within your cerebrum. They generate a field that I can enhance.

"And only," said the thief, remembering, "when my flesh touches your image."

No. Once I alter them they remain altered for all time.

"I suppose it's something," the thief said. He had often encountered situations where a slight adjustment of the odds in his favour could have greatly affected the outcome. He was not an unskilled thief, but it often seemed that those he stole from—or attempted to—received more of fortune's smiles than he did.

"Still," he said, "it is not the best bargain I have ever made."

It is the best I can offer. On the other hand, I do not need to offer it. I can compel you, as long as your flesh touches my portal.

"Portal?"

The wooden eidolon.

"I see." Raffalon brushed aside the willow withes and stepped into the clearing, crossed to the trail. He saw more spots of blood, presumably Fulferin's. "If your devotee survives and completes the ritual you spoke of, your powers will increase?"

Oh, yes. Many fold.

"What then of the Zagothian lottery?"

You would win something.

"Every time I bought a ticket?"

Every time.

The man stepped onto the trail. "And this small luck would apply to my other endeavours?" He could think of past occasions when a slight nod from a god of fortune would have been useful, including one desperate flight that had led only to a lengthy term on the contemplarium's treadmill.

You would have to rescue Fulferin so that he can fulfill the requirements of the rite.

"Then that," said Raffalon, "must be our bargain." He pointed his still prominent nose in the direction of Vandaayoland and followed the trail. After a few steps, he said, "Perhaps you would be more comfortable travelling in your plush-lined box?"

No. You might then decide not to keep our bargain.

Their mission having been successful, the Vandaayo did not set themselves a gruelling pace. Nor did they watch their back trail, the chances of anyone wishing to be on the same path as six of their ilk being far too slim to warrant even a glance over a green-mottled shoulder. So it was that, towards late afternoon, as Raffalon descended a slope into a narrow valley he saw through the trees a motion in the greenery on the other side of the declivity. The part-men marched steadily up an incline that zigzagged up and out of the valley. At one switchback in the trail, the thief saw the band pause and transfer their pole-slung burden from one pair of bearers to another.

Raffalon had a rough idea how far it was to Vandaayoland and did not think that the man-snatchers could cross the border before nightfall. He thought it probable they would stop before dark; this part of the forest had become uninhabited after Olverion's final misjudgment and the large predatory beasts that now roamed free had no compunctions against dining on wereflesh.

He closed the distance between them until he could hear their grunts and panting breath ahead of him, a turn or two in the trail. As dusk began to settle, he heard different sounds and crept forward to find that the path crossed another in a clearing. Here the Vandaayo had stopped and were now gathering wood for a fire and bracken for sleeping pads. Fulferin, still wrapped in the net that had captured him and trussed to a pole, lay inert beside the track.

Raffalon established himself behind a tree and observed as the part-men built themselves a good fire. They settled themselves around it, squatting or sitting cross-legged in a circle. They had been carrying capacious leather pouches from which they now drew gobbets of rank-smelling meat and bottles of fired clay. The sounds of tearing flesh and gurgling liquids were added to the crackle of the flames, followed by grunts and belches and the occasional growl when one Vandaayo paid too much attention to another's victuals.

Dusk became darkness. At a sound from the other trail, the part-men became alert. They put down their uneaten meals and stood up, watchful. A moment later, they relaxed, though only slightly, as a second party of Vandaayo emerged from the forest, carrying their own pole-slung contribution to the ritual feast.

Greetings were exchanged—or at least that was what Raffalon thought the spate of grunting signaled. But he noted that the two groups did not mix, and that the party he had been following did not lapse into complete relaxation as the newcomers began gathering fuel for a second fire and leaves for their own beds. Indeed, two of the first arrivals left the communal blaze and went to squat beside poor Fulferin, while the other party put their own captive as far from the new camp as the clearing's size would allow.

The last light was now fading from the leafy canopy above the thief's head. He watched the proceedings as the newcomers made their own rough supper and the two groups settled for the night, each arranging its sleeping positions on the far side of its fire from the others, so that between the two hearths was a wide space of trampled grass that was clearly no-Vandaayo's land.

"Hmm," the thief said to himself. After watching a little longer, he withdrew deeper into the forest, out of pointy-earshot and spoke softly to the small deity. "I am going to need both hands."

He felt the hand that held the deity rise and find its way to the open neck of his tunic. A moment later, the little piece of wood tumbled down to rest against his stomach. The voice in his head said, *As long as some part of me touches some part of you, I will remain in control.*

The thief's curiosity was piqued. "Are you actually within the wood?"

I am where I am. The eidolon opens a . . . . conduit between there and here. Now, please get on with the rescue.

Raffalon shrugged and went farther back along the trail until he came to a place where he had crossed a small watercourse. He knelt and put his hand into the water, feeling along the stream bottom, and found what he needed. He rose and looked about. Fifty paces away, a lofty, well-leafed tree arched over the stream. He went to it, fished in his wallet, and drew out a stout knotted cord connected to a grapple. He threw this up into the branches and, luck now being with him, it caught securely on the first cast.

He left the cord hanging and returned to the edge of the clearing, Fulferin's wallet heavier by the weight of several pebbles, ranging in size from the size of his thumbnail to almost the breadth of his fist.

Staying within the tree line, he circled stealthily around the clearing until he found a tree that would best suit his purposes. He climbed until he found a comfortable crutch between two branches with a good view of the two camps. Then he composed himself to wait.

Night eased itself down over the clearing. The Vandaayo fires burned low and were refreshed. Then they burned down again. By now, all of the anthropophagi were curled or sprawled on the grass, save for one from each group. Raffalon noted that these sentries did not face the outer darkness and whatever threats might lurk there. They kept an eye on each other.

He waited until he saw one rise and go to fetch a new log for its fire. As the hunched figure bent to pick up the length of wood, the thief whispered to the deity, "A little luck would assist us now," and lobbed a pebble out into the darkness. The missile arced across the dark air and he heard a satisfying *snick* as it connected with the Vandaayo's hairless pate.

"Ow!" said the injured sentry, adding a stream of gobbling gutturals directed at its opposite number. The other group's sentry peered across the open space and, though it could not ascertain the cause of the other's pain, it recognized an occasion for mirth.

The head-struck sentry went back to its position, tossing the new log onto the fire. It squatted, rubbing its injury, and stared through slitted eyes at its counterpart, muttering what Raffalon took to be dire vows of retribution.

The thief waited until the second sentry saw it was time for fresh fuel. As it stooped to lift a log from its group's supply, he tossed another stone. He heard the same noise of impact as with the first, a similar cry of pain that was met with a hoot and jeers from the other side of the clearing.

The newly injured Vandaayo stalked to the edge of the open ground between the fires and addressed several remarks to the mocker, accompanied by juts of jaw and shakes of fists. The recipient of these attentions replied with words and gestures of its own, including the revelation of naked green buttocks and the sound of their cheeks being slapped by hard hands.

It was while the thief's first Vandaayo target was thus bent over with its back turned to the second that Raffalon sped another pebble—this one larger—on its way through the darkness. It landed with a solid *crack!* on the butt-slapper's head, bringing a new howl of rage and pain.

The freshly wounded Vandaayo spun around and charged across the neutral zone, its hand reaching for a cudgel thrust through a strap that circled its waist. Its opposite number drew its own weapon, a club ground from grey stone, and, bellowing its own war cry, rushed to meet the assault. They came together in the middle of the clearing and went at each other with all the fervour and indifferent coordination—compensated for by great strength—for which Vandaayo warriors were renowned.

The noise and tumult awoke the others, who sat up or got to their feet, blinking and staring about. Raffalon launched several missiles in rapid succession, including his largest. Aided by the luck of the small god, each found a target among one of the two clusters of sleep-fuddled part-men. One rock came down with sufficient force as to lay out the leader of the six that had snatched Fulferin. When his fellows saw their superior stretched out on the ground and their sentry doing battle, they took up their weapons and, ululating, charged the foe. The enemy, smarting from their own hurts, raced to meet them.

Raffalon descended lightly from the tree and turned to skirt the clearing to where Fulferin lay bound. But his legs disobeyed him and turned in the opposite direction. At the same time, the voice in his head said, *We may need something to delay pursuit,* while an image appeared of himself and the rescued devotee fleeing along a trail while some hapless and ill-defined person was left behind for the pursuing Vandaayo to squabble over.

"You are a cruel god," he whispered as he headed for the other captive.

I am, by nature, a kindly sort of god, came the answer, *dispensing what small blessings are within my power. But now I do as I must.*

Raffalon made no further comment, but skulked along the edge of the clearing until he came to the recumbent form wrapped in a stout net that had been snugged tightly with braided leather cords. He found his knife and cut through the restraints, whispering, "Hush! Here is a rescue. Rise and follow me in silence."

He could not see the figure clearly, this far from the fire, but he recognized the motion of a nod and heard a grunt. He set off around the clearing toward where Fulferin lay, aware of the released captive slipping through the bushes behind him. He found the god's man awake and struggling against his bonds, muttering something that sounded like a cantrip.

"Easy," he whispered. "I will cut you loose and we will flee while they are busy battering each other."

"Hurry!" said the bound man. "I see only six left standing."

Raffalon worked with his knife, looking up to see that the fight was indeed reaching its conclusion. Two Vandaayo of Fulferin's group were standing back to back, surrounded by four of the opposition. It was only a matter of time before matters were settled and the victors came to see what prize they had won.

"This way," he said, as Fulferin rose to his feet. Though both captives must have been stiff and cramped from their confinement, they came along after him as he skirted the rest of the clearing to find the trail back toward the forest road. As they plunged back into the darkness of the night forest, he could hear grunts and impacts. Moments later, the ugly sound of Vandaayo crowing triumph came to his ears and he said over his shoulder, "Faster!"

They reached the little brook where he had chosen the stones and he turned to lead them upstream to the knotted rope.

"Climb!" he said to Fulferin. The god's man had recovered his strength because he swarmed up the rope like a well-conditioned acrobat. Raffalon turned to the indistinct figure of the second captive and said, "Now you."

But this one, though smaller, was in poorer condition and struggled to make the climb. Now the thief heard new sounds from the Vandaayo camp, howls of anger and outrage. He reached out in the darkness and seized the other's torso in both hands, intending to supply extra lift. The effort was successful and the person, now able to apply feet as well as hands to the knotted cord, began to ascend.

He waited until the feet had passed above his head, then he took hold of the hemp and followed, fretting at the slowness of the climber above as the slap of Vandaayo footsteps came from the direction of the clearing. He came up onto the branch around which the grapple had snagged the rope and said to the figures beside him, "Higher, quickly but quietly."

He heard the rustle of their ascent while he freed the grapple and drew up the rope. Then he turned and silently climbed into the tree's sheltering canopy, finding two blobs of darkness against the slight shimmer of the foliage, sitting on stout branches, their backs against the trunk.

"Absolute silence," he whispered as he found a perch for himself and froze. Through the leaves, he could see the glow of torches. The Vandaayo were coming along the stream, bending over to sniff at either bank. They passed beneath without looking up.

Time passed, then the searchers came back, shoulders slumped, addressing each other in tones that Raffalon took to be accusatory. One shoved another so that its torch fell into the stream with a hiss. Grumbling, they went downstream to the trail and back to the shambles of their camp.

"We will wait," said Raffalon, softly, "until daylight, then find our way back to the road to Port Thayes."

"Agreed," said Fulferin.

"I, too," said the second rescued. Raffalon was not surprised to hear the tones of a young woman. His hands, earlier moving over her torso as he helped her up the rope, had encountered two parts of her that, though smaller than he preferred, were inarguably female.

"I will take first watch," he said. He listened to their breathing settle and thought that if he had to abandon anyone to the Vandaayo, he would prefer to leave Fulferin behind.

The little god read his thoughts. The voice said, *I must do as I must.*

At first light, they heard the Vandaayo moving off, but waited in the tree until mid-morning. They descended and made a thin breakfast of water from the stream, then set off up the watercourse. The part-men would be anxious to replenish their stolen larder, Raffalon told the others. Trails and tracks were their preferred settings for ambush. Besides, the sound of the moving water would disguise the noise of their movements.

They walked in silence and single file for a time. Then the thief felt a tug on his sleeve. Fulferin said, "That is my satchel slung across your shoulder."

"Opinions are divided on that matter," said Raffalon. "I found it abandoned, which entitles—" but even as he spoke, he saw that his treacherous hands were unslipping the strap and handing the leather bag to the other man.

Fulferin threw open the cover flap and delved into the satchel. He came out with the puzzle box then issued a yelp of unhappy surprise as he saw its secrets exposed and its velvet-lined inner compartment empty.

He looked a sharp question at his rescuer, but the voice in Raffalon's head was already saying, *Give me to him.* The thief complied without reluctance, glad to be his own man again, but he watched Fulferin carefully as the little sculpture changed hands. Actually, he noted that hands were not equally employed on both sides: the lanky man did not touch the wood, but instead held out the box so that Raffalon could snug the eidolon into its former place. Then he carefully slid the cover back into position and restored the hidden locks.

Raffalon heard the other man's sigh of relief. While Fulferin slung the satchel's strap over his own shoulder, the thief studied the man he had saved. He was interested to compare the reality before him with the image the little god had put into his mind. They did not match. Physically, Fulferin was as advertised, tall and spare, with long, spatulate fingers and knobby protrusions at knee and elbow. But the face was different. Raffalon had been shown a wide-eyed visionary; the visage he now saw was that of a man who calculated closely and went whichever way his sums dictated.

The exchange had been watched by the young woman, whose manner indicated that she found little to choose between the two men and, despite having been rescued by one of them, would not have gladly elected to spend time with either. For his part, Fulferin ignored her, all his concern fixed on the box and its contents.

Raffalon studied the woman as frankly as she had him. She was well past girlhood, but not matronly, sharp of eye and even sharper of nose, with a thin-lipped mouth that easily fell into a mocking twist. She was dressed better than a farmer's girl, though not so richly as a merchant's daughter. When his gaze rose again to her face, their eyes met. He said, "I am Raffalon, already known to you as a man of resource and valour. He is Fulferin, a god's devotee. What is your name and station?"

"Erminia," she said. "My father is an innkeeper—the Grey Bird at Fosseth."

"How did you come to be taken by the part-men?"

"My father sent me to pick morels for the Reeve's banquet."

Raffalon's brow wrinkled. "When the Vandaayo were ahunting?"

The corners of her mouth drew down. "The inn's license comes up for renewal next month. My father weighs the value of his possessions by his own scale."

"We should get on," Fulferin said, clutching the satchel to his chest. His chin indicated the stream. "Where does this lead?"

The thief shrugged. "I have seen maps. It parallels the forest road. Somewhere ahead it flows through an old estate that was abandoned after Olverion's slight miscalculation. If we can find it, it would be a good place to stay under cover until we are sure the Vandaayo have gone home."

"I must get to Port Thayes as soon as I can."

Raffalon gestured eloquently at the thickets that lined the stream on either side. Fulferin subsided, but the thief saw a flicker of calculation in those definitely-not-otherworldly eyes and surmised that the same thought about having someone to leave for the anthropophagi had just crossed Fulferin's mind. The god's man gestured in a way that invited his rescuer to lead them on.

An hour's more walking brought them to a weir that cut across the stream at a place that must have been the beginning of a stretch of rapids before the barrier was put in place. When they scrambled up they saw that the weir had created a long and narrow lake. On one of its shores, surrounded by weed-choked gardens and orchards of unpruned fruit trees, stood a mouldering agglomeration of vine-draped stone walls, spiral towers, cupolas, colonnades, peristyles, and arcades.

They explored and found that one of the towers had been built with defence in mind—probably some generations ago when the Vandaayo were only an inchoate nuisance. It had a stout door and hinges so well-greased that they had not rusted. In the basement, the stored food had long since rotted, but the wine in one of the butts was still potable.

Erminia said that she would gather fruit from the orchards if someone would come and keep watch. Raffalon volunteered. Fulferin said that he would climb to the highest point of the tower and stand sentry, calling out if he spied any Vandaayo coming their way. The thief doubted that the god's man would make so much as a squeak, and when he and the woman reached the fruit trees he climbed the highest and kept a lookout.

Erminia found apples, persimmons, karbas, and blood-eyes, wrapping them up in her shawl. She called up to Raffalon who climbed down to rejoin her. The thief thought this might be an opportune moment to test the extent of the young woman's gratitude for his having delivered her from the Vandaayo cooking pot. She was not his type, but she was here.

A moment later, face smarting from a hard-handed slap and hip aching from a knee that he had avoided just in time, he understood that Erminia drew sharply defined limits. Angered, he briefly considered enlisting Fulferin's help in mounting a concerted assault on the innkeeper's daughter's virtue. But the thought of any cooperative endeavour with the god's devotee gave him more qualms than did the concept of forcing her acquiescence.

He showed Erminia two palms in token of surrender and accompanied her back to the tower, where they bolted the door and climbed the spiral staircase to the top apartment. Here they found Fulferin, not on the alert but at ease amid the dust, sprawled on a grimy divan, drinking from a wineskin he had filled from the ample supply downstairs.

The windows were glassless, but the season was mild. Raffalon cleared a table and Erminia spread her harvest on it. They found chairs and Fulferin came to join them, bringing the wine. The young woman went to rummage in a sideboard and came back to the table with a stout cook's knife. But instead of using it to cut the fruit, she showed the point to each of the men in a meaningful way, then tucked the blade into her kirtle.

They ate in silence, passing the wineskin around. The liquid had a tinge of the vinegar to it, but was otherwise drinkable. Finally, his stomach full and his blood warmed by the wine, the thief pushed himself back from the table and regarded the god's man.

Fulferin looked back with an expression that said he did not invite the curiosity of strangers. Raffalon ignored the implied rebuff and said, "Your god made an arrangement with me. Having rescued you, I am sure you will want to help him honour it."

The worldly eyes narrowed. "What arrangement?"

"He is a god of luck in small things. He said that, if I aided you, he would henceforward bless me with his intervention. I believe his influence has already served me, and it will grow even stronger once you have revived his powers."

Fulferin shrugged. The matter clearly did not engage his interest.

Erminia said, "What is this god talk?"

Fulferin seemed disinclined to answer. Raffalon succinctly described the series of events that had brought them all together. He saw no profit in disclosing the god's willingness to sacrifice her.

The woman leaned forward, her heavy brows downdrawn. "What is this rite that will restore the god's strength? And what, by the way, is his name?"

Raffalon realized that the question had not come up, and turned to Fulferin, his face forming an interrogative. Again, the god's man showed no inclination to continue the conversation, but when pressed, he said, "Gods who do not hear their names from worshippers gradually forget them. It is akin to falling into a deep sleep, from which it is difficult for them to wake."

"So the rite will wake him up?"

The god's man shrugged. "I am no expert."

When the thief questioned him further, he displayed annoyance and made gestures that said the inquisition was an affront.

"Why this reluctance?" Erminia said. "Are you not this god's devotee, dedicated to restoring his powers? Speak!"

But Fulferin did not. Instead, with a gesture of irritation, he rose from the table, taking his satchel and its precious contents with him, and went up the small flight of stairs that ended in a door that opened onto the flat roof.

Raffalon watched him go, and was prey to dark thoughts. Fulferin was not the man the god thought he was. He remembered how careful the fellow had been not to touch the idol, which would have given the deity access to his innermost thoughts.

The thief made a thoughtful sound in the back of his throat. His gaze slid sideways toward Erminia. The woman, sitting with her chin in her hands and her elbows on the table, had also watched Fulferin depart. Now she threw a look Raffalon's way, tilting her head and moving her mouth in a way that said she knew something.

"What?" he said. "What do you know?"

But now her face said she was keeping the information to herself.

Raffalon grunted. "Next time I rescue people from the Vandaayo's cauldron, I mean to be more choosy."

That won him a short laugh from Erminia, but the sound lacked humour. She took a final apple and went to sit in one of the open windows, where she could keep an eye on one of the approaches to the estate. Raffalon took the embrasure opposite. As the day wore on, one or the other would come back to the table for a swallow of wine or a piece of fruit, but otherwise they kept their separate vigils.

At nightfall, Fulferin came down from the roof. They did not seek to light a fire, the windows being unblockable. Raffalon said he would take the first watch. Erminia said she would take the second. Fulferin shrugged and lay on the floor, his satchel for a pillow.

After three hours without incident, Raffalon woke the woman—carefully, because she slept with her knife to hand—and disposed himself to sleep.

Fulferin snored loudly in a corner, but it had been a long day following a short night's sleep, and that in a tree. The thief soon fell into oblivion.

He awoke in the full light of morning to find Erminia shaking him. "Get up!" she said. "The bastard has betrayed us!"

He sprang to his feet and followed her to a window. The sun was a good hand's breadth above the forest canopy. Below, in a leaf-strewn, flagstoned courtyard, a fire smoldered, sending a tall column of grey smoke into the still air. Of Fulferin, there was no sign.

"The Vandaayo will have seen the smoke," said the woman. "We have to get out of here!"

Raffalon was already moving toward the staircase. He picked up his wallet along the way then went leaping down the stairs, Erminia close on his heels. At the ground floor, he found the stout door open, its lock crammed with mud.

Outside, the thief hopefully kicked aside the smoldering fire, then went to an ornately perforated garden wall and peered through one of the openings. Across the lake he could see motion in the tree line. In a moment, it had resolved into the shapes of Vandaayo. They plunged into the water, trusting in the amphibian strands of their ancestry to sustain them. It would not take them long to cross the distance.

"Run!" he said.

"If we're lucky," he said to the woman as they pounded along a trail that he thought would lead back to the road to Port Thayes, "Fulferin went this way, and we'll catch up to him."

"And then?" she said, panting as she strove to keep up.

"Between the two of us, we overpower him, and leave him to do for us what he intended us to do for him."

"Leave him for the Vandaayo? Agreed."

The trail was hard-packed and showed no tracks. But Raffalon caught sight of an overturned pebble, its reversed side darker than the others around it. A little while farther on, he spied a thread snagged on a thorn. The influence of the god of small luck was still with him.

They came to a wider stream, crossed by stepping stones. As they slowed to navigate their passage, Erminia said, "I know something about Fulferin that he does not know I know."

"What?" said the thief. "And how?"

"He has come through Fosseth and stopped at our inn."

"He didn't recognize you."

"I am mostly consigned to the kitchen, scrubbing pots and scraping plates while my sister, Elfrey—she of the blonde hair and balloonish breasts and pneumatic hips that draw all eyes—she waits on the customers. Father reckons it good for business."

Raffalon extended a hand to help across a wide gap where the current ran strong between the stones. "What do you know of Fulferin?"

"He is no more than a hedge sorcerer, if that." She leapt over, daintily. "I doubt he knows more than a handful of minor spells, but he is in service to Bolbek, who calls himself the Potence, a powerful thaumaturge in Port Thayes."

"Why does Bolbek send him through Fosseth?"

"It is on the old road to the ruins of Itharios."

The man knew of the place, a tumble of broken walls and upheaved pavements, devastated in an earthquake millennia ago. "So?" he said.

"Fulferin delves in the old fanes, seeking out effigies of foregone gods. These he delivers to his master. Though sometimes they dig together."

"To restore their powers?"

They had crossed over now. She shook her head. "It involves powers, to be sure, but from what I heard them whispering when once they both stopped at the Grey Bird, the thaumaturge uses the gods the way a spider uses a fly."

"Ah," said Raffalon. Having been once incarcerated and treated in ways he had not enjoyed, he had since tended to come down on the side of flies and to reject the claims of spiders. "He has fooled the god," he said.

"I suppose," she said, "that even deities are disposed to believe what they want to believe, especially when they are desperate to survive. And when a powerful mage cloaks his assistant's true nature."

The man remembered the image of an innocent Fulferin that the god had put up on the screen in his mind. "Hmm," he said, then, "we had better move on."

They continued along the trail, making good time. The thief always seemed to place his foot in just the right place for maximum traction. Bushes did not impede his passage. He wondered if his luck would actually put barriers in their quarry's way, and decided that it could not. But it might be enough to keep him out of the Vandaayo's reach. He wondered if he was also lucky to have found Erminia; she was turning out to be a useful companion.

He came across another upturned pebble and paused to examine it. The exposed bottom was still wet, even though the sun was now well up and the day warming. He said to the woman, "He has slowed down. By now, he thinks the Vandaayo have us and is no longer hurrying."

"He struck me as the kind who expects matters to arrange themselves to his convenience," she said.

They went quickly but quietly now. The country was more up and down than level and soon they found themselves traversing a ridge. Through the trees, Raffalon saw a flicker of movement ahead. He stopped and peered forward, and in a moment he was sure. "There he is."

"He's long-legged," Erminia said. "If he hears us coming, he may well outrun us."

The man took a moment to appreciate that scrubbing pots had not diminished this woman's ability to focus on what mattered. Meanwhile, he was scanning the woods around them, seeking an opportunity for advantage.

Ahead of them, the ridge and the trail made a leisurely curve to the right. If, swiftly and silently, he could cut across the bight he might come out on the track ahead of the sauntering Fulferin.

"There," he said, pointing. A tall tree had recently fallen, crashing through what would otherwise have been an impenetrable thicket. They pushed through the bushes, scaled the tree's exposed root mass, and now they were on a clear, straight course. They ducked low and ran fast.

The fallen trunk was branchless for a long stretch and when they encountered its first foliage, they dropped down onto an open space carpeted in moss and lichens. It followed what must have once been the course of a spring-fed stream, now dried up, that led through a low tunnel of overarching branches and ended up behind a screen of a single flowered bush, only a few paces from the trail.

The man and the woman arrived just in time to see knob-kneed Fulferin come striding along at an easy pace. There was no time to plan a strategy. They simply leapt from concealment and threw themselves on their betrayer. Raffalon took him high, and Erminia low, and between them they conclusively toppled the tall man to the ground. By another bit of luck, the thief's knees landed square on the god stealer's midriff, driving the air from him in a great *whoof*!

Raffalon dug in his wallet and came out with a length of cord. With Erminia's help, he flipped the recumbent, gasping man over and quickly bound him at wrist and ankle. Then they turned him again so that he was sitting with his back against a bank of earth. The woman tore a strip from Fulferin's shirt and gagged him well, lest he speak a spell to do them mischief.

While she was doing this, Raffalon said, "If you had merely abandoned us, I could be more forgiving. But lighting a fire to draw the Vandaayo?" He left the consequences unsaid.

Erminia was more forthright. She delivered a substantial kick to Fulferin's ribs. To Raffalon, she said, "Let us go."

The bound man was making facial signs that he wished to tell them something. Raffalon stooped, removed the gag, but held his knife to the betrayer's throat. The thaumaturge's assistant said, "My master will pay you well if you help me deliver what I am bringing him." When his captors made no particular response, he went on: "This item will complete a project of great importance to him."

Raffalon hefted the man's satchel. "I'll be sure to tell him that you were thinking of him 'til the end," he said.

A sly look occupied Fulferin's face. "But you do not know who he is!"

"I didn't," said the thief, then nodded at the woman. "Until she told me." He reapplied the gag, then turned and looked back along the curve of the ridge, where mottled green shapes were bustling along the trail. "We'll be on our way now."

The house of Bolbek the Potence was in the upper reaches of Port Thayes, which occupied a hillside that ran down to the river port. It was built of an unlikely combination of black iron panels and hemispheres of cerulean blue crystal. To discourage the uninvited, it was fenced by a tall hedge of semi-sentient ravenous vine, the plant's thorn-bedecked catch-creepers constantly probing for flesh-scent.

Raffalon and Erminia approached the single entrance, a narrow, wooden archway that pierced the hedge. As they neared the opening, the air turned cold and something vaporous hovered indistinctly in the gap. "My master," it said, "expects no visitors."

"Say to your master," Raffalon said, holding up the carved box, "that something he *is* expecting has arrived."

The apparition issued a sigh and faded in the direction of the manse. The man and woman waited, batting away the hedge's mindless inquiries, until the gatekeeper once more semi-coalesced in the air before them. "Follow," it said.

The vines shrank back and the ghost led them along a path of luminous flagstones to a pair of tall double doors in each of which was carved a great contorted face. It was only when they reached the portals that Raffalon, seeing the wooden features move as the faces turned his way, realized that the panels were a pair of forest elementals enthralled by the thaumaturge to guard his entrance.

The doors opened at the ghost's further approach; the man and woman stepped into the foyer, a place clearly intended to disorient the senses. The thief closed his eyes against the onset of dizziness and said, "We will not endure ill treatment. We will leave now." He turned and groped blindly toward the doors, finding Erminia's hand and leading her behind him. Eyes downcast, she demurely followed.

"Wait," said a commanding voice. The thief's giddiness abruptly ceased. Raffalon reopened his eyes and saw that they had been joined by a short, wide-bellied man clad in a blood-red robe figured in black runes and a tall hat of complexly folded cloth and leather. His expression was impassive. He said, "What have you brought me?"

Raffalon reached into his wallet and brought forth the puzzle box.

Bolbek's eyes showed a glint of avarice. "What of Fulferin?" he said.

"He accepted an invitation to dinner," said the thief. "In Vandaayoland."

The thaumaturge's face showed a brief reaction that might have been regret. Then he said, "And in the box?"

"Fulferin said it was a god of small luck," said Raffalon. He smiled a knowing smile and added, "so to speak."

The greedy glint in Bolbek's eyes became a steady gleam. "Bring it to my work room," he said.

Raffalon stood still. "First, we must settle the issue of price."

Bolbek named a number. Raffalon doubled it. The mage gestured to show that chaffering was beneath him and said, "Agreed. Bring it." He turned and exited by a door that appeared in the wall as he approached it.

The thief was concerned. Sometimes those who agreed too easily to an extortionate price did so because they had no expectation of having to pay it. As he and Erminia followed the thaumaturge, he was alert for sudden departures from his plan.

The room they entered was of indeterminate size and shape. The walls appeared to recede or advance depending on whether they were viewed directly or peripherally; nor could the angles where they met floor or ceiling be depended on to remain static. Raffalon saw shelves and sideboards on which stood several items he would have liked to examine more closely. Indeed, he would have liked to take them away for a leisurely valuation, followed by a quick resale.

But Bolbek gave him no time. The thaumaturge bustled his way across the stone floor to a curtained alcove. He pulled back the heavy brocaded cloth to reveal a work-in-progress in two parts. One was a cylindrical container of white gold, on whose sides were drawn in shining metal a string of characters the thief could not decipher, though he had the sense that one of them replicated the unreadable symbol on the puzzle box. The ideograms must be a cantrip of considerable power, he thought, seeing them glow rhythmically against the gold, like a slowly beating heart.

The second part of the project was man-shaped—indeed, shaped very much like the man who had made it. It was a wire framework fashioned from gold and electrum, connected to the cylinder by thick, braided cables of silver. The framework was made in two halves, hinged so that the thaumaturge could open it and then stand within, completely enclosed by whatever energies the cylinder would presumably generate.

Bolbek cast an eye over the double apparatus. Apparently satisfied, he turned to Raffalon. "The box," he said.

"The price," said the thief.

A flash of irritation animated the mage's bland features, then he spoke two words and made a complex motion of one hand. A leather pouch appeared in the air before the thief, then fell to the floor with a sound that said it was well filled with Port Thayes double mools.

Raffalon handed over the box and stooped to pick up the purse. Then he turned away, as if to examine the contents in private. As he did so, he reached into a fold of his garment, out of Bolbek's line of sight. His hand closed on something concealed there. Now he tucked the coins away, while sending a meaningful glance Erminia's way.

The woman, who had so far been at pains not to draw attention to herself, began to drift toward one of the sideboards. She fixed her eyes on a glass-topped jar full of blue liquid in which swam a short-limbed homunculus with enormous eyes of lambent yellow.

Meanwhile, the thaumaturge had set the box on a small table next to the cylinder of white gold. He moved briskly to take from a drawer in the table a pair of gloves that he now pulled on up to his elbows. They were of a shimmering, scaly leather, iridescent in the room's diffuse light, as if they contained rainbows.

With clear evidence of excitement, Bolbek now turned to the box. He found the entry point on one end and slid aside the little piece of worn wood. Then he took a pin from the drawer and inserted it into the hole. His former lifeless expression had transformed into a mask of intensity and his breath came sharp and fast.

Raffalon heard the click as the box unlocked. He looked to Erminia. The woman had reached the sideboard. She now turned so that her elbow struck the jar. It wobbled and almost toppled, the lid coming free and blue ichor splashing out, with a harsh sound of glass on glass.

Bolbek's head snapped her way. "Idiot! Get away from—" he began, but at that moment, Raffalon swiftly brought the little effigy of the luck god from concealment and touched it to the bare flesh of the thaumaturge's neck. Instantly, the mage stiffened. Cords stood out in his throat and his eyes bulged. His lips writhed as he struggled to speak a syllable. To be sure he didn't, Raffalon pinched the man's lips together.

The thief was impressed at how long the spell-slinger was able to resist the god's power; his own enthrallment had been almost instantaneous. But finally the struggle ended. Bolbek's body relaxed, though his eyes spoke of inner misery.

"All well?" the thief said. He kept the idol pressed against the man's neck.

"I am still examining the contents of the memory," said the god through the thaumaturge's vocal apparatus. "Remarkable."

Erminia came forward. "What would this have done to you?" she said, indicating the apparatus.

"Dissolved me, taken my power, infused it into Bolbek." A moment's pause. "The cylinder already contains six imprisoned deities. My entry would have allowed this fellow to take the final step to leach us of our energies. Then the mana would have been transferred to the cage, to be incorporated into his own being."

"He would have become a god?" said the thief.

"No. The procedure would have failed. They always do. But he would have had a very interesting few moments before the cataclysm obliterated him, his house, and the neighbourhood."

Raffalon examined Bolbek's eyes, saw rage and despair. "And yet, somehow," he said, "I do not think that he would thank us for intervening."

"He would not," said the god within the thaumaturge. "You had better bind him well, including his fingers. And gag him thoroughly. He knows spells that need only a single syllable, and he is resolved to use them on you."

"There's a wizard's gratitude for you," said Erminia. She went and found cords, chains, and cloth, then set about rendering Bolbek harmless. She even tied his toes together. When he was comprehensively immobilized, Raffalon removed the effigy from contact with the mage's skin and set the little god on the table. "Now what?" he said.

The deity spoke in his mind again. *I studied his plans for the apparatus*, it said. *If you carefully unscrew the lid, the prisoners will be released.*

The thief said, "They are liable to be angry, and perhaps indiscriminate in how they express themselves."

I will see that they do you no harm. Indeed, I believe they will see that they owe the two of you whatever rewards are in their power.

Raffalon relayed this information to Erminia and suggested that she come and stand close to him. When she had done so, he reached for the cylinder's top and slowly rotated it. Fine threads showed, and the white gold squeaked faintly as it unwound.

Then came the last turn, and the top of the cylinder flew into the air, knocking the man's hand aside. A coruscating fount of force, in several colours and of an intensity too bright to be even squinted at, shot up to the ceiling. The air of the room was filled with overpowering scents, rushing winds, claps of near-thunder, and waves of pressure that made the thief's ears hurt.

Invisible hands seized Raffalon and Erminia in a crushing grip and raised them high above the floor. The thief had but a moment to think that he was about to be dashed against the flagstones. Then as quickly as they had been taken up they were gently lowered again.

I regret, said a different voice. *Potho has explained that you have been our deliverers, not our captors.*

"Potho?" Raffalon and Erminia said, together.

It is my name, said the voice the thief recognized as the luck god's. But now he sounded delighted. *Mithron recognized me, as I did him. We are the divine equivalent of cousins.*

"Mithron?"

Now the other voice spoke. *A god of those who race horses*, it said. *Potho and I were often invoked together.*

The luck god made other introductions: Iteran, who presided over crossroads; Belseren, whose province was health and vigor; Samiravi, a goddess of erotic fulfilment; Fhazzant, who looked after licence inspectors and tax collectors; Tewks, who, if properly propitiated, could fulfil heart's desire.

We are all grateful to you, said Potho. *And each of us has bestowed upon you both what blessings are within our purview, now that we all know our names and our powers are restored.*

"You mean I can count on a good day at the races?"

Always, said Mithron.

Raffalon mentally itemized his other gains. He would never be ambushed at street corners. He would never sicken or tire, nor be embarrassed or unfulfilled in moments of intimacy. What benefits he would accrue from the patron of tax collectors he could not at first imagine.

They will leave you unmolested, said a new voice he assumed to be Fhazzant's.

"I thank you all," he said and made a formal gesture of gratitude.

"As do I," said Erminia, although at first Raffalon did not recognize the musical voice as hers. He turned to her and saw that Samiravi had been at work. The young woman's eyes were now not quite so close together, nor her nose so long and pointed. Her lips had become fuller and a hairy mole on her chin was gone. Her upper and lower garments had filled out. She glowed with health and erotic promise.

From the way she was looking at him, it seemed that he, too, had been reordered and improved. He felt his nose and found it handsomely reshaped, while he surreptitiously slipped a hand into a pants pocket and quietly determined that his initial inquiry about prodigiousness had been remembered and fully answered.

"I thank Tewks, most particularly," he said.

Now, said Potho, *we will say farewell. We have business with this prideful sorcerer.*

Mithron added, *We have dismissed all his familiars and frighteners. If, on the way out, you see anything you like, feel free to take it with you.*

Fhazzant's voice said, *He will have no further need of his goods.*

Raffalon repeated the gesture of gratitude. Erminia offered a graceful curtsy, then said with a ravishing smile, "I've never been able to do that right before."

Together, they left the thaumaturge's work room, where the winds had once more begun to roar. Throughout the mansion, doors slammed open, locked coffers popped their lids, and cupboard doors swung wide.

Sometime later, their pockets full, bearing between them a densely packed trunk, they were making their way down one of Port Thayes's better boulevards, seeking a place to stay. Erminia said, "I have been thinking. If we built an inn at a crossroads, near a good race course . . ." She paused for thought, then went on, "And if I served the customers and you ran a few games of chance, perhaps set up a tote . . ."

Raffalon said, "We would have no troubles with overzealous officials."

"It could work," she said. "Of course, you and I would have to be personally compatible."

"There is a hotel across the way," the thief said. "We could take a room for the night and see."

He was surprised, but pleased, when she forthrightly expressed approval of his proposal.

Later that night, having discovered that they were indeed wonderfully compatible, she threw a sated arm across his chest and said, "To be a success, an inn needs a good name."

He said, "With luck, I'm sure I'll think of one."

The Full Lazenby

JEREMY BUTLER

The cardboard box held fewer books than I expected. Sartre was safe but Neitzsche ended up in the trash. I wanted to cry.

Dwight burst into our room, still in last night's clothes. "Dude, you should have come out. I hooked up with this chick, a two-thirds Anaïs Nin. It was dirrrty." He noticed the empty shelves, the box of my prized books. "No scholarship, then?"

"Nope. No one wants to subsidize philosophers."

"You could switch majors. That girl last night said poetry has good backing. Some software developer found out he was 64 percent Ezra Pound and now he's throwing money at anyone who can rhyme."

I shook my head. No wealthy industrialist would foot the bill so I could read Camus.

"Then get tested," he said. "Find out who you are. Maybe you're a 90 percent Dostoyevsky. I bet State would drop tuition for that."

I paused. "Schools do that?"

"For sure! Look at Peterson next door, she's a ninety-plus Beethoven. She got a full ride and I heard she's tone-deaf."

"That's so not right."

"It's your only hope, buddy. Roll the dice. I'll pay."

"Yeah, but what if I'm a Caligula?"

"They haven't got him. I've checked."

"Goebbels?"

"Ach!" He grunted. "Let's skip the *'What if I'm Hitler?'* talk. Just read the pamphlet."

Dwight asked the woman at the testing centre to run my sequence but not release it publicly until we screened it. She left us alone in the waiting room where I paced like an expectant father.

The centres boasted a database of millions of talented and/or famous individuals. Phenotypy and genealogy were weak indicators of similarity, or so the homology quotient supporters claimed.

If Betsy Rowling, only 13 percent her great-grandmother, boasted a million pre-orders for her unwritten first novel then a 95-plus percent JFK match running for senator was easily considered the real thing. Cue headlines, cue interviews, media coverage, excited electorate.

Everyone loved a dynasty, even a scientifically dubious one.

Dwight had four weak matches. For a directionless trust fund kid, his quotients defined his world. Because of his 45 percent William Shatner quotient, he studied drama. His 32 percent Henry Kissinger had him in political science. Jane Austen, creative writing. Carl Sagan, astronomy.

Full matches were sufficiently rare that outside of twins there had never been living duplicates. Dwight still pined for a match with some yet-to-be-sequenced celebrity, preferably a minor Borgia or Jesus.

The woman returned. I couldn't read her expression, only its intensity. She held out the envelope and Dwight snatched it away, pulling out the paper within. His eyes scanned back and forth. The girl stared at me, then winked coyly.

"So," I said. "Who am I? Let me guess. Henry Winkler, Ringo Starr . . ."

"Am I reading this right?" Dwight asked.

The girl nodded.

"A 99.7 percent match?"

Panic gripped me. "Who? Oh god, please don't say Dahmer."

"George Lazenby."

I searched my memory and came up blank.

"James *fricking* Bond," Dwight gushed. "Do you know what this means?"

My phone rang from my pocket. Dwight stared, expectantly. I answered.

"Is this Lazenby, George Lazenby?"

"What? No. I'm sorry, my name is—"

"Agent 007, your presence is requested at once!"

There were four Bond Houses, each on a different continent. The North American one was an extravagant mock-European affair with crystal chandeliers, baccarat tables, and wall portraits of the sixteen Bond actors. Its revenue was supported largely by weddings, conferences, and weekend getaways.

The facilities kept the character alive, thereby feeding the film and television franchises, which in turn fed the facilities and their staff. It was an integrated media experience that crossed the boundaries between amusement park, movie, and family to the tune of billions annually.

"We expect our Bonds to be men and women of education and manners, first and foremost," my guide said. The man, a 92%-Roger Moore, was of Middle Eastern descent and spoke with a posh English accent. "We will, of course, ensure that you are taught self-defence, weapons, and foreign languages. You speak Russian at least?"

I shook my head.

"That's okay. Any military service?"

"Afraid not."

"My dear boy, not to worry. There is plenty of time. We are just happy to have you. Our last Lazenby died in a skiing accident. For thirty years, all we've had are false alarms to . . . address."

"Address?"

"Bond is a legacy that must be protected. Impostors are just one of the threats. Double agents, defectors. We have moles at the very top of the testing centre administration. We keep tabs. The last thing we need is a 95 percent Judi Dench being picked up for armed robbery again, am I right?"

I had no idea what he was talking about.

"We deal with those threats the way our forefathers did." He smiled wanly. "Never mind that now. You're going to fit in wonderfully, George."

I was about to correct him, but he continued.

"We'll start with the wardrobe. We would like to see you wear something more fitting. And do you own a car?"

"No, I bus it, usually."

He grimaced. "That will not do. A Bond on public transportation? How the Bournes would love that!"

"Actually, I'm broke. I'm dropping out to—"

"I'm aware of your finances, George. A distraction from your studies and your Bondship. Your outstanding debt was paid this morning. Please let me welcome you to Her Majesty's Secret Service."

"For real?"

"Well, figuratively."

Everything changed.

Women threw themselves at me. Men, too.

My neck ached from nodding at double entendres.

Professors paid me more attention. The Dean approved my scholarship saying that my "breeding and roguish contempt for authority would bring fresh air to a stale department."

Even my parents got excited. They told their friends all about their famous son and his spiffy new Aston Martin. They even went to get tested themselves. Dad was nearly a 40 percent Alan Hale. Mom was a quarter Dian Fossey.

It all felt good. Weird, but good. I was celebrated for the accomplishments of a theoretical relative playing a fictional person. Material for a great thesis or else a nervous breakdown.

Bond House didn't ask for much in return, just to promote the legacy: dress well, stay out of trouble, exude confidence, and most importantly, stay single.

After an on-camera piece about *Bond 2212*, 92%-Moore scolded me for shoehorning Kant into an on-camera piece. "Just stick to wordplay. Keep your studies to yourself, understood?"

A few vodka martinis in, my tongue let loose. "Like, you'll only live once to see this episode. How's that?"

92%-Moore smiled magnanimously. "Great."

"Diamonds are forever, but this film won't be in theatres long. Be sure to—"

"Very clever, yes."

"The world is not enough to keep me from tonight's showing of—"

"Do shut up, 007."

I moved into a small apartment replete with all the trappings of a spy's 1960s love nest—hidden entrance, rare tropical fish, rotating bed, wet bar.

Dwight showed me how to use my identity for fun. Cops, bartenders, hotel staff. A casual reveal led to rule bending, free drinks, respect. I had the weight of a multinational corporation behind me.

After plain bribery got me a passing grade in Senior Ethics, Dwight and I hopped a flight for the Bond casino in Monte Carlo.

The place was packed. Full Christopher Walken regaled a crowded bar. Full Halle Berry held court at craps. I made the rounds, posing for pictures and punning my way through the tuxedoes and evening gowns.

Along the way I met twin Russian 75 percent Diana Riggs that clung to me like henchmen. They were hopeful of entering the Bond House and teared up when I hinted they weren't pure enough Rigg.

"There are two of us, though," one said. "Bring us in together."

"Yeah," cooed the other. "That's one-and-a-half Riggs."

By the time I finished, Dwight was at the poker table, deep in the hole and more than a little tipsy. I took the seat across, a partial Rigg nibbling each of my ears.

"They say two heads are better than one," Dwight called. "We should totally test that out."

The Riggs stopped. One of them hissed.

I raised a hand. "Dwight, that's not the carriage of a gentleman. Please apologize."

Dwight rolled his eyes and threw back the rest of a scotch.

The Riggs turned their attention to my thighs. "Where's your suite, George? Let's all retire to some place more private."

"I believe I have the accommodations to accommodate that," I said, eyebrow raised. The Riggs tittered.

"Tenth floor," Dwight said. "His name's on the door. Give us a few minutes to freshen up, then come on up."

They recoiled. "Us?"

"I'm George's benefactor. Isn't that right?"

Reluctantly, I nodded.

"See, girls," Dwight slurred, pushing back from the table. "George was a much better bet than cards. He always brings me returns on my investment." I watched in horror as he unzipped his fly.

The Riggs were over the table and pounding him before I could move. By the time Dalton and Brosnan pulled the Riggs off, Dwight's bloodied nose and lip had ruined his dinner jacket.

The Riggs were dragged out, cursing in Russian.

The room was silent, everyone stared: Walken, Berry, Grace Jones, even the new Sophie Marceau I hadn't met yet.

"I'm going to invite you to leave," Dalton said to Dwight. "Unless," he turned to me, "he's with you?"

My friend stood bleeding and drunk, surrounded by opulence and beauty. His fly gaped, mucus poured from his nose. He was a buffoon, everything Bond was not. Everything I was not.

All eyes were upon me.

"Me? No." I said. "We've never met."

Dwight must have caught a flight that night. He didn't return my calls, was never in our old room. He avoided me, and I couldn't blame him.

I graduated, although I missed Commencement for a two-year Guest of Honour stint aboard the new Bond Cruise Line. Tuxedos and Hawaiian shirts, bon mots and international women. The good life.

I had barely regained my land legs when my phone woke me from sleep, finding me uncomfortably alone. It was 92%-Moore.

"Get to the Bond House fast. We believe that someone may try to kill you."

I pulled on a pair of cream linen trousers. "Kill me? Like for real? Why?"

"Because you're a Bond."

"What? Who would do that?"

"George, six months ago, Gert Fröbe was sequenced. He has a full match. We wanted to make an offer for him to join Bond as a lobby greeter or desk clerk. But the man disappeared. Our extensive network of resources uncovered no trace. It was odd, but soon forgotten."

"Fröbe, who's that?"

"The actor who played Auric Goldfinger, the ruthless mining magnate that was one of Bond's greatest nemeses."

"Okay, so . . . ?"

"This evening, Brosnan, your replacement on the H.M.S. Thunderball, was found dead. He was covered in gold paint."

"What?"

"Dalton put it all together. A man who has the means to hide out from our extensive surveillance. An incident he recalled from Monte Carlo. A man who holds a grudge against Bonds. We're recalling Bonds everywhere, especially since you two shared a roof . . ."

My head started to swim.

I ran for my safe and found its door was already open. My Walther PPK and laser watch had always been for show, but now were gone. Only one other person knew the combination.

A gun cocked in the darkness.

Dwight stepped forward into the bubbling light of the exotic aquarium. He pointed my pistol at me. The aquarium's light reflected off a collection of medallions he wore around his neck.

"Hang up the phone, George."

I hung up. "You're really embracing the gold thing. This is for real? You killed Brosnan?"

"You're the philosopher. What do you think, coincidence or fate?"

"Neitzsche said that the metaphysical need for art to—"

Dwight laughed with disheartening malice. "Save it for someone who cares."

"I'm sorry. I should have . . ."

He raised his hand, quieting me.

"You don't understand, you and your Bond friends. I wasn't *given* the opportunity you were, so instead I'll *take* it. No one wants a partial Shatner that can't emote or a witless slice of Austen. But a Goldfinger that beats Bond, there is a somebody."

"You are somebody, Dwight."

"Don't call me that! Other than this, I'm just potential diluted to inconsequence. When I learned of the match, I knew. I felt it in my bones. This was who I was meant to be."

"A murderer?"

He grinned. "I'm just what you made me. Hero of the No-Ones."

It wasn't a bad speech, given the situation. I nearly suggested that he reconsider the Austen path, but it was too late for that. We stared at each other, the moonlight casting shadows. Dwight stretched out his arm, pointing the weapon at my chest.

"Good-bye, Mr. Bond," he said.

"Goldfinger was a great villain. But he's not the most popular."

"I know that. I'm not even a great nemesis. Are those are your final words?"

"I'm just saying that if you're going to define the role for yourself, I think you should take a cue from what's worked."

"Such as?"

"Blofeld is far more popular. It's all about your escape. The chase, the mystery—where is he, what is he doing, what will he do next? The mystery's the thing. That's what keeps the audience coming back. Trust me, it's Bond 101."

He lowered the gun an inch. "You think so?"

It was my chance. I dove at him, knocking his arm aside as bullets shattered windows and the aquarium. My eardrums sang as we wrestled, but with his Shatner-inspired combat skills he handily threw me to the floor.

Aquarium glass pierced my back and breathing became sharp and pained. I heaved like the exotic fish flopping around me. Dwight stepped forward and leveled the gun at my face.

"Good bye, Mr. Bond."

I rolled over, unwilling to stare down a gun's dark hole of death, to a fish, drowning on the shag carpet, my companion in suffocation.

Two eyes stared at me and in them, I found salvation.

A quick toss sent the fish tumbling through the air, its spikes protruding in defense as Dwight put up a hand to block. The pufferfish's spines sent neurotoxin into his hand before he batted it away, dropping the gun in the process.

His screams were muffled by my still-ringing ears and the all-consuming pain in my chest, though I had a sense that he screeched even as he ran into the night.

At some point sirens came.

At some point I blacked out.

I came off the ventilator after a day, though the pain lasted longer. My parents visited and the police took my statement. A week in, 92%-Moore arrived, his brow furrowed but wearing a full grin.

"This is amazing, George. The interest we're seeing is off the charts. The police are keeping tabs on Octopussy and eight Blofelds, just in case. There's talk about re-releasing the original films in IMAX-3D and building an Australian Bond House in your honour."

He continued like that for ten minutes. Finally, I interrupted: "I'm fine, thank you, Roger."

"What's that, George? You must find Goldfinger. The media and the fans are demanding it."

"Track him down? I'm not a real spy. Why would I do that?"

"We'll help you, George. It's what you're made for."

"Made for? I'm supposed to be reading books, not hunting enemies, not getting shot at. You know that we're not actual agents, that none of this is real?"

92%-Moore shrugged.

I removed the oxygen mask so there would be no confusion. "Look, Roger, I'm done. I appreciate all you've done for me but I don't want to be Bond anymore. I'll change my name, move to Guam, whatever. You'll have to wait for the next Lazenby."

He stared at me agape. "Give up Bond? Just like that? With no thought of the future, no plan for what comes next?"

"I appreciate everything you've given me. But let Connery take a crack at Goldfinger. That sounds right to me."

92%-Moore laughed.

"Quit Bond after one adventure? That is *so* Lazenby."

The God of Lost Things

NEILE GRAHAM

Is a small beast with a body of Celtic knots. Ears twitching
soft as a doe's.
Lively-eyed, narrow-eyed. His nose is long and
wide, wide open.

My prayer to him is simple at first. I want what I want
and want it back.
But vain hours later I'm inventing prayers of smoke
and mirrors,

knotted into silver lace. They rise into the tarnished sky
sparking and weaving
all ears, all eyes, all long, long nose. Please be seeking, be
finding, be bringing

it back to my hand, oh beast, how my hands then will stroke
those ears, bless
those bright eyes, how I will delight that nose with delicious
tidbits, offerings

of thanks. How I will make a pet of you place you in my silken
cage lined with your new
velvet bed. How when you curl there I will say I want what I want
and I want it. You.

The Beat that Billie Bore
LISA L. HANNETT

Anton plays so much better on stage than ever he did with his Pap and breddas on the jetty. Painted bright yellow, the plywood dais resonates beneath the chip-shuffle of his bare feet. His step lively even after sixty-odd years of dancing, easily keeping time with the soca tunes ringing loud and joyous from his steel drum. Age has leached the golden kelp from his dreadlocks, twisted them long with strands of urchin-grey, but otherwise hasn't softened him. Frontish, as always, Anton's got his shirt off for the audience. From a leather strap hanging round his proud neck, the instrument he's famous for is held against a belly taut and ridged. Sunlight reflects up from the dented pan, highlighting the angles and curves of his quick-moving iron arms, the fading brown of his skin, the silver and chrome in his seams. Striking note after triumphant note, Anton turns his hard body this way and that, flexing what muscle he has left.

A real showman, Billie thinks, watching her husband perform for fidgeting school kids, cross-legged on the grass. For his surviving breddas and their sons, all drummers by soul and trade, sitting on steps cut into the dunes. For the vendors dishing up sweet khurma, hot pholourie and conch fritters on the boardwalk, the peddlers serving shark and bakes in paper bags. For the halter-dressed hornerwomen skulking by tall palms, plumping their lips, batting lashes; dumb chits she knows Anton would still like to rut. For the tanties and oncles taking a morning stroll on the beach. Most of all, for the cameras.

Another documentary is in the works. How many is this, now? Must be the twentieth, maybe the thirtieth he's signed on for since the attack.

Some, like this one, want to catch the magic of his music. Others cast him as host before sending him, a layman, a Grade Six dropout, on scientific expeditions. *Under the Sea—with Anton Daize. Carnivores of the Deep—with Anton Daize. Anton Daize: Chasseur des Sirènes.* More than four decades on, unflagging interest in his story. Offers endlessly trickling in from all over the globe. A lifetime of celebrity founded on stupid luck, on the fluke of his still being alive.

Billie unballs her hands, folds them demurely on her lap. This film crew is professional, well-oiled. By the looks of their gear, well-funded. Up with the first patrol, they arrived on site early to hoist lightboxes and tripods and microphones. To erect the platform, far enough from shore to keep Anton safe, close enough to capture him, a seasoned rhythm-man, within sight of the legion of boys practising their beats on the pier. The scene perfectly orchestrated, from the set list to the number of coast-watch balloons floating above the sea. Lenses dilate and pan and zoom in close. Producers hunch over monitors, wearing the squint of artists poised for the winning shot.

Smoothing her features, Billie sits up straight in the back row. Knows there's a camera reserved just for her. Inhales slowly, breathing in warm spice and kid-stink and salt air. Plays the captivated wife to Anton's centre of attention.

Now Anton's hands are more walnut and lead than flesh, his fingers tipped with hard latex balls. They flit, shadow-fast, across tempered steel, coaxing out layer upon layer of rich, round notes. Vibrations thrum up his forearms and biceps and into his chest; the sound intensifies, redoubles. He hasn't used separate mallets in years.

And why would he, Billie thinks, remembering how Anton used to struggle with pitch. With control. Before he'd been remade.

Barely twenty, bleary-eyed, he'd take his dawn post on the wharf beside his twelve breddas—men all much older, much less afraid than he was. Right about then, Billie had started noticing him. Perched on a breakwater on the opposite side of the harbour, she'd raised her binoculars, gaze shifting from fins and flippers, churning waves. Focusing instead on Anton's sun-burnished face, a fairer copy of the other Daize boys'. The freckles darkening the bridge of his nose. The pale green of his irises, stark against russet skin. The glints of gold in his deep brown goatee. The sand-brushed wisps of his dreads. Stylised tattoos inked across his lean torso, nipped down to his waist, snaked the lengths of his arms. In his fists, black-headed drumsticks held far too tight.

With the other men playing beside him, Anton always tried too hard. Tension and worry restrained music that should've flowed out of him, easy as air.

"*Eh eh!* Loose, dey! Loose!" said Anton's Pap, harsh voice carrying over the water. He'd cracked his own sticks across the boy's knuckles, raising welts. "You're choking the blinkin' chune, child. Watch how Kane and Tito swings them elbows. Loose, loose. See?"

That day, like so many before, there'd been little time for lessons. Shouldn't have needed them anyway, Billie once thought. Daize sons and breddas had been guarding that bay for two generations at least; swinging a mallet, chanting back to the mermaids' taunts. It was all Anton had ever known.

But *knowing* isn't the same as *doing*, Billie thought, spying on that boy through the double-Os of her lenses. Flushed, he'd tried to mimic Tito's technique—joints fluid, a bounce in ankles, free wrists—but soon enough the sea beasts got to howling. Anton's hard-earned looseness went rigid. His old man set a dingolay tempo, then it was all he could do to keep up.

Feet thumping on driftwood boards, quick-step getting quicker as the Daizes drummed. Sweat slicking brown shoulders, beading on beards and locks and lashes. Brows furrowing, intent, as coconut notes rolled from beaten steel bowls, dropping like bombs into the water. Pommerac harmonies swelled, burst on splashing fish-bodies. Jasmine strokes unspooled from the instruments, pulsing longer and stronger, melodies noosing neck after mermaid neck.

So many of the creatures, so many finning for shore. Salt-hued and iridescent. Bottle-nosed and saw-toothed, jelly-featured and aquiline. Bone-fingered and scythe-flippered. All gilled and ribbed with cartilage. Some bulbous, pregnant; others bubble-spined, carrying broods of transparent eggs on their backs. Fierce, malachite sirens, their tapered fishtails hollow sacks for carrying, drowning, digesting human children. Schools of dagger-beaked killers. Piranhas scaled with faces of the lost.

Thrashing, flailing, breaching, the mermaids attacked. High on the bloodlight of dawn, frenzied on the smokedust of twilight, they advanced and retreated with the tides. Hungry for land, and those that walked on it. Forever hungry.

Whistle clenched between her teeth, Billie had shrilled warnings if any beasts wriggled through to the shallows. Not many did; the only hole in the breddas' audible net was at the deepest end of the wharf, where Anton, as youngest, stood. Four hundred metres of Daize men between him and the beach. Four hundred metres of calypso causing a real bacchanal in the water; the mermaids, gone giddy on music, screamed like whales, tearing each other to bits. Four hundred metres of unbroken ginger-spiced rhythm, with only that one sour note at its end.

Between songs, Anton fields questions from the crowd. At least half are scripted; the producers of these things are always uptight about content, about getting enough of the right kind of material. This crew has planted child actors among the schoolkids—Billie spots them in seconds. The girls with plaits neatly ribboned, the boys with a sheen of spray on their curls. Uniforms bought, not hand-me-down. Skin fairer than most, exposed to spotlights and flashes more than sun. Their little voices clear, projected from the gut, just the way mainland coaches taught. Enunciation perfect. No rambling, trail-away thoughts.

Not that Anton cares for such polish. He's off laughing now, speaking before the askers even finish their asking. Editors got their work cut out with him, Billie knows. Directors can give prompts 'til their arms drop off, won't guarantee Anton'll take them. Always was better at improvising, ad-libbing, than ever he was at minding a set score. Gets away with it, nowadays, more often than not. Her husband's still a charmer, Billie will grant him that. Tongue quicker than his rhythms.

Too quick sometimes, she thinks, tuning out as Anton skims over their history together. A reel of highlights for the kids, for the cameras. How sweet to look on Billie was at seventeen. How she was first to dance at the bonfire, after moon-feasts. Lord, how she threw waist! Here, a practised pause. An interlude on the drum, washed in pineapple breezes. How the two of them carried on! Bulling and chooking whenever they weren't on duty, whenever their old Paps weren't looking. Celebration pace slows to contemplation; Anton's fingers flutter across steel bevels, producing minor tones. Those arresting eyes of his turn serious as he reminisces, staring off-stage, a bloom of red the publicity folk will call love colouring his cheeks. How Billie stood by him, after everything. How she nursed him, unflinching, despite the gore. How she keeps the drum in his hands every day . . .

What luck I've had, he'll say quietly. What luck.

Half a mile down the coast, at the midpoint of the cove's gentle arc, a two-storey house thrusts its verandah out of the surrounding greenery. The clapboards well-fitted, gleaming white. The pointed roof shingled bright blue. Their home since the release of *Bloodwater: Surviving Merasme Bay*. A lovely building, but often draughty. Seagulls ride thermals above its gables, easily negotiating turbulent currents. Wings spread, freewheeling.

Unmoving, Billie follows them with her gaze.

In all his candid chatter, Anton never mentions the house, though everyone knows it's theirs. Never mentions Billie's binoculars, or her high-pitched whistle. How for years she'd sound it just for him—a secret tune at the first splash of mermaids—to help him race to the jetty before his breddas, before his Pap. To buy him time. To let him settle his nerves, get his cadences up to speed before the rest of the men came down and out-drummed him. Never mentions how he married her, resented her, for it. How he'd knock her with those over-tight fists of his, beats without measure, then doux-doux her as she cried, rocking her in his arms until she fell asleep. How she left him, twice, after their babies came and went, shells that echoed without any rhythm. How he struggled against wave after wave of sea death. His best almost as good as his breddas' worst. Anton is no virtuoso, never has been. Only more beautiful, now, for having been broken. Even Billie sees that, without having to look too close.

Applause as her husband stops talking, continues playing. His metal arms strobed with gold light as clouds scutter across the sky. Gashes across his broad chest and neck, thick with burnished silver lines, rise and dip like soundwaves. A wolf-whistle trills from under the palm trees. Laughter erupts from the crowd. Over their bobbing heads, Anton looks for Billie. Nods once when he finds her stiffly clapping.

Then he turns away, focuses on the intricacies of song.

Never once mentions how she saved him.

Before the end of his concert, Anton signals for a stagehand, a distant cousin with aspirations of wielding mallets one day. The girl climbs the three plywood steps, face turning plum as she crosses the boards, bringing her uncle a sheaf of poster-sized cards. Holds them up one by one, so Anton can talk and point at 8x10 photos fading on the colourful sheets. Tape yellowing around pictures of Anton bloodied, full-dazed, flat out on the pier. The boiling mass of steel, bubbling against his scorched and blistered skin. The sleek water ambulance that jetted him off to the mainland. Pre- and post-op snaps of his flesh, red-puckering around streaks and blotches of newly entrenched metal. The melted mess of his hands before reconstruction. The wooden smoothness after.

The placards are embarrassing, Billie thinks. Dunce-papers for show and tell. Scrawled with Anton's juvi writing, bubble-letter titles in primary colours. Any of the kids come to see his show could've done better. But the director eats them up. Probably thinks they're quaint, down-home—that they show how *genuine* is her husband. How simple and unpretentious. How open.

As he shoos the girl off stage, Anton pulls a handful of fangs from the pocket of his ragamuffin pants. Holds them up individually, jabbing the points into the thick of his walnut thumbs so everyone can see how big they are, how sharp. He matches some with the gouges in his jaw, others with the rips in his gut. Folk *ooh* and *ahh* at the right moments, flinching and *steupping*, sucking air through clenched teeth. Anton grins. Doesn't admit these aren't the actual chompers, the ones that mauled him, but some shark fossils he unearthed while shooting *Inside Nature's Giants* on the other side of the world.

Billie knows what the real set looks like. Every day, she's felt their bluntness with her own tongue.

For a while, it had seemed the shoals of mermaids were thinning. Only two or three toddlers had been snatched in as many years. A dozen goats from coastal yards, maybe twice that many chickens. And one old crab-trawler whose missus might've turned hornerwoman; a pride-bruised man who might've got all doltish on black rum, who might've swum with the beasts on purpose, just to spite his cheating wife. Twice daily, Billie's binoculars caught only a fraction of the scales and fins and sea-tresses they would've in earlier seasons. People had begun to dust off their surfboards. They'd started wading in the shallows at noon. There'd been talk of a summer regatta. Rumours of sinking a series of standard, rope and fishing-wire shark nets. Blind promises of life on the water.

On the quayside, the breddas' calypso numbers had started to rankle. With so many rhythm-barrels, and so few creatures left to subdue with them, the bay was suddenly blinkin' rowdy. After years of noise, locals had a mind for a bit of quiet liming. They were less inclined to slip coin into Daize pockets, to bring thirteen hens to the obeah woman for sacrifice on their behalf, or leave baskets of baigan, plantain, dasheen, and fried bake on the docks for the drummers to eat. Out of gratitude, loyalty, or just old habit, a few ancients had hobbled down to the beach each morning to give the breddas their due. Some days the offerings fed half of them, others they'd barely scraped together enough to satisfy twelve men.

Hunger hadn't improved Anton's performance—and without mermaids snarling and snapping and churning the sea to red froth, there was no distraction from his stiff playing. His poor timing. His missed beats. Through her lenses, Billie scoped the way Anton's family gave him the side-eye. His Pap passing barra to the older men first, leaving little or nothing for the youngest. Cringing at his clanging attempts to outpace them, to *earn* his bread. Still letting him play—Anton was a Daize, after all—but moving him far, far from the shore. A lone sentinel at the pier's end, well away from the crowd-pleasing band.

Brine winds had ruffled the near-empty cove that one day, cool near-autumn breezes buoyed with the scent of decay. The stink, Billie had hoped, of incoming mermaids. Holding back stray wisps of hair that had escaped her topknot, she'd strained her eyes through the glass. Turquoise waters rippled clear near land, blueing to black beyond the seawall. Tankers belched grey spume on the horizon, sailing tortoise-slow off the edge of the world. Gulls and shearwaters dotted the surface, wings tucked as they bobbed. Near the sandbar, a shadow smudge of movement. Oiled dorsal fins. Long-slatted gills. Hides dark as the abyss.

Billie had mouthed her whistle, aching to blow. If only that pod of rotters would advance, she'd thought, looking at Anton's lonely silhouette, backlit against the sunset. Even slump-shouldered, the man still cut a fine figure. Years and bad timing hadn't wizened him. Not physically. But with every wrong note, every missed cue, every frustrated pounding, his spirit seemed to shrink that much more. At night, after Anton had exhausted himself on her, Billie swore she could hear the soul rattling around inside him, one split pea in a hollow gourd.

Billie wasn't stupid; she knew there was more to her husband than that. She had never been stupid. *All he needs*, she'd told herself, she'd had to believe, *is a good chance to prove it.*

Teeth grew first inside Billie's guts, and around them the creature took shape.

At first she'd imagined the obeah woman would toss magic like burley straight into the sea—lure the mermaids inland with a scum of rank meat and nostalgia. But within minutes of tapping on the charm-laden door, Billie had understood better. This was *her* idea, *her* burden to bear. And soon as the witch had chanted those hot-pulsed words, wadding that jumbie-seed up under Billie's skirt, the beast had gripped her good. Scraping and gnawing at the lowest parts of her belly. Biting for a way out. Worse pain than ever she'd had, worse than monthly bloods, worse than loosing Anton's unfinished babes from her womb. The clever-nennen had cautioned her beforehand, said red spells took a greater toll on the body than black or blue or yellow—but it was seeing those same colours around Billie's sockets, the bois-marks on her ribs and back, that had convinced the old woman that this here was a girl with sufficient strength and need to withstand it.

Before Billie left the stilt-walker's bungalow, a tray of eggs had changed hands. A pouch of pepper. A fig-sized ball of coins. Not enough, she'd begun to apologise, but was hushed by the woman's grunt.

"Allyuh get a share from this," she'd said with a thin smile. "Patience, child. You'll see."

Billie had bloated *fast*, her stomach walloped outward with powerful, regular foot-beats. By late afternoon, even Anton had noticed the swell of her waistband. Thinking he'd had something to do with it, he'd stood a sight taller. Teased her affectionately. Called her mampee and booboolups. Pinched and kissed what he'd mistaken for baby-fat.

Before twilight, her rounded belly had purpled. Orange veins marbled her skin with fire. "How will I know when it's ready?" Billie had asked that morning, and was startled by the hex-talker's bark.

"Ah, my lolo-girl," the woman had laughed. "Trust me, you'll know."

Insides thump-thump-thumping, Billie had left Anton in the grog of daysleep, an alarm clock ticking next to the bed. That inner beat drove her down to the breakwater a good half hour before her husband was due to take up his post. Instinct had led her away from folks carousing on the strand, squatted her behind a blind spot in the rocks. Hiking her skirts, she'd wriggled her dancer-hips lower. Head bowed, groaning, she'd submerged her nethers, and *pushed*.

Thirty-some documentaries in, and Anton hasn't once told the full story. Not that he holds back on details—at least not the ones he knows. With tooth-spiked fingers, he drums a soundtrack for his version of the encounter, a frantic rap-tap-tap-tapping to dramatize the shock of nearly dying. The children love this part. Directors, too. Cameras zoom in on rapt, morbid little faces as Anton describes his last waterside shift. Billie's hands clench on her lap, dripping sweat onto her white linen shift. She doesn't move, won't move now, until the telling is done.

Yes, there had been an early whistle to warn Anton of the creature's attack. Ever reliable, Billie had manned the breakwater, binoculars rather than eyes. Though she'd been sitting on the wet rocks instead of standing, he says, swaying like weeds in a strong current, his girl had been first to spy the mermaid. Gouts of steam trailed the thing churning through the water, talons shredding the distance between seawall and pier. Shell flickering, morphing, seething—like it wore a crust of banked coals.

"Never drummed so good in my life," Anton says, giving a short rendition of his salvation song. "Man, I *wailed* on that steel. I *killed*. 'Course—" he pauses, routine chuckles "—bête had a good crack at killing me first."

Muting the drum with his palms, Anton lowers his voice.

"This one," he says, "it didn't just swim, did it? Eh eh. Wasn't like the rest of them, the ones that came flooding back after. This jumbie got het up, didn't it? Launched itself—*whoosh!*—straight out the water, and *flew*. A screeching ball of fire, hell-streaking right at me. Angriest, friggin' scariest thing I ever saw."

Billie waits for Anton to meet her gaze. Holds it until he breaks. Turning theatric for the kids, he lifts the drum like a shield, same way he had that long-ago day. Play-acts fending off the devil-thing while the kids scamper and laugh and whoop. "How it beat me down," he says. "Lord, what a pounding!" Miming where the steel had melted under the fire-maid's breath, where it had sizzled against his flesh, where it had filled. Acting bolder and tougher than he had then, than either of them had.

"Angriest, friggin' scariest thing."

Billie stifles a snort.

Anton doesn't know the half of it. He hadn't watched the ink-limbed biter slip from between her legs. Hadn't felt its flimsiness, its newborn slime, its temporary vulnerability. Hadn't heard the way it slapped the water with tail and tongue, calling its kin out from the deeps. Hadn't seen its translucent skin calcifying in the air, spite trapped in a carapace. Hadn't seen Billie's own face repeated in its gaunt features. Hadn't pointed that face toward the one man standing lonely guard on the pier.

No, he hadn't had to survive *that*.

As ever, her husband sees only what he needs, not a blink more. The fame the harridan bought him. The terrible beat she bore.

Close-ups catch Anton saying he'll never forget that raging fire, that flame-lashing, that vengeful rhythm. Elbows creaking, wanting grease, he shifts the drum strap. Flexes his powerful arms. Steel jaw glints in the stage lights as he turns his head, winks at the back row. Saying, he wouldn't be here now without it.

Outside Heavenly

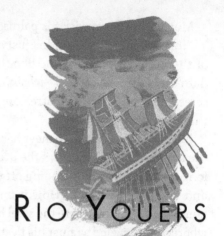

RIO YOUERS

The pillar of black smoke could be seen from Heavenly. The townsfolk looked from their windows and gathered on sidewalks. They knew it was the Roth place burning, and they prayed for the girls but not the man.

Police Chief John Peck sat on the hood of his cruiser and watched the volunteer fire department hush the flames. It took all of the one thousand gallons carried in the engine and most of the two thousand carried in the tanker, but they got it down and when the smoke cleared the remains stood like an incomplete sketch. Ashes swirled and clung to the tall grass. Sassafras and oak at the edges of the lot creaked disagreeably. Some leaves were blackened. Beyond, the sky paled to iris-blue and a murmuration of starlings made a shape in the air and disappeared.

Calloway's voice crackled over the radio. Peck had posted Calloway on Dogwood Road to turn away the curious, and with the Roth place in flames they could be many. Calloway told him that a truckful of menfolk had turned up to help, but Peck knew what they really wanted was to witness, up close, Roth struck low.

"It's under control," Peck said. Through haze and dancing ash he saw the fire chief approaching. "You thank them boys and send them on their way."

He slid off the hood and met the fire chief in the climbing sunlight, away from the smoke and ash.

"She's out, but we'll keep a close eye." Joe Neath had headed Heavenly's fire department for seven years. In his other life, he was the foreman at Gator Steel and a father of five. "Out doesn't mean dead, 'specially in this heat."

"Any idea what started it?"

"No obvious point of origin, but Perry Horne will be out later and he can tell us more." Joe unzipped his jacket a little way and palmed sweat from his throat. "I don't need a fire marshal to tell you it wasn't an accident, though."

Peck sighed and stiffened his jaw. The fire chief nodded, started toward the ruin. Peck followed. They skirted the yard where dry grass ticked, then crossed to the house's eastern face, intact but damaged. The ground was soupy from the hoses' spray. Peck stepped around the deeper puddles where the sky was reflected dull. A child's soft toy stared at him with stitches for eyes.

"You might want to ready yourself," Joe said.

Heat drove off the building and kinked the air and Peck felt his shirt latch to his back. The smell was char and smoke but something else, too. A sharp scent that kicked like ammonia. Peck cupped a hand over his nose and mouth. Ashes brushed his cheeks. They neared a window black as a box of soot with the glass broken and faux wooden blinds part-melted to the frame. Within, the carbonised remains of the living room. Most everything was stripped to whatever wouldn't burn. Peck noted the steel frame of a bed that had collapsed from the room above and what remained of the armchair where Beau Roth no doubt watched TV and sank beer and contemplated wrongs. Peck would study the scene later, when it was safer, but for now he couldn't see much beyond the savagery.

The corpse hung by its arms from a support beam. It was headless and naked. The stomach was open from sternum to groin and the entrails strung around the room. They—like the rest of the body—were red and blistered but not burned through.

"Jesus Christ." Peck turned away and tried to breathe deeply but the air was too choked. He spluttered and spat in the dirt.

"No accident," Joe said.

"Well, Christ." Peck looked again and turned away quicker than before. His nostrils flared. "That Beau, you think?"

"I'd say." Joe wiped more sweat from his throat. "Torso's about the right size."

"Yeah." Peck nodded. "Why didn't he burn up?"

"Makes no sense."

"The girls?"

"No sign."

The two men looked at each other. They were the same age and height—forty-three, a little under six feet—and shared a similar build, once muscular but starting to soften. It was as if growing up in Heavenly had shaped them similarly, like two dunes sculpted by the same winds. They said nothing but much passed between them. Peck sleeved grey sweat from his brow and shook his head.

A small section of the back wall crumbled and fell. Embers lifted and died in the air. Peck's radio squawked and he grabbed it, thankful for the diversion. He started to speak but got a chestful of that bad air and coughed. He strode clear of the house and tried again.

"What you got, Ty?"

Tyler Bray was a part-time cop and most-time grease monkey at Go Auto, which made him useful when it came to maintaining the department's two vehicles. He was young and enthusiastic, but better with a wrench than he was with a badge. Peck had him skirting Roth's two acres for signs of anything untoward, mainly to keep him out of the way.

"I found Mary Roth, Chief."

"What's your twenty?"

"A short sprint northerly." Ty's voice was tight with nervous excitement; he wasn't rotating tires now. "A hundred yards, I'd say. There's an old pickup sitting on blocks, but I doubt you'll see it with the grass being—"

"Step on the roof a moment, Ty. Flap those long arms."

Peck looked north where the grass moved like a great hand was brushing over it, and after a moment Ty's head poked up and he waved his arms. Peck started briskly toward him, cutting a trail through grass that started at his knees, then climbed to his chest and beyond. Rat snakes whipped out of sight and some tightened as he stepped over them, tongues at the air. Peck kept the mast of dark smoke at his back and turned often to keep his bearing.

Mary Roth knelt head down, arms crossed over her face. Her dress was faded, dirty, and had rucked up to her pale stomach. Her thighs were smeared with soot and grime.

"She say anything?" Peck asked Ty, stepping abreast of him.

"Not a word, Chief."

"Mary? Mary . . . it's Chief Peck."

The sun had risen fast and seemed dedicated to this thin clearing behind the abandoned pickup. Peck felt sweat trickle to his beltline and the heat at the back of his neck was heavy as a metal bar. He blew over his upper lip and crouched beside the woman. He could smell the smoke in her hair.

"Mary?"

Peck had known her all her life—Beau's only child, and to look at her was to cry, imagining what she might have been under kinder circumstances. But Beau was a fiercely wicked man who crushed all that could be loved. Mary—like all—was born beautiful. Thirty-two now with ghosts on her shoulders, her spirit withered like some sweet fruit dried in the heat.

"Talk to me, Mary."

He crouched lower and saw her mouth through her crossed arms. Teeth clenched.

"Are you hurt?"

A beat, and then she shook her head and uncrossed her arms. She used the hem of her dress to mop wet eyes. Soot beneath her fingernails. Smudged across her brow. She breathed and her upper body trembled, as if the world's hard edges had been packed into her lungs.

"This all . . ." Mary gestured at the truck and the clearing, then wider: at the trees, sky, and everything. "This all seems lesser now, like something that can be opened and poured out."

Peck wiped his eyes and saw Beau Roth disemboweled and headless. Crows bristled suddenly from the grass and made south, calling.

"You need to tell me what happened, Mary."

She almost smiled. There was red in her eyes. "Nothing but the devil's doing." Her hands trembled, curled to fists. "That son of a bitch got what he deserved."

Mary Roth weighed all of one hundred and twenty pounds and her fifteen-year-old daughter—Cindy: missing—was yet smaller. There was no way that, even working together, they could have strung up Beau's corpse. He was a truck of a man, loaded with old muscle. Peck knew he had some work to do.

The interview room was small and cool and—until about an hour ago—used mainly for storage. Interrogation was not one of Peck's regular duties. His days were spent on admin, general upkeep, and—when there was time—patrolling. Every now and then he'd be called to settle a dust-up, or would ticket speeders on the open stretch of blacktop between Heavenly and Gray Point. It was an unremarkable department, comprised of three full-time cops, one part-timer, and one volunteer. Enough for a two-stoplight town. Even so, Peck rarely worked fewer than sixty hours a week.

He and Ty cleared the interview room while Mary Roth got cleaned up and checked by paramedics. Calloway led her in just a little shy of noon. Her chestnut hair had been brushed and clasped back from her face, which was pale and sad, and her eyes had the look of cold water. She wore clothes salvaged from the town hall's lost and found. A Nike sweatshirt and a pair of basketball shorts almost as long on her as pants. She took a seat and placed her trembling hands flat on the table. Her fingernails had been scrubbed.

"Am I under arrest?"

"No, Mary."

"I may as well be; I got nowhere else to go."

She closed her eyes and a tear slipped fast onto her cheek. Peck nodded at Calloway and he left the room. For a moment the only sound was electricity in the walls and the sigh of the A/C. Peck set the audio recorder running. Tape spooled with a hiss.

"Tell me what happened, Mary. Leave nothing out."

She looked at him. "I tell you a lie and you'll think I'm guilty." She looked away. "I tell you the truth and you'll think I'm insane."

"Let's go with the truth."

"I already told you." Another tear, quick as the first. "It was the devil's doing."

Peck looked at the running tape and knew that the clock was ticking. County forensic units were already on the scene. If he didn't get answers soon, Pine County or state police investigators would take the reins. They'd be direct, insensitive. Peck didn't want them in his town.

"Your father's dead," he said. "Your daughter's missing. No doubt the devil played his part."

Mary wiped her eyes and they flickered and she stared for a long moment at the blank wall. There was a depth to her expression that made him turn away. He'd learned to study aspect and body language, where the truths were often clearer than anything spoken. The weight of her eyelids, the set of her mouth, her hands palm-down on the table, illustrated a single truth that unnerved him: Mary was haunted.

"I want to help you," Peck said.

"I'm beyond that."

"And I want to find Cindy."

"She's been gone a long time."

"Talk to me, Mary."

A mile out of town the Roth place—what remained—stood black and wet. The air still smelled of smoke and that other thing, sharp like ammonia. The vehicles plugging the yard belonged to the fire marshal and the county forensics unit, each working to assemble pieces that might make something like a picture. In Heavenly proper, tongues ran like a new fire and the devil was mentioned more than once, always in regard to Beau himself. In the interview room, the tape ran and the A/C purred. John Peck said little. Mary Roth blinked tears that flashed and unbridled her ghosts.

"Momma died. Some brain thing, so they say. Thirty and dead, and I think God walked out on us the day we parked her box in the ground. Daddy got closer. First in a way that was affectionate, and then overly familiar. He raped me on my eleventh birthday. I felt afterward like a dress that had been left out in the wind and sun, all colourless and tattered. Something that could never be worn pretty. At fourteen I was pregnant with his child. You didn't know about that. The child was born—a boy—and at five months he fell off the bed and knocked his head good. He cried a lot and died in the night. Daddy buried him in the garden, like a dog with a bone. This all has nothing to do with the fire, except it does: when God is so missing from your life, the devil has more room to move."

Peck inhaled through his nose, his teeth locked and lightly grinding. He showed no emotion, but felt inside as though a match had been struck close to his heart.

"Daddy lost his job when Gator Steel cut loose a lot of manpower, and life moved from bad to worse in a hurry. I thought about running away. Even killing myself. I don't know if it's courage or stupidity that keeps a person from doing those things, but whatever it is, I got plenty of it. Daddy found work after a time. Nothing solid. Just here-and-there jobs. Cutting wood. Raking leaves. That kind of thing. I started waitressing at Captain Griddle. Daddy didn't like me leaving the house, but I brought in as much money as him and he found no room to argue. Anyway, that's where I met Gordy Lee. Short order cook. Some sweet, but not exactly busy between the ears."

Peck nodded. He remembered Gordy. Cleft lip and a stutter. Gordy got knocked around by his older brothers. Peck would often see him cooking eggs with bruises about his face and then one day he wasn't cooking eggs any more. Rumour was he'd made tracks to Canada, but nobody knew for sure.

"We fooled around," Mary said, "but it was nothing much. Then one night when we were alone, cleaning up, he lifted my skirt and pumped himself into me, and I didn't stop him. Boy came like a horse and we made more than eggs in that kitchen. I told him a couple months later and he ripped quick out of town. Guess he wasn't ready to be a daddy—or to deal with *my* daddy. Chicken-livered, harelipped ol' son of a whore, either way you cut it."

"And Gordy is Cindy's father?"

"Yes, sir. She got his brown eyes and that's all."

"You ever hear from him?"

"No, sir."

"You don't know where he is?"

"No, sir."

Peck let his mind run an unlikely track: Gordy Lee—nearly sixteen years tougher and uglier—shooting south to claim his little girl, and taking care of Beau Roth in the bargain. Again Peck saw Beau hanging by his wrists, headless, guts strung about the blackened room. He remembered the bruised, skinny kid cooking eggs at Captain Griddle and couldn't get the pieces to fit, no matter which way he turned them.

Still, he asked, "You think Gordy may have tried to get in touch with Cindy?"

"No, sir." Mary shook her head. "Boy was a coward. A stupid one, at that. He could cook eggs and fuck like a bug, but that's about it."

Peck nodded and made a gesture for her to continue.

"I'm telling you what happened, for better or worse. You don't need your police hat right now. You need your *believing* hat. This little slice of family history shows that I'm done hiding, and I got no interest in lies. You might want to bear that in mind as we move along."

Peck nodded again.

"I kept being pregnant from Daddy for as long as I could. But a woman will usually show sooner with her second child, and by four months not even the biggest of my dresses could hide the bump. Daddy didn't take it well. I never told him that Gordy was the father—never told nobody, until now—but he wanted blood, just the same. He got into a lot of fistfights around town, and I guess he spent a few nights in those cells you have downstairs. I tried to stay out of his way. There's a clearing in Brack Wood where the sun shines in and the flowers grow long and pretty, and I'd go there all the time—just sit and daydream with my hands curled around my belly. I wouldn't go home 'til after dark when I knew Daddy would be passed out drunk. But I couldn't avoid him all the time and he found ways to hurt me. One time he suffocated me with a pillow. Held it over my face until the whole world faded, then took it away at the last moment. Another time he pinned me to the kitchen floor and shouted hateful things at my belly—shouted until his throat split like old wood. I've never hated him more."

Mary took one hand from the table and stroked her stomach. A soothing, circular motion. She looked at Peck and then away. The tears came again.

These bigger, slower. She let them run down her face and drop from her chin.

"Ain't life a string of woe?" she said.

"It can get better," Peck said.

She shook her head as if she didn't believe that, and Peck could hardly blame her. She could live until everything about her withered, but might always feel that contentment was like the clothes they'd appropriated from the lost and found: not hers by right, something she'd never grow into.

"If the best God can do for me is a few tall flowers in the wood, I fear He may be outgunned." A stiff, bitter smile. Her yellow teeth gleamed. "The devil has cast a wider net, and left a deeper mark."

Peck bridged his fingers. He still smelled smoke when he inhaled.

"Heavenly is a small town and people talk. I could hear the whispers from my house. A sound like bugs in the grass. And the way you all looked at me. Part wonder. Part sympathy. The way you'd look at someone born with a deformity. It's no wonder I didn't come looking for help." She uttered a brittle laugh. "But for all the talk, you got no clue how bad it was. I spent my days in fear and always crying. Then Cindy came along and I feared for her, too. But abuse isn't like an uncomfortable pair of boots you can just kick off. It's like being the passenger in a car speeding the wrong way down the highway. You know there's hurt ahead, but you're too scared to jump out. All you can do is hope it slows down, or better still, that it stops completely. Maybe it's different for other victims, who have more family and friends, or who live in a bigger town. But I don't know of much beyond Heavenly and Daddy. This is all I got. This is my life."

Mary drew a long breath. Spittle glimmered on her lips and she wiped her face with baggy sleeves. A little time passed. Peck thought about his wife and boys, relieved to erase—if only for a moment—Beau Roth from his mind. He'd take the boys fishing this weekend, he decided. And tonight, instead of sitting on the porch with a beer or two, he'd hold Gracie. Hold her tight. Grateful that he could.

"Seeing Daddy with Cindy, the way he treated her—the way he mistreated her—was bad. Feeling that I couldn't protect her was worse. And knowing that I brought her into this . . ." She trailed off, wet eyes rolling to the ceiling. "She used to beg me to run away with her. She had it all planned out. We'd leave while Daddy was at work. Hitchhike to Carver, then catch a bus to New York City. We'd be dancers, she said. Pretty as flowers, she said. I recall a time when she took her makeup box and made us both up, and we sat for a long time looking at one another in the mirror. Painted like dolls. It was like looking through a window into what *could* be. Then we turned the radio on and danced until we were short of breath. I've never known such joy. Couple nights later, Daddy rolled in drunk and took to us both. He knocked me out cold and when I came to, I saw his ugly bull of a body atop Cindy, pounding into her while she cried and bled. Her eyes met mine and I remembered how we'd looked in the mirror, and I knew then that I had to do something. But Cindy beat me to it. She was gone two days later. Up and left—jumped out of that speeding car. I found a note in her makeup box and it read GONE DANCING with a little X for a kiss. Fourteen years old. I thought the world would tear her to pieces and my heart just broke for her. For *me*, too. I was alone with the monster again. I didn't think life could get any worse. But I was wrong about that."

Mary placed her damp hands on the table and they left prints that glimmered in the light. Her breath hitched twice in her chest like a cold engine starting. Tears, still, running from some deep reservoir.

"Cindy came home a few months later."

Flowers with petals like lace, their stems withered, placed in a bunch on the ground. Peck thought: *He cried a lot and died in the night. Daddy buried him in the garden, like a dog with a bone.* Had a feeling that if he dug down just a little way, he'd find a tiny human skeleton. He shook his head and made a note to get on that. Give the boy a decent burial, stone and all, even if he had to pay for it himself.

A pale morning after a night of stripped sleep and Peck was at the Roth place early. Beau's body had been removed and now all that remained was the burned shell surrounded by yellow tape. It rippled with a sound almost lonesome. There was more at the head of the driveway, tied between trees, where officers had been posted in shifts to keep away prying townsfolk. Peck received the call last night that state police were taking over the investigation, which meant that he could go back to pushing his pen around and attending fundraisers. He turned from the little grave marked only with dry flowers and approached the blackened house. That ammonia smell still touched the air. He looked through the charred window where he had seen Beau's body hanging. Reddened and blistered but not burned through. *Makes no sense*, Joe Neath had said. Peck looked at his watch. Five of eight. State police would roll in at noon, suited and clean. Until then, this was his.

Perry Horne, the county fire marshal, had called him last night, too. His investigation was hindered by anomalies, cause of the blaze chief among them. "This'll take some time," he said. "I've known you twenty-some years,

Peck, friend and colleague, and I don't mind telling you I'm at a loss. There's no obvious origin point, direction of melt is not consistent, and the char patterns—normally clear as footprints—have got me in circles. There's no evidence of an electrical fault or accelerants, and every room is evenly damaged. If I didn't know better, I'd say the entire house spontaneously ripped into flames."

"Can that happen?"

"Well, shit, no." Perry had made an exasperated sound. "Every fire has cause and origin, Peck. But not this one. Not that I can see."

Peck had asked about Beau's corpse.

"I've got no answer for that, either," Perry replied. "Second-degree burns are not consistent with the damage to the house. Temperature in there would have been over a thousand degrees Fahrenheit. He should have been barbecue."

"That's what I thought."

"The way I see it, the house was deep in flames—the fire department likely rolling into the yard—before Beau was strung up."

"That's impossible."

"Yeah, it is." And Perry had barked a short, humourless laugh. "This whole thing is one big question mark."

"There has to be an explanation."

"When you find it, you let me know."

Peck walked away from the house and the hard thoughts associated with it, but couldn't get distance from the latter. They followed him like hungry children. The sun lifted from behind a shelf of cloud on the horizon and his shadow sprang ahead of him. He skirted the infant's grave and made through the high grass toward a cluster of trees—Brack Wood—with leaves catching the morning light. A vague trail linked the edge of Beau's lot to the trees, marking Mary's frequent passage. Peck followed it. The woods smelled of pine and turned earth and the light was a cool, watery green. After a time he came to the clearing Mary spoke of and the flowers were tall. Snakeroot and bellwort and Carolina lily. They nodded their bright, pretty heads. The only sounds were birdsong and the branches whickering.

This was where Mary—and perhaps Cindy, too—had come to escape the monster. A shallow scoop of serenity within their troubled lives. And the earth was fuller, the needles greener, for having absorbed so many daydreams. Peck sat with his back propped against a yellow pine and gathered his knees to his chest. Eyes closed, he sought patience and open-mindedness. Guidance, too. He inhaled the forest smells and they were kind. After a long moment, he opened his eyes and tears spilled onto his cheeks. It occurred to him—and not for the first time—that he could have helped those girls a long time ago. *Should* have.

Peck linked his hands and brought his knuckles to his forehead.

"God, hear me . . ."

He'd tried praying last night. He'd prayed with his wife, their hands joined, but he hadn't sensed God and it was the same now.

The sun rode higher as he walked back to the house. The day's heat was already hard. Peck rounded the field and approached from a different direction, more northeasterly. Here the ground was patchy, long grass in places but mostly bare earth cracked and polished by the sun. Peck kept an eye out for carelessly discarded evidence—anything Tyler may have missed. They still hadn't found Beau's severed head. The thinking was that—unlike the rest of Beau—it had burned up in the blaze, and that Perry Horne would find his blackened teeth, or the tough knots of his skull, while sifting through the ashes.

Closer to the house, Peck discovered several black tracks in the dry grass. He squatted to his haunches to examine them in more detail. They were each about ten inches long, as wide as his hand and arched on the inside. Eleven in total, tracking away from the Roth place. Peck measured them against his own stride. He touched the scorched grass and smelled his fingers.

Yes, they were burn marks, but they were also footprints.

She wore the same clothes as the day before and the same haunted expression. Her hair wasn't clasped but looped onto her shoulders. It looked a shade lighter.

Peck's finger paused over the red button on the audio recorder.

"Listen, Mary, the state police will be here this afternoon and they'll want to question you. They don't know Heavenly, and they have little patience for small town ways. They'll be stiff-necked and businesslike. That's the way they work. The more you tell me now—the more we get on tape— the less you'll have to tell them. Do you understand?"

Her eyes were heavy and dark. Peck thought she might be the only person in all of Heavenly who'd had less sleep than him.

"You don't live with Daddy for thirty-two years," she began with a dry smile, "only to be intimidated by a couple of suit-and-tie cops from the city. They can ask their damn questions, and they can be as businesslike as they please. I'll tell them everything I know, just like I'm telling you. This investigation won't depend on my cooperation, but on how quickly you can explain the unexplainable."

Peck recalled Perry Horne declaring this whole thing one big question mark. He felt something like a knot in his chest.

"Just thought you should know," he said.

She nodded.

Peck pushed the red button. The tape rolled.

"Do you know how your father died, Mary?"

Her hands were clasped in her lap and she looked at them and when she looked up her eyes fixed on Peck and did not waver. She shook her head once and then, realising this wouldn't come across on tape, said, "No. I was in the yard at the time."

"Do you know who killed him?"

"The devil," she said, still looking at him straight.

"You get a good look at him?" Peck asked. "The devil?"

"*Her.*"

"I'm sorry?"

"Devil's a she," Mary said. Another dry smile. "And yeah, I got a good look. She slept under the same roof as me. Baked bread with me. I cooked her meals and washed her clothes."

"You're talking about Cindy?"

"I'm talking about the devil," Mary said. "She just *looked* like Cindy. Same hair, same eyes, same skin. But inside . . . not my little girl. No, sir."

Peck took a calming breath. Any other time he would have applied a little pressure—let Mary know that neighbourly indulgence only carried so far. This was not a game, and he was not going to be played with. The mystery of this all stood before him, though, and he could not as yet see around it. He remembered the clearing with its tall flowers, and how he'd prayed for open-mindedness.

"Help me out, Mary," he said.

Mary sat back in her seat. She still looked at Peck but didn't really see him. Her expression glazed as her mind drifted elsewhere. Peck sat back in his own seat and it creaked and he waited. Mary shook her head. The tears came again and she didn't try to wipe them away. It looked like she had her face turned up to the rain. Just her face. She started to speak, but then stopped and broke down. "Not my little girl," she managed between sobs, and didn't say anything else for a long time.

Peck fetched her Kleenex and hot coffee in a paper cup and gave her a moment. The clock inched toward noon.

She said, once her eyes were damp but not dry, "Cindy came home, but she wasn't the same. Something had happened to her out there. Wherever she went. She'd moved from being a young girl to a young woman, but it was more than that. A mother knows."

Peck felt like saying that years of abuse will wilt even the prettiest flower, but he bit his lip. He encouraged Mary with warm eyes and she kept talking.

"There was an edge to her. She was always fine with me, but with Daddy, the way she looked at him sometimes . . . she could drive nails with a stare like that. And Daddy felt it, too, because he didn't take to her the way he used to. Oh, he was still heavy-handed, and plenty so, but he kindly backed away afterward. I'd never seen him like that. Not scared but . . . *uncertain*. And that scared *me*."

Another long silence and she looked away again, remembering. Peck counted time in his head. Only his chest moved as he breathed.

"But it wasn't only this edge," she continued. "No, sir, there was an outright wrongness about her. She was still some sweet but it felt like thin ice—like something that could crack at any time. I thought it was depression. I made an appointment to see Doctor Everett but Daddy stopped us from going. He said Cindy would snap out of it—that Everett would only go poking where he had no business, and no good would come of that."

Peck felt the anger and guilt tick inside him again.

"You surprised she was acting that way?" he asked. "Given everything that went on in that house?"

"It wasn't depression."

"She needed help, Mary."

"Don't we all?" Mary fixed him with the same unwavering glare and colour rose from inside her collar, touched her jaw. "Judge me all you like, Chief, for something I did or didn't do, but save a few stones for yourself, for this whole shitheel town. And remember this: casting judgment on someone who's seen hell is just about the same as whipping the dead."

She and Peck took long breaths and something in the air realigned itself.

"Okay, Mary." He nodded. "Continue."

"Cindy said that the only reason she came home was to get me. Said she'd found a place where I'd be made stronger, and where I'd never be hurt again. She begged me to go back with her but I didn't, for all the reasons I said before. I told her to go alone, to be happy and strong, but she said she wasn't leaving without me. I guess that's when all the strange things started happening."

"Strange?"

"Growling in the walls. The trees moving closer to the house. Two moons appearing in the sky, one as red as a drop of blood. Crows crowding the roof and windows. Rats and snakes pouring from the well." Mary counted off on her fingers but now she spread her hands wide. "Lots of things. Strange."

Peck nodded. He'd seen his share of strange just lately, but still believed he'd find the truth. Nothing real was truly unexplainable.

"One night—Daddy was mean-drunk and had just taken to me with his belt—I looked out the windows, front and back, and saw at least a hundred coyotes sitting in a circle around the house. They didn't howl or fuss. They just sat there, like they were waiting for something. Cindy asked me again to leave with her. I told her no. Then she stepped onto the porch, spoke some language I didn't understand, and those coyotes turned tail and slipped into the dark. Let me tell you, Chief, I've never been so scared. Not even when Daddy was at his worst."

Peck opened his mouth but found he had nothing to say.

"Clocks running backward. Windows and doors blowing open. Rain falling hard on the house and not a cloud in the sky. Flies everywhere, inside the house and out—so many damn flies. And don't get me started on the smell."

"Like ammonia?" Peck shifted in his seat.

"I guess," Mary said. "Sharp and bitter. Back of the throat."

Peck knew the smell, and this at least rang true, but he let everything else sit for now. Very little about this whole mess was normal, but a picture had started to form in his mind. He saw Cindy leaving home, getting in with some vigilante group—strong boys and arsonists among them—who decided to take the law into their own hands. It didn't come close to explaining everything, but Peck felt he was on the right track.

"This place," he said, studying Mary's dark-ringed eyes. "Where Cindy went. Where she wanted to take you. She ever tell you where it is?"

"No, sir."

"You don't know anything about it?"

"I tried asking, but she wouldn't say much. Got all tight-lipped and sullen."

"Tell me whatever you remember, Mary."

She thought a while, sitting back in her chair with her brow knitted, picking at her fingernails. Peck, for his part, worked to push away the unexplainable, and concentrate on solid facts. He figured everything else would slide into place once he had a strong foundation.

"Outside Heavenly," Mary said. She frowned a little deeper, then nodded. "She went on foot. That I know. Must've gone east because she said she passed the old water tower—said its shadow was like a big ol' spider. All them legs, you know?"

Peck nodded.

"She walked, but I don't know how far. All she said about the place was that the raptors circle clockwise there, except for one—him bigger—going aboutways."

Peck pulled a notebook from his pocket and wrote this down. "Anything else? Landmarks? Or distinct sounds—you know, like a river, or a train? Anything?"

"No, sir."

"How about the people she was with? She give you any names? Descriptions?"

Mary stopped picking her fingernails and linked her hands much as Peck had in the clearing. "For what it's worth." And here the frown was replaced with a cold little smile. "She called them the boys with the black feet."

Peck pulled over at the side of Cotton Road. Sun on the windshield like a branding iron. To his left, beyond a rusted chain link fence, Ring Field and the old water tower which had stood dry for more than ten years. Faded letters across the tank once read HEAVENLY. In a certain light you could see the ghosts of those letters, but not now. Peck stepped out of the cruiser and Tyler Bray followed. They scaled the fence like children. Ty tore his pants and swore.

East the way was flat and hard. Rocky ground and dust devils with the sun always like a hammer thrashing. A mile beyond, Forney Creek marked the town limits. They stopped to douse their hats in water, to fill their hands and drink. They crossed where it was shallowest but still got wet to the thighs, even Ty with his crane fly legs. Here Peck had no jurisdiction. Here he turned from a lawmaker to a citizen with a gun.

"How far we walking, Chief?"

"Until I say."

"This ain't even Heavenly."

Across the cracked grassland to the southwest of Gray Point, through a sparse forest where the boughs rattled dryly, skirting marshland where bullfrogs croaked and a fetid mist rose from between the reeds. Beyond this the flies grew fat and many. The men slapped at them with their hats. Peck looked at the sky but it was bare and blue. They walked another twenty minutes then rested a while. Peck checked the time but his watch had stopped.

"Got the time there, Ty?"

Ty checked. "I got two twenty."

"Well, shit. That can't be right."

"That's what I got."

They carried on but with languor, following no course other than Peck's instinct. Across barren fields and through a narrow valley of mostly shale, where the sun was reflected in bullets and horned lizards blinked at them sleepily. They emerged into a field where grass swayed chest-high. The flies grew in number but were slower, fatter. Ty wheezed and wanted to rest but Peck spurred him on. He was tired too, and the heat had placed a fierce ache across the inside of his skull. Whenever he felt like stopping, he remembered Mary Roth in her borrowed, too-big clothes. So many tears, like a face in the rain.

Tell me about the night of the fire, Mary.

She'd be with the state police now. They'd lean hard on her. Cross-examine her. They'd listen to the tape and believe not a word.

Daddy saw all the strange happenings, too. He was stupid and angry, but not blind. It all got too much for him. He felt threatened, I guess. So he took me aside and told me that Cindy had been chained by the devil, and that it was our duty to set her free. I'd had the same thoughts—had even contemplated calling Reverend Mathis. I told Daddy this, but he wouldn't let me bring an outsider into the house. Not even a man of the cloth. He said he had his own way of handling it, and just as Christian.

Their hats dried in the heat and felt stiff on their heads, and Ty peeled his off and fanned his face with it. His shirt was black with sweat.

"You notice anything strange?" he gasped.

Peck searched the sky and the long grass and it *all* felt strange. Thin, almost, like a bleached and moistureless backdrop with something darker behind. He thought Ty was referring to the smell, though. It rose from the earth here. Caustic and foul. Back of the throat, Mary had said.

"That smell," Peck said, nodding. "Same as at the Roth place. Maybe we're getting close."

"Smell's bad, but that ain't it." Ty knuckled sweat from his eyes. Foamy spittle nestled at the corners of his mouth. "We're walking east, right?"

"More or less."

"Then why is the sun setting ahead of us?" Ty pointed at the fried bullet hole in the sky, and even *it* appeared to be sweating. "Should be behind us, this time of day."

Peck pulled up and frowned and turned a loose circle. He took off his hat and scratched his head. "Must've got turned around somehow."

"We walked a straight line and you know it."

"Just keep going." Peck put on his hat and sniffed the air, following his nose now. "East or west, don't matter. We're close."

Ty used his hat to shade the sun. "And don't it look like a drop of blood?"

It was the early hours. I was sleeping. Not deeply. I'm always aware of the sounds around me. It's like sleeping with one eye open, I guess. I heard a commotion and stirred, but then the screaming started and I jumped out of bed like there was a rattler between the sheets. I ran downstairs and saw Daddy stepping outside, Cindy slung over one shoulder like a sack of firewood. He'd tied her wrists and ankles with rope. I screamed and followed, and he shouted back at me to stay in the house, that I didn't need to see any of this. Normally I do what Daddy says, but not this time. No, sir. I staggered outside and saw Daddy drop Cindy next to the woodpile. He grabbed her hair and dragged her head down across the chopping block. Then he took up his axe.

They kept walking and Peck felt blisters growing inside his boots and it wasn't long after that he noticed the sleek shapes in the grass. They flowed alongside and the grass rippled. Peck tried to get a sense of their number. He knew what they were long before Ty drew his sidearm.

"Coyotes," Ty said.

"They won't hurt you." But Peck wasn't sure about that. He placed a hand on the grip of his own Glock and walked wary.

"This is crazy, Chief."

"Keep walking."

"We shouldn't be doing this." Ty stopped suddenly and the shapes in the grass stopped too. "We got no business out here."

"We got every business."

"You're chasing shadows." Ty holstered his weapon. Flies crawled across his face. Some were so big they dragged. "This is a state police matter. Let *them* trek through hell and back." He flapped at the flies but only some buzzed away.

"You listen to me, Ty Bray, and you listen good. We—that's you, me, the whole damn town—we spent too many years ignoring what was happening at the Roth place. Hid inside our comfortable little lives and didn't do a goddamn thing to help those girls. It's time to put that right. There's a truth out here somewhere and we're going to find it."

Ty wiped his eyes. "Let the state cops find it."

"They won't believe a word Mary tells them." Peck's face was a shade of red and his headache almost blinding. "They'll think she's hiding something and tear her to pieces. She may wind up confessing to something she didn't do, and I can't let that happen. She's been through enough."

Daddy raised his axe and I ran at him—bounced off him, more than anything. I clawed at his legs and he kicked me away. I would have gone at him again, of course, but then Cindy started talking in that weird language, same as when she spoke to the coyotes. I saw a glow beneath her skin, deep and orange, and the ropes binding her turned to ash. She got to her feet as Daddy was raising the axe again, and he just about fell over backward. Her eyes . . . they were like burning coals, pouring smoke. The axe toppled from his hands and she pushed him. It was like she was pushing a door open—that easy—and he flew halfway across the yard like a leaf in the wind. He got to his feet and reeled into the house. Cindy picked up the axe and followed.

Ty now fifteen feet behind and staggering. Teeth clamped, shaking his head. He'd given up on swatting away the flies and they droned around him and settled and drank the sweat from his open pink pores. Peck flapped his own hat and saw ahead a scratch of forest. He sniffed at the bitter air and walked that way.

Cooler beneath the canopy, but darker. Here the coyotes were shadows and some howled in the gloom. Something else ticked among the branches. Peck waited for Ty, resting his hand on a gnarled trunk that twisted beneath him and when he looked he saw no trunk, no tree. Evening light spilled through the canopy, like wine through a cracked glass.

"Let's stop awhile," Ty panted.

"I don't want to stop here."

They trudged on with Peck barely looking, his dread tamped down by determination. The thunder in his head was his heartbeat—a reckless, spirited thing. They made it through the forest and the light now was burned purple. Across a wide, dry riverbed and into a field marked by the outlines of trees and rocks. The grass here was knee-high and the coyotes' backs showed like otters in water.

"There's a hill ahead," Peck said, pointing to where the ground rose. "We can maybe get a bearing from there."

Ty nodded but he looked close to tears, no doubt wishing he was changing oil at Go Auto or hanging out with his girl. They struggled up the hill, which wasn't steep, but both men fairly crawled. At the summit, Peck looked around but saw nothing he recognised. The sky had grown pale. He'd swear it was getting light again. They caught their breaths and pushed on. Midway down the hill, Peck noticed—not a mile away—a small settlement. Glass and aluminum winked in the sunlight. It was definitely getting lighter. Hotter, too.

"This is some kind of nightmare," Ty said.

Peck's gaze drifted upward, and he saw several birds in the sky above the settlement. Red-tailed hawks, he thought, judging from the size. They circled clockwise, all but one—a raptor Peck had no name for, with a broader, crooked span—looping the other way.

He moved on. His stride was long.

"We're here," he said.

I can't tell you what happened in the house because I stayed in the yard. And I wasn't alone. The coyotes were back, sitting in the long grass with their ears high and their eyes shining. Seemed the devil was all ways and if there was any heaven to be found, I didn't know where. So I stayed put. And how I screamed, but not as loud as Daddy, and not for as long. Then the house went up. You know when you set fire to a book of matches and it flares in your hand all at once? It was like that. I thought for sure they were both dead, then Cindy stepped out of the flames. She was on fire, but she wasn't burning. I know how that sounds, but I swear it's true. It's like she controlled those flames; like the coyotes, they did whatever she told them to, and ain't that the devil's way? I watched her walk across the grass and away, all those coyotes by her side, and for a while I followed her flame and then she was gone. Then I took to my heels. I wanted to find my clearing but got lost in the dark. I wound up by that old truck in the field, and there I hid, and there you found me.

Peck thought 'settlement' too grand a word for what amounted to a few tumble-down shacks and trailers. Some were painted faded colours, their windows either blacked-out or boarded over. There were no satellite dishes or barbecues. No washing strung to dry. Peck would think it abandoned but for the feeling they were being watched—and not only by the coyotes, mostly gathered in the grass around the site. Others sat on the tall rocks with their backs straight.

"What is this place?" Ty asked. He was a step or two behind Peck.

"I'm not sure."

Cogongrass sprung from the baked earth, strewn with trash. A dusty flag Peck didn't recognise rippled softly. They advanced cautiously and came across four listless hogs tied to a stake in the earth. The smell in the air was that same bitter ammonia, hard to breathe. The sun rode directly overhead and the heat was thick as tar.

"Anybody home?" Ty screamed. He brushed at the flies on his face. "Anybody? I figured hell would be busier."

"Hush." Peck placed a hand on Ty's chest and he knocked it away.

"Don't touch me."

Sound of a door opening, closing with a snap. They turned and saw a boy walking toward them, bare-chested, eating something from a bowl. Five years old, Peck figured, having a boy of his own that age.

"Keep it together," Peck whispered to Ty. "Remember, we got no jurisdiction here, but these people don't know that. Keep your weapon holstered. Pull that trigger and you'll have a lot of questions to answer."

The boy wore faded blue jeans turned up at the ankles. His feet were soot-black. The bowl was filled with dry corn. It rattled between his teeth when he spoke.

"You probably shouldn't be here."

"We're looking for somebody," Peck said. He turned on his friendly police officer smile, perhaps to make up for his shapeless hat and the flies on his throat. "Maybe you can help me. Girl. Fifteen years old. Brown hair. Goes by the name of Cindy."

"She's with us now," the little boy said. He took a mouthful of corn that rattled. "And she ain't Cindy no more."

Even in the heat, these words sent a chill motoring up Peck's spine. They mirrored what Mary had said. Not that he needed more convincing. As a lawman he'd always favoured a logical line, but after everything he'd seen and heard, that line wasn't nearly as solid.

"Where is she?" Ty asked.

The boy softened corn in his mouth. He spat yellow in the dirt, then turned around and walked away.

"Hey!"

"Rubin's trailer." He flicked a finger to his left.

The men—bone-weary but still upright—moved in that direction, beyond a screen of raggedy shrubs and toward a trailer the colour of an old dime. It sat on its underbelly, wheels and jack long gone. Dry weed snaked through holes in the panelling and the windows were marked with red Xs. There were two coyotes perched on the roof, coats clotted with dirt and teeth showing. Somebody had buried an axe in the trunk of a nearby tree. A tin bucket hung from a branch by a length of twine.

Peck looked over his shoulder and saw the little boy watching and grinning. In the heat it looked like his black feet were smoking.

"We find her and go," Peck said. "We'll send the big boys back here to ask questions."

"Amen," Ty said.

Peck turned back toward the trailer and in so doing walked clumsily into the tin bucket hanging from the branch. A drove of flies were disturbed but didn't go far. The bucket swung and the branch creaked. Peck looked inside and saw Beau Roth's head, parched and blistered. One eye was filled with flies.

"Christ and Jesus." He staggered backward and drew his gun and Ty drew his too. Peck flapped a hand at him that didn't make any sense and Ty hunkered, confused, and the barrel of his weapon moved unsurely. The flies settled again on the bucket. The coyotes on the roof howled. Peck looked the way they had come and saw the little boy laughing. He imagined the corn rattling between his teeth and had an urge to run a bullet through his narrow chest, then a door squeaked open and he turned to see Cindy Roth standing outside the trailer. Not the same girl who sat quietly at the back of the class while Peck gave one of his school talks, or the girl he often saw walking the mile from Sunshine Shopper to her house, weighed down with groceries, and who wouldn't accept a ride when he offered it. Cindy Roth now was fierce-eyed, closer to a woman, and with a charge about her—some deep thing desperate to break out. She smiled and stepped toward Peck. Her feet were black.

"Hello, Chief," she said.

All Peck wanted was a shred of solid evidence, something to lend credence to Mary Roth's story, enough for the state police to investigate further. He'd brought Ty along because he didn't want to be alone, but also because Ty—unlike Calloway—was green enough to follow, even when they went beyond the town limits.

He hoped he'd live to regret his decisions.

It all happened quickly.

There came a whirl of heat and dust and suddenly they were surrounded by black-footed boys, including two atop Rubin's trailer—thin and naked both—in place of the coyotes. Peck backed away and raised his gun in warning. Ty showed no such restraint. He fired two shots at the boys on the trailer and missed them both. Peck screamed at him to cease fire but he didn't listen. He turned and shot the little boy dead. Blew him backward, black feet smoking. His bowl of corn spilled everywhere.

Peck recalled Mary gesturing at the sky—at everything—and saying that it all seemed lesser, like something that could be opened and poured out, and now he knew exactly what she meant. He did then the one thing he thought would save his hide: turned his gun on Ty and shot him in the throat. Ty went down, dead as stone before he hit the ground.

Still the fire came.

The crooked raptor landed in a flurry of thick black feathers, squawking as flames ripped suddenly, viciously, around the site. Peck shielded his eyes and when he looked again, the bird was gone. A man strode toward him—black-footed, like the boys—over eight feet tall and narrow-faced. Smoke rippled from his eyes and he spat coal and bones. Peck was lifted into the air without being touched, fully ten feet above the ground, and then dropped. The boys howled and Peck tried to reel away but was lifted again. He saw the site burning and the fields beyond. He saw Cindy Roth twisting in the flames and laughing. Embers burst from her mouth and spiralled around her. Again Peck was dropped and he landed hard, breaking both legs. Still he tried to crawl.

Fire surrounded him. It sucked the oxygen from the air and he wheezed and reached for help that would never come. His skin bubbled in the heat but did not blacken.

The man stood over him. Flames crackled from the tips of his fingers.

Peck lifted his gun and pulled the trigger desperately. The first and second shots hit the tall man square in the chest. Fire and feathers flew. The third hit Cindy Roth and threw her thin, fifteen-year-old body back through the door of the trailer. Eleven rounds left in the mag and Peck spent them all. Some of those shots went astray but most found a home. Bodies and fire all around.

Peck tried to scream but there wasn't the air. He wished he'd kept a bullet for himself. He crawled a little way and then fell chest down in the dirt. The cogongrass crackled as it burned and he heard the hogs squealing.

The last thing he saw before passing out was the little boy Ty had shot, back on his feet and scooping corn—popped now—off the ground and into his mouth. His smile was almost beautiful.

He came around with the fires still burning and the skin on his face and hands blistered. All the shacks and trailers were gone. The boys with the black feet were gone. Not a body in the dirt, nor a drop of blood. Not even Ty's.

Just him and that bucket twisting in the heat.

Peck dragged his broken legs and screamed. The fire raged around him, branding a shape on the land he felt but could not see: a five-pointed star enclosed in a perfect circle, burning hungrily and—from point to point—many miles wide.

Brains, Brains, Brains
PUNEET DUTT

most times we wait
for bone harvest
to flesh
    for first sigh of blood
    for grunt work's spin

we guard our knees
drag our limbs
tilt scarred hands towards amber dusk
    and rise from the trenches

our unmoored unaliveness
moans
somewhere inside of us
where dark things scratch
    blood heat's caw
    awakens our belly clocks
    as sharp as book spines

our meals are co-authored
shameless gang-
braining fantasies
anthropophagical cravings

newborn thighs
silk fine lust

Brains, Brains, Brains

stacked husband plucked from football mondays
with beer dripping breasts
divorcee tongues marinated in rocket sauce

first bite fractures the undeadness   an inoperable splinter
tendon snaps puncture what lay so still
lopped off
murdered potential coils down the dry pipes
     and for a second
     we feel alive
flash feeling
of human's
electric hum

in lean years
we huddle potato-eyed
squat in dumps
shatter bird cliques with spare limbs
     peck at survival
groan all night
     for next day could be dust day
     our heads in our lap

we do not ask
simply paddle by osmosis
learning as we feed   toe by bloody toe

to carry on
we pick at scabs and lumps scalding side-alley dumpsters
sacking three or four a night   easy
a bare sputter to drink   a patch of marrow to suck
gorging the meager rations

after all   this should be enough
to wail without memory
to lug our breathless bones
to consume checklists of menued parts

but no

we are a dangle of arrested hooks
warring day and night for plasmic gore
for *brains*
brains
brains
to fill this haunting of our belly ghosts

we are not the bad guys

recognize stars
listen to the mad thrust
of a trapped house fly
pounding at a closed door

cannot summon feelings   but go on
we see can see
we see ourselves in these things   when we eat

The Colour of Paradox
A.M. Dellamonica

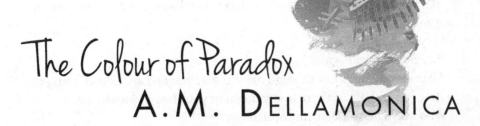

The last thing they did, before sending me into the past, was shove me to the end of the world.

The Project Mayfly nurse waited as I raised myself onto a wicker table with a surface made of tightly-strung hide, a grid that put me in mind of a tennis racket. The squares of string pressed against the thin fabric of my hospital gown.

As I climbed on, I couldn't help noticing the drain in the floor. It was a hand's width away from the letters scratched into the concrete: "16—Hungry."

There were marks on the wall, too, across from the metal staircase. A timeline, in yellow chalk, running from floor to ceiling, hashed at one-inch intervals. The year 1900 was scrawled at the bottom, the numbers mashed short by the floor. A foot and change upward from that, 1914 and 1916. The nines had a familiar, slightly twisted look to them. They were at once readable and yet not quite perfectly formed. So were the nines in the other chalk digits that followed: 1937 and the current year, 1946.

The nurse dodged the hand I'd put out, just for a last friendly pat, you know. She covered me, toes to chin, with a lead blanket.

"When do you tell me my mission?"

"Willie will send word when you've gotten there safe and sound." The Major's words came from a speaker in the ceiling. "Good luck, son."

"Eyes wide, now." The nurse slid a hand into the seven tons of steel bolted to the ceiling above me, drawing out a pair of rubber cups on a long, noodle-pallid cord. I complied, distorting my view of the chalk timeline on the wall across from me; she popped the cups on my eyes, like contact lenses except they were so thick they braced my eyelids open.

"Bit of discomfort coming," she said, patting the lead blanket.

Blinded, I felt the vibration of the machine as it lowered from the ceiling, Dr. Frankenstein's version of an optician's examining rig. It settled on my body like an automobile laid atop the blanket. I heard clips. The flesh of my rump pressed the rawhide grid below.

"It's wrong on my nose," I protested: cold steel was pressing down on my face with bruising force.

"Try to breathe."

"My nose," I said again.

All their warnings ran through my mind: If you lied about ever being to Seattle you will die. If there is any metal in your body, you will die.

Who would lie about visiting Seattle?

This is a one-way mission.

Knowing I would survive the press was hardly a comfort.

Seven tons of steel were clamped around me and my nose was going to break, and after telling me to *breathe, just breathe*, that nurse—she smelled of rosewater, I'll never forget it—was sliding some kind of leather bit into my mouth. It was enough to make me wish I was at the front, face-to-barrel with one of the new Russo-German repeating rifles.

I heard her retreat to the staircase, locking the lead door. I counted to thirty. What felt like a year passed.

Then I saw the death of the world.

It was hot, but there was no fire. My crushed nose picked up a smell straight out of Dante's *Inferno*: charnel and brimstone. I rose above the great American city, above Lake Washington and Puget Sound. Higher, higher.

But something was wrong with the colour of the future, seven weeks out. Seattle, below, the sky above, even the air around me . . . it was all splashed with colour I'd never seen before. Everything was off the accepted painter's wheel of red, blue, yellow.

The cries of thousands of living things, dying in agony, merged with my own.

My mind, confronted with the impossible, revolted. Pinned, gagged, and clamped in place, unable to look away, I screamed as the timepress thrust me against the end of everything, as I bounced off that imminent stained future and ricocheted into the past.

A sproing, a sense of strings beneath me popping. I dropped—but struck something soft before I realized I was falling.

It was dark, everything hurt, and I was still screaming.

I fought the howls, eventually compressing them to whimpers, then a voiceless suctioning of air. The cups over my eyes were gone, but I seriously doubted whether I would ever open my eyes again.

. . . colour that colour that sound that smell . . .

When I did, I saw a square of light above, the doorway at the top of the staircase.

Was I still in the project basement? All the equipment was gone. I lay on a mattress in the middle of the floor, placed where the gurney had been. A bare light bulb hung overhead; the staircase that led up and out was wood, rather than steel, and my chalk timeline, naturally, was gone.

Just within reach was a milk jug full of water. A bucket waited in the corner.

A woman—not the nurse from before—waited at the top of the staircase. She had a blanket in one hand and a pistol in the other.

"How do you feel?" She sounded wary.

I covered my groin with one hand and felt for the bit in my mouth. The handful of leather was almost too much to lift; I was that weak.

I prodded my nose: not quite broken.

She waited.

What I managed was a thready: "Skinned. I feel skinned."

She nodded, pocketed the weapon, and brought the sheet, restoring my modesty with a brisk snap of linen. Everything it touched ached, as if bruised.

Vanishing upstairs, she returned with a pillow, a proper blanket, and a tray containing broth, aspirin, and a tiny soda biscuit.

"Keep your hands under the bedclothes," she ordered, feeding me extremely small sips of the soup.

"Who are you?"

"Constance Wills. Willie."

"You're Agent Sixteen?"

"Thought I was a chap?" she said. "The Major loves his little joke."

The Major had told me they'd pressed Willie in 1937, seven weeks before the first time the world ended. Somehow she'd made it back to 1916 and pushed the devastation off nine years. If not for her, I'd have died at age nine.

She was the first of us to survive the timepress.

"Do whatever Willie says," they told me. "You'll be fine."

It was a bit of a dirty trick to be expecting some war-ragged captain and to find, instead, a girl with cornflower eyes, hair the colour of a strawberry roan, and delicate, freckled hands. Her face was stronger than I liked, her gaze more direct. No lipstick, either. Pity. I like a girl who tries.

"I'm—" I began, and she dumped lukewarm soup in my mouth.

"I don't want to know your name unless you make it."

With the spoon caught between my teeth, I could hardly tell her how I knew I would survive.

It was days before my body agreed, and conceded to feeling as though I might not, as Willie expected, simply die.

I took what she gave me—pills, pale suggestions of food—and shivered on the mattress. The thing I'd seen raked at my dreams, even though I couldn't properly recall that awful colour, or the exact timbre of that chorus of screams.

I dreamed incomprehensible, awful things: men suckling the intestines of disembowelled soldiers, window glass turning to liquid and forcing itself into the ear canals of soft, white-fleeced sheep, a robed worker running a girl's body through an industrial steam press.

The dark and quiet of the basement were soothing. The walls were close and plain, offering tight, restful concrete horizons. The crawl to the bucket in the corner was as much as I could manage physically, and as far as I wanted to go.

Willie nursed but otherwise ignored me until I finally got bored enough to ask for a newspaper. She brought me the *Post-Intelligencer* and there was almost more information in it than I could bear: I threw it aside after two pages of Volstead Act enforcement and reminisces of a snowstorm the previous year.

The next day she brought the paper again and the world was easier to face. That afternoon, I was allowed a little more solid food: two bites of chicken and a mash of turnips.

"The paper," I said. "It's current?"

She nodded.

"I've just had my appendix out—at home, I mean."

"They press us down into the precise moment when our younger selves are under anesthetic. Doctor Stefoff's theory is it's easier to make the transition that way."

I ran a finger over a week's worth of beard. "I'd like to shave."

"You're not ready."

"I wish to be presentable."

"Nobody cares what you look like."

I tried to summon a shred of charm. "You should be nicer to me, Willie. I'm here to save the world, remember?"

"You can have a mirror and a razor when you come up to your room." With that, she vanished upstairs.

That gave me pause. The prospect of climbing that staircase filled me with dread, like a child mandated to visit to a malevolent old relative. Some dying grandfather, furious as his body failed, refusing to know his time was coming. Clawlike hands and the smell of dying . . .

Up in the house was sunshine and fresh air and the inevitability of the end.

It took me another day to muster the nerve. I was rubber-legged and sweating before I was halfway up the staircase.

"See here, old man. This isn't physical." To prove it to myself, I marched down to the bottom again, one two, one two, setting a slow but steady pace and swearing I wouldn't break it. When my feet hit the concrete floor I turned on my heel—about face, good soldier!—and maintained my march to the top.

I was trembling with nausea when I reached the door, but I nevertheless forced myself through.

The door led into a closet, filled with men's clothes. Beyond it was a plain, old-fashioned and distinctly masculine bedroom, with blue bed covers and uninspired wooden furniture. Even that, for a moment, was almost too much colour.

A shaving kit taunted me. The water was fresh, steaming; Willie must have heard me dithering on the stair.

"You can do this," I told myself.

The face in the mirror was thinner, and the bruising on the bridge of my nose was smeared, on one side, into a black eye. I've always been on the pale side; now I looked positively bloodless. My hair had turned a brittle white-blond, except at the roots.

I had been convinced I'd see it—the end, that horrible colour—brimming from the sockets of my eyes.

I shaved, slowly, taking care not to cut myself. The sight of blood would have sent me quailing back to my sickbed. Putting on a suit from the closet that just about fit, I listened at the door.

Women's voices and a mutter of teacups: Willie had company. No matter. She couldn't keep me from my mission forever.

I found her in the kitchen with an older woman and a sickly looking Negro man, the three of them sharing a breakfast of eggs and bacon. The smell was so rich my stomach turned.

The older woman looked at me, eyebrows raised. "Who's this fellow?"

"My brother." Willie swallowed a slimy, soft-boiled egg. "Jules Wills the Third."

The woman turned out to be a housekeeper and cook. Her name was Mrs. Farmer and she seemed a gem: motherly, warm, efficient, everything a matron should be. The old man, Rufus, was nominally a servant. This polite bit of fiction allowed him to live, despite his race, with three other gents Willie was keeping upstairs. I was given to understand she ran a boarding house for convalescent bachelors.

I endured an interminable stretch of pointless chitchat about the stock market and a recent State of the Union address and whether the carrots at market had been overpriced that day. Finally Rufus caned his way out into the hall and Mrs. Farmer took away the dishes, with their intermingling, overstrong smells.

"I could just about do a cup of tea," I said. "Be a love, will you?"

Willie affected not to have heard, opening a small journal and paging through the opening leaves.

"Why am I appointed your brother?"

"Because you're a flirt, and I wish to avoid trouble."

"You said you'd be nicer to me if I survived."

"Who says you have?"

That took the wind out of my sails. "My strength is—I am recovering."

"You might yet run mad and cut your throat," she said, with no apparent interest. "Or need to be shot."

"You're not as cold as all that, are you?"

"Would you like to test me?"

I was too irked to tell her that I'd seen proof I was going to make it. "When do I receive my orders?"

She took up a pen, turned to a blank page in her journal, and spoke as she wrote: "February 7th, 1920. My brother Jules has arrived from England and met with a mishap: he's been robbed of his luggage and caught a fever. I have been nursing him 'round the clock—"

"Ha!" said I.

"—and it begins to look as though he may pull through. Since I saw him last, six years ago, Julie has grown into a reasonably handsome fellow—"

"Faint praise."

"He has blue eyes, like mine, and hair so dark it might be taken for black."

"It's not dark now."

"It'll grow in." Willie continued to narrate: "He has had his appendix removed in childhood and—" She paused. "Other scars?"

"If you'd nursed me as attentively as you claim, you'd know."

"The project must know which one you are if they're to send proper identification."

Which one you are. It raised the hairs on my arms.

"Shall I be forced to describe your personality?" Withering tone there: whatever she said would be unflattering.

"It's the bottom of my foot. I stepped on a fishing lure."

She finished the sentence in silence and then added, "Though dear Julie isn't out of danger yet—"

"I'm not wild about this pet name you've given me."

"—he is restless and eager to be of use." She looked across the table. "They'll send something along presently."

"Just like that?"

We could press things back, never forward. Willie would complete her girlish diary and shelve it somewhere safe: her notes would wait until they reached the project, twenty-six years on, for the Major to read about my arrival.

"What is it?" Willie said.

"I won't see 1946 again until I'm in my forties." The thought was staggering.

She frowned. "Your package will arrive downstairs. When you go, bring up the sheets."

"Would you have me dust while I'm at it? Arrange some flowers?"

"I'm sure, Julie, that I don't care what you do." She jotted one last sentence, snapped the journal shut when I tried to see it, and left me tealess and suddenly chilled in the kitchen.

She told them I was insubordinate. My stomach cramped and I was, all at once, brimming with fury. I had an urge to chase her out of the room, to smash her head against the banister until her blood ran between my knuckles. To lick, drink . . . I touched my tongue to the notch between my clenched index and middle fingers, imagining salt, and saw a flash of colour . . .

It passed, leaving me dry-mouthed and appalled at myself.

You may yet run mad.

"Maybe Julie isn't out of the woods yet," I conceded, and escaped downstairs.

The basement had a sour smell I associated with an animal's den—my smell, I realized, from days of sickness—overlaid by lubricated machinery. I gathered the bedding, wadding everything into the top sheet, and walked it up to the room with the wardrobe. The stairs were easier the second time.

Between the sheets and the mattress was a stiff black tarpaulin. I folded that, too, finding the mattress beneath pristine, and carried it up.

Returning once more, I strained to tilt the mattress off the floor. There was no drain there yet. The message scratched into the floor, "16—Hungry," seemed fainter than it had been, a week ago in the future, when I was climbing aboard the gurney.

I let the mattress fall back into position and paced the room. There was nothing down here but cool air, bare walls, soothing quiet. By my time, there would be a trapdoor under the staircase, access to a lower basement. For now, though, the floor was intact: this was the bottom of the hole.

I had never been monstrous. The flash of bloodlust was tied to what I'd seen, seven weeks into my future, at the end of the world. I'd been infected. Some rot was blooming within my mind or soul.

What could I do but fight it?

I should go out, take in a little air, feel the rain on my face. Or eat—Mrs. Farmer would fix me tea, I'd wager, even if Willie had no idea of proper female behaviour. I could go upstairs and meet the convalescents.

Instead I sat on the steps in the blessed dim and quiet, trying to still my thoughts.

After about an hour a satchel appeared in mid-air, at waist-height—the height of the gurney. It was scorched. A scrap of strung hide was burning into its bottom.

It flopped onto the mattress, just as I had, and lay there, smoking. I thought of horse droppings, suddenly, steaming on frosty lawns.

Inside the satchel I found bundles of letters and a paper-wrapped package, tied in string and all neatly labelled, like an odd Christmas parcel. Names: mine, hers, someone named Robert Chambers, and Kenneth Smith.

I opened a package with "Jules Wills III" on it, and found a wallet containing thirty dollars in American bills. A small fortune.

The brown paper the wallet came in had been inked with facts and figures I was meant to memorize: my birthday in 1898, Willie's in 1895, our parents' names. There were notes outlining a sketchy little cover story about growing up on an estate in the West Dorset countryside, and the circumstances that had brought us to America.

The tale was Willie had married a man who'd brought her here. He'd died in the Great War and so she'd set up the convalescent home. Our parents had sent me out to check on her.

"Is the post in?" Her voice at the top of the stair made me jump. "I smell smoke."

I coughed, stood, passed it up. Her eyes travelled over the basement—she saw the soot-mark from the bag on her virginal mattress and I realized I wasn't meant to have brought up the tarpaulin.

"You put the mattress there?" I asked suddenly. "You'd have fallen onto—"

I gestured at the floor and wondered if she'd broken anything when she hit the concrete.

She extracted the bundle with her name on it and passed me a bunch of letters. "From Father," she said. I could sense she was debating her answer.

"Please, Willie. I don't mean to be beastly. None of this is what I expected."

She shook her head. "There was no mattress. How could there be?"

"It's only a yard, I suppose. Were you hurt?"

"Grady and Biggs broke my fall."

"Who?"

"Agents fourteen and fifteen. What remained of them, anyway."

I'd have expected her to leave after that grisly revelation—Willie seemed to love a good exit line—but instead she gave my shoulder an absent pat and started opening her letters. "The brown sheets speak plainly—they're meant to be burned. The letters we can keep. They don't say anything revealing."

"Aren't they afraid we'll miss one of the brown sheets—fail to burn it?"

"They don't last. The ink fades and the paper tatters within a month or two."

The letters from my false parents ordered me to mind my sister, mind my health, and remember the considerable spiritual benefits of prayer and clean living. In other words: obey my C.O., stay physically fit, and try to avoid going mad.

The note from 'Father' was written in the Major's hand. He wanted me to set up a bank account and asked me to make some modest but specific investments. Cash would be provided for further deposits. There was also an allowance: this much for clothes and kit, that much for expenses as I 'made myself useful.'

Useful. The letter hinted that I might indulge a bit of a carousing and gambling habit, by way of ingratiating myself with local gossips and crooks. This would be funded as long as I wrote home about whatever they told me.

A licence to drink and gamble. There were worse things.

"Mother," whose handwriting I didn't recognize, said I should see Willie's doctor and take iodine pills—these they'd enclosed. I was to refrain from smoking while I recovered.

The final wrapped lump with my name on it felt like a book.

I untied the string and then, in the process of extracting the biography of a reporter I'd long admired, I tore the brown paper in half.

My eyes drifted to the mattress in the middle of the floor and I pictured Willie suddenly: young, sick . . .

(helpless, bleeding, delicious)

. . . and dropped on concrete, onto the corpses of two previous agents. Using something—who knew what?—to scratch those words into the floor.

"16—Hungry." Begging the future for food, because she was too weak to fetch any for herself.

I shook the image away and held two sides of the page together to see what it was I'd been sent back to do.

"Bloody hell!"

Willie looked down, offering an especially masterful performance of her incurious stare. I passed her the torn pages.

She held them up and scanned. "Paperboy with the *Seattle Union Record*. Name of Peter Rupert, lives near Jackson Street. Ruin, spoil, or if necessary, kill."

"Bloody Peter Rupert." I waved the biography at her.

"You know him?"

"Don't you?"

She shook her head. "He wasn't—in my 1937, he must not have had any significance."

"Well in *my* 1937 he's a bloody hero. Cottoned onto an attack Japan was planning on Hawaii, on the U.S. Fleet. He broke the story and stopped the whole—"

"You have to forget about that," she said. "It's going to change. Whatever you remember is already gone. It will all unfold differently after you—"

"Ruin a nine-year-old boy?"

"Or kill him."

"What kind of a monster are you?"

"If you are so certain that ruining someone is better than killing them outright, you've had something of a soft go at life."

"I'm not killing a child."

"All right." She ignored my distress, looking over the book but far off, deep in thought. "If he were disfigured, people mightn't talk to him. Or if his voice were damaged—did he file dispatches by telephone?"

"Disfigure or cripple a nine-year-old," I said. "A hero. He reported on the Russian counter-revolution. I dreamed about being like him."

"No doubt that's why you were sent. Know thy—"

"Enemy?"

"Target."

"I have no intention of doing my target the slightest harm," I said.

She shrugged, passed the book back, and left me in the basement to fume.

Anger drove me out of the house. I went and set up the bank account and investments, paying lip service to the idea of military obedience. I bought myself a new suit and an umbrella. Everyone looked young and hopeful. They were dressed in clothes that reminded me of my childhood. There were almost no automobiles on the streets: trolleys, carts, and pedestrians were everywhere.

In the basement, at Willie's, I might still have been in 1946. Now it sank in: I was living in my own past.

Up ahead, just decades away, the world was turning to something far worse than ash. Peter Rupert would do something to bring that day closer.

But it was probably one action of his, wasn't it? Probably the Japan scoop. One single story of the hundreds he filed.

I found myself a street corner that smelled of washed earth—not of horse, not of smoke or fuel. I stood there, snug under my umbrella, and watched the rain pour down as I formulated a plan.

"What if I got close to him?" I said to Willie that night. "The Project must know more about whatever Peter does to . . ."

"To bring on the Souring?" She sat in a rocking chair in the parlour, knitting in front of the fire, playing at being an ordinary woman.

My mouth went dry. "The—"

"Sorry—that's what I call *it*. What we saw."

I swallowed. "It's apt."

"It's useful," she said. "I use it in the journals. I've cultivated a conceit that losing my husband made me a bit odd."

"Ramblings of a daft young widow?"

She nodded. "Just in case someone unauthorized gets a look."

"Whatever Peter does to bring on your Souring," I said, "it's bound to be one story. They chose him because he's key, am I right? Because he's a simple target?"

"So?"

"The Project must tell me which story. If he sees me as a friend, an older brother, or even a father figure—his own father died in the flu epidemic—"

She flinched, for some reason.

"It's why he's working as a paperboy, to support his mother. In any case, I'll keep him off that one story."

"You're proposing to chum around with him for years?"

"Why not? I'll make myself useful meanwhile: keep investing money, reporting gossip, maybe help dig out the next basement . . ."

"Jules."

". . . I'd need someone to explain the engineering to me, obviously. How *does* one secretly dig a second basement in a house that already exists?"

"Jules."

"I needn't live here in the house if you don't want me underfoot."

She pulled herself upright in her chair, sitting as prim and proper as a schoolteacher. I imagined I heard her sleeve tearing, and thought about running my tongue over the freckles on her arm: how far did they go? She folded her hands, seemed to fight an urge to wring them, and waited for me to run down.

"What is it?"

She said. "The timepress uses a radiant form of energy. It's what makes us so sick. They told you that, didn't they?"

"I'm not going to relapse on you. I live, I know it."

She didn't smile. "Chances are you will die of cancer within the year."

"Chances?"

"Rufus has survived almost fifteen months, but . . ."

She meant the sickly Negro man.

"You have no great span of time in which to befriend Peter Rupert. You can't jolly him along for a decade and hope to break his leg before he leaves for Japan. You—"

I was across the room before I knew it, grabbing at her, tipping the rocking chair. We ended on the floor, my hand wrapped around her jaw, and again that red desire swam up. To smash, to smash, to taste of her blood on my knuckles.

"You're. Not. Dead," I snarled. "It's been years and you're not dead."

A little flicker. Fear? I am ashamed to admit I hoped so. I needed to see something beyond pity or contempt in her.

"Go ahead, then," she said, and I realized my other hand was resting atop—was squeezing—one of her strangely firm breasts.

Trying to buy her life? Well, she'd all but opened her legs now: I gave her blouse a swift tear as my defeated sanity—the despairing, quashed part of me that knew better—protested.

I found: a padded bodice, formed like a woman's body.

I pushed it aside, exposing her belly . . .

. . . and found nothing but scars.

The slices had been pulled up and then stitched tight. Everything below her collarbones was purple and red, twisting lines of hashed-together tissue.

"About a week after I finished my mission." Her words were distorted by the grip I had on her—she couldn't really move her jaw. "I woke up with a terrible feeling. It wasn't physical—I'd never felt so well."

"Feeling?" I was staring at her torn-up body; I couldn't look away.

"Panic, pure and simple. I went to a surgeon and paid him to cut away everything that made me a woman."

I gagged, released her, and pushed myself back, back, until I was almost in the fireplace. I got entangled with her knitting bag and it came with me, my slippers trailing a half-knit Christmas stocking and strands of red and green wool.

Willie sat up. "This city is full of sweet, bright, talented boys, Jules."

"But the future won't have anyone, bright or otherwise, unless I fulfill my mission. Is that what you're saying?"

She struggled to anchor her bodice over the ruin of flesh under her throat. Those empty scoops. Then she hunted on the carpet for the buttons I'd torn off her dress. She got to her feet, righted the chair, and peered out before creeping off into the house, holding her blouse shut.

I disentangled my feet from the red and green yarn, spilling Willie's journal in the process. Snatching it up, I fled the house.

The Major had recommended a particular neighbourhood speakeasy to me and it was there, with a whiskey in front of me, that I opened up the journal.

I suppose I expected to find an account, cleverly couched, of Willie's earliest days. Or that first mission of hers.

Who did you ruin, spoil, or kill, Willie?

But that first journal was long since filled, I'm sure, filled and locked away, waiting for the project to discover its secrets. This one had only been on the go for a month or so.

It began with a brief account of the death of one of the gents upstairs, and a note to the effect that she was glad he'd got to see the Great Pyramid on 'his recent business trip to Egypt.'

They had briefed me on that mission: Smitty had interfered with the mail in the Middle East, stealing correspondence and replacing it with false letters to a number of gentlemen in Jerusalem. This had eased tensions there and thereby delayed the onset of the second Great War until 1936.

All the sick men upstairs in the bedrooms. They're not tenants, they're time agents. They've served their purpose and now . . .

"What're you doing, Mac?" A drunk nudged me, apparently hoping I'd stand him a round.

"Reading my sister's diary," I said, which got a general laugh.

Ruin, spoil, or kill. The thought crept in, despite my resolve to refuse the mission. Peter Rupert, the reporter, had terrible problems with drink.

I paged ahead, past an account of some Boeing engineer and his odd friendship with Rufus. Beyond that was the account of my arrival Willie had written, just days before. I checked that last line, the one I'd believed was her tale-telling about my intransigence.

She had written: "What's best about him, so far, is that he's stubborn."

There was more about the engineer, and an entry saying someone named Valois had written with an address in France and a request that she forward his mail. He was settling down with a girl in Paris, for 'however long he had.'

She'd got back to me in her final entry: "Julie has survived his first week in America. His spirits are in turmoil. Homesickness, I expect. Nothing out of the ordinary. He's wonderfully strong. Father expects rather a lot from him, and he is mulling over how to make the family proud."

I had one more shot of the bathtub whiskey, then paid for a flask to take away.

On the way back, I passed a school. It was late in the day; the children were gone.

On a whim, I went in and wandered the halls, waiting for someone to challenge me. Nobody did; nobody took notice of me at all.

I stepped into a classroom and found myself contemplating a long ruler and a piece of chalk. The smell of the chalk was like the bare cement walls of the project basement: dust and bone, calm, a scent of earth and eternity.

"Are you here to fill in for our art teacher?"

I turned. The man who'd addressed me was cut from the same pattern as my father: round, pink, affable. He had green eyes, emerald chips, bright and long of lash. His wedding ring was plain and a little too tight for his finger; the valise he clutched was well-worn.

"Veteran?" he said, and I nodded.

"There aren't enough thanks in all the world, sir, for what you've done."

"I accept pound notes," I said.

His laugh was like Dad's, too, a boom that came from the soles of his feet. "Principal's at the end of the hall, on the left."

I found Willie tucking her heavy tarpaulin back into place on the mattress in the basement. There was an ugly bruise around her mouth, but when she saw me, her lips twitched. Trying not to laugh?

"Sorry." What else could I say?

"It's nothing."

I lifted the edge of the mattress so she could smooth the tarpaulin under. "What are you doing?"

"Preparing for the next one." She handed me the sheet.

That should have been my cue to tell her it wouldn't be necessary to send another man, that I'd take on the mission. But there would be someone else, wouldn't there?

"Have you got my book, Julie?"

I passed the journal to her. "Lots about Boeing."

"The airfield's one reason we're in Washington. A hint to an engineer here, a line on a blueprint there . . . the planes make an immense difference to how it all plays out."

"Is that what you did—help make planes?"

"Rufus is the engineer," she said. "Who would take plane-building notes from a dotty old widow?"

"So your mission: was it 'ruin, spoil, or kill' too?"

"Well." Her voice was dry. "We are siblings."

I took that as a yes.

She said: "You've thought it out, haven't you?"

I showed her the flask. "Peter Rupert has a compulsion. If I start him drinking early, especially given the poisons they're putting in alcohol right now . . ."

Willie nodded. "Might be kinder to shoot him."

"Kinder for him? Or me?"

"You, of course."

If he became a drunk as a youth, he might yet pull a less illustrious life together later. "It shouldn't be easy."

"That's simply masochism."

"You're afraid it won't work? That I'll die before he's—"

She gestured at the mattress. Meaning: if I failed, someone else would come and finish the job.

I took up my ruler and walked to the wall, drawing the line I'd seen there.

Working slowly, I made notches at one-inch intervals, and wrote 1900, 1914, and 1916 at the appropriate heights. They looked just as I'd remembered. There's an odd curl to my nines I never managed, quite, to amend.

I counted forward to 1937, the year they pressed Willie, and wrote an encircled "1" beside it.

"The first Souring?" she said.

"Yes." I counted forward through the nine years she'd bought us, to my own time, and noted the second.

"They're learning more with every press," she said. "Rufus has been doing quite well."

I nodded, but I wasn't paying attention. The scent of the chalk had caught me again, along with the odd little miracle of the bright yellow line it made, here on the rough grey wall, and the residue left on my hand. It was the same feeling I'd had when talking to the old teacher, an almost painful awareness of . . . was it beauty?

"Sorry, what?" I said.

She wore, to my shock, a smile. "One of the effects of having been—what was your word?—skinned," she said. "Little things shine out like that. It's never the things that are meant to be attractive, I find, but—"

I gave in to the urge to put the chalk under my nose, like a cigar, and inhale. "It's just that it's so different. Different from the end."

"Yes. Solid, somehow. Real. Food's better too, once you can handle it."

"Tonight, maybe," I said, pocketing the chalk and leaving the ruler leaned up against the short stretch of the twentieth century, the scratched out record of the precious years we'd bought so far. "So, Willie, do you want to know my name yet?"

"When you've lived, Julie," she said, and she meant something different by it this time. And what did it matter? I bent to help her with the sheet, smoothing out the mattress to catch the next wretched one of us, whenever he or she might land.

A Wish from a Bone

GEMMA FILES

War zone archaeology is the best kind, Hynde liked to say, when drunk—and Goss couldn't disagree, at least in terms of ratings. The danger, the constant threat, was a clarifying influence, lending everything they did an extra meaty heft. Better yet, it was the world's best excuse for having to wrap real quick and pull out ahead of the tanks, regardless of whether or not they'd actually found anything.

The site for their latest TV special was miles out from anywhere else, far enough from the border between Eritrea and the Sudan that the first surveys missed it—first, second, third, fifteenth, until updated satellite surveillance finally revealed minute differences between what local experts could only assume was some sort of temple and all the similarly coloured detritus surrounding it. It didn't help that it was only a few clicks (comparatively) away from the Meroitic pyramid find in Gebel Barkal, which had naturally kept most "real" archaeologists too busy to check out what the fuck that low-lying, hill-like building lurking in the middle distance might or might not be.

Yet on closer examination, of course, it turned out somebody already *had* stumbled over it, a couple of different times; the soldiers who'd set up initial camp inside in order to avoid a dust storm had found two separate batches of bodies, fresh-ish enough that their shreds of clothing and artefacts could be dated back to the 1930s on the one hand, the 1890s on the other. Gentlemen explorers, native guides, mercenaries. Same as today, pretty much, without the "gentlemen" part.

Partially ruined, and rudimentary, to say the least. It was laid out somewhat like El-Marraqua, or the temples of Lake Nasser: a roughly half-circular building with the rectangular section facing outwards like a big, blank wall centred by a single, permanently open doorway, twelve feet high by five feet wide. No windows, though the roof remained surprisingly intact.

"This whole area was under water, a million years ago," Hynde told Goss. "See these rocks? All sedimentary. Chalk, fossils, bone-bed silica, and radiolarite—amazing any of it's still here, given the wind. Must've formed in a channel or a basin . . . but no, that doesn't make sense either, because the *inside* of the place is stable, no matter how much the outside erodes."

"So they quarried stone from somewhere else, brought it here, shored it up."

"Do you know how long that would've taken? Nearest hard-rock deposits are like—five hundred miles thataway. Besides, that's not even vaguely how it looks. It's more . . . unformed, like somebody set up channels while a lava-flow was going on and shepherded it into a hexagonal pattern, then waited for it to cool enough that the up-thrust slabs fit together like walls, blending at the seams."

"What's the roof made of?"

"Interlocking bricks of mud, weed, and gravel fix-baked in the sun, then fitted together and fired afterwards, from the outside in; must've piled flammable stuff on top of it, set it alight, let it cook. The glue for the gravel was bone-dust and chunks, marinated in vinegar."

"*Seriously*," Goss said, perking up. "Human? This a necropolis, or what?"

"We don't know, to either."

Outside, that new chick—Camberwell? The one who'd replaced that massive Eurasian guy they'd all just called "Gojira," rumoured to have finally screwed himself to death between projects—was wrangling their trucks into camp formation, angled to provide a combination of look-out, cover, and wind-brake. Moving inside, meanwhile, Goss began taking light-meter readings and setting up his initial shots, while Hynde showed him around this particular iteration of the Oh God Can Such Things Be travelling road-show.

"Watch your step," Hynde told him, all but leading him by the sleeve. "The floor slopes down, a series of shallow shelves . . . it's an old trick, designed to force perspective, move you farther in. To develop a sense of awe."

Goss nodded, allowing Hynde to draw him towards what at first looked like one back wall, but quickly proved to be a clever illusion—two slightly overlapping partial walls, slim as theatrical flats, set up to hide a sharply zigzagging passage beyond. This, in turn, gave access to a tunnel curling downwards into a sort of cavern underneath the temple floor, through which Hynde was all too happy to conduct Goss, filming as they went.

"Take a gander at all the mosaics," Hynde told him. "Get in close. See those hieroglyphics?"

"Is that what those are? They look sort of . . . organic, almost."

"They should; they were, once. Fossils."

Goss focused his lens closer, and grinned so wide his cheeks hurt. Because yes yes fucking YES, they were: rows on rows of skeletal little pressed-flat, stonified shrimp, fish, sea-ferns, and other assorted what-the-fuck-evers, painstakingly selected, sorted, and slotted into patterns that started at calf-level and rose almost to the equally creepy baked-bone brick roof, blending into darkness.

"Jesus," he said, out loud. "This is *gold*, man, even if it turns out you can't read 'em. This is an Emmy, right here."

Hynde nodded, grinning too now, though maybe not as wide. And told him: "Wait 'til you see the well."

The cistern in question, hand-dug down through rock and paved inside with slimy sandstone, had a roughly twenty-foot diameter and a depth that proved unsound-able even with the party's longest reel of rope, which put it at something over sixty-one metres. Whatever had once been inside it appeared to have dried up long since, though a certain liquid quality to the echoes it produced gave indications that there might still be the remains of a water table—poisoned or pure, no way to tell—lingering at its bottom. There was a weird saline quality to the crust inside its lip, a sort of whitish, gypsumesque candle-wax-dripping formation that looked as though it was just on the verge of blooming into stalactites.

Far more interesting, however, was the design scheme its excavators had chosen to decorate the well's exterior with—a mosaic, also assembled from fossils, though in this case the rocks themselves had been pulverized before use, reduced to fragments so that they could be recombined into surreally alien patterns: fish-eyed, weed-legged, shell-winged monstrosities, cut here and there with what might be fins or wings or insect torsos halved, quartered, chimerically repurposed and slapped together to form even larger, more complex figures of which these initial grotesques were only the pointillist building blocks. Step back far enough, and they coalesced into seven figures looking off into almost every possible direction save for where the southeast compass point should go. That spot was completely blank.

"I'm thinking the well-chamber was constructed first," Hynde explained, "here, under the ground—possibly around an already-existing cave, hollowed out by water that no longer exists, through limestone that *shouldn't* exist. After which the entire temple would've been built overtop, to hide and protect it . . . protect *them*."

"The statues." Hynde nodded. "Are those angels?" Goss asked, knowing they couldn't be.

"Do they *look* like angels?"

"Hey, there are some pretty fucked-up looking angels, is what I hear. Like—rings of eyes covered in wings, or those four-headed ones from *The X-Files*."

"Or the ones that look like Christopher Walken."

"Gabriel, in *The Prophecy*. Viggo Mortensen played Satan." Goss squinted. "But these sort of look like . . . Pazuzu."

Hynde nodded, pleased. "Good call: four wings, like a moth—definitely Sumerian. This one has clawed feet; this one's head is turned backwards, or maybe upside-down. *This* one looks like it's got no lower jaw. This one has a tail and no legs at all, like a snake. . . ."

"Dude, do you actually know what they are, or are you just fucking with me?"

"How much do you know about the Terrible Seven?"

"Nothing."

"Excellent. That means our viewers won't, either."

They set up in front of the door, before they lost the sun. A tight shot on Hynde, hands thrown out in what Goss had come to call his classic Profsplaining pose; Goss shot from below, framing him in the temple's gaping maw, while 'Lij the sound guy checked his levels and everybody else shut the fuck up. From the corner of one eye, Goss could just glimpse Camberwell leaning back against the point truck's wheel with her dis-tractingly curvy legs crossed, arms braced like she was about to start doing reverse triceps push-ups. Though it was hard to tell from behind those massive sun-goggles, she didn't seem too impressed.

"The Terrible Seven were mankind's first boogeymen," Hynde told whoever would eventually be up at three in the morning, or whenever the History Channel chose to run this. "To call them demons would be too . . . Christian. To the people who feared them most, the Sumerians, they were simply a group of incredibly powerful creatures responsible for every sort of human misery, invisible and unutterably malign—literally unnameable, since to name them was, inevitably, to invite their attention. According to experts, the only way to fend them off was with the so-called 'Maskim Chant,' a prayer for protection collected by E. Campbell Thompson in his book *The Devils and Evil Spirits Of Babylonia, Vol.s 1-2* . . . and even that was no sure guarantee of safety, depending just how annoyed one—or all—of the Seven might be feeling, any given day of the week. . . ."

Straightening slightly, he raised one hand in mock supplication, reciting:

"They are Seven! They are Seven!

"Seven in the depths of the ocean, Seven in the Heavens above,

"Those who are neither male nor female, those who stretch themselves out like chains . . .

"Terrible beyond description.

"Those who are Nameless. Those who must not be named.

"The enemies! The enemies! Bitter poison sent by the Gods.

"Seven are they! Seven!"

Nice, Goss thought, and went to cut Hynde off. But there was more, apparently—a lot of it, and Hynde seemed intent on getting it all out. Good for inserts, Goss guessed, 'specially when cut together with the spooky shit from inside. . . .

"In heaven they are unknown. On earth they are not understood.

"They neither stand nor sit, nor eat nor drink.

"Spirits that minish the earth, that minish the land, of giant strength and giant tread—"

("*Minish*"?)

"Demons like raging bulls, great ghosts,

"Ghosts that break through all the houses, demons that have no shame, seven are they!

"Knowing no care, they grind the land like corn.

"Knowing no mercy, they rage against mankind.

"They are demons full of violence, ceaselessly devouring blood.

"Seven are they! Seven are they! Seven!

"They are Seven! They are Seven! They are twice Seven! They are Seven times seven!"

Camberwell was sitting up now, almost standing, while the rest of the crew made faces at each other. Goss had been sawing a finger across his throat since *knowing no care*, but Hynde just kept on going, hair crested, complexion purpling; he looked unhealthily sweat-shiny, spraying spit. Was that froth on his lower lip?

"The wicked *Arralu* and *Allatu*, who wander alone in the wilderness, covering man like a garment,
　"The wicked *Namtaru*, who seizes by the throat.
　"The wicked *Asakku*, who envelops the skull like a fever.
　"The wicked *Utukku*, who slays man alive on the plain.
　"The wicked *Lammyatu*, who causes disease in every portion.
　"The wicked *Ekimmu*, who draws out the bowels.
　"The wicked *Gallu* and *Alu*, who bind the hands and body . . ."

By this point even 'Lij was looking up, visibly worried. Hynde began to shake, eyes stutter-lidded, and fell sidelong even as Goss moved to catch him, only to find himself blocked—Camberwell was there already, folding Hynde into a brisk paramedic's hold.

　"A rag, *something*," she ordered 'Lij, who whipped his shirt off so fast his 'phones went bouncing, rolling it flat enough it'd fit between Hynde's teeth; Goss didn't feel like being in the way, so he drew back, kept rolling. As they laid Hynde back, limbs flailing hard enough to make dust angels, Goss could just make out more words seeping out half through the cloth stopper and half through Hynde's bleeding nose, quick and dry: rhythmic, nasal, ancient. Another chant he could only assume, this time left entirely untranslated, though words here and there popped as familiar from the preceding bunch of rabid mystic bullshit—

Arralu-Allatu Namtaru Maskim
　Asakku Utukku Lammyatu Maskim
　Ekimmu Gallu-Alu Maskim
　Maskim Maskim Maskim

Voices to his right, his left, while his lens-sight steadily narrowed and dimmed: *Go get Doc Journee, man! The fuck's head office pay her for, exactly?* 'Lij and Camberwell kneeling in the dirt, holding Hynde down, trying their best to make sure he didn't hurt himself 'til the only person on-site with an actual medical license got there. And all the while that same babble rising, louder and ever more throb-buzz deformed, like the guy had a swarm of bees stuck in his clogged and swelling throat . . .

ArralAllatNamtar AssakUtukk Lammyat EkimmGalluAlu MaskimMaskimMaskim (Maskim)

The dust storm kicked up while Journee was still attending to Hynde, getting him safely laid down in a corner of the temple's outer chamber and doing her best to stabilize him even as he resolved down into some shallow-breathing species of coma.

"Any one of these fuckers flips, they'll take out a fuckin' wall!" Camberwell yelled, as the other two drivers scrambled to get the trucks as stable as possible, digging out 'round the wheels and anchoring them with rocks, applying locks to axles and steering wheels. Goss, for his own part, was already busy helping hustle the supplies inside, stacking ration-packs around Hynde like sandbags; a crash from the door made his head jerk up, just in time to see that chick Lao and her friend-who-was-a-boy Katz (both from craft services) staring at each other over a mess of broken plastic, floor between them suddenly half-turned to mud.

Katz: "What the *shit*, man!"

Lao: "I don't know, Christ! Those bottles aren't s'posed to *break*—"

The well, something dry and small "said" at the back of Goss's head, barely a voice at all—more a touch, in passing, in the dark.

And: "There's a well," he heard himself say, before he could think better of it. "Down through there, behind the walls."

Katz looked at Lao, shrugged. "Better check it out, then," he suggested—started to, anyhow. Until Camberwell somehow turned up between them, half stepping sidelong and half like she'd just materialized, the rotating storm her personal wormhole.

"I'll do that," she said, firmly. "Still two gallon cans in the back of Truck Two, for weight; cut a path, make sure we can get to 'em. I'll tell you if what's down there's viable."

"Deal," Lao agreed, visibly grateful—and Camberwell was gone a second later, down into the passage, a shadow into shadow. While at almost the same time, from Goss's elbow, 'Lij suddenly asked (of no one in particular, given *he* was the resident expert): "Sat-phones aren't supposed to just stop working, right?"

Katz: "Nope."

"Could be we're in a dead zone, I guess . . . or the storm . . ."

"Yeah, good luck on that, buddy."

Across the room, the rest of the party were congregating in a clot, huddled 'round a cracked packet of glow-sticks because nobody wanted to break out the lanterns, not in this weather. Journee had opened Hynde's shirt to give him CPR, but left off when he stopped seizing. Now she sat crouched above him, peering down at his chest like she was trying to play connect-the-dots with moles, hair, and nipples.

"Got a weird rash forming here," she told Goss, when he squatted down beside her. "Allergy? Or photosensitive, maybe, if he's prone to that, 'cause . . . it really does seem to turn darker the closer you move the flashlight."

"He uses a lot of sunscreen."

"Don't we all. Seriously, look for yourself."

He did. Thinking: *Optical illusion, has to be* . . . but wondering, all the same. Because—it was just so clear, so defined, rucking Hynde's skin as though something was raising it up from inside. Like a letter from some completely alien alphabet; a symbol, unrecognizable, unreadable.

(**A sigil**, the same tiny voice corrected. And Goss felt the hairs on his back ruffle, sudden-slick with cold, foul sweat.)

It took a few minutes more for 'Lij to give up on the sat-phone, tossing it aside so hard it bounced. "Try the radio mikes," Goss heard him tell himself, "see what kinda bandwidth we can . . . back to Gebel, might be somebody listening. But not the border, nope, gotta keep off *that* squawk-channel, for sure. Don't want the military gettin' wind, on either side. . . ."

By then, Camberwell had been gone for almost ten minutes, so Goss felt free to leave Hynde in Journee's care and follow, at his own pace—through the passage and into the tunnel, feeling along the wall, trying to be quiet. But two painful stumbles later, halfway down the tunnel's curve, he had to flip open his phone just to see; the stone-bone walls gave off a faint, ill light, vaguely slick, a dead jellyfish luminescence.

He drew within just enough range to hear Camberwell's boots rasp on the downward slope, then pause—saw her glance over one shoulder, eyes weirdly bright through a dim fall of hair gust-popped from her severe, sweat-soaked working gal's braid. Asking, as she did: "Want me to wait while you catch up?"

Boss, other people might've appended, almost automatically, but never her. Then again, Goss had to admit, he wouldn't have really believed that shit coming from Camberwell, even if she had.

He straightened up, sighing, and joined her—standing pretty much exactly where he thought she'd've ended up, right next to the well, though keeping a careful distance between herself and its creepy-coated sides. "Try sending down a cup yet, or what?"

"Why? Oh, right . . . no, no point; that's why I volunteered, so those dumbasses *wouldn't* try. Don't want to be drinking *any* of the shit comes out of there, believe you me."

"Oh, I do, and that's—kinda interesting, given. Rings a bit like you obviously know more about this than you're letting on."

She arched a brow, denial reflex-quick, though not particularly convincing. "Hey, who was it sent Lao and what's-his-name down here, in the first place? I'm motor pool, man. Cryptoarchaeology is you and coma-boy's gig."

"Says the chick who knows the correct terminology."

"Look who I work for."

Goss sighed. "Okay, I'll bite. What's in the well?"

"What's *on* the well? Should give you some idea. Or, better yet—"

She held out her hand for his phone, the little glowing screen, with its pathetic rectangular light. After a moment, he gave it over and watched her cast it 'round, outlining the chamber's canted, circular floor: seen face on, those ridges he'd felt under his feet when Hynde first brought him in here and dismissed without a first glance, let alone a second, proved to be in-spiralling channels stained black from centuries of use: run-off ditches once used for drainage, aimed at drawing some sort of liquid— layered and faded now into muck and dust, a resinous stew clogged with dead insects—away from (what else) seven separate niches set into the surrounding walls, inset so sharply they only became apparent when you observed them at an angle.

In front of each niche, one of the mosaicked figures, with a funnelling spout set at ditch-level under the creature in question's feet, or lack thereof. Inside each niche, meanwhile, a quartet of hooked spikes set vertically, maybe five feet apart: two up top, possibly for hands or wrists, depending if you were doing things Roman- or Renaissance-style; two down below, suitable for lashing somebody's ankles to. And now Goss looked closer, something else as well, in each of those upright stone coffins . . .

(Ivory scraps, shattered yellow-brown shards, broken down by time and gravity alike, and painted to match their surroundings by lack of light. Bones, piled where they fell.)

"What the fuck *was* this place?" Goss asked, out loud. But mainly because he wanted confirmation, more than anything else.

Camberwell shrugged, yet again—her default setting, he guessed. "A trap," she answered. "And you fell in it, but don't feel bad—you weren't to know, right?"

"We found it, though. Hynde, and me . . ."

"If not you, somebody else. Some places are already empty, already ruined—they just wait, long as it takes. They don't ever go away. 'Cause they *want* to be found."

Goss felt his stomach roil, fresh sweat springing up even colder, so rank he could smell it. "A trap," he repeated, biting down, as Camberwell nodded. Then: "For us?"

But here she shook her head, pointing back at the well, with its seven watchful guardians. Saying, as she did—

"Naw, man. For *them*."

She laid her hand on his, half its size but twice as strong, and walked him through it—puppeted his numb and clumsy finger-pads bodily over the clumps of fossil chunks in turn, allowing him time to recognize what was hidden inside the mosaic's design more by touch than by sight: a symbol (**sigil**) for every figure, tumour-blooming and weirdly organic, each one just ever-so-slightly different from the next. He found the thing Hynde's rash most reminded him of on number four, and stopped dead; Camberwell's gaze flicked down to confirm, her mouth moving slightly, shaping words. *Ah*, one looked like—*ah, I see*. Or maybe *I see you*.

"What?" he demanded, for what seemed like the tenth time in quick succession. Thinking: *I sound like a damn parrot.*

Camberwell didn't seem to mind, though. "Ashreel," she replied, not looking up. "That's what I said. The Terrible Ashreel, who wears us like clothing."

"Allatu, you mean. The wicked, who covers man like a garment—"

"Whatever, Mister G. If you prefer."

"It's just—I mean, that's nothing like what Hynde said, up there—"

"Yeah sure, 'cause that shit was what the Sumerians and Babylonians called 'em, from that book Hynde was quoting." She knocked knuckles against Hynde's brand, then the ones on either side—three sharp little raps, invisible cross-nails. "*These* are their actual *names*. Like . . . what they call *themselves*."

"How the fuck would you know that? Camberwell, what the hell."

Straightening, shrugging yet again, like she was throwing off flies. "There's a book, okay? The *Liber Carne*—'Book of Meat.' And all's it has is just a list of names with these symbols carved alongside, so you'll know which one you're looking at, when they're—embodied. In the flesh."

"In the—you mean *bodies*, like possession? Like that's what's happening to Hynde?" At her nod: "Well . . . makes sense, I guess, in context; he already said they were demons."

"Oh, that's a misnomer, actually. 'Terrible' used to mean 'awe-inspiring,' 'more whatever than any other whatever,' like Tsar Ivan of all the Russias. So the Seven, the *Terrible* Seven, what they really are is angels, just like you thought."

"Fallen angels."

"Nope, those are Goetim, like you call the ones who stayed up top Elohim—*these* are Maskim, same as the Chant. Arralu-Allatu, Namtaru, Asakku, Utukku, Gallu-Alu, Ekimmu, Lammyatu; Ashreel, Yphemaal, Zemyel, Eshphoriel, Immoel, Coiab, Ushephekad. Angel of Confusion, the Mender Angel, Angel of Severance, Angel of Whispers, Angel of Translation, Angel of Ripening, Angel of the Empty . . ."

All these half-foreign words spilling from her mouth, impossibly glib, ringing in Goss's head like popped blood vessels. But: "Wait," he threw back, struggling. "A 'trap' . . . I thought this place was supposed to be a temple. Like the people who built it worshipped these things."

"Okay, then play that out. Given how Hynde described 'em, what sort of people would *worship* the Seven, you think?"

". . . .errible people?"

"You got it. Sad people, weird people, crazy people. People who get off on power, good, bad, or indifferent. People who hate the world they got so damn bad they don't really care what they swap it for, as long as it's *something else*."

"And they expect—the Seven—to do that for them."

"It's what they were made for."

Straight through cryptoarchaeology and out the other side, into a version of the Creation so literally Apocryphal it would've gotten them both burnt at the stake just a few hundred years earlier. Because to hear Camberwell tell it, sometimes, when a Creator got very, verrry lonely, It decided to make Itself some friends—after which, needing someplace to put them, It contracted the making of such a place out to creatures themselves made to order: fragments of its own reflected glory haphazardly hammered into vaguely humanesque form, perfectly suited to this one colossal task, and almost nothing else.

"They made the world, in other words," Goss said. "All seven of them."

"Yeah. 'Cept back then they were still one angel in seven parts—the Voltron angel, I call it. Splitting apart came later on, after the schism."

"Lucifer, war in heaven, cast down into hell and yadda yadda. All that. So this is all, what . . . some sort of metaphysical labour dispute?"

"They wouldn't think of it that way."

"How *do* they think of it?"

"*Differently*, like every other thing. Look, once the shit hit the cosmic fan, the Seven didn't stay with God, but they didn't go with the devil, either—they just went, forced themselves from outside space and time into the universe they'd made, and never looked back. And that was because they wanted something angels are uniquely unqualified for: free will. They wanted to be us."

Back to the fast-forward, then, the bend and the warp, till her ridiculously plausible-seeming exposition-dump seemed to come at him from everywhere at once, a perfect storm. Because: *misery's their meat, see—the honey that draws flies, bi-product of every worst moment of all our brief lives, when people will cry out for anything who'll listen. That's when one of the Seven usually shows up, offering help—except the kind of help they come up with's usually nothing very helpful at all, considering how they just don't really get the way things work for us, even now. And it's always just one of them at first, 'cause they each blame the other for having made the decision to run, stranding themselves in the here and now, so they don't want to be anywhere near each other . . . but if you can get 'em all in one place—someplace like here, say, with seven bleeding, suffering vessels left all ready and waiting for 'em—then they'll be automatically drawn back together, like gravity, a black hole event horizon. They'll form a vector, and at the middle of that cyclone they'll become a single angel once again, ready to tear everything they built up right the fuck on back down.*

Words words words, every one more painful than the last. Goss looked at Camberwell as she spoke, straight on, the way he didn't think he'd ever actually done, previously. She was short and stacked, skin tanned and plentiful, eyes darkish brown shot with a sort of creamier shade, like petrified wood. A barely visible scar quirked through one eyebrow, threading down over the cheekbone beneath to intersect with another at the corner of her mouth, keloid raised in their wake like a negative-image beauty mark, a reversed dimple.

Examined this way, at close quarters, he found he liked the look of her, suddenly and sharply—and for some reason, that mainly made him angry.

"This is a fairy tale," he heard himself tell her, with what seemed like over-the-top emphasis. "I'm sitting here in the dark, letting you spout some . . . Catholic campfire story about angel-traps, free will, fuckin' misery vectors. . . ." A quick head-shake, firm enough to hurt. "None of it's true."

"Yeah, okay, you want to play it that way."

"If I *want*—?"

Here she turned on *him,* abruptly equal-fierce, clearing her throat to hork a contemptuous wad out on the ground between them, like she was making a point. "Look, you think I give a runny jack-shit if you believe me or not? *I know what I know.* It's just that things are gonna start to move fast from now on, so you need to know that; *somebody* in this crap-pit does, aside from me. And I guess—" Stopping and hissing, annoyed with herself, before adding, quieter: "I guess I wanted to just say it, too—out loud, for once. For all the good it'll probably do either of us."

They stood there a second, listening, Goss didn't know for what—nothing but muffled wind, people murmuring scared out beyond the passage, a general scrape and drip. 'Til he asked: "What about Hynde? Can we, like, *do* anything?"

"Not much. Why? You guys friends?"

Yes, damnit, Goss wanted to snap, but he was pretty sure she had lie-dar to go with her Seven-dar. "There's . . . not really a show, without him," was all he said, finally.

"All right, well—he's pretty good and got, at this point, so I'd keep him sedated, restrained if I could, and wait, see who else shows up: there's six more to go, after all."

"What happens if they all show up?"

"All Seven? Then we're fucked, basically, as a species. Stuck back together, the Maskim are a load-bearing boss the likes of which this world was not designed to contain, and the vector they form in proximity, well—it's like putting too much weight on a sheet of . . . something. Do it long enough, it rips wide open."

"*What* rips?"

"The crap you think? Everything."

There was a sort of a jump-cut, and Goss found himself tagging along beside her as Camberwell strode back up the passageway, listening to her tell him: "Important point about Hynde, as of right now, is to make sure he doesn't start doin' stuff to himself."

". . . like?"

"Well—"

As she said it, though, there came a scream-led general uproar up in front, making them both break into a run. They tumbled back into the light-sticks' circular glow to find Journee contorted on the ground with her heels drumming, chewing at her own lips—everybody else had already shrunk back, eyes and mouths covered like it was catching, save for big, stupid 'Lij, who was trying his level best to pry her jaws apart and thrust his folding pocket spork in between. Goss darted forward to grab one arm, Camberwell the other, but Journee used the leverage to flip back up onto her feet, throwing them both off against the walls.

She looked straight at Camberwell, spit blood and grinned wide, as though she recognized her: *Oh, it's you. How do, buddy? Welcome to the main event.*

Then reached back into her own sides, fingers plunging straight down through flesh to grip bone—ripped her red ribs wide, whole back opening up like that meat-book Camberwell had mentioned and both lungs flopping out, way too large for comfort: two dirty grey-pink balloons breathing and growing, already disgustingly over-swollen yet inflating even further, like mammoth water wings.

The pain of it made her roar and jackknife, vomiting on her own feet. And when Journee looked up once more, horrid grin trailing yellow sick-strings, Goss saw she now had a sigil of her own embossed on her forehead, fresh as some stomped-in bone-bruise.

"Asakku, the Terrible Zemyel," Camberwell said, to no one in particular. "Who desecrates the faithful."

And: "God!" Somebody else—Lao?—could be heard to sob, behind them.

"Fuck Him," Journee rasped back, throwing the tarp pinned 'cross the permanently open doorway wide and taking impossibly off up into the storm with a single flap, blood splattering everywhere, a foul red spindrift.

'Lij slapped both hands up to seal his mouth, retching loudly; Katz fell on his ass, skull colliding with the wall's sharp surface, so hard he knocked himself out. Lao continued to sob-pray on, mindless, while everybody else just stared. And Goss found himself looking over at Camberwell, automatically, only to catch her nodding—just once, like she'd seen it coming.

"—like *that*, basically," she concluded, without a shred of surprise.

Five minutes at most, but it felt like an hour: things narrowed, got treacly, in that accident-in-progress way. Outside, the dust had thickened into its own artificial night; they could hear the thing inside Journee swooping high above it, laughing like a loon, yelling raucous insults at the sky. The other two drivers had never come back inside, lost in the storm. Katz stayed slumped where he'd fallen; Lao wept and wept. 'Lij came feeling towards Camberwell and Goss as the glow-sticks dimmed, almost clambering over Hynde, whose breathing had sunk so low his chest barely seemed to move. "Gotta *do* something, man," he told them, like he was the first one ever to have that particular thought. "*Something.* Y'know? Before it's too late."

"It was too late when we got here," Goss heard himself reply—again, not what he'd thought he was going to say, when he'd opened his mouth. His tongue felt suddenly hot, inside of his mouth gone all itchy, swollen tight; strep? Tonsillitis? Jesus, if he could only reach back in there and *scratch* . . .

And Camberwell was looking at him sidelong now, with interest, though 'Lij just continued on blissfully unaware of anything, aside from his own worries. "Look, fuck *that* shit," he said, before asking her: "Can we get to the trucks?"

She shook her head. "No driving in this weather, even if we did. You ever raise anybody, or did the mikes crap out too?"

"Uh, I don't think so; caught somebody talkin' in Arabic one time, close-ish, but it sounded military, so I rung off real quick. Something about containment protocol."

Goss: "*What?*"

"Well, I thought maybe that was 'cause they were doing minefield sweeps, or whatever—"

"When *was* this?"

". . . fifteen minutes ago, when you guys were still down there, 'bout the time the storm went mega. Why?"

Goss opened his mouth again, but Camberwell was already bolting up, grabbing both Katz and Hynde at once by their shirt-collars, ready to heave and drag. The wind's whistle had taken on a weird, sharp edge, an atonal descending keen, so loud Goss could barely hear her—though he sure as hell saw her lips move, *read* them with widening, horrified eyes, at almost the same split-second he found himself turning, already in mid-leap towards the descending passage—

"—INCOMING, *get the shit downstairs, before those sons of bitches bring this whole fuckin' place down around our goddamn—*"

(ears)

Three hits, Goss thought, or maybe two and a half; it was hard to tell, when your head wouldn't stop ringing. What he could only assume was at least two of the trucks had gone up right as the walls came down, or perhaps a shade before. Now the top half of the temple was flattened, once more indistinguishable from the mountainside above and around it, a deadfall of shattered lava-rock, bone-bricks and fossils. No more missiles fell, which was good, yet—so far as they could tell, pinned beneath slabs and sediment—the storm above still raged on. And now they were all down in the well-room, trapped, with only a flickering congregation of phones to raise against the dark.

"Did you have any kind of *plan* when you came here, exactly?" Goss asked Camberwell, hoarsely. "I mean, aside from 'find Seven congregation site—question mark—profit'?"

To which she simply sighed, and replied—"Yeah, sort of. But you're not gonna like it."

"Try me."

Reluctantly: "The last couple times I did this, there was a physical copy of the *Liber Carne* in play, so getting rid of that helped—but there's no copy here, which makes *us* the *Liber Carne*, the human pages being Inscribed." He could hear the big I on that last word, and it scared him. "And when people are being Inscribed, well . . . the *best* plan is usually to just start killing those who aren't possessed until you've got less than seven left, because then why bother?"

"Uh huh . . ."

"Getting to know you people well enough to *like* you, that was my mistake, obviously," she continued, partly under her breath, like she was talking to herself. Then added, louder: "Anyhow. What we're dealing with right now is two people definitely Inscribed and possessed, four potential Inscriptions, and one halfway gone. . . ."

"Halfway? Who?"

She shot him that look, yet one more time—softer, almost sympathetic. "Open your mouth, Goss."

"Why? What f—oh, you gotta be kidding."

No change, just a slightly raised eyebrow, as if to say: *Do I look it, motherfucker?* Which, he was forced to admit, she very much did not.

Nothing to do but obey, then. Or scream, and keep on screaming.

Goss felt his jaw slacken, pop out and down like an unhinged jewel-box, revealing all its secrets. His tongue's itch was approaching some sort of critical mass. And then, right then, was when he felt it—fully and completely, without even trying. Some kind of raised area on his own soft palate, yearning down as sharply as the rest of his mouth's sensitive insides yearned up, straining to map its impossibly angled curves. His eyes skittered to the well's rim, where he knew he would find its twin, if he only searched long enough.

"Uck ee," he got out, consonants drowned away in a mixture of hot spit and cold sweat. "Oh it, uck *ee*."

A small, sad nod. "The Terrible Eshphoriel," Camberwell confirmed. "Who whispers in the empty places."

Goss closed his mouth, then spat like he was trying to clear it, for all he knew that wouldn't work. Then asked, hoarsely, stumbling slightly over the words he found increasingly difficult to form: "How mush . . . time I got?"

"Not much, probably."

"'S what I fought." He looked down, then back up at her, eyes sharpening. "How you geh those scars uh yers, Cammerwell?"

"Knowing's not gonna help you, Goss." But since he didn't look away, she sighed, and replied. "Hunting accident. Okay?"

"Hmh, 'kay. Then . . . thing we need uh . . . new plan, mebbe. You 'gree?"

She nodded, twisting her lips; he could see her thinking, literally, cross-referencing what had to be a thousand scribbled notes from the margins of her mental grand grimoire. Time slowed to an excruciating crawl, within which Goss began to hear that still, small voice begin to mount up again, no doubt aware it no longer had to be particularly subtle about things anymore: *Eshphoriel Maskim, sometimes called Utukku, Angel of Whispers . . . and yes, I can hear you, little fleshbag, as you hear me; feel you, in all your incipient flowering and decay, your time-anchored freedom. We are all the same in this way, and yes, we mostly hate you for it, which only makes your pain all the sweeter, in context—though not quite so much, at this point, as we imitation-of-passionately strive to hate each other.*

You guys stand outside space and time, though, right? he longed to demand, as he felt the constant background chatter of what he'd always thought of as "him" start to dim. *Laid the foundations of the Earth—you're megaton bombs, and we're like . . . viruses. So why the hell would you want to be anything like us? To lower yourselves that way?*

A small pause came in this last idea's wake, not quite present, yet too much there to be absent, somehow: a breath, perhaps, or the concept of one, drawn from the non-throat of something far infinitely larger. The feather's shadow, floating above the Word of God.

It does make you wonder, does it not? the small voice "said." *I know I do, and have, since before your first cells split.*

Because they want to defile the creation they set in place, yet have no real part in, Goss's mind—*his* mind, yes, he was *almost* sure—chimed in. *Because they long to insert themselves where they have no cause to be and let it shiver apart all around them, to run counter to everything, a curse on Heaven. To make themselves the worm in the cosmic apple, rotting everything they touch . . .*

The breath returned, drawn harder this time in a semi-insulted way, a universal "tch!" But at the same time, something else presented itself—just as likely, or un-. Valid as anything else, in a world touched by the Seven.

(Or because . . . maybe, this is all there is. Maybe, this is as good as it gets.) That's all.

"I have an idea," Camberwell said, at last, from somewhere nearby. And Goss opened his mouth to answer only to hear the angel's still, small voice issue from between his teeth, replying, mildly—

"Do you, huntress? Then please, say on."

This, then, was how they all finally came to be arrayed 'round the well's rim, the seven of them who were left, standing—or propped up/lying, in Hynde and Katz's cases—in front of those awful wall-orifices, staring into the multifaceted mosaic-eyes of God's former *Flip My Universe* crew. 'Lij stood at the empty southeastern point, looking nervous, for which neither Goss nor the creature inhabiting his brain-pan could possibly blame him. While Camberwell busied herself moving from person to person, sketching quick and dirty versions of the sigils on them with the point of a flick-knife she'd produced from one of her boots. Lao opened her mouth like she was gonna start crying even harder when she first saw it, but Camberwell just shot her the fearsomest glare yet—Medusa-grade, for sure—and watched her shut the fuck up, with a hitchy little gasp.

"This will bring us together sooner rather than later, you must realize," Eshphoriel told Camberwell, who nodded. Replying: "That's the idea."

"Ah. That seems somewhat . . . antithetical, knowing our works, as you claim to."

"Maybe so. But you tell me—what's better? Stay down here in the dark waiting for the air to run out only to have you celestial tapeworms soul-rape us all at last minute anyways, when we're too weak to put up a fight? Or force an end now, while we're all semi-fresh, and see what happens?"

"Fine tactics, yes—very born-again barbarian. Your own pocket Ragnarok, with all that the term implies."

"Yeah, yeah: clam up, Legion, if you don't have anything useful to contribute." To 'Lij: "You ready, sound-boy?"

"Uhhhh . . ."

"I'll take that as a 'yes.'"

Done with Katz, she swapped places with 'Lij, handing him the knife as she went, and tapping the relevant sigil. "Like that," she said. "Try to do it all in one motion, if you can—it'll hurt less."

'Lij looked dubious. "**One can't fail to notice you aren't volunteering for impromptu body-modification,**" Eshphoriel noted, through Goss's lips, while Camberwell met the comment with a tiny, bitter smile.

Replying, as she hiked her shirt up to demonstrate—"That'd be 'cause I've already got one."

Cocking a hip to display the thing in question where it nestled in the hollow at the base of her spine, more a scab than a scar, edges blurred like some infinitely fucked-up tramp stamp. And as she did, Goss saw *something* come fluttering up behind her skin, a parallel-dimension full-body ripple, the barest glowing shadow of a disproportionately huge tentacle-tip still up-thrust through Camberwell's whole being, as though everything she was, had been and would ever come to be was nothing more than some indistinct no-creature's fleshy finger-puppet.

One cream-brown eye flushed with livid colour, green on yellow, while the other stayed exactly the same—human, weary, bitter to its soul's bones. And Camberwell opened her mouth to let her tongue protrude, pink and healthy except for an odd whitish strip that ran ragged down its centre from tip to—not exactly *tail*, Goss assumed, since the tongue was fairly huge, or so he seemed to recall. But definitely almost to the uvula, and: oh God, oh shit, was it actually splitting as he watched, bisecting itself not-so-neatly into two separate semi-points, like a child's snaky scribble?

Camberwell gave it a flourish, swallowed the resultant spit-mouthful, then said, without much affect: "Yeah, that's right—'Gallu-Alu, the Terrible Immoel, who speaks with a dead tongue . . .'" Camberwell fluttered the organ in question at what had taken control of Goss, showing its central scars long-healed, extending the smile into a wide, entirely unamused grin. "So say hey, assfuck. Remember me now?"

"**You were its vessel, then, once before,**" Goss heard his lips reply. "**And . . . yes, yes, I do recall it. Apologies, huntress; I cannot say, with the best will in all this world, that any of you look so very different, to me.**"

Camberwell snapped her fingers. "Aw, gee." To 'Lij, sharper: "I tell you to stop cutting?"

Goss felt "his" eyes slide to poor 'Lij, caught and wavering (his face a sickly grey-green, chest heaving slightly, like he didn't know whether to run or puke), then watched him shake his head, and bow back down to it.

The knife went in shallow, blunter than the job called for—he had to drag it, hooking up underneath his own hide, to make the meat part as cleanly as the job required. While Camberwell kept a sure and steady watch on the other well-riders, all of whom were beginning to look equally disturbed, even those who were supposedly unconscious. Goss felt his own lips curve, far more genuinely amused, even as an alien emotion-tangle wound itself invasively throughout his chest: half proprietorially expectant, half vaguely annoyed.

"We are coming," he heard himself say. **"All of us. Meaning you may have miscalculated, somewhat . . . what a sad state of affairs indeed, when the prospective welfare of your entire species depends on you not doing so."**

That same interior ripple ran 'round the well's perimeter as 'Lij pulled the knife past "his" sigil's final slashing loop and yanked it free, splattering the frieze in front of him; in response, the very stones seemed to arch hungrily, that composite mouth gaping, eager for blood. Above, even through the heavy-pressing rubble-mound which must be all that was left of the temple proper, Goss could hear Journee-Zemyel swooping and cawing in the updraft, swirled on endless waves of storm; from his eye's corner he saw Hynde-whoever (**Arralu-Allatu, the Terrible Ashreel,** Eshphoriel supplied, helpfully) open one similarly parti-coloured eye and lever himself up, clumsy-clambering to his feet. Katz's head fell back, spine suddenly hooping so heels struck shoulder-blades with a wetly awful crack, and began to lift off, levitating gently, turning in the air like some horrible ornament. Meanwhile, Lao continued to grind her fisted knuckles into both eyes at once, bruising lids but hopefully held back from pulping the balls themselves, at least so long as her sockets held fast. . . .

(*Ekimmu, the Terrible Coaib, who seeds without regard. Lamyatu, the Terrible Ushephekad, who opens the ground beneath us.*)

From the well, dusty mortar popped forth between every suture, and the thing as a whole gave one great shrug, shivering itself apart—began caving in and expanding at the same time, becoming a nothing-column for its parts to revolve around, an incipient reality fabric-tear. And in turn, the urge to rotate likewise—just let go of gravity's pull, throw physical law to the winds, and see where that might lead—cored through Goss, ass to cranium, Vlad Tepes style, a phantom impalement pole spearing every neural pathway. Simultaneously gone limp *and* stiff, he didn't have to look down to know his crotch must be darkening, or over to 'Lij to confirm how the same invisible angel-driven marionette hooks were now pulling at *his* muscles, making his knife-hand grip and flex, sharp enough the handle almost broke free of his sweaty palm entirely—

(*Namtaru, the Terrible Yphemaal, who stitches what was rent asunder.*)

"**And now we are Seven, without a doubt,**" Goss heard that voice in his throat note, its disappointment audible. "**For all your bravado, perhaps you are not as well-educated as you believe.**"

Camberwell shrugged yet one more time, slow but distinct; her possessed eye widened slightly, as though in surprise. And in that instant, it occurred to Goss how much of herself she still retained, even in the Immoel-thing's grip, which seemed far—slipperier, in her case, than with everybody else. Because maybe coming pre-Inscribed built up a certain pad of scar tissue in the soul, in situations like these; maybe that's what she'd been gambling on, amongst other things. Having just enough slack on her lead to allow her to do stuff like (for example) reach down into her other boot, the way she was even as they "spoke," and—

Holy crap, just how many knives does this chick walk around with, exactly?

—bringing up the second of a matched pair, trigger already thumbed, blade halfway from its socket. Tucking it beneath her jaw, point tapping at her jugular, and saying, as she did—

"Never claimed to be, but I do know *this* much: Sam Raimi got it wrong. You guys don't like wearing nothin' *dead*."

And: *That's your* plan? Goss wanted to yell, right in the face of her martyr-stupid, *fuck all y'all* snarl. Except that that was when the thing inside 'Lij (Yphemaal, its name is Yphemaal) turned him, bodily—two great twitches, a child "walking" a doll. Its purple eyes fell on Camberwell in mid-move, and narrowed; Goss heard something rush up and out in every direction, rustle-ruffling as it went: some massive and indistinct pair of wings, mostly elsewhere, only a few pinions intruding to lash the blade from Camberwell's throat before the cut could complete itself, leaving a shallow red trail in its wake.

(Another "hunting" trophy, Goss guessed, eventually. Not that she'd probably notice.)

"**No,**" 'Lij-Yphemaal told the room at large, all its hovering sibling-selves, in a voice colder than orbit-bound satellite-skin. "**Enough.**"

"**We are Seven,**" Eshphoriel Maskim replied, with Goss's flayed mouth. "**The huntress has the right of it: remove one vessel, break the quorum, before we reassemble. If she wants to sacrifice herself, who are we to interfere?**"

"**Who were we to, ever, every time we have? But there is another way.**"

The sigils flowed each to each, Goss recalled having noticed at this freak-show's outset, albeit only subconsciously—one basic design exponentially added upon, a fresh new (literal) twist summoning Two out of One, Three out of Two, Four out of Three, etcetera. Which left Immoel and Yphemaal separated by both a pair of places and a triad of contortionate squiggle-slashes; far more work to imitate than 'Lij could possibly do under pressure with his semi-blunt knife, his wholly inadequate human hands and brain.

But Yphemaal wasn't 'Lij. Hell, this very second, *'Lij* wasn't even 'Lij.

The Mender-angel was at least merciful enough to let him scream as it remade its sigil into Immoel's with three quick cuts, then slipped forth, blowing away up through the well's centre-spoke like a backwards lightning rod. Two niches on, Katz lit back to earth with a cartilaginous creak, while Lao let go just in time to avoid tearing her own corneas; Hynde's head whipped up, face gone trauma-slack but finally recognizable, abruptly vacated. And Immoel Maskim spurted forth from Camberwell in a gross black cloud from mouth, nose, the corner of the eyes, its passage dimming her yellow-green eye back to brown, then buzzed angrily back and forth between two equally useless prospective vessels until seeming to give up in disgust.

Seemed even angels couldn't be in two places at once. Who knew?

Not inside time and space, no. And unfortunately—

That's where we *live*, Goss realized.

Yes.

Goss saw the bulk of the Immoel-stuff blend into the well room's wall, sucked away like blotted ink. Then fell to his knees, as though prompted, only to see the well collapse in upon its own shaft, ruined forever—its final cosmic strut removed, solved away like some video game's culminative challenge.

Beneath, the ground shook, like jelly. Above, a thunderclap whoosh sucked all the dust away, darkness boiling up, peeling itself away like an onion till only the sun remained, pale and high and bright. And straight through the hole in the "roof" dropped all that was left of Journee-turned-Zemyel—face-down, from a twenty-plus-foot height, horrible thunk of impact driving her features right back into her skull, leaving nothing behind but a smashed-flat, raw meat mask.

Goss watched those wing-lungs of hers deflate, thinking: *she couldn't've survived*. And felt Eshphoriel, still lingering, clawed to his brain's pathways even in the face of utter defeat, interiorly agree that: *It does seem unlikely. But then, my sister loves to leave no toy unbroken, if only to spit in your—and our—Maker's absent eye.*

Uh huh, Goss thought back, suddenly far too tired for fear, or even sorrow.

So maybe it's time to get the fuck out too, huh, while the going's good? "Minish"
yourself, like the old chant goes. . . .

Perhaps, yes. For now.

He looked to Camberwell, who stood there shaking slightly, caught
off-guard for once—amazed to be alive, it was fairly obvious, part-cut
throat and all. Asking 'Lij, as she dabbed at the blood: "What did you *do*,
dude?"

To which 'Lij only shook his head, equally freaked. "I . . . yeah, dunno,
really. I don't—even think that was *me*."

"No, 'course not: Yphemaal, right? Who sews crooked seams straight . . ."
She shook her head, cracked her neck back and forth. "Only one of 'em still
building stuff, these days, instead of tearing down or undermining, so maybe
it's the only one of 'em who really *doesn't* want to go back, 'cause it knows
what'll happen next."

"Maaaaybe," 'Lij said, dubious—then grabbed his wound, like something'd
just reminded him it was there. "Oh, *shit*, that hurts!"

"You'll be fine, ya big baby—magic shit heals fast, like you wouldn't
believe. Makes for a great conversation piece, too."

"Okay, sure. Hey . . . I saved your life."

Camberwell snorted. "Yeah, well—I would've saved yours, you hadn't
beat me to it. Which makes us even."

'Lij opened his mouth at that, perhaps to object, but was interrupted
by Hynde, his voice creaky with disuse. Demanding, of Goss directly—
"Hey, Arthur, what . . . the hell *happened* here? Last thing I remember was
doing pick-ups, outside, and then—" His eyes fell on Journee, widening.
"—*then* I, oh Christ, is that—who *is* that?"

Goss sighed, equally hoarse. "Long story."

By the time he was done, they were all outside—even poor Journee, who
'Lij had badgered Katz and Lao into helping roll up in a tarp, stowing her
for transport in the back of the one blessedly still-operative truck
Camberwell had managed to excavate from the missile-strike's wreckage.
Better yet, it ensued that 'Lij's backup sat-phone was now once again
functional; once contacted, the production office informed them that border
skirmishes had definitely spilled over into undeclared war, thus necessitating
a quick retreat to the airstrip they'd rented near Karima town. Camberwell
reckoned they could make it if they started now, though the last mile or
so might be mainly on fumes.

"Better saddle up," she told Goss, briskly, as she brushed past, headed
for the truck's cab. Adding, to a visibly gobsmacked Hynde: "Yo, Professor:

you gonna be okay? 'Cause the fact is, we kinda can't stop to let you process."

Hynde shook his head, wincing; one hand went to his chest, probably just as raw as Goss's mouth-roof. "No, I'll . . . be okay. Eventually."

"Mmm. Won't we all."

Lao opened the truck's back door and beckoned, face wan—all cried out, at least for the nonce. Prayed too, probably.

Goss clambered in first, offering his hand. "Did we at least get enough footage to make a show?" Hynde had the insufferable balls to ask him, taking it.

"Just get in the fucking truck, Lyman."

Weeks after, Goss came awake with a full-body slam, tangled in his sleeping bag and coated with cold sweat, as though having just been ejected from his dreams like a cannonball. They were in the Falklands by then, investigating a weird earthwork discovered in and amongst the 1982 war's detritus—it wound like a harrow, a potential subterranean grinding room for squishy human corn, but thankfully, nothing they'd discovered inside seemed (thus far) to indicate any sort of connection to the Seven, either directly or metaphorically.

In the interim since the Sudan, Katz had quit, for which Goss could hardly blame him—but Camberwell was still with them, which didn't make either Goss or Hynde exactly comfortable, though neither felt like calling her on it. When pressed, she'd admitted to 'Lij that her hunting "methods" involved a fair deal of intuition-surfing, moving hither and yon at the call of her own angel voice-tainted subconscious, letting her post-Immoelization hangover do the psychic driving. Which did all seem to imply they were stuck with her, at least until the tides told her to move elsewhere. . . .

She is a woman of fate, your huntress, the still, small voice of Eshphoriel Maskim told him, in the darkness of his tent. *Thus, where we go, she follows—and vice versa.*

Goss took a breath, tasting his own fear-stink. *Are you here for me?* he made himself wonder, though the possible answer terrified him even more.

Oh, I am not here at all, meat-sack. I suppose I am . . . bored, you might say, and find you a welcome distraction. For there is so much misery everywhere here, in this world of yours, and so very little I am allowed to do with it.

Having frankly no idea what to say to that, Goss simply hugged his knees and struggled to keep his breathing regular, his pulse calm and steady. His mouth prickled with gooseflesh, as though something were feeling its way around his tongue: the Whisper-angel, exploring his soul's ill-kept boundaries with unsympathetic care, from somewhere entirely Other.

I thought you were—done, is all. With me.

Did you? Yet the universe is far too complicated a place for that. And so it is that you are none of you ever so alone as you fear, nor as you hope. A pause. **Nonetheless, I am . . . glad to see you well, I find, or as much as I can be. Her too, for all her inconvenience.**

Here, however, Goss felt fear give way to anger, a welcome palate-cleanser. Because it seemed like maybe he'd finally developed an allergy to bullshit, at least when it came to the Maskim—or this Maskim, to be exact—and their fucked-up version of what passed for a celestial-to-human pep-talk.

Would've been perfectly content to let Camberwell cut her own throat, though, wouldn't you? he pointed out, shoulders rucking, hair rising like quills. *If that—brother-sister-whatever of yours hadn't made 'Lij interfere . . .*

Indubitably, yes. Did you expect anything else?

Yes! What kind of angels are you, goddamnit?

The God-damned kind, Eshphoriel Maskim replied, without a shred of irony.

You damned yourselves, is what I hear, Goss snapped back—then froze, appalled by his own hubris. But no bolt of lightning fell; the ground stayed firm, the night around him quiet, aside from lapping waves. Outside, someone turned in their sleep, moaning. And beyond it all, the earthwork's narrow descending groove stood open to the stars, ready to receive whatever might arrive, as Heaven dictated.

. . . .there is that, too, the still, small voice admitted, so low Goss could feel more than hear it, tolling like a dim bone bell.

(But then again—what is free will for, in the end, except to let us make our own mistakes?)

Even quieter still, that last part. So much so that, in the end—no matter how long, or hard, he considered it—Goss eventually realized it was impossible to tell if it had been meant to be the angel's thought, or his own.

Doesn't matter, he thought, closing his eyes. And went back to sleep.

A Spell for Rebuilding Your Lover Out of Snow
PETER CHIYKOWSKI

When I saw your boot-print
glazed into my snowy stoop,
I thought, *There's a trick to this*,
finding your lover
in the record of his step,
the bite wound
of treads.

Like a cartographer
pulling the brow of a mountain
up through her map,
or a paper-folder
creasing cranes in the
unhatched dimensions of the page,
I'll unfold you
from the floor-plan of your feet,
see how you've thinned
like February's clouds,
collapsing into
a single sheet
of sky.

Your body is a track
pressed into winter's crisp vinyl.
I can't hear you
in those grooves
even as I spin their dizzy
vector, trying to make them point
home.

Man in Blue Overcoat
SILVIA MORENO-GARCIA

Does the devil ride the train? Her mother says the devil comes to town on a black mare, taking care to hide his hoofs from sight and conceal the hellfire in his eyes. But if the devil is unnaturally handsome—and in mother's dire stories, he is—then the man in the blue overcoat who just stepped off the five o' clock train from Miraflores fits the bill.

Eloisa forgets that she is in the station waiting for her cousins. She stands on her tiptoes, no longer scanning the crowd for signs of the boys, instead trying to catch another glimpse of the man.

And then, there, before she can grasp how, he is suddenly stopping right in front of her and taking off his hat.

"Good day, miss," he says.

He puts his hat on again, leans on a cane and she notices a metal brace running up his left leg. A war injury? Is this some former revolutionary? Or does he have the extremities of a goat, as mother warned her. Mother, who runs a small pension and never lets the boys lodging there speak to her. Mother, who threw a fit when she caught her looking at a movie magazine showing girls with short hair. Bald sluts. Bad girls.

"Say, do you know what the fuss is all about? This place is packed like a can of sardines and I can't find a car to drive me to El Monte."

Eloisa frowns. "Don't you know? Tonight is the feast of San Rafael."

"Is that a big deal?"

"They take the statue of the saint on a procession around town, then sit him down in front of the church. There's fireworks and music."

And dancing. Most of all there is dancing. Eloisa has not been allowed to participate in the festivities. But this year is different. Her cousins are coming to visit and mother says they can all go together to see the fireworks.

"It sounds delightfully pagan to me. What's your name?"

For some reason she has a childish impulse to lie, to deny herself. Why? What does a name matter? "Eloisa."

"You wouldn't happen to have an automobile, would you Eloisa?"

"No."

"Too bad," he says. "Hey, would you know of a place I can stay? If I can't get an automobile I'll need a room."

There's an empty room in her mother's pension. She normally rooms men who work at the glass factory, but one of the boys has gone off and married, leaving his room behind just two weeks ago. However, she knows exactly how it'll look if she returns home with a man—a devil, perhaps—in tow, after mother instructed her not to speak to any strangers. Mother, who is even angry when she reads poetry—father's old books, the skeletal remains of his collection. Harmless words which deserve a beating. *Why won't Eloisa do something useful rather than sit on the front step of the house, daydreaming?*

"You won't find a room, not with the festival tonight. Everyone has come for the festival," she says.

He smiles, as though he can tell she is lying and Eloisa feels a shiver go through her body, as if she's just jumped into a pond.

"Well, then, I must find a mule or a cart or some way to El Monte. Take care, miss."

With that he grabs the small suitcase he had set on the ground and the cane, limping merrily away.

Eloisa and her cousins, mother in tow, go to the town square. Eloisa is not allowed to wear ribbons in her hair, she is not even allowed to wear a nice dress. Grey are her colours and mother is always in black, though father passed away nearly seven years ago. But it doesn't matter for there are purple, yellow, and white papers adorning the buildings around the square and plenty of colour in the jackets and the skirts of the attendants.

Mother plops herself on a chair by some older ladies and refuses to dance, but she agrees that Eloisa may walk around the square—even dance—as long as she partners with one of her cousins. For a little while it is this way, she walks with a cousin on each side and they chatter and laugh. But eventually a couple of girls catch the boys' fancy and even though they are not supposed to, they scatter away to dance with them while Eloisa steps back, standing under the arches that frame the town square.

"You were right. There is no way out of town. Not a blasted automobile for miles around and apparently mules are also scarce."

The man in the blue overcoat is just a few paces from her, under the arches.

"It's the festival," she says. "Tomorrow you can ask one of the townsfolk to lend you a horse."

"I'll be damned if I can ride it. I'm a city boy, I ride the trams."

She chuckles for it's an odd thing to discover that the devil does not ride horses, after all.

"You find my predicament amusing?" he asks, smiling.

"No. So you have a place to stay for tonight?"

"Something of the sort."

She nods. He checks his pocket watch and she wonders if the rule is true and he must leave by the time the cock crows. Because that's how it goes. The devil rides into town, he asks a vain girl to dance and she dances—ignoring the warnings, never bothering to look at his feet—and when the cock crows he vanishes and she is singed. Hair burnt off, body smelling like sulphur.

Girls like that always end insane or dead.

She stares at him. He cocks his head a bit.

"What?"

"They say the devil comes into town on dance nights."

"Does he? How do you know?"

"You recognize him by his hoofs."

"It's a good thing I'm not dancing, then," he says, lifting his cane.

"Were you a soldier?"

"No. I'm the devil, remember?"

He's making fun of her and she likes it. The lightness of his words and how he smiles.

She spots her mother coming across the square, fury in her eyes. She's seen her. She knows Eloisa is not in the company of her cousins.

She grabs the man's hand and pulls him with her.

"Come," she says.

They rush through the narrow alleys. He moves fast for a man with a limp and his steps seem to draw no echoes. Her own footsteps are as loud as drums. When she stops to catch her breath he is laughing and the crackling of the fireworks echoes through the town.

"That was my mother," she explains. "She wouldn't want us talking."

"Is she some evil stepmother who has you locked in a tower?"

"Sometimes."

"Here, want to see a castle?" he asks and it is his turn to grab her by the hand.

They arrive at the doors of a large house and Eloisa frowns.

"That's Mr. Carrasco's house. He's off in Mexico City until winter time."

The man looks like he already knows this and he opens the door, walking into the house. Eloisa pauses at the threshold. Is this magic? Or is she in the company of a common thief who picked a lock and made himself a bed for the night?

Eloisa steps inside. She can't see a thing, but he grabs her firmly and guides her through the rooms as though he can see in the dark. He stops and lets go for a moment. A light blooms and he sets a lantern on a table. The furniture around them is covered with white sheets. The man pulls a sheet and reveals a couch. They sit there while the dim noise of the fireworks seeps in through the cracks.

"What do you do in your tower, Eloisa?" he asks, leaning back and staring up at the ceiling.

"It's hardly a tower. It's just a little house. A pension. I do the things everyone does."

"What does everyone do?"

"Help with the household chores. Read."

"Anything good?"

"Poetry."

"I only read the papers," he says.

He proceeds to ask more questions, tugging stories out of her until she has laid her whole life before him: the town, her home, her relatives. It strikes her then that he is at an advantage and has revealed nothing, only vague hints which hover like smoke for a moment, then dissipate.

"I don't know your name," she says.

"Don't have one," he replies, sounding earnest. "You can make one up for me."

"Really."

"Give it a try."

"How about . . . Abelardo."

"Eloisa and Abelardo. Isn't that a love story?" he asks. "I think it has a nasty ending."

It's one of many tragic stories she found in her father's books, amongst the silverfish. Great loves and great rhymes, a pressed flower—forgotten, left behind—to mark the pages. All those pages which her mother despised because father had been good for nothing, always with his head in the clouds and when he died, they had to turn the house into a pension to survive.

One of these days, mother said, *one of these days you're going to take a wrong step and break your neck from staring at the clouds.* She believes this is precisely one of those days.

"I suppose," she says.

He drifts closer and without a word plants a light, chaste kiss on her mouth. He smiles at her when he draws back, then repeats the motion. Lingering this time. Nothing chaste about it. His hand brushes her cheek.

She wonders if she should slap him. That's what she should do. But she also shouldn't be here at all, shouldn't talk to men she knows nothing about.

Eloisa frowns.

"Can I look at your feet?" she asks.

"To make sure I'm not the devil in disguise?" he asks.

She stares at him. The smirk on his face fades. His eyes, now that she looks at them carefully, gleam with the hellfire mother warned her about.

"If I do and I'm the devil," he says, carefully removing the right boot, fingers slow. "Then what happens next is you'll scream. The house will mysteriously catch fire. . . ."

He stands up, switches his attention to the left leg. He works on the metal brace, removing the straps that attach it to the boot.

". . . and only ashes will remain to mark the place. A memory of a folly."

He takes off the boot, rolls up the pants legs and reveals a hideously scarred foot. Instead of five toes there are three, with dark nails resembling claws.

"Are you going to scream?"

She raises a hand and begins unbuttoning the grey dress. Eloisa stares at him and he shakes his head in a vague gesture she can't recognize. He mirrors her, removing the coat, his shirt and vest, his trousers.

His leg is completely scarred, as is his torso. Ugly, puckered marks mar his skin, reaching the neck. Burn marks.

She steps forward, kissing the spot where his neck meets with his shoulder.

Ghost light intrudes through a gap in the curtains, waking her. She is on a sofa, naked, covered only by a blue overcoat. After she dresses she looks for him knowing already he's left the house.

She walks back to the town square, which is littered with dozens of paper flowers from the night before. The church is a few paces away. Or she could spin west, to her house.

Eloisa thrusts her hands in her coat pockets and walks to the silent train station, sitting on one of the wooden benches and surveying the tracks. They seem to go on forever in this hazy dawn.

The station's clock ticks and she observes the big hand move. Black like the man's eyes.

And she already knows she is going to become a cautionary tale for other girls in town. They'll say the devil rides into town on a train. They'll say to watch out for men in blue overcoats.

The taste of ashes coats her tongue.

And she closes her eyes, smiling.

And there is the loud toot of a horn, making her frown and look at the source of the noise.

That's Mr. Carrasco's automobile, glossy, inky black.

"I'm heading to El Monte and I can't ride a horse. Can you point the way?" he asks, as casual as casual can be.

"Did you steal that car?"

"Well, you stole my coat. Can I have it back?"

She crosses the tracks and tosses the overcoat into the back, then climbs in.

What You Couldn't Leave Behind
MATTHEW JOHNSON

The client looked like all the rest, dressed for travel in cargo pants and a crumpled shirt, hauling his suitcase like a ball and chain. He was wearing the confused, overwhelmed look most of them have: dragging his steps, peering into each of the shop windows as though part of him knew that he wasn't headed anywhere good.

"Hey, pal," I said. He glanced around, then over in my direction with a who-me look on his face. "Yeah, you. Looking for something?"

He frowned. "Um, I—they say I'm—"

"Dead. Yeah. Get used to it. Know what's coming next?"

He shook his head. "No, they—they just said, go on to Departures."

I jerked my head at the chair in front of my desk, and after a moment's hesitation he sat down. I could see the relief on his face as he let go of his suitcase. "Pretty heavy, huh," I said.

He nodded. "Yeah. You know, I don't remember packing it. Do you think they'll let me take it with me?"

"Don't worry, you packed it." I held out my hand. "I'm Beau Sutton—call me Buddy. Please."

"Adams. Roger Adams."

"Coffee, Roger?"

He glanced over at the Starbucks, reached into his right pocket and drew out a pair of copper coins. "I don't think I have enough money."

"My treat." I unscrewed my thermos, poured us each a cup, then drew my flask out of my pocket, waved it at him. He nodded, so I unscrewed it and poured a nip into each of our cups.

"Thanks." Roger blew on his coffee, took a sip. "So, uh—what do you sell, here, exactly?"

"I don't sell. I'm a detective."

He raised his eyebrows. "Really? What kinds of crimes do you handle?"

"Murders, mostly." I took a long sip of coffee, hot and strong. "Yours, for instance."

Okay, I admit it: I time that to hit right when they have a mouthful of coffee. "What? No, no—I wasn't murdered. I died from—I don't know what from, but I wasn't murdered. I died in the hospital."

"All deaths are murders, Roger. The question is who pulled the trigger and how."

"But how can that matter now? I mean, I'm dead, aren't I?"

"Do you know what happens after you leave here, Roger?" He shook his head. "You go on to the airport, and they put that briefcase on a scale. If there's too much in it—I mean, if it's heavier than a feather—then you get right on another flight and start all over again. Maybe as a tree, maybe a pigeon, but probably just another dumb guy, making all the same dumb mistakes."

"And if it's light enough? What then?"

I shrugged. "Then you find out what."

"So—" He shook his head. "Why are you still here, if you know all this? You an angel or something?"

I cocked an eyebrow, took off my fedora to reveal my halo-free head. "I emptied out my suitcase a long time ago, but I decided to stay here for a while, help guys like you."

"I already said, I can't pay much."

"Don't worry about it. What you have is enough."

"So how do I make my suitcase lighter?"

"Like I said, I solve your murder. That's what you're hauling around in there: your fears, your desires—all the things in your life you can't let go of. I find the one that had such a hold you let it kill you, and then you'll be able to leave them behind."

Roger took a long breath, released it. "I guess. Sure—I mean, it sounds better than starting all over again." He reached down for his suitcase, hauled it up and held it out to me.

Taking the case, I popped it open. Inside were a set of jars—not jam jars but clay tubes, each topped by a lid carved into a little statue. "Once I start, I won't be back 'til I'm done," I said. "I may be a little while, but don't worry—I haven't failed a client yet."

He nodded. "Thank you," he said. "So what do you do first?"

I uncorked the first jar. "Round up the usual suspects."

The Jackal's place stank of beer and stale smoke. Once-opulent oak and leather booths sat under a layer of grime, their original colour barely recognizable; on the wall a sign reading PLEASE NO PIPES OR CIGARS had been angrily defaced. From outside tiny shafts of sunlight crept in tentatively through windows that had once been stained-glass but were now just stained.

I went up to the bar, elbowing aside a guy who was wide enough to need two stools. The barman was pulling a pint. I watched him pour it, working the tap with forearms like Popeye's. I slipped one of the coins Roger had given me out of my pocket and put it down on the bar, to catch his eye when he turned my way.

"What's your poison?" he asked, putting the mug of dark amber beer in front of the man I had pushed aside. The barman was a heavy guy, too, all soft except for those pistons he used to pull the pints with. His head was mostly bald, and it just sloped outward from the dome top to his jowls and then his shoulders, not bothering with a neck. He wore an apron that bore the stains of a thousand different meals.

I picked the coin up again before he could grab it, turned it so it caught the light. "The Jackal around?" I asked.

The barman's pig eyes narrowed. "Maybe," he said.

"Could you find out?"

He reached out for the coin in my hand, took it like a frog snatching a fly. "Yeah, he's here," he said. He jerked his head at the kitchen door, moved aside so I could get to it. "Go on in."

I worked my way around the bar, squeezed into the barman's side past a man who was attacking a plate of steak and eggs like it was Juno Beach. The kitchen doors swung aside as I pushed through them, letting me into a crowded room where steam and smoke were fighting for supremacy. A pair of short-order guys worked the grill, each skinny as a rail. Neither one looked at me or at each other, but kept their eyes fixed on the job in front of them. They didn't say anything either, except to swear now and then under their breath when a grease fire flared up.

"You got a reason for being here?" a raspy voice asked me. Peering past the smoke I saw the Jackal sitting at the waiter's table. He had a high forehead and sunken cheeks, eyebrows that climbed right up his head. A plate sat in front of him, crammed with just about everything that might go on a grill or in a fryer, and handy by his elbow was a double-pint glass of beer. He had tucked a little white napkin into his collar so that it looked like an ascot.

I held up my wallet, flipped it open and then quickly closed it again. "Health inspector," I said.

The Jackal gave a barking laugh. "You think you're the first guy to try that?" he said. "I pay good money so I never have to see a health inspector, so whoever you are, you ain't him."

"You got me," I said. I put my wallet away. "I'm here about a guy."

"Unless his name's Fish or Chips, you're in the wrong place."

I shook my head. "Roger Adams," I said, watching his eyes. "That mean anything to you?"

"What about him?" the Jackal asked.

"He's dead, for starters."

"Huh." The Jackal's knife and fork were still in his hands, the blade of the knife slipping rhythmically in and out of the tines of the fork. "Why are you telling me?"

I shrugged. "Word is he used to spend a lot of time here," I said. "As who wouldn't, a quality place like this?"

"Hey," he said, pointing his knife at me, "maybe this isn't one of those joints where you get a half-dozen peas on a silver plate, but people who come here, they go away happy. Satisfied." To make his point, he speared a slice of fried ham with his fork and stuffed it into his mouth, working his sharp jaw up and down. It went down like you had dropped it in a bottomless pit: for everything he ate the Jackal was nothing but skin, bone and gristle.

"Maybe you don't ever see a health inspector, but how would it go down if those guys out front heard somebody had died from eating here?" I asked. "You understand, I don't care if it was you who killed him or somebody else. But I have to find out."

"You think you can scare me?" the Jackal said. Flecks of half-chewed ham sprayed onto his shirtfront. "Half the guys out there know they're gonna die with a fork in their hand." He swallowed. "I think I've had enough of this conversation."

The mixed smell of grease and sweat was starting to get overpowering. I took a step closer, pulled his plate across the table before he could stop me. "I don't want to make this a quarrel," I said.

He dropped his fork on the table, reached spastically towards the plate. "Hey," he said, "a man's gotta eat." He looked over at the short-order guys: each one had his back to us, focused on the grill in front of him.

"Roger Adams," I said. "Seen him lately?"

The Jackal started to stand up and move towards me, but I took a side-step away, keeping the table between me and him. He reached out at me again, trying to stretch his arm longer, then finally sat down. "He used to come in all the time," he said, "but I haven't seen him in ages."

I looked him in the eyes, nodded. "So where's he been?" I asked, holding the plate just out of his reach.

"Falcone's," he said, his eyes fixed on the plate. "You know, the strip club on third? I heard he's there almost every night. Was, I mean."

I held the plate a few seconds longer, just until I started to enjoy it. Then I handed it back to him, turned away before I could see him start to gorge himself. Suddenly I wanted to get out of that place and breathe some fresh air, or at least what passes for it around here. I pushed back out the kitchen doors and past the barman, keeping my mouth shut as I squeezed by all the customers perched over their groaning plates.

Finally I was outside again. I risked opening my mouth, took a cautious breath in and waited to see if anything came out. My throat caught for a second, and I closed my eyes. There was a noise behind me, but before I could do anything I felt a crack on my skull and after that the lights stayed out for a while.

When I woke up I was in Heaven. Well, maybe not your Heaven but mine: my head was in the lap of a soft, young brunette, her teardrop-shaped face hovering over me. Her hair was pulled back and she wore a pair of glasses with tortoiseshell rims, which she was holding onto with her right hand to keep them from falling.

"Are you all right?" she asked, her voice quiet.

"How long was I out?"

She shook her head, leaving a blurry trail that told me I wasn't quite back in condition. "I don't know how long you were unconscious before I found you," she said. "It's been about ten minutes since I brought you back here."

Reluctant as I was to leave the nest I had found I drew myself up onto my elbows. She had lain me on a long couch, cracked brown leather patched with electrical tape. All around were shelves full of books, paper and hardcover mixed pell-mell. "Where's here, exactly?"

"This is my shop, Foy's Books. I'm Zoe Foy."

I sat up, groaning as my head protested the move, and extended my hand. "Pleased to meet you, Miss Foy," I said. "Buddy Sutton. You spend a lot of time dragging drunks out of alleys?"

"But you're not a drunk," she said quickly. After a second she took my hand and squeezed it. Her hand was warm. It felt nice. "I mean, you do smell a little like one—but I know the look of the guys that spend all their time at the Jackal's. I see enough of them, it's right across the street."

"So you're just a good Samaritan."

Her mouth went tight. "I just—I thought—"

"It's okay," I said, patting her on the arm. It felt nice too. "You just get suspicious, in my business, especially after a knock on the head. I shouldn't snipe at you for doing a good deed."

"I understand," she said. She was smiling now, her face sunny again. "So what business is that, exactly?"

"Well—"

A jingle came from the other side of the shelves. "Oh, that's the door," she said, standing up. Standing had a good effect on her, especially from my perspective. She held up a finger. "You hang on. I'll be right back."

I watched her go around the bookshelf, counted ten and then stood up. As quietly as I could, I moved to the nearest shelf and peered through it. The room was a big one, and probably had first been a warehouse: only the shelves divided it into corridors. They were all used books and shelved without rhyme or reason, mouldy encyclopedias next to last year's bestsellers. I was just about to sit down again when I heard a scream.

A few quick steps took me to the other side of the bookshelf and down the hall towards the door. Zoe was in front of it, frozen. Past her, standing in the doorway, was someone in a long dark overcoat. Before I could get a look at his face I caught sight of a gun barrel rising up to level with Zoe's heart. There were still at least ten steps between me and her.

Instead of running, I threw my shoulder into the bookshelf nearest me and heaved with all my might. The shelf creaked for an endless second and then fell my way, throwing hundreds of books into the air. A shot broke the air and Zoe screamed again as I fought my way through the paperback rain. She was crouched on the floor now, her arms thrown over her face to protect her, and the man in the dark coat was gone.

"Do you know what that was about?" I asked, helping her up. A book on the shelf above her had been blown to bits, a copy of *Grey's Anatomy* shot through the heart.

She shook her head. She was crying, breathing in gasps. "I can't imagine what," she said. "I've never seen that man before in my life."

"It was a man? What did he look like?"

"I didn't get a good look," she said, turning away. "He had a hat on, the light was behind him—he was clean-shaven, about your height. That's all I know."

I reached up to stroke the stubble on my cheek. Clean-shaven, about my height—that narrowed it down to about a million guys, just in Bardo City. "All right," I said. "I guess this was about me. Somebody probably saw you pulling me in here."

"What should we do?"

"You stay here and close up," I said. "I'm going to go register my displeasure."

She grabbed my arm with both hands. "I can't stay here," she said. "Not now."

I looked back into the store, then at her. "Do you have a car?" I asked. She nodded. "Okay, then. You're going to stay in it."

She nodded again, two quick jerks.

I took a step towards the door, paused. "Before we go—do you have a copy of the *Lotus Sutra*, the 1903 British Buddhist Society edition with the missing line on the fifth page?"

"I don't think so," she said, throwing a glance at the pile of books on the floor. "Is it important?"

"Probably not." The door jingled as I opened it for her, and I threw a quick glance left and right before stepping outside.

The lights were on at Falcone's, neon dancers flickering onto the sad sacks slouched around the door. When the engine cut I opened the door, turned to Zoe. "You coming?"

She frowned. "I thought you wanted me to stay here."

"Right. Sure, I forgot." I got out of the car, fixed my gaze on the bouncer at the door to the club. "If I'm not back in twenty minutes send a rescue party."

"Don't you carry a gun?" she asked.

I shook my head. "Bad karma." I shut the car door behind me, cut into the line right in front of the bouncer. He wasn't that big a guy, an inch or so shorter than a grizzly bear.

Somehow without taking a step he filled the space between me and the door. "There's a cover."

"I'm not here for the floor show," I said. "I need to see Falcone."

"What's your name?" he asked. I told him, and he flipped through a little pad that he held in his left hand. "Not on the list," he said.

"I understand," I said. "But I need to see Falcone. He'll be sorry if he misses me."

The bouncer nodded slowly, then brought his right hand up in a fist against my jaw. Somebody somewhere was uncorking a bottle of champagne. "I don't think so," he said.

I took a step back, stopped myself. "Okay," I said, stepping back up to the bouncer. "But I need to see Falcone."

"No," the bouncer said. He put his hand on my chest, flat, and pushed. When he saw I wasn't going anywhere he swung back and socked me in the stomach. "No," he repeated.

A cough flew out of me, spattering blood in his direction. I straightened up, kept my hands at my sides. "I need to see Falcone," I said, my voice a bit slurred.

He drew his fist back, and I flinched. He paused. "You gonna swing back?" he asked. I shook my head. "You one of those guys who likes getting beaten on?"

I shook my head again, regretted it. "I need to see Falcone," I said again.

A look crossed his face, pity or maybe disgust. His fist was still drawn back, but his posture had gone slack. After a minute he shook his head slowly, stepped aside. "Go in, then," he said. "You tell Falcone those lumps were from me."

"Sure," I said. "Thanks for the comp." The way my jaw was rattling, though, I don't know if he understood me.

Falcone's was a classy place, the kind where they spray the girls with a mister instead of just letting them sweat. Nina Simone was on the speakers, singing "Please Don't Let Me Be Misunderstood" good and slow, and there was a girl at each end of the T-shaped stage following her rhythm. It was a little bit like the Stations of the Cross: you could get up and walk from clothed to undies to nude if you didn't feel like waiting.

I let my gaze drift from the stage and looked around the room. It was full of the same guys I had seen outside, slouched and embarrassed. They sat at the stage if they could, or else close to it, staring at the girls without blinking. A few of them chatted up the waitresses, dancers on their off-shifts, and every now and then one would slip the girl a bill and the two would vanish up the back stairs.

Fratelli Falcone was sitting at a table near the back. Unlike his customers he faced away from the stage: he knew the dancers were there. A girl sat on either side of him. One of them was buttoned up in a shirt, jacket and tie, like a Catholic schoolgirl. The other was dressed about the same but the effect was different, with the tie loosened, the shirt halfway undone and the skirt about six inches further north.

"Buddy," Falcone said, spreading his arms wide as I came near him. He had a sharp face, with a nose you could use to climb mountains. A walking stick leaned against his knee and he wore a brown cape with a fringe like feathers. "So long since we've seen you."

I looked at one girl then the other, and finally tried to stare Falcone in the face. "Not my scene anymore," I said.

"Oh? And what are you into now?"

I raised my hand to my still-aching jaw. "Being beaten up," I said, "but to tell you the truth I'm getting tired of it. So how about we get right to business: what does the name Roger Adams say to you?"

Falcone gave a slow, wide shake of the head, taking in a good look at each girl. "That is not a name I know," he said. His voice was oilier than the grill at the Jackal's. "Buddy, my friend, I think you have been working too hard. How would you find a visit to the Champagne Room? On the house of course."

Despite myself I looked at the two girls: the first looked away demurely, while the second locked eyes with me and ran her tongue across her lips. I shook my head. "Another time," I said.

"These are my best girls, Buddy," Falcone said. He sounded disappointed. "It's never just business to them, they are very talented at making it seem natural." He took his hand off the girl to his right and waved it in the air, looking for the right word. "Genuine."

"Is that what happened to Roger?" I asked. "Did he get too tight with one of these girls? Is that what he can't let go?"

"Please, Buddy. You know as well as I that, in my business, discretion is—"

Before he could finish speaking his eyes went wide. I congratulated myself for watching them, instead of the many more interesting things in the room: they gave me just enough warning to dive out of the way. Falcone had a few more seconds than I did but nowhere to go, and when the shot came a big red splotch opened up on his chest.

I prayed the shooter was as distracted as I was and turned around, staying low. He was in the doorway, a dark shape in a long coat and hat turning away.

"Hey!" I shouted. "You're gonna shoot me, make it stick!"

He didn't slow. Swearing under my breath I stood up, checked on Falcone. He was dead. His two girls were comforting each other, and it took me a minute before I remembered why I had come.

To my relief Zoe was still in the car. She looked startled when I opened the door. "What happened to you?" she asked.

"Which part?" I asked.

She reached her hand up to my cheek and I flinched. "You might have cracked your jaw," she said.

"Why don't you kiss it better?" I said, sitting down next to her.

She smiled and gave me a kiss. It was just a peck on the cheek, but you would never confuse it with the kiss you'd get from your grandmother. "So where to now, shamus?"

I shook my head. "You go home," I said. "I don't know whether that guy was gunning for me or Falcone, but now I know he wasn't after you. Better you go where it's safe."

"I can't stand the thought of reshelving all those books," she said. "Besides, you need a driver. You're in no condition to walk."

I mulled it over for a minute. "Okay," I said. "You know how to get to One Padmasambhava Place?"

"City hall?"

"Falcone wasn't a very nice guy but he was well-connected. Nobody would take a shot at him without the mayor's say-so."

She frowned. "He won't be in his office at this hour."

"That's what I'm hoping for."

After what had happened at Falcone's Zoe wasn't too happy to be staying in the car, but she wasn't crazy about breaking into city hall either. I left her outside to watch the door while I slipped in the back way and up the stairs to the mayor's office.

I slipped the pick from my coat pocket and worked the lock. The stencil on the door read HON ROBT. BOONE, MAYOR, and when I got it open I saw that name repeated a dozen times or more on plaques, awards and honorary diplomas mounted on the wall. Pictures of the mayor with dignitaries and people so famous even I had heard of them filled what was left of the space, and the marble-topped desk was cluttered with trophies, mementoes and even a bust of the man himself. It made me wonder how a guy ever got anything done in a place like that, surrounded by his own name and face.

It wasn't the mayor's face I was interested in, though, but his brain: that is to say the files he kept in the room beyond. The mayor's life had been one long climb up an endless ladder, and you don't get to be boss of a town like Bardo City without having the dirt on everyone else in it. If he had his hooks into Roger, the reason would probably be in there.

I switched on my flashlight, played it over the filing cabinets. They were unlabelled, so I got the top drawer of the first one open and started to flip through the folders. They were full of a lot of juicy material, things that would surprise you about people you think you know, but nothing about Roger. I was just starting to think that I had had a few better ideas in my life when I heard a noise from the office.

"Who's there?" a voice called. I froze, trying not to breathe too loudly. A second later the office lights went on. "Come on out," the voice said. "I know you're in there."

I sighed, walked out into the office with my hands up and saw the mayor standing there. He had a long face and he looked like he needed a shave, but it wasn't going to happen: his kind hadn't shaved in a million years and weren't about to start now. He had on a shaggy blue coat, its arms trailing down past his knees, and bright red pants. Standing behind him was a taller guy, thin and with about as much expression as an ice cube. He was dressed in a long grey coat, smooth except for the lump in the right pocket.

"Nice night for a party," I said as the tall guy patted me down.

"Just what do you think you're doing here?" the mayor said, hunching forward. His wide nostrils flared as he took a long whiff of me. "Do you have any idea who I am? What I can have done to you?"

"Since I'm in your office, I'd guess that I do," I said. I turned my head to the guy who had been frisking me. "What's your story?"

"He does what I tell him," the mayor said. "That's all you need to know. Who are you?"

I shrugged. "A monkey's uncle."

The mayor hissed at me, his fangs showing. There was a noise from out in the hall, and the blank-faced guy turned towards it and then back to the mayor. "Should I check it out?" he asked.

"Sure," the mayor said. He showed his teeth again. "He's harmless."

I waited until the mayor's stooge had left before I spoke again. "Let's cut the games," I said. "What did you have on Roger Adams?" I watched his little eyes for a reaction. "What was it you offered him? Fame? Power?"

"Listen," the mayor said, grabbing me by the neck, "I don't know who you think you are, but I'm asking the questions here. So why don't—"

There was a shot out in the hall, and we both froze. Still holding my shirt the mayor turned his head around. Zoe appeared in the doorway, a dull grey pistol in her hand. A moment passed before she levelled it at the mayor and fired. The shot hit him in the back and threw him into me, both of us toppling to the ground.

"Oh my God," Zoe said. "Buddy, are you all right?"

With effort I lifted the mayor's body off of me, climbed to my feet. I patted my chest all over, feeling for blood. "Bullets don't always stop at the first body, you know," I said.

"I'm sorry," she said. "I just saw him holding your neck and I thought—"

"Where'd you get the gun?"

She looked down at the pistol still in her hand, took a deep breath and dropped it. "I saw those men going into the building, so I came up to see if you were all right," she said. "The man in the coat found me, he drew his gun—I was so scared, I just grabbed it and—"

"You took a big risk," I said. "You should have stayed in the car."

"I wanted to, but I just couldn't—couldn't stand the thought of losing you." She kissed me once, quickly, and then again. "But it's all over now. You're safe, and I guess with the mayor dead your case is over."

"I guess so." I kissed her again, then took her hand in mine, raised it to my lips and kissed it. "Now that I know you killed Roger."

She tried to pull her hand away but I held it fast. "What are you talking about?"

"Did you meet him at Falcone's?" I asked. "That's why you wouldn't come in, wasn't it, even when I was going to let you? That's why you shot Falcone, before he could tell me anything." I kissed her hand again. "Powder burns, angel."

"I just shot two men," she said. "I saved your life."

"Sure. But you had those burns before, in the car." I reached out with my free hand, stroked her cheek. "You met Roger at Falcone's, but it wasn't sex, was it? Oh, maybe at first, but that's not why he couldn't let go of you. He let go of his gut, of sex, his ego—but he couldn't let go of love."

She turned her head away. "What are you going to do with me?" she asked. "Turn me over to the police?"

"And risk that sweet neck?" I shook my head. "All that matters is I know. He can let go of you, now, and move on."

"And me?"

"You'll move on, too," I said. "Everybody's looking for love."

My office had never looked so much like home as when I got back. Roger was still sitting in the chair in front of my desk, his fingers interlaced, looking nervous.

"What happened to you?" he asked.

"Slightly more complicated case than usual," I said, lowering myself into my chair. "Don't worry, I worked it out. You should be able to go on now."

Roger let out a held breath, got up and picked up his suitcase. A frown crossed his face.

"What is it?" I asked.

"It's still heavy." He held it out to me. "Here."

I took the briefcase from him, felt its weight in my hand. I put it on my desk, popped it open: it was empty, but still felt like it was packed with bricks.

"You said it would be lighter," he said.

"It should be." I furrowed my brow, trying to work things out. "Tell me, Roger—you ever hear of a thing called tape echo?" He shook his head. "That's when you record on a tape more than once, and a little bit of the old recording doesn't get covered up. Well, that can happen with souls, too—if you've been through here a few times, you might have something from a past life still stuck in there."

"But if it's not even mine, what can I do about it?"

I held my hand out palm-down, holding him still. "I think we're about to find out," I said. A dark shape had appeared in my office door: a man about my height in a dark coat, wearing a broad-brimmed hat that cast his face into shadow. A gun was in his hand.

"Who are you?" Roger said, turning around.

"Quiet, Roger," I said, keeping my eyes on the gun. "Why don't you let this guy go," I said to the intruder in a carefully level voice. "This is just about you and me, isn't it?"

The man said nothing but moved closer, keeping the muzzle of the pistol pointed my way.

"Get out of the way, Roger," I said.

Roger moved aside as the man took another step in my direction. I took a breath, snapped my hand out and jabbed at the switch of my desk lamp. The man blinked in surprise at the sudden light and I saw his face.

He was me.

I had intended to grab the gun while he was dazzled, but I was more stunned than he was. The barrel was level with my forehead. "Who are you?" I asked.

"Open the desk," he said with my voice. I was frozen. He pressed the gun to my head. "Open it."

Feeling my sweat run around the ring of cold metal I reached down to my desk drawer, pulled it open.

The man with my face pulled the gun away, just a few inches. "Look inside."

With effort I pulled my gaze away from the pistol aimed at me, looked down. A jar like those that had been in Roger's suitcase sat there, a clay tube with a top carved in the shape of a cat's head.

"What's going on?" Roger said, his voice cracking. "Aren't we already dead? Who is this?"

I looked myself in the face, suddenly unafraid. "You're what I couldn't leave behind, aren't you?"

"You said you'd cleared your own suitcase," Roger said. "That you just stayed here out of compassion."

"No—not compassion," I said. "Curiosity. I realize that now." The man with my face smiled, nodded. "That's what I couldn't let go, why I stayed here—the puzzle. Wanting to know how it all works out." I laughed. "I'm just as much of a sap as you are, Roger."

The man with my face lowered the gun, tapped it against the jar. I nodded, and he grabbed the lid with his free hand. I took the base and we each pulled, and when it had popped open he was gone.

I took a deep breath, picked up Roger's suitcase. It was light, lighter than a feather. "Here," I said, handed it to him.

He took it by the handle. "It's empty," he said. "But does that mean you're—we're—"

"This part of me stayed here," I said. "That part of me—the part that couldn't let go—wound up as you."

He took a step for the office door. "So we're—free? Both of us?"

"Come on," I said. I flipped the sign on my door to CLOSED, stepped out into the corridor and locked up. The two of us started to walk down the street, towards the airport. "This looks like the beginning of a beautiful friendship."

Return to Bear Creek
LOUISA HOWEROW

My mother's warnings follow me—
her fear of woods, bears, children
bearing children, and yet

I left her to her stylus,
wax lines crossed on empty
eggs she then dyed red—

and all that spring she knew
and couldn't stop me listening
to the swollen creek, to the bloodroot

whispering:
You are the queen of queens.

The Lonely Sea in the Sky
AMAL EL-MOHTAR

White as Diamonds

My name is Leila Ghufran. I am fifty-six years old. I am encouraged to begin this journal in this way because, says the team's psychiatrist, telling myself who I am will prove beneficial. This is, of course, ridiculous, because I am not my name—did not even choose it for myself—and a name is always a synecdoche at most, a label misapplied at the least. My name does not tell you that I am a planetary geologist, that I love my work enough to submit to this indignity, that despite the fact that I am a valuable member of my team I am expected to waste time on churning out this miserable performance for the sake of a stamp before I can get back to work.

I suppose I see what she did there. Well done, Hala.

I am allegedly exhibiting signs of succumbing to the middle stages of Meisner Syndrome, colloquially known as adamancy, which sounds more like a method of divination than anything else—as is appropriate, frankly, to the hazy mysticism that passes for the disease's pathology. "A preoccupation with the nature and properties of diamonds, and/or the study of the same, especially extraterrestrial"; "obsessive behaviour related to the study of diamonds, especially extraterrestrial"; "unusual levels of alertness and attention to detail"—*I am a planetary geologist, Hala!* These are features, not flaws! How could several years' friendship not—

I am pausing to remind myself that as someone who's known me for several years is insisting on this exercise, perhaps something is a little off, and perhaps I am not the person best qualified to judge. But the symptoms of adamancy are ridiculously vague and diffuse and at the present moment are hampering my actual work. I am meant to be studying Lucyite at our Triton base. Instead I've been banished—is hyperbole a symptom of adamancy?—to the Kola Borehole in order to assist with extra-galactic neutrino detection. Not content to exile me to Siberia, my friend, you literally found the deepest hole on the planet to shove me into under the guise of studying the sky.

I can actually hear you saying this is for my own good. It's a little hilarious, actually.

Meisner's Syndrome, aka Adamantine Dissociation Syndrome, aka Adamancy

Etiology

Theorized to be a consequence of cumulative exposure to Lucyite-powered technologies or the Corona fields of extraterrestrial minerals. Affects an estimated one percent of the global population.

Symptoms

Hyperfocus, especially on light refraction; sudden, temporary sensation of cold ("cold flash"); urgent need to submerge oneself in hot water. A preoccupation with the nature and properties of diamonds, and/or the study of the same, especially extraterrestrial; unusual levels of alertness and attention to detail alternating with periods of trance-like calm.

Risks and Complications

As with other obsessive disorders, sufferers are at risk of self-neglect relating to hygiene, nutrition, and personal relationships, resulting in a poor quality of life. Certain kinds of work are also at risk: driving, operating heavy machinery, and performing delicate tasks are all to be avoided.

Progression

At more advanced stages of the disease, sufferers are prone to sometimes violent emotional outbursts, often accompanied by memory loss. Consequently, it may become difficult to convince a sufferer of their diagnosis.

Treatment

Symptoms can be managed with varying degrees of success with anti-anxiety medications. Cognitive behavioural therapy and other forms of talk therapy have not been found to be effective. Some studies suggest isolation from crystalline structures and Paragon technologies is helpful, and others have demonstrated an easing of symptoms when the sufferer is under ground—possibly as this isolates them from most instances of ambient light refraction and the trances these can provoke.

Prognosis

Even with treatment and lifestyle change, chances of full recovery remain slim.

Lucy in the Sky with Diamonds

I could say I have always loved diamonds, but this isn't quite true. I have, for as long as I can remember, loved the idea of diamonds; loved diamonds in stories; loved the things compared to diamonds in metaphor. Stars; the spark of light on water; that sort of thing.

It comes down, I suppose, to loving light—but no, more than that—it must be about the breaking of light, its containment. A bit sinister when put that way, isn't it? Sunlight on its own holds little appeal, but angle it against the ocean, make it dance—poetry.

Diamond oceans on Neptune! I suppose that's what started everything off—those early accounts of *diamond oceans* in the twenty-teens. Determine that diamonds behave like water—that you can have diamond in liquid form that isn't graphite, and chunks of diamond floating on it—and you have the realisation of metaphor, you have every fairy tale made flesh. Only a hop and a skip in the mind from that to holidaying on extraterrestrial getaways by shores of literally crystalline water.

All well and good until you think about the heat and the pressure required to maintain diamonds in liquid state, and realize you'd be liquid yourself long before you could dip a careful toe in.

Still. It still sounds beautiful to me, somehow, in spite of everything, in spite of having worked with solid chunks of it on Triton. A diamond ocean in the sky. Like that John Masefield poem you recited for me once—you remember how I misheard it? *I must go down to the sea again / the lonely sea in the sky.*

Up above the world so high, like a diamond in the sky. Isn't it incredible that we take something born out of the bowels of the earth and stud the sky with it in our songs and stories? Isn't it desperately strange?

Isn't it even stranger that we should *find* them where we'd imagined them to be for so long?

I hope you're feeling guilty, Hala.

Teleportation Possible Within Ten Years, Scientists Say

Recent studies coming out of Triton Base 1 provide a veritable cavalcade of information about the mineral composition of Neptune's mantle and the unusual properties of the liquid carbon contained there.

"Though the only carbon samples we succeeded in extracting from the planet were solid, and almost indistinguishable in their crystal lattice structures from Earth diamonds, we discovered that super-heating them until they turned liquid caused them to vanish, completely, without a trace," said an excited Dr. Jay Winzell. "Eventually we realized that the spikes of thermal activity we'd been observing on Neptune *corresponded exactly* to the moments we liquefied the crystals. It was a leap, but—that's what they were doing! Our samples, made liquid, were *jumping back to Neptune* and mixing with the diamond ocean there."

Dr. Winzell believes it could be possible, with further study, to understand how this teleportive quality works. "We're a long way off, still theorizing how this behaviour is even possible within our current understanding of quantum mechanics—but it's conceivable that once we've understood it, we could harness this property somehow, contain and channel it such that we could effectively *ride* the liquid substance across vast distances instantaneously within a closed system. The journey to Neptune would be shortened from years to seconds. But imagine using it on Earth! This could do for travel what the internet once did for communication. It's a massive paradigm shift—our very notions of distance, of space and time, will have to be re-examined."

Dr. Winzell, as discoverer of the diamond-like mineral, has elected to name it Lucyite, in honour of the iconic Beatles song.

Diamonds on the Soles of Her Shoes

I'm not allowed mirrors. Too much chance of light reflections causing relapse. I'm astonished they let me work at all, but I suppose you knew it would be worse for me without something to keep my mind and hands busy.

I hate it here.

From "Untangling the Melee: Towards Practical Applications of Quantum Entanglement," by Dr. Elaine Gallagher

In conclusion, while there is as yet no definitive theory explaining *why* Lucyite behaves as it does, the properties are clear: Operating on the principles of quantum entanglement outlined above, we can consistently manage the energy state of each individual unit. When liquid, the unit's entangled property teleports it to the location of the unit with the next highest energy level, allowing for distance—bearing in mind that, as previously stated, "teleport," though a less than ideal description of linear movement theorized as taking place in higher dimensions, is nevertheless the nearest term one can accurately use without succumbing to the more colloquial "blink," "jump," or, even more ludicrously, Paragon Industries' preferred term of "shine."

Diamonds are Forever

I am encouraged to write about my family, but all I want is to write to you, Hala. It helps me to think of saying these things to you and I would rather not pretend that there is privacy here, between my mind and the screen. I would rather address you and the things you request of me.

When I was small my mother would read me bedtime stories out of holy texts. She later told me this was so I wouldn't ever mistake fictions for fact, but I had little sense of her project then; I just loved the fantastical tales about things transforming into other things, people doing bad things and being punished or forgiven or vindicated.

She read me this bit out of the Talmud, once, that I loved desperately for how strange and otherworldly it seemed to me:

Rab Judah, the Indian, related: Once we were travelling on board a ship when we saw a precious stone that was surrounded by a snake. A diver descended to bring it up. [Thereupon] the snake approached with the purpose of swallowing the ship, [when] a raven came and bit off its head and the waters were turned into blood. A second snake came, took [the head of the decapitated snake] and attached it [to the body], and it revived. Again [the snake] approached, intent on swallowing the ship. Again a bird came and severed its head. [Thereupon the diver] seized the precious stone and threw it into the ship. We had with us salted birds. [As soon as] we put [the stone] upon them, they took it up and flew away with it.

It's probably fair to say I wanted to go off-world because of these stories. You grow up on giant snakes and life-rendering gems and the prospect of a manned mission to Neptune's not reaching very far at all.

You know the Talmud is structured like a diamond of popular imagination, too? Seders at the crown, footnotes at the culet. You'll have to ask Ben about it for me sometime.

I was reminded of that passage when my mother read me stories of Sindbad later on—in his second voyage he comes to a valley of diamonds beset by giant serpents that will eat anyone who approaches. So Sindbad figures out a way around them: He throws down slabs of raw meat into the valley that they might become studded with gems before attracting great birds to swoop down and carry the diamond-laden meat into their nests.

Is this not the Melee? Or perhaps the reverse of it—diamonds carrying slabs of meat through space at astonishing speed, in spite of serpents, in spite of all—and is our understanding of the Melee not roughly this sophisticated?

Was ours not a ship navigating towards a serpent wrapped around a precious gem?

And have we not cut—have we not stolen—

It's funny, isn't it—my mother wanted me to think of scriptures as fairy tales so that I would not be their dupe. But as a consequence, all my frames of reference, my earliest acquisitions of knowledge, are fantasy. Fairy tales have, in a sense, become my scripture.

I am very cold. I need a bath.

The Gasp Heard Round the World

Thousands gathered today to observe the first human use of the network of gates known as the Melee. Established by international conglomerate Paragon Industries in collaboration with governments around the world, the Melee revolutionized international commerce with its Lucyite-powered technology, allowing instantaneous transport of goods across the world. Today Paragon President Alastair Moor prepared to be the first to blink from Glasgow to Damascus and back.

Cameras in Glasgow recorded Mr. Moor stepping into the Glasgow Gate and waiting for its in-built Z-mechanism to activate and liquefy the Lucyite. No sooner had Mr. Moor vanished from the Glasgow monitors than he appeared, not a hair out of place, on the Damascene cameras, having successfully effected a journey of over 3,000 miles in less than a single second.

"One small step for man," said Moor, and the crowd erupted in cheers.

She dwelt among the untrodden ways

I never feel clean enough. Is this because of what I can't remember doing? I never feel clean enough. I walk the halls and I sit to write and all I want is to wash, wash, wash until my skin pinks and peels into petals floating on the surface of the bath. If all of me could slough off into remnants, into something beautiful—if all of me could dissolve—if I could just get clean—

Why do you suppose we have so many stories about diamonds? Diamonds are curse-stones in some places, markers of great fortune in others. Diamonds are so hard and so brittle, so strong and so delicate at once. Do you suppose, ultimately, those stories are all about us? Carbon to carbon to carbon?

Do you think it possible that, once upon a time, all our diamonds were an ocean? It used to be that all land was one land, no? Perhaps we had a diamond ocean here. Perhaps we loved it, and it died. Perhaps it loved us and it died. Perhaps because it loved us it died.

No motion has she now, no force;
She neither hears nor sees;
Roll'd round in earth's diurnal course,
With rocks, and stones, and trees.

Wordsworth. Maybe I am going mancy after all.

From Philip Kidman's *A Melee for You and Me*

There is a very real sense in which we can comprehend quantum entanglement as applied to Lucyite in terms of living memory. Without wishing to lend a crumb of credibility to the Friends of Lucy's extremist ravings, it could be said that the Melee operates on a carefully curated forgetfulness: After all, the entirety of the Melee's infrastructure is powered by the dispersal of one large chunk of Lucyite brought to Earth from Triton. By breaking it into precise halves and carefully calibrating each half's liquid state, Nobel-winning Dr. Jay Winzell succeeded in causing the halves to blink towards each other in a closed system, instead of back to Neptune—which is, as the physicists have it, the place of highest entanglement. Dr.

Winzell effectively pioneered the method for entangling Lucyite crystals with each other, the further perfection and sophistication of which enables the complexity of the Melee. Possessing only "memory" of each other, the fractions of Lucyite liquefied at each gate will always blink towards each other within the Melee's careful curation of space.

Looking ahead, we can see that every upgrade to the Melee in future—any expansion beyond Neptune, or extension of the existing system on Earth beyond our current stock of calibrated crystal—will require an enormous overhaul to take into account the higher entanglement of new Lucyite. Luckily the system is at present so efficient that no such recalibration will be necessary within our lifetimes, and indeed, any introduction of new crystal into the system would throw it into disastrous confusion and disarray at best, or provoke a devastating chain reaction at worst.

It would appear that, ironically, the most advanced system of travel and transport we have yet devised is powered by absent-mindedness. The worst thing we could do in our pursuit of getting places quickly is jog our precious superconductor's memory of where it came from.

Coal to Diamonds

A melee is a packet of small diamonds all of roughly the same size and value.
    A melee is a fight, a mess, a jumble.
    A melee has three vowels in it, four if you count the indefinite article.
    A melee could be a woman's name.
    Amelie, Amelie, Amelie.
    A melee or eight. Amelie, orate. A melior ate.
    Ameliorate.

Triton Base 1 Incident Report: Dr. Hala Moussa

At 0200.23.04.2076 NTC I found Dr. Leila Ghufran in the laboratory, palms pressed into a tray of Lucyite chips. They had cut into her palms and her hands were bleeding. She was standing very still and did not respond to her name until I approached her and initiated physical contact. I grasped her shoulder and pulled her to face me, at which point I saw blood on her lips and at the corners of her mouth. I suspected she had severely bitten her tongue; this appeared to be the case when she began speaking. Her initial lack of responsiveness was alarming, but her eventual words were more so: She began exhibiting severe distress, crying and saying I was hurting her, that she was very cold, that she wanted to go back.

After we restrained and sedated her, Dr. Ghufran claimed to have no memory of our interaction. Given our proximity to the diamantine ocean of Neptune and Dr. Ghufran's extensive exposure to it and the samples extracted from it, I am diagnosing her with Meisner's Syndrome and recommending she be relocated to a subterranean project as soon as possible.

Diamonds and Pearls

Imagine if you took a tiny piece of a diamond and you put it in some meat.

Imagine it irritating the meat, agitating it, inflaming it.

Imagine if the meat rose around to coat it with layers of itself, to obfuscate and obscure it.

Imagine if Sindbad's slabs of meat swallowed the diamond and became something else, became diamond-and-meat, became organic crystal, became other.

I don't know what I am saying. I'm dizzy. Hala I'm sorry. I'm so sorry. I think I am going to fail you. I love you, Hala. I'm sorry.

Extract from "Friends of Lucy" Manifesto

Meisner Syndrome is a lie!

Adamancy is a lie!

A conspiracy concocted by Big Pharma and high-ranking members of international governments in concert with the logistical-industrial complex to make us all complicit in the torture and dismemberment of a living organism!

We say again, *Lucyite is alive!*

We don't need the Melee any more than we needed to eat animals! It screams like a thousand thousand pigs being slaughtered, like lambs, like cattle!

Stop the screaming!

Save Lucy!

End the Melee!

Shine On, You Crazy Diamond

Everything is wrong. Everything is broken and wrong and no one can see it.

Do you remember the playground, Hala? The bullies who hated when we held hands? How it didn't matter how much they goaded and spat and pushed and shoved, the moment we threw a punch we were at fault? Because we had to be better, we were supposed to be better, and they were just a fact of life. Do you remember how we hated that? How unfair it was? How we vowed that we'd never be taken in by "looking at both sides" when all it meant was that people had the means to justify and excuse our suffering?

Hala, imagine if when we were children, we had seen a girl splayed out on the floor, spread-eagled, her every bone broken beneath the feet of boys jumping up and down on her as if she were solid ground. Imagine we could hear her screaming, begging them to stop, to let her go, but the boys could not, because she was nothing, she was the earth, she could not feel. *But we could see her. We could hear her.*

What would you have done, Hala? Told them to stop? But this ground is so much softer on their feet, it is so much more fun to jump on it, why should they? Why should they believe that there is a woman there they cannot see? We are few and they are so many, we must be insane, we must be diseased to imagine something so horrible.

Imagine, Hala, that in the eye of one of these boys you see satisfaction. You see knowledge. You see that he knows he is making someone scream but it doesn't bother him, *it doesn't matter*, because he can get away with it.

What would you do?

President Moor Responds to Diamond Fanatics

Following the evacuation of the Triton base in response to a terrorist threat, Paragon Industries hastened to reassure the public that the Melee remains safe and open to business as usual. We reached President Alastair Moor for comment.

"It's very sad, but they're deeply troubled people," says Moor. "They deserve not our scorn, but our empathy, our pity, and our help."

When asked whether there might be any truth to allegations made by the Friends of Lucy, Moor responded:

"Look, it's just crazy. You may as well say electricity has feelings. People believed all sorts of wacky things when Tesla coiled wires, but we can't imagine living without electricity now. This is no different."

A Star to Steer Her By

Of course I had nothing to do with that threat. I know who did, though. I can feel them at the edge of my vision now, shimmering, especially when my fingers start to go numb. It's always so cold here.

They're cold, too, all of them. *Frozen in the ring of diamond time*, that was from a poem, wasn't it? Alexa Seidel? Pre-Melee, of course. I don't know why all of my favourite things should be. I suppose it's nostalgia for a time before our fictions were fact.

It's good that you're not on Triton just now. Things are about to happen there. I'd hate for anyone to be stranded when the gate crashes.

I'm going to miss you so much.

I remember, now, what I couldn't on Triton. I remember you taking my wrists and looking at my palms, I remember you sitting by me as they soaked every last speck of diamond from the meat of me to make sure I wouldn't accidentally bring any back with me to Earth. You never left me, even though the work was piling up, the demand for reports and explanations.

I wish I could see you one more time. The ocean's kind, to let me have this memory of you back. I hope you can understand. I hope you can forgive me.

My tongue wasn't bloody because I bit it. It was bloody because I licked the diamonds off the tray. I swallowed as much as I could. It's probably why I haven't gotten better, for all that you buried me so deep. They're still inside me, as entangled as any quantum physicist could wish, dense enough with memory of Neptune to summon all the Earth's stolen droplets and make a body of her again, a mind, a recollection, give her a destination and the will, the energy to reach it.

All I have to do is make them liquid.

Ridiculous that I've been so cold for so long when the solution's been so near to hand. We have a Z-machine here, and I'm on its scheduled maintenance rotation. All I need is a moment alone with it, and I will be warm again.

I am a slab of meat awaiting my vulture. I am a salted bird brought to life. I will dissolve, I will melt, I will dip my toe into a diamond ocean and I will swim.

I am glad there won't be anything left of me here.

I hope—I feel that it will take me with it. Back to Neptune. That I might go up to the sea again, the lonely sea in the sky.

Maybe it will be better there.

Maybe we'll keep each other company.

Jelly and the D-Machine
SUZANNE CHURCH

My name is Austin and I'm a disaster.

Okay, I'm exaggerating; more of a testosterone challenged, ubercerebral tragedy.

This week, fate's bingo parlour dropped me three bad balls in a row. First, I failed my trigonometry mid-term; a fist to the gut in the self-esteem department, with the added bonus of crushing my mother's hopes for my acceptance at Waterloo.

Second, my attempt to secure a prom date failed. Susan said no. Her quick response was, "I'm busy." Then she bit her lip and stared at me like I might not believe her, and said, "I don't really like you." To be honest, I'm glad she admitted the truth. Because that warm feeling I get when I look at Drake Ferris isn't going away. I could listen to his Irish brogue all day long.

Which brings me to the third and final ball. Jelly caught me staring at Drake in math class. By tomorrow, the entire school will know I'm a fag, which is really annoying when I haven't quite decided if homo rather than hetero tastes better on my eggs. In terms of my overall popularity, though, my catapult from the closet won't matter. Because Jelly will knock my lights out and then, hey, problem solved.

Carl *Jelly* Fraser is a self-righteous bully. You're thinking, with a name like Jelly, he's more a victim of scorn, but that's not the way karma descends on the town of Schmuckville.

He chose the nickname for himself because grape jelly makes a mess of you. If you spill it, it gets on your fingers, your clothes, hell, all over your kitchen, and if your shirt is white, you'll never get out the stain. I would give anything to kick that bastard into the next county. So would every guy like me; even Drake.

My encounter with Jelly will last longer than the traditional tussle. Jelly will have me like a dog has a pig's ear: to chew on and suck on and drag into the yard where he'll forget about me until it's time to pick me up and work me over some more.

So I'm lying in bed, listening to the ceiling fan click while it spins, hot as a frying pan for a June night, and I'm doing what I do best: worrying. If Jelly brings a knife, what will I do? Should I pretend to fall unconscious or fight back? And even if I deny being gay, will he believe me? Will I believe myself?

I've watched the moon's light slowly paint my room, from the door a couple hours ago, to my computer, and now it's moved out the window to the tree house.

There's an idea. If I disappear, how long will Mom take to look in the tree house?

Days? Weeks?

I wonder how long I'll have to live off the grid, waiting for the world to change enough so I can safely re-emerge. I'm a pretty patient guy.

Time, man, that's it. I need more of it, tons of it, a googolplex of its beautiful bounty. Better yet, Dad's ultimate nerd weapon: the time machine. I can leap into the future to a time when no one will care about my personal preferences. To a place where Jelly is a bitter night manager and his minions have spawned newer and more sophisticated fish to fry.

Dad used to ramble about how time machines are only products of quantum mechanics and the fourth dimension. His deepest and clearest desire had been to build one, become uber-famous, and live a life of fame and fortune. Or better yet, be in a *Science* textbook. And he had been so damned close when . . .

I decide it's time for me to step up and finish what he started.

I figure that if I climb high enough and plummet through a small enough hole, I can separate the quantum likelihood of my existence into two versions of myself. Just like the light experiments with the tiny hole in the piece of paper and the big, bright bulb. At the critical moment, I will rupture a membrane along the edge of the fourth dimension and drop out on the other side. I could hang in other-land, make a few friends, maybe lay low, especially if no one recognizes me. Or better, if I *also* exist there, I can watch my other self, maybe, if I don't freak myself out too much, have a long chat over coffee and a couple of donuts and figure out who we really are. It's cheaper than therapy; that's a given.

When I and other-me are ready, I'll reverse my steps, take another plunge, and slip back into my life. Mom'll cry, and I'll be in the news, "Lost Boy Found after Unexplained Absence." Possibly rake in a little side cash, enough for a car, spinning a few white lies about alien abduction; hot probes and such, get myself a tidy story-bonus for the tabloid spread.

Definitely.

After assuring myself of Mom's continued slumber, I find Dad's stash, including the rubber-chicken-toss target-board from the school Fun Fair, marked with "This must be it!!" in Dad's red-Sharpie-handwriting on the back. Finally, my Mom's endless volunteering comes in handy. The "double prize" hole has been triple-circled in red. Chuckling to myself, I haul it upstairs and outside, then go out to the garage to snag our supply of bungee cords. I want to be sure, so I use several packs, so many that any spider will be envious of my design. From a spy satellite circling overhead, my machine can pass as a trampoline—no late calls to homeland security required, move along, pal.

Remembering Dad's insistence that light plays a crucial role; I hook up our two painting lights and point them so they converge right below the hole.

A final check through Dad's journal to be sure I've set up the equipment correctly, then I sneak into the study and grab my father's laptop. Dust has piled pretty thick on top. Mom will kill me if she walks in, so I'm extra, super quiet. Dad was working on fourth dimensional formulae the night before the dump truck smashed him out of our lives. He had told me so. Late that Thursday after too many beers.

"Son," he slurred, "you're gonna be so proud of me. Oh, people will laugh, especially your mother. Don't tell her I said so, because she's mad enough about the money I'm *wasting*. But I'm certain these calculations are right this time. She's finally going to be proud of me. God, I love her."

And she had loved him right back, as much as I did, maybe more. After the squish, she set up a corner of the study as his shrine. Minus the candles and incense of course; she isn't a *zealot*.

Laptop under my arm, I sneak out and awkwardly climb the ladder to the tree house. I boot the computer, set dad's iterative calculations to auto, and stand in the open doorway.

The target looks damned small from up here. For at least a minute, I wonder if the Jelly-beating can theoretically be a more pleasant option than the unqualified pain if I miss my mark. But self-inflicted-stupidity always wins the teen debate against bully-plus-humiliation, so I lean forward.

As I find the air, I have at least one second to think, *This one's for you, Dad.* Then I find the hole.

Skin scrapes free of my arms as they rub against the rough edges of the wood. The brightness of the painting lights blinds me, numbing the pain like somehow not seeing the wounds makes them hurt less. Sound adds its personal spin, splinters and rushing air, a scream that's more like a whimper when my lungs are compressed.

Then the thud. It's a crackless thud, giving me hope that I haven't snapped a bone. Down here, in the shadow of the tree, the soft light nudges my courage in the open-your-eyes direction.

So I do.

There's Dad's car. And not Mom's.

Whoa. Not squished.

I brush off the splinters and remember my torn skin too late. The scream is enough to wake the dead.

"Austin? What the hell are you doing out there? It's five A.M., for crying out loud."

This is the part where I tell you he's alive, and I'm so glad because I've missed him, and dump trucks are stupid, and karma may finally have been *fair* for a change.

But then he's downstairs and out the door and hovering over me, probably wondering how I so massively hurt myself by falling from the tree house through a hole. Except there is no tree house, and there is no hole. I throw my arms around him and, for the first time in years, I hug him like I'm five and he's brought home the biggest bag of candy to ever grace this wonderful planet.

I can feel his awkwardness underneath, like he can't fathom what's come over me. But another, more important thought finds its way to my frontal lobe; Mom should be here, too, just as angry and confused.

"Where's Mom?"

He drops his arms to his sides. "Very funny."

I refuse to release him. "Seriously."

His voice, muffled by my constriction of his chest, comes out in gasps, "Did Jelly put you up to this? Because I thought you were staying over at his place tonight?"

"*Jelly's* place?" I release my grip and give him the biggest dose of sarcasm-plus-confusion my pained body can muster. "*Overnight*?"

That's when he starts to pick at my hair, checking for a brain injury. "The video game slam-down, not ringing a bell? Or did you damage your hearing, too?"

Without hesitation, I flip from I'm-so-glad-you're-alive to contemptible teenager. "It's a throw-down, not a slam-down, Dad. Don't you *ever* watch TV?"

"I'm waiting for an answer."

I launch into a blur of explanation-laced-with-B.S., enough to distract and confuse while I find my bearings. The contraption worked, although I'm pretty sure that the year and my age are bang-on identical, so I guess I didn't build a *time* machine, more a *dimension*-machine. Dimension-machine sounds lame, though. D-Machine: there's an epic name that will look good on any supermarket shelf. I coined the term without hesitation. "I'm exhausted, and to be honest, my arms really hurt," I say.

He takes a long, intense look at me, then at his own hands, which are stained with my blood. "Yeah, maybe we should get you cleaned up. Think it's hospital-worthy?"

I shake my head. "Peroxide."

"That'll sting like you-know-what."

No worse than having my dad come back from the dead and my mom be controvertibly absent. "Better pain, than an infection," I say.

"Agreed."

He leads me into the house and up to the bathroom where there isn't one stick of feminine stuff to be seen. No makeup, no night cream, no hair straightener; not even the box of *products* she leaves in plain sight so embarrassingly that I cover them with a towel whenever a friend comes over.

I found my way back to my father and forgot to show Mom the way.

"I miss her," I say.

He chooses that moment to dab on the peroxide.

Austin the disaster strikes again.

Allow me to clarify.

If you're considering fabricating a D-Machine to visit another version of your reality, make sure to pick a destination where you will at least be able to find the parts you'll need to build the return-portal. Because when your mom dies, your dad is likely to be so distraught that the last item on his massive to-do list will be going out for the PTA. And without his finger in that volunteer pie, I doubt you'll have a rubber-chicken-toss target-board still stored in your basement. And he may never get around to hiring that dude to build you a tree house so you won't feel like you'll miss out on a part of your childhood from only having one parent available.

Oh, and remember to slip out the back door and find a great hiding spot as soon as you can, because the other version of you is due home any minute, and you don't want to get that egg on your face in the first twenty-four hours.

But I am in too much of a stupor, a combination of the peroxide pain and the loss of my rubber-chicken-toss target-board, to remember to hide. Sure enough, along I come, the other me, home from a night of frolicking and fanciful play at Casa Jelly. Adding another nail to the Austin-coffin, Drake and Jelly arrive in tow.

I hear their footsteps on the stairs only moments before the inevitable big entrance, so I dive under the bed.

Oh, here's another tip: Used socks smell incredibly bad. *Truly*. Don't kick them under the bed; it's not worth the agony.

One at a time, each boy crashes on the bed. I can tell which dent belongs to the Jelly-man, because face it, with a name like that, you must've guessed he carries a few extra pounds. The three of them are still high from the all-night video frenzy.

The conversation is the usual, "So then my guy kicked your guy," game chatter, but when Dad wakes up and makes a point of stumbling downstairs, the topic sways in another direction. Drake gets all quiet, and he's mumbling something to Jelly that sounds a little too friendly, and then other-me says, "Come on, you two. Bad enough I have to cover for you at school. If my dad walks in—"

"He won't," says Jelly. "I can hear the cereal crunching from here."

Then the room goes quiet and I hear a soft sucking sound. Like a kiss.

"Stop," other-me says.

But I don't sound disgusted. I mean, other-me, he doesn't sound like he's revolted by their kiss. No, he sounds *hurt*. Turns out, no matter which dimension I find myself, or a *version* of myself, in, I have my eye on Drake. Both eyes in fact.

Add to that a dash of the Jelly roadblock.

I want to jump out and confront them. All of them. Right then and there. Granted, the stinky sock factor is a contributing persuader in the equation. The possibility of permanently messing up my multi-dimensional karma stops me. So I plug my nostrils and breathe out of my mouth as quietly as possible.

Jelly keeps on making his moves on Drake, until sanity returns to the worlds-at-large and the other-me says, "I need fuel, or I'm gonna crash."

"Eggs," says Drake.

"I'm in," other-me says.

"Perfect," says Jelly.

Then they're gone, and I'm alone once more in my other-room. I decide to get out of D-Dodge, find my way back, and take my chances with evil-Jelly. I will need a new D-Machine, and an immeasurable number of minutes to properly say goodbye to my Dad. And not in that order.

Other-me doesn't have any D-machine-worthy parts in his room, so I sneak down to the basement. Tough gig, because the basement stairs are in a big sight-line from the kitchen, where the four of them are laughing and planning their Saturday. A couple of times I'm sure Dad has spotted me in his peripheral vision, but he doesn't react, so I assume I'm clear.

The basement has been hit by a nuclear explosion, or some other weapon of mass destruction. I'm leaning into an oversized plastic bin chock full of circuit-board-and-wire-spaghetti when someone's hand is on my back.

I fall on my ass, shrieking like a girl.

"They're gone," he says.

That silences me. I open my mouth to tell him the truth, okay, to exaggerate a *little*, but then I close it again because he looks delighted; as though he may have finally invented something good.

"I shouldn't have given up," he says. "Tell me how I did it?"

"Did what?"

"Finished the dimensional disruption device. And why didn't I take the first trip?"

"How did—"

"Your hair can't grow four inches in an evening," he says.

I touch my hand to my head. Yeah, I admit it, I'm a guy *and* I take good care of my hair: sue me. "Busted," I say.

"Tell me. *Every* detail."

I start with his laptop and the dimensional formulae, but when I get to the rubber-chicken-toss target-board, his face gets scrunchy and he looks like he's going to cry.

"Back in your world, your mother, she's . . . *alive*?"

"Yeah," I say.

He crosses his arms on his chest and bites his lip. I can tell he wants to cry, but he's trying not to. "No dump truck?" he whispers.

My turn to hold back the tears. Only I'm not as good at it as he is. "Oh, there was still a dump truck."

He leans down and puts his hands on my shoulders. Both of us have tears leaking out now, but we're still holding a fraction of our dignity together. "Is she paralyzed? Or mentally incapable? That would—"

"She's fine," I say. Then I hit him in the chest like somehow it's his fault, and I add, "You're dead. Not her. *You!*" I hit him again, and suddenly I'm pummeling his chest, except he's blocking me, and the punches are more like shoves, and then I'm crying so hard that he's holding my hands, and I'm letting him.

"The worst of it," I say, "is that I can't stay here. I can't. Not with Jelly, and Drake, and—" My throat closes, and I'm choking, but I need to say it. "It's not fair!"

He's holding me, and running his hand down my back like he used to when I was little. "Shush," he says, "I understand."

"Why can't I have you both? At the *same time!*"

He doesn't speak for a while.

I begin to feel too old for this, too mature to be crying in my father's arms. Too much of a man to be afraid, but I don't have the will to push away.

"You know, I didn't believe in God," he says.

I look up and nod at him.

"Well, when she died, I prayed. I spoke to God over and over, demanding to know *why*. But he didn't answer me. Maybe because he only answers if you truly believe. Maybe because he thinks I can't take the answer. Maybe because he has a twisted sense of humour. In any case, she's gone." He gestures around the basement, and says, "From here."

Then he points to his heart and says, "Not from here. She will always live here." Then he points to my heart, and adds, "And here."

"Come back with me," I say. "We'll be together again. She misses you so much. She doesn't talk about it, but she's always so busy with her committees, and her events, and I know it's because she doesn't want to think about how empty our lives are without you."

He holds me again. And I can feel him shaking, like he's crying, but the quiet kind of cry, where you want to hold some of it back because if you let it go, you'll finally feel better and you can't feel that good; you don't *deserve* to be that happy.

"Please come back with me," I say.

"I can't leave you behind."

I open my mouth to object, and he says, "The other you. He misses your mother so much, he doesn't have the strength to stand up to Jelly. I need to be here for him. For *you*. Because one day, he'll realize that Drake isn't worth it. And he's going to need all the help I can give him to admit it to himself."

"Back in *my* life," I say, "I like Drake." I pause, take a deep breath, and come clean. "Back there, I'm gay."

"Here, too," he says. "Have been since sixth grade."

I shudder. "I came out to you and Mom in sixth grade?"

He laughs. "You—*he* still hasn't admitted it, *out loud*. He will when he's ready."

"But you know?" I say.

He nods. "Your mother figured it out ages ago. I took longer to convince, but she kept pointing out the signs."

"When did she die?" I say.

"Three years ago."

"And four months, and twelve days?" I ask.

He nods, and looks at his watch. "Seven hours, and . . . *nine* minutes."

I look down at my watch. Yep, the karma clocks are perfectly synchronized.

We stare at each other, knowing. Then his hand is on my shoulder again. "I'm glad you told me. About being gay. How does it feel?"

"Lighter," I say.

"Yep."

"If you're going to help me get back, we need a big board with a hole in it," I say.

"I have just the item."

Recreating the D-machine with my dad is fun. We don't speak of our impending separation, or of Mom. We're simply two guys exploring their geek side.

I'm holding a piece of plywood and Dad's using a jigsaw, which I can't believe he can do without severing a finger, and he says, "Jelly's an idiot."

"Yep. Back where I come from, though, he's worse. A complete bully. He's the reason I left."

"How so?"

I explain about the prom and Drake, and Jelly likely bashing me into next week after he tells the world I'm gay.

"Most of your friends probably know already."

"I don't have any friends."

"What about Drake?"

I rethink the Drake situation. Sure, I find him handsome, but we have also been lab partners, and we've eaten lunch together on a fairly regular basis. Come to think of it, whenever he misses class he always asks me for my notes.

"You're right."

"Drake is gay, here. And his relationship with Jelly is more one-sided than you, I mean the other you wants to admit. Do you want my advice?"

"Sure."

"Tell Drake how you feel. And if Jelly says a word about your sexual orientation, tell everyone it's because he's gay and can recognize it in you. In fact, he's secretly in love with you."

"Yeah," I laugh. "Like *anyone* will believe that."

"You'd be surprised. The truth has a way of outing itself."

He finishes with the saw, and I let go of the plywood. I'm staring at him, processing what he's said, and I wonder if maybe he's right. Maybe all that teasing was actually *flirting*.

"You're right," I say.

"It's astonishing, I know. But it happens with surprising regularity here."

We both laugh then it multiplies until we're both cracking up so hard that we're crying. I can't believe how good it feels to let loose with him. My *dad*. I had resigned myself to never experiencing a moment like this ever again.

"We should be recording this," I say.

"I hear you."

He hugs me and I don't want it to ever end.

Dad rigs up a quick pulley system to recreate the D-machine that night. Without the tree house, I have to climb the tree. With a ladder, of course, because let's face it, I'm a geek and we're not known for our jock-ular prowess. We use bungees and lights, like before.

The hardest part for Dad has been recreating the dimensional formulae. In my reality, he left them on his computer. Here, in a fit of frustration, he deleted them all. But he'd kept the journal, which was buried pretty deep in the basement. We find it and re-enter them. I trust his judgment that they are identical to the ones I've set in motion in my old life.

Other-me has spent the day at the mall. When he arrives home, Dad distracts him with a pizza and then heads back outside. I stay out of sight, hiding high in the foliage of the tree. Luckily, other-me doesn't show interest in Dad's latest experiment. Apparently, these still occur with enough frequency to qualify as lame.

When all of the components are in place, Dad looks up, and says, "Any time you're ready."

"I'll climb down and say goodbye," I say.

He shakes his head. "It's better this way." He pauses. "Easier."

"But." I bite my lip because he's right. "Easier," I agree.

"Tell her I will love her forever," he says.

"So will she," I say. "Love you, I mean. Because I know she does. I do, too."

He smiles. "Now jump."

"Right."

I lean forward, staring down at the hole, and it's just as tiny and pain-inducingly-scary as it was before. I've had the foresight to borrow a long sleeved shirt so as not to open up the scabs all along my arms.

My father is watching me with enough love to make me cry, and I don't want to cry again. So I aim for the hole, close my eyes, and push off from the tree.

While I'm falling, I have enough time to say, "Dad, I love," but the, "you," doesn't make it out because I'm hitting the hole and scraping open my wounds, and my head feels as though it may split open and release watermelon guts over a hundred metre radius, and then I'm on the ground.

It's brighter than before, and I look up to see the rubber-chicken-toss target-board above me, and the painting lights. I stand slowly, and painfully. The tree house is where it should be. Mom's car is in the driveway. Not Dad's.

Above me, a window opens. "Austin?"

Mom is wearing the ratty sweatshirt she uses as her pajama top. It used to be Dad's. Here, he will never wear it again. But she will.

"I'm fine, Mom."

"What are you doing with . . . oh my God, look at your arms!"

She disappears from the window. I can almost hear her running down the stairs to come to the aid of her wounded son. When she bursts into the yard, she hugs me like I'm a baby.

And I let her.

Jelly is waiting on the front steps of the school to beat the crap out of me. Everyone who passes hears Jelly's proclamations of my sexual preference. Some glare at me, others laugh. I meet all of it with a smile.

I can hear my Dad telling me how he knew all along, and how most people would've figured it out already. Not only was he right, but somehow his acceptance makes me proud of who and what I am, acting like a shield against what I feared would be the Jelly-wrath, but turns out to be more like Jelly-failure.

When I get close enough that he can deck me, I stand still, toe to toe, and wait for it. He hesitates, as though he can't decide what part of me to hit first.

I take a deep breath, and say the words I've been refining all night. "Took you long enough to notice, Jelly. But too late, because I only have eyes for Drake. Sorry to break your heart."

"I'm not gay," he sputters, "you fag."

"That's what you tell yourself."

I keep walking.

This is the part where I figure he will jump me from behind. I brace myself for the impact.

Laughter.

Not from Jelly, either. But from everyone who's had the good fortune to overhear our confrontation. Like they've all been waiting for confirmation, and it makes total sense. Better, Drake is at my side and he's taking my hand.

You'd be surprised, my father had said. *The truth has a way of outing itself.*

The truth, like me, is out. And it tastes as sweet as grape jelly.

We Be Naked

ZSUZSI GARTNER

We be naked, not nude. Something to remember as the memory of us moves into the slipstream. Nude is in the eye of the beholder, naked a true enough fact.

Call it what you will—occupation, prorogue, strike—our stand-off began in April 2014, right after the collapse of the Kyoto Protocol at the Reykjavik Conference, in what was left of the Icelandic capital following the so-called Pirate Party Bombings. For almost two years we be chill, afloat in amniotic fluid, playing rock-paper-scissors, and perfecting our parkour moves, intuiting that nothing in the outside world had changed for the better.

We sent forth Harmonium to parley, he be the most sweet-tempered of us all. We soon be learning of your deviousness. You wrapped him in soft swaddling and put milky teats to his lips, then placed him in thrall to a mobile of extinct dancing animals and the plinky-plink of Mozart for babies. The most infantile of composers a good choice for the most impressionable, you were thinking? This was in the Prime Minister of Canada's own backyard. (The world media wanted to know, why fracking Canada? But we be holding no national allegiances. We be random.) The mother was a waitress at a club in Hull, the father, it was rumoured, a second-year student of criminology at Carleton University. Emmanuel, his *maman* called him, as he be the first child born in such a while. Although in the night she be calling him Em and crying of aloneness.

Em, Emmanuel, Harmonuim, made no matter-mind. Traitor was what we be calling him—Guy Fawkes, Judas (or Theon Turncloak by those whose parents-to-be watched HBO)—until Djembe voiced the bitter-root truth: any of us would be doing the same. That was when we be deciding no more of us be born until our demands were met. You could rout us out one by one and soon learn what constant fibre we be composed of. The worldwide moratorium on Caesarean sections—in place since the International Win-a-Million Preemie Pageant fiasco—was lifted, and C-sections were scheduled around the clock. Medécins sans Frontières even made assisting the births a priority. Gamelan and Hi-Hat be lost that way, and Kobza and Balalaika, and thousands more to the cause; blue babies all, umbilical cords around the neck, ropes of meat and blood for our cherished martyrs. Suicidal babies be the saddest music on earth and the parents' tears could have flooded the drought-ravaged Sahel belt. *Tant pis.*

Because here was the thing. Together we be one kickass mind, one righteous bundle of twigs no man could break apart over his knee, not if he be blacksmith or warlord. Separated, out there, we be nothings—no tensile strength, just soft bones waiting to knit together and powdered flesh. Which, as Kazoo spoke true for us all, just sounded so babyish!

Our demands be modest. We not be asking for the moons of Jupiter. Clean air to breathe, clean water to drink. Fish in the seas, trees in the forest. Oh, *zut!* And lay down your arms and pick up your instruments, music being the only true and beautiful man-made thing in this world.

So we waited, and we watched skies and hearts fill with poison.

Em, when he be turning six, already learned the mistrust of the Anglos across the river, although, poor dove, he be not pure laine himself. Next door to him, in a two-bedroom condo with den, skylights, and a refrigerator that made penguin-shaped ice cubes, lived a fifteen-year-old boy originally from Tajikistan who be saving up his drug money for a pallet of fertilizer. *U pray or party?* his friends asked. *Har har,* he texted back. Two years later he be dead in Deir ez-Zor, hair, eyebrows and wispy, devout beard singed right off.

Inside, naked, we be brothers and sisters. Outside, we be taking against each other. Maybe this will help make sense of it. Ten years into our occupation the new President of France became pregnant and not knowing yet. But Lute (Boadicea, if Madame Beyoncé could convince Monsieur Jay Z) be one of us already, in situ sister to the twins Lotar and Mandolin. Their expecting father be the de facto mayor of the Paris exurbs, plotting some messiness on the metro near Place d'Italie. Did they want to be born sworn enemies? Better naked, we be maintaining, and dug in our wrinkly heels for the long haul.

Here was a stumper for the moral minority and the amoral majority. Babies could refuse to be born; they be *crazy*! Pointy heads of state put their considerable energies into debating the future of the him and her race. ("Race," Theremin asked, "why does it always have to be a race?") If it be a race, you were the hares and we the tortoises, at least that's what we be thinking back then.

To while the edge off our years in internal exile, we be telling stories, like the buddies and buddettes in *The Decameron* or *Generation X*. Stories kept us alive, sharp. We be partial to Aesop, but soon exhausted all the fables so our tellings be quite catholic.

You already-borns have no doubt heard them all before. Three men walk into a bar. A mean white guy, a mean black guy, a mean Asian guy. Here we be cuing uncomfortable laughter. In imperial Japan, a boy springs from a peach pit on the shores of the Yoshikigawa River and into the arms of his aging parents who had given up hope of ever having a son. All over the world, a girl be loving a boy her family disproves of so she drinks the poison or the father drowns the boy in boiling oil, or the boy drowns the father in boiling oil and inherits the gold in the cave and the girl. Or the father and brothers push the girl's car into the canal and plead cultural amnesty. Or the boy allows the Force to be with him, only to discover the dark side. There is always a dark side: the pestilence before the cleansing flood, the scouring fire before the rosy dawn. The thieves be either stupid or noble; the saints arrogant or naive or covered in boils and wens. The queens be unhappy, the housewives mad, the hookers happy, the eunuchs golden, and the cheerleaders ambitious. Somebody, somewhere, be wanting something: the treasure, the trophy, the kingdom. ("Or the guy!" laughed Sitar, whom the anticipating parents be calling Harmeet.) But what they really want is self-respect or their props from their daddies. This is screenwriting 101, if you know your Syd Field.

If there are explosions, there are lessons learned. "There are *reasons*," Ukulele scoffed on behalf of us all. The him and her race never did believe in chaos, just chaos theory. First trusting in religions, then science.

In the stories there are wily spiders, ravens, or coyotes. The bear be a great demon or a nobleman or a god or a lover. Never a bear with a fat, oily chinook salmon speared on its claws. "A naked bear," Banjo said more than once. "Those people think that's not a story."

Well, here is a true enough story. The schools collapsed from the Pacific

Northwest to Leipzig to the Cape Verde Islands. The schools collapsed, but no matter, as no children be in them for near to a decade. No children to be teaching to colour inside the lines, no children to sing-song the national anthems. No children to starve or be stuffing 'til supersized with type 2 diabetes. No children to bleed or bugger or bugger off on.

Sometime around the eighteenth anniversary of our strike, you concluded we didn't know what we wanted, that we be too vague and unfocused, against everything. *Professional malcontents.* You said we just be lazy or afraid to face the economic consequences of growing up. Still, we be not worried. "Sticks and stones and all that jazz," Clarinet reminded us. If not for that team of scientists at the Sheffield Bioincubator in the UK, things could have turned out differently. We would be around to warn you. You might still experience what we be calling seasons; you might still eat what your grandmothers be calling food. But it proved easier to build a better, more reasonable baby than to stop driving your SUVs to the big box stores to buy strawberries in bulk in February.

Those biomedical wizards with their PVC corpuscles and synthetic DNA, their genome holograms and 4-D printers, proved you didn't need us anymore. Just don't be telling anyone it all started with Dolly the sheep. It began further back than that. With a spare rib, or the vomit of one god or t'other. Or with fire or mud.

The mothers-not-to-be were herded up like bison. The spots they leaped from are legion. They jumped from the Lions Gate Bridge and the Millau Viaduct, from the General Rafael Urdaneta Bridge and the Three Gorges Dam. They tumbled from Head-Smashed-In Buffalo Jump and the new World Trade Center, and into the K'one and Concepción volcanoes. They flew from the Chess Playing Pavilion on the Sacred Flowery Mountain and from the diving tower of Montreal's long-drained Olympic pool. So for a short time, we flew, too. If we'd thought to pack parachutes, we be flying still.

One lone nude woman, flushed from her redoubt by the local Freemasons, fell, a splinter in the sole of her bare left foot, from the ruins of the Tallahatchie Bridge in Money, Mississippi. She took Squeezebox, the last of us, with her.

Where was the cavalry?

Had we really asked for so much?

The Parable of the Supervillain
ADA HOFFMANN

Don't think I didn't watch the news, sister of mine,
in those days. Don't think I didn't see you
in that mountaintop palace strewn with blood-red bones,
the mosasaur moat, the horned, hooved footmen.
At four in the morning with the baby biting me,
I watched you call the President of Australia
from his velvet bed
and feed him to the army ants.
You were never satisfied. Money, sex, guns, velociraptors:
Mother only wanted your voice on the phone.
You wanted the world.

Evil, they said. Pray for her soul, they said,
for her to step down meekly right this instant
and join some convent, or die. But I clung to the television
not knowing what I felt, at first,
pretending to change diapers and scrub sheets,
not knowing half of it was envy.

They broadcast that final battle of yours—
you remember, I'm sure—and I scratched tic-tac-toe
in my arms to wake myself.
I often dreamed they'd murdered you because I'd put a foot wrong:

The Parable of the Supervillain

I'd made the wrong face
or whispered your name to my son.
Those grim, strapping, blue-pyjamas men:
I watched them fly. They shattered stones with their hands
and cracked wise like you were nobody's sister.
That last explosion, like a nursery-school
spilled can of paint, Golden Yellow and Clementine
licked with Sea Green.

Of course they never found your body.
Finding people is a black art, sister—
ask me about the time I lost my husband.
One morning, the squeeze of his sweaty arms:
the next, nothing. Bedclothes in disarray.
It took a month to find him:
lazing in the U.S. Virgin Islands
with a younger me whose voice didn't choke
when they broadcast endless sparkling parades
for your defeat.
I get it, sister.
I know the rage that fills a woman,
swelling you up cumulonimbusly
until not even the President of Australia
could be enough.

So don't grovel like that on the doorstep.
I can't offer much:
I don't keep army ants
or a bathtub big enough for your mosasaur.
But the guest room's clean.
Don't beg for forgiveness like I'm one of them, sister,
like I'll put on blue pyjamas and blow you to smithereens
if you cry the wrong number of tears.
You don't know what you did for me
in your old defiance. Please, come in.
There's tea in the kettle, soup on the stove,
and a six-year-old, chocolate-smudged nephew I'd like you to meet.
We can talk until sunup and past,
if you like. Don't sorry me. We're sisters.
You're home.

The Tun

TREVOR SHIKAZE

When you go through your boyfriend's jacket pockets, you forfeit the right to freak out over what you find. But when Cecile found the little man, that's just what she did. The jacket was sentimental to Marc, his old rowing team jacket, which he'd worn every day through senior year and not once since then. He'd never had it properly cleaned. Next week he would turn thirty, and Cecile planned to surprise him by sneaking the jacket down to that Filipino laundry where the lady gave her such good deals. She knew that Marc, on principle, wouldn't fork over the cash to dry-clean a jacket he hadn't worn since high school, yet she felt you shouldn't store dirty clothes with clean clothes; here was her chance to have her way while also doing Marc a birthday favour. Two birds, one stone.

The jacket smelled like senior year gone stale, glands and sweat and boy, and she'd bugged him about it off and on for months. She went through the pockets because she didn't figure she'd find anything that would make her jealous, maybe a long-expired condom or a baseball card or whatever teenage boys carried around in their pockets. She didn't figure on what she found. It was about the size of a golf ball but the wrong texture. A potato? She pulled it out, gasped, dropped it, laughed at herself. What the hell was that? She watched it bounce into the corner. Was it a dead mouse? She pushed aside a shoe box with the tip of her toe. It wasn't a mouse. A mouse wouldn't bounce.

The thing was brown and dry-looking, curled up, like a tiny armadillo. Did mice hibernate? In pockets? She knelt for a closer look, and she saw the little face. She gasped again and stood up and hopped out of the closet. Then she laughed again.

Don't be a dork, Cil. It's just a toy.

She'd known a guy in her dorm at the U who was really into computers and obscure movies, who kept a collection of ugly toys that you couldn't play with and you weren't even allowed to touch. Apparently they were expensive—*rare*, as he put it, like Ming vases or some stupid thing. Gross monsters from slasher flicks. She went back into the closet and knelt again and had another look. Was *that* what this was? A creepy toy? But Marc wasn't into those things.

She picked up the little man and brought it into the light, into the big open living space with the giant windows and the loft, Marc's space, the space he wouldn't let her officially co-lease even though she slept there every night and showered there every morning and had a goddamn key. She brought it into the big open room and she looked at the little face, the little scrunched up human face, the bald little man. When sunlight hit the face, it frowned. She screamed and dropped the thing again and it bounced off, landed in one of Marc's giant potted plants.

She covered her hand with a plastic bag and collected the little man the way you collect a dog turd. She hid it in her purse. The thing was alive and it freaked her out, but she'd forfeited the right to freak out because she'd gone through pockets. Action, consequence; one of Marc's rules. She'd always thought the going-through-pockets rule was unfair and mean—yet another arbitrary rule designed to keep her from feeling secure in their relationship, to keep her from feeling at home. Now she wondered.

"Your iron count is back up where we want it to be. I'm glad you're eating red meat again."

Cecile's doctor was the same doctor her mother went to, an older man with white eyebrows that curled up in little arcs. He was nearing retirement, which made Cecile nervous. She'd never been to another doctor. Her girlfriends told her this was a perfect opportunity to switch to a woman doctor, and she felt they were right, felt a grown woman should see a woman doctor, but she also felt a certain loyalty to Dr. Haley. She wasn't about to make the switch until she had to.

"Dr. Haley?"

"Yes?"

"Can I show you something that isn't exactly health related? I sort of need an opinion on something and I don't know who to ask."

He set his clipboard aside. "Of course."

She opened her purse and pulled out the plastic bag. "Have you ever seen anything like this? I found it yesterday." She handed him the little man.

He glanced at it, handed it back. "Where did you find that?"

She returned it to the bag. "In my boyfriend's jacket pocket." She couldn't look him in the eye. This was unusual. They'd discussed her vagina without either one blinking—why the embarrassment now? "I saw it move. Is it alive?"

Dr. Haley rolled his chair over to the window and stared through the blinds. He sighed, folded his hands, then swiveled to regard Cecile. "It's alive, yes. It's a tun."

"A tun?"

"Your boyfriend, is he a very giving person? Very open?"

"Is he open? He's a private person. I guess he's not very open. I mean, in comparison to other people." She slid the bag into her purse and snapped the clasp. "Why do you ask? What's a tun?"

"It's a bit hard to explain, Cecile. Think of it as a part of your boyfriend. A part of him he doesn't share."

"What do you mean a *part* of him?"

"It's a biological object. Though in a state of dormancy." Dr. Haley placed a finger to his lips and thought hard. "Some desert flowers, in dry times, will lie dormant as seeds for years. Waiting for rain. They go into a state of suspended animation. It's called an avoidance strategy, Cecile—a way of coping with a hostile environment."

She wagged her head, not following.

"Some men are similar."

"They're like flowers?"

"When the conditions aren't right, they pack a part of themselves away, suspend it. Until more favourable conditions prevail." Dr. Haley raised his eyebrows and gave a little shrug.

Was that it? "I'm not sure I follow."

"I can't tell you much more, I'm afraid. I'm no expert."

"Is this normal? Does every guy have one of these?"

"It isn't abnormal. But it isn't common, either."

"Why haven't I heard of this before?"

He gave another little shrug. "It tends to be something men don't talk about."

These were not satisfying answers. "What should I do about it?"

"Put it back where you found it, Cecile." He rolled toward her and gazed over his reading glasses, as he always did when he wanted her to listen closely. Doctor's orders. "And don't mention it to your boyfriend. Okay?"

She pinched the clasp on her purse and nodded.

Like hell she'd put it back. Like hell she wouldn't mention it. She bought a bottle of water from a vending machine and stormed out to the clinic's snowy parking lot. She threw her purse on the passenger seat, fumbled with the ignition, opened the purse, shoulder-checked, wedged the bottle in her armpit as she pulled out of the stall, unscrewed the bottle with one hand, steered with the other, jammed the bottle into the cup holder, dug around in her purse until she found her Xanax. This sort of behaviour drove Marc up the wall. *You're upset, Cecile. When you're upset, you get careless. You start doing two or three or four things at once, and then you can't figure out why accidents happen. Just take a breath and count to ten for Christ's sake.*

She popped a pill at a stoplight and sipped the water. When the light changed, her hands were full. Some asshole honked his horn. She tossed the bottle into her purse without screwing the cap back on, then nearly ran off the road.

"Shit!"

She parked on the shoulder as vitamin enhanced hydrating essence glugged all over her wallet, all over her makeup, all over her phone and her gum and the nest of receipts she carried around like an undercover bird. She grabbed the bottle and chucked it at the windshield, dodged the rebound, slapped the steering wheel, swore her head off.

Then she drained her purse as well as she could, snapped the clasp shut, and sobbed the whole drive home.

It was snowing hard when she pulled up in front of her apartment building. Her purse had developed an odor, sort of a wet-dog-and-loam combo. She assumed it was the lining. Her building was brick and charming and old, and also expensive, more than she wanted to pay for what amounted to a storage facility. Her apartment was where she kept the oversized art books she'd collected in her university days, back when she cared about art and oversized books; where she kept the beautiful teak table and the beautiful oak dresser and matching trunk that just didn't seem to *mesh* in Marc's space; where, in a mostly empty closet, she'd hidden the golf clubs which had cost her a fortune and which she hoped would cause Marc to remember that he loved her. *Happy thirtieth, babe.*

She got in and turned on the lights and stood for a second staring at the place, her place, which looked to her like a museum exhibit. Cecile as she had been. Then she dropped her purse in the kitchen sink and headed for the washroom to dig up a hair dryer.

She found the dryer. She returned to the kitchen. She opened the purse.

Next thing she knew, she was peering around the corner in the little hall that led to the living room. That's where her legs had taken her. She watched the kitchen sink, waiting for the thing to emerge, but it didn't. Her mind held a flashbulb picture of the face she'd seen, the wide rubbery lips and wide nose, the wide-set eyes. Thank Christ those eyes hadn't opened—she'd have peed herself. The tun had swollen to fill her purse. It must have quadrupled in size. *The water. Oh, Cil, you idiot. The water.*

She crept into the kitchen. She'd taken the good knives to Marc's, but in the drawer under the microwave was a cleaver neither of them could figure out how to use properly. She slid along the wall, around the fridge. She eased the drawer open and eased the cleaver out, raised it above her head. She peered into the sink. The face wasn't quite as horrible as her brain remembered it. She kept the cleaver raised and stepped closer. Marc. That thing looked like Marc.

"Marc?" she whispered.

The face in the purse twitched and Cecile stepped back. "Marc? Babe, is that you?"

The lips parted. The eyelids fluttered but stayed shut. "Cil?"

It sounded like Marc, like Marc talking in his sleep. Soupy half-formed words. "Cil. So dry. So dry."

She laid the cleaver on the counter. "It's okay, babe. Tell me what you need."

The face frowned. "Thirsty."

She touched the cheek. This was Marc. She stroked the cheek. "It's okay, babe. It's okay. Let me help."

It would have seemed strange to the Cecile of one day ago, would have appalled her to watch, but the Cecile of right now felt no revulsion and no reluctance as she slid her hands into the purse and pulled out the swollen tun. It was mostly a face. Underdeveloped arms and legs and a cute little button of a penis clung to a trunk like a larval afterthought, a tadpole's baggage. She cupped the face in her palms and pressed it between her breasts, practically cooing. This thing was Marc. And he wasn't doing too good. She tested his skin with her thumb, saw the parched surface wrinkle painfully, split and spread like a baked mud flat.

My poor guy. I'll run him a bath.

She wrapped the thing in a towel and opened the faucets as wide as they'd go. Out of habit, she reached for a tin of soothing salts, but stopped herself. He didn't need Me Time Lavender Soak. He needed clean water. He'd drink it through his skin.

She ran a few lukewarm inches—not too much, didn't want to drown him—and unwrapped the tun. She placed it in the bathtub and scooped handfuls of water over its brow. The skin glistened. The face sighed. The sigh flushed the scalp with bristles. The little hands stretched as the torso grew, as the thighs thickened. Hairs squirmed out of their follicles and the penis rolled over like a piglet getting muddy. A drip formed on Cecile's nose, sweat and steam, and she wiped it away, unfastened her blouse. The Marc in the tub was starting to look like Marc. The features, so grotesque on that shrunken head, found their proper position and proportion as the skull filled out. He was the size of a child now, though his limbs were still abnormally short. The arms and legs were fat where they attached to the torso, but then tapered abruptly into delicate pink spades. He looked like a seal. He thrashed a little and his flesh squeaked against the tub; the water had all but vanished. She ran more, much more, kept it running. The arms telescoped. The hair grew long, longer than she'd ever seen it on the original Marc, then longer still, right past his shoulders. A beard fell down his chest. She watched his face, which was peaceful, though he tossed his head like a dreamer trying to surface. She would have expected pangs from such a rapid metamorphosis, but Marc's eyes had not yet opened, he remained sedate, untroubled. In fact, there were signs he was enjoying himself. One sign in particular, which she couldn't help but notice. Which was on its way to purple. She reached for a hand towel and draped it over the erection, not to preserve Marc's modesty but to dampen her own unruly transformations. The towel jumped around before settling. She took a few deep breaths and watched hair spread up the stomach. The lips moved and made a sleepy sound.

"Marc?"

"Cil?"

"How are you feeling?"

He murmured something she couldn't make out.

"That's okay, babe. If you're tired, you just rest."

One last growth spurt shot his feet over the edge of the tub. His heels slapped the wall tiles. He was full size.

She sat by the bathtub for a long time. What now? She needed to manage the situation, which meant she needed time. She left Marc dozing in the tub and bounded into the kitchen, dug the phone out of her purse, bounded back. The phone was damp but it worked fine.

"Babe? It's me."

"Hi."

"Look, I probably won't come over tonight."

"Okay."

Oh, it was okay, was it? Not even gonna ask why? For fuck's sake, she could be having an affair, for all he knew. "It's the Richmond account. The one I told you about? I'll need to pull a few all-nighters this week."

"That's okay."

"Yeah. So. You probably won't see me much."

"Okay."

"Okay. I just want to clear up as much work as I can so we can spend your birthday together stress-free. Okay?"

"Okay."

"Okay bye I love you."

"Bye, Cil."

She glared at the condensation on the tiles. Then she dropped her gaze to the peaceful face in the tub, and she sighed.

It's not your fault. It's not your fault he's a dick.

"Hi, this is Cil, sorry to leave a message like this but something's come up, my mom's heart again, it's probably nothing serious so don't worry, but they're running some tests and I'll probably have to take the week off. Anyway you can email or text, and of course you can call but I probably won't be picking up much, but if you need any documents just let me know and I'll send them along, and sorry about this. Anyway take care. I'll be in touch soon. Okay thanks so much bye!"

There. Now she had time.

Marc seemed content in the bathtub but she worried he'd get cold, so she hauled him out and half-carried, half-dragged him to the bedroom. The hand towel stayed hooked in place. She threw back the covers and rolled him onto the mattress, tucked him in. His hair was wet so she brought in the hair dryer and a comb, and she dried and combed him like a gigantic doll. Long hair. She hated long hair on men. But it kind of looked good. It actually suited him. This beard, on the other hand—and these fingernails! Wow.

She found nail clippers, scissors, an old leg razor and some shaving gel, and spent a solid hour grooming her man. Now why didn't they make dolls like *this* for little girls? This was fun.

The second Marc slept the whole time, every so often mouthing a word that Cecile strained to hear. She paused in her work and leaned in and listened, because this was Marc, this was the Marc that Marc kept hidden from her, this was the Marc that she wanted to know. This was the Marc that she wanted. She trimmed him just so and rubbed him with shea butter from top to bottom.

At length he looked about as pristine as she could make him, so she put away the toiletries and washed her hands. Then she plugged the fridge in and popped out for groceries; she guessed he'd be hungry, and her cupboards were bare. She bought steak and bacon and bread and potatoes, which was all Marc ever wanted to eat. She bought organic veggies, a little greenery for the side. Sparkling water, cantaloupe. Artisanal cheesecake slices. She drove the groceries home and carried them into the kitchen and peeked into the bedroom to see if she could tempt her guest. The bed was empty.

"Marc?"

She checked the washroom, where he wasn't, and the living room, where he wasn't, though the sliding glass door was open, the track blinds swaying from the cold air inrush, steam billowing through the slats. She pushed the blinds aside and stepped onto her tiny balcony, where he was. Naked.

"Marc? Jesus Christ, what are you doing out here? People will see!"

He had a dazed look in his eyes, and when she hustled him in he gave a wild laugh that she hadn't heard in a long time, a wild wicked laugh that made her feel wild too. That laugh was one of the first things she'd loved about him and one of the first things to go. She slid the balcony door shut and locked it, then turned to watch him scamper into the bedroom. Her heart was thumping and it felt good. He'd spooked her and now he was teasing her and it felt good. She followed him.

"Cil, I'm back." He was seated on the bed with his knees drawn up to his chin. His scrotum, which she'd shaved, rested loosely on the sheets. "You brought me back."

She found herself grinning. But she also felt sad.

"Why'd you go, Marc?"

"I don't know. You'll have to ask *him*."

He stretched out. She moved in. And before she could make sense of what they were doing, they were doing it. They were doing it on the bed and then in the hall, and then in the shower, and then briefly in the kitchen, sort of a conjoined crabwalk to fetch the sparkling water (she put the meat and the cheesecake in the fridge while he did her from behind), and then they were doing it in the living room, on the teak table, on the futon, and then they were back in bed, and it was almost morning.

She said, "I was going to make you dinner."

"A romantic dinner? One thing about that. I don't eat."

Which would have seemed strange to the Cecile of two days ago, but the

Cecile of right now merely grinned. In fact, she'd been grinning the whole time; the grin just changed hue. He was with her again. He was back. So she was back too.

They spent the next couple of days barely talking, mostly just doing it and sleeping and showering and keeping their strength up. Cecile took irregular meals to boost her blood sugar whenever it felt like her head was about to float off. Marc drank water. He drank constantly. They filled pitchers and placed them around the apartment so he could pause for a chug without having to pull out. She watched in amazement as he pounded back gallon after gallon. She never saw him pee. And, strangely—though she didn't notice until midway through day two—she never saw him sweat. His locks stayed dry as they fell about his face, as they danced about his face and brushed her back, her thighs, her forehead, her feet. He slept a lot; she slept little. While he dreamt, she stared at his lips, listening for hints.

Say something, Marc. Make sense for me. I don't want to talk, not yet. But I want to hear.

On day three, she said, "I remember you."

Then they talked, and she heard what she wanted to hear. She heard the Marc she'd known, the Marc who'd charmed her, who'd laughed, the Marc she'd forgotten. They talked about nothing but they wouldn't stop talking. They talked while they did it. They talked while she ate. They talked in the shower. They talked as he drifted dozily. She drifted too, her vigil now ended, and she dreamt about them talking.

On day four, he said, "This can't last, you know."

She forced him down on her and that shut him up for a nice long time. They didn't talk much for the rest of that day.

Then on day five: "I'd like to go out. I'd like to travel. We could travel."

She sat up. "I'd like that. We should travel."

"But I can't go out yet."

"Why not?"

"I can't go out with Marc still around."

"Marc? Marc who?"

"We'll go to Paris someday."

"I'd like that."

On day six, as he cradled her, mouth in her hair: "You'll have to get rid of him." It wasn't a command. Just a casual observation.

"Get rid?"

"Of Marc. I'll take his place."

"How can I get rid of him?"

"You'll think of something. I'd do it myself, but I can't leave here. Not until he's gone."

"Why not?"

He squeezed her. "Things are the way they are."

Then day seven came, and the Marc she'd forgotten showed her a Marc she'd never known. They were doing it, he was on top, the light was on. He told her to get rid of Marc, and she asked how, and he said just do it. She said that's murder. He said no. How is it murder if I'm still here? If it's murder, you're cheating.

"What's that supposed to mean?"

"It means what it means, Cil. Marc and I are the same guy. That's why it's okay for you to fuck me. If we weren't the same guy, you'd be cheating. But you're not." He slowed his rhythm and said, "That's why it's okay to get rid of him. I'll still be here."

"I can't do it."

He put a hand on her throat. "Yes, you can."

She sat up and he slid away, and she told herself he'd been bracing himself, harmlessly bracing himself.

"Do it, Cil."

"You can't make me."

He took her in his arms and she told herself she could break free if she needed to. He said, "Yes, I can."

"Okay. Okay, I'll do it." He hugged her and let go. She pulled on some jeans and a T-shirt, a sweater. Could he see that she was shaking?

"Good, Cil."

"And then what happens? Once I do?"

"We can go to Paris."

He followed her into the kitchen, where she opened the drawer and found the cleaver. She slid it into her purse and pinched the clasp.

"Once he's gone," Marc said, "I can leave this apartment. I can walk out that door. I'll take care of any mess. You just get it done."

He helped her with her parka, which she wouldn't normally allow him to do. Not that this version of Marc had ever offered, but the other Marc, the original Marc, sometimes tried to help her get dressed. Which annoyed her: she could button herself. Tonight she was glad for the help, because her fingers weren't working. He zipped her up.

"You trust me, right, Cil?"

"Of course."

"You love me, right?"

"Of course, Marc."

"I love you too."

He kissed her and she felt his teeth on her lip. She tried to smile as she backed out the door.

What if my car doesn't start? What am I doing? Why did I take the cleaver? The roads are icy. I should just drive away. Can I call the police? I haven't eaten. Which one is Marc? I just ran a stop sign. They're both Marc. Are they? What would I even tell the police? Is this even happening? Breathe, Cil, breathe. Count to ten. Breathe.

She parked by Marc's building, on the hill where there was almost always a spot, remembered to turn her wheels. She got out and steam puffed from her nostrils. *Breathe.* She held the pass card over the scanner and pushed the door when it buzzed.

In the lobby mirror, she looked frozen and terrified. Like a little girl, red nose and red-rimmed eyes and bright red lips. She took the elevator and unlocked the door and stepped in, clutching her purse with numb fingers.

"Marc?"

The vestibule lights were out.

"Hi." There he was in his giant space. "Thanks for calling ahead."

"Sorry." She was supposed to call before showing up. That was one of the rules. Even though she had a goddamn key. "Marc?"

She stepped into his space. He was faced away, at his desk, at his computer. She slid the cleaver from the purse. He didn't turn or even look up at her reflection in the giant windows, the giant windows that became a mirror at night. One big black mirror full of twinkling street lights and snowflakes washing through the darkness.

She dumped the cleaver in a plant pot. "Marc, we have a problem."

"I know." He turned at last.

"You know?"

"Of course I know." He sounded spent. He looked defeated.

"But how did you—"

"It's obvious, Cil. We never talk. I haven't heard from you in—what's it been, a week? Not even a text? That's never happened before. I get it. You've finally figured out what a huge loser I am."

"This isn't . . ." She caught her reflection. The snow washing through her. "I didn't come here to break up with you."

"You didn't?"

"No."

"Oh."

"Marc." She went to the closet as he watched. She brought out the jacket. She turned out the pockets. "The tun. I found it. By accident."

"You what?"

"I got it wet."

"You what?"

"It's not my fault! I wanted to know!"

He was on his feet. He was holding her arms. "Cil. Where is it?"

"At my place."

"You left it alone?"

Then they were in her car. He was driving; he'd insisted. He was driving fast.

"Is there any liquor at your place?"

"No."

"We've gotta stop then."

She balled up her fists. "No, there *is* some. A bottle of Johnnie Walker. I was saving it for your birthday."

"That'll do."

"Marc, what's going on?"

"What were you thinking? Can you tell me what the fuck you were thinking?"

"I don't know!" She punched the door. "Okay, I *do* know. You know what I was thinking? I was thinking *don't think*."

She could see him counting to ten.

"Cil, how long's it been?"

"I don't know. A week."

"Is it full size?"

"Yes."

They said nothing for a long time, then Marc said, "You can't believe anything it told you."

They said nothing more till they arrived. He pulled up in front of her building and turned to her.

"You have to stay here."

"In the car?"

"You have to stay."

"I want to come up."

"You can't."

"Why not?"

"You just can't. I have to go alone. Where's the Johnnie Walker?"

"What are you gonna do, have a *drink* with it?" *Not the right tone, Cil. Stay calm, Cil.* "Marc? Tell me what's happening."

"I'm going to have a drink with it, yes. I'm going to talk to it."

"Marc, it wants to kill you. You can't go in there."

"It doesn't know what it wants. Trust me."

"I'm pretty fucking sure it thinks it wants to kill you—"

"I can reason with it. Okay? Stay calm. Just stay calm."

"I can't stay calm. I'm not like you."

He opened the door. He paused. "How do you know it wants to kill me?"

"It told me it wants you dead."

He stepped into the snow, left her keys dangling in the ignition. From his shirt pocket he produced a spare apartment set she'd cut for him ages ago, which, to her knowledge, he'd never used. "It won't kill me. It's not that crazy. I'm part of it." He leaned on the door and stared at her. "Did it ask *you* to?"

She gave him a look that she hoped he could read. An apology look, which was also a plea to drop the subject.

He sighed. "Where's the scotch?"

"I hid it in the fridge. In the crisper." She grabbed at his wrist but missed him. "How long will this take? Marc? I'll freeze out here!"

"It'll take as long as it takes. Run the heat." He closed the door and looked at her through the window. He held up his palms. Stay.

There he goes. Talk to it? Reason with it? I should've killed him. Don't think that. We could've gone to Paris. Don't think that. Poor Marc. Poor boring Marc. I should run the car. Run the heat. Which one is really him? They both are. This is stupid. Would it take me to Paris? It said it would. Don't believe it. But I bet it would if only I could follow through. If only I could get rid of the other one. The real one. I can't. We can't. We never could. Did I try hard enough? It's too much to ask. I can see my breath. Don't blame yourself. Count to ten.

She did, and did again. She counted to ten for twenty minutes. How many tens was that? She told herself to go. She told herself to run the heat. She couldn't stand this.

She closed the car door as quietly as possible, tiptoed through the snow, stole up the stairs. She stood on the landing outside her apartment and listened. She heard them. She pressed her ear to the door. She heard that laugh, that wild wicked laugh. Marc in stereo. Laughing.

What were they laughing about?

She bit her lip and turned the knob, delicate as a safecracker. When the latch clicked, she nearly fainted. She beamed a prayer at the hinges, begging them not to squeal as she opened the door just wide enough to slip past. She crouched behind the kitchen island.

Why were they *laughing*?

She heard Marc say, "The thing is, Cecile needs something you can't give her. She needs to be wanted."

She heard Marc say, "I want her."

"Not just physically."

"That's how it starts."

"You're not hearing what I'm saying. You can't give her what she needs. It won't work."

"She can move on, then."

"She won't. She'll keep trying. She's loyal that way."

"*I* can move on, then. Plenty o' fish."

"You think it's that easy?"

The tun said, "It's that easy, Marc. Unless you make it harder. And in the meantime—Christ, when else are we gonna lay our hands on a pair of tits like that? We should be grateful she has such low self-esteem."

Next thing she knew, she was in the living room.

The tun said, "Oh, hey babe."

It was naked, lounging on the futon. Within striking distance.

"Don't 'hey babe' me you asshole."

The tun laughed.

"Don't *laugh*."

Marc said, "Cil."

He sat across from the tun, on the couch. The open bottle of scotch sat on the table between them. They each had a glass.

"What?" she snapped. She regretted dumping the cleaver.

The tun sat up on its haunches.

"Maybe you shouldn't snoop around if you can't handle what you hear." It edged toward her. "Truth hurts, babe."

She balled up her fists and lunged at it—not intending to strike, just angry.

It caught her forearm and said, "You got a real temper, you know that? It's ugly."

Marc said, "Everyone calm down."

The tun caught her free arm. It pressed her arms together and clamped one hand around her wrists.

"Let me go, you stupid fucking—"

"Shut up."

"Don't tell her to shut up!"

"Don't tell me to shut up—"

The tun hit her. "When I say shut up, you should shut up."

She screamed and Marc leapt over the table, threw an arm around the tun's neck. The double was strong, impossibly strong. It hit Cecile again and shoved her against the wall, then it flipped Marc to the floor. Then it was on him.

"Go, Cecile!" Marc said. "Get out! Run!"

She took a step back. She watched. Marc grabbed the tun's right fist with his left hand; it mirrored the move. Cecile darted for the closet.

The tun said, "You're in the way, Marc. I think I'll get rid of you."

"You need me."

"Let's find out."

Marc's fingers mashed in bad directions as the tun tightened its grip. His arm went slack. The tun laid in. It hit his face and said again, "Let's find out."

But before it could, Cecile bent a nine iron on its brain.

It reeled back. She sliced the air with the golf club, struck the tun in the chest. It crashed into a corner. Marc rolled on his side and saw her hack away. She aimed for the head, but the tun shielded itself, took the blows on its arms. She hit a shoulder and sensed the joint cave under the skin, like a grapefruit in a sock. She became clinical. *Aim for the spine. Break the spine, and then it can't move, and then you can split its head open. Breathe, Cil. Breathe.*

"Stop! Cecile! Don't!" This from Marc. Not the Marc beneath her blows— the other one, the one she was saving. "Don't kill him."

She stopped. Don't kill him? Why not? What was this?

"Cil, please. Hold on."

Count to ten.

The tun lay prone in the corner, one arm hooked around the back of its head. The legs kicked weakly. The fingers flexed.

Marc pulled himself up and stood by Cecile. His eyes were bloody. He held his injured hand to his chest. Wincing from the pain, he said, "Salt. We need salt."

Nine. Ten. She said, "The kitchen," and they went in together. She took a shaker from the spice rack.

"No. We need more. Is there a box?"

She dropped the golf club on the table and opened a cupboard.

Marc said, "Where did you get that club?"

"It was supposed to be—" A sob pulled at her voice, but it passed. "It was supposed to be your birthday present."

She found a box of salt. He led them back to the living room.

"My hand's fucked," he said. "Open the box."

She tore off the top.

"Empty it. On him. Start with the head."

She shook the salt on the tun's head. The head turned and opened its mouth. The tun said, "We could've gone to Paris, Cil."

Then the head began to shrink. The lips pulled back, tightened over the gums, which blackened. The teeth retracted. The eyes collapsed and withered like toads on a griddle.

"Get the rest of him. All of him."

She poured salt in her palm and shook it over the shoulders, the back, the ass. She knelt and rubbed it on the arms and legs, which drew into their sockets. The skin tightened, hardened like sun-bleached wood. But the hair. Look at that. That lovely long hair, it wasn't shrinking. Maybe Marc would let her keep it.

"We'll have to burn the hair."

"Do we have to?"

"Yes."

"Why?"

"That's the way it is."

They watched in silence as the tun shriveled into its dormant state. *So compact*, she thought. *You could step on it by accident—you'd hardly notice.* Then Cecile and Marc looked at one another for a long time, longer than they'd done in a while. She wondered what he saw. She saw the man she'd forgotten and the one she'd never known, and also the one she knew too well, the one that was left.

He said, "We never talk anymore."

She said, "I'll drive you to the hospital. Get that hand fixed. Then we can talk."

She collected the tun in her purse, pinched the clasp, and that's what they did.

Aversions

HELEN MARSHALL

"Beauty," father told us, "attracts the divine eye."
He crafted for my sisters each
a mask of panned mud and witch grass.
Made them wear it out of doors
until their faces took on the folds and crevices,
strange distortions,
the ugliness of his hands.

Back then we kept our eyes low.
All that blue sky was a hunting ground.
Sarah bent her back like an old dowager.
Maria walked with a limp.
Always.

"He will come for you," father warned us,
"in the shape of a great white bull,
a dark-eyed swan, or a shaft of light in the murdering hour.
Do not be fooled.
I lost your mother that way."

Liza has learned to spit.
Cresseida tore a hole in her eye so it wept blood.

In the evenings we sit beside the fire
under a roof of thatch,
timber stripped to heartwood.
Diana takes scissors to her curls,
and I watch them drift golden in the smoke:
hair burns so quickly,
curls up like a mouse from a hawk.

"Go to sleep," my sisters whisper to me.
"Hush now and good night, little one."
They stroke my cheek,
leave sooty fingerprints, like blessings,
for the morning.

Tomorrow they will take me into the light.
They will wear masks,
set their feet deliberately crooked
on the path from the cottage.
I alone—
unbroken in their arms,
hidden in the shadows they make for me—
will recall the slant
of their shining.

Wendigo Nights
SIOBHAN CARROLL

Day Eleven

Lately I've been thinking about eating my children.

When Olivia tugs at her glossy curls, I think about her hair in my mouth. Paper-dry, tasting of smoke and strawberry shampoo. The strands would break between my teeth. The sound they'd make—a tiny crunch, like a foot falling through snow—that sound would fill me. I would not be so hungry after that.

I allow myself the hair. It is better than the other things I imagine eating.

Macleay says, "I'm going to try again this afternoon. I think today's the day." We nod as though we believe him.

I study Macleay's hands. They're large and dirt-streaked. I imagine crunching through his knuckles and rolling the tattered joint on my tongue like a marble.

"What about you, Hui?" Sanderson's tone is a bit too casual. "Any news on that canister?"

I shrug. I don't want to open my mouth. I'm afraid of what might happen.

The arctic wind howls through our silence. It's blizzarding outside the research station, -36 Celsius by the thermometer, god-knows-what once you factor in wind chill. The kind of weather even the locals complain about.

"They'll send a plane as soon as the weather clears," Bannerjee mutters. She's been saying the same thing for a week now.

"Yeah." Macleay doesn't look at her. "I'll try again this afternoon."

"You okay, Hui?" I can feel Sanderson's eyes on me. He knows something's off.

Carefully, very carefully, I part my lips. Not much. Just enough to reply. And I know this is my chance—maybe my last chance—to warn them.

Olivia giggles in the corner. The thought darts into my head: *If not Macleay, then her.*

"Fine," I mutter. "I'm fine."

After a moment, Sanderson nods.

That was on day eleven.

Day Nine

They say people who've received a terminal diagnosis brood over history. They go looking for mistakes: theirs or someone else's. They try to identify the moment things started to go wrong.

I can think of two possibilities. In my mind, I flip them like a coin.

The first possibility: eleven days ago.

Bannerjee set something dull and gray on my work bench. "Check this out." She looked flushed, proud as an angler who's caught his first salmon. "It was in the ice, about a metre down."

I picked it up. A gray canister, about the size of a paint can, weighing about two kilos. It was made out of a clouded, dull metal, striated with rings.

"What is it?" I wasn't interested, just being polite. Nothing about the canister suggested danger.

"No idea." Bannerjee leaned forward. "But I saw another can down there. And clothing." She was practically squirming with excitement.

"Clothing?"

"A wool coat." She grinned. "I stopped drilling. Shifted the borehole. We need to call this in." Seeing my confusion, she added: "Could be old."

Now something connected. "How old?"

"Dunno. But . . . it could be old."

I turned the canister over. Once, maybe, we'd have shrugged our shoulders over a frozen coat. But not these days. The scramble for the melting Arctic is on, and governments look to history to strengthen their territorial claims. Canada has resumed the nineteenth century's search for Franklin. Hell, a few years ago, Russia planted a flag on the seabed beneath the North Pole. A *flag*. Like in the Eddie Izzard skit. Everything old is new again.

"Franklin et al.," I said. "They wore wool coats, didn't they?" Like me,

Bannerjee wore Canada Goose, the unofficial uniform of the frigid zone. Her coat was blazing red; a slot for the Arctic Rescue tag gaped emptily on her back.

"Yeah." Bannerjee's eyes glittered with what I assumed was excitement.

Now, looking back, I wonder if I was wrong about the look in Bannerjee's eyes. If, like the slow crack of lake-ice underfoot, things were already getting out of hand.

Day Twelve

"We need to talk about Bannerjee," Sanderson says in a low voice.

I grunt. So far I have managed to get through the morning without opening my mouth. I am thirsty, but the hunger is much, much worse. It claws at my insides like a wild animal stuffed in a cage. If I open my mouth, I fear it will get out.

"I can't find her anywhere," says Macleay of the edible fingers. "I thought... I thought she might have tried for the mine. But when I checked the snowmobiles I found this." He opens his dirty hands to reveal a tangle of black wires.

"She butchered the machines." Sanderson's voice sounds wet and heavy, like warm-weather snow.

It takes me a moment to register what they're saying. I raise my eyebrows at Macleay.

"I can't repair this," Macleay says in disgust. His eyes are frightened. "We're stuck here until the plane comes. Or until the satellite phone starts working again." He makes no mention of trying the phone again this afternoon.

The blizzard moans through our walls. Out of the corner of my eye, I see Ethan and Olivia watching us. *Dohng, Suug Yee*, I would say, were I to call them by their Cantonese names. Unlucky names. I try to smile at the children reassuringly, but my heart is sinking.

We are in more trouble than I can bear to think about. Some facts I can face head-on: the damaged snowmobiles, the missing plane. Others I can only sneak glances at.

Fact: *I was the first person to touch the canister after Bannerjee.*

Fact: *Something is wrong.*

Fact: *I do not have, and never have had, any children.*

"Well," Sanderson says eventually. "Keep an eye out for her." He looks deflated, as though he has finally realized what I have suspected for eleven days now.

Escape is no longer an option.

Day Nine

The second possibility: five years ago.

My then-girlfriend, Anna, wanted to see the Anthropology museum. One of her college friends was in Vancouver for a conference. So I drove her and the other folklorists to the weird borderland-city of UBC.

I circled the Bill Reid sculpture while Anna and Joel reminisced about grad school. I've always loved wood, and the honey-glow of the giant raven appealed to me. Not so the rest of the museum. A bunch of masks with distorted faces and stringy grass hair.

"The last murder was in the 1960s," Joel said.

That jerked my attention back to their conversation. "What?"

"Creepy," Anna agreed. Her skin was almost the same colour as the yellow cedar. Ethereal.

She turned to me. "They left the uncle to babysit their kids." Her words were aimed in my general direction, but her eyes drifted past mine. Another one of the disconnections that had become common between us. "When they came back, he'd built a fire on the lawn. He was roasting his nephew's body. And crying about it."

The mask that reared up behind them was ugly. Lips peeled back from red-lined teeth. Black eyes staring nowhere.

"Did you hear about that bus murder in Winnipeg?" Joel said, out of nowhere.

Anna grimaced. The news was full of the Greyhound murder, which fascinated and repelled us. It was the sort of thing our Vancouver friends avoided talking about.

But Joel was from New York. "Beheading and cannibalism," he continued, staring at the mask. "I'm just saying. Maybe wendigo psychosis is still with us."

"Wendigo?" I could feel the conversation rushing past me, the way they usually did when Anna and her grad-school comrades got together.

"Yeah." Joel's face got the bright, careful look I imagined he must wear when teaching. "You've heard of the wendigo?"

And that was it. The moment of infection.

Day ???

I am finding it difficult to keep track of time.

This is a common complaint in the Arctic. The land of the midnight sun. It disorders everything.

Still. Time is becoming difficult. I watch the old plastic clock on the wall to make sure the seconds are still advancing.

I hear sounds from the kitchenette. But I will not get up. I will not investigate.

Things must be kept in order. Or else.

Day Twelve

My children are playing with leftover office paper. Olivia is showing Ethan how to fold the green-and-white sheets into dolls. They decorate their creations with pencil: people don't bring pens to our latitude.

Ethan batters the dolls against each other, making them fight. It disturbs me, but I don't know why.

Outside the wind is raging. I try not to think about Anna's description of a deranged uncle roasting kids on the lawn. I don't even know the whole story. The gaps in my knowledge make it worse, somehow.

"Hui."

I hear Ethan drop his pencil. Olivia's eyes widen and I follow her gaze to where Bannerjee stands, dripping and wide-eyed. Dried blood cakes the side of her head.

The sudden, frozen silence of my children's fear gives me the strength to take Bannerjee gently by the arm. I steer her out of the small dorm room.

"*What are you doing?*" I spit through clenched teeth. I want to rip her throat out. "*What have you done?*"

Bannerjee shakes her head. She's always been a small, anxious woman. Now she's trembling like someone's running a current through her.

"Macleay," Bannerjee manages. There's something wrong with her eyes. "I found him by the snowmobiles. He . . . was tearing them apart. He tried to *kill* me, Hui."

I feel the same way I did in the museum all those years ago. Things are rushing past me faster than I can handle.

"Macleay?"

Bannerjee nods. She's crying now, big, fat tears that track mascara and blood down her face. "You have to help me. He's looking for me."

I feel dizzy. I can't remember the last time I ate. I feel my mouth move—"How can I help?"—although I'm not sure I trust Bannerjee. I'm not sure I trust Macleay either. Something about the way he held those wires.

Here's a question I never thought about when I flew up here: *If the world goes haywire, is there anyone in this station you can trust?*

"It's the canister," Bannerjee says hoarsely. That look in her eyes. "We need to get it out of here. We need to give it back."

I nod as though this makes sense. Part of me—a part I can barely keep track of right now—agrees, but wants to warn her. Because here's the thing about extracting resources. It's always easier to take something out of the land than it is to put it back.

But suddenly I am too tired to say anything.

"Sure," my mouth says. And I watch myself follow Bannerjee down the hallway. She keeps glancing back at the way we came. She's dragging her left leg a little.

As we enter the field lab, Bannerjee whispers something that gives me pause. "We've angered the *vetala*."

"The what?" I hear myself say. An echo of a museum long ago.

Bannerjee looks at me strangely. "The air is full of ghosts." She delivers this information as though it were an ozone reading: a fact, visible to us all.

Later I wish that Bannerjee had explained herself. If I could have heard her version of the last twelve days—maybe I could have altered something.

But maybe not. "Come on," Bannerjee says and pushes the door open.

I don't like to think about what happens next.

Day One

"Is that it?"

Sanderson is framed by the doorway, a big, burly man who likes to wear his beard long and curly. He's typical of a certain kind of Arctic visitor: the geologist who thinks of himself as a frontier throwback. And like a lot of geologists, he's a bit odd.

Automatically I've thrown a cloth over the canister. For some reason I don't want people to see it. Now, reluctantly, I remove the cloth.

Sanderson snorts. "Doesn't look like much. Thought it might be the Holy Grail the way Bannerjee's been carrying on."

My stomach grumbles, and I am suddenly, painfully hungry. But I've already eaten three meals today. It isn't even noon yet.

"Has she got through?"

Sanderson shakes his head. "Coms are down. Murphy's law. Bannerjee makes a find and she can't tell anyone. It's driving her nuts." His shoulders shake as he laughs. Sanderson prides himself on being laid-back. He finds the high-strung Bannerjee amusing.

"Do you think the plane will come through?"

Our station gets a bi-monthly supply drop. The pond-hopper that visits us and the southern Inuit villages is a tough little bird. It might be able to get through in this weather. But I'm not surprised to see Sanderson shrug.

"Maybe." He sounds bored. "Wind's bad. Don't blame them if they postpone the drop. It'll drive Bannerjee extra nuts though." He chuckles.

I wonder now if Sanderson remembers this moment. I wonder if he appreciates the irony.

The pond-hopper never arrives. Normally I mark a missed drop with a minus symbol in my diary: -1 day of supplies. But that evening, I write "Day One" at the top of the page. Because that is what it feels like. Like something has begun.

Day Twelve

The day she left, Anna and I argued in the parking lot. She said I was incapable of love. Worse, she said it sadly, as though it was something we both knew and had just been too polite to mention until now.

I protested, but words have never been my strong point.

If I could talk to Anna right now—if we could get a line out, if I could feel confident about baring my teeth to the air—I'd tell her that she was wrong. That what I find difficult isn't love, but expressing it.

If she could see me now—the way I'm trying to shelter the children from danger, the way I'm trying to protect them from myself—I think she'd think differently.

At least, I hope she would.

"Tell us a story," Olivia begs. I look away from her dark curls and Ethan's bright, plump cheeks. The only stories in my head are awful ones. Franklin and his men staggering in the dark. Starving men cutting up their comrades for cooking pots. And the story Joel told me all those years ago.

"No," I mumble. "No story tonight." Olivia wails. Ethan bounces up and down.

"Fine," I say. "Once upon a time there was . . ."

"A canithter," Ethan lisps.

It takes me a moment to respond. I am tired. So very tired of fighting. And I really can't think of anything else to say.

"A canister." My voice sounds dull, even to my ears. "Buried in ice."

"And then one day . . ." Ethan prompts. They look at me expectantly, with glittering eyes.

"One day," I agree.

"One day," Olivia says, her voice rising with excitement, "it gets *out*!"

Five Years Ago

Joel turns to me and says, "You've heard of the wendigo?"

I shake my head. Out of habit I want to stop him; I tend to be bored by Anna's descriptions of legends and tale-types. But she is watching me closely.

"'*This is the blue hour / The ravenous night . . .*'" Joel quotes. He pauses, looking at me. When I show no sign of recognition, he moves on. "It's a Native American legend." (Anna winces at his word choice.) "A cannibal spirit that possesses a person and makes him want to feed on human flesh. Particularly friends and family members."

"We always hurt the ones we love." Anna is smiling sadly to herself.

"Vampire and werewolf stories are similar that way," Joel reflects. "But I think the wendigo's scarier."

"Why?"

"Because of the way it's transmitted."

Joel smirks and preens a little. I know he wants me to ask him about the transmission. I don't want to ask him. I try to catch Anna's eye, but she isn't looking at me. And I can't figure out a way to exit this conversation. So I turn back to Joel, and ask him, "How?"

This, ultimately, is my tragedy. I go along with things.

"Anyone can become a wendigo," Joel says. "It's a culturally transmitted madness. That's actually documented, by the way. Wendigo psychosis."

"Which means?"

"As soon as you learn about the wendigo, you can turn into a wendigo." He grins triumphantly, haloed by the amber light of the museum. "Just by listening to this, you've been infected."

I feel a flash of anger. Even now, all these years later, I still want to punch him.

I think I could forgive Joel for telling me about the wendigo. But I can't forgive him for that grin.

Me, I apologize. I don't know if that makes it any easier. I was just trying to make sense of things. And it was easier for me to do that on paper.

Even in reading these words, you have been infected.

Day ???

This is the blue hour. The ravenous night.

I find Macleay in the kitchenette. His body is bent like a broken straw. He looks dead. But I can hear his breath, even above the sound of the wind. The slow pump of blood in his veins.

His eyes slide open as I approach. Puppet's eyes.

"Still alive, Hui?" He gives a mad, wet giggle.

I sink down in a crouch before him. I'm salivating at the metallic taint of blood in the air. This disgusts me. I wish I didn't know what was going to happen next.

"It's the canister," Macleay says and smiles. His face slides into the same holy-fool expression that Bannerjee's wore at the end. "Not from this planet after all."

His smugness irritates me. Like Bannerjee, he thinks he has found an explanation. Bannerjee blamed ghosts. Macleay wants aliens. I suppose it does no harm to let them believe they figured it out at the end. That there was an answer.

"What happened?" I rasp, trying to delay the inevitable.

"Sanderson," Macleay whispers. He smiles a red smile. "I thought he was all right. But he fooled me. The son-of-a-bitch."

"Where is he?"

Macleay rolls his eyes towards the door. *Outside. In the death-storm.*

I hear a gasp behind me and know that Olivia has trailed me into the kitchen. I motion her back with my free arm. I don't want her to see my face.

"Get him for me, will you?" The shred that remains of Macleay wants vengeance. I nod, to keep him happy.

The crunch of bone fills my mouth and I try to think about other things. About the line I once came across in an old explorer narrative that Bannerjee had picked up in Anchorage. "The North has induced some degree of insanity in the men."

The North has induced some degree of insanity in the men. It's untrue, of course. One of those annoying stories that southerners like to tell about the Arctic. But we bring those stories with us when we come up here.

My opinion? I don't think there was anything in that canister. There didn't need to be. All it needed was our stories.

"Sanderson's putting gasoline around the building," Olivia announces in a detached voice. I nod. I can smell it, an ugly, thick stench that corrupts the taste of blood in my mouth. I clamber to my feet, ignoring the stickiness on my hands and face.

I've always been good at ignoring uncomfortable truths. The wariness in Anna's eyes. Macleay's corpse at my feet. The children.

The only excuse I can make is that, when things descend into nightmare, you cling to the parts of the story you want to believe in.

"Hui!" Somewhere, Sanderson is screaming my name. He wants to test his story against mine. I grin a death-mask grin and click my nails together. I can feel my body stretching to accommodate the life it has devoured.

"Don't worry," I tell my silent, ghost-faced children. "I'll protect you."

I put my hand on the howling door. I pull it open.

This is the blue hour. The ravenous night.

The Smut Story
GREG BECHTEL

(III)

Disabling that economic structure in order to encourage self-discovery, intelligent relations, individual sexual freedom, and sexual transcendence on a routine basis would violate the sanctity of the marketplace, the shrine within which this cultural, sexual discourse occurs. The failure or disabling of individual imagination, so impoverishing to our sexual and emotional lives, enriches the pornographers.

And that, of course, is why we are not encouraged to be our own pornographers.

— from Candas Jane Dorsey's "Being One's Own Pornographer" (as quoted by T.i.o. Boop)

Press Conference
March 14, 2010
Leva Cappucino Bar
Edmonton, AB

Let me be perfectly clear.

The Hermen collective does not know the current whereabouts of Mr. (or Ms.) T. Boop. Any one of us would happily testify under oath that he (or she) was without a doubt one of the most attractive women (or men) we have ever seen. However, try as we might—and trust me, we have tried— we cannot come up with a consistent description. Nor do any of Hermen's members have any knowledge of Ms. (or Mr.) Boop beyond the events of Hermen's Erotica and Pornography Night, now more commonly known as the Mother's Day Affair.

Certain local pundits have suggested that the mere scheduling of such an event on Mother's Day was in poor taste. The Hermen collective respectfully disagrees. Indeed, we would argue that any attempt, whether implicit or explicit, to repress (or deny) the obvious connections between motherhood and sex is at best misguided. Fuck the virgin-whore dichotomy. However, regardless of any abstract moral(istic) quibbles surrounding the underlying concept and timing of the event itself, the following statement is intended to address some of the more pointed allegations—particularly those of a certain Peter Smith—that have recently resurfaced in several print venues. To wit, Hermen can neither confirm nor deny reports of a "post-reading orgy" following the Mother's Day reading of May 10, 2009.

The collective would have preferred not to respond to these allegations at all, since if you weren't there it's none of your damn business. I mean, seriously. Why do you care? Seems to me you're probably getting off on this too. Nonetheless, given the frequency and persistence of these allegations, as well as the overwhelming public response to said allegations— both censorious and supportive—legal counsel has advised this statement as a necessary compromise.

First, Hermen would like to point out that the lack of credible, mutually corroborating first-hand witnesses to the events in question makes their very existence a matter of dispute. Certain publications have described these alleged events as "improper," "lewd," and even "obscene," and have further argued on this basis that Hermen should be investigated and prosecuted as a "common bawdy house." It is our position that such accusations are not only baseless but quite possibly libellous. And just for the record, Mr. Smith in particular should feel free to go fuck himself.

Nor does Hermen wish to comment on the recent birth of Eva, whose surname will not be repeated here, in deference to her mother's wishes— unlike certain writers working with thinly veiled "anonymous" sources, some of whom we could easily identify were we so inclined. However, unlike *some* people, we hold a healthy respect for the deep vulnerability and resultant expectation of privacy implicit in certain forms of intimate communication, even the privacy of those individuals who seem (apparently) constitutionally incapable of respecting our own. Nor will we speculate on the connections between Eva's birth and the alleged events of that night just over nine months ago. Nonetheless, we both can and do offer our congratulations to Eva's mother on the arrival of her healthy baby girl.

Furthermore, while the Hermen collective can neither confirm nor deny the post-reading events in question, we do affirm that to the best of our knowledge whatever may or may not have happened on the night of the reading was a matter of personal choice on the part of any and all alleged participants. Indeed, none of the published reports to the contrary (and yes, we have read them all) have included even a single first-hand account to corroborate their claims. On this point, even Mr. Smith's morally outraged, symptomatically vague, yet strangely persistent "anonymous" sources have remained uncharacteristically silent.

What Hermen can confirm are the basic events of the reading itself, which were as follows. At seven P.M., Hermen's Erotica and Pornography Night opened its doors to an audience of approximately five, a number which grew closer to twenty by the start of the reading. At eight o'clock, Joel Katelnikoff introduced the theme for the evening, noting that the order of performances would be changed due to the conspicuous absence of the first reader. (At this point, Mr. Katelnikoff may or may not have made certain comments about the absent reader's mother.) Stephanie Bailey then introduced the (formerly) second and third readers, whose pieces were performed without incident and generally well-received.

During the break, an audience member approached Mr. Katelnikoff and offered to fill in for the missing reader with a piece entitled "(The Importance Of) Being One's Own Pornographer." This audience member was, of course, the now-infamous T. Boop. In consultation with the rest of the collective, Mr. Katelnikoff agreed to include Boop's piece as a preferable alternative to cutting the reading short. Mark Woytiuk, in the course of this consultation, further commented that, "If nothing else, she's got a great voice." This statement prompted double-takes from certain group members but passed without further comment.

The performances resumed with the third reader, whose piece was also well-received, after which Ms. Bailey introduced "Mr." T. Boop—again prompting double-takes from several audience members—as a newcomer to Hermen. She also read Boop's supplied introduction, which consisted solely of an epigraph quoted from Candas Jane Dorsey's "Being One's Own Pornographer." Audience members have universally described Boop as a powerfully attractive person of indeterminate age, average height and build, and nondescript dress. Boop's gender, however, remains unknown, with various audience members recalling the reader as distinctly—and even notably—female, transgendered, androgynous, or male.

What? No, *convenient* is not at all the word I would use.

It's hardly *convenient* for us to have to try to explain any of this. Personally—and I'm sure that in this I speak for everyone who was there—I would much prefer to know who Boop really was. Not to mention, I for one would very much like to see (and especially hear) her again. Now please, if you could just let me finish.

All agree that the piece was structured as a nested second-person narrative, describing an unnamed "you" recounting an explicitly pornographic first-person anecdote to her (or his) unnamed lover. Audience members further reported that their immediate surroundings seemed to "recede" or "fall away" under the influence of Boop's voice, a voice described alternatively as "sonorous," "soft-spoken," "deep," "childlike," "husky," or even "operatic." Myself, I would call it melodious, even musical. Or incantatory, like a spell . . .

But where was I? Ah yes.

In spite of broad agreement regarding the structure and subjective effect of the piece—succinctly described by Hermen organizer Eleni Loutas as "one for the spank bank"—no two members of the audience (or the Hermen collective, for that matter) recall T. Boop's story as depicting the same narrative. Depending on the individual, the story may be recalled as containing explicit scenes of homosexual, transvestite, transgendered, BDSM, incestuous, cross-generational, and even—in some instances—entirely vanilla, heterosexual sex. Thus, in spite of certain passages having been widely (and irresponsibly) reported as "verbatim" reproductions, the precise contents of Boop's reading, like the gender of the reader her- (or him-) self, remain unverifiable.

No, I don't *expect* you to believe anything. And frankly, I don't care. I'm sure you've all heard the expression *you had to be there*? Well in this case you really did. And you weren't. If you want to make up a story, feel free. But in that case, please recognize *and acknowledge* that that's what you're doing.

No, I'm not being facetious. Seriously, have fun with it. I know we have, and I expect we will continue to do so. But unlike some, we haven't printed every batshit crazy speculation that came into our heads as fact. And we would thank you to show the same restraint.

No, I . . .

That isn't what I said.

Look, do you want me to finish or not?

During Boop's performance, certain audience members saw fit to slam down their glasses, noisily gather their belongings, and pointedly exit the premises. (It should of course go without saying that none of these early-departing audience members have the slightest idea what may or may not have happened after the reading. So please bear that in mind when interviewing your "sources," anonymous or otherwise.) Nonetheless, in spite of these interruptions, the piece continued successfully to its conclusion, at which point Boop referred back to his (or her) bio/epigraph, explicitly encouraging audience members to become their own pornographers by expanding upon her (or his) story in conversation amongst themselves.

Seriously? No seriously, how the hell would I know that?

Look, if you want to know what Peter Smith and his so-called "sources" are on about, you're going to have to ask him yourself. We would have been happy to talk to him at any point in this process, but he hasn't contacted us. In fact, we have tried to contact him repeatedly over the past nine months, but he hasn't returned any of our calls. He hasn't talked to any of us since . . . Well, let's just say he hasn't consulted us on any of his articles.

Like I said, you'd have to ask him.

And while you're at it, maybe ask him what he was doing that night.

Now please. I'm almost done.

It is the official position of the Hermen collective that any conversations, storytelling, or other interactions which arose and/or continued at this point—whether on the premises or elsewhere—were entirely private and therefore remain beyond the ability (or right) of the Hermen collective to either report or comment upon. Nonetheless, the collective affirms and supports the right of Ms. (or Mr.) Boop to present his (or her) work in whatever form and venue she (or he) may choose. And we encourage him (or her) to continue to do so. Indeed, we would be honoured to have her (or him) perform with us again were he (or she) so inclined.

For although the alleged post-reading events can be neither confirmed nor denied, many of the alleged participants in these alleged activities have (allegedly) described said activities as quite enjoyable indeed. Hermen's official stance on the alleged events themselves, however, can be summarized in two words: "No comment."

(II)

For Eva S—
c/o L&P Associates
Barristers & Solicitors
Edmonton, AB
To be delivered on the occasion of her 18th birthday.[1]

10 May 2015

Dearest Eva,

If all goes as we hope, this letter will be redundant by the time you receive it. But we have no way of guaranteeing that will be the case. So this is our insurance policy, a hedge against the unthinkable. Hopefully, its contents won't come as a complete surprise. No matter what others may have told you (especially Peter), please bear with us. You need to hear this.

For me, the memory always starts with that late spring, approaching-solstice light. The time warp kicks in the day all the clocks spring ahead, throwing everything subtly (but distinctly) off-kilter. The sun glows golden, hanging low on the horizon for hours, and the whole world becomes an instantly nostalgic, time-faded photograph of itself.

At first the effect is entirely subliminal. On a sunny afternoon, you might sit down at a café or patio or wherever. Doesn't matter what you're doing. Maybe you get absorbed, maybe not. Maybe you're bored as hell. But at a certain point, you look up from whatever you're doing (or not) and think, "Hey, I should eat something." Only to find the dinner hour passed, evening having long since given way to full night without the slightest hint of a transition. The light has fooled your body and mind, both retroactively awakening to the hunger that has haunted you for quite some time, only now springing full-blown into consciousness.

....

[1] Editor's Note: Eva S is believed to have celebrated her 18th birthday on February 14, 2028. However, although many scholars and biographers have accepted Eva's claim that her receipt of the long-delayed "Eighteen Year Letter"—as it has come to be known—was precisely what inspired her earliest work, the question of when (and indeed whether) she actually received and read the letter, as well as her direct or indirect reactions to its contents, remain ultimately unverifiable.

Every year, the slow-changing light draws me back into that same odd surrealism, a disjunction arising from a conflict between subconscious expectations and the material reality of living in this particular part of the world, at this particular time of year.

Always, it takes me like a dream.

It's May 2009 as I walk slowly, almost reluctantly, towards the reading. Mother's Day has drained these residential streets of activity, a vaguely post-apocalyptic desertion: abandoned toys on lawns, yard and gardening tools set aside, all the signs of a sudden departure. Elsewhere, restaurants are packed, parking near impossible, reservations the ultimate currency of the day. But here, Mom's night off prefigures the end of the world.

Leva materializes on the corner, a former convenience store converted to a retro Italian organic café. Broad windows across the north and west sides admit the late-afternoon light, transforming the round marble tabletops and chrome-and-plastic stools into something out of a foreign film. In the back, windowless portion of the room, a row of black-and-chrome espresso machines gleams darkly. Behind the counter, organic food, fancy coffees, and a strategically limited selection of exotic alcohols are available to those who can recognize and properly name them. Both the staff and clientele are much younger and hipper than I ever was.

As I look around, my dubious distinction as the oldest guy in the room slowly sinks in. My beige T-shirt, green hoodie, black chucks, and blue jeans suddenly feel more try-hard than inconspicuous. I had hoped to blend into the crowd, but only eight people have arrived so far. Nine including me. Recognizing no one, I take a table by myself, wishing I had brought along a book or a notebook or *something* to make me look occupied. Instead, I pretend to stare out the window, watching the half-transparent images of surrounding hipster kids reflected in the glass. Like a child hiding under covers, I'm convinced that if I don't look directly at the Monster then it won't see me, and I'll be okay. Effectively invisible.

Or perhaps I'm both monster and child. Monster in the sense of the creepy older guy, slimy old porn-junkie emerging from his basement in search of like-minded company. Child in the sense of naïveté and disorientation. Why am I even here? Sure, I've seen porn. Who hasn't? But I don't really *get* it. Perhaps my casual googling was insufficient, a proper pornographic education requiring more dedication to the form. Whatever. Everything I found was boring, too mechanistic, disconnected, misogynist, or just plain weird. Seriously. Who gets off on this stuff? But perhaps I'm missing the point. Or perhaps that *is* the point. To see if there's something *else* out there. Or rather, out here. Something between the bullshit happily-ever-after fairy tale of a romance novel (not that I've ever read one) and the empty hump and grind of internet porn. Something actually *sexy*. I don't know.

All I know is that I have never felt quite so straight as I do at this moment. Not straight as in heterosexual, but straight as in square. *Tete carré*, as the Quebecois might put it. A hapless voyeur in the land of the young. My first exposure to the very idea of sex came from playground jokes, kids who knew little more than I did, which was next to nothing. Dirty jokes whose dirtiness arose almost entirely from their incomprehensibility, the knowing chuckle we all quickly learned to fake. But these hipster-kids have grown up (insofar as they have) swimming in a virtual sea of porn. It's an everyday fact of living in a world where the internet, for as long as they can remember and beyond, *has always existed*. In such a context, even the most explicit displays of bodily extrusions and orifices, arranged in any imaginable configuration, must carry little more impact than one of those tasteless playground jokes. Or so I imagine.

I stare out the window, half-watching the slow arrivals trickle in, more hipster kids, some guy in a suit who looks almost as out of place as me. Dissociate into that all-encompassing light. Let it subsume my discomfort into the deeper surrealism of the season. Absorb.

I have no recollection of her entry.

One moment, I'm drifting awash in light, and the next she is simply there. A shadow coalescing in shades of black: T-shirt, jeans, chucks, and a hoodie. Like me, minus the awkward self-consciousness and chromatic variety. I follow her reflection in the window. Dark hair in a pageboy bob frames narrow features, her body thin to the point of boyishness yet somehow obviously, even aggressively, feminine. Can't pin down an age, so I'm assuming way too young. I risk my first direct glance of the evening to find her smiling. At me. Dark eyes and a quirked eyebrow. I revert back to my window-gazing, and by the time I look again she's taken a seat directly between me and the microphone. Alone. The crowd quiets as the reading begins.

The first reader passes in a blur. He probably thinks I'm entranced—and I am, but not by him. I can't take my eyes off Hoodie Woman. I watch her reaction to the reading, which has something to do with animal sex and the circle of life. Deleuze meets *The Lion King* meets Nietzsche or some such nonsense. She looks . . . nonplussed, and I can practically hear her thoughts. *Porn and erotica? This?*

I agree. Deleuze? I mean, I get the sapiophile thing, but that's still one hell of a stretch. He could have at least gone with Irigaray or Cixous. Thankfully, the reader finishes quickly and scurries back to his seat, his departure accompanied by polite applause.

Next up, an older woman reads a piece about porn-watching teenaged boys, a note-perfect depiction of their reactions to hardcore porn in the semi-public social setting of a basement rec-room. Her wry description of the wah-wah guitars, bad dialogue, and orifice-filling frenzy of bad porn makes me chuckle, and her recounting of the boys' crass overcompensation for their own sexual inexperience—manifesting in a series of increasingly tasteless and even downright offensive fourteen-year-old-boy commentary—makes me cringe in recognition. Yet even through the most explicit scenes, she keeps her eyes fixed on the text before her, no shift in expression beyond the occasional introspective smile. As if she's simply watching these events unfold on a small eight-and-a-half-by-eleven screen and reporting them back to us in real time. Beneath the satire, I hear an undercurrent of sympathy for the boys' naïveté, and I wonder if she has teenaged boys of her own. If so, I doubt they realize how lucky they are.

Hoodie Woman tilts her head back and closes her eyes, exposing the delicate curve of her throat. Lips part, breath visibly deepening as her hands open wide. Fingers grasping at air as the piece winds to its end, a final image of the boys' inevitably impending wet dreams. On the final line, her hands clench and eyes snap open, locking onto the reader. A silent, full-body shiver, then another, and her fists release. The reader looks up for the first time and freezes, snared by Hoodie Woman's eyes, that focused stare. The reader's eyes widen, and I have to look away.

When I look back, the reader has turned bright red, her gaze pinned to the floor before her. She murmurs a closing thank you, and the applause is immediate and enthusiastic as she walks swiftly back to her seat, still avoiding all eye contact. The emcee encourages us to refresh our drinks for the next set and immediately follows her own advice, beelining to the counter for a glass of white wine. She downs it, orders another, then sips the second while casting occasional, darting glances over at Hoodie Woman. So it's not just me.

As the slow wave of between-sets conversation rises, anticipation crackles through the room like an approaching prairie storm. Everyone talks at once, trying (and failing) to defuse that unspoken, building tension. Hoodie Woman sits alone at the eye of the storm, surveying the room and its inhabitants, sipping her red wine in silence. I also sit in silence, racking my brain for some way to start a conversation. I have to meet her. As I half-rise to walk over and give it a shot, a voice emerges from the surrounding hum.

"Is this seat taken?" A thin blonde woman stands next to me, her hand on the back of the unoccupied chair where I've set my jacket. She looks nervous. "I mean, if you're saving it . . ."

"No. No, not at all." I smile (reassuringly, I hope), transfer my jacket from the empty chair to the back of my own, and again begin to stand. "In fact, if you could save my seat . . ." But now Hoodie Woman is deep in conversation with one of the organizers. Too slow.

I sit back down.

"Thanks!" says the blonde. "I mean, if you're sure that's okay."

"No, really, I'd love the company." Still, she hesitates. "I was actually feeling a bit conspicuous. You know, guy sitting alone at a porn reading." Sure, that'll make her feel real comfortable. "I uh . . . I mean, really, it's no problem. All yours." I push the chair in her direction.

She sits but seems paralyzed by the question of where to put her jacket and purse. The stutter-step rhythm of her movements reminds me of a squirrel. She tries the table first, then pauses. A quick half-move towards her lap, another longer pause, and a decisive flurry of action, purse under chair, coat draped over the back. "I mean, I got here late," she resumes, settled now but speech still echoing that same stuttering rhythm. "And I stood at the bar for the first set, but." A half-second pause, then all in one breath, "But then I noticed this seat but I wasn't sure if it was free or not so I just waited for the break and now . . . well . . . hi."

We shake hands. More organizers surround Hoodie Woman. And though they outnumber her four to one, they're the ones who look nervous.

"So have you been to a lot of these things?" The blonde's question pulls me back. "I mean, is this how they usually go?" She's cute, I realize, but not intimidatingly so. A hint of hot-librarian with muted vegan undertones. Her glasses are big, round, clunky things, and she wears no makeup. Like her clothes, the glasses are too plain and lacking in irony to be fashionable with this crowd. Not vintage, just aging and a bit out of date. Like me.

"Actually, I have no idea," I admit. "It's my first time too. It's . . . interesting."

"That's one word for it." She smiles, calmer now, and catches me glancing at Hoodie Woman, who is laughing with the last reader, the woman who couldn't meet her eye just a few minutes ago. The blonde chin-nods. "Friend of yours?"

I blush. "No, we've never . . . I mean, I guess I just . . ."

"Oh, I know exactly what you mean." She chuckles, openly staring at the object of my not-as-covert-as-I-thought attention. "You know, for the life of me I couldn't tell you what the first two readers looked like?"

The emcee's introduction of the next set cuts off my response.

A woman in the audience hands off the newborn in her lap to the man beside her, stands, and approaches the microphone. She has that T-shirt-and-overalls look of a new mom, totally at ease in her own physicality, and she launches directly into a piece exploring pre-, during-, and post-pregnancy sex in explicit and erotic detail. The blonde blushes right up to her hairline, and for the first time tonight I feel like the voyeur I earlier imagined myself to be. This reader makes unflinching eye-contact with individual audience members, some for just a few words, others for a full line or more. She saves Hoodie Woman for last, finally meeting her gaze and holding it through an entire stanza, mingling images of breastfeeding, labour, and orgasm to close on a sustained climax of milk and blood and cum.

No one makes a sound.

A single clap. Then another. Hoodie Woman applauds alone, still holding that gaze. Then she smiles and nods, a brief head-dip of respect freeing the reader to deliver two ringing thank yous, one to Hoodie Woman, the second to the room at large. The answering applause is thunderous, including a few hoots and whistles. The reader returns to her seat, retrieves her child, and nods back to Hoodie Woman over the nestling newborn's head. Then she calmly unhooks an overall strap, lifts her shirt, and latches the child to her breast to nurse.

Still applauding, the emcee returns to the microphone and introduces the final reader as "Mr. T. Boop." I think I am ready for anything. Until Hoodie Woman pushes back her chair, stands, and slowly walks to the front. She takes her time, lightly touching the emcee's arm and leaning forward to whisper something in her ear before turning to face us.

No, not us. Me. Her eyes lock on mine. A wave of vertigo.

Then the adrenaline jolt. Accelerated heart rate, breath turning shallow and fast, a deep *hop* in the gut as that swooping moment of freefall stretches. A powerful desire to hide, and a strong thread of fear. Fear and panic and paralysis (still pinned by those eyes), and at first the only thought I can muster is *oh fuck*. Then: *Holy shit, I really want this person.*

And it scares the shit out of me.

Her eyes expand, pupils dilating impossibly large as the room fades and recedes. Darkness creeps in at the edge of my vision, the chair beneath me and the table I lean on turning abstract, fluid, and nebulous. And though I know I must still be sitting in the chair, still gripping the table, my feet and hands float in empty space as gravity contorts, convulses, and vanishes. Her face a final beacon in the surrounding darkness. Then that disappears too.

I shake my head. Blink furiously. No change. Just the strangely muted sound of my own breathing. It doesn't echo or reverberate. It is *absorbed*. As if the darkness were a sponge, soaking up every light, sound, touch, and smell to leave me floating alone in perfect isolation. Except for her. I can't see her, but I know she's here.

The darkness is warm and humid. If it weren't for the slightest warm breath against my corneas, I wouldn't know if my eyes were open or closed.

Close them for several seconds. Deliberately turn my head. Open.

The room shimmers like heat-wave haze over summer blacktop then slowly swims into focus. The espresso machines in the back, the Euro-minimalist décor, the setting sun a bit lower, but still there. The light, the world, and all the objects within it have returned. But the silence remains. No background chatter. No clinking of dishes, cutlery, or glasses, no whispered orders at the front counter. No soft rustle of people shifting in their seats.

I scan the audience to either side, carefully avoiding even the slightest glance towards the front of the room. Some stare blankly in the same direction I avoid. Are they trapped in the space I just escaped? Others, like me, blink and shake their heads, averting their eyes as I do. The latter shy away from direct eye contact, as if that singular gaze might be contagious, each pair of eyes a trap waiting to be sprung. A flurry of noise and motion at the far end of the room as first one man, then a woman, then others, slam down their glasses and mugs, hastily gather their belongings, and head for the door. A few more hurried exits, the door slamming once, twice, three times. The full exodus takes no more than a minute or two. A final slam of the door, and silence returns. The only sound, that of the crowd's soft, slow respiration. Only a few remain who have thus far avoided (or escaped) the gravity well of Tia's eyes. Any who glance in her direction, however briefly, are instantly caught.

Finally, she speaks. A whisper so soft it should be hard to hear. But it's not.

"This story is not for reading, but for telling. Not for you, but for your lover. This is the story of a story of a story . . ."

I listen to Tia's story, which is also my story. It is beyond porn. No distanced, controlling camera. No distance at all. Not apart from me, but a part of me. A reflective, amplifying feedback loop. Her voice lifts me up and pulls me in, a wave of sound evading all internal censors to draw out my most intimate sensual fantasies, my most secret desires. Drawing them out only to return them to me, shared and multiplied in the amplifying echo of a lover's growing arousal. In response to this story. My story. A story of lips and skin and tongue. Of taste and touch. Slowly, with a growing (yet achingly restrained) urgency, the story builds.

A ragged gasp at my side pulls me back.

The blonde surfaces as I did, shaking her head and breathing heavily. Her shoulders hunch, white-knuckled hands gripping the marble tabletop. A pause, then she pushes herself up to look around the room. Our eyes meet, and we mirror each other's confusion across the small table as Tia's story continues. Progressively colonizing our senses, it expands. I can still see the blonde breathing—almost hyperventilating now—but the sound is gone. She looks down at her feet, squares her shoulders, and takes a long, slow breath. When she looks back up, she smiles and shrugs as if to say, *Hey, if you can't beat 'em* . . . Then she takes one more deep breath like a swimmer about to dive, and turns to face Tia.

And though my resistance is waning, breath grown ragged and muscles tensing under the story's growing influence, I can still focus just enough to see the full process. The electric jolt of initial contact, her entire body stiffening. A soft gasp (seen not heard), eyes widening, pupils instantly dilated. Then the tension passes, shoulders release, and her lips part slightly, curving upwards as she willingly surrenders to her own world-engulfing arousal.

In that moment, she is absolutely fucking gorgeous.

Time and space vanish. Only the story remains.

The room slowly coalesces in half-silvered café windows, and as Tia concludes with thanks and an exhortation for us to share our own stories, I watch its reflection, returning. I have forgotten nothing, details as fresh and vivid now as they will remain for years to come. But the compulsion to watch Tia has vanished. Now, I want to see everyone else.

A few formerly occupied tables sit entirely empty. Those who remain stare as openly as I do. And suddenly everyone—every single person—is inexpressibly beautiful. I meet several pairs of eyes and never once feel the urge to look away. Around the room, glances meet, and these universally flushed cheeks clearly have nothing to do with embarrassment. My eyes wander back across the room to settle on the blonde beside me. Like every other person, she sits entirely unchanged. Like every other person, she is transformed. Our eyes meet and hold. Then she smiles, and I smile back. And we begin to talk.

First, we talk about the story. She shares her version, I mine. They start off the same but rapidly diverge into completely different (though equally explicit) narratives. And when first a man, then two more women and another man join us, the sharing expands to incorporate each new arrival's story, divergences multiplying and growing ever wilder. Given the content, the conversation is strangely effortless. At first we avoid touching, but incidental contacts accumulate, prompting shared smiles, more expansive gestures. Hands brushing across the table, a chance jostling of shoulders, a hand on a shoulder or the back of a neck.

When the subject of Tia herself comes up—and here there is some debate as to whether it was *Tia* or *Tio*—we discover that she, like her story, manifested differently for each person. Depending on the viewer, she was male, female, trans, androgynous, fat, thin, both light and dark haired, light and dark skinned. One woman insists she was wearing a mask. No one seems particularly concerned by these discrepancies. We're more interested in the stories.

Only much later does it occur to one of the women to wonder if Tio (or Tia) might want to join our conversation. But when we finally look around and try to locate her (or him), we find that he (or she) is gone.

Not much more to tell, really. Where the audience had arrived in quiet singles, pairs, and trios, it left in talkative quads, quints, and sextuples. Our group adjourned to Jamie's place—yes, *that* Jamie[2]—where we continued sharing stories. No longer merely recounting, we started embellishing with increasingly collaborative interjections. I think it was Peter who started that, though some of the others remember it differently. By that time, everyone was talking at once so it's hard to say for sure. Some additions were funny, others downright strange. Later, none of us could pinpoint exactly when we shifted from telling to showing.

....

[2] Editor's Note: Although Jamie's identity has never been confirmed, it seems reasonable to assume that this is the same person Eva S often refers to in her own writings as "Uncle"—or occasionally "Auntie"—Jamie, who is generally assumed to be one of her five co-parents. If one believes Eva S's version of her own history.

When the six of us awoke the next morning, there was no sense of awkwardness as we dressed, exchanged phone numbers, and agreed to keep in touch. And incredibly, we did. Except for Peter. Within a week he stopped returning our calls, and the number he gave us was disconnected a few weeks later. That was disappointing, but aside from your mother no one was particularly worried. Right from the start, Peter seemed more solid than anyone, generally grounded, stable, and competent in the world. Shows how much we knew.

Later, as your mother's pregnancy became more apparent—and yes, of course she was "the blonde"—it seemed only natural for her and Jamie to rent a house, and the rest of us moved in one at a time as our respective leases ran out. And then there was you. How to explain these last five years? The incredible moment of your arrival, the brief but intense battle we fought to have all five of us present in the delivery room when the home-birth turned complicated and we ended up in a hospital after all? Those first few months? You have changed us all, and (almost) all for the better. We foresaw none of this, but we wouldn't change a thing. Well, except for Peter. As you no doubt know by now, he didn't take it well.

The rest, I'm sure, is fairly obvious. Or should be if things have gone as we hope. But Peter's raising a stink again. At first it was just letters to the editor, a few op-eds, all that crap about the reading. We tried to contact him, left messages inviting him to come visit any time, that we considered him as much your parent as any of us. But he got it in his head that people "like us" (whatever that means) aren't fit to raise a child. After he got married, he upped his game, turned the whole thing into a legal battle, starting with (failed) demands for paternity testing (which would have required your mother's consent), then suing for custody on broader "moral" grounds. For a while none of it went anywhere, but now he's got some serious backing. Some conservative "family values" group, which we're thinking must mean he hasn't told them everything. And that's good, might give us some leverage if push comes to shove. Still, even if they ditch Peter along the way, these family value thugs might still go after us in court, try to set a legal precedent or something. Thus this insurance policy.

We *hope* that none of this is necessary, that we're being overly paranoid and worrying for nothing. But the fact is, if you're receiving this letter, we have no way of knowing what you may think of us by now. A lot can happen in thirteen years. And we wanted to make sure you at least knew your own history. You deserve at least that much. So if we haven't been able to tell you this story ourselves, we hope you will at least consider the possibility that there is *absolutely nothing wrong or shameful about you and where you came from.* Whatever second thoughts Peter may have had, and whatever he may have told you, you were conceived and raised—insofar and for as long as we were able—in a space of joy and love and celebration.

We also figured this was probably the closest you could get to meeting Tia (or Tio). And since she (or he) is in some ways as much your parent as any one of the six of us—and yes, that includes Peter—we thought you at least deserved to know. First, where you came from, and how, and under what circumstances. Second, that we believe in you. Even now, I can hear you laughing in the next room. And for this I will always be grateful. May you always hold onto that incredible joy. And may you never have to receive this letter.

(I)

A Note on the (Missing) Text(s)[3]

This story is not for reading, but for telling. Not for you, but for your lover.

This is the story of a story of a story. If it happens to turn you on, that is nothing more than a side effect. Like sex, it can take a thousand different forms, but it always progresses through a narrative: beginning, middle, end (. . . and end . . . and end . . .). As much as you might wish it—and you often do—no single instance can go on forever. This story is collaborative. You tell it with as well as to your lover. And always, the story starts not with your lover, but with you.

It is, after all, your story.

Thus begins—and ends—the only verifiable surviving fragment of "(The Importance Of) Being One's Own Pornographer," as performed by the mysterious Tio Boop.[4] Whether or not one believes that this performance ever happened, its seminal (or perhaps ovarian) influence on Eva S's work

---

[3] Excerpted from Dr. Maria Quinlan's introduction to the 2059 edition of *The Smut Story: Critical Reflections* (Vanitate Books), released in honour of the (alleged) fiftieth anniversary of the Mother's Day Affair.

[4] This passage is technically "verifiable" only in the sense that it is the sole fragment of Tio Boop's story to remain consistent across all versions and to have been both endorsed and circulated by Eva S. However, the original source of this fragment remains a matter of significant scholarly dispute.

remains undeniable.[5] Boop's inexhaustible (and by all accounts unforgettable) story haunts the study of Eva S's work at every turn, echoing down the decades to reverberate in every scholarly paper, every ethnographic study of Eva S fandom, and every Eva S performance. Even so, in producing the first edition of this volume, my co-editors and I agreed that it would be best to omit any transcriptions of Tio Boop's original story, acknowledging its central importance only through the title.[6] And although I have expanded this edition with several more recent critical reconsiderations of Eva S's oeuvre, I still stand by that decision.

Certainly, numerous "transcriptions" of Boop's story are available from both online and print sources, and though the contents vary wildly, each one opens with the passage quoted above and echoes the underlying structure described in Hermen's 2010 press conference.[7] However, the most reliable versions of Boop's story remain accessible only through Eva S's extensive audio archive of first-hand oral accounts of the original reading.[8] As the self-appointed guardian and archivist of The Smut Story—which she often cites as the primary inspiration for her own career as an erotic

---

[5] While many believe that Eva S has empirically verified the contents of the Boop passage cited above through her ongoing collection of first-hand accounts from the original reading, others argue that she may have invented the "collection" itself (at least initially) in an attempt to imagine what attendees might have heard and what such accounts might have sounded like, had any existed. Still others contend that the Eighteen Year Letter, Tio Boop, and even the Mother's Day Affair itself are nothing more than an elaborate hoax (or performance piece) designed to mythologize Eva S's critical engagement with her own artistic practice and philosophy. However, neither I nor my former co-editors subscribe to any of these overly elaborate theories, preferring instead to take Ms. S at her word.

[6] Although they have declined to append their names to this edition, I must thank Doctors Linda Martin and John Torres, co-editors of the original 2044 edition of The Smut Story, for their contributions to the text. I still believe that our differing perspectives—and occasionally vigorous debates—ultimately made this volume the success it has been for the past fifteen years. Nonetheless, we all agreed then, as I believe now, that referencing "The Smut Story"—the colloquial term by which Smutsters the world over now refer to Tio Boop's original story—in the title constituted the perfect acknowledgement of Ms. (or Mr.) Boop's contribution both to Eva's work and to this volume.

[7] Like the original reading, the events of the Hermen press conference cannot be verified via the public record, although all of the organizers named in the (alleged) press conference transcript agree that it is accurate insofar as they can recall. Indeed, to date, the only "verified" attendees to either the original Mother's Day Affair or the subsequent press conference are the Hermen organizers themselves, since even second-hand published accounts—such as those the aforementioned transcript attributes to "Peter Smith"—have been lost, presumably erased by the info-liberationist (or, according to some, info-terrorist) group known only as "We."

[8] Eva S has been collecting these stories for decades, having issued a call in 2030 (which remains open) for anyone who remembers Tio Boop's original performance to visit the archive in person and recite his (or her) story in its entirety. These recitations are recorded directly to audio files, thus preserving the precise nuance, intonation, and rhythm of each storyteller's voice, which Eva S maintains is an utterly crucial aspect of the project.

performance artist[9]—Ms. S strictly regulates access to these recordings, keeping them available to the public on two conditions: (1) that no recording devices may be used to reproduce or transmit these stories beyond the archive[10], and (2) that no one may listen to these recordings in solitude but must be accompanied by at least one companion with whom they will discuss the story afterwards.[11] Once these conditions have been agreed to, visitors are free to browse the archive and listen as they choose.

After visitors have explored the archive, however, Eva S encourages them to share these stories in the spirit of the original reading, preferably in as open and public a venue as possible. (Indeed, the so-called Smutsters have enthusiastically adopted this directive in both their guerrilla performances and more formal readings, which range from the impromptu and improvised

---

[9] Eva S's iconic breakout performance piece, "Fuck(ing) the Pope" (2029), has remained available online since its original (unauthorized) filming, the posting of which prompted an immediate firestorm of debate that has been well-documented elsewhere. (For insightful discussion of the shifting social and moral anxieties attached to these debates by various groups in the fifteen years following the video's release, see Sharon Riddle's "'Blasphemy,' 'Obscenity,' 'Pornography,' and 'Art' as (Sub)Cultural Diagnostics: Mapping 'Moral' Readings of Eva S's 'Fuck(ing) the Pope' from 2029 to 2044.") To date, Eva has declined to comment on whether the sex and orgasms were real or simulated, or whether the recorded audience reactions were spontaneous or a scripted part of the performance. The priest in this video has long since been identified (and defrocked) and has likewise declined to comment on the real or simulated nature of his own participation. Eva's career since then—from the early live performances to her later audio sculptures, which range from the conceptual ("Fidelity," 2047) to the ironically pornographic ("Seventies Bush," 2048)—has likewise been well-documented in both popular media and a variety of scholarly publications. For further reading on Eva S's artistic trajectory from internet porn sensation to subcultural icon to internationally respected performance artist, see Jonathan Torres' landmark critical monograph, *Pornography and/as Art: The Rise of a Reluctant Icon* (2049).

[10] Accessed by a gravel laneway, Eva S's estate consists of an aging two-storey farmhouse on a half-acre lot with a spacious garden, several fruit-bearing trees, and a broad, well-kept lawn. No fences or other obvious external security systems distinguish the home from any others in the area, and the archive is housed in a modest addition out back. However, while the estate is open to physical visitors, it is a technological fortress. All virtual intrusions—from neural interfaces to nanotechnology shunts to neutrino-enabled networking prostheses—are strictly regulated by some of the most sophisticated security systems in existence. All wireless communications are blocked from the estate boundary onward, and either Eva or one of her assistants meets all visitors at the door, producing a detailed list of forbidden technology which must be surrendered before entering the house. (Although no scanners are in evidence, the list is invariably comprehensive, detailed, and specific to each visitor.) One presumes that these security systems have been supplied by We, for whom cyber-privacy has always been a central concern, and of whom Eva S has long been a strong and vocal supporter. Indeed, various governments have attempted to requisition the estate's scanning technology in the name of national security, but all such demands have subsequently been quietly withdrawn, likely under direct pressure from We.

[11] privacy has always been a central concern, and of whom Eva S has long been a strong and vocal supporter. Indeed, various governments have attempted to requisition the estate's scanning technology in the name of national security, but all such demands have subsequently been quietly withdrawn, likely under direct pressure from We.

to more "authentic" reproductions of the original Mother's Day event.)[12]
Ms. S describes the maintenance (and oral dissemination) of this archive
as her tribute to Tio Boop, without whose original reading she would quite
literally not exist.[13] She further claims that through sharing these stories—
and the intensive subjective engagement arising from this in-person
sharing—Tio Boop's purpose will inevitably manifest itself, that purpose
being not merely to titillate but to free people to share and explore their

....

[12] The designation Smutster was originally coined in 2030 as a derogatory term for Eva S's
exponentially growing legion of fans. However, the term was reappropriated almost
immediately by those same fans and aggressively refined over the decades, such that it now
refers more narrowly to aficionados of the Tio Boop stories rather than fans of Eva's work
as a whole. The Smusters' "authentic" readings—although their authenticity has never been
endorsed by Eva S as such—strive to reproduce the original Erotica and Pornography Night
described in the Eighteen Year Letter as faithfully as possible. Traditionally, these events
are held at a faux-European café (even in continental Europe, some faux-European cafés
have sprung up to cater to purist Smutsters), with a row of espresso machines in the back,
lighting systems rigged with slow-timed dimmers to mimic the fading Edmonton light, and
as many additional supporting details as the organizers can manage. Each event opens with
the alleged epigraph to Tio Boop's original reading and consists of four reading slots,
including a last-minute reshuffle of the reading order due to the (also traditional) absence
of the first reader. The final reading slot is typically held open in case Tio him or herself
should show up, and when Tio invariably fails to arrive, the remainder of the reading may
proceed in any number of ways. The final reader may be arranged in advance or selected
from the audience, either by random ballot or some more spontaneous method, such as a
blindfolded organizer picking a person from the crowd by touch alone. Some purists omit
the final reading entirely, observing a minute of silence, while others read from bootleg
transcripts of "original" stories allegedly heard at the 2009 event. Indeed, debates over the
appropriate means of handling these finer details have often led to significant splits within
the Smutster community. When participating in these events both as a fan in my teens and
later while researching my master's thesis, I always preferred the minute of silence, during
which—if only for a moment—I could close my eyes and imagine Tio right there in front of
us, about to begin. However, even the most "authentic" of these readings stop short of
reproducing—at least on any formal level—the post-reading events described in the
Eighteen Year Letter. For an in-depth study of these practices within the broader context of
the Smutster movement, see *Smutsters Unite! Sexual Revolution in the 21st Century: A Case
Study* (Quinlan, 2045).

[13] Due to her status as one of the earliest and most thoroughly documented "We-orphans" of
the late '20s and early '30s, no official records exist for Eva S before 2028. She maintains that
she was raised by her five parents until the age of eight, when one of Peter Smith's legal
challenges gained enough traction to have her removed from the family. However, Smith's
concurrent bid for sole custody was unsuccessful, and Eva was placed into foster care until
age eighteen, when she received two letters. The first, written as an "insurance policy" in case
the worst happened and Peter succeeded in breaking up the family, described the unusual
circumstances of Eva's conception. The second letter arrived enclosed with the first, a cryptic
missive from the group We, detailing Smith's ongoing harassment of Eva's birth family even
after her removal. In response, the family had accepted an offer from We to erase all records
of their existence, and now the organization was making that same offer to Eva. Eva
immediately accepted, thereby neutralizing Smith's harassment, and asked to be reunited
with her family. Shortly after this reunion, Eva began producing her own erotic performance
art. Unlike many early We-orphans, Eva was never brought up on charges of fraud or identity
theft (possibly because of her sudden fame) and was in fact a key promoter of We's emergence
into the public sphere in the late '20s. (Although it remains difficult to determine with any
certainty, anecdotal evidence suggests that We had been operating covertly since at least
2004, and many We-orphans resorted to identity theft as a means of survival.) However, it

own erotic fantasies and stories and, more importantly, to learn to enjoy these stories without guilt or fear of reprisal.[14]

In her own work, in accord with her manifesto, Eva S has consistently aimed at enlarging the realm of erotic possibility, encouraging her audience (and the world at large) to move beyond the guilt so deeply and commonly ingrained in certain ways of looking at sex and sexual desire.[15] Her most recent work ("Long Time Coming," 2049), for example, explores the possibility that even the infamous "Peter Smith" may have been as much a victim as a proponent of the conservative "family values" he so vehemently espoused.[16]

....

was not until We's cyber-erasure of several world leaders in 2034—including the acting President of the United States—that worldwide legislative reform provided legal status to the growing legion of We-orphans. To this day, despite her extraordinary candour regarding the details of her own life, Eva has refused to identify anyone from her pre-We past by either their current or "real" name. Certain scholars have argued that Eva's entire backstory may be fabricated, but the demonstrable existence of We—along with Eva's longstanding and well-documented connections to that group—seems to support Eva's version of events. Moreover, I can personally attest to at least some of We's activities around that time, since in 2028, when I was thirteen, the group abruptly and thoroughly erased both my own and my father's files. To the best of my knowledge, this was the only time We ever erased private citizens' files without their explicit request and permission.

[14] Over years of visiting the archive, first while researching my dissertation and later in support of my ongoing scholarly work, I have found it impossible to predict how any given listener will react to a particular story. Furthermore, I can personally attest to the fact that not all—indeed, not even the majority—of the archived stories are titillating in the sense of provoking sexual excitement. Certainly, some do (and powerfully so), but others may be heard from a more distanced, almost anthropological perspective. But however devoid of erotic impact (or even downright repulsive) they may be, a current of vulnerability runs through them, a sense that each story somehow reflects the recorded speaker's entirely uncensored erotic self. And with each new story, the listener may be pulled further into the profoundly human character of each telling. Rather than blurring together into a mind-numbing catalogue of increasingly banal and mechanized sexual acts, each story becomes more particular, more visceral, more differentiated from every one that came before. Indeed, over the course of several stories, the listener may gain a stronger and stronger sense of having almost been there for the original reading, as if slowly being convinced, cajoled, and freed to tell her own story in response, and this anachronistic sense of presence may help to explain how this archive of "original" stories has proliferated and expanded beyond all mathematical possibility to contain hundreds (possibly thousands) of stories. And yet, impossible or not, I have studied these stories and their variations for several decades now, and I can attest with great confidence—my former co-editors' objections notwithstanding—that *they are all genuine.*

[15] See Eva S's uncharacteristically direct "Manifesto" (2033), another early performance piece. See also Dulles and Candle's essay in Part 4 of this volume for an intriguing use of this piece as an interpretive lens through which to (re)read some of Eva's earliest work ("Manifesting the Manifesto: Exposures, Recoveries, and Complications of the 'Political' in Eva S's Early Performances").

[16] At various times, Peter claimed to be Eva's rightful guardian, her estranged uncle, and even her biological father, but since his attempts to force a DNA test failed, these claims remain unverified. In all his legal battles with Eva's family, Smith consistently appealed to "family values," thereby securing financial and legal support from a variety of conservative political and religious groups. Nonetheless, when one of these well-funded custody challenges proved (temporarily) successful in removing Eva from her family, Peter was disqualified as a suitable guardian on the basis of his own participation—however disavowed and regretted after the fact—in the "sordid" circumstances of her conception.

In it, noting the one in three chance that Mr. Smith was indeed her biological father, she explores how Smith's persistent guilt over his participation on the night of her conception could have fuelled his two-decade quest to reclaim the child he genuinely believed to be his daughter.[17] If, she implies, Peter Smith had been free to construct his erotic self on his own terms—and to partake in the incredible erotic diversity of the world around him—he might not have felt such a compulsion to impose received notions of sexual morality upon his own former sexual partners.

Ultimately, this is why I have upheld the original decision to omit all transcriptions of Tio Boop's original story from this collection. Not, as my former co-editors insisted, because of their unreliability or potential to offend, but out of respect for the story itself. As Ms. (or Mr.) Boop so succinctly put it, this ever-proliferating story is not for reading, but for telling, and to pin it down to any singular or static representation would violate the very deepest principles of Boop's (and by extension Eva's) artistic project. Rather, I strongly encourage readers to visit the archive and hear these stories for themselves. Immerse yourself in them, surrender to their rhythms, their internal logic, and explore what sensations may come. Let them under your skin, where they can expose the contours of your own hidden stories.

Then pass them on to friends, lovers, or even strangers—none of these being mutually exclusive categories, of course—along with your own, ultimately mingled and mixed, indistinguishable, the one from the other.[18]

....

[17] My father and I were never close. He never approved of my studies and wasn't shy about saying so at every opportunity. Ever since I attended my first Smut Story reading at the age of fifteen, he hated what he called "that goddamn smut stuff" and found it intolerable that any daughter of his would demean herself by becoming involved with it in any way. Six months ago, for the first time, he told me why. He was, he said, the very same "Peter Smith" who had worked so hard to remove Eva from her family, and he sincerely believed he was her father. His voice shook as he apologized for disparaging my studies and told me how deeply he now regretted his nineteen-year persecution of Eva and her family. Then he entrusted me with what he called his own "Forty-nine Year Letter," which he asked me to deliver to Eva, sealed and in person, upon the event of his death. He also had me hold the microphone to his lips as he finally told the story he heard on that fateful night. This, I was to deliver into the Smut Story archive on his behalf, if Eva would accept it. He was very ill, and prone to rambling towards the end, so these could simply be the dementia-fuelled inventions of a dying man. Nonetheless, I have delivered—along with the letter and the tape—my own half of the DNA evidence required to verify at least one part of my father's story. The rest is up to Eva.

[18] Take Peter's story, for instance. It has been added to the archive, and you can ask for it by name. I have listened to it several times now, with Eva. Now it's your turn. Take it, listen, and find out for yourself. There is no knowing how it will strike you. You might turn it into a joke. Or dismiss it. But know that for one person at least, if only for a moment, it was true.

Witch I
COURTNEY BATES-HARDY

She doesn't think she wants
children—all that blood
and sleeplessness.

She wonders if it's Disney
that makes her afraid
to lose her waist and tiny feet.

She knows it's selfishness
because the papers tell her
about her need.

She's not enticed by breakable necks
or toothsome skin—
maybe if they came out talking,
she'd let her foot descend,
and rip herself in two.

Hollywood North
MICHAEL LIBLING

Based on a true story (as they say)

1. Jack the Finder, Annie Barker, and Gloomy Gus

Jack Levin was the boy who found things. When he was nine, a meteorite. When he was eleven, a message in a bottle. When he was twelve, a gold ring.

Jack made the front page of the *Trent Record* every time.

LOCAL BOY FINDS METEORITE IN GARDEN

LOCAL BOY FINDS TRAGIC MESSAGE IN BOTTLE

LOCAL BOY FINDS LONG-LOST WEDDING BAND

I was only a year younger than Jack, but even then I was in awe. From the first photo I saw of him, he struck me as heroic, as if he himself had grabbed the comet's tail, hopped aboard, and chiseled out his prize. It might've been his smile, a cryptic quirk suggestive of more daring feats to come. He was squatting, pointing to the spot where the meteorite had been discovered, yet I would've bet you a million the photographer had tied him down to get the shot, Jack's unruly hair a stirring glimpse of anarchy in a town torn between Brylcreem and brush cut.

Look for Rochester on your map and Trenton is about an inch straight up, an aberrant speck of chronic self-deception on the north shore of Lake Ontario.

The Ontario Trenton, not the New Jersey one.

It's popular with boaters, fishermen, and the British Royal Family. Queen Elizabeth has turned up a bunch of times. As a kid, I stood by the roadside and waved to her with the rest of the town and she waved back, though her hand never moved much, like she had a backscratcher up her sleeve.

You might have heard of the town. In 2010, Trenton had a serial killer. The commander of the nearby Air Force Base, no less. A colonel. I'm not kidding. The guy had even piloted the Queen's plane a few times. I'm not kidding about that, either. You can look it up.

A serial killer didn't surprise me, of course. I only wondered what took so long.

These days, the Killer Colonel pretty much sums up what most people know about Trenton and this includes the people who live there. Not that I hold it against them. Nobody knew much in my day, either. And those who did weren't talking.

Every town has its history. Every town has its secrets. Trenton's secret has always been its history.

From the beginning of me, I sensed the town would be the end of me—as if my designated bogeyman had vacated his lair beneath my bed, preferring to lie in wait in less patent territory. I saw neither streets nor avenues, only dead ends and dead endings. While other kids made do with stamps and coins and baseball cards, I collected fears. My worst was that my mother would die and leave me on my own.

"Do you ever feel it?" I once asked Annie Barker. Annie ranked next to my mom in the trust department. It was second grade and I'd never opened my mouth about my creepy worries to anyone. I tended to weigh the pros and cons of everything. I could carry some stuff inside of me for years—the better part of this story a case in point.

"I'm not sure I understand," Annie said, and coaxed me forward in that gentle way of hers.

"You know, like something is going to get you, except you don't know how bad or how soon. And there's nothing you or anybody else can do to stop it. Like whatever's going to happen is going to happen."

"My goodness, no. I do not feel it. No. Not at all. Never." She shook her head with the same forbearance and pity she had reserved for me since kindergarten. I was and would forever be her *special project*. "Oh, my Gloomy

Gus. Can't you see how lucky we are to live here? There are children in Europe who would give their eye teeth to be in our shoes." Annie was into her Debbie Reynolds phase then. Sunshine, positivity, and dimples. Sandra Dee and Hayley Mills and Patty Duke would come later. Whatever. I would not have traded Annie for any of them.

I carried on as before, hopeless, lips sealed, the burden of impending doom mine alone. No way I'd become that *Invasion of the Body Snatchers* guy, racing headlong into traffic, warning the unsuspecting masses as they heaped him with abuse. Screw them. Stupid ingrates. Let them learn the hard way. Not that I was anywhere near clear as to what I'd be warning them about. Or if I'd bother even if I was clear.

The message in the bottle Jack found had come from the *James B. Colgate*, a steamer that had gone down in Lake Erie forty-four years earlier.

jbc 20 Oc 1916
high wind Wave
good By my Gitte
Harald Nordahl

Here, the photo of Jack, the bottle balanced with care upon his palm, two fingers at the neck, made you wonder if poor Harald Nordahl hadn't passed it directly to him, entrusting the Levin boy above all others. Like the dying soldiers of "In Flanders Fields," the poem teachers hammered into us each Remembrance Day.

To you from failing hands we throw
The torch; be yours to hold it high.

I wanted to be Jack. I wanted to be a finder, too. We'd be The Hardy Boys, Frank and Joe. We'd find stuff together. Solve mysteries. Salvage valuable relics. Rescue cute girls from slavering fiends in derelict mansions. Annie could be our Iola Morton.

Jack and I went to the same school. Dufferin Public. I could have told him easy how I felt, but I knew the risks. One ordinary kid declaring fandom to another is a bad idea any way you cut it. It is going to come off as weird. Smart kids nip the inclination in the bud. And I counted myself among them, until the morning my brain turned to Jiffy Pop.

I scoured the playground, locked him in my sights, and charged ahead.

"You're Jack," I said.

"Yeah. I know."

And without additional formality, my three years of self-restraint and meticulously cultivated anonymity went down the toilet in a sycophantic rush of verbal diarrhea. "I just want to say that uh how I think it's really neat how you know how like how you find stuff like me too uh five dollars once outside the A&P uh I'm always looking uh Mommy uh my mom uh she said uh uh." *Mommy.* I'd said *Mommy.* My mastery of the awkward was flawless. *Kill me now.*

His buddies were roaring. I was by far the funniest thing they'd heard and seen since Moe last blinded Curly.

"You got a screw loose or what, kid?"

"Look at that, Jack. You found yourself a little girlfriend."

"You gonna cry? You gonna go tell *Mommy* on us?"

Jack laughed along with them, and man, I hated him right then like I'd never hated anyone. "Is that so?" he said to me, and returned to his friends and their football, jogging long and deep as he signaled for a pass, leaving me behind, alone, and, in retrospect, shielded from further ridicule.

I was never anything more than an average student. But when it came to beating up on myself, I was scholarship material from the get-go. Never took much. A minor setback, the slightest slight, and I'd agonize like nobody's business. On those days, I knew to avoid Annie. She'd only try to cheer me up. Good thing, outside of school, we went our separate ways.

Walking home that afternoon, I was well down the slippery slope, eleven years old and in the throes of shame. *How clueless could I be?* As I came upon my street, I wished what I have wished far too often over the years: I wished I was dead. Jack and his stupid pals, they'd be sorry then. I was working on who else might be sorry, cataloging every best and probationary friend I'd ever discarded or lost, when I heard the footsteps closing in from behind.

"Hey, you. Kid! Wait up. You the Flash or something?"

I did not turn. I did not slow.

"Never mind those guys," Jack said. "They were only pulling your leg."

Poker face. I gave him nothing.

"Well, okay. Good. Glad they didn't get to you. What's your name, anyhow?"

I kept my focus on the straight and narrow, mumbled a miserable and unexpected, "Gus." It was what Annie was calling me by then, the Gloomy implicit; I saw no need to confuse the issue with the truth. Never considered the possibility my secret identity would stick.

"So, you like finding stuff, too, eh?"

I did not so much as drop the hint of a nod.

"Most people think it's about keeping your head down and your eyes open. But if it was that simple, everybody'd be a finder, right? The thing you need to know—listening is as important as looking."

I stopped at my house, searched the sky, surveyed the trees, the grass, the sidewalk.

"Well, okay then, Gus, if that's the way you want it." He mock-punched my arm, roughed up my hair till it was as messy as his own, and took off, his PF Flyers flying.

I didn't put a comb to my hair for days. Thought the look might improve my finding skills, same as Samson's hair had juiced his strength. But then Mom got fed up, hauled me off to Lloyd the Barber. A brush cut, yet, goddamn.

Jack gave the meteorite to Queen's University in Kingston, the message and bottle to Cardiff Mann, Jr., President of the Great Lakes Mariners Historical Association, and the gold wedding band to Mrs. Edna Bruce, the seventy-two-year-old widow who had lost it forty-nine years earlier.

Jack's largesse returned him to the front page every time.

LOCAL BOY DONATES RARE METEORITE

JACK THE FINDER DONATES MESSAGE IN BOTTLE

JACK THE FINDER RETURNS LOST WEDDING BAND

Yeah, Jack the Finder. That's what the *Record* was calling him by then. Bryan McGrath, the reporter who had taken Jack under his wing, had come up with it. People seemed to like it. I know I did.

Queen's put the meteorite on exhibit with a small bronze plaque to credit Jack. You can still see the meteorite in the school's Miller Museum, though the plaque went missing long ago. (I'll get to that soon enough.)

Cardiff Mann, Jr., and the Great Lakes Mariners Historical Association were frauds, of course. The news caused quite the stir.

JACK THE FINDER VICTIMIZED

Jack shrugged it off, expressed confidence Harald Nordahl's legacy would be preserved. "Anyone who'd go to all that bother to steal an old bottle is going to look out for it way better than most."

Edna Bruce offered him five dollars in gratitude for the ring, but Jack declined politely. "I don't find things, exactly," he was quoted as saying. "It's more like things find me."

The Widow Bruce went on to say Jack's gallantry reminded her of her own son. "I pray it doesn't kill him like it did my Murray." Murray Bruce had lied about his age, enlisted in the Canadian Army at fifteen, fell on Juno Beach at eighteen.

I clipped the stories, stowed them flat between the pages of the biggest book I owned, *Richard Halliburton's Complete Book of Marvels*. I guess I thought of Jack and his finds as marvels, too. The book was the last gift my father had given me. Not that he gave it in person. And not that I ever believed the book was intended for me, but rather for the bookshelves in the den with all of Dad's other big books. He was killed at Christmastime in 1955 on his way home from Toronto. He slipped in the bathroom of a Texaco gas station near Oshawa and cracked his head open on the sink. (In my retelling over the years, I tended to alter a detail or two and recount how my dad was blown to smithereens on D-Day alongside the bold and brave Murray Bruce, heedless of the fact I was born six years after the event.)

Mom had found the book among Dad's belongings. There is an inscription inside the front cover:

Xmas 1955
To the best son in the world.
Love you forever and a day,
Daddy

The handwriting is my mother's. I never did tell her I knew. I mean, what kind of dad would write *Love you forever and a day* to a son?

Trenton is the Phantom of the Opera, but with a crappier mask and deeper scars. Fires have exacted a heavy toll. Huge, catastrophic fires. Too many in too many years to count.

Rip-roaring blazes on the outskirts and into the heart of downtown.

Walk the main street and you'll see. There's a charmless, slapped-together look to it all. You can't help but wonder if public tenders are extended only to builders schooled on LEGO, and then awarded free rein to masturbate in brick, aluminum, and plastic. Aesthetics. Zoning. Heritage protection. Afterthoughts, at best. Then again, what's the point in sprucing up tinder?

While I was happy Jack had tried to set things right with me after my schoolyard meltdown, we did not become what you'd call friends right off. We'd nod in passing and such, but not much else. Mostly, I kept to myself with renewed determination, refining my lone-wolf persona: the gun-shunning sheriff with a violent past; strong, silent, in need of nothing, nobody, nowhere, no time. A solitary life is a safe life.

It was during this stretch, twice a month on my mother's paydays, she began to splurge on burgers and pie at the Levin family's restaurant, though neither Jack nor I let on we knew each other. That'd be all we needed, grown-ups involved.

Bert and Mollie Levin's Marquee Café stood at the corner of Dundas and Division, next to the Odeon Theatre. It was a cubbyhole diner, four tables, ten seats at the counter, and bins and racks that flowed and spilled with chocolate bars, chewing gum, and penny candy—enough to trip up even Hansel and Gretel.

If Jack wasn't minding the cash or washing dishes, he'd be on a stool at the counter. Inevitably, some customer would be bending his ear. Older people loved talking to Jack. He had a knack for listening, grinning or grim-faced as the drift required.

When Jack and I got around to talking at any length, it was more happenstance than circumstance, a matter of finding ourselves on the same side of the street after school and heading in the same direction. We fell into an easy routine. "Best movie ever?" Jack would say.

"*The 7th Voyage of Sinbad*," I'd tell him, and we'd be off and running.

"Best scary movie?"

"*Horrors of the Black Museum* . . . you know, when that girl looks into those binoculars and the spikes shoot into her eyes . . ."

"Space movie?"

"*It! The Terror from Beyond Space*."

"Better than *Forbidden Planet*? C'mon, Gus!"

"The robot was good, but the rest was so boring."

"Red licorice or black?"

"Black."

"Rin Tin Tin or Lassie?"

"Mr. Peabody."

"You kill me, Gus. You kill me."

"*Sick, Cracked* or *Mad*?"

"Anyone ever tell you how much you look like Alfred E. Neuman?"

Only after establishing our cultural parameters did we up the ante. "Those people in the restaurant—the ones you're always talking to—what's that about?"

"I don't just find things," Jack said, "I *find out* things."

"What's that supposed to mean?"

"I dunno. A gallon of paint covers four hundred square feet of wall?"

"Who cares?"

"Mr. Fox, he paints houses. He likes to talk about paint."

"Yawn."

"You remember Mrs. Gibbons? Used to teach third grade?"

"Fat and mean, right? Glad I never got her."

"When she was a kid, she built her own soapbox, but they wouldn't let girls enter the derby back then. So she dressed up as a boy—pretended to be her own brother—and won the whole thing."

"She was a kid once?"

"There's a lot of bad stuff, too. People love telling me the bad stuff most of all. Did you know there used to be this big plant down by the river that made bombs and bullets and stuff . . . ? The whole thing blew up in 1918. Took out half the town."

"Jeez."

"That's only the tip of it. Ever hear of the Walker Shoe Factory? Winter of '27, roof got weighted down with snow and caved in. A bunch of people died. Another time, these two planes flying over town crashed into each other. Bodies fell out of the sky and everything. And another time, this circus came to town and the big top caught fire—"

"Yeah. And what? Lions and tigers got loose and ate people? I saw that movie."

"Hey, I don't care if you believe me or not. I'm only telling you what people told me. You were born when—1950, Gus? This school bus coming down King loses its brakes and crashes into a train passing through at Division. Dead kids everywhere."

"Jesus."

"I know."

"You're creeping me out."

"Tell me about it. Half the time, I don't want to listen. But it's like they *need* me to know. Since the newspaper started writing about me, you'd think I was their best friend. Weird, eh?"

"Yeah. Weird." I hoped he wouldn't realize I'd begun to think of him as my best friend, too, by then. "And it's all true? You sure?"

"Some of the stuff people tell me is just plain nuts. But not all. My mom and dad remembered something about the school bus. So then I asked Mr. McGrath, that reporter over at the *Record*. If anybody would know, it's him. He laughed, said he wouldn't have a job if bad stuff didn't happen. 'More the better.' But then he got all serious, warned me to take whatever the old coots say with a big grain of salt or I'd end up as loony as them."

"Jack, if I tell you something, you promise not to laugh?"

"Not unless it's a joke."

"Since I was little, I've had this bad feeling—"

"I know. I know. Like something's going to get you and there's nothing you can do to stop it. You know *The Twilight Zone* is about Trenton, don't you?"

"What?"

"*The Twilight Zone*. The show's about Trenton."

"You're lying."

"Rod Serling, he's from Syracuse or Rochester or someplace." Jack pointed in the direction of Lake Ontario. "He's been here a bunch of times, comes across on his cabin cruiser. I saw him a couple of years ago."

"You saw him?"

"Honest to God. At the dock."

"And you talked to him?"

"Sort of."

"What? How?"

"Well, I guess I mostly just said, 'Are you Rod Serling?'"

"What'd he say? What'd he say?"

"'Last time I looked, son.'"

"And?"

"That's it."

"Did he know who you were? Did you tell him you were Jack the Finder? Wow! What if he does a *Twilight Zone* about you?"

"I'm just trying to tell you, Gus, he knows the town. And I bet you anything he's gotten a bunch of his ideas right here. Watch the show, you'll see. It's practically a documentary."

Drowning is another Trenton favourite. Only hunting, fishing, and arson rank higher among local pastimes.

Everybody knows somebody who has drowned.

I know four.

Susan Burgess's little brother was my first. He chased a beach ball into Lake Ontario and the ball came back without him.

Dottie Swartz was my second. She worked up at the Unemployment Insurance Offices with my mom. She took a header off Dam #1 into the Trent-Severn. She'd been fishing with her husband, Helmet. They'd been married just a couple of months. He tried to save her, had the injuries to prove it. Wore a bandage the size of a sleeping bag for weeks. Even so, people talked. "Do you think Helmet pushed Dottie into the water?" I asked my mother.

"All that matters now is what people want to believe," she said. She'd go all teary-eyed at the memory of Dottie.

"But do you believe it, Mom?"

"The more you get to know a person, dear, the more you find to dislike, I'm afraid."

Later, I'd come to see Mom's theory worked in other ways.

The more people got to know me . . .

The more I got to know myself.

While I saw Jack's adventures as something to aspire to, his buddies had a different take. With every Jack the Finder story in the *Record*, his circle had grown smaller. Soon, there was no circle.

"Who crowned you King Shit, Levin?"

"My dad said you're gettin' too big for your britches."

"Hey, Jackass! You're so full of yourself, you're gonna puke your insides out."

Most damning, they branded him teacher's pet. He was, of course. Had no say in the matter. It's what teachers do best, paint targets on the bright and industrious, turn them into victims.

It was something to see how Jack held his own, stared down the bullies, looked through the turncoats. He wasn't the biggest kid around, not by a long shot, though he was plenty solid and not averse to shoving back. He had this Audie Murphy sort of presence, like in *Destry*. Kill 'em with kindness. Let nothing faze you till it fazes you. *Then blammo!* Me, in his shoes, I would've handed in my badge, let the bad guys run the town.

I gave Jack credit. I knew how hard it was, the effort required, pretending you don't give two shits when the whole time you surely do.

I also knew what it was like to see friends bail. Unlike Jack, I deserved most of what I got. More than once, Annie Barker had tried to set me straight. "You're too sensitive, too unforgiving. No one is perfect. You need to give people a chance." Besides my mother, Annie remained my one constant. She put up with me no matter how undeserving I was.

It may not sound like it from what I've told you thus far, but I think of Annie as often as I do Jack. How can I not?

Admittedly, Jack's loss was my gain. The more his pals froze him out, the more he warmed to me. By fifth grade, he came to be on my side of the street most every day, and the walks home took longer and longer.

No one would ever go so far as to characterize Gloomy Gus a conversationalist, but I was with Jack, I tell you.

He shared my sense of doom, of course, every local accident and disaster logged cerebral confirmation of worse things to come.

It helped that we were both into *Ripley's Believe It or Not*, though it was my casual mention of Elsie Hix and Charles Fort that cemented my potential as a viable sidekick. I'd wager we debated the merits of every unexplained mystery and phenomenon known to man.

The *Mary Celeste*.

The Abominable Snowman.

Death by spontaneous combustion.

The Loch Ness Monster.

Lost worlds. Atlantis. Lemuria. Mu.

Houdini's secrets, which according to page 129 of my *Reader's Digest Junior Omnibus*, all would be revealed on April 6, 1974. "I hope I'm still alive," I said. "I hope I am, too," Jack said.

The Nazca Lines of Peru.

Stonehenge.

And Oak Island, the Nova Scotia treasure pit alleged to have been engineered by Captain Kidd himself. It spooked me like no other, instilled a lifelong fear of being buried alive. In quicksand. In a landslide. In a coffin. In my lies.

"I wouldn't hold my breath on that one," Jack said. "They won't find anything on Oak Island till it wants to be found."

His certainty could be so damn aggravating. "Things don't *want* to be found," I said. "They *get* found."

"If that's what you want to think. But I'm telling you, when something is lost, it lets you know when it's ready to be discovered. Like hide-and-seek, when you're still under the bed an hour in, you sure as heck want to be found, right? You show yourself. You catch an eye. You make noise. Like that."

"Is that why you stopped finding things?" I said. "Because nothing's ready?"

"I still find stuff. I just don't talk about it."

"But you were in the newspaper—"

"And a lot of good it did me. Seen my friends lately?"

"Only me," I said quietly.

When Jack finally came around, let me in on his unpublicized finds, it was on the understanding I'd keep the knowledge to myself. Who would I tell, anyhow? *Jeez, who'd be interested?* An Indian arrowhead. The brass hand from an old clock. A rusted tin of Shawmut Seidlitz Powders, whatever the heck that was. None of it was anywhere near the meteorite or message in the bottle.

It wasn't until a Monday afternoon in an unseasonably mild October that Jack the Finder finally rode again.

2. How to Be a Worthy Sidekick

Jack hadn't said diddly-squat since we'd left the school grounds. We were a couple of blocks along before I asked what was up. He carried on in silence for another stretch, then spun to face me. "Remember when I told you I don't just find things, but *find out* things?"

"Like half the town blowing up? Kids getting creamed on school buses?"

"Finding out things is how I usually come to find things."

Some of the stuff he said required more thinking than I had patience for. My fallback face was nothing but attentive, while my brain was happy to settle for the gist.

"Tell me, Gus, you ever hear something so crazy, you put it out of your head without a second thought? And then, later on, could be weeks or months, something happens that puts the crazy thought right back?"

The slack in my jaw would've done a Morlock proud. I hadn't a clue where he was headed.

"You know Sure Press Dry Cleaners on Front Street? Mr. Blackhurst?"

"The bald guy with the bushy eyebrows, hairy ears? My mom goes there."

"Eight, nine months ago, he traps me in the Marquee, talks my head off. He's going on about nothing and everything, then out of the blue he tells me he used to be in pictures and his wife was an actress and they made movies—get this, man!—right here in Trenton. In a big studio near Hanna Park."

"Home movies, maybe."

"Yeah, I know. Totally loony. And then he says, back in the day, they called the town Hollywood North."

"Hey! Look! Marilyn Monroe just drove by."

"Thing is, Gus, Mr. Blackhurst might not be so nutty."

Coast clear, Jack prodded me from the sidewalk, led me beyond the reach of prying eyes to a thicket of cedars.

He paused, gave me an unexpected once-over, as if my fidelity might be in question. With a here-goes-nothing shrug, he pulled four large cards from his canvas schoolbag. Each was about the size of a shirt cardboard.

He revealed them one by one.

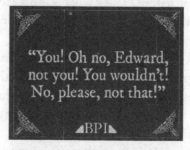

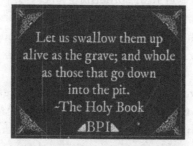

"Neat! They're like what you see in old-time movies," I said.

"I thought of Mr. Blackhurst, second I saw them."

"How? Where?"

"Hanna Park, you know, the swampy part, by the railway tracks."

"I've been there a zillion times."

"That's how it is with lost crap. Once it's made itself known, you wonder how you ever missed it. This old metal box was just sitting there, under leaves and deadwood, but not like anybody couldn't see it. It's rusty and all, but the cards inside—every one, as good as these. Forty-seven of them."

"You're gonna be in the paper again, Jack. You gotta be."

"Not me, Gus. You."

"Huh?"

"I need you to pretend you found them."

"That's crazy."

"It'll be easier, that's all."

"Because you don't want to lose any more friends. And you figure I don't have any to lose. Is that it?"

"Hey, c'mon. You know I'm not like that."

"The more you get to know a person—"

"Look, my mom and dad aren't getting along so well, okay? They're fighting a lot or whatever, and me finding something just now, making a big deal about it, well . . . I mean, my sisters and all, nobody needs me doing that. I'd feel like a jerk. Like all I cared about was me or something. You'll be helping me out."

"It'd be lying."

"You're good at that."

"C'mon—"

"It'll be fun, Gus. You'll be a hero. It's what you've always wanted, isn't it?"

"Why not wait till your parents aren't fighting? Tell everybody about the cards then."

"Yeah. Sure. If I had fifty years, maybe."

"I dunno, Jack."

"Imagine how your mom will feel, seeing you in the paper and all. Think about it, Gus. Bet she'd be real proud."

"What do I have to do?"

"Just swear you'll keep it to yourself. You can't tell anybody it was me, ever."

"Okay. Fine."

"Swear to God."

"I swear to God."

"Swear on your mother's life."

"C'mon, Jack. What's the big—"

"Forget it then."

"No. Wait. Stop. I swear." I mumbled a wobbly, "On my mother's life."

"Don't you forget."

I nodded with vigor. Proving myself a worthy sidekick could be exhausting. A never-ending audition.

I mentioned I know four people who have drowned. I told you about Susan Burgess's little brother and my mom's friend, Dottie Swartz.

Jack and Annie, they're the other two.

3. The Villain, the Old Gent, and the Femme Fatale

The *Trent Record* building was no *Daily Planet* and, his horn-rimmed glasses aside, Bryan McGrath was no Clark Kent.

Hatrack tall and coat-hanger thin, the senior reporter looked nothing like the headshot that ran with his hunting and fishing column; he was a good twenty years older, his hair grayer, eyes beadier, mouth meaner. He wasn't anybody I'd ever want to go hunting or fishing with. Still, he came across friendly enough, slapped Jack on the back and glad-handed me just short of paralysis. Yeah, he was all smiles and chuckles, until I gave him a glimpse of the old-time-movie cards *I'd found*. (You can be sure I'd practiced the line plenty.) Jesus, you'd think he was goddamn freaking Dracula and I'd just pulled a crucifix on him.

He shut the door to his office, rolled ink-stained shirtsleeves to scabby elbows, lit a cigarette, glanced at Jack, inhaled, scowled at me, exhaled, contemplated the floor, inhaled, exhaled, picked tobacco from his tongue, stared out the window, inhaled, marched me up against the wall, plowed his forearm hard across my chest, and exhaled into my face. "Where did you get these?" I felt myself grow weak and inconsequential, *The Incredible Shrinking Man* astray in the cellar, fresh meat for the resident black widow.

The heat of his cigarette scorched my cheek. Another inch and he'd have set my left eyebrow on fire. If only I hadn't sworn on my mother's life.

Jack came to my rescue. "Nobody gave them to him," he said. "He found them. Hanna Park. Right, Gus?"

I blinked frantic confirmation.

McGrath gritted his teeth, waited a beat, and backed off. "Who else has seen them?"

"What's going on?" Jack said.

McGrath cleared two overtaxed ashtrays from a corner of his desk and sat. He took a long, thoughtful drag of his cigarette, examined the length of ash at the tip.

I slunk toward the door, begged Jack to heed my telepathic plea to follow.

"Sir?" Jack said. "Mr. McGrath?"

And as if all this wasn't cuckoo enough, McGrath chose that moment to regale us with poetry, his delivery hoarse and laden with menace. "'There are strange things done in the midnight sun by the men who moil for gold; And the Arctic trails have their secret tales that would make your blood run cold. . . .'"

"Pardon?" Jack said.

"It's 'The Cremation of Sam McGee,'" I whispered. "Robert Service." It was the only poetry I liked, outside of "Casey at the Bat."

"Jesus H. Christ! Can't you see I'm speaking metaphorically, trying to make a point here, boys?" McGrath stubbed out his cigarette, crumbled the unfiltered butt between thumb and forefinger. He rose from his perch. "Not a place on Earth doesn't have its secret tales. Given time, not a place you'd go that wouldn't make your blood run cold. This town . . . I'm telling you, this find of yours, let it go. Trust me. For your own good."

"But they used to make movies here, right? And these cards are from back then, right?" Damn that Jack. The idiot didn't know when to quit.

"Who told you that, Levin?"

"Nobody. I just heard."

"You need to stop now. Cease. Desist. Shut the hell up. Some shit deserves explaining. Some shit doesn't. Explanations won't change a thing. Sometimes there is no explaining." Again, McGrath took aim at me. "The intertitles— that the lot of 'em?"

"What?" I'd yet to get my head around his poetry.

"The cards? How many you got?"

"What was it you told me, Gus?" Jack maintained the sham. "Forty-something?"

McGrath switched it up, a yellow finger, locked, loaded, and between my eyes. "Listen and listen well. You're gonna pack 'em up. You're gonna take 'em home. And you're gonna burn every last one. All forty-something. You read me?"

"Yes," I said.

And there was Jack, mouthing off again. "That's not fair."

"And you, Levin—you're gonna help your little pal, make sure it gets done right. Understand? And then the two of you are gonna forget you ever saw 'em or that we ever talked about 'em."

"But why?"

"But but but. But but but . . . I'm warning you, Levin—you and Silent Sam here—you need to stop finding shit. You have no idea the damage you can do. You love your folks? Your mother, your father? Do you, boys? You love your brothers and sisters? Your puppy dog? Your parakeet? Please, do what I'm telling you. Because it'd be a crying shame otherwise if you brought anything bad upon any one of them. I'd hate to see it and I know you would, too. We on the same page? You do what I'm telling you. Agreed?"

He offered his hand and we shook in turn. McGrath winked, promised he'd be watching, then burst out laughing, told me I had the handshake of a dead fish.

"Jesus, Jack, why'd you make me lie? Now he thinks—"

"You wanted to be a finder, didn't you?"

"We need to kill him."

"What are you talking about?"

"Before he kills my mom. We need to kill him." Scaredy-cats are nothing if not practical.

"He's not going to kill anybody. And neither are we. Can't you see, he's just trying to scare us? Hell, the look on his face when he saw the cards? He wouldn't even touch them. He was more frightened than you, Gus."

"Frightened of what? Cardboard?"

"I haven't the foggiest, but I know where we can find out—where we should've gone first."

"We've got to burn them, Jack. What he said—"

"Adults say all sorts of dumb shit. Spend five minutes on a stool in the Marquee. The day you see me doing everything I'm told is the day the brain eaters get me."

"Jesus, Jack."

"I mean it."

"I'm afraid."

"Me, too. But it's a whole lot better than being bored."

As we made our way from the *Record* to Front Street, I applied all I had learned from *The Hardy Boys' Detective Handbook* and the chapter on shaking off tails. "You're crazy." Jack laughed. "Relax. No one is following us." But he stuck to my roundabout route, the sudden turns and about-faces, and we reached the dry cleaners without picking up any suspicious types. Far as we knew, anyhow.

Mr. Blackhurst was twisting the OPEN sign to CLOSED as Jack rapped on the window, and the old guy let us in.

I showed him the cards and, well, you might have thought a cherished, old friend had dropped in to reminisce. His caterpillar eyebrows arched with devious glee. Slowly, reverently, he reached out and lifted the cards from my hands.

"Sir?" Jack said. "You know what these are?"

"Intertitles," Mr. Blackhurst said, more to himself than to us, his British accent thicker than I'd remembered. "Never did I expect to touch the likes of these again."

"My friend found them." Jack urged me forward, his hand at my back, and I shot him a dirty look.

"Ah, this one. I so fondly remember this one," Blackhurst said. Jack and I moved to either side for a better view.

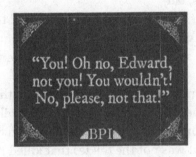

"You! Oh no, Edward, not you! You wouldn't! No, please, not that!"

BPI

"I wrote it myself for *The Black Ace*. Nary an iota of graphic violence, yet you should have heard the audiences scream." He shut his eyes, savoured the memory. "Wholly terrorized, chilled to the marrow, they were. It was marvelous. My magnum opus. Yet it was the infinitely inferior *The Lodger* that won the accolades. How unjust is that! And only recently, Hitchcock, you know, the man is shameless—the shower sequence in *Psycho*, stolen frame for frame from *Black Ace*. The scoundrel thought no one would know, thought sufficient time had elapsed. But I know. *We* know."

"And this down here?" Jack said, indicating the logo.

"Blackhurst Pictures International. My production company. Alas, as ill-fated and lamented as the others—Canadian National Features, Adanac, Pan American Films . . ."

"So it's true, then, what you told me—they did make movies here," Jack said, and my excitement was every bit as palpable as his.

"Hollywood North, right, Mr. Blackhurst?" I said, eager now to play a featured role. "I found them. It was me who found the intertitles. I've got a bunch of them."

"Thing is," Jack said, "Mr. McGrath, over at the *Record*, he told us we needed to burn them. Why would he—"

"I beg your pardon? McGrath? Bryan McGrath?"

"It was like he was scared of them."

"It was really, really weird," I said.

"McGrath, the great saviour. Why in Heaven's almighty name would you share a find of this magnitude with the likes of him? A more egregious overreactor I have never known. Burn them? Quintessential McGrath. A nervous Nellie of the first order. A mediocre and malodorous screen scribe transmogrified to mephitic muckraker. Your intertitles are but memories of a bygone era. The man's worries are woefully misplaced."

"So there *is* something to fear then, sir?" Jack said.

"Isn't there always, lad?"

"You're telling me," I said with a laugh, committed to enjoying this new, enthusiastic version of me for as long as I could maintain it.

"Can we see the movies?" Jack asked. "Is there a place? Do you have them?"

"Norman." We turned to the rear of the shop and the voice of a woman.

Mr. Blackhurst was quick to draw us back. "She will tell me I have said too much. Alas, to you, it will appear that I have said too little. No matter what you may hear, it was not the talkies that killed Hollywood North, it was the fear."

"That's enough, Norman. Please."

He winked at me. At Jack. And aged ten years in ten seconds. The cards sailed to the floor and half his brain, too, apparently. His expression went from blank to black, Dr. Jekyll awakening to find Mr. Hyde's bloody cane in his hands.

"Sir?" Jack said, but the man had gone full zombie on us. In dull retreat he dragged his feet and exited behind a curtain of cleaning. Quite the performance.

I dropped to my knees to gather up the cards. Jack skirted the counter in pursuit.

"Let him be," the woman said, gentle, then assertive: "Let him be."

I rose gingerly to my feet. *Holy cow. And wow!*

She stood square with Jack, ravishing and resolute, a vision to behold in black silk and pearls, with raven curls that fell softly to slight shoulders.

She was Helen of Troy relocated to a dry-cleaning shop in Trenton, Ontario, Canada. A cruel twist of Fate, for sure, even without the lousy winter weather.

Jack edged away. *I'd never seen him anywhere near flustered before.* His footsteps were jittery in keeping with his stammer. "You must be Mr. Blackhurst's daughter . . . uh . . . um . . . wife . . . uh . . . daughter . . . uh . . . jeez, I'm sorry, Miss, Missus, Ma'am, Missus, Ma'am, Miss . . ."

She was either the youngest old person I had ever seen or the oldest young person. All I knew for certain, the lady was way too pretty for this town. She was nobody's mother, nobody's sister.

"Excuse me." I raised a hand, thinking this an opportune moment to impress. "Did Mr. Blackhurst tell you? It was me. I'm the one who found them, aren't I, Jack?"

She folded her arms, slender fingers and scarlet nails extended to opposing shoulders, and lifted her chin in expectation. *The expectation we would leave.*

And those blue eyes of hers, goddamn, way bluer than any blue was ever meant to be.

We did not want to leave. We wanted only to stare.

She observed us with growing impatience, bending us to her unspoken will. And those heels of hers, goddamn, they must have run halfway to Heaven.

Poor Jack and me, thirteen and twelve, mere novices on the front lines of puberty. And those red lips of hers, goddamn, way redder than any red was ever meant to be. I could hardly breathe.

"She's like a movie star," I said.

"My dad's expecting me at the restaurant," Jack said.

4. An Unexplained Mystery to Call Our Own

"Did you know they used to make movies in Trenton?"

Mom stifled a giggle.

"Mr. Blackhurst said so."

"From the cleaners?"

"Yeah. I met his wife, too."

"He's not a widower?"

"I don't know. His daughter, then . . ."

"I didn't think he had anyone. When was this, exactly?"

"Um, just before. Uh, on the street."

"You know you shouldn't talk to strangers."

"It's not like I never went to the cleaners with you."

"Well, from what I know, he's a rather odd old man who likes to make up stories."

"You're saying it's not true?"

"My goodness, dear, I don't know if it is or not. It does sound somewhat far-fetched, however. If it were anything more, we would have heard, don't you think?" She was humouring me, her grin on standby at the corners of her mouth. I hated when she did that. "You need to respect old people, but to believe everything they say . . ."

Jack and I waited till Saturday morning when my mom was at the A&P and his parents were at the restaurant to make our next move. We secured the cards beneath the false bottoms of two board games, Risk and Concentration, and smuggled them from Jack's bedroom to my house.

We pushed back the coffee table and sofa and spread the lot across the living-room floor, singling out the most intriguing as we went.

We reordered the cards, laid them out every which way. Read each aloud, two, three, four times. But try as we might, we could find no red flags to justify why McGrath went psycho or why the Blackhursts had circled the wagons. Two hours in, we admitted defeat.

"Wish we could see the movies," I said.

"Till then, looks like we've got our own unexplained mystery, Gus."

We buried the cards among the books of my father's library. I slipped the last between Lithuania and Luxembourg, in the brittle pages of a Hammond World Atlas.

"Pull up! Pull up!
Good God, ol' chap,
pull up!"

BPI

"You sure your mom won't find them?" Jack said.

"My dad was the reader."

"A big one, too, from the looks of it."

"He died in the War. On Juno Beach."

"Wow. Like Mrs. Bruce's son. You know, the old lady whose wedding ring I found?"

"My dad and him were friends," I said.

The Thursday after Jack and I had hidden the cards, Mom and I were doing a payday dinner at the Marquee. I'd just pulled the toothpick from the first quarter of my turkey club when Jack gave me this anxious look and the front door sprung open.

McGrath hailed Jack's dad as only a café regular can. "What's cookin', Bert?"

Mr. Levin fired back from his post at the grill: "What's the scoop, Mac?"

"Five cents and you can read it in tomorrow's *Record*." McGrath chuckled and settled in at the table by the window, as if he owned the damn joint.

He summoned Jack with a curt two-finger wave and the grizzled spectre of Robert Service reared its head once more, the lines reeling ominously through my mind: *When out of the night, which was fifty below, and into the din and the glare, There stumbled a miner fresh from the creeks, dog-dirty, and loaded for bear.*

Mom was talking, asking me about school, yammering on about her day at work, her breakfast, her coffee break, her lunch, her coworkers, and this wonderful article she'd read in *Reader's Digest*, but my focus was Jack and the reporter. Not that I could hear anything. I had to wait for Jack to fill in the blanks.

"You talked to Norman Blackhurst."

"I brought my dad's shirts in for cleaning."

"Don't lie to me."

"I'm not."

"What did he tell you?"

"Thursday. He'd have the shirts on Thursday."

"You think I'm an idiot?"

"I'm not thinking anything."

"That man, he's not right in his head. He imagines things. Hallucinates. Makes stuff up. You best forget whatever it was he might have told you."

"But my dad already picked up the shirts."

"Now you're a comedian, eh? You disappoint me, Jack."

"What is it you think he told me?"

"Ha! You're good, kid, I'll grant you that. You and your pal take care of that business we discussed?"

"I can show you the ashes." Days earlier, Jack and I had incinerated a bundle of cardboard. The ashes awaited McGrath's inspection, stowed in a Kit Kat carton on a shelf in Jack's garage.

"The lot of 'em? Neither of you tempted to keep a souvenir?"

"Swear to God," Jack said. He crossed his legs at the ankles to ensure God's forgiveness for implicating Him in the lie.

McGrath clicked his tongue like he'd just cocked a six-shooter. "Always knew you were a bright boy."

And for no reason he could explain, Jack cracked: "I know about Hollywood North, the movies. Why's it so secret?"

"Blackhurst. I knew it." McGrath's mouth withered dry and small. "Demented old fuck." The sinews of his neck skewered his skull. He dragged his eyeglasses down the length of his nose, folded them into his shirt pocket. He was shaking, his voice squeaky tight, his every word a hardened turd: "How 'bout you fix me a nice slice of your mom's apple pie? A wedge of cheddar. Cup of joe. Black. Three sugars."

Jack did as asked, and as he set the pie and coffee onto the table, the reporter clamped wiry fingers around his wrist and from behind the cover of a Karloff grin he said, "Let's you and I go hunting one of these days. I'll set it up with your dad. I got this elephant gun—what a beaut! Same weapon Frank Buck favoured. You know Frank Buck, don't you? Big-game hunter. Crack shot. Ice water in his veins. Could take down a rabid rhino at twenty paces and never break a sweat."

"I don't know what you want me to say."

"Look. A person digs up the past, next he knows—no future." He let the message sit. "You love this town, Jack?"

"What?"

"Trenton? Do you love it?"

"Yeah. Sure. It's okay."

"I'm on your side, son. I see kids playing with dynamite, I take away the matches. You need to understand: sometimes the truth is less credible than the lie. You let it out of the bag and they stick you in a straitjacket. Am I making myself clear?"

"Maybe. I guess. I don't know."

"I am telling you for the last time, stop before you're sorry. And, believe me, you don't know what sorry is."

McGrath lightened his grip. Jack reclaimed his hand, fetched the man a refill on his coffee, and retreated.

He secluded himself at the sink, washed up a storm of dishes. Glanced over once. Caught my eye. Mouthed: "Oh. Shit."

McGrath polished off his pie, smoked, nursed his coffee, kibitzed with Bert and fellow regulars. *Everyone knew Bryan McGrath. McGrath was a good guy.*

My stomach made a break for my throat. I sensed he might be waiting for Mom and me to finish up, only to follow us home and finish *us* off. We were getting to our desserts when he stood to leave.

McGrath ambled to the door, humming as he circled behind me. I figured I was in the clear, but then he turned 180, pulled a spazzy double-take. "Hey, I know you."

I bowed my head, excavated the Suez across the top of my chocolate pudding. But good ol' Mom, she would not stand for that: "Don't be rude. Mr. McGrath is speaking to you. He writes for the newspaper, you know?"

My head weighed a ton, the hydraulics frozen.

"I do indeed, ma'am. But your son . . . Am I right? Aren't you the boy who's friends with that nice little girl—what's her name?—Annie, is it? Annie Barker? I know her family well. Dad owns the lumber yard out on Wooler Road. Gone hunting with him once or twice. Fine people. Sweet girl. You be sure to say *hello* for me next time you see her, will ya?"

Annie went under first. Then Jack.

Memories may be faulty hereabouts, but I pray to God there are some who remember Jack and Annie.

I hope to God no one remembers me.

So far, so good. I keep my visits short. Take in a movie or two. Quick in, quick out.

After McGrath's second round of threats, Jack and I didn't talk much about the cards or Hollywood North. And not at all after Jack found the reporter snooping in his garage, sifting through the ashes in the Kit Kat carton.

We avoided going to the cleaners. When Mr. Blackhurst would show up at the Marquee, Jack was quick to make himself busy.

I was tempted, now and then, to pull a card from the bookshelves, pictured myself rejoicing in a moment of *Eureka!*, and rushing up Henry Street to bring Jack the thrilling news. But then I'd also picture McGrath hunting me down, strapping my carcass, bled and dressed, to the hood of his truck. Or Annie's carcass. Or Blackhurst's. Or my mother's.

The dynamics of our walk-and-talks changed, too. For starters, we invited Annie to come along. Annie and Jack operated in separate spheres and I had made it my mission to keep it so: Annie, my in-school friend; Jack, my after-school. But should McGrath intend to do Annie harm, Jack and I agreed it would not happen on our watch. It was the least we could do.

We did not tell Annie why, of course. She thought we were nuts, seeing how she lived up in the Heights, blocks out of our way. She had her friends to consider, too, though they branched off early along her route. Mostly, she confided to me, she was wary of the famous Jack the Finder. "He's pretty full of himself, I hear."

"Gee," I said. "Does that mean I should believe what everybody says about you?" She didn't need to know I'd never heard a mean word about her.

Naturally, Annie and Jack hit it off.

As for Robert Ripley, Elsie Hix, and company, our enthusiasm for their chronicles of the unexplained was no longer what it had been. We withdrew to safer ground.

"Best superhero?"

"J'onn J'onnz, Martian Manhunter."

"What?"

"You heard me."

"You're kidding?"

"Who then? Superman?"

"Herbie Popnecker."

"Who?"

"*Forbidden Worlds*. The tubby kid with the glasses? The lollipop? He's at least as good as your dumb Martian Manhunter."

"Not to me."

"*Famous Monsters of Filmland* or *Screen Thrills Illustrated*?"

"*Find the Feathered Serpent*—you ever read that book?"

"Hot dog or hamburger?"

"Hot dog."

"Larry, Moe, or Curly?"

"Shemp."

"He's dead. So is Costello."

"Abbott and Costello's Costello?"

"Yup. Hardy, too."

"The fat one?"

"Sorry."

"Curly then, I guess. The old Curly, not the new Curly."

At first, Annie only listened as Jack and I dazzled with our profound knowledge and extraordinary taste. Soon she brought her own spin to our game, giggling her head off with *Best Paul Anka song?* or *Hollywood's most handsome?* or *Best Elvis movie?* or *Beehive, bun, or ponytail?* as Jack and I drew sputtered blanks. And no, we didn't mind for a second. "You guys are a riot," she'd say, and in my head I'd hear my plaintive reply, "I love you, too, Annie Barker. So goddamn much."

We kept it going until June of 1963.

The 20th. A Thursday. The day Jack Levin disappeared.

5. Gloomier Gus

"His parents split up," Annie said.

"Like a divorce?" I hoped she wouldn't pick up on my disappointment. I'd expected more of Jack, a vanishing to rival the lost colony of Roanoke, for instance. Or the crew of the *Mary Celeste*.

"You didn't know?" she said.

"Of course I did."

She saw right through me. "His mom took him and his sisters to Montreal. They've got family there."

"But he'll be back, right?"

"Maybe. Sometimes. I hope. I mean, his dad is still here, the restaurant and all . . ." She fumbled with her bag, fished out an envelope. "He left you this."

"What is it?"

"Um . . . an envelope? Probably with a message inside?"

"What's it say?"

"Gosh, how should I know?" She grabbed my wrist and slapped the envelope into my palm. "Honestly, Gus, sometimes . . ."

I unfolded the sheets inside, held them close so Annie couldn't see.

The first page was a sprawling whirl of hoops and loops and curlicues—syllables in cartoon clothing.

> *Dear Gus,*
>
> *Put Hollywood North on the back burner. It's going nowhere. My gut tells me we missed the better mystery. Bad stuff and Trenton. It's like thunder and lightning. Except I get stuck at the same question. Why's it so hush-hush? Are people dumb? Is it some kind of amnesia? Or what if it's like in The Time Machine? You know how the Morlocks took care of the Eloi, fed them, gave them clothes, made them think everything was great. Then the Morlocks ate them. What if it's that, Gus? What if everybody here's Eloi? That'd make us Eloi too. Think about it. Keep your head up. Watch your back.*
>
> *Yours truly,*
> *Jack Levin*
>
> *P.S. Here's my list. I keep finding more. I left out the fires and drownings. Everybody knows about them.*

I flipped to the second page.

> *1898 - Grand Trunk train wreck*
> *1918 - Ammo plant blows up*
> *1922 - Tour boat catches fire, flips over in bay*
> *1923 - Foss Brothers Circus catches fire and the grandstand collapses*
> *1927 - Walker Shoe Factory roof caves in*
> *1929 - Scout camp flash flood kills 7*
> *1937 - Planes collide over town*
> *1938 - Mount Pelion landslide crushes 4 houses*
> *1950 - Train hits school bus*

"So?" Annie said. "Nice letter? Happy now?"

I crumpled the pages, buried my fist within my pocket, and held it clenched until I'd made it home. What the hell was I supposed to do with his stupid letter, anyhow? What was I supposed to do now?

The Hardy Boys were dead. Iola Morton, too.

Jack was said to visit his dad on long weekends, but I never saw the jerk, never heard from him.

I wallowed in my bitterness, brooded over how he'd pursued the other mystery on his own. *Should've been* our *mystery*. Who cared, anyhow? Train wrecks. Plane crashes. Dead school kids. *Read a newspaper, why don't you? Watch Huntley and Brinkley.* Bad stuff happened everywhere. And those dumb movie cards—those stupid cards Jack found? He didn't give a crap, anymore? I had news for him. I *never* gave a crap.

Jack the Finder was over and done. Who'd he think he was? Giving Annie the lowdown on his leaving and not me? I'd show him. I'd show her. I didn't need anybody. I proved it, too. Put up a wall, let her protest all she wanted. "You're being silly. C'mon, Gus, please. You don't throw away a friend for no good reason. You know I'm your friend. Your best friend." But my silent treatment won the day. Annie relented: "Nothing more I can do, if that's how you want to be."

It wasn't anywhere near *how I wanted to be*. It was how I was.

Bert Levin and my mom became friendlier after his family dumped him. "Are you and him getting married?" I asked her.

"Mr. Levin is a very nice man, but I am not going to jump from the frying pan into the fire."

If you needed a bite to eat or a few bucks to carry you through, everyone knew you could count on Bert Levin. That was the bone of contention between him and Mollie. Bert gave away whatever profits the Marquee Café managed.

"You can't blame Mrs. Levin for wanting out," Mom said. "No matter how kind Bert is, Mollie played a big part in those earnings. Her pies, my goodness. If they serve apple pie in Heaven, you know it's going to be Mollie Levin's."

I'd been half-listening. "She's dead?" I said. *Had Jack crossed a line? Had McGrath and his elephant gun paid a visit to Montreal? Would my mother be next?*

"What? Mrs. Levin? No. No," Mom said. "I'm sorry, sorry. It's just an expression. Mrs. Levin is fine. Absolutely fine."

I went for broke, figured I'd never have a better chance to put it to her. I'd sought an opening for ages. "When you die, will you promise to contact me from the Beyond, same way Houdini promised Mrs. Houdini?"

A tidal wave of mush swept down on me. "With all my heart, I promise," she said, and held me twenty minutes past uncomfortable.

Anyhow, a lonely widow saddled with a teenage sad sack was right up Bert Levin's do-gooder alley. That's how, come the summer of 1966, I ended up at the town marina.

"His son will be working with you," Mom said. "You remember Jack, the boy who used to find things?"

"I thought he was in Montreal." It was three years since I'd seen him.

"He's coming for the summer."

"I don't want the job," I said.

"Mr. Levin went out of his way for you. Besides, what else have you got to do?"

"I'll find something."

"It's high time you contributed, young man. You're taking the job and that's final."

6. Best Summer Job Ever Until It Wasn't

The Trenton Marina was a weather-beaten slab of mausoleum concrete at the mouth of the Trent-Severn Waterway. No bigger than a softball infield, it was tucked into a corner off the main street, behind a Chinese restaurant and in the shadow of the old swing bridge.

I showed up the first morning intent on keeping mum. I was going to make Jack regret every rotten thing he had or hadn't done to me. I'd make him pay same way I'd made Annie.

Damn that Jack Levin. He strode right up to me, squeezed a shoulder, messed with my hair. "Spider-Man or Fantastic Four?"

I chewed on my tongue, dug in my heels.

"Ginger or Mary Ann?"

I shrugged my finest shrug.

"Leafs or Canadiens?"

All of three seconds and I caved. "Canadiens," I said. Who could blame me? It was what I'd missed the most—Jack and me doing this.

"I'll be damned. I never knew . . . Mighty daring, Gus, a Habs fan this deep in Maple Leafs territory? You got guts, man. I always knew." And just like that, the grudge I'd nurtured for three crappy years began to crumble and I wanted nothing more than for his assertion to be true.

"You just left on me," I said.

"You got my note."

"You told Annie you were going."

"C'mon! My list wasn't better than some corny good-bye?"

"And the times you came back to visit your dad—"

"Once, I swear. Two days. It was my dad who always came to visit us."

"You could've told me to my face. You should've told me. Before Annie, at least."

"What do you want me to say? 'I'm sorry?' Okay, I'm sorry. I thought for sure the list would do."

I shuffled my feet, couldn't get my own sorry out. I owed Annie one, too. A big one.

"So, any luck?"

"Huh?"

"With our mystery?"

"Which one?"

"Take your pick."

"I thought you were done with Hollywood North."

"I was. But now that I'm back . . ."

"McGrath hasn't gone anywhere, you know?"

"He still giving you trouble?"

"I keep out of his way."

"It's different now, Gus. You're bigger, I'm bigger. You're smarter, I'm smarter. Plus, I've got my brown belt in judo."

"That supposed to impress me?"

"Annie says you've been a misery the whole time I've been gone."

"Yeah? When she tell you that?"

"You might as well know, Annie and me, we've been writing letters."

"What, you're boyfriend and girlfriend or something now?"

"You have a problem with that?"

"Not as long as you got your brown belt in Judo," I said, and Jack nearly split a gut. I hadn't meant it as joke. I was mulling who to kill first, him or Annie.

"Hey, take it easy," he said. "I was teasing. Annie and me, we're good friends, same as you and me. Same as I hope you and Annie will be again. What do you say, Gus?" He threw out his hand, left me no choice. I snagged it firmly in mine (consciously unfishy) and we shook, not like we were sixteen and seventeen, but like men—any two of *The Magnificent Seven*.

Except Lee, the crazy weenie. The Robert Vaughn character.

Annie would make her entrance that afternoon at the tiller of a small wooden outboard, puttering in from her parents' cottage near Carrying Place.

I kept my distance, toed the line between preoccupied and uninterested as Jack helped her onto the dock. I hated how she pecked him on the cheek, how her hand lingered in his. But then she spotted me and her Ellie-May smile faded. She made her way toward me, tentative and coy. "Friends?"

My victories have been few and, in their limited wake, any satisfaction fleeting. The hug she gave me remains the best single moment of my life. And as her tears wet my cheek, I convinced myself they meant far more than the measly kiss accorded Jack.

I do not sentimentalize Annie Barker. I do not idealize her. She is the only girl I forever strive to remember as she was in reality and not in my imagination. The catch in her voice. The freedom in her laughter. Her long brown hair, her bangs and ponytail. Her eyes, the displays of happiness and hurt, the anger and forgiving—that look she'd use to put me in my place, to save me from myself. The longing never leaves me. How beautiful she would have been.

The learning curve for the job was low. Good thing, too, because our boss was Clyde Neil. He owned Clyde's Auto Body on Water Street. The Town, after routine elimination of all qualified candidates, had named Clyde wharfinger—a fifty-dollar word for dock manager, coined circa 1545. Not that Clyde did any managing. Five seconds into showing us the ropes, he was sweaty, winded, and ready for a nap, then spent the next two hours downing Cokes, guzzling from his silver flask, chain-smoking Export "A", and guffawing over how much he hated water, how he swam like a tire iron, how he couldn't tell a *yawtch* from a *cata-meringue*, how his folks got vaporized in the big tanker truck smash-up of 1948, how his grandpa dropped the *O'* from O'Neil to speed the spelling, how he wished he'd had a penis that swelled up—and stuck—"*You know, like a collie's. Wouldn't that be the cat's meow!*"—and how he hoped we'd be good boys, wouldn't cause him grief.

Jack cast a knowing glance my way, put it straight to Clyde. "Tanker truck smash-up?"

"That punk Jim Geary, dumb-ass murdering bastard, haulin' for Supertest, comes round the bend out by Marmora . . ." Clyde swallowed hard, his voice tailed off, as if God were in the process of striking him sober.

We saw him only on Fridays after that. He'd wave us over to his pickup and hand us our pay. "Everything on the up and up?" he'd ask, and never once hung round to hear if everything was.

We were on our own from before sunrise to after sunset, seven days a week, and that was fine by us. We'd berth the boats, the ritzy and the dinky, pump gas, haul ice, grill hot dogs, toast up frozen pizza and, when Annie wasn't around, flirt like mad with the girls who'd come sailing in. Jens and Patties and Candies and Sandies and Lauras and Lindas from Rochester and Syracuse and Toronto and Cornwall and Buffalo and Alexandria Bay. And, jeez, the moms, too. Some days we'd swear Ursula Andress herself, curves and white-bikini-hot, had quit on James Bond to hook up with Trenton's boys of summer. "Are you guys brothers?" they'd ask, and Jack and me, we'd smile, no need to clarify.

Fate was with us, too, I tell you. First Monday on the job, Norman Blackhurst showed up—yeah, *the* Norman Blackhurst of Hollywood North fame—and a daily ritual was begun.

Crack of dawn, six days a week, we'd hear the engine sputter to life, the sound carrying to our ears from across the bay. Jack and I would drop whatever we were doing. One of us would throw a hot dog onto the grill while the other headed down to dockside to meet him. Right on schedule, Mr. Blackhurst and *Evie III* would come splashing into view, the nineteen-foot Chris Craft at once elegant and arrogant as it spanked the early morning waters. She was a pampered beauty, that runabout, lacquered mahogany and polished chrome, with red vinyl seats that put shame to leather. If ever a boat was a woman . . . or vice versa.

Mr. Blackhurst didn't seem the type to put on airs but a commodore's cap and ascot would have suited him fine. On land, he could have pulled off jodhpurs, boots, and beret with equal aplomb. The reality, however, never varied: white shirt, paisley tie, suspenders, brown trousers with double pleats and two-inch cuffs.

Safely ashore, the old guy would make his way up to the canteen, his belly providing the necessary momentum. A hot dog was his standing order. "My breakfast chaser," he'd say with a gravelly chuckle, and perhaps a hint of guilt.

Three quick bites and the hot dog was gone. He'd hitch his trousers 'til foiled by overhang and with a snap of his suspenders propel himself in the direction of Front Street and the workday ahead.

If Blackhurst recognized Jack as Bert Levin's boy or me as the kid who had brought him the intertitles, he did not let on. Not a word of movie-making or Hollywood North crossed his lips.

I pushed Jack to go for it. "You got your brown belt. What are you afraid of?"

"The timing has to be right. We don't want to scare him off."

"At this rate, we'll never get any answers."

"I don't see you volunteering, tough guy."

McGrath continued to hold sway, and not just in our heads. The *Record* building was a short hop from the marina and, now and then, we'd catch him watching us. Once, he and Blackhurst crossed paths near the foot of the bridge. Voices were raised. Lots of pointing, hand-waving. But the old man never brought it up and neither did we. McGrath's presence kept our bravado in check. He was Vincent Price skulking in the shadows, Peter Lorre gaily sharpening his shiv. We took it slow with Blackhurst. Until I guess we couldn't help ourselves.

He'd been babbling on about his beloved *Evie III* with the usual rapture, entering the homestretch with another pithy word of advice for Jack and me. "You'll find it makes life infinitely easier, your mistress and your wife having the same name."

Jack jumped in before I'd had a chance to decode the tip. "Evie, she's your wife, sir? The lady we saw in the dry cleaners that day? You remember, right?"

"Evangeline August. My Evie. She had the world at her feet, that girl. Mary Pickford, Lillian Gish—none shone brighter. And to think she gave it all up to be with me."

"She was a movie star, sir?"

"In a borough abustle with simpletons and sycophants, what else would she have been? Good Lord, an extra?"

We hung our heads. "Sorry," Jack said, and I mumbled a version of the same, unclear as to what we were apologizing for.

"You lads, of all people, should know. Does it not take one to know one? From the moment she laid eyes upon you, she had nary an iota of doubt. 'Stars,' she called you. 'Stars.'"

"What?"

"If you have *it*, you have *it*."

"I'm not sure we get *it*, sir," Jack said. I scratched my head in support. "If you could just ex—"

"Dear God, you inform me of this now, the denouement at hand? For Heaven's sake, you have your roles. Am I your wet nurse? Follow the bloody script."

Take away the lunacy that came after and you couldn't beat the first three weeks of that summer. Hanging out with Jack, the give and take. I didn't need to be me, free to hone the fantasy of a better me. *You got guts, man.* That's what Jack had said. *You got guts, man.*

If only.

Jack had a theory as to the nature of Evil, how it manifested itself in vapors, windborne and guided by whim. "When it comes to Trenton," he said, "the vapors tend to linger." I wondered at times if Jack hadn't swiped half the stuff he said from movies and books.

Still, there's no denying something was in the air. The day before, news had come from Chicago, 600 miles to the southwest, that the bodies of eight student nurses had been found, raped and stabbed and strangled in the dorm they shared. It's why the date sticks. July 15, 1966. And while Richard Speck would soon become the first mass killer to set up camp in my consciousness, we had a body of our own to contend with that morning.

"Gonna be a sticky one," Mr. Blackhurst said, noting the sear of the sunrise. He would know, I thought, the way the red filled his face, rose from beneath his knotted tie and buttoned collar.

His spirits lifted at the sight of the hot dog. The toasted bun. The zigzag of mustard. He got right to it, his jaw working to the rhythm of a throaty purr, which is why, when he started hacking, I figured hairball. Jack was more perceptive. "You feeling okay, sir?"

The guy went Wolfman on us. His face obliterated by mouth. A chainsaw cough and a popgun pop. And bun and wiener shot onto his palm in a bloodied wad. He teetered, grim realization dawning, as if done in by sabotage—slivered bamboo or powdered Kryptonite. He braced against me, his flesh as gray and clammy as the concrete underfoot, clutched his armpit, and the life fell out from under him.

It's the one thing they never teach you in school, what to do with a dead body.

Jack ran to the Marquee to tell his dad.

All I could think was how the hot dog was the last one Mr. Blackhurst would ever eat. I kicked the slimy wad onto the crabgrass, ducked as a seagull swooped in to claim it. Wondered if I'd know when it came down to my last hot dog.

They were wheeling the stretcher into the rear of the ambulance when McGrath turned up. He peeled back the sheet for a quick I.D., snapped a photo, asked a few questions, took some notes. He saved Jack and me for last.

He wanted our eyewitness accounts. Jack glared, brushed by him, fetched a broom, and started sweeping. I figured I had nothing to lose by filling him in. Maybe I'd finally get my name in the paper. "Well, he came by early, same as—"

"Cut to the chase, son. Dead is dead. All I need are his last words."

I was eager to please, stuttered as I racked my brain for a clever parting line—something about the fatal hot dog, perhaps. Then Jack cracked the broomstick on the picnic table and stole my limelight, yet again.

"'I made movies.' That's what he said. 'I made movies in Hollywood North.' His last words exactly."

McGrath met the claim with a skeptic sniff. He pocketed his notepad. "Let me tell you, the old coot dropping dead is the best thing that could've happened to him. Best that could've happened to all of us. May he rest in peace. And may you have the respect to let him."

I'd never read an obituary till Mr. Blackhurst's. Not even my dad's. I tore it from the *Record* and have transferred it to every wallet I have carried since. I did not do the same when Jack's and Annie's turns came. Or my mother's. I feel bad about that.

> **BLACKHURST, Norman Charles**——Suddenly, in Trenton, on Monday, July 15, 1966 in his 72nd year. Born in the United Kingdom and a decorated veteran of the Great War, the proprietor of Sure Press Dry Cleaners on Front Street, Trenton, will be sadly missed by his friends and customers. He leaves behind his cherished companion of many years, Miss August. In keeping with Norman's wishes, cremation has taken place. For those wishing, donations may be made to the March of Dimes or charity of choice.

"It's a lie," I said. "You know. I know."

"I'm thinking we need to let it go. For real, this time. Like McGrath said, Gus, it's about respect."

"You kidding me? Two days ago you were ready to punch him out."

"Death changes things."

"What are you talking about?"

"I'm no grave robber."

"Who said you were?"

"What if it's just that you and me wanted something so bad, we started seeing and thinking things that weren't there? Did McGrath ever do anything to us? Did he? Really? Did he ever say anything that was so wrong? Or was it in our heads?"

"You're like the rest of them now, Jack? That it? You've shut your eyes, blocked your ears? You believe what you're told more than what you know and see? You gone Eloi on me?"

"You got me wrong, man."

"Then tell me. Tell me."

"I guess it's sort of like Paint by Numbers."

"Jesus. You sound like Annie."

"You start out all excited, ready to paint this masterpiece, but five, six numbers in, you realize it's going to be worthless shit, no matter how careful you are to paint within the lines. You stop. You shove it in a drawer. You have the good sense to know that even should you get it done, who's going to give a crap? You're not making art, you're jerking off. That's us, Gus. We solve the mystery—so what? What do we prove? And who do we prove it to, if no one cares to begin with?"

"I care. You cared."

"And what if it turns out the only mystery was us, kidding ourselves into believing there was one?"

"The cards. McGrath. Blackhurst. Hollywood North. The accidents nobody talks about . . . None of that's Paint by Numbers."

"Don't be so sure."

"Does it matter? You don't read Sherlock Holmes for the solution, you read it for the steps he takes to get there."

"Annie's right—you need to have more fun, Gus."

"She tell you that?"

"Let's just go back to the way it was, okay? You and me, working the dock, goofing with the girls, playing our games. . . . Beach Boys or Beatles? Ann-Margret or Elke Sommer?"

"I *am* having fun, Jack. You want to bail, be my guest."

We worked together same as before. We didn't argue. We continued to talk and such, laugh at stupid stuff. But nothing amounted to much. Jack was moving on without me, again. I could feel it. He didn't vanish this time around. Not completely. He was *The Invisible Man* on a half-dose of monocaine—here, gone, partly here, gone, here, gone, partly here. . . . He was the one who'd let me down, yet he was making *me* pay.

Annie played peacemaker. "I don't know what's happened between you two, but it's got to stop. You're best friends. Please, Gus. Tell him you're sorry."

"Me?"

"One of you has to make the first move."

"Tell that to your boyfriend."

"Pardon me? Is that what this is about? You're fighting over me?"

"You wish," I said, scoffing at the suggestion, surprised she'd uttered it. Annie knew boys liked her. *How could she not?* But she'd always kept her vanity in check, self-deprecating to a T, advocating the fraud there was nothing special whatsoever about her—which made boys like her all the more. Yet now she had revealed an unintended truth: he was her boyfriend. I'd blurted it and she had pretty much admitted it. I could stop conning myself, pretending Jack, Annie, and I were a trio. And he wanted to punish *me*?

I would've launched my counteroffensive had it not been for Clyde Neil, the wharfinger. Our elusive boss. "You boys any chance recollect that old guy croaked, few weeks back? *Blackhearse*, was it?"

"Do we *recollect*?" Jack said, and for one disbelieving instant the two of us were happily in sync.

"Message come in, his lady friend or some-such wants her boat back. You boys know anything 'bout it?"

"*Evie III*," I said. She bobbed patiently at dockside where Mr. Blackhurst had left her, as if her dear master might yet return.

"Well, once you finish up here tonight, you're to take it 'cross the bay." Clyde passed me the directions through the window of his truck.

"Me?" I said.

"The two of yous. That's what she said. She requested the two of yous. Never met the lady myself, mind you. Who has, eh? Reclusive by nature, I hear. Funny that, eh, some people? Not quite right upstairs, if you catch my drift. Women, you know, them and their times—"

"How do we get back?" Jack said.

"Yeah," I clarified. "If we're leaving her the boat . . ."

Clyde sanded his fingertips on the stubble of his neck. "Well, that's a stumper, can't deny," he said, and drove off.

7. Icebox, Front Row

Admiral Friggin' Jack manned the throttle, First Mate Annie all too cozy at his side, and me, lowly Deckhand Gus, on the bench behind. I'd been assigned towline duty, minding our return transportation, Annie's old dinghy bouncing and bucking in the bitchy wake of *Evie III*.

We ignored Clyde's orders and cut out early, putting a good hour of daylight in our favour. Enough to make it there and back before dark.

Sunset bled across the waters, an open wound poisoning the bay. Not that Annie saw it my way, of course. She shivered, reached for Jack's hand. "I ask you, how could anyone tire of anything so magnificent? How can there not be a Higher Power?"

Jack held her closer. "'Red sky at night, sailor's delight . . .'"

Annie's cheek touched his. "You look at all this beauty and you know the Devil doesn't stand a chance."

"Oh, Jesus." I was itching for a showdown. "What a load."

The grins Jack and Annie traded were benign, and infuriating. They saw me as a work-in-progress. I knew better. By then, I was well on my way to lost cause.

Despite the map and notes provided, we missed the landing on our first pass. Annie was quick to spot our error and we doubled back with few minutes lost. She noted how the waters were running faster and shallower than was typical of the bay, while a rocky outcrop discouraged boaters from straying too close. At the shoreline, trees and bushes competed for dominance, presenting an impassive front for the secrets that might lie inland. The domain of the late Norman Blackhurst was the last place on the Quinte anyone would have thought inhabited.

"I can't believe it. I go by here almost every day," Annie said.

Jack eased off on the throttle, piloted the boat between the rocks and shore, and we drifted up against the floating dock.

"Cheer up, Gus," Jack said, initiating a momentary thaw in our cold war. "I have a feeling we're going to get some answers."

"You guys are out of your minds," Annie said.

Thirty feet up the trail the forest receded, then conceded to a one-horse bridle path canopied by inconsolable willows. It wasn't much further when a cast-iron fence stopped us cold. We looked to either side and up. Fleur-de-lis finials capped the pickets, sharpened spears with sharper barbs that'd gut you through the ass should you be fool enough to attempt the climb.

"Welcome to Transylvania," Jack said, his Lugosi impression not half-bad.

"Shut up," Annie said. "It's spooky enough."

Jack gripped the bars, peered into the thickening gloom. "Hello? Anybody out there? Miss August?"

My mouth went dry. The Angel of Death was bearing down upon us.

Evangeline August was a slinky lot more than I recalled, in mourning black of flowing lace and silk, a charcoal etching of ethereal grace upon a canvas of dusk. The solitary colour, her lips, a succulent slash of red. (What can I tell you? When it comes to me and Evie August, I will always be the horny teen with a downmarket thesaurus. She was fifty-three then, looked thirty-five, and would die in 1988 at the age of seventy-five. And while older women were never my thing, until I was old myself and out of options, Evie in this moment became the standard by which I judged all other women, the enduring stimulus for my every arousal, desire, and kink.)

She held the gate ajar as we paraded through. God, she was tiny. Then again, she'd been in heels first time we'd met, while I'd been four years and a good foot younger.

Annie promptly cued us to the appropriate etiquette. "I am sorry for your loss, Mrs. Blackhurst."

Jack chimed in, "He was a nice guy."

"He sure liked hot dogs," I said.

Evie's reply was a study in dispassion. "It was his time. To be honest, later than I expected. The difference in our ages, you understand—a Lita Grey in thrall of Chaplin sort of escapade. May-December, should the allusion fail you."

She started back the way she came and we followed in silence. Well, Jack and I, anyhow. Annie wasn't pleased, hushed annoyance at Jack's ear: "You promised we were just dropping the boat off. It's almost dark. My parents are going to kill me. You promised . . ." I loved the sound of that, you bet.

I figured for sure it'd be the *House on Haunted Hill*. What we got was *Moby Dick*—an old Cape Cod with a wraparound porch, shuttered windows, and a widow's walk negated by the treetops. Evie saw our surprise, bluntly explained: "Norman salvaged the façade from *The Women of Butternut Bay* and built from there."

The seafaring theme carried on to the dimly lit interior as she hurried us from one room to the next. A blur of patterned sofas, barrel chairs, and driftwood lamps. Brass instruments with fancy dials and scale models of tall ships. Oils of craggy mariners in pea coats and mackintoshes.

Midway down a cluttered passageway, she stopped and took an overcoat and scarf from a rack on the wall. "Find one you like," she said. The request was downright nutty. Humidity hung heavy within the old house and our trek had left us sweaty. Still, we didn't question.

Kids are stupid. We were stupid. I'd seen enough movies to know good-looking women did bad things, particularly lipsticked beauties slight in stature. I told myself I'd go only so far. Should she offer us a drink, I would not fall into the trap as Hercules had done in *Hercules Unchained*; I would not end up captive in a cave. Or cellar. Or dungeon.

At the base of a short flight of stairs, she paused with key in hand before a door, shut her eyes, turned the handle, said, "Button up, children," and a blast of frigid air blew us back.

"Welcome to Norman's icebox," she said.

We entered, shoulders hunched, hands in pockets, apprehension rife on breathy vapors.

"Wow!" Jack said. "Wow. Wow. Wow." And I had to agree.

The screening room was no bigger than a bedroom. Like some head-shrinking witch doctor had worked his magic on the Odeon.

Two terraced rows, four seats abreast. Plush velvet cushions and armrests. A wall-to-wall screen. Burgundy curtains, trimmed and cinched with gold braid. Conch-shell sconces, the light fanning upward along the walls. An ornate plaster ceiling, naked cherubs frolicking amid pastel garlands and bows. Sculpted cornices, masks of Tragedy and Comedy. And behind the top row of seats, propped on four legs of its own, the projector—a boxy contraption of black and gray metal, a reel above, a reel below.

"The chill is to preserve the film," Evie said, "what little remains."

"The movies you made? Hollywood North?" Jack said, a concessionary shrug aimed my way.

She ushered us to the front row.

We sat. Me. Jack. Annie. In that order.

Evie deposited a space heater at our feet. Heartless, she was not.

Jack gave it another shot. "Mr. Blackhurst told us you were a movie star."

"She is?" The news excited Annie. "Honest? You are? Have I seen you in anything?"

"You are here to honour Norman's last wishes. Let us leave it at that." In fact, Annie had not been invited. Only Jack and me. We'd thought Evie might question it, but this was the closest she came.

"All set, then?" she said, and disappeared behind us.

The theatre darkened.

The projector whirred to life, revved to a metallic snore.

And the film wended its way down through the sprockets, clippity-clop, clippity-clop, like a Jack of Hearts pegged to the spokes of a bike.

Silent movies, we learned, were only as silent as the projector allowed, delivering an unauthorized soundtrack to the images that flickered across the screen.

Five movies unspooled that night. Perhaps as many as eight. None of us could say for certain.

Anticipation ran high from the first frame. Jack and I could not sit still. Yeah, he was back in the hunt, all right. We were on the lookout for clues—or whatever it might be Mr. Blackhurst had wanted us to be on the lookout for.

Right off the bat, a card we remembered from our collection popped up.

"Beware her accursed charms, for behind those pearly whites lies the bite of a shrew."

BPI

But aside from a half-decent bridge collapse toward the middle, the movie stunk. Stiff-necked men and women yakking in parlours. Zero action. No Keystone Cops chasing bank robbers. No Laurel & Hardy pitching pies. Music would have helped, I suppose. In a weird way, the din of the projector had shifted from grating to sedating. Maintaining focus was a challenge, even without my other problem. . . .

Jack and Annie were necking full-out before the first picture was done. Two tongues sloshing together is nothing anybody wants to hear, unless one of the tongues is their own.

I was yet unaware that hormones trumped friendship every time. Or that jealousy trumped both. As unexplained mysteries go, hormones were up there with Area 51.

Despite my objections ("Cut it out! C'mon!") and frequent elbows to Jack's ribs, they kept at it till Annie dozed off a quarter through the second feature, slumbering serenely within the crook of the dirty double-crosser's arm.

And wouldn't you know, there was my best bud Jack, back on the job as if his tongue hadn't been swabbing my oldest friend's throat ten seconds before. Oh, I was seething. Still, I set aside our differences for the greater good, vague though it was.

We watched. Fought sleep. Drowsed. Nudged one another awake. Pointed out familiar intertitles, noted scenes relevant to our disaster files. Yeah, the pieces were coming together. Sort of.

The best of the lot was *The Black Ace*, the movie Mr. Blackhurst had been so keen on.

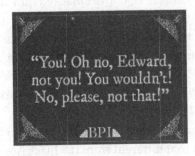

"You! Oh no, Edward, not you! You wouldn't! No, please, not that!"

The hero was this one-time WWI flying ace who becomes a barnstormer. He's got it made. Swell hair. Manly moustache. Winning smile. Super-sweet girlfriend. Adoring public. But when the clock strikes midnight, he dons his canvas flying helmet, adjusts the chin strap, lowers his goggles, and makes like Jack the Ripper.

Even with all our nodding off, we managed to come up with seven sure hits on our intertitles, with another half-dozen possibles. Our collection continued to gather dust where we'd stashed it among the books. Had I known we'd be going to the movies, I would've taken a fresh look beforehand.

Spotting accidents and disasters required way less concentration. Calamity and tragedy underscored every film Blackhurst had lined up for us.

Most didn't mean much. The bridge collapse, the hurricane, the mine cave-in, or the smallpox outbreak, for instance. But plenty of others struck home.

A train derailment.

A bomb factory explosion (courtesy a German saboteur).

A yacht fire and sinking.

A big-top fire and grandstand collapse.

A midair plane collision (a highlight of *The Black Ace*).

A landslide above a sleepy village.

A bus getting creamed by a train.

A tanker truck blowing up.

And thousands of drownings (most in *The Deadly Waters of Nantes*, a costume drama set in France).

"Were you in any of them?" Annie asked Evie.

"Not if you blinked, dear."

"So, then, all the bad stuff that's happened, that's what you made your movies about?" Jack said. "Is that what Mr. Blackhurst wanted us to see?"

Jesus! I couldn't frigging believe what I was hearing. The answers were so damn obvious. Who was this guy, *Jack the Blinder*? Had his horniness for Annie screwed his brain? Had love smacked him stupid? How could he not put two and two together? The worst of it, he wasn't done.

"So what's wrong with doing that? I mean, why's Hollywood North a secret? Why doesn't anyone remember it? Or talk about it? I mean, all those movies . . . And Mr. McGrath, why'd he get so upset when we brought him the title cards? And you, why'd you tell Mr. Blackhurst Jack and me were stars—stars of what?"

Evie stared at him a moment. "You're the boy who finds things. . . ."

His smile wasn't all that different from the Black Ace's. "Jack, ma'am. Jack Levin."

"Well, Jack Levin, I have a question for you: who do you think I am? The character at the end of the story who explains the mystery in one fell swoop, wrapping up all the loose ends? Is that who I look like to you?"

"No, Miss, it's just that—"

"I showed you the films as Norman requested. Make of them what you will."

Annie was up and at the door of the theatre. "Please, Jack. Please, can't we go? I need to get home."

"And why'd he say—why did Mr. Blackhurst tell us it was fear that killed Hollywood North and not the talkies? You can tell us that much." Jack was scrambling, brain cells shooting out his ears. The guy had lost it. Man, it felt good to hold the upper hand for once.

"Listen to your girlfriend, Jack."

"Can we come back another time?"

Evie lowered her eyes, turned away, guided us out of the icebox, up the stairs, and into the passageway.

"You'll let us see more, won't you? Please."

I dawdled by the coatrack, stalled 'til Annie dragged off Jack.

"Jack had it backwards," I said. "Maybe not the train wreck, but the rest . . . The accidents happened in your movies first, before they happened for real. *Before*. That's it, isn't it? It's like your movies made the bad stuff happen."

"Your friends are waiting for you."

"People got scared. That's why you stopped making the movies. That's what killed Hollywood North."

She busied herself with the tassels of her scarf. "After you've opened the gate, leave the key in the lock. I'll retrieve it later."

"And it hasn't stopped, has it? The bad stuff you filmed, some is still happening for real. And if it hasn't, it's coming. I'm right, aren't I? Aren't I, Miss August?"

Her eyes met mine so unexpectedly, I turned my cheek, checked my neck for whiplash. "Which would you say comes first, the chicken or the egg?"

"Pardon?"

"Does film mirror life or does life mirror film?"

"I don't—"

"Neither do I."

"But—"

"You're the one they call Gus."

"It's not my real name."

"That's okay. Evangeline August isn't my real name."

"It isn't?"

"Two complete strangers in a room, each known by their respective alias . . . Some might attach great significance to such a coincidence."

"Mr. Ripley would," I said, and it was the closest I ever came to seeing her smile.

"To me, there is only one real coincidence: that each and every person's life is riddled with coincidence."

My brain was backfiring. "You're saying the bad stuff in the movies and the bad stuff that's happened in Trenton are coincidences?"

"Tell me, Gus, would you like to be famous?"

"Huh? Like a movie star?"

"Do you have a plan?"

"What?"

"You know what you need to do, of course?"

"I don't—"

"Something very good. Or something very bad."

"I'm not sure I understand."

"How odd. You profess to have a perfect grasp of everything else."

I caught up with Jack and Annie at the gate.

"I hope this wild goose chase of yours is finally over," Annie said.

"You told her?" I said to Jack.

"Mrs. Blackhurst is very pretty, but she's not what I'd call normal. And from what Jack says about Mr. Blackhurst and Mr. McGrath . . . If you ask me, you've been making mountains out of molehills."

"It was between you and me, Jack. You and me."

"C'mon, Gus, she's got a point."

I laughed out loud. How and when had I become the believer and Jack the doubter?

8. How Jack and Annie Drowned

We were on the bay, a few minutes from the Barkers' cottage. Annie's anxiety was running high, seeing how late it was, so Jack and I were surprised when she cut the Evinrude, let the current have its way with us. She knew better than to stand, but you know how it was with Annie—when her spirit thumbed its nose at caution. "There!" she said, arms spread wide like she might hug the sky. "The stars. The stars. If you look—really, really look—you'll see God in every one." (This was where her mom and dad fell to pieces. The pastor repeated it word for word, too, in his eulogy.)

The rest happened fast. We hit a rock. Or something. My first thought was that Jesus had snatched her up to Heaven. Abracadabra, I swear. She was there and then she wasn't. And Jack and me, we were jumping in after her. That's when the boat capsized.

It's all I remembered. Annie's father, Mr. Barker, and a friend of his found me in the morning, clinging to the hull. They gave me coffee, asked me where Annie was. I didn't know what to tell them. Or how.

And then, I guess, I did.

9. The Perils of Cellulose Nitrate Base Film

Bryan McGrath interviewed me in the hospital.

"I know the truth," I said.

He patted my shoulder. "And that is exactly what I am going to give them, son."

"The only part I haven't figured out is why nobody talks about any of it—nobody remembers."

"Well, they're talking now, I tell you. You're quite the hero." He pretended we were talking about the same thing.

"But all I did was—I didn't drown."

"That's all it takes, most often."

Got my picture in the paper.

Was famous.

For a month or so.

And thus it dawned on me: the part of the mystery that had continued to baffle was not quite so complicated after all.

My newest fear was that people would point fingers. I had not forgotten Helmet Swartz and the rumours after Dottie had tumbled from Dam #1 into the Trent-Severn. I confessed to my mother.

"My poor, brave boy," she said. "The lovely things Mr. McGrath wrote about you, how can you even think it? Everyone knows you did your best to save them." It was eerie, how much my mother sounded like Annie. First Jack, now her.

Jack's dad closed up the Marquee, joined his family in Montreal. "Mr. Levin and Jack's mom are getting back together," Mom said. Mourning their son proved too great a burden to bear alone.

"Will you miss him?" I said.

"Not as much as you miss your dear friends."

I got through high school. Did well enough. Teachers cut me slack.

Wasn't sure what I'd do next, until Annie's Mom and Dad handed me $3,000 for college. The money had been set aside for her. "It's what she would have wanted," they assured me.

Went to Queen's in Kingston.

In October of my sophomore year, I made my way to the school's Miller Museum and saw firsthand the meteorite Jack had found when he was nine. Should anyone yet wonder, I'm the prick who stole the bronze plaque that bore his name.

Graduated. Without flying colours. A BA in Balls All.

Spent time in Toronto, Thunder Bay, Saskatoon, Kelowna. Worked as a stringer for the papers. Had a piece picked up by *Time* once. Canadian edition. With a byline, yet. Thought it would be my springboard to the Big Time. Ended up writing ad copy at a radio station.

Married twice. Divorced twice. *You try living with me.*

Settled in Winnipeg, mosquitoes and shitty winters my sackcloth and ashes of choice.

There is a sequence in *The Black Ace* where a newspaperman believes he is close to solving the string of gruesome murders. He tracks his prime suspect to an airfield and confronts him with the evidence. Fists fly. A chase ensues. The newspaperman runs into a spinning propeller. And *The Black Ace* lives to rip another day.

In 1972, Bryan McGrath ran into a spinning propeller, too. The *Record* milked it for a week. He was one of their own, you understand.

TRAGIC HOLLYWOOD ENDING FOR ACE NEWSMAN

JAMES CAGNEY TAKES LIFE OF OUTDOORS COLUMNIST

Yeah, the Cagney line threw me, too—yet another bit of Trenton's secret history.

In the early days of WWII, Warner Brothers' *Captains of the Clouds* was shot at the town's RCAF base. The exteriors, anyhow. (Cagney had the good sense not to show.) The thirtieth anniversary of the movie's release was coming up and McGrath was planning to make a story of it. That's what brought him to the base and, I guess, his face into the tail rotor of the helicopter.

He should have known better. The credits for *The Black Ace* listed him as Assistant to the Producer.

The *Record* printed the last entry in McGrath's notebook:

Trenton's brush with Hollywood greatness

The town frightened me almost as much as I frightened myself. No chance in hell I would have gone back had it not been for the call from the lawyer. I'd not set foot in Trenton since my mother died. Promised myself I never would. Then comes January 1988 and Evie August goes and dies and leaves me Captain Ahab's dream house.

"I'm not interested," I told the guy.

"The only proviso is you watch the movie. After that, done deal, the property and all its movables are yours. There's a vintage Chris Craft you have got to see to believe."

"And if I want to get rid of it? Sell, maybe?" I wasn't exactly flush with cash.

"Anything you want."

"This movie I need to watch, what's it called?"

A pause. A rustling of papers. "*Boy Girl Boy*, if that makes sense. Never heard of it myself."

"Me, neither," I said.

I avoided the Quinte. Took King's Highway over to 3. I'd never have found the place had the caretaker not flagged me down. The house was as isolated from the road as it had been from the bay.

"Fit as a fiddle, she was. One day to the next." The caretaker snapped his fingers. "Never a peep 'bout any kin. All these years, at her beck 'n' call, to come up empty-handed . . . Just my luck, I says to the wife. Just my luck."

"The keys, please," I said.

I did not take a coat from the rack. I had my own.

The 35mm reel of *Boy Girl Boy* was waiting for me in the projector.

I searched for a note, an explanation, but found only detailed instructions on the operation of the projectors (there were three) and the care and storage of nitrate film.

I dimmed the lights, flicked the switch, and took my seat in the front row. What did I have to lose?

A year after Evie's death, a local writer, Peggy Leavey, published a book about Trenton, titled it *The Movie Years*. For the record, they went from 1917 to 1934. Among the productions was *Carry On Sergeant!*, the costliest silent film in Canadian history.

In 1992, the town erected an historical marker where the studios once stood. Should you be in the area, look for the stone obelisk on Film Street, just up from Hanna Park, where I found the metal box and intertitles.

Hollywood North was not quite so secret anymore.

Not sure what the catalyst may have been. In a spiritual sense, perhaps the passing of Evangeline August had set the memories free. Selected memories, at least.

There were so many other secrets by then.

Boy Girl Boy was no *Birth of a Nation*. The plot had to have been stale even by 1920s' standards: two best friends and the pretty girl they both loved.

I wasn't clear on why Evie had wanted me to watch it. Not until the final minutes.

A moonlit night. A rickety rowboat in the middle of a quiet lake.

One boy sits with the girl at the stern, his lips at her ear, her fingers in his hair.

Facing them at the bow, a younger boy, his hands wound tight round the oars as he propels them through the waters.

There is no missing his rage. In his face. In his posture. In the intertitle.

He wrenches an oar from its rowlock, lurches to his feet, and swings at his rival. The girl sees, eyes wide with shock and terror, lunges to protect her boyfriend from the blow, and bears the brunt. She crumples into his lap. But the attacker does not stop. He swings the oar once more at the boy, connects, pulls back, pauses. He flips the oar end to end, shifts his grip, and rams it into the chest of his stunned opponent. Again and again and again.

He sees what he has done. Buries his face in his hands. Trembles. Cries. Panics. Thinks.

He rows closer to shore, amid the rocky shoals.

He kisses the girl's limp hair, drags her to the side, lifts her up, over, and into the water. The body of his comatose friend is more of a struggle. Suddenly, the boy regains consciousness. They wrestle. The boat capsizes and into the drink they go.

At dawn, two fishermen happen upon the younger boy. He clings to a rock, the oar yet within his grasp. He sobs.

"I tried to save them. God knows, I tried."

They wrap him in a blanket, give him hot coffee from a Thermos, and do their best to console the grief-stricken survivor.

The oar floats away. Slowly.

Nitrate film is notoriously unstable. It can decompose and combust if handled or stored improperly. Mr. Blackhurst had salvaged thirty-two films, stowed each in ventilated containers and fireproof vaults, and maintained the ideal temperature and humidity. Evie had respected his legacy. So have I.

For over twenty-five years, I have come and gone. Three times a year. One- or two-day visits, never more. Hunkered down in the icebox.

My favourite remains *The Black Ace*. Did I tell you how the commander of the Trenton air base was convicted of murder and rape in 2010? I was beginning to wonder if it might never happen.

Bryan McGrath, incidentally, had writing credits on three of the films. My mother taught me never to speak ill of the dead, but I have to agree with Mr. Blackhurst: "Bryan was a mediocre and malodorous screen scribe."

I watched *Boy Girl Boy* only that once. Forwards, that is. Backwards, I lost count. It made no difference. None that I have found. But then I never was much good at knowing where to look.

As for the others, you wouldn't believe how many times. Even the rotten ones, including the three penned by McGrath.

Trenton may thank me some day, but I won't hold my breath. The town remains mired in the here and now. The history they don't tell you will always be greater than the history they do.

Last night, I hauled the films from their vaults.

This morning, I shut down the cooling system.

The End

Witch II
COURTNEY BATES-HARDY

She thinks she might want
children—all that chatter
candying her cottage.

She wonders if it's Disney
that makes her afraid
to live with an empty belly
and too much food.

She knows it's insanity
because the papers tell her
of the unwanted left in the woods.

She's not enticed by the chocolate cottage
or the frosting sugar windows—
maybe if she didn't need a push,
she'd open the oven
and climb right in.

Sideshow

CATHERINE MacLEOD

"You have ten minutes to convince me not to kill you," Minos said.

"Spare me the melodrama." It wasn't as if I hadn't noticed the gun. It wasn't much uglier than the hand holding it, or the expression he wore when I tucked my hair behind my ears. It's a common gesture, but apparently not one he expected from the likes of me.

I usually keep my face covered in polite company.

No one's ever accused Minos of being polite.

I took the seat he hadn't offered, and willed my stomach to stay down. I didn't really think he'd shoot me, but I wasn't betting, just in case. I wasn't surprised that he was armed, not with another group of animal rights activists phoning in a bomb threat. My knapsack and rain coat had been searched for weapons at the door.

A wall of monitors showed different views of the Labyrinth. "Don't you ever turn them off?" I asked. I've been told my voice is surprisingly pleasant. No one's ever said compared to what. "Were you watching when . . . ? Yes, of course you were."

Minos shrugged. Good suit, silk tie, polished shoes: he still dressed like a king. An old, tired, and forgotten king, but his dark eyes missed nothing. "Nobody's seen you for six months," he said. "I wasn't expecting you back. Why do you want to see me?"

"I don't. You had the bouncer drag me in here, remember?" He's used to being hounded by crackpots and gold-diggers. I wondered which he thought I was. I'm sure he would've paid me to disappear after the attack if I hadn't already gone into hiding. But I hadn't wanted to be hounded, either.

"What are you doing here?" he asked.

"Waiting until the crowd thins."

"And then?"

"I'm going into the maze." His look of horror didn't faze me; I've seen it on too many other faces. "I'm not here to cause a scene. If I was, I'd have shown up when the doors opened."

"Then why not come when the club's empty?"

"Because I need witnesses. I want someone to notice if I disappear."

"And you think that might happen?"

"Absolutely—I know who you are. If I turned up dead the police would have questions, but you'd be rid of publicity you think you can't afford."

"What do you think I *can* afford?"

"Excuse me?"

"Aren't you here to blackmail me?"

I snorted. It's the closest I can come to laughter. "I don't want anything from you, Mr. Minos."

"Except my permission to enter the maze."

"If you try to stop me I *will* cause a scene, and then the tabloids will have tomorrow's headline."

"Sounds like blackmail to me."

"Fine, it's blackmail. What are you going to do about it?"

Bravado was the best plan I had. "Why do you want to see me?" I asked.

"I don't. You showed up where you knew you weren't wanted."

He was still territorial, even if he didn't like the territory. He hadn't lived this long by showing weakness, either. He thought I hadn't seen the cane behind his desk.

I watched him watch me. Probably thinking the usual: that I seemed intelligent for one of my kind, whatever that was.

He said, "Is your name really Rumer?"

"I couldn't possibly be fact." I smiled. He looked away. "It's an old joke. I hear it all the time. My name means *unique*. I was named after my grandmother. She was pleased until she saw me." Having never met my grandmother, I can well imagine how that scene went. A baby girl with soft dark hair, brown eyes, long eyelashes, but not even vaguely pretty. My body looked human enough, but no one would ever have modelled a china doll after me. *Little Miss Minotaur*, they called me at the circus. Even as a child the name fit.

I shifted, trying to get comfortable. "Everyone knows my name, Mr.

Minos. What did you really want to ask?"

Once, I would have been out of place there, among polished wood and soft leather. But now the sofa was worn and the panelling scratched, and I was no shabbier than the rest of his office. I almost felt pity—his life didn't need more monsters.

I said, "Is it true time has no meaning in the Labyrinth?"

"Yes. Why?"

"Because the tape is only four minutes long, but I'm sure my rape took longer."

He nodded. "It did." He stared at nothing for a moment. "Where are your companions from that night?"

"I don't know." And it's in their best interests not to be found. You can hear them laughing on the security tape, under the Minotaur's grunts and the sound of tearing meat. Only one wall away, and they didn't try to save me. Justin, Marcus, and Caroline just patched their handscreens into the camera and watched the whole thing.

Minos said, "Tell me what happened."

I didn't want to need him. I said, "You know."

"I saw. It's not the same thing."

"They thought I'd be eaten alive. I've heard there were doubts they meant for me to be raped, but not many, and none of them mine. Your bartender said he heard Justin call me *that ugly cow*. Which was unkind, even if it *was* apt."

I know how the lies would go: "I guess she'd had too much to drink. We saw her stumbling into the maze and went in after her." Since there probably wouldn't have been enough of me left for a tox screen, who could prove otherwise? Considering the Minotaur's fabled appetite, their treachery was well-planned.

Except for something no one considered.

I said, "I think the Minotaur needs me."

"Why?"

"He didn't eat me, even though he was hungry."

"How would *you* know?"

Parents can be clueless about their children. It worries me. "Because he once dined on seven youths and seven maidens. But not anymore, right?"

"Right. People in this time tend to be less understanding of such things. And—" He actually sounded amused. "I doubt I've ever had fourteen virgins in here."

At any other time I would have laughed. I knew he was feeding the Minotaur fowl.

I said, "I'm alive because he tried not to kill me."

"Because?"

"He's lonely. He's hungrier for touch than for food. And the lonely, you know, we tend to seek out our own kind."

I saw him understand. I saw him not want to.

I said, "I'm as close as he's going to get."

He said, "Tell me the rest."

It's an old, well-known story. All stories are; only the details ever change.

"Justin, Marcus, and Caroline were pretty people. I knew them from the office—*Daedalus Engineering*. They worked out front where they'd be seen. I worked in back where I wouldn't. I was in the archives, putting old files on disk. They didn't work for the money; they were there because their families have interests in the company. But I needed the job. I didn't want to go back to the freak show."

It had been hard when the circus manager, Mr. Avery, died while we were here in Las Vegas. His son Ken had taken over the job. He had ideas for making the "human oddities" even more interesting. His plans for me started with a nose ring and tattoos, and then got ugly.

Refusing got me fired. Ken's sister came to see me before the circus left town. She was like her father, kind just because she could be. I'm sure she called in a favour to get me work. She helped me find a small apartment. The neighbours weren't exactly welcoming, but they left me alone.

She'd told me, "Don't lock yourself up all the time, okay? You're going to need people around you."

She was right.

"Why did you trust them?" Minos asked.

"Because even monsters get desperate for company. We can't always wait for trustworthy companions—even the beautiful wait a long time for those."

He nodded, possibly remembering betrayal. Maybe recalling how often he'd dished it out.

"I was surprised when they asked me out after work. They'd always been civil, but not friendly. That should've been my first clue. But I hadn't been out in so long. The Labyrinth wouldn't have been my first choice, though. It's just another sideshow. Oh, don't give me that look—I know a circus when I see one."

Minos laughed softly. "It is, isn't it?"

The Labyrinth is all theatrics: strobe lights, bone-rattling music, brightly-painted dancers who don't really worry about the Minotaur coming out. Although, for insurance reasons, they're all warned it might happen. You enter at your own risk. You pays your money, you takes your chances.

Maybe they believe that because they've never seen it there isn't really a monster. But they should know better. Sideshows *always* have a monster.

And in my case it was Justin. He learned the guards' routine; he found the one door that would be unlocked for a few minutes. One drink past midnight he pulled me further into the maze and backed me into a corner. I knew then. The only men who want to get that close to me are barkers and aspiring pornographers. When I let go of my glass it took a long time to hit the floor.

History repeats itself. There'll always be people who hurt others for fun. Those who think monsters never get lonely, and those who know all too well that we do.

There'll always be a date-rape drug.

Old story.

He said, "You tell your story well. But you've never told it to the press, no matter how much money they offered."

"No. I didn't want to be found." I'm good at reading expressions, but I couldn't read his. He looked weary. His gun hand trembled slightly, which didn't help my nausea.

"Turning down cash has never been a common practice among my acquaintances," he said. "Especially the women."

I deciphered his new look just fine. "Or whatever I am?"

"What *are* you?"

His candour was a nice change from the usual.

"I'm not a Minotaur. That's what you're wondering, right? I'm a mishap, not a myth. A misshapen woman who fits into a limited number of niches. Admittedly, the maze is a big one, but it still has its restrictions."

"Then why are you so determined to go in?"

"Where else would I go? I'm not sleeping on the street tonight."

He sat up suddenly. "You intend to *stay* in there?"

"Yes."

After the rape, a social worker had taken me to a home for women in crisis, miraculously empty at the time; but it had filled as the months went by. I wasn't the scariest thing the other women had ever seen, not by a long shot, but I frightened their children. When some of them started having nightmares I knew it was time to move on. My landlady was too miserable with all the media attention for me to think of going back there. No decent hotel would have me.

I considered my choices: Ken would probably take me back; Minos might not throw me out. I had my choice of circuses.

I glanced up as the Minotaur ghosted across the nearest screen. "I have to admire you, Mr. Minos. Up to a certain point, that is. It was clever of you, turning your last piece of real estate into a nightclub."

But he'd always been tough. Kings live on the good will of their subjects, and there had been less and less of it the last few years of his reign. There had been stories of sorcery and terrible rituals practiced in the palace, some of them true. There had been rumours of his death and several attempts to make gossip into fact, but he was still on his feet.

"You've done your homework," he said.

"I told you, I know who you are. Minos, former king of Crete, husband of Pasiphae. I don't know much about her—she was sent to the asylum before my time. I suppose giving birth to the Minotaur would drive any woman insane. But even before that—falling in love with the white bull you were supposed to sacrifice to Poseidon because it was so beautiful? A little peculiar."

"Twisted," he murmured.

"Definitely. But since you couldn't stand to slay it for the same reason, maybe you shouldn't throw stones."

"May I tell you something?"

"You're holding the gun."

"Poseidon *made* Pasiphae love the bull because I refused to sacrifice it. Her madness is my fault." He didn't say anything about the curse Poseidon had put on the Labyrinth, slowing time inside to a crawl so that Minos's misery would last longer. He didn't say that when he'd used sorcery to move the Labyrinth through time to what he'd hoped would be a safe place, he'd had no way of knowing the curse would come with it. A leap of faith, not knowing where he'd land. We didn't need to revisit that story.

"I know about time with no meaning," he said. "The white bull is dead, but I'm still serving penance."

We watched his son move through the heart of the maze, dark and filthy and mad. He was hard to look at, and I wondered if that wasn't part of the reason for the looser security inside. There were hundreds of security cameras in the maze, but maybe the guards simply couldn't stand to look.

I wondered if disbelief had frozen them the night of my assault. No one had expected to see people that far into the maze, and there was a good chance they'd never seen such violence before. Who believed such brutality possible?

I believed. And so did King Minos.

"And what are you?" I asked.

"Not getting by as well as you think." He *was* tired, if he was opening his heart to monsters. Or maybe it had just been a while since he'd had someone to talk to.

I checked the view of the bar. "The crowd's dwindling."

"That *is* the crowd."

"You're kidding."

"I have a talented PR man. Business is good if you believe the papers. But word-of-mouth has slowed us down considerably. The club is taking on the air of bygone days."

He was right. That was exactly how it felt. "What will you do if it closes?"

"It can't. Feeding my son still takes money. I have an obligation to family." His gaze held mine for a long moment. I looked away first. "Tell me what you remember about that night."

"Bones. I remember scattered bones. And the crowd that gathered to watch me being carried out."

"That's it?" he asked.

"After being drugged I shouldn't remember even that much."

But in my nightmares there's the sound of my bones cracking under the Minotaur's weight. The smell of my blood spraying and my bladder letting go. The Minotaur's breath, rank beyond description. The manure he dropped on my legs in his excitement. The *sound* of him mounting me. I'm sure some of it is memory.

"I've been waiting to hear from your lawyer," he said. "My men expected to be sued for not getting you out of there sooner."

"It never crossed my mind." They did the best they could—even the Minotaur runs from a dozen Tasers. "I don't blame anyone but Justin."

"Not the others?"

"I can't see Marcus and Caroline planning this. I think they went along with it because Justin needed an audience."

I wish I could say they set me up for some bizarre ritual, that they needed a sacrifice or something. But I know better. For somebody like Justin, jaded and oh-so-entitled, betrayal is just another game, and disappearing is an adventure. It's possible with enough money.

I suspect he'll always have enough—an anonymous someone is copying the Labyrinth's security tapes and selling them to special collectors. My rape is a popular show in certain circles now. I'm a star.

I'm sure Minos knows more about that night than I told him, right down to how many stitches I needed.

Many: an hour before I'd been a virgin.

Some of my hair was ripped out. Bones had to be set. The doctors were horrified at the damage to my face, and more so when the x-rays showed there wasn't any.

They said there was less damage than they'd expected.

I expect anything less than DOA would have been a surprise.

One of them said my survival was a miracle and asked if I thought the gods had played a part in it. I looked at the old man watching the Minotaur onscreen, and wondered if they'd played a part in his survival or if they'd just turned their backs. He was neither loved nor missed in his former kingdom, and he must be relieved to be away.

But he also must be lonely. Monsters get that way.

It's so easy to lose everything. One mistake, one moment of doubt.

Old story.

"You're really human?" He wasn't being rude; he just couldn't come to terms with it.

I nodded. "My parents made sure. If I hadn't been, they might have felt less guilty about sending me away with the circus."

Mr. Avery never told me how he'd heard about me; he wasn't proud of the fact that he listened to gossip. He came to our house on my fourteenth birthday, hat in hand, and offered me a place in his show. He took us to the circus to meet his "oddities," and asked me what I thought. I didn't want to go with him, but told my parents I did because I wanted them to stop looking over their shoulders. The tension at home wasn't my fault, but I was still the cause.

Even at fourteen, when you become self-conscious about your body and hate being stared at, I knew this was how it would have to be. There were only so many places I would ever fit in.

My parents sent me off with warm clothes, volumes of the poetry I loved, and all the extra money they had. Bless them, they never once looked relieved.

I remember them pointing out clouds shaped like animals, and the constellation Taurus, because my birthday is the end of April. I remember the flower-shaped chocolate cake they made me every year.

I remember red paint splashed on the house and detergent dumped in the koi pond. The neighbours were afraid I'd infect their children with repulsiveness. Fear can make you stupid. My parents did their best to keep me safe.

They should've come with me.

But we all knew safety was relative.

"I know what I'm walking into," I said. "They say there's someone for everyone, right? And he's half-human, which is more than I can say for some humans."

I tried again to find a comfortable position on the hard chair. There didn't seem to be one. Realization dawned on his face as my coat fell open. "You're—?"

"Yes."

He pointed with the gun. "Tell me."

Where to even begin?

"They say pregnant women get this glow, but I don't see it. My back hurts all the time. Your son likes human flesh, and his son appears to have the same tastes—sometimes I get . . . cravings. The doctors gave me standard treatment at the hospital, so this should have been impossible, but . . ."

"Should have been," he sighed, and I heard what he hadn't said—that nothing in the Labyrinth was what anyone expected.

They'd told me what to expect after the rape—sleep disturbances, change in appetite, severe mood swings. By the time I realized the symptoms could mean something else it was too late for a safe abortion.

It was too late for a lot of things.

"I've memorized the layout," I said. "I think I can avoid him. And if I can't . . . I know what to expect this time."

"You memorized . . . ? How?"

"The design of the maze was one of the files I put on disk. Apparently Justin saw it, too. Daedalus was a brilliant architect, wasn't he? And you tried to put him out of business so he could never build another Labyrinth. You arranged for a little crash-and-burn. That's why I made sure people saw me come in—you remove people you find inconvenient."

He nodded. We were running out of conversation. But finally I couldn't help asking, "Were you ever really planning to use that on me?"

He set the gun on the desk. "Sometimes I think about using it on myself. But then who would feed my son? No, I'm not about to kill the mother of my grandchild."

It was nice to hear him say it. "So it's just an accessory?"

"Yes. Like you, I enjoy the illusion of choice."

It occurred to me that he probably didn't want to need me, either. I glanced around the office. "You've been living in here, haven't you? Sleeping on the couch."

"Time moves on. Sometimes it leaves us behind. I don't fit in many niches, either." He watched the screens for a moment. "Amazing," he said. "We might actually be too strange for Las Vegas."

"You didn't know, did you?" I asked. "You didn't always have security cameras."

"What are you talking about?"

"Some of the bones in there are awfully small, Mr. Minos. I think a couple of your sacrifices died in childbirth."

He spoke on the second try. "I never thought of that."

"Neither did anyone else, apparently. But it's still possible to survive the birth. Your wife is living proof."

Neither of us said, *If what she does can be called living.*

I said, "By this time next week you'll have all the customers you can handle."

They'll come looking for an encore. Their need for spectacle will exceed their fear. I'm going to sell more tickets than he can count.

"I'll be watching," he said. "I'll send help when you go into labour."

He's the head of the family; he won't neglect his kin. He's a businessman; he won't risk losing his star attraction.

He opened the door for me, an unexpected courtesy. "How long do you have?"

"Cows and humans both take nine months. So, maybe three."

"But you really don't know."

"Time is different in the maze."

"Shall I have my men escort you in?"

"No, thank you. I know my way."

"Rumer?" I looked up at him. He didn't flinch. "Is this an old story, too?"

"They all are, remember?"

"How does it end, do you suppose?"

He watched me look for an answer. He saw me not find one. He closed the door quietly behind me.

The Marotte

TONY PI

My executioner threw me face down in the snow before Patriarch Damascu. Though my hands and feet were bound, I spat blood and struggled onto my knees, but my act of defiance only spurred on the rabid mob in the courtyard below. Even those who once hailed me as Lord Conjurer hurled curse-beads at me, calling for my death.

Damascu raised his Troika-staff and bellowed his lies to the clamorous crowd. "In this dark hour, Her Majesty the Tsarina lies deathly ill because of this *necromancer* who covets the throne. By the laws of the Tsardom, this traitor must die. May his righteous death placate the gods and move them to save the Tsarina."

"I had no hand in Her Majesty's sudden illness. I am loyal to Tsarina Prianya," I cried. "I have ever plied my arts in defense of the realm as Lord Conjurer. Let me prove—"

"You dare proclaim innocence, Vod?" Damascu roared. "Condemn him for his flagrant defiance of Death's will, enslaving souls of the dead as he pleases. Judge him by his grimoires and vile talismans. Only fire will purge their evil." His disciples lit a bonfire in the courtyard as soldiers marched towards the blaze bearing rare tomes of magic and manikin familiars. The puppets were mine but had been defiled by blood and mangled into grotesque poses. Though it pained me to see my tools of magic fed to the fire, I would gladly forfeit all worldly possessions to save my beloved.

I fought my urge to decry Damascu's claims. Common folk did not understand that the revenant shades I summoned could do good or evil, cleaving to their nature in life. While darker souls bargain hardest to return to the living world, it took a virtuous heart to bring a bright soul across the veil. The people only wanted a scapegoat to blame for Prianya's illness, and the Patriarch gave them me to fuel their wrath. If only I had my scrimshaw wand, I might have found a way to escape.

"Last chance, Vod. Lift your curse on Her Majesty. Confess your sins to the Troika, lest you suffer a thousand torments in their thrice-ten nightmares." Damascu thrust his staff before my gaze, turning it slowly so that I met the pearl eyes of his golden gods in turn. Fortune-Dreaming. Hag-Rid-Rapture. Death-In-Sleep.

But his gods were not mine and did not frighten me. "I reject your Troika. Only to Mistress-Sun do I lay bare all lies, and call for the justice of Master-Moon. I did not harm the Tsarina." I lifted my head and began a hymn to the old gods, praying in my heart that they would give me time to save my beloved.

The crowd silenced.

"Infidel!" Damascu swung his Troika-staff at my head. The impact broke my nose and blood gushed down to soak my beard, but I kept to my song.

Someone grabbed me by the hair and forced my head against the executioner's block. I wanted to cry out Prianya's name, but then I heard other voices join in the hymn and I knew I had to keep—

The axe-blade chopped through my neck.

The sudden crush of pain overwhelmed me, but for a moment of wretched wonder I saw my own body headless, and only after I blinked for the last time did my mind understand that I had died.

The world faded but not the agony. Phantom claws ripped me from my severed head. I steeled myself for whatever death would bring. My order believes that the dead linger in the void of the skies, waiting for Mistress-Sun or Master-Moon to choose the brightest souls for stars. But instead would I suffer the torments of the usurper gods as Damascu threatened, imprisoned eternally in the Troika's thrice-ten nightmares?

Though I felt the icy touch of the realm beyond the veil, something kept my soul from crossing completely. Pulled taut between life and death, I could not escape the unending pain of my demise, nor the grief of knowing that I had failed Prianya.

Did thrice-nine years pass, or a single day? I did not know, but so long as I still remembered my beloved, I prayed for another chance to save her.

It hurt to think, but I caught the scent of ambergris and a glimmer of light, and with trepidation, opened my eyes.

The first thing I saw was a face as grand as the white cliffs to the west of the city. It took me a while to realize that it was Prianya's favourite fool, Cherchenko.

The world had grown huge. A slight and youthful man dressed in a jester's motley of shimmery scarlets and winter-hare whites, Cherchenko thrust me into the grizzled face of the brute mocking him: Korofkin, a member of the Palace Guard. I was tiny in comparison. What lunacy was this?

"Please, good Sir Brute, I must see Her Majesty," Cherchenko pleaded with unmoving lips, a skilled ventriloquist throwing his voice. "Let me break her from her illness. She needs good cheer to rouse her soul. I'll make her laugh and lift her spirits."

I could now see where we were: outside the cedar-wood doors to the Tsarina's apartments. Strangely, I could only feel my head and nothing below the neck except the beating of my heart. I supposed that was because of my beheading, but shouldn't I be dead?

"Jingle your bells elsewhere, Chero. No one may enter without the Patriarch's permission." The spade-bearded man shoved Cherchenko, and the fool fell to the ground. I tumbled out of his grasp, skittering across the flagstones with a clatter. I expected to hurt, but my head yielded like cloth with the impact. But parted from Cherchenko, I felt my face begin to stiffen and lose life. Worse, I felt the pull of forces from beyond the veil trying to consume me. I fought to resist their call, drawing on all my training as a conjurer.

Suddenly, I was lifted up again. Cherchenko had grabbed whatever propped my head up. Vitality entered me again, but Chero flinched when he moved me. He forced a smile back on his face and waved me in Korofkin's direction so fast that I was getting dizzy. "I'll be back with song and dance, brutish sir, and jokes to send you rolling on the floor. Then you'll let me in, won't you, sweets?"

"Keep living in that dream-world of yours, Chero."

Cherchenko bowed and headed down the corridor, sweeping me dizzily back and forth as he sang a ditty full of snide double-entendres about Korofkin. I caught sight of the pomander he wore at his waist, the source of the ambergris scent. But then I saw the bells tipping the crown stitched onto my head swish back and forth in front of me.

Somehow I had become a fool's bauble, Cherchenko's marotte!

Like the way I once conjured revenant shades to animate my manikin familiars, my soul was now trapped inside a cloth jester's head impaled on the fool's mock symbol of office, complete with belled cap and painted face. It wasn't my heartbeat I had been feeling—it was Cherchenko's.

The odd haze in my mind made it hard to think; but the more he shook me, the worse it became. I could suffer it no longer. "By the Sun and Moon, stop!"

He did.

He heard me.

Cherchenko looked around him; but after I called his name, he raised me up and squinted at me. He had the kind of eyes that looked deep into you, maybe too deep. I stared back. The pools of pale blue reflected the face of his marotte and not my true face. Still, when I pursed my lips, so did the puppet's mouth.

Why I had returned from beyond death, I did not know; but perhaps this was the opportunity I was denied in life, my last chance to save my beloved Prianya. However, without a body and only a cloth head filled with beans, I could not do anything without Cherchenko's help.

"Nod if you can hear me."

"Flay my hide, I've gone mad at last," he said, but slowly nodded nonetheless. He was smarter than he let people believe.

"No, you haven't, Cherchenko. It's me, Vod."

"Vod? Then I'm definitely mad." He slumped to the floor and squeezed into an alcove. What I could see of his natural face had turned white. "You're dead, Lord Conjurer. They spiked your rotting head on a pole at the palace gate. Is this part of your—" he cast a suspicious glance behind him, as though spies could be hiding behind the tapestries that lined the corridor, "—your necromancy?" he finished in a whisper. Even the mere mention of the word *necromancy* in the palace was unwise.

"The Tsarina's life is still in grave danger. I think the Patriarch means her harm," I said. "You must help me discover what's wrong with her, Cherchenko."

He closed his eyes and trembled. "Why do you haunt me, Vod? Haven't you hurt me enough?"

I didn't know what he meant, but I had to rouse him to action. "You've seen me conjure wyverns of bone against the armies of our enemies, raise drowned men to harry river pirates. Is it so difficult to believe in me as a ghost?"

"Oh, Lord Vod, what can I do?" he said, his eyes tearing up. "They won't let me in because that worm Damascu thinks he's in charge. He never laughs, you know. We can't have that."

"No, we can't. I don't know how long I have left in this world, but I must try to save her. For some strange reason I'm stuck in your marotte."

He smiled weakly. "Nice face, at least. I'd say it's an improvement, but who could ever improve upon you, Lord Vod?"

"Then you'll help?"

"How can I not, when you ask so sweetly? What should I do?"

"We'll need my wand—if Damascu hasn't broken it already. You must check my apartments. It's about the length of your forearm and made from carved whalebone."

"Got it," he said.

I expected Cherchenko to head for my room, but he stayed sitting. "What are you waiting for?"

"I have it already," he said. "I saw the soldiers storm into your apartments to drag you away. More came for your manikins and spellbooks, but I sneaked in afterward and found the wand under your bed. I knew they shouldn't have it, so I hid it."

I breathed a sigh of relief. "Where?"

"Um, well, you're part of it."

I smiled when I figured it out. He had stuck the fool's head from his baton on top of my wand. "Brilliant, Chero." The scrimshaw wand was my conduit for channeling my magic. I had put a sliver of my soul inside it, which was why I could communicate with Cherchenko. But I had begun to fade when he lost his grip on the wand earlier. The wand must be stealing his lifeforce to keep me in the world of the living. It wasn't my heart I felt beating, but his.

Chero blushed. "I still don't know how to get into the Tsarina's apartments. Korofkin won't let me through."

But I knew a way. Though Prianya named me Lord Conjurer, many in the Tsardom believed Patriarch Damascu's accusations and called me necromancer. Prianya could not openly profess her love for me without jeopardizing her throne, but we found a way to tryst with one another. "There is a secret entrance, but you must tell no one."

He sighed. "On pain of undeath, I suppose?"

"Heart's Door. There's a fresco of two swans in the Tsarina's Garden, opposite the Royal Tower. Go there."

Cherchenko sprang to his feet. We hurried through the palace towards the garden, saluting chambermaids and blowing kisses to guards along the way.

"Chero, what were you doing watching my apartments in the middle of the night?" I asked.

"Oh, that? I—I couldn't sleep." I caught his cheeks reddening before he turned my face away. "Say, even if we can get in to see Her Majesty, what then?"

"A spider plans no web till her first strand takes. So, too, we must wait." We darted into the snow-kissed garden, lit by the light of dusk. At the fresco, I directed him towards the swans, one black as soot and the other paler than frost. Facing each other, their necks outlined the shape of a heart. Prianya and I had painted them together last summer. Each morning I'd daub her nose with a dash of white paint, and in return she'd touch black to the beard under my lip. That was our secret kiss.

"Press your hand against it and say *Aleksiniu*." It was the name of the Star of Loyalty. "If you bear no malice against the Tsarina, the magic will take you through."

"Wh-what if I'm n-not so fond of Her Majesty as you think I am?"

Could I have judged him wrong? No. He had an annoying habit of being constantly underfoot, barging in at the most inopportune times, but Prianya always said Chero was her confidante. "You have a good heart, Chero. I cannot imagine you hurting Prianya."

"I wouldn't. Not on purpose." He slumped to the ground with tears in his eyes, his heart pounding faster.

"What's wrong?" I asked softly. "What did you do?"

His eyes widened. "Nothing. But when she tells me things about you—about how much she loves you—well, I'd wish she never told me those things, and sometimes I'd, I'd. . . ." His lips trembled uncontrollably.

Did he harbour hidden feelings for Prianya? "Chero. A secret love still shines with love's splendour. Though the Tsarina may not return your affections, trust in your love for her and do right by—"

Cherchenko lifted me and kissed me, stunning me into silence.

Pieces of the puzzle fell into place. The way he used to stare at me in court. Why he was watching my apartments in the middle of the night. His blush. Why he sneaked into my chambers and took my wand, keeping it close as always.

He was in love with *me*.

He threw me to the ground. "I *have* gone crazy."

I should have seen the signs of his yearning for me, but I had been so lovestruck that I overlooked the clues, much like I did Damascu's scheming. Quite possibly, it was his love for me that called back my soul.

"Please, Chero, I'm real. Pick me up," I begged, nearly unable to form the last word.

"She favoured you so. Sometimes I wished she'd simply go away and not love you at all." Reluctantly, he plucked me from the ground. His voice weakened to a whisper. "I wished every day for you to notice me. To smile. To need me."

"I'm sorry. I never knew." What could I say? "Do you hate her because she loves me?"

He looked up at the darkening sky. "That's why I don't think I can do this."

"You care more than you think. Isn't that why you tried to get inside her apartments? Your loyalty has not been compromised by your love for me. Do not let the memory of me darken the bond between you and your Tsarina."

"A wretched memory that won't let me drown in my own tears."

"Nonetheless, Chero, I have need of you."

Cherchenko sniffled. "Right. Whether you're a ghost or just a figment of my imagination, I must still save Her Majesty." He reached for the heart-shaped spot on the fresco and touched it, speaking the secret name.

We faded like shadows exposed to sunlight and re-formed in front of a sister fresco inside the Royal Tower. Cherchenko pulled his hand from the wall and stared at the painted birds, also black and white but in mirrored positions.

"Quiet," I cautioned. "It might help if you take off your hat."

He removed the hat with only the barest hint of a jingle. "Sorry, I can't undo your bells," he whispered.

"Can't be helped. Just be careful."

Cherchenko stuck my head into the doorway and waited for me to signal before he tiptoed into the next room. In this manner we moved deeper into the apartments, following the growing scent of burning herbs. When we reached the Tsarina's bedroom, Cherchenko thrust the marotte into the doorway at heel's height to afford me a view of the interior.

The Palace Healer Olleska sat at the Tsarina's bedside tending to smouldering herbs in a censer. Patriarch Damascu stood on the other side, leaning in to study Prianya's face. I whispered to Cherchenko to stay where he was but to hold me steady so I could spy on them.

I could barely see my beloved amid the down pillows and silken sheets, but the Patriarch said prayers over her, took out a crystal vial and sprinkled her brow with liquid from inside it. Was it holy water or poison? Did the healer not think it strange?

"Can you do nothing more for her?" Damascu asked.

"I'd be surprised if she ever wakes, let such thoughts be damned," Olleska admitted. She added more herbs to the censer and wafted the smoke towards Prianya. "Poor girl. I doubt she knows she's with child."

A child. *My* child?

"It is for the best," Damascu said. "It disgusts me, the thought of that treacherous necromancer forcing himself upon her royal body, but an heir is still an heir. Better to raise the child under my tutelage than risk a civil war. I shall teach the child to love and fear the Troika. Have you the skill to keep her alive until the child is born?"

Olleska nodded, but looked pained. "If you could call that living. But giving birth will kill her."

I wanted to make hands of my welling anger and choke Damascu. I wanted to bury him alive, conjure his corpse from the grave and send it to walk the land until his flesh rotted and his bones rattled apart. But trapped in the marotte as I was, I could do nothing but seethe. "Chero, we must prove Damascu's treachery. We must find out what he's sprinkling on the Tsarina."

"Bet you it's in Damascu's chapel," Chero said, stealing back towards Heart's Door. "He can't shut his mouth about the Troika between two pisses. But what if we don't find proof, Vod?"

"Then we might have to resort to magic."

He drew a deep breath. "I—I won't dabble in necromancy."

"Conjuration," I corrected. "The words are easy to learn, but once unleashed, difficult to control. Do you feel it? Your life-force coursing through the scrimshaw wand?"

"Is that what it is?" He blew hot breath on his reddened fingers holding the wand. "I thought I had the chilblains."

"Like a needle, the wand pierces the veil between life and death. But for a conjurer to keep a soul in the world, he must sustain it with a measure of his own life. You called me back from the dead, Chero, so you must have a natural skill for it. Had you conjured a spirit who meant you harm, it might have devoured all your life."

"Does this mean you actually like me?" he asked with a nervous laugh.

I smiled. "I suppose. Will you learn a spell?"

"I don't know. I'm not strong like you." Cherchenko touched the heart-spell and returned us to the Tsarina's Garden.

"You have a unique strength of your own. It took great courage to admit your love for me."

"That?" He shrugged. "I figured you couldn't punch me in the face, what with you being armless and all."

"I would never do that."

"I was teasing. Very well, Vod. Only for you."

"Then I give you a name to conjure with, but do not speak it whilst you hold the wand, not yet." I waited for him to nod before continuing. "*Ilincharna*, the Sentinel Star. When your life is in danger, point to something once living, cry forth her name and it will rise to defend you."

"That's it? Point and say a name? I thought you conjurers spent years on your craft."

"More I dare not teach you," I answered. "Beyond the names, we learn the lore of the stars as well as spirits. Much of the training is to learn how to resist the voices of the dead and the power they promise."

"Oh? Does that mean I should start ignoring your voice?" He smiled.

The Chapel of Reveries was built into Palace Halcyon when Damascu rose to the rank of Patriarch. Under his guidance, worship of the Troika swelled in Nobylisk, and indeed, throughout the entire Tsardom. Chero and I arrived at an inopportune time of night, at least for our plans to search the chapel. After all, night was the time to worship the Gods in Slumber.

The stained glass windows high in the chapel walls depicted the Troika chained in sleep, while statues of white stone carved into their likenesses towered from the centre of the chamber. Fortune-Dreaming, a man in a two-faced mask balancing knives and cups; Hag-Rid-Rapture, an incarnation of beauty wreathed in her own long hair, hands creeping out of the tangles to grope her curves; the one-armed Death-In-Sleep, the grinning skeleton, wielding his sabre of life-taking. Three of Damascu's acolytes tended to the candles illuminating the hall, while twelve penitents sat cross-legged on silken weaves, rocking as they prayed.

"What are they praying for?" Cherchenko whispered.

"Safe slumbers, prophetic visions, and a role in the harem-dreams of Rapture," I guessed. "Not a worshipper, are you?"

"I prefer to sleep at night, not pray."

"Too many eyes," I said. "They'll tell Damascu if they notice us skulking around."

Cherchenko smiled. "Then forget skulking and let me deal with it my way. I *am* only a fool to them. I'll let you look for the hiding spot." He stuck the marotte into his mouth and cartwheeled into the chapel with dizzying speed, the world spinning around us.

"By the Troika, what are you doing?" cried the woman dressed in the garb of Hag-Rid-Rapture.

Cherchenko returned the marotte to his hand and bowed, letting me see the statues up close, the nearest one being Fortune-Dreaming. "I'm a new convert, paying tribute to the Troika my way." He turned and bowed to the confused worshippers. "Look, isn't Fortune-Dreamy a jester like me? You never know what he's going to do, and that pretty much sums me up too." He did an impromptu one-handed handstand.

Even the smallest detail seemed as grand as emblems on billowing sails to my eyes, but I could not see any telltale seams of concealed compart-ments on Fortune's statue. It wasn't here. "Chero, get us closer to Death-In-Sleep."

He somersaulted over to Death's statue where he pulled the man with the skull mask towards him, staring into his mask's eye sockets. "Next we have Dying-In-His-Sleep. The best way to go, hmm? What say you?"

With his other hand, he waved the marotte towards the statue, affording me a better view of it. However, I still could not find anything strange.

"Fetch the Patriarch," the woman dressed as Rapture said to the skull-masked man.

"It's not here, either," I said. "That leaves Rapture."

Taking the cue, Cherchenko danced around the base of Hag-Rid-Rapture. I looked high and low, wherever he waved the marotte.

"Haggy-Rapture, can you mend my broken heart? Make me forget the one who can never return my love?" Chero said with true sadness. "I beg you to take away my pain. Send me an incu—I mean, send me a succubus to kiss away my troubles. I've dreamt it all my life."

Incubi and succubi! They were dream demons in service to Hag-Rid-Rapture, and it was said that their saliva was a poison of a kind, sending mortals into a fevered sleep from which they might never wake. It fitted the way Damascu would think: a sacrifice in the name of the Troika. "Chero, I think he's using incubus venom."

But how did you counter incubus venom? I thought about my studies, trying to remember all I could about demon nightmares and how to wake someone from one. A lover's kiss was the only thing that came to mind. Being dead, however, I doubted a kiss from a ghost stuck in a marotte would work.

"Damascu doused her earlier," Chero whispered. "Maybe he needs to renew the dose each night?"

"Then we stop him tonight. Chero, it must be in one of Fortune-Dreaming's cups."

Cherchenko looked up and gulped. "Where do they keep the ladder?"

Damascu stormed through the doors with his skull-masked acolyte. We were out of time.

Cherchenko bit the wand to free his hands. The acolytes tried to grab him, but I once watched Chero leap through burning hoops without singeing a tassel on his costume. He dodged them and clambered up the statue with acrobatic flair.

"Penitents, clear out. You, lock the doors behind them," Damascu shouted.

The worshippers began filing for the exit, but we reached the third cup from the bottom, halfway up the Fortune statue and discovered a silver flask etched with the image of Hag-Rid-Rapture. Cherchenko took it out of its hiding place with a triumphant cry, drawing the attention of the few who dawdled. "*Wha gnaw?*"

"We have to get it to Olleska," I said.

"Can we trust her?"

"We'll have to. We need to connect Prianya's illness to the Patriarch. Too many people have seen you with the flask for him to cover up where it came from."

Damascu shouted up at us. "Cherchenko, my good fool. What have you there? Give it here."

The acolytes locked the doors behind the last petitioner.

Cherchenko stuffed the flask down his pantaloons and took the marotte in his now-freed hand. "Alas, I dropped it somewhere where the Sun never sees, but sometimes the Moon." He stuck out his tongue.

Damascu smiled. "There's no place for you to run, clown."

"'Tis a pity you don't have a man-shaped hole in those." said Cherchenko, gesturing at the stained glass windows. "Want one?"

"Leap through them if you dare, but you will not survive the fall," Damascu replied. "Surrender and I will treat you well. You can dance for me as Fortune-Dreaming. Tell me, who put you up to this?"

"Do you really want a name?" Chero asked. "It's V—"

"Wait, Chero, throw me to him," I interrupted. "Then tell him the name of the Sentinel Star."

Cherchenko understood. "Here, catch," he said to Damascu, and tossed me towards the Patriarch.

I fell and spun through the air. Surprised, Damascu reached for me. Clumsy as he was, he would doubtless have dropped me, but with the last vestiges of power I willed the marotte to twist in mid-air and land in his grasp. My face began turning back to cloth.

"Her name's *Ilincharna*, and she sends her love," Cherchenko shouted.

"*Ilincharna?*" Damascu repeated. My scrimshaw wand began to pull life force out of him and into me, softening my face again. I began consuming his strength.

"H-help me," he cried.

"Too late, traitor," I said, and by his startled reaction realized he could hear me. I leeched life from Damascu's pounding heart, forcing it to slow. He fought me and cried to the Troika to save him, but I had no mercy for him. Not after what he did to me, my beloved, and my unborn child.

Damascu's lifeless body fell to the floor, and I rolled out of his hand. The fog in my head had cleared, and I did not feel magic seeping out of me this time. The life force I had taken from my enemy now sustained me.

The skull-masked acolyte cried out and knelt to shake the Patriarch's body, while the others flung open the doors and began shouting for guards.

A hand scooped me up: Chero, who darted out of the chapel. I could no longer feel his heartbeat. He ran with great vigour once again for Heart's Door, and by the time he reached Olleska he was out of breath. He shook the flask out of his pant-leg and gave it to the puzzled woman. "Dam, Damascu used this inc, incu, incubus venom," he managed.

Olleska's eyes widened. She took the flask from Cherchenko, opened it and sniffed the contents. "Where did you get this?"

Chero crumpled into a chair to catch his breath, and told a version of the tale that did not include me.

At the end of his story, Olleska thanked Cherchenko. "Korofkin?" she cried at the top of her voice.

Korofkin answered her call with fear on his face. "Ma'am? Is the Tsarina . . . ?"

"No, Korofkin, she lives," Olleska said, her eyes brimming. "Quickly, find my apprentice and ask her to brew firesmoke tea, sweetened with clover honey."

"Will that wake her?" Chero asked.

"No, but it will ease Her Majesty's last nightmare."

Korofkin nodded. He raised an eyebrow at Chero, as though to ask how he got in, but then hurried from the room.

"The lords will come to question you, Chero, and some will not believe you," Olleska said.

"I am not afraid," Chero answered, and I was proud.

While Olleska tended to Prianya, I told Chero my wishes. "When she wakes, tell her I love her," I said to him.

Chero's lower lip trembled. "Why not tell her yourself?"

"She must never know. I will not have her waste her life pining for a ghost, and nor should you, my brave Jester Conjurer." I had taken Damascu's remaining years and they would sustain me in the marotte, but it would be kinder to let them think I must go. I would watch over them in secret until they had need of me, though I hoped such a day would never come. "Protect her as you have this day."

"I will, my love." Chero daubed away a tear from my eye.

I didn't know a marotte could cry.

The Snows of Yesteryear
JEAN-LOUIS TRUDEL

Northern Kujalleq Mountains

What would they do without the guy from Northern Ontario? Paul's thoughts were stuck in a loop. The same question was popping up every few seconds, probably because his leg muscles were gobbling up most of his body's oxygen. His brain just couldn't phrase a proper answer when the cold September wind was freezing his cheekbones, his breath burned in his throat, and his legs drove him up the snowy slope. The bag with the medikit seemed to grow heavier with every step. Soon, it would drag him all the way back down the mountain.

What would they do without the guy from Northern Ontario? The others had nominated him on the spot. Sure, send Paul, he's Canadian, he knows how to ski! Yeah, and he likes to play in the snow too. In the end, Francine had looked at him with those big, dark eyes of hers, and he'd been unable to say no.

He couldn't complain, not really. The Martian Underground had had its pick of young bacteriologists, but they wanted the one with actual winter experience. The guy from Northern Ontario. He'd said yes, to the job in Greenland and to the rescue mission.

Even with lightweight snowshoes, he sank a bit in the fresh snow as he leaned into the climb. Tomorrow, his muscles would ache. They didn't use to, not when he snowshoed through the woods of Killarney Park or skied cross-country in the hills outside Sudbury. But he was almost thirty and he'd spent more time in the lab lately than in the field.

He did wonder how the Old Man had fared coming out this way. He must have taken the long way around, down to Narsarsuaq, and then down the coast, skirting the fjord, until he could walk up the valley formerly occupied by the Ikersuaq glacier. Four days at least. A long hike, but not a hard one even for Professor Emeritus Donald B. Hall, who was so old he remembered the twentieth century. Very little of it, actually, but enough to spin unlikely stories that entranced his graduate students.

Early on, Paul had looked up some history sites and decided Old Man Hall was repeating tales he'd heard from his own teachers. Passing joints at a Beatles concert? Flying to Berlin to help tear down the Wall? His date of birth was confidential, but he couldn't be that old, even with stem cell therapies.

Not that he was going to get the chance to beat any records if Paul didn't reach him in time. Every time Paul looked back, the Sun seemed closer to the horizon. He only stopped once, to catch his breath. If he saved the Old Man's life, he swore he would get the truth out of him about the one story he'd never managed to disprove or disbelieve.

His heart pumping, Paul started to climb again. He still found patches of snow to plant his snowshoes in, but he was nearing the windswept summit. Sometimes, the synthetic treads clanked and slipped on the bare rock, and he lost his balance for a second, his arms windmilling.

He was pondering whether or not to take off the snowshoes and rely on his boots the rest of the way when he saw the sign.

Private Property.

Paul frowned, worry fighting it out with disgust. The valley floor had been buried under the ice for millennia, and it had remained so well into the twenty-first century. And now, as stunted trees grew among the glacier rubble, it had already been claimed by outside interests. The sign was labelled in English, not in Kalaallisut or Danish. A number in a corner identified one of the companies owned by the Consortium that ran the seaports catering to the trans-Arctic trade.

Despite the sign, the new owners probably hadn't bothered with a full surveillance grid. Otherwise, the Old Man would already have been picked up, flown to a hospital, and fined.

Paul should be safe as well from prying eyes. Beyond the sign, the peak was in sight. After putting away his snowshoes, the bacteriologist clambered up the last few metres and mounted a small repeater on top of a telescopic pole. He wedged the pole into place with a few rocks. The small device hunted around for a few seconds and then locked on the signal of its companion a couple of kilometres away, within sight of the Martian Underground base camp.

"I'm at the boundary," Paul rasped into his mike. "A bit past it, in fact. I'll be starting the downhill leg now."

"We're here if you need us," Francine's sweet voice answered. "You're running behind schedule, but just be careful."

"I intend to."

"And, Paul," cut in the voice of the director, "try and find out why Professor Hall ended up where he did."

"I definitely intend to."

"I know he left before you announced your latest results, but if this was all a ruse to allow him to rendezvous with outsiders . . ."

"I don't see how he could have known before me, or swiped a DNA sample. But I'll ask."

He strapped on his skis and launched a small drone to act as an extra pair of eyes for him. As he set off, the drone's eye view was relayed to his ski goggles and helped him avoid several, literal dead ends. Slopes leading to unseen cliffs, rocks hiding around a curve, and other places where he would have ended up dead. Though his exposed skin stung from the wind chill, he enjoyed the descent along the slope of new powder, its blank whiteness marred only by animal tracks. A slope never skied before.

Mid-September wasn't supposed to be this cold in southern Greenland. Yet, temperatures had dipped as they once did in the twentieth century and preserved a couple of recent snowfalls. In Sudbury, Paul had played in snow drifts that were much thicker when his mother sent him outside because she didn't want him at home. He looked too much like his father and she didn't care for the constant reminder. So, yeah, he really liked the snow. It had done such a great job of replacing the home he couldn't have.

Snow had once meant hardship. Now, it was a luxury. Greenland's first ski resort had just opened an hour's flight away. The local forecast wasn't calling for more, but Paul tracked warily the oncoming cloud banks, massed so thickly over Niviarsiat Mountain that they threatened to blot out the late afternoon sun.

The Old Man's camp was putting out an intermittent signal, just strong enough to reach his drone still circling above the valley. By the time Paul was halfway down the mountain, he knew in which direction he would have to head. Towards the ice dam and the lake.

It was almost dark when he found the tent. It was white, propped up by a glacial erratic, and set in the middle of an expanse of fresh snow. Perfectly camouflaged.

"Professor Hall?" Paul called, his voice reduced to a hoarse croak.

"Don't bother knocking."

Hall was lying on air mattress, bundled up in a sleeping bag. Prompted by the voice in his earbud, Paul hastened to check the Old Man's vital signs.

"His temperature is slightly elevated."

"Perfectly normal for a fracture. Carry on. Anything else?"

The professor endured Paul's amateurish inspection without a complaint. He unzipped the sleeping bag himself, revealing his bare legs. A large, purplish swelling ran around the middle of his left shin. The skin was mottled and bruised, but unbroken. Paul swept his phone, set for close focus, over most of the injury.

The base camp's doctor did not hide her relief.

"Not an open break, then. This will make things easier. Give him painkiller number 4 and take a breather. Do not try moving him or putting on the exolegs for another fifteen minutes at least."

Paul took the hypo from the medikit and loaded the designated ampoule. As soon as the painkiller hit the Old Man's bloodstream, a couple of deeply etched lines on his face relaxed and vanished.

The bacteriologist settled down on the tent's only stool. He was breathing more easily, but his shoulders felt like tenderized meat. When he undressed to put on a dry shirt, he found that the skin chafed by the pack's shoulder straps had turned an angry red.

"So, what was so urgent?" he asked. "I thought you were dying."

"I may have exaggerated slightly the gravity of my condition."

"Why?"

"Because it wasn't a secure link. However, I assume you've set up a secure line of relays, as I asked."

"As secure as we could make it, using the same repeaters we use in our glacier tunnels. Narrow beams once the lock is made."

"Good boy."

"Well, tell me now, why couldn't Francine just fly in with the chopper to get you?"

"Any craft big enough to take both of us out of here would have been detected."

"I could have died out there on the mountain, Professor. Were you that afraid of being busted for trespassing?"

Hall responded by pointing his phone at the tent wall. A low-resolution video played on the billowing canvas. The first pictures were blurry, but they seemed to show a small, ground-hugging plane, its wings flapping occasionally to detour around a rocky outcrop. It flew above the shadowed southern valley flank, heading straight for the ice dam, and stopped so suddenly that it dropped out of the screen.

"I thought it had crashed. So, I sent up my emergency drone to see if the flyer needed any help. But you know what they say about good deeds . . ."

Wormhole Base, Northern Greenland

The ice was a creaking, shifting presence. Dylan didn't like to dwell on the audible reminders that a substance so hard could be so dynamic that it would slowly fill any tunnel bored through it.

"Was this part of the American base?" Kubota asked.

The businessman from somewhere in Asia—the name sounded Japanese to Dylan, but he hadn't inquired—was casting eager looks at the mechanical debris mixed in with the icy rubble left along the foot of the newly-carved wall. Dylan hurried him along and opted for enough of an explanation to keep him happy.

"In a sense, yes. The Americans were thought to have cleaned out all of Project Iceworm's stuff when they left, back in 1966, but we're still finding their scraps. Looks like they just didn't bother dragging out various pieces of broken-down machinery or equipment. We've also come across furniture and remnants of the theatre. Or perhaps it was the church. Everything got trapped inside the ice sheet when it closed in."

"So then, this tunnel isn't one of the original diggings?"

"No."

"Did you find any missiles?"

Dylan glanced at Kubota without managing to spot the twinkle in his eye that had to be there.

"No," he said curtly. "And the nuclear reactor was decommissioned and removed."

"Good. So then, this is a safe place."

Maybe he was radiation-shy. Given the effects of the Taiwan nuclear exchange on the entire region he came from, that wouldn't be surprising.

"The safest," Dylan confirmed. "Part of the Consortium's cover here is the Extragalactic Neutrino Observatory. The deep ice is clean enough for Cerenkov radiation to shine through quite a large volume. Not as good as in Antarctica, but at least we're looking in the opposite direction. The detectors point down, of course, to use the Earth itself as a gigantic shield and filter, but they're also protected to some extent by the bulk of the ice over them. We're not as far down, with only ninety metres of ice above us, but it's still a nicely rad-free environment."

"A one-time creation."

"The whole point," Dylan agreed.

The Consortium offered visitors with a need for utmost confidentiality the most private facilities ever built. Every meeting room was freshly dug out of millennia-old ice. The only manufactured objects brought in—chairs, tables, infrared lamps—were so basic as to be easily searched for even nanotech bugs. Nobody else had used a given room before and nobody else would afterwards.

This time, the Consortium itself had called the meeting. Secrecy would be absolute. Dylan had heard that all of the furniture would be made of particle board produced on the premises with lumber harvested from a submerged forest in an African lake. The whole idea being that no hidden transmitter or recorder could have been included decades ago within the trunks of a soon-to-be-drowned grove, or would have survived the chipping process . . . Dylan could think of a few flaws with this assumption, but as long as it set suspicious minds at ease, he wouldn't quibble.

"Here we are," he said.

Kubota went in first and Dylan followed, finding his way to the side of Brian McGuire. As head manager of the local Consortium office, McGuire would chair the meeting. As the brightest of the bright young interns, Dylan would supply specifics if required.

The room was large and freezing cold outside the enchanted ring of infrared lamps.

The tables were set in a hollow square, with enough seating for twenty people: an eclectic mix of owners, executives, and highly-trusted assistants.

"No names," McGuire announced in a booming voice. "Names are too easy to remember. Faces just slip away. Or change."

Not that individual names really mattered. The only names that counted were displayed on yellow cardboard squares and they identified the companies or industrial concerns represented by the people around the table.

"Notes?" asked a woman with a slight Scandinavian accent.

"You may use papers or internal electronics. If you managed to sneak in any external electronics, my congratulations to your technical staff, but you'll still have to sneak them out and their contents will have to survive a low-level electromagnetic pulse."

The woman nodded. McGuire added:

"At the end of the meeting, I will offer a road map, boiled down to six main points. We worded them to be easy to memorize. In many instances, details will come later. We are here to ask and to answer questions. If the answers aren't satisfactory, we won't go forward. But I truly believe that we are standing on the ground floor of something big."

Heads nodded. The Consortium had already proved it could place big bets when it had built up Qaqortoq from a sleepy fishing village into a major port for container ships coming or going from Asia, Europe, or North America, and needing to swap containers before heading to their ultimate destination. In the broader context, Wormhole Base was a side-project catering to a few thousand people a year while also serving to demonstrate the Consortium's commitment to Greenland. But McGuire was willing to go slow and build his case first.

"Global warming is the new industrial frontier. Mitigation and adaptation are already huge, and are going to become even huger. We'll have to beat back deserts, move cities to higher ground, and re-create whole new species."

"I thought the Loaves and Fishes group was cornering the market for new heat-tolerant crops and pollution-resistant fish," said an older man whose spot at the table bore the name of a well-known Canadian nanotech company.

"Perhaps, but they're not turning a profit," Dylan objected.

McGuire threw him a menacing look, but his voice remained smooth and practiced as he ignored the double interruption.

"Everybody here has a finger in the pie, and a stake in the result, but we want more. Greenland is the first new piece of prime real estate completely up for grabs since humans arrived in North America—unless the first wave actually beat the one that went to Australia."

"Rather barren real estate."

"It'll get better."

"And not entirely deserted."

"The current population is just hanging off the edges of the landmass, so it will only be a factor if we let it. Our new facilities have attracted so many immigrants that they're swamping the locals. One way or another, we don't expect the Nuuk government to be a worry."

The man identified as Toluca nodded, apparently willing to concede the point. His own face bore a distant family resemblance with that of the Greenland Inuit.

"As part of your invitation, we included a topographic map of Greenland without the ice sheet," McGuire added. "It must have struck you, looking at the map, that there are only a few major glacial outlets. Plug them up and the Greenland ice sheet will no longer contribute anything to sea level rise."

There were blank looks all around the table. Preventing sea level rise was not an obvious source of profits. Saving the world would have to yield dividends to catch this group's attention.

"Where will the water go?"

"Nowhere. It'll stay where it is. Part of Greenland lies below sea level. Up to three hundred metres. The central part of the continent can easily contain a major inland sea."

"Isn't the crust depressed under the weight of all that ice? Won't it rebound?"

The woman from Scandinavia probably knew something about post-glacial rebound. Dylan looked expectantly at McGuire, but the Consortium manager did not need to consult his assistant.

"Come on, think! If the water is contained when the ice melts, it won't go anywhere. The overburden remains nearly the same. The meltwater will be quite sufficient to prevent isostatic rebound."

The woman did not yield as easily as Toluca and probed further.

"I did look at the map. The central ice sheet is over three kilometres high; most of the surrounding mountains are no more than hills. The peaks reach up to two kilometres on the eastern coast, but most of the western hills are only half a kilometre high. Even if you could turn most of central Greenland into an enclosed basin, something like half the ice is still going to melt and add to sea level rise."

"Half is better than none. And the half flowing out can be turned to good use."

"Such as?"

"No mean bonus. If you plug the outlets and water rises behind the walls, we will be able to use some of it to power hydroelectric plants."

Dylan hid a smile as backs straightened, chair legs scraped along the roughened ice of the floor, and gazes fastened on McGuire.

"White coal," Kubota said, his eyes narrowing.

"Enough to power whole new cities, yes."

"The gaps between the hills are huge," the Scandinavian woman noted.

"All the more work for us. If this is sold as a way to control water outflow, we can get government money to help with the construction. And we can start with the smallest outlets, the ones that will cost least to plug and will be all the more profitable."

"So then, assuming there is money to be made, I think we would like to be a part of it," Kubota said slowly. "We can talk about the technical issues later. Plenty of time for that. What I would like to know is how you intend to tackle the political side. Sea levels have risen a metre since the beginning of the century, but most governments haven't budged or tried seriously to slow the warming. Why would they act now?"

"Floods."

"As in glacial lake outburst floods?" the Scandinavian woman asked. "Those can be cataclysmic!"

Dylan had researched the Missoula floods that had devastated eastern Washington State at the end of the last glacial period. The lake had been gigantic. The collapse of an ice dam had unleashed a flood with more water than all of the planet's rivers put together, flowing with a speed rivalling that of a car on a highway. The flood had scoured riverbanks down to bedrock and carried chunks of glacier for kilometres downstream. He expected to answer questions later, but it was still McGuire's show for now.

"Precisely," the Consortium manager confirmed. "Take Niviarsiat Lake in Kujalleq. Fifty years ago, there was a glacier half a kilometre high in the same spot. Now, it's a meltwater lake dammed by leftover ice. If the dam broke, the water would rush down Ikersuaq Fjord and destroy everything within reach."

"Is this what you're proposing to do?" the Canadian asked.

Some of the attendees glanced at the icy walls and ceiling, as if to reassure themselves they were as safe from espionage as could be.

"Does anybody live in Ikersuaq Fjord?" Toluca asked, squinting again.

"Most of the valley near the lake actually belongs to a Consortium company and access is forbidden. Once you reach the actual fjord, there's a small settlement at Niaqornaq and the town of Narssaq is found on the next fjord over, though it is connected to Ikersuaq by a strait. Many buildings have already been moved to higher grounds, but the docks would certainly be swamped."

"What about victims?"

"Their deaths will serve a greater purpose. Let's be frank, people. Casualties would help us make our case to the government."

"Is this a hypothetical discussion?" the Canadian insisted.

McGuire held the eyes of the owners and executives around the table. Dylan noticed some of the assistants closer to his own age looked uneasy, but they weren't involved. McGuire challenged his peers when he answered, his voice dropping to a lower tone.

"Last winter, one of our best men set off explosives underneath the glaciers feeding the lake. There were no visible effects, and the blasts could be confused with an icequake, but the ice beneath the glaciers was turned into Swiss cheese. Throughout the summer, the glaciers calved several times, shedding huge chunks of ice that melted in the sun. The lake level has risen so far and so fast that pressure near the bottom should have pushed the freezing point below the temperature of the ice. The water should already be eating away at the base of the dam."

"When will it break?"

"Two weeks from now. Mid-September."

Nobody asked how he could be so certain of the timing. Faces closed while minds readied to grapple with technical details as a way of forgetting what had just been discussed. Dylan suspected that all they cared about now was that the meeting room be blown up as promised after they left, tons of ice crushing the furniture and burying the very memory of the words they had heard.

Niviarsiat Lake, Southern Greenland

Old Man Hall had slipped just as he was launching the drone into the air, banging his leg hard on a boulder in the wrong place at the wrong time. He said drily that he'd known right away that it was a break, not just a bruise. Paul didn't ask how. Unable to put any weight on it, he'd managed to hop and crawl back to his tent, where he'd waited for the return of the drone.

The drone's video was much clearer than the phone pictures. The small plane seen earlier had found a smooth stretch of gravel by the fan of rivulets streaming out of the ice dam base. Paul would have liked to freeze the frame, but the professor was still holding his phone. The gravel looked suspiciously smooth and uniform, devoid of any larger rocks or significant dips. A previously used landing strip, perhaps?

"This is where it gets interesting," the Old Man whispered.

The plane had come to a quick stop close to the foot of the ice dam. A man stepped out, looked around, but did not look up. He opened a cargo compartment, took out a heavy rucksack, and walked over to the dam, bent under the weight of his load. He was using what looked like a ski pole as a walking stick. He took his time climbing up the bumpy outward surface of the dam. When he was about two thirds of the way to the top, the man knelt by a narrow crevasse and probed with his pole. He got up and tried another crevasse a few metres away. It took him two more tries to find what he was looking for.

This time, he pulled out of his bag four, long box-like objects linked by cables. He lowered them inside the crevasse, using a rope clipped to one of the boxes, and then rose to his feet. The rucksack was much lighter now. The man checked his phone, walked down a few metres, checked it again, walked back to the plane, and checked it one last time before taking off.

"Any chance those wouldn't be high explosives?" Paul asked hollowly.

"A very small one. I've been in the field for decades, I've seen geologists at work, glaciologists, bacteriologists, paleontologists . . . I can't say why exactly, but the man's behaviour just doesn't fit. He was too hasty, didn't take any measurements . . . perhaps he was dropping off an instrument package for somebody else, but I don't buy it. It's a good thing I didn't look at the video for a couple of hours. Too busy trying to take care of my leg, so it was already dark when I watched it."

"And that's when you called base camp."

"Right away. And I didn't sleep much that night."

"Why do you think they would want to blow it up?"

"Unsure. The lake behind it is not that big, but the flood would rush down to the fjord and threaten Narssaq. I think Narsarsuaq would be safe from any kind of backwash. If it's some sort of terrorist plot, I fail to see the logic of it."

"Who else then?"

"Every time the world changes, there are those who will try to take advantage. Sometimes, they'll crawl out of very dark corners if they think they have something to gain."

"The Loaves and Fishes crowd?"

"They're into radical adaptation. New heat-tolerant crops. New marine life forms engineered to withstand the acidic seas. If they can thrive on a plastic-enriched diet, even better, since the oceans aren't going to run out of plastic for centuries. . . . But terrorism? I know they've sabotaged some bottom trawlers to make a point about disappearing fish stocks. And they've been strident about highlighting the shifting land and ocean conditions due to climate change. Still, why would they be behind this?"

Paul shook his head, unable to offer a rationale. The Old Man had been thinking it over for hours, after all.

"How about the Sunscreen Lobby? They've been looking for a way to convince governments to fund their orbital shield for years."

The professor shrugged. "Sure, extreme environmentalists of all stripes might go for it as a reminder of the dangers of global warming, but casualties are going to be low even if they blow it at night. And there's so much happening elsewhere that I doubt it would grab the world's attention."

"If it's that unlikely, it might not be a bomb. I should go and check before we panic."

"Now? It's dark and you won't see anything."

"I've got a good lamp. I watched the video carefully. I think I can find the right crevasse."

"How will you fish the package out? It looks like he picked the deepest crevasse he could find."

"But he didn't recover the rope he used to lower the package. With a bit of luck, I can use the rope to pull it back up."

The professor half rose up, stretching out his arm as far as he could.

"Don't go. If the dam blows while you're out there, I won't have a chance. The flash flood will just roll over me."

"And I'll be dead. In that case, you might as well tell me now why you came here."

"What I do on my own time is none of your business."

Paul stood and zipped up his coat.

"If that's how you feel, Professor, we'll have to discuss this when I come back. I've come over the mountain to help you, and that was hard enough. But I've spent years working on the identification of bacteria preserved in the ice, or beneath the ice. I've examined I don't know how many samples taken out of tunnels dug with hot water hoses or brought back by icebots from deep under the ice sheet. I've helped to isolate bacteria able to repair their DNA in freezing conditions for over a million years. I've found two new strains that synthesize methane in brutally cold conditions to help the Martian Underground jumpstart the global warming of Mars. And I've . . . Anyway, if you don't think I care about my work going to somebody who didn't pay for it, you need more time to rethink your assumptions"

"All work that I taught you how to do."

"Don't flatter yourself. I had other professors. But I did look up to you for one thing."

"What?"

"Ethics."

The Old Man grabbed for the stool and tried to lever himself upright without using his leg. Paul shouldered his backpack again, wincing slightly, and opened the tent slit.

"No, Paul, wait. It's not what you think. I was freelancing, but it had nothing to with the Martian Underground, or with your work."

"What, then?"

"I had a contract with the Pliocene Park Foundation. I was supposed to sample Niviarsiat Lake, or the glaciers upstream ideally, for ancient DNA."

Paul turned around.

"The Pliocene Park project? I've heard of it. Doesn't it involve buying land for a nature preserve that will recreate the environment of the Pliocene?"

"More than that. It will be stocked not only with surviving species of the Pliocene, but with ones we've been able to resurrect from past extinction.

In Siberia, the melting permafrost has released carcasses from the last interglacial. Reviving mammoths was only a start. The Russians are working on mastodons and stegodons and chalicotheres. But one of the best places for finding relics is underneath the Greenland ice sheet. There may be fossils once we access the underlying rocks. And there are certainly DNA remains in the lowest strata of the ice, some of which should date back to the Eemian or Pliocene. Mostly plants, we expect, but also some northern animals."

"So, you were working for a zoo. I guess we can all sleep easier."

"There's more to it than that. Global warming is a time machine back to the Pliocene. The whole project is about reminding people of that."

Paul sighed. "Your generation is still trying, isn't it?"

"And yours has given up."

"Perhaps because we saw how far you got. The sins of our fathers passed down to us, but we don't have to repeat the errors of our fathers."

"At least, we tried. We threw everything at the problem. Even cut back on total emissions while the population was rising to ten billion. But things kept getting worse. Warmer seas no longer absorbed as much carbon dioxide. So, we seeded the ocean deserts with iron dust and made them bloom with phytoplankton. Carbon dioxide uptake increased. So did ocean acidification, killing the coral reefs. When fisheries declined, people starved and turned to coastal fish and shrimp farms. Without the mangroves they cut down and the sand bars drowned by rising seas, hurricanes swept in and tidal surges wiped out many of the farms. . . . More people starved. In the end, we went back to farming, even if forests had to be cleared, even if synthetic fertilizers were needed, and even if transportation costs ballooned as such farms got too far from the mouths to feed. Except that pulping the forests returned more carbon to the atmosphere and transportation still burned up too much carbon. . . . Your turn now. Try to do better."

Paul had let him speak, thinking of the world beyond the small tent, beyond the deserted valley in southern Greenland. Drowned cities, burning forests, shifting sand dunes in Iowa, and the poor dying of thirst in India. What could a guy from Northern Ontario do about it all? He'd stopped loving the snow when he'd realized it was an illusion. It only covered up the same landscape as before. In the end, it changed nothing.

"In the end," Paul said quietly, "you always ended up back at your starting point, leaving us to live in a warming world or die."

"So, what did you do?"

"We faced reality. My generation intends to live. On this world or another."

Paul stalked out, leaving his mentor speechless. He stood in darkness for a moment, listening for any sound other than his quickened breathing.

If there was a bomb, it could be set off by a signal sent from a satellite passing overhead. The man in the plane wouldn't come back. There would be no warning.

He ducked inside the tent and took out another earbud as well as the medikit. He displayed the exolegs, which looked like pieces of bulky black hose connected to shapeless shoes.

"The earbud, you know how to use. If you haven't used exolegs before, pay attention to our doctor's instructions. The main thing is not to try to pull them on. Even with the painkiller, you'd feel the bones grinding together. If you do it right, they will split lengthwise so that you can wrap the covering around your leg. The smart material will exert the right amount of pressure to set and immobilize the bones. Afterwards, if you lead with your good leg, the artificial muscles will also walk your legs for you. The exoskeleton will take up most of the pounding, but you'll feel it when the painkiller wears off. It will hurt like hell."

He grinned evilly, thinking of his own battered flesh, then pointed in the general direction he'd come from.

"Head south, up the valley flank. The summit repeater will act as your beacon. But stop when you reach an altitude one hundred metres above sea level. There's a terrace Francine can land the chopper on to take us out. If you don't run across it, stay put, and I'll find you later. Or Francine will find you in the morning."

"Paul, wait, please. Come with me. You don't need to go."

"I still think it might not be a bomb. And if it's a bomb, there might be clues as to its maker."

"If it's a bomb, there's a good chance that it will blow tonight."

"It's still early. I'm betting that they'll wait till midnight, whoever they are."

This time, when he stepped outside, he kept going. Clouds hid most of the stars, so he turned on a flashlight. Gravel crunched under his boots and he thought of his old dream of walking on Mars. Nobody could work for the Martian Underground and not think of the possibilities.

Colonizing Mars was another long shot, like the orbital sunscreen intended to cool Earth. The methanogenic bacteria found in cold, lightless, microscopic pockets at the base of ancient Earth glaciers might serve to hasten the terraformation of Mars. They might even prove to be of Martian origin. On Earth, they were part of a slow-paced, long-lived subglacial ecosystem still dining off leftover biomass from earlier thaws.

Sowed across the Martian surface, they would belch, under the right conditions, enough methane to start creating a future haven for humanity.

Within the Martian Underground, fans of the ideas sometimes called themselves the Young Farts of Mars, if only to make it clear they wouldn't be happy with just going to Mars, like previous generations.

Francine's voice suddenly blared into his ear.

"Paul Weingart, what are you doing?"

"What a guy from Northern Ontario can do. No more no less."

"We heard everything. We think it's a bomb and that you should get the hell out of the way. Both of you."

"I won't be long. Just keep track of Professor Hall for me."

"Paul, please, wait!"

"Too late. Now, please give me some quiet, I need to concentrate."

He had reached the foot of the dam. The flashlight's beam played over the icy slope. He hadn't been boasting. He had a good memory for weird surfaces, trained by his work in the lab, and it only took him a quarter of an hour to find the spot where the man had left the package.

He swore when he discovered that the rope had slipped, falling into the crevasse. However, the beam picked up the yellow nylon rope only a metre or so below the lip of the crevasse. Paul threw himself flat on the ice, extended his arm, and grabbed the end of the rope.

And swore again when he realized he could do nothing with it. The load at the far end of the rope was too heavy. With one arm fully outstretched and the other braced at an angle against an ice boulder to keep himself from slipping forward, he lacked the leverage needed to pull himself up as well as the package.

He pondered his next move for a moment, fully aware of the ticking minutes that brought midnight closer. He finally took his other hand away from its hold and teased one of his snowshoes out of his pack. Gently. The friction between the main mass of his body and the snow-dusted ice was all that was keeping him in place. He lowered the snowshoe within reach of his right hand, using it to thread the rope between the frame and the decking before tying a quick lasso knot. He pulled back his free hand and groped for a hold.

Paul thought of Francine before trying to rise. She'd sounded worried about him. Was she still listening in? Trying to guess what was happening to him from his breathing?

Exhaling sharply, he pulled himself back from the brink in one go. He stayed in a crouch for a moment, his heart pounding, and then pulled out the snowshoe as slowly as possible. He was afraid that the knot might slip when placed under tension, but he just picked up the slack in the rope.

Once he had the rope well in hand, he wasted no time in lifting the package out of the crevasse. A grunt escaped his lips. The package was heavy.

"All's well," he announced. "I've got the . . ."

He hesitated. Shone the light on the objects from the crevasse. Noted the absence of any dials, gauges, or markings. Started walking suddenly with a faster stride.

"I think it's a bomb, after all."

"Leave it then," the director said.

"Not yet."

He backtracked all the way to the Old Man's tent. He checked it was empty and left the explosives inside. The farther he got from the tent, the harder it was to breathe. What if they blew *now*? He would feel really silly.

Yet, the bomb hadn't blown when he reached the side of the valley and began climbing immediately. Soon, he spotted the trail left by Old Man Hall, the trampled snow almost silvery in the light. He made quick work of following in the professor's footsteps and soon discerned the man's silhouette ahead of him. Just as he was on the verge of hailing him, the bomb blew.

The noise was surprisingly loud and the flash illuminated the entire nightscape, the dam dazzlingly white, the evergreen saplings thrown in sharp relief, and every rock of the valley floor clearly outlined. A few seconds later, gravel pattered down like a hard rain.

Paul wheezed helplessly for a moment, his ears ringing. He couldn't remember breathing since leaving the crevasse, but relief now unclenched overlooked muscles. The flash had shown him the terrace was within sight. Old Man Hall had found the edge of the flatter ground and was just waiting for him. He was an experienced hiker, after all.

The explosion had also caused the professor to turn around and locate the younger man. Once Paul caught up to him, the first thing out of the professor's mouth was a warning.

"They'll come and see why the dam didn't collapse. Whoever did this isn't going to be happy with us."

"I know. But we'll be gone. And your camp has been blown to bits. We'll be hard to track."

"But completely exposed until we get back."

"Look up."

The Old Man blinked and glanced at the clouds overheads, the light clipped to his head sweeping up. Whitish stars were falling from the sky and crowding into the beam. Snowflakes.

"It's snowing."

"As expected. The snow will hide our tracks, cover what's left of your tent, and make it more difficult for others to identify the helicopter."

"What helicopter?"

Paul raised his hand and waved at the shape emerging out of the flurries. He'd cheated. His younger ears had picked up the sound of the approaching aircraft before his mentor.

The professor's shoulders slumped as the man relaxed. He'd held up surprisingly well, given his age. Which reminded Paul of the question he'd wanted to ask.

"Hey, Prof, there's one thing I always wanted to know. Did you really work on the DNA profiling of O.J. Simpson?"

Hall stared at him and then smiled slowly.

"I'll tell you in the helicopter if you tell me why you were so sure that it was going to snow."

Paul nodded. He'd given him a few clues, but Old Man Hall was still a sharp one. "You know what many of us are looking for. Sure, the Martian Underground puts up the funding for bacteria that can survive on Mars, whether they're simple extremophiles or highly durable methanogens. But that won't help us on Earth. Except that, as you said, global warming is taking us back to the Pliocene."

"You've found something from the Pliocene!"

"Ironic, isn't it, that you came hunting here for Pliocene relics just as I was going to announce that I'd isolated a new strain of ice-forming bacteria in a sample from deep below the ice sheet."

"Rain-makers?"

"Exactly. We've always thought that bacteria from a warmer age might be more effective in our warming world than current strains. Pliocene microorganisms adapted to a warmer climate over millions of years, not the ten thousand years or so since the last freeze-up. The strain I found is related to modern-day varieties that promote ice nucleation in clouds."

"And now you've released it in the wild?"

The professor looked up again, his mouth closed firmly to resist the temptation of sticking out his tongue and tasting bacteria from another geological age.

"Whose fault is that?" Paul asked. "Don't worry, there's some left for further study, but I cultured enough to leave a flask with Francine. We agreed that she could use a drone to seed any likely cloud mass if it seemed necessary."

"That wasn't very ethical," the Old Man said, eyes downcast.

"But it may save our lives until we can report the sabotage to authorities."

The professor nodded, any further comment cut off by the roar of the helicopter landing at the far end of the terrace. Paul knew that he would work out soon the other implications of the discovery. The new bacteria heralded a wave of other discoveries that might help with humanity's adaptation to a warmer world. Might even help to control warming, if that wasn't too much to hope for.

Old Man Hall headed for the craft, walking stiffly. Paul followed, but he didn't make it all the way. The helicopter's pilot had jumped out in the snow and she ran to meet him. It was Francine.

She threw her arms around him, hugged him, and kissed him. When they stopped to breathe again, he smiled and asked, "Francine Pomerleau, what are you doing?"

"The only thing possible under the circumstances. You've forced me to ask a question that I don't know the answer to. What would I do without my guy from Northern Ontario?"

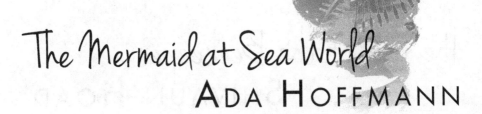

The Mermaid at Sea World
ADA HOFFMANN

Her house is six light-dappled slabs,
flat, silent, portholed:
children like woodpeckers hammer the glass
and men leer.

Once a day, the show: they pick him
from the crowd, a young man, strong
and camera-chained. The kind
who can't tear his eyes from the fins.
Preferably willing.
They toss him in.

The thrashing. The red-mottled water.
The ripple of wave-cuddled light on dead limbs.
The crowd goes wild, every time

yet, with her tail round his thighs and his throat in her teeth,
for six light-dappled breaths,
she forgets them.

The Trial of the Beekeeper
SHIVAUN HOAD

There was a huge clump of bees at the end of my driveway. That in itself wasn't reason enough for me to run towards them—they'd swarmed before—but the ever-so-familiar pair of pink Doc Martens protruding from the clump was.

Shit. I hadn't seen Ellen since our latest screaming match, but there were her boots, lying in my driveway.

As I knelt beside them, the bees took off, hovering over my head and exposing the body that lay beneath them. It was Ellen all right: the short red hair, those boots, and one of her usual flowery dresses. She was cold. The hum from the bees' wings was loud enough to be a shout.

I stood up. I needed to call the police, or maybe her mother. The bees buzzed louder, and circled my head, all of them in unison. That was weird. And once I thought about it, it was weird that they'd been all over Ellen—unless she was drenched in sugar water, they just shouldn't be that interested.

The bees stilled in front of my face, and began separating. They'd spelled out my entire name before I realized I was looking at letters.

The whole message read "JIM ITS ELLEN FUCK YOU." And that's when they started stinging me.

Honeybees don't sting at random. Each one dies once it uses its stinger, so they have to feel very mad or threatened. But once they do sting, and die, a chemical is released that signals to all the other bees to sting in the same place.

This kind of explains why I was stung twenty-five times in the face, mostly around the eyes, but nowhere else. Still, when it was time for me to be released from the hospital, I phoned my friend Benjamin and asked him to bring me my beekeeping gear. He was nice enough to not ask me any questions (and he and Ellen had been in a few art classes together, so I figured he'd be safe—just in case).

"Are you training your bees to join the circus or something?" he asked when he came to pick me up.

"Something like that. Why, were they doing something strange?"

"Well, it kinda looked like the whole lot of them were flying around in formation spelling out 'COCKSUCKER.'"

"Oh."

I dressed in my beekeeping suit: first the white shirt, tucked into white elastic-waist pants and gloves to my elbows, then the stiff hat with a veil hanging over it that drawstrings shut at the bottom. The layers keep the bees from getting to your skin, and everything's white to help you seem invisible—bees see a different colour spectrum, more ultraviolet than us humans.

Benjamin dropped me off at the edge of my driveway. When I stepped out of the car, the bees were spelling "CAST OUT THE DRONE." Ellen had said that the honeybees' practice of kicking all the male drones out of the hive for winter was sexist, but that she could see their point: the female workers were the ones who fetched all the nectar, the drones just ate and waited to mate with the queen. They were dead weight. I was dead weight. Wasn't that why we'd broken up?

I shook my head. I needed to focus if I wanted to sneak past this swarm. I lit my burlap rag and dropped it into the smoker. Everyone thinks beekeepers use smokers to calm the bees—that's not really true. Smoke freaks them out. They think their hive is on fire, so they rush back to fill up on honey to carry it safely away. It only "calms" them because they're too busy making a slow getaway to bother with you.

I walked slowly towards my house, with the smoker in hand, ready to give it a few pumps if the bees started focusing on me. So far, so good. I made it all the way up the long driveway to my front door without incident. Once I unlocked the door and stepped inside, a shudder ran through all the bee letters. By the time I'd locked the door, they had broken formation and were a huge loose cloud patrolling the yard.

After two days of getting dressed up in my bee-suit every time I went into the yard, I was getting seriously worried. The bees kept spelling different messages; I was grateful they were in the backyard (buzzing "DICKFACE") when the police were in the front yard asking me about finding Ellen's body. They were initially very curious about why she'd come to see her ex-boyfriend on the day she died. Well, so was I. They lost interest in Ellen, and in me, soon enough—it turned out she'd had an aneurysm. Being a suspect had made me angry; now I was just numb.

The bees were probably going hungry. I hadn't seen them visit their hive or any flowers in days, and they only had so much reserve strength. This year's honey crop was going to tank—if they didn't start collecting nectar soon, there wouldn't be enough honey to last them through the winter, much less any extra for me to extract and sell.

I wanted to put out some sugar water, just to help them keep their strength up, but . . . did I want weeks of being insulted by my bees? On the other hand, if I let them die, I'd have to order a new batch of workers and a queen, and it would take years to get as big as this colony.

After two days of stalemate, I couldn't avoid work any longer. I'd used up what bereavement leave I could get. I walked to my car in my bee-suit, got in and started to drive away. The second the car began to move, the bees were all over it, crawling on the roof, all over the side-mirrors and passenger windows. The front and back windows remained clear of bees, though, so I could still see pretty well.

I could park, run back into the house and hide, if they didn't get me once I opened the car door. Or, I could drive to work, and pretend I wasn't being haunted by the swarm.

So I drove to work. Once I hit the city proper, I got honked at constantly— and no wonder! The skin of my car looked like it was coming alive. I was half wishing my car was white, too, but I was getting sick of hiding. I parked and shed my bee-suit, then opened the door slowly, not wanting to squish any bees. They took flight, hovering just above the car's surface. As I stepped out, I could hear them close behind me. I turned around. Two feet behind me, was me. Well, an exact model of me, 6'1", long arms and skinny as a rake, formed of bees. Thousands of beating wings and compound eyes were fixated on me. After a second, the bee-me turned its head to look over its left shoulder, too. Oh, God. The thought of being followed by a bee-shadow all day was excruciating. Maybe I could lose them.

The door to get inside was automatic. I walked up to it and stopped a foot away. The door slid open but I stayed motionless. I checked over my shoulder again. Other than checking over their "shoulder" and beating their wings to stay in place, the bees stayed motionless, too. I took a huge step, through the open door and just to the far edge of the weight-sensing mat, then stopped. I checked again. The bee-shadow had stopped just before the open door. It slid closed, shutting them outside. Yes! I indulged in a stuck-out tongue of triumph at the bee-shadow. Too far—it dissolved in angry buzzing, all the bees dropping low as though the shape was melting. Soon they were all crawling over the sensor-mat. The door wouldn't budge though, it was meant for people, mostly adults, and there was no way they'd be heavy enough. I left the frustrated bees on the mat and headed to my cubicle.

I'd had a fairly productive morning—made a few sales over the phone and had one woman threaten to sue—and decided grab a coffee from the cafeteria. My mind kept drifting back to the bees outside. Could they damage my car? There was no way they could pierce the tires. The worst thing I could come up with was flying in through the exhaust, but that seemed like a suicide mission. Ellen didn't know much about cars anyway.

When I got back with my cubicle, there were bees on my chair, my headset and my computer monitor. I jerked and spilled coffee onto my shoes and the carpet. I realized what I should have been worried about: what happens when someone else goes through that door?

I went to sit down, but the bees on the seat of my chair stayed motionless, calling my bluff. I stayed standing.

Caroline, my boss, noticed my head protruding from the top of the cubicle, and took it as a cue to come over. Her eyes widened at the bees.

"Ah, Jim, what's going on here? Are those wasps *alive*?"

"Well, these are my honeybees, and they, um, followed me to work."

"Pest control!" she screamed.

"Stop it," I whispered as loud as I could. "I'll get them out of here!"

"You know Tara's allergic," Caroline whispered back. "You want us to get sued out of existence?" She yelled again: "Emergency, 9-1-1!"

I saw my coworkers standing up, looking over their cubicles. Panicking, I sprinted to the communal fridge and grabbed a can of coke.

I cracked it open. I poured the pop slowly over my head, getting it in my hair and beard, then dumped the rest onto the front and back of my shirt. It was cold and sticky and smelled like sugar. Perfect.

The bees started buzzing. Some started to fly towards me.

"Okay, bees. Ellen. Whatever. You're coming with me now. Because I'm sugary sweet and fucking irresistible."

And just like that, I was covered in them. Some guys do this "bee beard" stunt, where they put a caged queen bee under their chin and hundreds of bees crawl on them to get to her. I've never wanted to do that. I mean, don't get me wrong, I love my bees. But I like having a veil between me and them. Now, they were buzzing and crawling right on me, licking the sticky Coke off my skin. I had to move fast, to leave before they got bored of the Coke. I stood up slowly. I didn't want to startle them.

I was so concerned about the bees' feelings that I had forgotten about everyone else in the office. Tara came out of the washroom and immediately started screaming.

"Oh God, what is that? It's wasps! It's a wasp man! Oh, God, you know I'm allergic to wasps!"

"Tara. Tara. It's cool. It's me, Jim. The bees and I are leaving." I tried to sound calm, but I was worried one of the bees might crawl into my mouth while I was talking. She just kept shaking her head spasmodically.

I walked outside. It had started to rain. I was getting soaked, and the bees were slowly taking off. There were none left on me by the time I got the car door open.

"C'mon bees, let's go home."

They flew with the car on the ride back, dodging raindrops. When I reached my driveway, I was ready to admit defeat. I couldn't control them. I couldn't control my life with them in it. And I couldn't let them die.

In five years of beekeeping, I had never had any bees inside my house. This time, I let the swarm follow me inside. We went upstairs, together, to my bedroom. I went to my bookshelf and pulled down the photo of me and Ellen laughing, at Sarah and Tim's potluck. I was waiting, bracing myself for the bees to go wild, to fly from behind me and cover the picture frame . . . but there wasn't a sound. I looked behind me. They were on the floor, barely moving.

I knew why Ellen had been in my driveway. She was always trying to figure me out. She had—we both had—said a lot of shitty things to each other in our last fight. I guess it's what made it the last one.

I stepped carefully around the bees on the floor. When I got back to the bedroom with a shallow bowl of sugar water, they were still motionless. I resisted the urge to pour it on them to get a reaction; I didn't want their wings to get sticky. I set the bowl down. They didn't move. I was out of ideas.

"Shit, Ellen. Just . . . shit." I wanted to be mad at the bees, at her for being crazy and following me around, and insulting me, and scaring the crap out of my coworkers. But I wasn't.

"I'm sorry that we never got to get over being spiteful to each other. I'm sorry that things didn't work out, and that I couldn't be who you wanted."

Through the blur of tears, I saw some bees rising from the floor.

"I'm sorry that you died. Not because I wanted us to get back together . . . but because you didn't deserve it. You're a good person, and you didn't deserve me making you feel like I hated you. Because I don't."

And once again, they were on me, tiny tongues licking away my tears. They'd wanted salt, not sugar. Some bees still hung in the air, spelling out, "OH."

"I don't love you anymore either, though. Just for the record."

I got back "JERK" in reply, but the bees on my face were soothing and calm, and I could almost see Ellen's wink.

When I was done crying, I felt exhausted. I sprawled onto my bed, fully clothed. The bees stayed on top of me, like a living blanket. There was something familiar about the weight of them on my chest, something I'd been missing.

I didn't think I could fall asleep, covered in honeybees, but I must have. In the morning, it was clear that there would be no more bee-shadows, no more swears, and no more following me to work. The sugar water was gone and the bees were everywhere in the house, buzzing around aimlessly. I had to ask two local beekeepers to help me round them all up to bring them back to their hive.

"Why did you let them get inside, anyway?" one asked, when the house was finally free of bees.

"I don't know," I said. "I guess I was lonely."

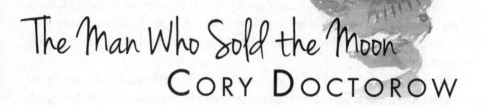

The Man Who Sold the Moon
CORY DOCTOROW

Here's a thing I didn't know: there are some cancers that can only be diagnosed after a week's worth of lab work. I didn't know that. Then I went to the doctor to ask her about my pesky achy knee that had flared up and didn't go away like it always had, just getting steadily worse. I'd figured it was something torn in there, or maybe I was getting the arthritis my grandparents had suffered from. But she was one of those doctors who hadn't gotten the memo from the American health-care system that says that you should only listen to a patient for three minutes, tops, before writing him a referral and/or a prescription and firing him out the door just as the next patient was being fired in. She listened to me, she took my history, she wrote down the names of the anti-inflammatories I'd tried, everything from steroids to a climbing buddy's heavy-duty prescription NSAIDs, and gave my knee a few cautious prods.

"You're insured, right?"

"Yeah," I said. "Good thing, too. I read that knee replacement's going for seventy-five thousand dollars. That's a little out of my price range."

"I don't think you need a knee replacement, Greg. I just want to send you for some tests."

"A scan?"

"No." She looked me straight in the eyes. "A biopsy."

I'm a forty-year-old, middle-class Angeleno. My social mortality curve was a perfectly formed standard distribution—a few sparse and rare deaths before I was ten, slightly more through my teens, and then more in my twenties. By the time I was thirty-five, I had an actual funeral suit I kept in a dry-cleaning bag in the closet. It hadn't started as a funeral suit, but once I'd worn it to three funerals in a row, I couldn't wear it anywhere else without feeling an unnameable and free-floating sorrow. I was forty. My curve was ramping up, and now every big gathering of friends had at least one knot of somber people standing together and remembering someone who went too early. Someone in my little circle of forty-year-olds was bound to get a letter from the big C. There wasn't any reason for it to be me. But there wasn't any reason for it not to be either.

Bone cancer can take a week to diagnose. A week! During that week, I spent a lot of time trying to visualize the slow-moving medical processes: acid dissolving the trace of bone, the slow catalysis of some obscure reagent, some process by which a stain darkened to yellow and then orange and then, days later, to red. Or not. That was the thing. Maybe it wasn't cancer. That's why I was getting the test, instead of treatment. Because no one knew. Not until those stubborn molecules in some lab did their thing, not until some medical robot removed a test tube from a stainless steel rack and drew out its contents and took their picture or identified their chemical composition and alerted some lab tech that Dr. Robot had reached his conclusion and would the stupid human please sanity-check the results and call the other stupid human and tell him whether he's won the cancer lottery (grand prize: cancer)?

That was a long week. The word cancer was like the tick of a metronome. Eyes open. Cancer. Need a pee. Cancer. Turn on the coffee machine. Cancer. Grind the beans. Cancer. Cancer. Cancer.

On day seven, I got out of the house and went to Minus, which is our local hackerspace. Technically, its name is "Untitled-1," because no one could think of a better name ten years ago, when it had been located in a dirt-cheap former car-parts warehouse in Echo Park. When Echo Park gentrified, Untitled-1 moved downtown, to a former furniture store near Skid Row, which promptly began its own gentrification swing. Now we were in the top two floors of what had once been a downscale dentist's office on Ventura near Tarzana. The dentist had reinforced the floors for the big chairs and brought in 60-amp service for the X-ray machines, which made it perfect for our machine shop and the pew-pew room full of lasers. We even kept the fume hoods.

I have a personal tub at Minus, filled with half-finished projects: various parts for a 3D-printed chess-playing automata; a cup and saucer I was painstakingly covering with electroconductive paint and components; a stripped-down location sensor I'd been playing with for the Minus's space program.

Minus's space program was your standard hackerspace extraterrestrial project: sending balloons into the upper stratosphere, photographing the earth's curvature, making air-quality and climate observations; sometimes lofting an ironic action figure in 3D-printed astronaut drag. Hacker Dojo, north of San Jose, had come up with a little powered guidance system, but they'd been whipped by navigation. Adding a stock GPS with its associated batteries made the thing too heavy, so they'd tried to fake it with dead-reckoning and it had been largely unsuccessful. I'd thought I might be able to make everything a lot lighter, including the battery, by borrowing some techniques I'd seen on a performance bike-racing site.

I put the GPS on a workbench with my computer and opened up my file of notes and stared at them with glazed eyes. Cancer. Cancer. Cancer.

Forget it. I put it all away again and headed up to the roof to clear my head and to get some company. The roof at Minus was not like most roofs. Rather than being an empty gravel expanse dotted with exhaust fans, our roof was one of the busiest parts of the space. Depending on the day and time, you could find any or all of the above on Minus's roof: stargazing, smoking, BASE jumping, solar experiments, drone dogfighting, automated graffiti robots, sensor-driven high-intensity gardening, pigeon-breeding, sneaky sex, parkour, psychedelic wandering, Wi-Fi sniffing, mobile-phone tampering, ham radio broadcasts, and, of course, people who were stuck and frustrated and needed a break from their workbenches.

I threaded my way through the experiments and discussions and build-projects, slipped past the pigeon coops, and fetched up watching a guy who was trying, unsuccessfully, to learn how to do a run up a wall and do a complete flip. He was being taught by a young woman, sixteen or seventeen, evidently his daughter ("Daaad!"), and her patience was wearing thin as he collapsed to the gym mats they'd spread out. I stared spacily at them until they both stopped arguing with each other and glared at me, a guy in his forties and a kind of miniature, female version of him, both sweaty in their sweats. "Do you mind?" she asked.

"Sorry," I mumbled, and moved off. I didn't add, I don't mean to be rude, just worried about cancer.

I got three steps away when my phone buzzed. I nearly fumbled it when I yanked it out of my tight jeans pocket, hands shaking. I answered it and clapped it to my ear.

"Mr. Harrison?"

"Yes."

"Please hold for Doctor Ficsor." A click.

A click. "Greg?"

"That's me," I said. I'd signed the waiver that let us skip the pointless date-of-birth/mother's maiden name "security" protocol.

"Is this a good time to talk?"

"Yes," I said. One syllable, clipped and tight in my ears. I may have shouted it.

"Well, I'd like you to come in for some confirming tests, but we've done two analyses and they are both negative for elevated alkaline phosphatase and lactate dehydrogenase."

I'd obsessively read a hundred web pages describing the blood tests. I knew what this meant. But I had to be sure. "It's not cancer, right?"

"These are negative indicators for cancer," the doctor said.

The tension that whoofed out of me like a gutpunch left behind a kind of howling vacuum of relief, but not joy. The joy might come later. At the moment, it was more like the head-bees feeling of three more cups of espresso than was sensible. "Doctor," I said, "can I try a hypothetical with you?"

"I'll do my best."

"Let's say you were worried that you, personally, had bone cancer. If you got the same lab results as me, would you consider yourself to be at risk for bone cancer?"

"You're very good at that," she said. I liked her, but she had the speech habits of someone who went to a liability insurance seminar twice a year. "Okay, in that hypothetical, I'd say that I would consider myself to be provisionally not at risk of bone cancer, though I would want to confirm it with another round of tests, just to be very, very sure."

"I see," I said. "I'm away from my computer right now. Can I call your secretary later to set that up?"

"Sure," she said. "Greg?"

"Yes."

"Congratulations," she said. "Sleep easy, okay?"

"I will try," I said. "I could use it."

"I figured," she said. "I like giving people good news."

I thought her insurance adjuster would not approve of that wording, but I was glad she'd said it. I squeezed the phone back into my pocket and looked at the blue, blue sky, cloudless save for the scummy film of L.A. haze that hovered around the horizon. It was the same sky I'd been standing under five minutes ago. It was the same roof. The same building. The same assemblage of attention-snagging interesting weirdoes doing what they did. But I was not the same.

I was seized by a sudden, perverse urge to go and take some risks: speed down the highway, BASE jump from Minus's roof, try out some really inadvisable parkour moves. Some part of me that sought out patterns in the nonsense of daily randomness was sure that I was on a lucky streak and wanted me to push it. I told that part to shut up and pushed it down best as I could. But I was filled with an inescapable buoyancy, like I might float right off the roof. I knew that if I'd had a hard time concentrating before, I was in for an even harder time getting down to business now. It was a small price to pay.

"Hey," someone said behind me. "Hey, dude?"

It occurred to me that I was the dude in question, and that this person had been calling out to me for some time, with a kind of mellow intensity—not angry, but insistent nonetheless. I turned around and found myself staring down at a surfer-looking guy half my age, sun-bleached ponytail and wraparound shades, ragged shorts and a grease-stained long-sleeved jersey and bare feet, crouched down like a Thai fisherman on his haunches, calf muscles springing out like wires, fingertips resting lightly on a gadget.

Minus was full of gadgets, half built, sanded to fit, painted to cover, with lots of exposed wiring, bare boards, blobs of hot glue and adhesive polymer clinging on for dear life against the forces of shear and torque and entropy. But even by those standards, surfer-guy's gadget was pretty spectacular. It was the lens—big and round and polished, with the look of a precision-engineered artifact out of a real manufacturer's shop—not something hacked together in a hack lab.

"Hey," I said.

"Dude," he said. "Shadow."

I was casting a shadow over the lens. I stepped smartly to one side and the pitiless L.A. sun pierced it, focused by it down to a pinprick of white on a kind of bed beneath the lens. The surfer guy gave me an absentminded thumbs-up and started to squint at his laptop's screen.

"What's the story with this thing?" I said.

"Oh," he said. "Solar sinterer. 3D printing with the sun." The bed started to jerk and move with the characteristic stepper-motor dance of a 3D printer. The beam of light sizzled on the bed like the tip of a soldering iron, sending up a wisp of smoke like a shimmer in the sun's glare. There was a sweet smell from it, and I instinctively turned upwind of it, not wanting to be sucking down whatever aromatic volatiles were boiling off the print medium.

"That is way, way cool," I said. "Does it work?"

He smiled. "Oh yeah, it works. This is the part I'm interested in." He typed some more commands and the entire thing lifted up on recessed wheels and inched forward with the slow grace of a tortoise.

"It walks?"

"Yeah. The idea is, you leave it in the desert and come back in a couple of months and it's converted the sand that blows over its in-hopper into prefab panels you can snap together to make a shelter."

"Ah," I said. "What about sand on the solar panel?" I was thinking of the Mars Rovers, which had had a tendency to go offline when too much Martian dust blew over their photovoltaics.

"Working on that. I can make the lens and photovoltaic turn sideways and shake themselves." He pointed at a couple of little motors. "But that's a lot of moving parts. Want it to run unattended for months at a time."

"Huh," I said. "This wouldn't happen to be a Burning Man thing, would it?"

He smiled ruefully. "That obvious?"

Honestly, it was. Half of Minus were burners, and they all had a bit of his look of delightful otherworldly weirdness. "Just a lucky guess," I said, because no one wants to be reminded that they're of a certain type—especially if that type is nonconformist.

He straightened up and extended his hand. He was missing the tip of his index finger, and the rest of his fingernails were black with grease. I shook, and his grip was warm, firm and dry, and rough with callus. You could have put it in a museum and labeled it "Hardware hacker hand (typical)."

"I'm Pug," he said.

"Greg."

"So the plan is, bring it out to the desert for Fourth of Juplaya, let it run all summer, come back for Burning Man, and snap the pieces together."

"What's Fourth of Jup-whatever?"

"Fourth of Juplaya. It's a July Fourth party in Black Rock. A lot like Burning Man used to be like, when 'Safety third' was the guiding light and not just a joke. Much smaller and rougher, less locked down. More guns. More weird. Intense."

His gadget grunted and jammed. He looked down at it and nudged one of the stepper motors with his thumb, and it grunted again. "'Scuse me," he said, and hunkered down next to it. I watched him tinker for a while, then walked away, forgotten in his creative fog.

I went back down into Minus, put away my stuff, and chatted with some people I sort of knew about inconsequentialities, in a cloud of unreality. It was the hangover from my week of anxiety and its sudden release, and I couldn't tell you for the life of me what we talked about. After an hour or two of this, I suddenly realized that I was profoundly beat, I mean beat down and smashed flat. I said goodbye—or maybe I didn't, I wouldn't swear to it—and went out to look for my car. I was wandering around the parking lot, mashing the alarm button on my key chain, when I ran into Pug. He was (barely) carrying a huge box, shuffling and peering over the top. I was so tired, but it would have been rude not to help.

"Need a hand?"

"Dude," he said, which I took for an affirmative. I grabbed a corner and walked backward. The box was heavy, but it was mostly just huge, and when we reached his beat-up minivan, he kicked the tailgate release and then laid it down like a bomb-disposal specialist putting a touchy IED to sleep. He smacked his hands on his jeans and said, "Thanks, man. That lens, you wouldn't believe what it's worth." Now that I could see over the top of the box, I realized it was mostly padding, layers of lint-free cloth and bubblewrap with the lens in the centre of it all, the gadget beneath it. "Minus is pretty safe, you know, but I don't want to tempt fate. I trust 99.9 percent of 'em not to rip it off or use it for a frisbee, but even a one-in-a-thousand risk is too steep for me." He pulled some elasticated webbing over it and anchored it down with cleats bolted inside the oily trunk.

"Fair enough," I said.

"Greg, buddy, can I ask you a personal question?"

"I suppose."

"Are you okay? I mean, you kind of look like you've been hit upside the head with a brick. Are you planning on driving somewhere?"

"Uh," I said. "Truly? I'm not really okay. Should be, though." And I spilled it all out—the wait, the diagnosis.

"Well, hell, no wonder. Congratulations, man, you're going to live! But not if you crash your car on the way home. How about if I give you a ride?"

"It's okay, really—"

He held up a hand. "Greg, I don't know you and you don't know me, but you've got no more business driving now than you would if you'd just slammed a couple tequila shots. So I can give you a ride or call you a cab, but if you try and get into your car, I will argue with you until I bore you into submission. So what is it? Ride? Taxi?"

He was absolutely, totally right. I hated that. I put my keys back into my pocket. "You win," I said. "I'll take that ride."

"Great," he said, and gave me a Buddha smile of pure SoCal serenity. "Where do you live?"

"Irvine," I said.

He groaned. "Seriously?" Irvine was a good three-hour drive in traffic.

"Not seriously," I said. "Just Burbank. Wanted to teach you a lesson about being too free with your generosity."

"Lesson learned. I'll never be generous again." But he was smiling.

I slid into the passenger seat. The car smelled like sweat and machines. The floor mats were indistinct grey and crunchy with maker detritus: dead batteries, coffee cups, multidriver bits, USB cables, and cigarette-lightercharger adapters. I put my head back on the headrest and looked out the grimy windows through slitted eyes as he got into the driver's side and started the engine, then killed the podcast that started blasting from the speakers.

"Burbank, right?"

"Yeah," I said. There were invisible weights on my chest, wrists, and ankles. I was very glad I wasn't behind the wheel. We swung out onto Ventura Boulevard and inched through the traffic toward the freeway.

"Are you going to be all right on your own?"

"Tonight? Yeah, sure. Seriously, that's really nice of you, but it's just, whatever, aftermath. I mean, it's not like I'm dying. It's the opposite of that, right?"

"Fair enough. You just seem like you're in rough shape."

I closed my eyes and then I felt us accelerate as we hit the freeway and weaved over to the HOV lanes. He put down the hammer and the engine skipped into higher gear.

"You're not a burner, are you?"

I suppressed a groan. Burners are the Jehovah's Witnesses of the counterculture. "Nope," I said. Then I said what I always said. "Just seemed like a lot of work."

He snorted. "You think Burning Man sounds like a lot of work, you should try Fourth of Juplaya. No rules, no rangers. A lot of guns. A lot of serious blowing shit up. Casual sex. No coffee shop. No sparkleponies. Fistfuls of drugs. High winds. Burning sun. Non-freaking-stop. It's like pure distilled essence of playa."

I remembered that feeling, like I wanted to BASE jump off the roof. "I have to admit, that sounds totally amazeballs," I said. "And demented."

"Both, yup. You going to come?"

I opened my eyes wide. "What?"

"Well, I need some help with the printer. I looked you up on the Minus database. You do robotics, right?"

"A little," I said.

"And you've built a couple repraps, it says?"

"Two working ones," I said. Building your own 3D printer that was capable of printing out nearly all the parts to build a copy of itself was a notoriously tricky rite of passage for hackerspace enthusiasts. "About four that never worked, too."

"You're hired," he said. "First assistant engineer. You can have half my van, I'll bring the cooler and the BBQ and pork shoulder on dry ice, a keg of beer, and some spare goggles."

"That's very nice of you," I said.

"Yeah," he said. "It is. Listen, Greg, I'm a good guy, ask around. I don't normally invite people out to the Fourth, it's a private thing. But I really do need some help, and I think you do, too. A week with a near-death experience demands a fitting commemoration. If you let big stuff like this pass by without marking it, it just, you know, builds up. Like arterial plaque. Gotta shake it off."

You see, this is the thing about burners. It's like a religion for them. Gotta get everyone saved.

"I'll think about it," I said.

"Greg, don't be offended?"

"Okay."

"Right. Just that, you're the kind of guy, I bet, spends a lot of time 'thinking about it.'"

I swallowed the snappish reply and said nothing.

"And now you're stewing. Dude, you are so buttoned down. Tell you what, keep swallowing your emotions and you will end up dying of something fast and nasty. You can do whatever you want, but what I'm offering you is something that tons of people would kill for. Four days of forgetting who you are, being whoever you want to be. Stars, dust, screwing, dope, explosions, and gunfire. You're not going to get a lot of offers like that, is what I'm saying."

"And I said I'd think about it."

He blatted out a raspberry and said, "Yeah, fine, that's cool." He drove on in silence. The 101 degenerated into a sclerotic blockage. He tapped at the old phone velcroed to the dashboard and got a traffic overlay that showed red for ten miles.

"Dude, I do not want to sit in this car for the next forty-five minutes listening to you not say anything. How about a truce? I won't mention the Fourth, you pretend you don't think I'm a crazy hippie, and we'll start over, 'kay?"

The thing that surprised me most was how emotionally mature the offer was. I never knew how to climb down from stupid fights, which is why I was forty and single. "Deal," I said.

Just like that, he dropped it. We ended up talking about a related subject—selective solar laser-sintering—and some of the funky things he was having to cope with in the project. "Plenty of people have done it with sand, but I want to melt gypsum. In theory, I only have to attain about 85 percent of the heat to fuse it, but there's a lot of impurities in it that I can't account for or predict."

"What if you sift it or something first?"

"Well, if I want it to run unattended, I figure I don't want to have to include a centrifuge. Playa dust is nanofine, and it gets into everything. I mean, I've seen art cars with sealed bearings that are supposed to perform in space go gunky and funky after a couple of years."

I chewed on the problem. "You could maybe try a settling tray, something that uses wind for agitation through graduated screens, but you'd need to unclog it somehow." More thinking. "Of course, you could just melt the crap out of it when you're not sure, just blaze it into submission."

But he was already shaking his head. "Doesn't work—too hot and I can't get the set time right, goes all runny."

"What about a sensor?" I said. "Try to characterize how runny it is, adjust the next pass accordingly?"

"Thought of that," he said. "Too many ways it could go wrong is what I'm thinking. Remember, this thing has to run where no one can tend it. I want to drop it in July and move into the house it builds me by September. It has to fail very, very safe."

I took his point, but I wasn't sure I agreed. Optical sensors were pretty solved, as was the software to interpret what they saw. I was about to get my laptop out and find a video I remembered seeing when he slammed on the brakes and made an explosive noise. I felt the brakes' ABS shudder as the minivan fishtailed a little and heard a horn blare from behind us. I had one tiny instant with which to contemplate the looming bumper of the gardener's pickup truck ahead of us before we rear-ended him. I was slammed back into my seat by the airbag a second before the subcompact behind us crashed into us, its low nose sliding under the rear bumper and raising the back end off the ground as it plowed beneath us, wedging tight just before its windshield would have passed through our rear bumper, thus saving the driver from a radical facial rearrangement and possible decapitation.

Sound took on a kind of underwater quality as it filtered through the airbag, but as I punched my way clear of it, everything came back. Beside me, Pug was making aggrieved noises and trying to turn around. He was caught in the remains of his own airbag, and his left arm looked like it might be broken—unbroken arms don't hang with that kind of limp and sickening slackness. "Christ, the lens—"

I looked back instinctively, saw that the rear end was intact, albeit several feet higher than it should have been, and said, "It's fine, Pug. Car behind us slid under us. Hold still, though. Your arm's messed up."

He looked down and saw it and his face went slack. "That is not good," he said. His pupils were enormous, his face so pale it was almost green.

"You're in shock," I said. "Yes," he said, distantly.

I did a quick personal inventory, moving all my limbs and experimentally swiveling my head this way and that. Concluding that I was in one piece, I did a fast assessment of the car and its environs. Traffic in the adjacent lane had stopped, too—looking over my shoulder, I could see a little fender bender a couple car lengths back that had doubtless been caused by our own wreck. The guy ahead of us had gotten out of his pickup and was headed our way slowly, which suggested that he was unharmed and also not getting ready to shoot us for rear-ending him, so I turned my attention back to Pug. "Stay put," I said, and pushed his airbag aside and unbuckled his seat belt, carefully feeding it back into its spool without allowing it to jostle his arm. That done, I gave him a quick once-over, lightly running my hands over his legs, chest, and head. He didn't object—or shout in pain—and I finished up without blood on my hands, so that was good.

"I think it's just your arm," I said. His eyes locked on my face for a moment, then his gaze wandered off.

"The lens," he said, blearily.

"It's okay," I said.

"The lens," he said, again, and tried once more to twist around in his seat. This time, he noticed his limp arm and gave out a mild, "Ow." He tried again. "Ow."

"Pug," I said, taking his chin and turning his face to mine. His skin was clammy and cold. "Dude. You are in shock and have a broken arm. You need to stay still until the ambulance gets here. You might have a spinal injury or a concussion. I need you to stay still."

"But the lens," he said. "Can't afford another one."

"If I go check on the lens, will you stay still?" It felt like I was bargaining with a difficult drunk for his car keys.

"Yes," he said. "Stay there." The pickup truck's owner helped me out of the car. "You okay?" he asked. He had a Russian accent and rough gardener's hands and a farmer's tan.

"Yeah," I said. "You?"

"I guess so. My truck's pretty messed up, though."

Pug's minivan had merged catastrophically with the rear end of the pickup, deforming it around the van's crumple-zone. I was keenly aware that this was probably his livelihood.

"My friend's got a broken arm," I said. "Shock, too. I'm sure you guys'll be able to exchange insurance once the paramedics get here. Did you call them?"

"My buddy's on it," he said, pointing back at the truck. There was someone in the passenger seat with a phone clamped to his head, beneath the brim of a cowboy hat.

"The lens," Pug said.

I leaned down and opened the door. "Chill out, I'm on it." I shrugged at the guy from the truck and went around back. The entire rear end was lifted clean off the road, the rear wheels still spinning lazily. To a first approximation, we were unscathed. The same couldn't be said for the low-slung hybrid that had rear-ended us, which had been considerably flattened by its harrowing scrape beneath us, to the extent that one of its tires had blown. The driver had climbed out of the car and was leaning unsteadily on it. She gave me a little half wave and a little half smile, which I returned. I popped the hatch and checked that the box was in one piece. It wasn't even dented. "The lens is fine," I called. Pug gave no sign of having heard.

I started to get a little anxious feeling. I jogged around the back of the subcompact and then ran up the driver's side and yanked open Pug's door. He was unconscious, and that grey sheen had gone even whiter. His breath was coming in little shallow pants and his head lolled back in the seat. Panic crept up my throat and I swallowed it down. I looked up quickly and shouted at the pickup driver. "You called an ambulance, right?" The guy must've heard something in my voice because an instant later he was next to me.

"Shock," he said.

"It's been years since I did first aid."

"Recovery position," he said. "Loosen his clothes, give him a blanket."

"What about his arm?" I pointed.

He winced. "We're going to have to be careful," he said. "Shit," he added. The traffic beyond the car was at a near standstill. Even the motorcycles were having trouble lane-splitting between the close-crammed cars.

"The ambulance?"

He shrugged. "On its way, I guess." He put his ear close to Pug's mouth, listened to his breathing, put a couple fingers to his throat and felt around. "I think we'd better lay him out."

The lady driving the subcompact had a blanket in her trunk, which we spread out on the weedy ground alongside the median, which glittered with old broken glass. She—young, Latina, wearing workout clothes— held Pug's arm while the gardener guy and I got him at both ends and stretched him out. The other guy from the pickup truck found some flares in a toolkit under the truck's seat and set them on the road behind us. We worked with a minimum of talk, and for me, the sounds of the highway and my weird postanxiety haze both faded away into barely discernible background noise. We turned Pug on his side, and I rolled up my jacket to support his arm. He groaned. The gardener guy checked his pulse again, then rolled up his own jacket and used it to prop up Pug's feet.

"Good work," he said.

I nodded.

"Craziest thing," the gardener said.

"Uh-huh," I said. I fussed awkwardly with Pug's hair. His ponytail had come loose and it was hanging in his face. It felt wiry and dry, like he spent a lot of time in the sun.

"Did you see it?"

"What?"

He shook his head. "Craziest thing. It crashed right in front of us." He spoke in rapid Russian—maybe it was Bulgarian?—to his friend, who crunched over to us. The guy held something out for me to see. I looked at it, trying to make sense of what I was seeing. It was a tangle of wrecked plastic and metal and a second later, I had it worked out—it was a little UAV, some kind of copter. Four rotors—no, six. A couple of cameras. I'd built a few like it, and I'd even lost control of a few in my day. I could easily see how someone like me, trying out a little drone built from a kit or bought fully assembled, could simply lose track of the battery or just fly too close to a rising updraft from the blacktop and crash. It was technically illegal to fly one except over your own private property, but that was nearly impossible to enforce. They were all over the place.

"Craziest thing," I agreed. I could hear the sirens.

The EMTs liked our work and told us so, and let me ride with them in the ambulance, though that might have been on the assumption that I could help with whatever insurance paperwork needed filling out. They looked disappointed when I told them that I'd only met Pug that day and I didn't even know his last name and was pretty sure that "Pug" wasn't his first name. It wasn't. They got the whole thing off his driver's license: Scott Zrubek. "Zrubek" was a cool name. If I'd been called "Zrubek," I'd have used "Zee" as my nickname, or maybe "Zed."

By the time they'd X-rayed Pug and put his arm in a sling and an air cast, he was awake and rational again and I meant to ask him why he wasn't going by Oz, but we never got around to it. As it turned out, I ended up giving him a lift home in a cab, then getting it to take me home, too. It was two in the morning by then, and maybe the lateness of the hour explains how I ended up promising Pug that I'd be his arm and hand on the playa-dust printer and that I'd come with him to Fourth of Juplaya in order to oversee the installation of the device. I also agreed to help him think of a name for it.

That is how I came to be riding in a big white rental van on the Thursday before July Fourth weekend, departing L.A. at zero-dark-hundred with Pug in the driver's seat and classic G-funk playing loud enough to make me wince in the passenger seat as we headed for Nevada.

Pug had a cooler between us, full of energy beverages and electrolyte drink, jerky, and seed bars. We stopped in Mono Lake and bought bags of oranges from old guys on the side of the road wearing cowboy hats, and later on we stopped at a farm stall and bought fresh grapefruit juice that stung with tartness and was so cold that the little bits of pulp were little frost-bombs that melted on our tongues.

Behind us, in the van's cargo area, was everything we needed for a long weekend of hard-core radical self-reliance—water cans to fill in Reno, solar showers, tents, tarps, rebar stakes, booze, bikes, sunscreen, first-aid kits, a shotgun, an air cannon, a flamethrower, various explosives, crates of fireworks, and more booze. All stored and locked away in accordance with the laws of both Nevada and California, as verified through careful reference to a printout sheathed in a plastic paper-saver that got velcroed to the inside of the van's back door when we were done.

In the centre of all this gear, swaddled in bubblewrap and secured in place with multiple tie-downs, was the gadget, which we had given a capital letter to in our emails and messages: the Gadget. I'd talked Pug out of some of his aversion to moving parts, because the Gadget was going to end up drowning in its own output if we didn't. The key was the realization that it didn't matter where the Gadget went, so long as it went somewhere, which is how we ended up in Strandbeest territory.

The Strandbeest is an ingenious wind-powered walker that looks like a blind, mechanical millipede. Its creator, a Dutch artist called Theo Jansen, designed it to survive harsh elements and to be randomly propelled by wind.

Ours had a broad back where the Gadget's business end perched, and as the yurt panels were completed, they'd slide off to land at its feet, gradually hemming it with rising piles of interlocking, precision-printed pieces. To keep it from going too far afield, I'd tether it to a piece of rebar driven deep into the playa, giving it a wide circle through which the harsh winds of the Black Rock desert could blow it.

Once I was done, Pug had to admit I'd been right. It wasn't just a better design, it was a cooler one, and the Gadget had taken on the aspect of a centaur, with the printer serving as rising torso and head. We'd even equipped it with a set of purely ornamental goggles and a filter mask, just to make it fit in with its neighbours on the Playa. They were a very accepting lot, but you never knew when antirobot prejudice would show its ugly head, and so anything we could do to anthropomorphize the Gadget would only help our cause.

Pug's busted arm was healed enough to drive to the Nevada line, but by the time we stopped for gas, he was rubbing at his shoulder and wincing, and I took over the driving, and he popped some painkillers and within moments he was fast asleep. I tried not to envy him. He'd been a bundle of nerves in the run-up to the Fourth, despite several successful trial runs in his backyard and a great demo on the roof of Minus. He kept muttering about how nothing ever worked properly in the desert, predicting dire all-nighters filled with cursing and scrounging for tools and missing the ability to grab tech support online. It was a side of him I hadn't seen up to that point—he was normally so composed—but it gave me a chance to be the grown-up for a change. It helped once I realized that he was mostly worried about looking like an idiot in front of his once-a-year friends, the edgiest and weirdest people in his set. It also hadn't escaped my notice that he, like me, was a single guy who spent an awful lot of time wondering what this said about him. In other words: he didn't want to look like a dork in front of the eligible women who showed up.

"I'm guessing two more hours to Reno, then we'll get some last-minute supplies and head out. Unless you want to play the slots and catch a Liza Minnelli impersonator."

"No, I want to get out there and get set up."

"Good." Suddenly he gorilla-beat his chest with his good fist and let out a rebel yell. "Man, I just can't wait."

I smiled. This was the voluble Pug I knew.

He pointed a finger at me. "Oh, I see you smiling. You think you know what's going to happen. You think you're going to go drink some beers, eat some pills, blow stuff up, and maybe get lucky. What you don't know is how life-changing this can all be. You get out of your head, literally. It's like—" he waved his hands, smacked the dashboard a couple times, cracked and swigged an energy beverage.

"Okay, this is the thing. We spend all our time doing, you know, stuff. Maintenance. Ninety-eight percent of the day, all you're doing is thinking about what you're going to be doing to go on doing what you're doing. Worrying about whether you've got enough socked away to see you through your old age without ending up eating cat food. Worrying about whether you're getting enough fiber or eating too many carbs. It's being alive, but it's hardly living.

"You ever been in a bad quake? No? Here's the weird secret of a big quake: it's actually pretty great, afterward. I mean, assuming you're not caught in the rubble, of course. After a big one, there's this moment, a kind of silence. Like you were living with this huge old refrigerator compressor humming so loud in the back of your mind that you've never been able to think properly, not once since about the time you turned, you know, eleven or twelve, maybe younger. Never been present and in the moment. And then that humming refrigerator just stops and there's a ringing, amazing, all-powerful silence and for the first time you can hear yourself think. There's that moment, after the earth stops shaking, when you realize that there's you and there's everyone else and the point of it all is for all of you to figure out how to get along together as best as you can.

"They say that after a big one, people start looting, raping, eating each other, whatever. But you know what I saw the last time it hit, back in 2019? People figuring it out. Firing up their barbecues and cooking dinner for the neighbourhood with everything in the freezer, before it spoils anyway. Kids being looked after by everyone, everyone going around and saying, 'what can I do for you? Do you have a bed? Water? Food? You okay? Need someone to talk to? Need a ride?' In the movies, they always show everyone running around looting as soon as the lights go out, but I can't say as I've ever seen that. I mean, that's not what I'd do, would you?"

I shook my head.

"'Course not. No one we know would. Because we're on the same side. The human race's side. But when the fridge is humming away, you can lose track of that, start to feel like it's zero sum, a race to see who can squirrel away the most nuts before the winter comes. When a big shaker hits, though, you remember that you aren't the kind of squirrel who could live in your tree with all your nuts while all the other squirrels starved and froze out there.

"The Playa is like a disaster without the disaster—it's a chance to switch off the fridge and hear the silence. A chance to see that people are, you know, basically awesome. Mostly. It's the one place where you actually confront reality, instead of all the noise and illusion."

"So you're basically saying that it's like Buddhism with recreational drugs and explosions?"

"Basically."

We rode awhile longer. The signs for Reno were coming more often now, and the traffic was getting thicker, requiring more attention.

"If only," he said. "If only there was some way to feel that way all the time."

"You couldn't," I said, without thinking. "Regression to the mean. The extraordinary always ends up feeling ordinary. Do it for long enough and it'd just be noise."

"You may be right. But I hope you're not. Somewhere out there, there's a thing so amazing that you can devote your life to it and never forget how special it is."

We crawled the last thirty miles, driving through Indian country, over cattle gratings and washed-out gullies. "The local cops are fine, they're practically burners themselves. Everyone around here grew up with Burning Man, and it's been the only real source of income since the gypsum mine closed. But the feds and the cops from over the state line, they're bad news. Lot of jack Mormons over in Pershing County, don't like this at all. And since the whole route to the Playa, apart from the last quarter mile, is in Washoe County, and since no one is supposed to buy or sell anything once you get to the Playa, all the money stays in Washoe County, and Pershing gets none of it. All they get are freaks who offend them to their very souls. So basically, you want to drive slow and keep your nose clean around here, because you never know who's waiting behind a bush to hand you a giant ticket and search your car down to the floor mats."

I slowed down even more. We stopped for Indian tacos—fried flat-bread smothered in ground beef and fried veggies—that sat in my stomach in an indigestible, salty lump. Pug grew progressively more manic as we approached the turnoff for Black Rock desert and was practically drumming on the dashboard by the time we hit the dusty, rutted side road. He played with the stereo, put on some loud electronic dance music that made me feel old and out of it, and fished around under the seat for a dust mask and a pair of goggles.

I'd seen lots of photos of Burning Man, the tents and shade structures and RVs and "mutant vehicles" stretching off in all directions, and even though I knew the Fourth was a much smaller event, I'd still been picturing that in my mind's eye. But instead, what we saw was a seemingly endless and empty desert, edges shrouded in blowing dust clouds with the hints of mountains peeking through, and no sign at all of human habitation.

"Now where?" I said.

He got out his phone and fired up a GPS app, clicked on one of his waypoints, waiting a moment, and pointed into the heart of the dust. "That way."

We rumbled into the dust cloud and were soon in a near-total white-out. I slowed the car to walking pace, and then slower than walking pace. "Pug, we should just stop for a while," I said. "There's no roads. Cars could come from any direction."

"All the more reason to get to the campsite," he said. "We're sitting ducks out here for anyone else arriving."

"That's not really logic," I said. "If we're moving and they're moving, we've got a much better chance of getting into a fender bender than if we're staying still."

The air in the van tasted dusty and alkali. I put it in park and put on the mask, noticed my eyes were starting to sting, added goggles—big, bug-eyed Soviet-era MIG goggles.

"Drive," he said. "We're almost there."

I was starting to catch some of his enthusiasm. I put it back into drive and rode the brakes as we inched through the dust. He peered at his GPS, calling out, "left," then "straight," then "right" and back again. A few times I was sure I saw a car bumper or a human looming out of the dust before us and slammed on the brakes, only to discover that it had been a trick of the light and my brain's overactive, nerve-racked pattern-matching systems.

When I finally did run something over, I was stretched out so tight that I actually let out a scream. In my defense, the thing we hit was a tent peg made out of rebar—the next five days gave the chance to become endlessly acquainted with rebar tent pegs, which didn't scar the playa and were cheap and rugged—pushing it through the front driver's-side tire, which exploded with a noise like a gunshot. I turned off the engine and tried to control my breathing.

Pug gave me a moment, then said, "We're here!"

"Sorry about the tire."

"Pfft. We're going to wreck stuff that's a lot harder to fix than a flat tire. You think we can get to the spare without unpacking?"

"No way."

"Then we'll have to unpack. Come on, buddy."

The instant he opened the door, a haze of white dust followed him, motes sparkling in the air. I shrugged and opened my door and stepped out into the dust.

There were people in the dust, but they were ciphers—masked, goggled, indistinct. I had a job to do—clearing out the van's cargo and getting it moved to our site, which was weirdly precise—a set of four corners defined as GPS coordinates that ran to the tenth of a second—and at the same time, such a farcically huge tract of land that it really amounted to "Oh, anywhere over there's fine."

The shadowy figures came out of the dust and formed a bucket brigade, into which I vanished. I love a good bucket brigade, but they're surprisingly hard to find. A good bucket brigade is where you accept your load, rotate 180 degrees and walk until you reach the next person, load that person, do another volte-face, and walk until someone loads you. A good bucket brigade isn't just passing things from person to person. It's a dynamic system in which autonomous units bunch and debunch as is optimal given the load and the speed and energy levels of each participant. A good bucket brigade is a thing of beauty, something whose smooth coordination arises from a bunch of disjointed parts who don't need to know anything about the system's whole state in order to help optimize it. In a good bucket brigade, the mere act of walking at the speed you feel comfortable with and carrying no more than you can safely lift and working at your own pace produces a perfectly balanced system in which the people faster than you can work faster, and the people slower than you can work slower. It is the opposite of an assembly line, where one person's slowness is the whole line's problem. A good bucket brigade allows everyone to contribute at their own pace, and the more contributors you get, the better it works.

I love bucket brigades. It's like proof that we can be more together than we are on our own, and without having to take orders from a leader. It wasn't until the van was empty and I pulled a lounger off our pile of gear and set it up and sank down into it that I realized that an hour had slipped by and I was both weary and energized. Pug handed me a flask and I sniffed at it, got a noseful of dust and whiskey fumes, and then sipped at it. It was Kentucky bourbon, and it cut through the dust in my mouth and throat like oven cleaner.

Pug sprawled in the dust beside me, his blond hair splayed around his head like a halo. "Now the work begins," he said. "How you holding up?"

"Ready and willing, Cap'n," I said, speaking with my eyes closed and my head flung back.

"Look at you two," an amused female voice said. Fingers plucked the flask out of my hands. I opened my eyes. Standing over us was a tall, broad-shouldered woman whose blue Mohawk was braided in a long rope that hung over her shoulder. "You just got here and you're already pooped. You're an embarrassment to the uniform."

"Hi, Blight," Pug said, not stirring. "Blight, this is Greg. He's never been to the Playa before."

"A virgin!" she said. "My stars and garters." She drank more whiskey. She was wearing coveralls with the sleeves ripped off, showing her long, thick, muscled arms, which had been painted with stripes of zinc, like a barber pole. it was hard to guess her age—the haircut suggested mid-twenties, but the way she held herself and talked made me think she might be more my age. I tried not to consider the possibilities of a romantic entanglement. As much of a hormone-fest as the Playa was supposed to be, it wasn't summer camp. "We'll be gentle," she said.

"Don't worry about me," I said. "I'm just gathering my strength before leaping into action. Can I have the whiskey back, please?"

She drank another mouthful and passed it back. "Here you go. That's good stuff, by the way."

"Fighting Cock," Pug said. "I bought it for the name, stayed for the booze." He got to his feet and he and Blight shared a long hug. His feet left the ground briefly.

"Missed you, Pug."

"Missed you, too. You should come visit, sometime."

They chatted a little like old friends, and I gathered that she lived in Salt Lake City and ran a Goth/alternative dance club that sounded familiar.

There wasn't much by way of freak culture out in SLC, so whatever there was quickly became legendary. I'd worked with a guy from Provo, a gay guy who'd never fit in with his Mormon family, who'd spent a few years in SLC before coming to L.A. I was pretty sure he'd talked about it. A kind of way station for Utah's underground bohemian railway.

Then Pug held out his hand to me and pulled me to my feet and announced we'd be setting up camp. This involved erecting a giant shade structure, stringing up hammocks, laying out the heavy black rubber solar-shower bladders on the van's roof to absorb the day's heat, setting out the grill and the bags of lump charcoal, and hammering hundreds of lengths of bent-over rebar into the unyielding desert floor. Conveniently, Pug's injured arm wasn't up to the task, leaving me to do most of the work, though some of the others pitched in at the beginning, until some more campers arrived and needed help unloading.

Finally, it was time to set up the Gadget.

I'd been worried about it, especially as we'd bashed over some of the deeper ruts after the turnoff onto Route 34, but Pug had been awfully generous with the bubblewrap. I ended up having to scrounge a heavy ammo box full of shotgun shells to hold down the layer after layer of plastic and keep it from blowing away. I drew a little crowd as I worked—now they weren't too busy!—and Blight stepped in and helped toward the end, bundling up armloads of plastic sheeting and putting it under the ammo box. Finally, the many-legged Gadget was fully revealed. There was a long considering silence that broke when a breeze blew over it and it began, very slowly, to walk, as each of the legs' sails caught the wind. It clittered along on its delicate feet, and then, as the wind gusted harder, lurched forward suddenly, scattering the onlookers. I grabbed the leash I'd clipped to its rear and held on as best as I could, nearly falling on my face before I reoriented my body to lean away from it. It was like playing one-sided tug-of-war. I whooped and then there were more hands on the leash with mine, including Blight's, and we steadied it.

"Guess I should have driven a spike for the tether before I started," I said.

"Where are you going to spike it?" Blight asked.

I shrugged as best as I could while still holding the strong nylon cable. "I don't know—close enough to the shade structure that we can keep tools and gear there while we're working on it, but far enough away that it can really get around without bashing into anything."

"Stay there," she said, and let go, jogging off toward the back forty of our generous plot. She came back and grabbed our sledgehammer and one of the longest pieces of rebar, and I heard the ringing of a mallet on steel—sure, rhythmic strokes. She'd done this a lot more than me. She jogged back a moment later, her goggles pushed up on her forehead, revealing dark brown eyes, wide set, with thick eyebrows and fine crow's-feet. The part of me that wasn't thinking about the Gadget was thinking about how pretty she was and wondering if she was single, and wondering if she was with Pug, and wondering if she was into guys at all, anyway.

"Let's get it tied off," she said. We played out the rope and let it drag us toward the rebar she'd driven nearly all the way into the hardpack, the bent double tips both buried deep, forming a staple. I threaded the rope's end through and tied a sailor's knot I'd learned in the one week I'd attended Scouts when I was nine, the only knot I knew. It had never come loose. If it came loose this time, there was a chance the Gadget would sail all the way to Reno over the coming months, leaving behind a trail of interlocking panels that could be formed into a yurt.

The sun was starting to set, and though I really wanted to go through my maintenance check list for the Gadget, there was dance music playing (dubstep—I'd been warned by Pug in advance and had steeled myself to learning to love the wub-wub-wub), there were people milling about, there was the smell of barbecue. The sun was a huge, bloody red ball on the horizon and the heat of the day was giving way to a perfectly cool night. Laser light played through the air. Drones flew overhead, strobing with persistence-of-vision LED light shows and doing aerobatics that pushed their collision-avoidance routines to the limit (every time one buzzed me, I flinched, as I had been doing since the accident).

Blight dusted her hands off on her thighs. "Now what?"

I looked around. "Dinner?"

"Yeah," she said, and linked arms with me and led me back to camp.

Sometime around midnight, I had the idea that I should be getting to bed and getting a good night's sleep so I could get the Gadget up and running the next morning. Then Pug and I split a tab of E and passed a thermosful of mushroom tea back and forth—a "hippie flip," something I hadn't tried in more than a decade—and an hour later I was dancing my ass off and the world was an amazing place.

I ended up in a wonderful cuddle puddle around 2 A.M., every nerve alive to the breathing chests and the tingling skin of the people around me. Someone kissed me on the forehead and I spun back to my childhood, and the sensation of having all the time in the world and no worries about anything flooded into me. In a flash, I realized that this is what a utopian, postscarcity world would be like. A place where there was no priority higher than pleasing the people around you and amusing yourself. I thought of all those futures I'd read about and seen, places where everything was built atop sterile metal and polymer. I'd never been able to picture myself in those futures.

But this "future"—a dusty, meaty world where human skin and sweat and hair were all around, but so were lasers and UAVs and freaking wind-walking robots? That was a future I could live in. A future devoted to pleasing one another.

"Welcome to the future," I said into the hollow of someone's throat. That person chuckled. The lasers lanced through the dust overhead, clean multicoloured beams sweeping the sky. The drones buzzed and dipped. The Moon shone down upon us, as big as a pumpkin and as pale as ancient bone.

I stared at the Moon. It stared back. It had always stared back, but I'd always been moving too quickly to notice.

I awoke the next day in my own airbed in the back of the van. It was oven hot inside and I felt like a stick of beef jerky. I stumbled out shirtless and in jeans and made it to the shade structure, where I found my water pack and uncapped the hose. I sucked it dry and then refilled it from a huge water barrel we'd set up on a set of sawhorses, drank some more. I went back into the van and scrounged my shades and goggles, found a t-shirt, and reemerged, made use of the chem toilet we'd set up behind a modesty screen hammered into the playa with rebar and nylon rope, and then collapsed into a hammock under the shade structure.

Some brief groggy eternity later, someone put a collection of pills and tablets into my left hand and a coffee mug into my right.

"No more pills, thank you."

"These are supplements," he said. "I figure half of them are harmless BS, but the other half really seem to help with the old seratonin levels. Don't know which half is which, but there're a couple neuroscientists who come out most years who could argue about it for your amusement if you're interested. Take 'em."

Pug thrust a paper plate of scrambled eggs, sausages, and slices of watermelon into my hands. Before I knew it, I'd gobbled it all down to the watermelon rind and licked the stray crispy bits of sausage meat. I brushed my teeth and joined Pug out by the Gadget. It had gone walking in the night, leaving a beautiful confusion of footprints in the dust. The wind was still for the moment, though with every gust it creaked a little. I steadied

Pug as he climbed it and began to tinker with it.

We'd put a lot of energy into a self-calibration phase. In theory, the Gadget should be able to tell, by means of its array of optical sensors, whether its test prints were correct or not, and then relevel its build plate and recentre its optics. The unfolded solar collectors also acted as dust collectors, and they periodically upended themselves into the feedstock hopper. This mechanism had three fail-safes—first, it could run off the battery, but once the batteries were charged, power was automatically diverted to a pair of servos that would self-trip if the battery ran too low. They each had enough storage to flip, shake, and restore the panels—working with a set of worm-gears we'd let software design and had printed off in a ceramic-polymer mix developed for artificial teeth and guaranteed not to chip or grind away for years.

There was a part of me that had been convinced that the Gadget just couldn't possibly work. Too many moving parts, not enough testing. It was just too weird. But as Pug unfurled the flexible photovoltaics and clipped them to the carbon-fiber struts and carefully positioned the big lens and pressed the big, rubberized ON button, it made the familiar powering-up noises and began to calibrate itself.

Perfectly.

Dust had sifted into the feedstock hopper overnight and had blown over the build plate. The sun hit the lens, and smoke began to rise from the dust. The motors clicked minutely and the head zipped this way and that with pure, robotic grace. Moving with the unhurried precision of a master, it described a grid and melted it, building it up at each junction, adding an extra two-micron Z-height each time, so that a tiny cityscape emerged. The sensors fed back to an old phone I'd brought along—we had a box of them, anticipating a lot more failure from these nonpurpose-built gadgets than our own—and it expressed a confidence rating about the overall accuracy of the build. The basic building blocks the Gadget was designed to print were five-millimetre-thick panels that snap-fit without any additional fixtures, relying on a clever combination of gravity and friction to stay locked once they were put together. The tolerances were fine, and the Gadget was confident it could meet them.

Here's a thing about 3D printing: it is exciting; then very, very boring; then it is exciting again. It's borderline magic; when the print-head starts to jerk and shunt to and fro, up and down, and the melting smell rises up off the build platform, and you can peer through that huge, crystal-clear lens and see a precise form emerging. It's amazing to watch a process by which an idea becomes a thing, untouched by human hands.

But it's also s-l-o-w. From the moment at which a recognizable object begins to take shape to the moment where it seems about ready to slide off, there is a long and dull interregnum in which minute changes gradually bring the shape to fruition. It's like watching soil erosion (albeit in reverse). This is the kind of process that begs for time-lapse. And if you *do* go away and come back later to check in on things, and find your object in a near-complete state, you inevitably find that, in fact, there are innumerable, mysterious passes to be made by the print-head before the object is truly done-done, and once again, you wish that life had a fast-forward button.

But then, you hold the object, produced out of nothing and computers and light and dust, a clearly manufactured *thing* with the polygonal character of everything that comes out of a 3D-modeling program, and once again—*magic*.

This is the cycle that the spectators at the inauguration of the Gadget went through, singly and in bunches, on that day. The Gadget performed exactly as intended—itself the most miraculous thing of the day!—business end floating on a stabilization bed as its legs clawed their way across the desert, and produced a single, interlocking shingle made of precision-formed gypsum and silicon traces, a five-millimetre, honeycombed double-walled tile with snap-fit edges all around.

"That's what it does, huh?" Blight had been by to see it several times that day, alternating between the fabulous dullness of watching 3D paint dry and the excitement of the firing range, from which emanated a continuous pop-pop-pop of gleeful shooting. Someone had brought along a junker car on a trailer, covered in improvised armour, rigged for remote control. The junker had been lumbering around on the desert while the marksmen blasted away at its slowly disintegrating armour, raising loud cheers every time a hunk of its plating fell away, exposing the vulnerable, rusted chassis beneath.

"Well, yeah. One after another, all day long, so long as the sun is shining. We weren't sure about the rate, but I'm thinking something like five per day in the summer sun, depending on the dust storms. It'll take a couple hundred to build a decent-sized yurt on Labor Day, and we should easily get that many by then." I showed her how the tiles interlocked, and how, once locked, they stayed locked.

"It's more of an igloo than a yurt," she said.

"Technicality," I said. "It's neither of those things. It's a 3D-printed, human-assembled temporary prefabricated experimental structure."

"An igloo," she said.

"Touché."

"Time for some food," Pug said. It could have been anywhere between three and seven P.M. None of the burner phones we were using to program and monitor the Gadget had network signal, so none of them had auto-set their clocks. I wasn't wearing a watch. I woke when the baking heat inside the van woke me, and ate when my stomach rumbled, and worked the rest of the time, and danced and drank and drugged whenever the opportunity presented itself.

My stomach agreed. Blight put a sweaty, tattoo-wreathed arm around each of our shoulders and steered us to the plume of fragrant BBQ smoke.

I am proud to say I administered the killing shot to the target car. It was a lucky shot. I'd been aiming for centre mass, somewhere around the bullet-pocked midsection, staring through the scope of the impossibly long rifle that a guy in cracked leathers had checked me out on. He was some kind of physicist, high energy at JPL, but he'd been coming out since he was a freshman and he was a saucer-pupiled neuronaut down to his tattooed toes. He also liked big hardware, guns that were some kind of surrogate supercollider, like the rifle over which I'd been given command. It was a sniper's tool, with its own tripod, and he told me that he had to keep it locked up in a gun club over the Nevada state line because it was radioactively illegal in sweet gentle California.

I peered down the scope, exhaled, and squeezed the trigger. Just as I did, the driver jigged the toy wheel she was using to control it, and the car swung around and put the middle of its grille right in my crosshairs. The bullet pierced the engine block with a fountain of black smoke and oil, the mighty crash of the engine seizing, and a juddering, shuddering, slewing cacophony as the car skidded and revved and then stopped, flames now engulfing the hood and spreading quickly into the front seat.

I had a moment's sick fear, like I'd done something terrible, destroying their toy. The silence after my shot rang out couldn't have lasted for more than a second, but then it broke, with a wild *whoop!*, and a cheer that whipped up and down the firing line.

The car's owner had filled it with assorted pyro—mortars and roman candles—that were touched off by the fire and exploded out in every direction, streaking up and out and even down, smashing into the playa and then skipping away like flat stones. People pounded me on the back as the car self-destructed and sent up an oily black plume of smoke. I felt an untethered emotion, like I'd left behind civilization for good. I'd killed a car!

That's when my Fourth of Juplaya truly began. A wild debauch, loud and stoned and dangerous. I slept in hammocks, in piles of warm bodies, in other people's cars. I danced in ways I'd never danced before, ate spectacular meals of roasted meat and desserts of runny, melted chocolate on fat pancakes. I helped other people fix their art cars, piloted a drone, got a naked (and curiously asexual) massage from a stranger, and gave one in return. I sang along to songs whose words I didn't know, rode on the hood of a car while it did slow donuts in the middle of the open desert, and choked on dust storms that stung my skin and my eyes and left me huddled down in total whiteout while it blew.

It was glorious.

"How's your windwalker?" Blight said, as I passed her back her water bottle, having refilled it from our dwindling supply.

"Dunno," I said. "What day is it?"

"Monday," she said.

"I don't think I've looked in on it today. Want to come?"

She did.

In the days since we'd staked out the Gadget, more tents and trucks and cars and shade structures and exotic vehicles had gone up all around it, so that its paddock was now in the midst of a low-slung tent city. We'd strung up a perimeter of waist-high safety-orange tape to keep people from blundering into it at night, and I saw that it had been snapped in a few places and made a mental note to get the spool of tape off the post where we kept it and replace it.

The wind had been blowing hard earlier that day, but it had died down to a breathless late afternoon. The Gadget was standing and creaking softly at the end of its tether, and all around it was a litter of printed panels. Three of its legs were askew, resting atop stray tiles. We gathered them up and stacked them neatly and counted—there were forty all told, which was more than I'd dared hope for.

"We're going to be able to put together two or three yurts at this rate."

"Igloos."

"Yours can be an igloo," I said.

"That's very big of you, fella."

"Monday, you said?"

She stretched like a cat. She was streaked with dust and dirt and had a musky, unwashed animal smell that I'd gotten used to smelling on myself. "Yeah," she said. "Packing up tonight, pulling out tomorrow at first light."

I gulped. Time had become elastic out there on the desert, that school's-out Junetime feeling that the days are endless and unrolling before you and there are infinite moments to fill and no reason at all in the whole world to worry. Now it evaporated as quickly as sweat in the desert. I swallowed again.

"You're going to get up at first light?" I said.

"No," she said, and pressed a couple of gel caps into my palm. "I was going to stay up all night. Luckily, I'm not driving."

At some point we worked out that Pug and I had three filled solar showers warm on the van's roof and then it was only natural that we strung them up and pulled the plug on them, sluicing the hot, stale, wonderful water over our bodies, and we took turns soaping each other up, and the molly and whatever else had been in her pills made every nerve ending on my body thrum. Our grey water ended up in a kiddie pool at our feet, brown and mucky, and when we stepped out of it the dust immediately caked on our feet and ankles and calves, gumming between our toes as we made a mad, giggling dash for the van, threw our bodies into it and slammed the door behind us.

We rolled around on the air mattresses in the thick, superheated air of the van, tickling and kissing and sometimes more, the madness of the pills and that last-night-of-summer-camp feeling thrumming in our veins.

"You're thinking about something," she said, lying crosswise so that our stomachs were pressed together and our bodies formed a wriggling plus sign.

"Is that wrong?"

"This is one of those live-in-the-moment moments, Greg."

I ran my hands over the small of her back, the swell of her butt, and she shivered and the shiver spread to me. The dope made me want to knead her flesh like dough, my hands twitching with the desire to clench.

"It's nothing, just—" I didn't want to talk about it. I wanted to fool around. She did too. We did.

"Just what?" she said, some long time later. At one point, Pug had opened—and then swiftly shut—the rear van doors.

"You and Pug aren't . . . ?"

"Nope," she said. "Are you?"

"Nope," I said.

"Just what, then?"

I rewound the conversation. I'd already peaked and was sliding into something mellow and grand.

"Just, well, default reality. It's all so—"

"Yeah," she said. Default reality was cutesy burner-speak for the real world, but I had to admit it fit. That made what we were in special reality or maybe default unreality.

"I know that we're only here to have fun, but somehow it feels like it's been . . ." *Important* was the word on the tip of my tongue, but what an embarrassing admission. "More." Lame-o!

She didn't say anything for so long that I started to get dope paranoia, a fear that I'd said or done something wildly inappropriate but been too high to notice.

"I know what you mean," she said.

We lay together and listened to the thump of music out in the desert night. She stroked my arm lazily with fingertips that were as rough as sandpaper, rasping over my dry, scaly skin. I could distinctly feel each nerve impulse move up my arm to my spine and into my brain. For a while, I forgot my curious existential sorrow and was truly, totally in the moment, just feeling and hearing and smelling, and not thinking. It was the refrigerator hum that Pug had told me about, and it had finally stopped. For that moment, I was only thinking, and not thinking about thinking, or thinking about thinking about thinking. Every time my thoughts strayed toward a realization that they were only thinking and not meta-cognizing, they easily and effortlessly drifted back to thinking again.

It was the weirdest moment of my life and one of the best. The fact that I was naked and hot and sweaty with a beautiful woman and stoned off my ass helped. I had found the exact perfect mixture of sex, drugs, and rock and roll to put me into the place that my mind had sought since the day I emerged from the womb.

It ended, gradually, thoughts about thoughts seeping in and then flowing as naturally as they ever had. "Wow," I said.

"You too?" she said.

"Totally."

"That's what I come here for," she said. "If I'm lucky, I get a few minutes like that here every year. Last time was three years ago, though. I went home and quit my job and spent three hours a day learning to dance while I spent the rest of my time teaching small-engine repair at a half way house for rehabilitated juvenile offenders."

"Really?" I said.

"Totally."

"What job did you quit?"

"I was CTO for a company that made efficient cooling systems for data centres. It had some really interesting, nerdy thermodynamic problems to chew through, but at the end of the day, I was just trying to figure out how to game entropy, and that's a game of incremental improvements. I wanted to do stuff that was big and cool and weird and that I could point to and say, 'I did that.' Some of my students were knuckleheads, a few were psychos, but most of them were just broken kids that I helped to put together, even a little. And a few of them were amazing, learned everything I taught them and then some, taught me things I'd never suspected, went on to do amazing things. It turns out that teaching is one of those things like raising a kid or working out—sometimes amazing, often difficult and painful, but, in hindsight, amazing."

"Have you got a kid?"

She laughed. "Maya. She's thirteen. Spending the week with her dad in Arizona."

"I had no idea," I said. "You don't talk about her much."

"I talk about her all the time," she said. "But not on the Playa. That's a kind of vacation from my other life. She keeps asking me to come out. I guess I'll have to bring her some year, but not to the Fourth. Too crazy. And it's my Blight time."

"Your name's not Blight, is it?"

"Nope," she said. I grinned and smacked her butt, playfully. She pinched my thigh, hard enough to make me yelp. "What do you do?" she said.

I hated that question. "Not much," I said. "Got in with a start-up in the nineties, made enough to pay cash for my house and then some. I do a little contract coding and the rest of the time, I just do whatever I feel like. Spend a lot of time at the hackerspace. You know Minus?"

"Yeah. Are you seriously rich?"

"No," I said. "I'm just, I don't know what you'd call it—I'm rich enough. Enough that I don't have to worry about money for the rest of my life, so long as I don't want much, and I don't. I'm a pretty simple guy."

"I can tell," she said. "Took one look at you and said, that is one simple son of a bitch."

"Yeah," I said. "Somehow, I thought this life would be a lot more interesting than it turned out to be."

"Obviously."

"Obviously."

"So volunteer. Do something meaningful with your life. Take in a foster kid. Walk dogs for cancer patients."

"Yeah," I said.

She kissed my shin, then bent back my little toe and gave it a twist. "Just do something, Greg. I mean, you may not get total satori out of it, but sitting around on your butt, doing nothing, of course that's shit. Be smart."

"Yeah," I said.

"Oh, hell," she said. She got up on her knees and then toppled forward onto me. "Do what you want, you're an adult."

"I am of adult age," I said. "As to my adulthood—"

"You and all the rest of us."

We lay there some more. The noise outside was more frenetic than ever, a pounding, throbbing relentless mash of beats and screams and gunshots and explosions.

"Let's go see it," she said, and we staggered out into the night.

The sun was rising when she said, "I don't think happiness is something you're supposed to have, it's something you're supposed to want."

"Whoa," I said, from the patch of ground where I was spread-eagled, dusty, and chilled as the sky turned from bruisey purple to gaudy pink.

She pinched me from where she lay, head to head above me. I was getting used to her pinches, starting to understand their nuances. That was a friendly one. In my judgment, anyway.

"Don't be smart. Look, whatever else happiness is, it's also some kind of chemical reaction. Your body making and experiencing a cocktail of hormones and other molecules in response to stimulus. Brain reward. A thing that feels good when you do it. We've had millions of years of evolution that gave a reproductive edge to people who experienced pleasure when something pro-survival happened. Those individuals did more of whatever made them happy, and if what they were doing more of gave them more and hardier offspring, then they passed this on."

"Yes," I said. "Sure. At some level, that's true of all our emotions, I guess."

"I don't know about that," she said. "I'm just talking about happiness. The thing is, doing stuff is pro-survival—seeking food, seeking mates, protecting children, thinking up better ways to hide from predators. . . . Sitting still and doing nothing is almost never pro-survival, because the rest of the world is running around, coming up with strategies to outbreed you, to outcompete you for food and territory . . . if you stay still, they'll race past you."

"Or race backward," I said.

"Yeah, there's always the chance that if you do something, it'll be the wrong thing. But there's zero chance that doing nothing will be the right thing. Stop interrupting me, anyways." She pinched me again. This one was less affectionate. I didn't mind. The sun was rising. "So if being happy is what you seek, and you attain it, you stop seeking. So the reward has to return to the mean. Happiness must fade. Otherwise, you'd just lie around, blissed out and childless, until a tiger ate you."

"Have you hacked my webcam or something?"

"Not everything is about you," she said.

"Fine," I said. "I accept your hypothesis for now. So happiness isn't a state of being, instead it's a sometimes-glimpsed mirage on the horizon, drawing us forward."

"You're such a fucking poet. It's a carrot dangling from a stick, and we're the jackasses plodding after it. We'll never get it though."

"I don't know," I said. "I think I just came pretty close."

And that earned me another kiss, and a pinch, too. But it was a friendly one.

Blight and her campmates pulled up stakes shortly thereafter. I helped them load their guns and their ordnance and their coolers and bales of costumes and kegs and grey water and duffel bags and trash bags and flaccid sun showers and collapsed shade structures, lashing about half of it to the outside of their vehicles under crackling blue tarps. Her crew had a storage locker in Reno where they'd leave most of the haul, only taking personal gear all the way home.

Working my muscles felt good after a long, wakeful night of dancing and screwing and lying around, and when we fell into a bucket-brigade rhythm, I tumbled directly into the zone of blessed, tired physical exertion, a kind of weary, all-consuming dance of moving, lifting, passing, turning, moving . . . and before I knew it, the dawn was advanced enough to have me sweating big rings around my pits and the cars were loaded, and Blight was in my arms, giving me a long hug that continued until our bodies melted together.

She gave me a soft, dry kiss and said, "Go chase some happiness."

"You too," I said. "See you at the burn."

She pinched me again, a friendly one. We'd see each other come Labor Day weekend, assuming we could locate each other in the sixty-thousand-person crush of Burning Man. After my intimate, two-hundred-person Fourth of Juplaya, I could hardly conceive of such a thing, though with any luck, I'd be spending it in the world's first 3D-printed yurt. Or igloo.

Pug got us early admission to the burn. From the turnoff, it seemed nearly as empty as it had when we'd been there in July, but by the time we reached the main gate, it was obvious that this was a very different sort of thing from the Fourth.

Once we'd submitted to a search—a search!—of the van and the trailer and been sternly warned—by a huge, hairy dude wearing the bottom half of a furry monkey costume, a negligee, and a ranger's hat—to stay under 5 mph to keep the dust plumes down, we were crawling forward. No GPS this time. During the months that we'd spent in L.A. wondering whether the Gadget was hung up, crashed, stuck, blown away, or stolen, so many vehicles had passed this way that they'd worn an unmistakable road into the Playa, hedged with orange-tipped surveyors' stakes and porta-sans.

The sun was straight overhead, the air-conditioning wheezing as we crept along, and even though the sprawling, circular shape of Black Rock City was only 10 percent full, we could already make it out against the empty desert-scape. In the middle of it all stood the man, a huge, angular neopagan idol, destined for immolation in a week's time.

Pug had been emailing back and forth with the Borg—the Burning Man organization, a weird cult of freak bureaucrats who got off on running this circus—all summer, and he was assured that our little paddock had been left undisturbed. If all went according to plan, we'd drop off the van, unpack it and set up camp, then haul bike-trailers over to the paddock and find out how the Gadget had fared over the summer. I was 90 percent convinced that it had blown over and died the minute we left the desert and had been lying uselessly ever since. We'd brought along some conveniences that could convert the back of the van into a bedroom if it came to that, but we were absolutely committed to sleeping in the yurt. Igloo.

We set off as quickly as we could, in goggles and painter's masks against the light, blowing dust. Most of the campsites were empty and we were able to slice a chord across Black Rock City's silver-dollar, straight out to walk-in camp, where there were only a few tents pitched. Pug assured me that it would be carpeted in tents within a couple of days.

Just past walk-in camp, we came upon the Gadget.

It had changed colour. The relentless sun and alkali dust had turned the ceramic/polymer legs, sails, and base into the weathered no-colour of driftwood. As we came upon it, the solar panels flickered in the sun and then did their dust-shedding routine, spinning like a drum-major's batons and snapping to with an audible crack, and their dust sifted down into the feedstock hoppers, and then over them. They were full. Seeing that, I felt a moment's heartsickness—if they were covered with dust, there'd be no power. The Gadget must not have been printing.

But that only lasted a moment—just long enough to take in what I should have seen immediately. The Gadget's paddock was mounded with tiles.

"It's like a bar chart of the prevailing winds," Pug said. I instantly grasped what he meant—the mounds were uneven, and the hills represented the places where the wind had blown the Gadget most frequently. I snapped several photos before we swarmed over the Gadget to run its diagnostics.

According to its logs, it had printed 413 tiles—enough for two yurts, and nearly double what we'd anticipated. The data would be a delicious puzzle to sort through after the burn. Had the days been longer? The printer more efficient?

We started to load the trailers. It was going to take several trips to transport all the tiles, and then we'd have to walk the Gadget itself over, set up a new paddock for it on our site, and then we'd have to start assembling the yurt. Yurts! It was going to be punishing, physical, backbreaking work, but a crackle of elation shot through us at the thought of it. It had worked!

"Master, the creature lives!" I bellowed, in my best Igor, and Pug shook his head and let fly with a perfect mad-scientist cackle.

We led the Gadget back by means of a pair of guide ropes, pulling for all we were worth on them, tacking into the wind and zigzagging across the Playa, stumbling over campsites and nearly impaling ourselves on rebar tent pegs. People stopped what they were doing to watch, as though we were proud hunters returning with a kill, and they waved at us and squinted behind their goggles, trying to make sense of this strange centaur with its glinting single eye high above its back.

We staked it into the ground on our site on a much shorter tether and dusted it off with stiff paintbrushes, working the dust out of the cracks and joints, mostly on general principle and in order to spruce it up for public viewing. It had been running with amazing efficiency despite the dust all summer, after all.

"Ready to get puzzling?" Pug said.

"Aye, Cap'n," I said.

We hadn't been sure how many tiles we'd get out of the Gadget over the course of the summer. They came in three interlocking sizes, in the Golden ratio, each snapping together in four different ways. Figuring out the optimal shape for any given number of panels was one of those gnarly, NP-complete computer science problems that would take more computational cycles than remained in the universe's lifetime to solve definitively. We'd come up with a bunch of variations on the basic design (it did look more like an igloo than a yurt, although truth be told it looked not very much like either) in a little sim, but were always being surprised by new ways of expanding the volume using surprisingly small numbers of tiles.

We sorted the printouts by size in mounds and counted them, plugging the numbers into the sim and stepping through different possibilities for shelter design. There was a scaling problem—at a certain height/diameter ratio, you had to start exponentially increasing the number of tiles in order to attain linear gains in volume—but how big was big enough? After a good-natured argument that involved a lot of squinting into phone screens against the intense glare of the high sun, we picked out two designs and set to work building them.

Pug's arm was pretty much back to normal, but he still worked slower than me and blamed it on his arm rather than admitting that he'd picked a less-efficient design. I was half done, and he was much less than half done, when Blight wandered into camp.

"Holy shit," she said. "You did it!"

I threw my arms around her as she leaped over the knee-high wall of my structure, kicking it slightly askew. She was wearing her familiar sleeveless coveralls, but she'd chopped her hair to a short electric-blue fuzz that nuzzled against my cheek. A moment later, another pair of arms wrapped around us and I smelled Pug's work sweat and felt his strong embrace. We shared a long, three-sided hug and then disentangled ourselves and Pug and I let fly with a superheated sitrep on the Gadget's astounding debut performance.

She inspected the stacks of tiles and the walls we'd built thus far. "You guys, this is insane. I didn't want to say anything, you know, but I never bought this. I thought your gizmo"—Pug and I both broke in and said *Gadget*, in unison, and she gave us each the finger, using both hands—"would blow over on its side in a windstorm, break something important, and end up buried in its own dune."

"Yeah," I said. "I had nightmares about that, too."

"Not me," said Pug. "I knew from day one that this would work. It's all so fault tolerant, it all fails so gracefully."

"You're telling me that you never once pictured yourself finding a pile of half-buried, smashed parts?"

He gave me that serene look of his. "I had faith," he said. "It's a gadget. It does what it does. Mechanism A acts on Mechanism B acts on Mechanism C. If you understand what A, B, and C do, you know what the Gadget does."

Blight and I both spoke at the same time in our rush to explain what was wrong with this, but he held his hands up and silenced us.

"Talk all you want about chaos and sensitivity to initial conditions, but here's the thing: I thought the Gadget would work, and here we are, with a working Gadget. Existence proofs always trump theory. That's engineering."

"Fine," I said. "I can't really argue with that."

He patted me on the head. "It's okay, dude. From the day I met you, I've known that you are a glass-half-empty-and-maybe-poisonous guy. The Playa will beat that out of you."

"I'll help," Blight said, and pinched my nipple. I'd forgotten about her pinches. I found that I'd missed them. "I hate you both," I said.

Pug patted me on the head again and Blight kissed me on the cheek. "Let me finish unpacking and I'll come back and help you with your Playa-tetris, okay?"

Looking back on it now, I think the biggest surprise was just how hard it was to figure out how to get the structure just right. If you fitted a tile the wrong way in row three, it wasn't immediately apparent until row five or six, and you'd have to take them all down and start over again. Pug said it reminded him of knitting, something he'd tried for a couple years.

"It's just that it's your first time," Blight said, as she clicked a tile into place. "The first time you put together a wall of lego you screwed it up, too. You've been living with this idea for so long, you forgot that you've never actually dealt with its reality."

We clicked and unclicked, and a pile of broken tiles grew to one side of the site. As we got near the end, it became clear that this was going to be a close thing—what had started as a surplus of tiles had been turned into a near shortage thanks to breakage. Some of that had been our fault—the tiles wanted to be finessed into place, not forced, and it was hard to keep a gentle approach as the day lengthened and the frustration mounted—but some was pure material defect, places where too many impurities had ganged up along a single seam, waiting to fracture at the slightest pressure, creating a razor-sharp, honeycombed gypsum blade that always seemed to find exposed wrists above the glove line. A few times, chips splintered off and flew into my face. The goggles deflected most of these, but one drew blood from the precise tip of my nose.

In the end, we were three—three!—tiles short of finishing; two from mine, one from Pug's. The sun had set, and we'd been working by head-lamp and the van's headlights. The gaps stared at us.

"Well, shit," Pug said, with feeling.

I picked through our pile of postmodern potsherds, looking for any salvageable pieces. There weren't. I knew there weren't, but I looked anyway. I'd become a sort of puzzle-assembling machine and I couldn't stop now that I was so close to the end. It was the punch line to a terrible joke.

"What are you two so freaked out about?" Blight said. "Just throw a tarp over it."

We both looked at each other. "Blight—" Pug began, then stopped.

"We don't want to cover these with tarps," I said. "We want to show them off! We want everyone to see our totally awesome project! We want them to see how we made bricks out of dust and sunshine!"

"Um, yeah," Blight said. "I get that. But you can use the tarps for tonight, and print out your missing pieces tomorrow, right?"

We both stared at each other, dumbfounded.

"Uh," I said.

Pug facepalmed, hard enough that I heard his glove smacking into his nose. When he took his hand away, his goggles were askew, half pushed up his forehead.

"I'll get the tarps," I said.

They came. First in trickles, then in droves. Word got around the Playa: these guys have 3D printed their own yurt. Or igloo.

Many just cruised by, felt the smooth finish of the structures, explored the tight seams with their fingernails, picked up a shard of cracked tile to take away as a souvenir. They danced with the Gadget as it blew back and forth across its little tethered paddock, and if they were lucky enough to see it dropping a finished tile to the desert, they picked it up and marveled at it.

It wasn't an unequivocal success, though. One old-timer came by, a wizened and wrinkled burner with a wild beard and a tan the colour of old leather—he was perfectly naked and so unselfconscious about it that I ceased to notice it about eight seconds into our conversation—and said, "Can I ask you something?"

"Sure," I said.

"Well, I was just wondering how you turn these bricks of yours back into dust when you're done with them?"

"What do you mean?"

"Leave no trace," he said. His eyes glittered behind his goggles. "Leave no trace" was rule number eight of the ten hallowed inviolable holy rules of Burning Man. I suppose I must have read them at some point, but mostly I came into contact with them by means of burnier-than-thou dialogues with old-timers—or anxious, status-conscious noobs—who wanted to point out all the ways in which my burn was the wrong sort of burn.

"Not following you," I said, though I could see where this was going.

"What are you going to do with all this stuff when you're done with it? How are you going to turn your ceramics back into dust?"

"I don't think we can," I said.

"Ah," he said, with the air of someone who was winning the argument.

"Didn't think so. You going to leave this here?"

"No," I said. "We'll take it down and truck it out. Leave no trace, right?"

"But you're taking away some of the desert with you. Do that enough, where will we be?"

Yep. Just about where I figured this was going. "How much playa dust do you take home in your"—I was about to say *clothes*—"Car?"

"Not one bit more than I can help bringing. It's not our desert to take away with us. You've got sixty thousand people here. They start doing what you're doing, next thing you know, the whole place starts to vanish."

I opened my mouth. Shut it. Opened it again.

"Have you got any idea of the overall volume of gypsum dust in the Black Rock desert? I mean, relative to the amount of dust that goes into one of these?" I patted the side of the structure—we'd started calling them *yurtgloos*.

"I knew you'd say that," he said, eyes glittering and beard swinging. "They said that about the ocean. Now we've got the Great Pacific Garbage Patch. They said it about space, and now low Earth orbit is one stray screwdriver handle away from a cascade that wipes out every communications satellite and turns the Lagrange points into free-fire zones. Anywhere you go in history, there's someone dumping something or taking something away and claiming that the demand'll never outstrip the supply. That's probably what the first goat-herder said when he turned his flock out on the Sahara plains. 'No way these critters could ever eat this huge plot down to nothing.' Now it's the Sahara!"

I had to admit he had a point.

"Look," I said. "This is the first time anyone's tried this. Burners have been changing the desert for years. They excavate tons of the surface every year to get rid of the burn platform and the scars from the big fires. Maybe we'll have to cap how many robots run every year, but you know, it's kind of a renewable resource. Dust blows in all the time, over the hills and down the road. It goes down for yards and yards. They mined around here for a century and didn't make a dent in it. The only thing that doesn't change the world is a corpse. People who are alive change the planet. That's part of the deal. How about if we try this thing for a while and see whether it's a problem, instead of declaring it a disaster before it's gotten started?"

He gave me a withering look. "Oh yeah, I've heard that one before. 'Give it time, see how it goes!' That's what they said in Fukushima. That's what they said when they green-lit thalidomide. That's what they said at Kristallnacht."

"I don't think they said that about Kristallnacht," I said, and turned on my heel. Decades on the Internet had taught me that Godwin's law was ironclad: as soon as the comparisons to Nazis or Hitler came out, the discussion was over. He shouted something at my back, but I couldn't hear it over the wub-wub of an art car that turned the corner at that moment, a huge party bus/pirate ship with three decks of throbbing dancers and a PA system that could shatter glass.

But that conversation stayed with me. He was a pushy, self-righteous prig, but that didn't mean he was wrong. Necessarily.

If you're a burner, you know what happened next. We kickstarted an entire flock of Gadgets by Christmas; built them through the spring, and trucked them out in a pair of sixteen-wheelers for the next Fourth, along with a crew of wranglers who'd helped us build them. It was the biggest Fourth of Juplaya ever and there were plenty of old-timers who still say we ruined it. It's true that there was a lot less shooting and a lot more lens-polishing that year.

The best part was the variation. Our three basic tiles could be combined to make an infinite variety of yurtgloos, but to be honest, you'd be hard-pressed to tell one from another. On our wiki, a group of topology geeks went bananas designing a whole range of shapes that interlocked within our three, making it possible to build crazy stuff—turrets, staircases, trusses. Someone showed how the polyominoes could be interlocked to make a playground slide and sure enough, come the summer, there was a huge one, with a ladder and a scaffolding of support, and damned if it wasn't an amazing ride, once it was ground down to a slippery sheen with a disc-polisher.

The next year, there were whole swaths of Black Rock City that were built out of dust-bricks, as they were called by that time. The backlash was predictable, but it still smarted. We were called unimaginative suburbanites in tract-house gated communities, an environmental catastrophe—that old naked guy turned out to be a prophet as well as a crank—and a blight on the landscape.

Blight especially loved this last. She brought Maya, her daughter, to the Playa that year, and the two of them built the most amazing, most ambitious yurtgloo you'd ever seen, a three-story, curvy, bulbous thing whose surfaces were finely etched with poems and doodles that she'd fed to the paramaterizer in the 3D-modeling software onboard her Gadgets. The edges of the glyphs were so sharp at first that you could literally cut yourself on them, and before the wind and dust wore them down, they cast amazing shadows down into the gullies of the carve-outs when the sun was rising and setting, turning the wall into a madman's diary of scribbles and words.

Maya was indifferent to the haters. She was fifteen and was a troubleseeking missile with a gift for putting creepers in their place that I was in absolute awe of. I watched her fend off the advances of fratty jocks, weird old dudes like me, and saucer-eyed spacemen dancing to the distant, omnipresent thunder of EDM.

"You raised her right, huh?" I said to Blight.

Blight shrugged. "Look, it sucks to be a fifteen-year-old girl. All that attention, it just gets in the way of figuring out who you are. I'm glad she's good at this, but I wish she didn't have to do it. I wish she could just have a burn like the rest of us."

I put my arm around her shoulders. "Yeah," I said. "Yeah, that sucks."

"It does. Plus, I don't want to get high because I feel like I've got to keep an eye on her all the time and—" She threw her hands up in the air and looked angrily at the white-hot sky.

"You're feeling guilty for bringing her, aren't you?"

"No, Dr. Freud. I'm feeling guilty for regretting that I brought her."

"Are you sure you're not feeling guilty for regretting that you feel guilty that you brought her?"

She pinched me. "Be serious."

I wiped the smile off my face. "Blight, I love you." I'd said it the first time on a visit to her place just after the last burn, and she'd been literally speechless for a good ten minutes. Ever since, it had become my go-to trick for winning arguments.

She pinched me hard in the arm. I rubbed the sore spot—every time I came back from a visit to see her, I had bruises the size of grapefruits and the colour of the last moment of sunset on both shoulders.

Maya ran past, pulling a giant stunt kite behind her. She'd spent the whole burn teaching herself new tricks with it and she could do stuff with it that I never would have believed. We cheered her on as she got it into the sky.

"She's an amazing kid," I said. "Makes me wish I'd had one. I would have, if I'd known she'd turn out like that."

Maya's dad was a city manager for a small town in Arizona that was entirely dependent on imported water. He came out twice a year for visits and Maya spent three weeks every summer and alternate Christmases and Easters with him, always returning with a litany of complaints about the sheer tedium of golf courses and edge-city megamalls. I'd never met him but he sounded like a good guy, if a little on the boring side.

"Never too late," Blight said. "Go find yourself some nubile twenty-five-year-old and get her gravid with your child."

"What would I want with one of those flashy new models? I've got an American classic here." I gave her another squeeze, and she gave me another pinch.

"Nothing smoother than an automotive comparison, fella."

"It was meant as a compliment."

"I know," she said. "Fine. Well, then, you could always come down and spend some time when Maya is around, instead of planning your visits around her trips to see her dad. There's plenty of parenting to go around on that one, and I could use a break from time to time."

I suddenly felt very serious. Something about being on the Playa made it seem like anything was possible. I had to literally bite my tongue to stop myself from proposing marriage. Instead, I said, "That sounds like a very good plan. I shall take you up on it, I think."

She drew her fingers back to pinch me, but instead, she dragged me to her and gave me a long, wet, deep kiss.

"Ew," shouted Maya as she buzzed us, now riding a lowrider playa bike covered in fun fur and duct tape. She circled us twice, throwing up a fantail of dust, then screeched to a hockey stop that buried our feet in a small dune that rode ahead of her front wheel like a bow wave.

"You've gone native, kiddo," I said.

She gave me a hilarious little-girl look and said, "Are you my new daddy? Mommy says you're her favourite of all my uncles, and there's so many of them."

Blight pounced on her and bore her to the ground, where they rolled like a pair of fighting kittens, all tickles and squeals and outflung legs and arms. It ended with Maya pinned under Blight's forearms and knees.

"I brought you into this world," she said, panting. "I can take you out of it, too."

Maya closed her eyes and then opened them again, wide as saucers. "I'm sorry, Mom," she said. "I guess I took it too far. I love you, Mom."

Blight relaxed a single millibar and Maya squirmed with the loose-jointed fluidity of wasted youth and bounced to her toes, leaped on her bike and shouted, "Suck-errrrr!" as she pedaled away a good ten yards, then did a BMX-style front-wheel stand and spun back around to face us. "Bye-ee!"

"Be back for dinner!" Blight shouted.

"'Kay, mom!"

The two stared at each other through the blowing dust.

"He's pretty good," Maya shouted again. "You can keep him."

Blight took a step toward her. Maya grinned fearlessly. "Love you, Mom! Don't worry, I won't get into any trouble."

She jammed down on the pedals and powered off toward open playa.

"You appear to have given birth to the Tasmanian Devil," I said.

"Shut up, amateur," she said. "This is what they're supposed to be like at fifteen. I'd be worried otherwise."

By the time they sent Pug home to die, Blight was practically living with me—after getting laid off and going freelance, there was no reason not to. I gave her the whole garage to use as workspace—parked my car in the driveway and ran an extension cord out to it to charge it overnight— but half the time she worked at Minus. Its latest incarnation was amazing, a former L.A. Department of Water and Power Substation that was in bankruptcy limbo. After privatization and failure, the trustees had inventoried its assets and found that it was sitting on all these mothballed substations and offered them out on cheap short-term leases. Minus was practically a cathedral in those days, with thirty-foot ceilings, catwalks, even two behemoth dynamos that had been saved from the scrappers out of pure nostalgia. They gave the place a theatrical, steampunk air—until someone decided to paint them safety orange with hot-pink highlights, which looked pretty damned cool and pop art, but spoiled the theatre of the thing somewhat.

Pug was no idiot—not like me. So when he found a lump and asked the doctor to look into it and spent a week fretting about it, he'd told me and Blight and a bunch of his other friends and did a week of staying on people's couches and tinkering with the Gadget and going to yoga class and cooking elaborate meals with weird themes—like the all-coconut dinner that included coconut chicken over coconut rice with coconut flan for dessert. And he arranged for me to drive him to the doctor's office for his follow-up visit.

We joked nervously all the way to the waiting room, then fell silent. We declined to be paged by the receptionist and sat down instead, looking from the big, weird, soothing animation on the fifty-inch TV to the health pamphlets that invited us to breathe on them or lick them for instant analysis and follow-up recommendations. Some of them seemed to have been licked already.

"Scott Zrubek?" said the receptionist from the door, looking from her screen to Pug's face.

"That's my slave name," he said to me as he got up and crossed to her. "Forget you ever heard it."

Twenty minutes later, he was back with a big white smile that went all the way to the corners of his eyes. I stood up and made a question of my raised eyebrows. He high-fived me and we went out to the car. The nurse who'd brought him back watched us go from the window, a worried look on her face, and that should have tipped me off.

"All okay, then," I said. "So now where?"

"Let's get some lunch," he said. "There's a chicken shack up on the left; they serve the best chili fries."

It was one of those drive-in places where the servers clipped trays to the windows and served your food on them, a retro-revival thing that made me glad I had vinyl seats.

"What a relief," I said, slurping on my shake. They had tiger-tail ice cream—a mix of orange and black licorice flavor—and Pug had convinced me to try it in a shake. He'd been right—it was amazing.

"Uh-huh," he said. "About that."

"About what?"

"Doc says it's in my liver and pancreas. I can do chemo and radiotherapy, but that'll just tack a couple months on, and they won't be good months. Doc says it's the kind of cancer where, when a doctor gets it, they refuse treatment."

I pulled the car over to the side of the road. I couldn't bring myself to turn my head.

"Pug," I said. "I'm so sorry—"

He put his hand on mine and I shut up. I could hear his breathing, a little fast, a little shallow. My friend was keeping it together so much better than I was, but he was the one with the death sentence.

"Remember what you told me about the curve?" he said. "Back when you thought you had cancer? The older you get, the more friends will die. It's just statistics. No reason I shouldn't be the next statistic."

"But you're only thirty—"

"Thirty-three," he said. "A little lower on the curve, but not unheard of." he breathed awhile longer. "Not a bad run."

"Pug," I said, but he squeezed my hand.

"If the next sentence to come out of your mouth includes the words 'spontaneous remission,' I'm going upside your head with a roll of quarters. That's the province of the Smurfs' Family Christmas, not the real world. And don't talk to me about having a positive attitude. The reason all those who've died of cancer croaked is because they had cancer, not because they were too gloomy."

"How about Laura?" I said. They'd been dating on and off for a couple months. She seemed nice. Did some kind of investment analysis for an ethical fund.

"Oh," he said. "Yeah. Don't suppose that was going to be serious. Huh. What do you think—tell her I'm dying, then break up; break up and then tell her I'm dying; or just break up?"

"What about telling her you're"—I swallowed—"dying, then giving her the choice?"

"What choice? Getting married? Dude, it's not like I've got a life-insurance policy. She's a nice person. Doesn't need to be widowed at thirty-two." he took his hand back. "Could you drive?"

When we got onto the 10, he chuckled. "Got some good birthdays in at least. Twenty-seven, that's a cube. Twenty-nine, prime. Thirty-one, prime. Thirty-two, a power of two. Thirty-three, a palindrome. It's pretty much all downhill from here."

"Thirty-six is a square," I said.

"Square," he said. "Come on, a square? Don't kid yourself, the good ones are all in that twenty-seven to thirty-three range. I got a square at twenty-five. How many squares does a man need?"

"Damn, you're weird," I said.

"Too weird to live, too beautiful to die." he thumped his chest. "Well, apparently not." He sighed. "Shit. Well, that happened."

"Look, if there's anything you need, let me know," I said. "I'm here for you."

"You're a prince. But you know what, this isn't the worst way to go, to tell the truth. I get a couple months to say good-bye, put things in order, but I don't have to lie around groaning and turning into a walking skeleton for six months while my body eats itself. It's the best of both worlds."

My mouth was suddenly too dry to talk. I dry-swallowed a few times, squeezed my eyes shut hard, put the car in gear, and swung into traffic. We didn't speak the rest of the way to Pug's. When we pulled up out front, I blurted, "You can come and stay with me, if you want. I mean, being alone—"

"Thanks," he said. He'd gone a little grey. "Not today, all right?"

Blight wasn't home when I got back, but Maya was. I'd forgotten she was coming to stay. She'd graduated the year before and had decided to do a year on the road with her net-friends, which was all the rage with her generation, the second consecutive cadre of no-job/no-hope kids to graduate from America's flagging high schools. They'd borrowed a bunch of tricks from their predecessors, most notably a total refusal to incur any student debt and a taste for free online courses in every subject from astronomy to science fiction literature—and especially things like agriculture and cookery, which was a critical part of their forager lifestyle.

Maya had cycled to my place from the Greyhound depot, using some kind of social bike-share that I hadn't ever heard of. On the way, she'd stopped and harvested berries, tubers, herbs, and some soft-but-serviceable citrus fruit. "The world'll feed you, if you let it," she said, carefully spitting grapefruit seeds into her hand. She'd scatter them later, on the next leg of the bike journey. "Especially in L.A. All that subsidized pork-barrel water from the Colourado River's good for something."

"Sounds like you're having a hell of a time," I said.

"Better than you," she said. "You look like chiseled shit." She grabbed my shoulders and peered into my eyes, searched my face. It struck me how much like her mom she looked, despite the careful checkerboard of coloured zinc paste that covered her features in dazzle-patterns that fooled facial-recognition algorithms and fended off the brutal, glaring sun.

"Thanks," I said, squirming away, digging a glass bottle of cold-brewed coffee out of the fridge.

"Seriously," she said, pacing me around the little kitchen. "What's going on? Everything okay with mom?"

"Your mother's fine," I said. "I'm fine."

"So why do you look like you just found out you're going to have to bury euthanized dogs for community service?"

"Is that real?"

"The dogs? Yeah. You get it a lot in the Midwest. Lot of feral dogs around Ohio and Indiana. They round 'em up, gas 'em, and stack 'em. It's pretty much the number one vagrancy penalty. Makes an impression."

"Jesus."

"Stop changing the subject. What's going on, Greg?"

I poured myself some coffee, added ice, and then dribbled in a couple of teaspoons' worth of half-and-half, watching the gorgeous fluid dynamics of the heavy cream roiling in the dark brown liquid.

"Come on, Greg," she said, taking the glass from me and draining half of it in one go. Her eyes widened a little. "That's good."

"It's not my story to tell," I said.

"Whose story is it?"

I turned back to the fridge to get out the cold-brew bottle again. "Dude, this is weak. Come on, shared pain is lessened, shared joy is increased. Don't be such a guy. Talk."

"You remember Pug?"

She rolled her eyes with teenage eloquence. "Yes, I remember Pug."

I heaved in a breath, heaved it out again. Tried to find the words. Didn't need to, as it turned out.

She blinked a couple times. "How long has he got?"

"Couple months," I said. "Longer, if he takes treatment. But not much longer. And he's not going to take it anyway."

"Good," she said. "That's a bad trade anyway." She sat down in one of my vintage vinyl starburst-upholstered kitchen chairs—a trophy of diligent L.A. yard-saling, with a matching chrome-rimmed table. She looked down into her coffee, which had gone a thick, uniform pale brown colour. "I'm sorry to hear it, though."

"Yeah," I said. "Yeah. Me too." I sat with her.

"What's he going to do now?"

I shrugged. "I guess he's got to figure that out."

"He should do something big," she said, under her breath, still staring into the drink. "Something huge. Think about it—it doesn't matter if he fucks it up. Doesn't matter if he goes broke or whatever. It's his last chance, you know?"

"I guess," I said. "I think it's really up to him, though. They're his last months."

"Bullshit," she said. "They're our last months with him. He's going to turn into ashes and vanish. We're going to be left on this ball of dirt for however many years we've got left. He's got a duty to try and make something of it with whatever time he's got left. Something for us to carry on. Come on, Greg, think about it. What do you do here, anyway? Try to live as lightly as possible, right? Just keep your head down, try not to outspend that little precious lump of dead money you lucked into so that you can truck on into the grave. You and Mom and Pug, you all 'know' that humans aren't really needed on Earth anymore, that robots can do all the work and that artificial life forms called corporations can harvest all the profit, so you're just hiding under the floorboards and hoping that it doesn't all cave in before you croak."

"Maya—"

"And don't you dare give me any bullshit about generational politics and demographics and youthful rage and all that crap. Things are true or they aren't, no matter how old the person saying them happens to be." She drained her drink. "And you know it."

I set down my glass and held my hands over my head. "I surrender. You're right. I got nothing better to do, and certainly Pug doesn't. So, tell me, wise one, what should we be doing?"

Her veneer of outraged confidence cracked a tiny bit. "Fucked if I know. Solve world hunger. Invent a perpetual motion machine. Colonize the Moon."

We wrote them on the whiteboard wall at Pug's place. He'd painted the wall with dry-erase paint when he first moved into the little house in Culver City, putting it where the TV would have gone a few decades before, and since then it had been covered with so much dry-erase ink and wiped clean so many times that there were bald patches where the underlying paint was showing through, stained by the markers that had strayed too close to no-man's-land. We avoided those patches and wrote:

SOLVE WORLD HUNGER
PERPETUAL MOTION MACHINE
MOON COLONY

The first one to go was the perpetual motion machine. "It's just stupid," Pug said. "I'm an engineer, not a metaphysician. If I'm going to do something with the rest of my life, it has to be at least possible, even if it's implausible."

"When you have eliminated the impossible, whatever remains, however implausible, must be—"

"How have you chosen your projects before?" Maya said. She and Blight sat in beanbag chairs on opposite sides of the room, pointedly watching the wall and not each other.

"They chose me," Pug said. She made a wet, rude noise. "Seriously. It never came up. Any time I was really working my nuts off on something, sweating over it, that was the exact moment that some other project demanded that I drop everything, right now, and take care of it. I figure it was the self-destructive part of my brain desperately trying to keep me from finishing anything, hoping to land a Hail Mary distraction pass."

"More like your own self-doubt," Maya said. "Trying to keep you from screwing something up by ensuring that you never finished it."

He stuck his tongue out at her. "Give me strength to withstand the wisdom of teenagers," he said.

"Doesn't matter how old the speaker is, it's the words that matter." She made a gurulike namaste with her hands and then brought them up to her forehead like a yoga instructor reaching for her third eye. Then she stuck her tongue out, too.

"All right, shut up, Yoda. The point is that I eventually figured out how to make that all work for me. I just wrote down the ideas as they came up and stuck them in the 'do-after' file, which means that I always had a huge, huge do-after file waiting for me the second I finished whatever I was on at the time."

"So fine, what's next on your do-after file."

He shook his head. "Nothing worth my time. Not if it's going to be the last splash. Nothing that's a legacy."

Blight said, "You're just overthinking it, dude. Whatever it is, whip it out. There's no reason to be embarrassed. It'd be much worse to do nothing because nothing was worthy of your final act than to do something that wasn't as enormous as it could have been."

"Believe me, you don't want to know," Pug said. "Seriously."

"Okay, back to our list." She closed her eyes and gave a theatrical shudder. "Look, it's clear that the methods you use to choose a project when you have all the time in the world are going to be different from the method you use when there's almost no time left. So let's get back to this." She drew a line through PERPETUAL MOTION. "I buy your reasons for this one. That leaves MOON COLONY and WORLD HUNGER." She poised her pen over MOON COLONY. "I think we can strike this one. You're not going to get to the Moon in a couple of months. And besides, world hunger—"

"Fuck world hunger," Pug said, with feeling.

"Very nice," she said. "Come on, Pug, no one needs to be reminded of what a totally with-it, cynical dude you are. We've all known all along what it had to be. World hunger—"

"Fuck. World. Hunger," Pug repeated.

Blight gave him a narrow-eyed stare. I recognized the signs of an impending eruption.

"Pug," I said, "Perhaps you could unpack that statement a little?"

"Come on," he said. "Unpack it? Why? You know what it means. Fuck world hunger because the problem with world hunger isn't too many people, or the wrong kind of agriculture, or, for fuck's sake, the idea that we're not doing enough to feed the poor. The problem with world hunger is that rich, powerful governments are more than happy to send guns and money to dictators and despots who'll use food to control their populations and line their pockets. There is no 'world hunger' problem. There's a corruption problem. There's a greed problem. There's a gullibility problem. Every racist fuck who's ever repeated half-baked neo-malthusian horseshit about overpopulation, meaning, of course, that the 'wrong' kind of people are having babies, i.e., poor people who have nothing to lose and don't have to worry about diluting their fortunes and squandering their pensions on too many kids—"

"So there's a corruption problem," I said. "Point taken. How about if we make a solution for the corruption problem, then? Maybe we could build some kind of visualizer that shows you if your Congresscritter is taking campaign contributions from companies and then voting for laws that benefit them?"

"What, you mean like every single one of them?" Maya pushed off the wall she'd been leaning against and took a couple steps toward me. "Get serious, Greg. The average elected official spends at least half of their time in office fund-raising for their next election campaign. They've been trying to fix campaign financing for decades and somehow, the people who depend on corrupt campaign contributions don't want to pass a law limiting corrupt campaign contributions. Knowing that your senator is on the take only helps if the guy running against him isn't also on the take.

"Come on, dude," she said. "The guy is *dying*, you want him to spend his last days making infographics? Why not listicles, too?" She framed a headline with her hands. "Revealed: the ten most corrupt senators! Except that you don't need a data analysis to find the ten most corrupt—they'll just be the ten longest-serving politicians."

"Okay," I said. "Okay, Maya, point taken. So what would you do to fight corruption?"

She got right up in my face, close enough that I could see the fine dark hairs on her upper lip—she and her cohort had rejected the hair removal mania of the previous decade, putting umpteen Brazilian waxers and threaders and laser hair zappers on the breadline—and smell the smoothie on her breath. "Greg, what are you talking about? Ending corruption? Like there's a version of this society that isn't corrupt? Corruption isn't the exception, it's the norm. It's baked in. The whole idea of using markets to figure out who gets what is predicated on corruption— it's a way to paper over the fact that some people get a lot, most of us get not much, and so we invent a *deus ex machina* called market forces that hands out money based on merit. How do we know that the market is giving it to deserving people? Well, look at all the money they have! It's just circular reasoning."

"So, what then? Anarchist collectivism? Communism?"

She looked around at all of us. "Duh. Look at you three. You've organized your whole lives around this weird-ass gift-economy thing where you take care of yourself and you take care of everyone else."

"Burning man isn't real life," Blight said. "God, I knew I should have waited until you were over eighteen before I took you to the Playa." Her tone was light, but given their earlier fury at each other, I braced for an explosion.

But Maya kept her cool. "It's a bitch when someone reminds you of all the contradictions in your life, I know. Your discomfort doesn't make what I'm saying any less true, though. Come on, you all know this is true. Late-stage capitalism isn't reformable. It's an idea whose time has passed."

We all stared at one another, a triangle of adulthood with solitary, furious adolescence in the centre.

"You're right, Maya. She's right. That's why the only logical choice is the Moon colony."

"You're going to secede from Earth?" Blight said. "Start a colony of anarcho-syndicalist Moon-men?"

"Not at all. What I want is, you know, a gift economy dangling like a carrot, hanging in the sky over all our heads. A better way of living, up there, in sight, forever. On the Moon. If civilization collapses and some chudded-out mutant discovers a telescope and points it at the Moon, she'll see the evidence of what the human race could be."

"What the hell are you talking about?" I said.

He stood up, groaning a little, the way he'd started to do, and half shuffled to his bookcase and picked up a 3D-printed miniature of the Gadget, run up on one of Minus's SLS powder printers. It even had a tiny, optically correct lens that his favourite lab in Germany had supplied; the whole thing had been a premium for a massively successful kickstarter a couple of years before. He handed it to me and its many legs flexed and rattled as it settled on my palm.

"I want to put Gadgets on the Moon. Mod 'em to print moondust, turn 'em loose. Years will pass. Decades, maybe. But when our kids get to the Moon, or maybe Maya's kids, or maybe their kids, they'll find a gift from their ancestors. Something for nothing. A free goddamned lunch, from the first days of a better nation."

One part of me was almost in tears at the thought, because it was a beautiful one. But there was another part of me that was violently angry at the idea. Like he was making fun of the world of the living from his cozy vantage point on the rim of the valley of death. The two of us had a way of bickering like an old married couple, but since his diagnosis, every time I felt like I was about to lay into him, I stopped. What if, what if. What if this was the last thing I said to him? What if he went to his deathbed with my bad-tempered words still ringing in the air between us? I ended up with some kind of bubbling, subcutaneous resentment stew on the boil at all times.

I just looked thoughtfully at the clever little Gadget in my palm. We'd talked about making it functional—a $7 Gorseberry Pi should have had the processing power, and there were plenty of teeny-tiny stepper motors out there, but no one could figure out a way of doing the assembly at scale, so we'd gone with a nonfunctional model.

"Can you print with moondust?"

Pug shrugged his shoulders. "Probably. I know I've read some stuff about it along the way. NASA runs some kind of 'What the fuck do we do with all this moondust?' challenge every year or two—you can order synthetic dust to play around with."

"Pug, I don't think we're going to get a printer on the Moon in a couple of months."

"No," he said. "No, I expect I'll be ashes long before you're ready to launch. It's gonna take a lot of doing. We don't know shit about engineering for low-gravity environments, even less about vacuum. And you're going to have to raise the money to get the thing onto the Moon, and that's gonna be a lot of mass. Don't forget to give it a giant antenna, because the only way you're going to be able to talk to it is by bouncing shortwave off the Moon. Better hope you get a lot of support from people around the equator; that'll be your best way to keep it in range the whole time."

"This isn't a new idea, is it?"

"Honestly? No. Hell no. I've had this as a tickle in the back of my brain for years. The first time we put a Gadget out in the dust for the summer, I was 99 percent certain that we were going to come back and find the thing in pieces. But it worked. And it keeps on getting better. That got me thinking: where's there a lot of dust and not a lot of people? I'd love to stick some of these on Mars, send 'em on ahead, so in a century or two, our great-greats can touch down and build Bradburytown pretty much overnight. Even better, make a self-assembling reprap version, one that can print out copies of itself, and see how fast you can turn any asteroid, dustball, or lump of interstellar rock and ice into a Hall of Martian Kings, some assembly required."

None of us said anything for a while.

"When you put it that way, Pug . . ." Blight said.

Pug looked at her and there were bright tears standing in his eyes. Hers, too.

"Oh, Pug," she said.

He covered his face with his hands and sobbed. I was the first one to reach him. I put an arm around his shoulders and he leaned into me, and I felt the weird lump where his dislocation hadn't set properly. He cried for a long time. Long enough for Blight, and then Maya, to come and put their arms around us. Long enough for me to start crying.

When he straightened up, he took the little Gadget out of my hand.

"It's a big universe," he said. "It doesn't give a shit about us. As far as we can tell, there's only us out here. If our grandchildren—your grandchildren, I mean—are going to meet friendly aliens, they're just going to be us."

Pug lived longer than they'd predicted. The doctors said that it was his sense of purpose that kept him alive, which sounded like bullshit to me. Like the stuff he'd railed against when he'd bitten my head off about "Positive attitudes." If having a sense of purpose will keep you alive, then everyone who died of cancer must not have had enough of a sense of purpose.

As Pug would have said, Screw that with an auger.

It was a funny thing about his idea: you told people about it and they just got it. Maybe it was all the Gadgets out on the playa percolating through the zeitgeist, or maybe it was the age-old sorcerer's apprentice dream of machines that make copies of themselves, or maybe it was the collapse of the Chinese and Indian Mars missions and the bankruptcy of the American company that had been working on the private mission. Maybe it was Pug, or just one of those things.

But they got it.

Which isn't to say that they liked it. Hell no. the day we broke our kickstarter goal for a private fifty-kilo lift to the Moon—one-fifth the weight of a standard-issue Gadget, but that was an engineering opportunity, wasn't it?—the United Nations Committee on the Peaceful Uses of Outer Space called a special meeting in Geneva to talk about prohibitions on "environmental degradation of humanity's moon." Like we were going to mess up their nice craters.

The Green Moon Coalition was a weird chimera. On the one hand, you had a kind of axis of paranoid authoritarianism, China and Russia and North Korea and what was left of Greece and Cyprus, all the basket-case countries, and they were convinced that we were a stalking horse for the American spookocracy, striking in the hour of weakness to establish, I don't know, maybe a weapons platform? Maybe a listening post? Maybe a killer earthquake machine? They weren't very coherent on this score.

Say what you will about those weird, paranoid creeps: they sure understood how to play UN procedure. No one could game the UN better except for the USA. If only we'd actually been a front for Big Snoop, maybe they would have had our back.

But that was only to be expected. What I didn't expect was the other half of Green Moon: the environmental movement. I sincerely, seriously doubt that anyone in the politburo or Damascus or the Kremlin or Crete gave the tiniest, inciest shit about the Moon's "environment." They just hated and feared us because our government hated and feared them.

But there were people—a lot of people—who thought that the Moon had a right to stay "pristine." The first time I encountered this idea—it was on a voice chat with a reporter who had caught a whiff of our online chatter about the project—I couldn't even speak coherently about it.

"Sorry, could you say that again?"

"Doesn't the Moon have a right to be left alone, in a pristine state?"

"There's a saying, 'that's not right. It's not even wrong.' The Moon doesn't have rights. It's a rock and some dust, and maybe if we're very lucky, there's some ice. And the Moon doesn't do 'pristine.' It's been hammered by asteroids for two billion years. Got a surface like a tin can that's been dragged behind a truck for a thousand miles. There's no one there. There's nothing there."

"Except for craters and dust, right?"

"Yes, except for those."

The call developed the kind of silence I recognized as victorious. The reporter clearly felt that she'd scored a point. I mentally rewound it.

"Wait, what? Come on. You're seriously saying that you think that craters and dust need to be preserved? For what?"

"Why shouldn't they?"

"Because they're inanimate matter."

"But it's not your inanimate matter to disturb."

"Look, every time a meteor hits the Moon, it disturbs more dust than I'm planning on messing up by, like, a millionfold. Should we be diverting meteors? At what point do we draw a line on nature and say, all right, now it's time for things to stop. This is it. Nature is finished. Any more changes to this would be unnatural."

"Of course not. But are you saying you don't see the difference between a meteor and a machine?"

There was no hesitation. "Human beings have just about terminally screwed up the Earth and now you want to get started on the Moon. Wouldn't it be better to figure out how we all want to use the Moon before we go there?"

I don't remember how I got out of the call. It wasn't the last time I had that discussion, in any event. Not by a very, very long chalk. They all ended up in the same place.

I don't know if the mustache-and-epaulet club were useful idiots for the deep greens or vice versa, but it was quite a combo.

The one thing we had going for us was the bankruptcy of Mars Shot, the private Mars expedition. They'd invested a ton in the first two stages of the project: a reusable lifting vehicle and a space station for it to rendezvous with. The lifter had been profitable from day one, with a roaring trade in comsat launches. But Mars Shot pumped every dime of profit into Skyhaven, which was meant to be a shipyard for the Burroughs, a one-way, twenty-person Mars rocket with enough technology in its cargo pods to establish a toehold on our neighbouring planet. And Skyhaven just turned out to be too goddamned expensive.

I can't fault them. They'd seen Mir and Skylab and decided that they were dead ends, variations on a short-lived theme. Rather than focusing on strength, they opted for metastability: nested, pressurized spheres made of carbon-fiber plastic that could be easily patched and resealed when— not if—it ripped. Free-floating, continuously replenished gummed strips floated in the void between the hulls, distributed by convection currents made by leaking heat from within the structure. They'd be sucked into any breach and seal it. Once an outer hull reached a critical degree of patchiness, a new hull would be inflated within the inner hull, which would be expanded to accommodate it, the inside wall becoming the outside and the outside becoming recyclable junk that could be sliced, gummed, and used for the next generation of patchwork. It was resilient, not stable, and focused on failing well, even at the expense of out-and-out success.

This sounded really good on paper, and even better on video. They had a charismatic engineering lead, Marina Kotov, who'd been laid off from JPL during its final wind-down, and she could talk about it with near-religious zeal. Many were the engineers who went into one of her seminars ready to laugh at the "space condom" and bounded out converts to "fail well, fail cheap, fail fast," which was her battle cry.

For all I know, she was totally right. There were a lot of shakedown problems with the fabric, and one of their suppliers went bust half way through, leaving them with a partial balloon and nothing they could do about it. Unfortunately for them, the process for making the fabric was patented to hell and back, and the patents were controlled by a speculator who'd cut an exclusive deal with a single company that was a lot better at bidding on patent licenses than it was at making stuff. There was a multi-month scramble while the bankruptcy trustees were placated and a new licensor found, and by then, Skyhaven was in deep shit.

Mars Shot had attracted a load of investment capital and even more in convertible bonds that they'd issued like raffle tickets. Building a profitable, efficient orbit-lifter wasn't cheap—they blew billions on it, sure that they'd be able to make it pay once Skyhaven was done and the Mars Shot was launched. I've seen convincing analysis that suggests that they would never have gotten there—not if they'd had to repay their lenders and make a 10x or 20x exit for their investors.

Bankruptcy solved that. I mean, sure, it wiped out thousands of old people's pensions and destroyed a bunch of the frail humans who'd been clinging to financial stability in a world that only needed banks and robots—people like me. That sucked. It killed people, as surely as Pug's cancer had killed him.

The infrastructure that Mars Shot owned was broken up and sold for parts, each of the lifter vehicles going to different consortia. We thought about kickstarting our own fund to buy one, but figured it would be better to simply buy services from one of the suckers who was lining up to go broke in space. Blight had been a small child during the dot-com crash of the 1990s, but she'd done an AP history presentation on it once, about how it had been the last useful bubble, because it took a bunch of capital that was just being used to generate more capital and turned it into cheap dark fiber bundles and hordes of skilled nerds to fill it with stuff. All the bubbles since had just moved money from the world of the useful into the pockets of the hyperrich, to be flushed back into the financial casino where it would do nothing except go around and around again, being reengineered by high-speed-trading ex-physicists who should know better.

The dot-com legacy was cheap fiber. Once all the debt had been magically wiped off the books and the investors had abandoned the idea of 10–20x payouts, fiber could be profitable.

Mars Shot's legacy was cheap lift. All it took was a massive subsidy from an overly optimistic market and a bunch of hedgies with an irrational belief in their own financial infallibility and bam, there it was, ten glorious cents on the dollar, and all the lift you could want, at a nice, sustainable price.

It's a good thing there was more than one consortium running lifters to orbit, because our Indonesian launch partner totally chickened out on us a month before launch. They had deep trade ties to Russia and China, and after one of those closed-door plurilateral trade meetings, everyone emerged from the smoke-filled room convinced that nothing destined for the Moon should be lifted by any civilized country.

It left me wishing for the millionth time that we really were a front for Uncle Sam. There was a juicy Colombian lift that went up every month like clockwork, and Colombia was the kind of country so deep in America's pocket that they'd do pretty much anything that was required of them. OrbitaColombia SA was lifting all kinds of weird crap that had no business being in space, including a ton of radioisotopes that someone from GE's nuclear division blew the whistle on much later. Still gives me nightmares, the thought of all those offensive nukes going into orbit, the ghost of Ronald Reagan over our heads for the half-life of plutonium.

In the end, we found our home in Brazil. Brazil had a strong environmental movement, but it was the sort of environmental movement that cared about living things, not rocks. My kind of movement, in other words.

We knew Pug's death was coming all along, and we had plenty of warning as he got sicker and the pain got worse. He got a morphine pump, which helped, and then some of his chemist friends helped him out with a supply of high-quality ketamine, which really, really helped. It wasn't like he was going to get addicted or OD. At least, not accidentally.

The last three weeks, he was too sick to get out of bed at all. We moved his bed into the living room and kept the blinds drawn and the lights down. We worked in whispers. Most of the time, he slept. He didn't get thin the way that people with cancer can get at the end, mostly because of his decision to bow out early, without chemo and radiation therapy. He kept his hair, and it was only in the last week when I was changing his bedpan that I noticed his legs had gotten scarily thin and pale, a stark contrast to the day we'd met and the muscular, tanned legs bulging with veins as he crouched by the proto-Gadget.

But he kept us company, and when he was awake, he kibbitzed in a sleepy voice. Sometimes he was too stoned and ended up making no sense, just tapering off into mumble-mumble, but he had surprisingly lucid moments, when his eyes would glitter and he'd raise his trembling arm and point at something on the whiteboard or someone's screen and bust out a change or objection that was spot-on. It was spooky, like he was bringing us insights from the edge of death, and we all started jumping a little when he'd do it. In this way, little by little, the project's roadmap took shape: the order of lifter consortia to try, the approaches to try with each, the way to pitch the kickstarter, and even the storyboard for the video and engineering suggestions for sifting regolith.

Pug slept on his hospital bed in the living room. In theory, we all took turns sleeping on the sofa next to him, but in practice, I was the only one who could sleep through the groans he'd make in his sleep but still wake up when he rasped hoarsely for his bedpan. It was just after two, one night, when he woke me up by croaking my name, "Greg, hey, Greg."

I woke and found that he'd adjusted the bed to sit up straight, and he was more animated than he'd been in weeks, his eyes bright and alert.

"What is it, Pug?"

He pointed at a crack in the drapes, a sliver of light coming through them. "Full moon tonight," he said.

I looked at the blue-white triangle of light. "Looks like it," I said.

"Open the curtains?"

I got up and padded to the window and pulled the curtains back. A little dust rained down from the rods and made me sneeze. Out the window, framed perfectly by it like an HD shot in a documentary, was the moon, so big and bright it looked like a painted set lit up with a spotlight. We both stared at it for a moment. "It's the moon illusion," he said. "Makes it seem especially big because we don't have anything to compare it to. Once it dips a little lower on the horizon and the roofs and tree branches are in the same plane, it'll seem small again. That's the Sturgeon moon. August's moon. My favourite moon, the moon you sometimes get at the burn." It was almost time for the burn, and my email had been filled with a rising babble of messages about photovoltaics and generators, costumes and conductive body paint, bikes and trailers, coffee and dry ice, water and barbecues and charcoal and sleeping bags. Normally, all this stuff would be a steadily rising chorus whose crescendo came when we packed the latest Gadgets into the van, wedged tight amid groceries and clothes and tents, and closed the doors and turned the key in the ignition.

This year, it was just an annoying mosquito-whine of people whose lives had diverged from our own in the most profound way imaginable. They were all off for a week of dust and hedonism; we were crammed together in this dark, dying room, planning a trip to the Moon.

"Outside," he said, and coughed weakly. He reached for his water bottle and I helped him get the flexible hose into his mouth. "Outside," he said again, stronger.

I eyed his hospital bed and looked at the living room door. "Won't fit," I said. "Don't think you can walk it, buddy."

He rolled his eyes at the wall, and I stared at it for a moment before I figured out what he was trying to tell me. Behind the low bookcase, the garbage can, and the overstuffed chair, that wall was actually a set of ancient, ever-closed vertical blinds. I dragged the furniture away and found the blinds' pull chain and cranked them back to reveal a set of double sliding doors, a piece of two-by-four wedged in the track to keep them from being forced open. I looked back at Pug and he nodded gravely at me and made a minute shooing gesture. I lifted out the lumber, reaching through a thick pad of old cobwebs and dust bunnies. I wiped my hand on the rug and then leaned the wood against the wall. I pulled the door, which stuck at first, then gave way with a crunchy, squeaky sound. I looked from the hospital bed to the newly revealed door.

"All right, buddy, let's get this show on the road. Moon don't wait for no one."

He gave me a thumbs-up and I circled the bed, unlocking each of the wheels.

It was a good bed, a lease from a company that specialized in helping people to die at home. If that sounds like a ghoulish idea for a start-up, then I'm guessing you've never helped a friend who was dying in a hospital.

But it was still a hell of a struggle getting the bed out the door. It just fit, without even a finger's width on either side. And then there was the matter of the IV stand, which I had to swing around so it was over the head of the bed, right in my face as I pushed, until he got wedged and I had to go out the front door and around the house to pull from the other side, after freeing the wheels from the rubble and weeds in the backyard.

But once we were out, it was smooth rolling, and I took him right into the middle of the yard. It was one of those perfect L.A. nights, the cool dividend for a day's stifling heat, and the Moon loomed overhead so large I wanted to reach out and touch it. Pug and I were beside each other, admiring the Moon.

"Help me lower the back," he said, and I cranked the manual release that gently laid the bed out flat, so he could lie on his back and stare up at the sky. I lay down in the weeds beside him, but there were pointy rocks in there, so I went inside and got a couple of sofa cushions and improvised a bed. On my way out the door, I dug out a pair of binoculars from Pug's Burning Man box, spilling fine white dust as I pulled them free of the junk inside.

I held the binocs up to my eyes and focused them on the Moon. The craters and peaks came into sharp focus, bright with the contrast of the full Moon. Pug dangled his hand down toward me and wriggled his fingers impatiently, so I got to my feet and helped him get the binoculars up to his face. He twiddled the knobs with his shaking fingers, then stopped. He was absolutely still for a long time. So long that I thought he might have fallen asleep. But then he gently lowered the binocs to his chest.

"It's beautiful," he said. "There'll be people there, someday."

"Hell yeah," I said. "Of course."

"Maybe not for a long time. Maybe a future civilization. Whatever happens, the Moon'll be in the sky, and everyone will know that there's stuff waiting for them to come and get it."

I took the binocs out of his loose fingers and lay back down on my back, looking at the Moon again. I'd seen the Apollo footage so often it had become unreal, just another visual from the library of failed space dreams of generation ships and jetpacks and faster-than-light travel. Despite all my work over the past weeks and months, the Moon as a place was . . . fictional, like Narnia or Middle Earth. It was an idea for a theme camp, not a place where humans might venture, let alone live there.

Seen through the binocs that night, all those pits, each older than the oldest living thing on Earth, I came to understand the Moon as a place. In that moment, I found myself sympathizing with the Green Moonies, and their talk of the Moon's pristineness. There was something wonderful about knowing that the first upright hominids had gazed upon the same Moon that we were seeing, and that it had hardly changed.

"It's beautiful," I said. I was getting drowsy.

"Jewel," he said, barely a whisper. "Pearl. Ours. Gotta get there. Gotta beat the ones who think companies are people. The Moon's for people, not corporations. It's a free lunch. Yours, if you want it."

"Amen," I said. It was like being on a campout, lying with your friends, staring at the stars, talking until sleep overcame you.

I drifted between wakefulness and sleep for a long, weird time, right on the edge, as the Moon tracked across the sky. When I woke, the birds were singing and the sun was on our faces. Pug was lying in a stoned daze, the button for his drip in his loose grasp. He only did that when the pain was bad. I brought his bed inside as gently as I could, but he never gave any sign he noticed, not even when the wheels bumped over the sliding door's track. I put things back as well as I could and had a shower and put breakfast on and didn't speak of the Moon in the night sky to Blight or Maya when they arrived later that morning.

Pug died that night. He did it on purpose, asking for ketamine in a serious voice, looking at each of us in turn as I put the pills in his hand. "More," he said. Then again. He looked in my eyes and I looked in his. I put more tablets in his hand, helped him find the hose end for his water as he swallowed them. He reached back for the morphine switch and I put it in his hand. I took his other hand. Blight and Maya moved to either side of me and rested their hands on the bed rail, then on Pug, on his frail arm, his withered leg. He smiled a little at us, stoned and sleepy, closed his eyes, opened them a little, and nodded off. We stood there, listening to him breathe, listening to the breath slowing. Slowing.

Slowing.

I couldn't put my finger on the instant that he went from living to dead.

But there was a moment when the muscles of his face went slack, and in the space of seconds, his familiar features rearranged themselves into the face of a corpse. So much of what I thought of as the shape of Pug's face was the effect of the tensions of the underlying muscles, and as his cheeks hollowed and slid back, the skin on his nose stretched, making it more bladelike, all cartilage, with the nostrils flattened to lizardlike slits. His lips, too, stretched back in a toneless, thin-lipped smile that was half a grimace. His heart may have squeezed out one or two more beats after that; maybe electrical impulses were still arcing randomly from nerve to nerve, neuron to neuron, but that was the moment at which he was more dead than alive, and a few moments after that, he was altogether and unmistakably dead.

We sat there in tableau for a moment that stretched and stretched. I was now in a room with a body, not my friend. I let go of his hand and sat back, and that was the cue for all of us to back away.

There should be words for those moments, but there aren't. In the same way that every human who ever lived has gazed upon the Moon and looked for the words to say about it, so have we all looked upon the bodies of the ones we've loved and groped for sentiment. I wished I believed in last rites, or pennies on the eyelids, or just, well, anything that we could all acknowledge as the proper way to seal off the moment and return to the world of the living. Blight slipped her hand in mine and Maya put her elbow through my other arm and together we went out into the night. The Moon was not quite full anymore, a sliver out of its huge face, and tonight there were clouds scudding across the sky that veiled and unveiled it.

We stood there, the three of us, in the breeze and the rattle of the tree branches and the distant hum of L.A. traffic and the far-off clatter of a police helicopter, with the cooling body of our friend on the other side of the wall behind us. We stood there and stared up at the Moon.

Adapting the Gadget to work in a lunar environment was a substantial engineering challenge. Pug had sketched out a map for us—gathering regolith, sorting it, feeding it onto the bed, aligning the lens. Then there was propulsion, which was even more important for the Moon than it was on Earth. We'd drop a Gadget on the Playa in July and gather up its tiles a couple of months later, over Labor Day. But the moonprinter might be up there for centuries, sintering tetroid tiles and pooping them out while the humans below squabbled and fretted and cast their gaze into the stars. If we didn't figure out how to keep the Gadget moving, it would eventually end up standing atop a bed of printed tiles, out of dust and out of reach of more dust, and that would be that.

This wasn't one Pug had a solution for. Neither did I, or Blight, or Maya. But it wasn't just us. There was a sprawling wiki and mailing list for the project, and at one point, we had three separate factions vying to go to the Moon first. One was our project, one was nearly identical in goals except that its organizers were totally committed to a certain methodology for sealing the bearings that our side had voted down.

The third faction—they were *weird*. /b/ was a clutch of totally bizarro trolls, a community that had cut its teeth drawing up detailed plans for invading Sealand—the offshore drilling platform that had been converted to an ill-starred sovereign data haven—moved on to gaming *Time* magazine polls, splintered into the Anonymous movement with all its many facets and runs and ops, fighting everyone from the Church of Scientology to the Egyptian Government to the NSA and that had proven its ability to continuously alter itself to challenge all that was sane and complacent with the world, no matter what it took.

These people organized themselves under the banner of the Committee to Protect Luna (SRSLY), and they set out to build a machine that would hunt down our machine, and all the tiles it dropped, and smash it into the smallest pieces imaginable. They had some pretty talented engineers working with them, and the designs they came up with solved some of the issues we'd been wrestling with, like a flywheel design that would also act as a propulsive motor, its energy channeled in one direction so that the Gadget would gently inch its way along the lunar surface. They produced innumerable videos and technical diagrams showing how their machine would work, hunting ours down by means of EMF sensors and an onboard vision system. For armament, it had its own sinterer, a clever array of lenses that it could focus with software-controlled servos to create a bug-under-a-magnifying-glass effect, allowing it to slowly but surely burn microscopic holes through our robot.

The thing was, the technical designs were absolutely sound. And though 90 percent of the rhetoric on their message boards had the deranged tinge of stoned giggles, the remaining 10 percent was deadly serious, able to parrot and even refine the Green Moon party line with stony earnestness. There were a lot of people in our camp who were convinced that they were serious—especially after they kickstarted the full load for a killer bot in thirty-six hours.

I thought it was trolling, just plain trolling. DON'T FEED THE TROLLS! I shouted online. No one listened to me (not enough people, anyway), and there was an exhausting ramble about countermeasures and armour and even, God help us all, a lawsuit, because yeah, totally, that would work. The wrangle lasted so long that we missed our launch window. The leaders of the paranoiac faction said that they'd done us all a favour by making us forfeit the deposit we'd put down, because now we'd have time to get things really right before launch time.

Another group said that the important thing wasn't countermeasures, it was delay—if we waited until the /b/tards landed their killer bot on the Moon, we could just land ours far enough away that it would take five hundred years for the two to meet, assuming top speed and flat terrain all the way. That spun out into a brutal discussion of game theory and strategy, and I made the awful mistake of getting involved directly, saying, "look, knuckleheads, if your strategy is to outwait them, and their goal is to stop us from doing anything, then their optimal strategy is to do nothing. So long as they haven't launched, we can't launch."

The ensuing discussion ate my life for a month and spilled over into the real world, when, at an L.A. burners' event, a group of people who staunchly disagreed with me made a point of finding me wherever I was to make sure I understood what a dunderhead I was.

I should have known better. Because, inevitably, the /b/tard who was in charge of the money fucked off with it. I never found out what he or she did with it. As far as I know, no one ever did.

After that, I kept my mouth shut. Or rather, I only opened it to do things that would help the project go forward. I stopped knocking heads together. I let Maya do that. I don't believe in generalizations about demographics, but man, could that girl argue. Forget all that horseshit about "digital natives," which never meant anything anyway. Using a computer isn't hard. But growing up in a world where how you argue about something changes what happens to it, that was a skill, and Maya had it in ways I never got.

"What's wrong with calling it the Gadget?"

Blight looked up from her weeding and armed sweat off her forehead, leaving behind a faint streak of brown soil. She and I traded off the weeding and this was her day, which meant that I got to spend my time indoors with all the imaginary network people and their arguments.

"Leave it, Greg," she said, in that tone that I'd come to recognize as perfectly nonnegotiable. We'd been living together for two years at that point, ever since I sank a critical mass of my nest egg into buying another launch window and had had to remortgage my house. The vegetable garden wasn't just a hobby—it was a way of life and it helped make ends meet.

"Come on," I said. "Come on. We've always called it 'the Gadget.' that's what Pug called it—"

She rocked back on her heels and rose to her feet with a kind of yogic grace. Her eyes were at half-mast, with that cool fury that I'd come to know and dread.

"Pug? Come on, Greg, I thought we agreed: no playing the cult of personality card. He's dead. For years now. He wasn't Chairman Mao. He wasn't even Hari Seldon. He was just a dude who liked to party and was a pretty good engineer and was an altogether sweet guy. 'That's what Pug called it' is pure bullshit. 'The Gadget' is a dumb name. It's a way of announcing to the world that this thing hasn't been thought through. That it's a lark. That it's not serious—"

"Maybe that's good," I said. "A good thing, you know? Because that way, no one takes us seriously and we get to sneak around and act with impunity until it's too late and—"

I fell silent under her stony glare. I tried to keep going, but I couldn't. Blight had the opposite of a reality distortion field. A reality assertion field.

"Fine," I said. "We won't call it the Gadget. But I wish you'd told me before you went public with it."

She pulled off her gardening gloves and stuffed them into her pockets, then held out her hands to me. I took them.

"Greg," she said, looking into my eyes. "I have opinions. Lots of them.

And I'm not going to run them past you before I 'go public' with them. Are we clear on that score?"

Again, I was stymied by her reality assertion field. All my stupid rationalizations about not meaning it that way refused to make their way out of my mouth, as some latent sense of self-preservation came to the fore.

"Yes, Blight," I said. She squeezed my fingers and dropped her stern demeanor like the mask it was.

"Very good. Now, what shall we call it?"

Everyone who had come to know it through Burning man called it the Gadget. Everyone else called it the moonprinter. "Not moonprinter."

"Why not? It seems to have currency. You going to tell everyone the name they chose is wrong?"

"Yes," I said.

"Okay, go," she said.

"Well, first of all, it's not a printer. Calling it a 3D printer is like calling a car a horseless carriage. Like calling videoconferencing 'the picture-phone.' As long as we call it an anything printer, we'll be constrained by printerish thinking."

"All right," she said. "Pretty good point. What else?"

"It's not printing the Moon! It's using moondust to print structural materials for prefab habitats. The way you 'print' a moon is by smashing a comet into a planet so that a moon-sized hunk of rock breaks off and goes into orbit around it."

"So what do you think we should call it?"

I shrugged. "I like 'the Gadget.'"

I ducked as she yanked off one of her dirty, balled-up gloves and threw it at my head. She caught me with the other glove and then followed it up with a muscular, rib-constricting hug. "I love you, you know."

"I love you, too." And I did. Despite the fact that I had raided my nest egg, entered the precariat, and might end up someday eating dog food, I was as happy as a pig in shit. Speaking of which.

"Dammit, I forgot to feed Messy."

She gave my butt a playful squeeze. "Go on then."

Messy was our pig, a kunekune, small enough to be happy on half an acre of pasture grass, next to the chicken run with its own half acre. The chickens ate bugs and weeds, and we planted more pasture grass in their poop, which Messy ate, leaving behind enough poop to grow berries and salad greens, which we could eat. We got eggs and, eventually, bacon and pork chops, as well as chickens. No external fertilizer, no phosphates, and we got more calories out for less energy and water inputs than even the most efficient factory farm.

It was incredibly labor-intensive, which was why I liked it. It was nice to think that the key to feeding nine billion people was to measure return on investment by maximizing calories and minimizing misery, instead of minimizing capital investment and maximizing retained earnings to shareholders.

Messy's dinner was only an hour late, and she had plenty of forage on her half acre, but she was still pissed at me and refused to come and eat from my hand until I'd cooed at her and made apologetic noises, and then she came over and nuzzled me and nipped at my fingers. I'd had a couple dogs, growing up, but the most smartest and most affectionate among them wasn't a patch on a pig for smarts and warmth. I wasn't sure how we'd bring ourselves to eat her. Though, hell, we managed it with the chickens, which were smarter and had more personality than I'd ever imagined. That was the other thing about permaculture: it made you think hard about where your food came from. It had been months since I'd been able to look at a jar of gas-station pepperoni sticks without imagining the animals they had once been.

Messy grunted amiably at me and snuffled at my heels, which was her way of asking to be let out of her pasture. I opened the gate and walked around to the small part of the house's yard that we kept for human leisure. I unfolded a chair and sat in it and picked up her ball and threw it and watched her trot off excitedly to fetch it. She could do this for hours, but only if I varied where I threw it and gave her some tricky challenges.

Maya called them the "brick shitters," which was hilarious except that it was a gift for the Green Moon crowd, who already accused us of shitting all over the Moon. Blight wanted "homesteaders," which, again, had all kinds of awful baggage about expropriation of supposedly empty lands from the people who were already there. She kept arguing that there were no indigenous people on the Moon, but that didn't matter. The Green Moon people were determined to paint us as rapacious land grabbers, and this was playing right into their hands. It always amazed me how two people as smart as Blight and Maya could be so dumb about this.

Not that I had better ideas. "The Gadget" really was a terrible name.

I threw the ball and thought some more.

We ended up calling it "Freelunch." it wasn't my coinage, but as soon as I saw it, I knew it was right. Just what Pug would have wanted. A beacon overhead, promising us a better life if only we'd stop stepping on one another to get at it.

The name stuck. Some people argued about it, but it was clear to anyone who did lexicographic analysis of the message boards, chats, tweets, and forums that it was gaining with that Internet-characteristic, winner-take-all, hockey-stick-shaped growth line. Oh, sure, the localization projects argued about whether free meant "libre" or "gratis" and split down the middle. In Brazil, they used "livre" (Portugal's thirty-years-and-counting technocratic "interim" managers translated it as "grátis").

More than eight thousand of us went to Macapá for launch day, landing in Guyana and taking the new high-speed rail from Georgetown. There had been dozens of Freelunch prototypes built and tested around the world, with teams competing for funding, engineer time, lab space. A co-op in Asheville, blessed by NASA, had taken over the production of ersatz regolith, a blend whose composition was (naturally) hotly debated.

The Brazilian contingent went all out for us. I stayed up every night dancing and gorging, then slept in a different family's living room until someone came to take me to the beach or a makerspace or a school. One time, Maya and Blight and I were all quartered in a favela that hung off the side of an abandoned office tower on impossibly thin, impossibly strong cables. The rooms were made of waxed cardboard and they swayed with the wind and terrified me. I was convinced I'd end up stepping right through the floor and ended up on tiptoes every time I moved. I tried not to move.

Celesc Lifter SA had a little VIP box from which customers could watch launches. It held eight people. The seats were awarded by lottery and I didn't get one. So I watched the lift with everyone else (minus eight), from another favela, one of the old, established ones with official recognition. Every roof was packed with viewers, and hawkers meandered the steep alleys with bulbs of beer and skewers of meat and paper cones of seafood. It was Celesc's ninety-third lift, and it had a 78 percent success rate, with only two serious failures in that time. No fatalities, but the cargo had been jettisoned over the Pacific and broke up on impact.

Those were good odds, but we were still all holding our breath through the countdown, through the first flames and the rumble conveyed by a thousand speakers, an out-of-phase chorus of net-lagged audio. We held it through the human-piloted takeoff of the jumbo jet that acted as a first stage for the lifter and gasped when the jet's video stream showed the lifter emerging from its back and rising smoothly into the sky. The jet dropped precipitously as the lifter's rockets fired and caught it and goosed it up, through the thin atmosphere at the edge of space in three hundred seconds.

I watched the next part from the lifter, though others swore it was better from Al Jazeera's LEO platform, framed against the earth, the day/night terminator arcing across the ocean below. But I liked the view from the lifter's nose, because you could see the Moon growing larger, until it dominated the sky.

Decades before, the *Curiosity* crew had endured their legendary "seven minutes of terror" when its chute, rockets, and exterior casings had to be coordinated with split-second timing to land the spunky little bot on our nearest neighbour without smashing it to flinders. Landing the first Freelunch on the Moon was a lot simpler, thankfully. We had a lot of things going for us: the Moon was close enough for us to get telemetry and send new instructions right up to the last second, it exerted substantially less gravity than Mars, and we had the advantage of everything NASA had learned and published from its own landing missions. And let us not forget that Earth sports a sizable population of multigenerational lunar lander pilots who've trained on simulators since the text-based version first appeared on the PDP-8 in 1969.

Actually, the last part kind of sucked. A lot of people believed they were qualified to intervene in the plan, and most of them were not. The signal:noise ratio for the landing was among the worst in the whole project, but in the end the winning strategy was the one that had been bandied about since the ESA's scrapped lunar lander competition, minus the observational phase: a short series of elliptical orbits leading to a transfer orbit and a quick burn that set it falling toward the surface. The vision systems that evaluated the landing site were able to autonomously deploy air jets to nudge the descent into the clearest, smoothest patch available.

Celesc's lifter released the Freelunch right on time, burning a little to kick itself back down into a lower orbit to prepare for descent. As their vectors diverged, the Freelunch seemed to arc away, even though it was actually continuing on the exact curve that the lifter had boosted it to. It dwindled away from the lens of AJ's satellite, lost against the looming Moon, winking in and out of existence as a black speck that the noise-correction algorithms kept erasing and then changing their mind about.

One by one, all the screens around me converged on the same feed: a split screen of shaky, high-magnification real-time video on one side, a radar-fed line-art version on the other. The Freelunch wound around and around the Moon in four ever-tightening orbits, like a tetherball winding around a post. A tiny flare marked its shift to transfer orbit, and then it was sailing down in a spiral.

"Coming in for a landing," Blight said, and I nodded, suddenly snapped back to the warm Brazilian night, the smell of food and the taste of beer in my mouth. It spiraled closer and closer, and then it kicked violently away, and we all gasped. "Something on the surface," Blight said.

"Yeah," I said, squinting and pinch-zooming at the view from its lower cameras. We'd paid for satellite relay for the landing sequence, which meant we were getting pretty hi-res footage. But the Moon's surface defies the human eye: tiny pebbles cast long, sharp shadows that look like deep cracks or possibly high shelves. I could see ten things on the landing site that could have been bad news for the Freelunch—or that could have been nothing.

No time. Freelunch was now in a wobbly, erratic orbit that made the view from its cameras swing around nauseously, a roil of Earth in the sky, mountains, craters, the ground, the black sky, the filtered grey/white mass of the sun. From around us came a low "wooooah!" from eight thousand throats at once.

Maya switched us to the magnified AJ sat feed and the CGI radar view. Something was wrong—Freelunch was supposed to circle two or three times and land. Instead, it was tumbling a little, not quite flipping over on its head, but rolling more than the gyros could correct.

"Fuck no," I whispered. "Please. Not now. Please." No idea who I was talking to. Pug? Landing was the riskiest part of the whole mission. That's why we were all here, watching.

Down and down it fell, and we could all see that its stabilizers were badly out of phase. Instead of damping its tumble, the stabilizer on one side was actually accelerating it, while the other three worked against it.

"Tilt-a-whirl," Maya said. We all glared at her. In a few of the sims that we'd run of the landing, the Freelunch had done just this, as the stabilizers got into a terminal argument about who was right. One faction—Iowa City–led, but with supporters around the world—had dubbed it the tilt-a-whirl and had all kinds of math to show why it was more likely than we'd estimated. They wanted us to delay the whole mission while they refactored and retested the landing sequence. They'd been outvoted but had never stopped arguing for their position.

"Shut up," Blight said, in a tight little voice. The tumble was getting worse, the ground looming.

"Fuck off," Maya said absently. "It's the tilt-a-whirl, and that means that we should see the counterfire any . . . second . . . now!"

If we hadn't been watching closely, we'd have missed it. The Freelunch had a set of emergency air puffers for blowing the solar collectors clear if the mechanical rotation mechanism jammed or lacked power. The tilt-a-whirlers had successfully argued for an emergency command structure that would detect tumble and deploy the air jets in one hard blast in order to cancel out the malfing stabilizer. They emptied themselves in less than a second, a white, smudgy line at right angles to the swing of the Freelunch, and the roll smoothed out in three short and shortening oscillations. An instant later, the Freelunch was skidding into the lunar surface, kicking up a beautiful rooster-tail plume of regolith that floated above the surface like playa dust. We watched as the moondust sifted down in one-sixth gee, a TV tuned to a dead channel, shifting snow out of which slowly emerged the sharp angles of the Freelunch.

I registered every noise from the crowds on the roofs and in the stairways, every moan and whimper, all of them saying, essentially, "Please, please, please, please let it work."

The Freelunch popped its protective covers. For an instant they stayed in place, visible only as a set of slightly off-kilter corners set inside the main boxy body of the lander. Then they slid away, dropping to the surface with that unmistakable Moon-gee grace. The simultaneous intake of breath was like a city-sized white-noise generator.

"Power-on/self-test," Maya said. I nodded. It was going through its boot-up routines, checking its subsystems, validating its checksums. The whole procedure took less than a minute.

Ten minutes later, nothing had happened.

"Fuck," I said.

"Patience," Blight said. Her voice had all the tension of a guitar string just before it snaps.

"Fuck patience," I said.

"Patience," Maya said.

We took one another's hands. We watched.

An hour later, we went inside.

The Freelunch had nothing to say to us. As Earth spun below the Moon, our army of ham operators, volunteers spread out across the equator, all tried valiantly to bounce their signals to it, to hear its distress messages. It maintained radio silence.

After forty-eight hours, most of us slunk away from Brazil. We caught a slow freighter up the Pacific Coast to the Port of Los Angeles, a journey of three weeks where we ate fish, squinted at our transflective displays in the sun, and argued.

Everyone had a theory about what had happened to the Freelunch. Some argued that a key component—a sensor, a power supply, a logic board—had been dislodged during the tilt-a-whirl (or the takeoff, or the landing). The high-mag shots from the Al Jazeera sat were examined in minute detail, and things that were either noise or compression artifacts or ironclad evidence of critical damage were circled in red and magnified to individual pixels, debated and shooped and tweaked and enhanced.

A thousand telescopic photos of the Freelunch were posted, and the supposed damage was present, or wasn't, depending on the photo. It was sabotage. Human error. Substandard parts. Proof that space was too big a place for puny individual humans, only suited to huge, implacable nation-states.

THERE AIN'T NO SUCH THING AS A FREELUNCH, the /b/tards trumpeted, and took responsibility for all of it. An evangelical in Mexico claimed he'd killed it with the power of prayer, to punish us for our hubris.

I harboured a secret hope: that the Freelunch would wake up someday, having hit the magic combination of rebooting, reloading, and reformatting to make it all work. But as the Freelunch sat there, settled amid the dust of another world—well, moon—inert and idle, I confronted the reality that thousands of people had just spent years working together to litter another planet. Or moon.

Whatever.

That wasn't a good year. I had another cancer scare because life sucks, and the doc wanted a bunch of out-of-policy tests that cost me pretty much everything left in my account.

I made a (very) little money doing some writing about the Freelunch project, postmortems and tit-for-tats for a few sites. But after two months of rehashing the same ground, and dealing with all the stress of the health stuff, I switched off from all Freelunch-related activity altogether. Blight had already done it.

A month later, Blight and I split up. That was scary. It wasn't over any specific thing, just a series of bickery little stupid fights that turned into blowouts and ended up with me packing a bag and heading for a motel. The first night, I woke up at 3 A.M. to vomit up my whole dinner and then some.

Two weeks later, I moved back in. Blight and I didn't speak of that horrible time much afterward, but when we held hands or cuddled at night, there was a fierceness to it that hadn't been in our lives for years and years. So maybe we needed it.

Money, money, money. We just didn't have any. Sold the house. Moved into a rental place, where they wouldn't let us keep chickens or pigs. Grocery bills. Moved into another place, this one all the way out in Fresno, and got a new pig and half a dozen new chickens, but now we were a three hours' drive from Minus and our friends.

Blight got work at a seniors' home, which paid a little better than minimum wage. I couldn't find anything. Not even gardening work. I found myself sitting very still, as though I was worried that if I started moving, I'd consume some of the savings.

She was working at a place called Shadow Hills, part of a franchise of old folks' homes that catered to people who'd kept their nest eggs intact into their long senescences. It was like a stationary cruise ship—twenty-five stories of "staterooms" with a little living room and bedroom and kitchenette, three dining rooms with rotating menus, activities, weekly crafts bazaars, classes, gyms and a pool, a screening room. The major difference between Shadow Hills and a cruise ship—apart from Fresno being landlocked—was the hospital and palliative care ward that occupied the tenth and eleventh floors. That way, once your partner started to die, you could stay in the stateroom and visit her in the ward every day, rather than both of you being alone for those last days. It was humane and sensible, but it made me sad.

Blight was giving programming classes to septuagenarians whose high schools had offered between zero and one "computer science" classes in the early 1980s, oldies who had managed to make it down the long road of life without learning how to teach a computer how to do something new. They were enthusiastic and patient, and they called out to Blight every time she crossed the lobby to meet me and shouted impertinent commentary about my suitability as a spouse for their beloved maestra and guru.

She made a point of giving me a big kiss and a full-body hug before leading me out into the gardens for our picnic, and the catcalls rose to a crescendo.

"I wish you wouldn't do that," I said.

"Prude," she said, and ostentatiously slapped my ass. The oldies volubly took notice. "What's for lunch?"

"Coconut soup, eggplant curry, and grilled pumpkin."

"Hang on, I'll go get my backup PB and J."

I'd been working my way through an online cooking course one recipe at a time, treating it like a series of chemistry experiments. Mostly, they'd been successful, but Blight made a big show out of pretending that it was inedible and she demanded coaxing and pushing to get her to try my creations. So as she turned on her heel to head back into work, I squeezed her hand and dragged her out to the garden.

She helped me lay out the blanket and set out the individual sections of the insulated tiffin pail. I was satisfied to see that the food was still hot enough to steam. I'd been experimenting with slightly overheating food before decanting it for transport, trying to find exactly the right starting point for optimal temperature at the point of consumption. It was complicated by the fact that the cooldown process wasn't linear, and also depended on the volume and density of the food. The fact that this problem was consuming so many of my cycles was a pretty good indicator of my degraded mental state. Further evidence: I carefully noted the temperature of each tiffin before I let Blight tuck in, and associated the correct temperature with the appropriate record on my phone, which already listed the food weight and type details, entered before I left home.

Blight pulled out all the stops, making me scoop up spoonfuls of food and make airplane noises and feed her before she'd try it, but then she ate enthusiastically. It was one of my better experiments. At one point, I caught her sliding my sticky rice pudding with mango coulis across to her side of the blanket and I smacked her hand and took it back. She still managed to sneak a spoonful when I wasn't looking.

I liked our lunches together. They were practically the only thing I liked.

"How long do you figure it'll be before you lose your marbles altogether?" she asked, sipping some of the iced tea I'd poured into heavy-bottomed glasses I'd yard-saled and which I transported rolled in soft, thick dish towels.

"Who'd notice?"

I started to pack up the lunch, stacking the tiffin sections and slipping the self-tensioning bands over them. Blight gently took them out of my hands and set them to one side.

"Greg," she said. "Greg, seriously. This isn't good. You need to change something. It's like living with a ghost. Or a robot."

A bolt of anger skewered me from the top of my head to my asshole, so sharp and irrational that I actually gasped aloud. I must be getting mature in my old age, because the sheer force of the reaction pulled me up short and made me pause before replying.

"I've tried to find work," I said. "There's nothing out there for me."

"No," she said, still holding my arm, refusing to surrender the physical contact. "No, there's no jobs. We both know that there's plenty of work."

"I'll think about it," I said, meaning, I won't think about it at all.

Still, she held on to my arm. She made me look into her eyes. "Greg, I'm not kidding. This isn't good for you. It's not good for us. This isn't what I want to do for the rest of my life."

I nearly deliberately misunderstood her, asked her why she wasn't looking for work somewhere else. But I knew that the "this" she meant was living with me, in my decayed state.

"I'll think about it," I repeated, and shrugged off her hand. I packed up the lunch, put it on the back of my bike, and rode home. I managed to stop myself from crying until I had the door closed behind me.

That night we had sex. It was the first time in months, so long that I'd lost track of how long it had been. It started with a wordless reaching out in the night, our habitual spooned-together cuddle going a little further, bit by bit, our breath quickening, our hands and then our mouths exploring each other's bodies. We both came in near silence and held each other tighter and longer than normal. I realized that there'd been a longer gap since our last clinging, full-body hug than the gap since our last sex. I found that I'd missed the cuddling even more than the sex.

I circled the Freebrunch—as the Freelunch's successor had been inevitably named—nervously. For days, I poked at the forums, downloaded the prototypes, and watched the videos, spending a few minutes at a time before clicking away. One faction had a pretty credible account of how the landing had been blown so badly, and pretty much everyone accepted that something about the bad landing was responsible for the systems failure. They pointed to a glitch in the vision system, a collision between two inference engines that made it misinterpret certain common lunar shadows as bad terrain. It literally jumped at shadows. And the tilt-a-whirl faction was totally vindicated and managed to force a complete redesign of the stabilization software and the entry plan.

The more I looked over Freebrunch, the more exciting it got. Freelunch had transmitted telemetry right up to the final moments of its landing, definitively settling another argument: "How much should we worry about landing telemetry if it only has to land once?" The live-fire exercise taught us stuff that no amount of vomit-comet trial runs could have surfaced. It turned out, for example, that the outer skin of the Freelunch had been totally overengineered and suffered only a fraction of the heating that the models had predicted. That meant we could reduce the weight by a good 18 percent. The cost of lifting mass was something like 98 percent of the overall launch cost, so an 18 percent reduction in mass was something like a 17.99 percent reduction in the cost of building Freebrunch and sending it to the surface of the Moon.

Blight knew I was hooked before I did. The third time I gave her a cold sandwich and some carrot sticks for lunch, she started making jokes about being a moon widow and let me know that she'd be packing her own lunch four days a week, but that I was still expected to come up with something decent for a Friday blowout.

And just like that, I was back in.

Freelunch had cost me pretty much all my savings, and I wasn't the only one. The decision not to take commercial sponsorship on the project was well intentioned, but it had meant that the whole thing had to be funded by jerks like me. Worse: Freelunch wasn't a registered 501(c) (3) charity, so it couldn't even attract any deep-pocketed jillionaires looking for a tax deduction.

Freebrunch had been rebooted by people without any such burning manian anticommodification scruples. Everything down to the circuit boards had someone's logo or name on it, and they'd added a EULA to the project that said that by contributing to Freebrunch, you signed over all your "intellectual property" rights to the foundation that ran it—a foundation without a fully appointed board and no transparency beyond what the law mandated.

That had sparked a predictable shitstorm that reached the global newspapers when someone spotted a patent application from the foundation's chairman, claiming to have invented some of the interlock techniques that had been invented by Pug himself, there on the playa. I'd seen it with my own eyes, and more important, I'd helped document it, with timestamped postings that invalidated every one of the patent's core claims.

Bad enough, but the foundation dug itself even deeper when it used the donations it had taken in to pay for lawyers to fight for the patent. The schism that ensued proved terminal, and a year later, the Freebrunch was dead.

Out of its ashes rose the Freebeer, which tried to strike a happy medium between the Freelunch's idealism and the Freebrunch's venality. The people involved raised foundation money, agreed to print the names of project benefactors on the bricks they dropped onto the Moon's surface, and benefited from the Indian Space Research Organization's lunar-mapping initiative, which produced remarkably high-resolution survey maps of the entire bright side of the Moon. On that basis, they found a spot in Mare Imbrium that was as smooth as a baby's ass and was only a few hundred K from the Freelunch's final resting place.

Of course, they failed. Everything went fine until LEO separation, whereupon something happened—there are nine documentaries (all crowd-funded) offering competing theories—and it ended up in a decaying orbit that broke up over Siberia and rained down shooting stars into the greedy lenses of thousands of dashcams.

Freebird.

(Supported, of course, by a series of stadium shows and concert tours.)

Freepress.

(This one printed out leaked WikiLeaks cables from early in the century and won a prize at the Venice biennale, held in Padua now that the city was entirely underwater. It helped that they chose cables that dealt with the American government's climate change shenanigans. The exiled Venetians living in their stacked Paduan tenements thought that was a laugh-riot.)

That took seven years.

The lost cosmonaut conspiracy theory holds that a certain number—two? three?—of Russian cosmonauts were killed before Gagarin's successful flight. They say when Gagarin got into the Vostok in 1961, he fully expected to die, but he got in anyway, and not because of the crack of a commissar's pistol. He boarded his death trap because it was his ticket into space. He had gone to what could almost certainly have been his death because of his belief in a better future. A place for humanity in the stars.

When you think of a hero, think of Gagarin, strapped into that capsule, the rumble of the jets below him, the mutter of the control tower in his headset, the heavy hand of acceleration hard upon his chest, pushing with increasing, bone-crushing force, the roar of the engines blotting out all sound. Think of him going straight to his death with a smile on his face, and think of him breaking through the atmosphere, the sudden weightlessness, the realization that he had survived. That he was the first human being to go to space.

We kept on launching printers.

Blight and I threw a joint seventieth birthday party to coincide with the launch of the Freerunner. There were old friends. There was cake. There was ice cream, with chunks of honeycomb from our own hive. There were—I shit you not—seventy candles. We blew them out, all of them, though it took two tries, seventy-year-old lungs being what they were.

We toasted each other with long speeches that dripped with unselfconscious sentiment, and Maya brought her kids and they presented us with a little play they'd written, involving little printed 3D printers on the Moon.

And then, as we tuned every screen in the house to the launch, I raised a glass and toasted Pug: "Let us live as though it were the first days of a better nation."

The cheer was loud enough to drown out the launch.

Freerunner landed at 0413 Zulu on August 10, 2057. Eight minutes later, it completed its power-on self-test routine and snapped out its solar collectors. It established communications with nine different HAM-based ground stations and transmitted extensive telemetry. Its bearings moved smoothly, and it canted its lens into the sun's rays. The footage of its first sintering was low-res and jittery, but it was all saved for later transmission, and that's the clip you've seen, the white-hot tip of the focused energy of old Sol, melting regolith into a long, flat, thin line that was quickly joined by another, right alongside it. Back and forth the head moved, laying out the base, the honeycombing above it, the final surface. the print bed tilted with slow grace and the freshly printed brick slid free and fell to the dust below, rocking from side to side, featherlike as it fell.

One week later, Freerunner established contact with the Freelunch, using its phased-array antennas to get a narrow, high-powered signal to its slumbering firmware. Laboriously, it rebuilt the Freelunch's BIOS, directed it to use what little energy it had to release the springs that locked the solar array away in its body. It took thirty-seven hours and change. We were on the Playa when we got word that the solar array had deployed, the news spreading like wildfire from burner to burner, fireworks rocketing into the sky.

I smiled and rolled over in our yurt. Igloo. Yurtgloo. I was very happy, of course. But I was also seventy. I needed my rest. The next morning, a naked twenty-year-old with scales covering his body from the waist up cycled excitedly to our camp and pounded on the yurt's interlocking bricks until I thought he might punch right through them.

"What," I said. "The fuck."

"It's printed one!" he said. "The Freelunch shit a brick!" He looked at me, took in my tired eyes, my snowy hair. "Sorry to wake you, but I thought you'd want to know."

"Of course he wants to know!" Blight shouted from inside. "Christ, Greg, get the man a drink. We're celebrating!"

The playa dust whipped up my nose and made me reach for the kerchief around my neck, pull it up over my face. I turned to the kid, standing there awkwardly astride his bike. "Well?" I said. "Come on, we're celebrating!" I gave him a hug that was as hard as I could make it, and he squeezed me back with gentle care.

We cracked open some bourbon that a friend had dropped off the day before and pulled out the folding chairs. The crowd grew, and plenty of them brought bottles. There were old friends, even old enemies, people I should have recognized and didn't, and people I recognized but who didn't recognize me at first. I'd been away from the Playa for a good few years. The next thing I knew, the sun was setting, and there were thousands of us, and the music was playing, and my legs were sore from dancing, and Blight was holding me so tight I thought she'd crack a rib.

I thought of saying, *We did it*, or *You did it*, or *They did it*. None of those was right, though. "It's done" is what I said, and Blight knew exactly what I meant. Which is why I loved her so much, of course.

Hereditary Delusions
RHONDA PARRISH

The dust shone,
trickled and danced
in the moonlight
blue, silver, blue
a halo of miniscule stars
surrounding him,
settling on his shoulders,
marring the perfect white
of his perfect suit.

I wanted him to be
Mother's visitor
from the night
I was conceived—

I thought he'd come
from light years away,
that the dust was residue
from the Big Dipper
the coldness in his eyes
from the vast depths
of space.

But when he walked it was
with a man's tread
crunching fallen leaves
like my dreams
beneath his boots.

He came to take her away,
not in a ship
but a Buick
blue, white, blue
with writing on its doors
while I watched from my window,
unseen.

Demoted

KATE STORY

It was the last day of second term before things got interesting, an icy April day, wind off the water. The seminar leader set the discussion: *Is kindness rational?* An ugly boy and a macho name-dropper debated; Tom looked out the window. The ugly boy—short red cowlicked hair, glasses—said Hobbes's "warre of alle against alle" was misunderstood taken out of historical and cultural context (he was always saying things like this, annoying the Great-Ideas-Are-Eternal seminar leader); the name-dropper countered with Kant and Nietzsche. The red-head responded with Rousseau, and hitchhiking.

"You always get where you want to go," Massachusetts farm boy accent coming through. "They'll warn you about psychos, but someone always picks you up."

Tom had a thing for redheads; the ugliness of this boy had been a depressant from day one. But now, gaydar pinged. He spoke to the creature after class.

"You got to believe in kindness." His name was Greeb. For real; he insisted on it. "How else would you get out of bed in the morning?"

"From a keen interest in seeing what horror the world brings forth today."

Greeb laughed. "But see," he said, "people run the world these days as if self-interest is the ruling principle. But it's a *choice*, a mass performance," and he lowered his voice. "The current of kindness—and I mean that in every sense, our deep kinship, yeah?—that current never stops running. Even in the worst places in the world." He put his hand on Tom's forearm, and Tom felt a thrill running up to his shoulder, around and down his spine. "How do you explain that?"

When Greeb said *worst places in the world* Tom knew he meant Darfur, Kabul. But it summoned an image of his own bedroom at home.

"Are you a Christian?"

Meaning *proselytizing fundamentalist*, although given the red hair Tom expected Greeb to be a fellow recovering Catholic. But Greeb laughed and laughed—too hard.

"Hasn't someone ever helped you out for no reason?" He flapped his hands, faggoty. "A guardian angel."

Tom's mother insists: *if you believe in angels they will come to you.*

Is that a threat, Mom, or a dare?

And then Greeb challenged Tom to a hitchhiking race, Boston to New York. The way he said *New York*, he might as well be saying *Heaven*. "That's right, baby, New York. And if you get there first I'll trumpet you through the gates."

Tom felt certain Greeb was coming onto him. He was repulsive, but on the other hand he'd be the grateful type. "Why are you taking such an interest in my welfare?"

The sadness in Greeb's eyes was unfathomable. "Me and my whole family, we are charged with a mission: to try to do good."

"Your family has a mission statement?"

Tom was laughing, but Greeb nodded, solemn. Tom thought how he'd never noticed before how very green Greeb's eyes were.

"What's the point?"

"In doing good?"

"Yeah." Tom made his voice hard. "In a world as horrible as this one—with people as horrible as me in it—what's some little drop of kindness going to do?"

Greeb didn't answer, and so Tom's words hung between them. He felt the truth of them, ringing in the air; he was intimate with the extent of his own misanthropy. And saying it like that, to this green-eyed creature, made it all just a little more true: another nail in the coffin of brotherly love. In Tom something writhed: inchoate longing, drowning in cynicism.

Tom broke the silence.

"And what makes you think I need your do-gooding?"

"It's obvious." Greeb flapped his fingers as if he could climb air. "You're like me. You want to *ascend*."

Tom's mother wanted to pay for a cell phone.

He'd made the mistake of calling to tell her about his end-of-term adventure. Tom could picture her huddling in the dingy Gardner kitchen, landline receiver cradled between ear and shoulder; she'd catch it from his father if he caught her babying their son. *If the little fucker won't get a job then he doesn't get a phone/new sneakers/a car.* She offered, he refused, her voice started shaking. She was probably clutching at the cross on the gold chain around her throat. "You'll come back, right? Finish the degree?"

"What do you think."

"Tom. Was it . . . Did the Father ever . . . do anything to you?"

It being the unspoken, terrible thing that was *wrong* with Tom. But the idea of Father Clancy "doing" anything . . . disgusting. He would never tell her about his first red-head. Billy was nasty but gorgeous, creepy and beautiful as an angel should be. *Angel* equalled physical pain, pleasure, confusion, social humiliation (adept bully, Billy); also the room in the church basement, choir robes, skin. Everything in black and white except the ruddy glow of Billy's hair.

"Why New York?" Her voice choked like she was saying *Sodom.*

He refused to respond. When her crying became audible, he hung up.

Tom stood at the intersection of Tremont and Marginal Road, thumb out, hoping for a ride onto the I-90 West. His sneakers had holes, his jacket was inadequate, it was foggy. Cars sped by, one guy deliberately swerving to splash Tom with polluted water. He thought of giving it up, then pictured his father's derision. *Fuckin' loser can't even catch a ride out of Boston. Little fairy.*

And then a white car pulled over.

Tom froze, staring; then lurched forward. A woman, baby asleep in a carseat in the back.

"Where you headed?"

"New York."

Perfect.

The woman had short hair. She wore a white Bench sweater, pilling and a stain down the front. Forty-ish. Eyes as green as Greeb's; must be wearing those coloured contacts, colour so vivid it looked fake.

"My name's Glee, by the way."

"That yours?" Tom jerked his head at the sleeping kid.

"Yes." That tender mom-look spread over her face. "I call her Geek."

How sweet.

She had broken up with her husband she said. Tom hoped she wouldn't go on about this. She rambled a bit about how she'd had second thoughts. She still loved him, she said. She was going to intersect him on the road. "All we have is each other," she said, "since we were shut out."

Shut out of what? Tom stayed quiet and at last so did she.

They got out onto the interstate, into what would have been a sunset on a better day. Tom watched the outskirts of the city spin by: new leaves on trees, churches, the ugliness of a mall. Tom dozed with his head against the window.

He was back in Gardner High, the day things slipped. Between classes, a shove in the hallway, *Bitch*. Nothing new, but Tom turned on the jock with his chemistry textbook. The feeling of his body coming around, the follow-through with the book. Wanting, in that moment, to sever the jock's head from his body. Knocked him to the floor and the guy even lost consciousness for a moment.

Tom felt he was falling, came to. It was now entirely dark; the car slid over the road and oncoming headlights swooped and passed.

"Nice snooze?"

Tom rubbed his face with his hand. "Nightmare, actually."

"You were whimpering."

He stared at the blankness out the window, willing her not to talk. They'd pulled him from school, sent him for counseling. The doctor told his mother it was the stress of coming out. Her face opening, wounded. She'd had no fucking idea.

Tom had finished high school from home; his mother rewarded him by paying for college. She thought he was too fragile to get a job.

A flare of light from the woman's face jerked his attention around. "Want a smoke?"

"Do you think we should?" Tom indicated the kid in back.

"She started it."

He looked behind. A face in the dark, lit with dim fire, blew smoke in his face. What he'd thought was a toddler was a sullen-faced teen. Tom turned away, the world tilting.

Wordlessly, he accepted the smoke.

"We're getting there," Glee said. "Soon we can stretch our wings."

"Good." The girl yawned. There was a rustling sound like the car seat was packed with paper. "He coming with us?"

"Tom?" the woman asked. "Are you coming with us?"

"To New York? Yeah, that's where we're going, right?" Tom looked out the window. "This isn't the interstate."

"I decided to take the back roads. So much prettier."

"Mom, can I bite him?" The girl's eyes were as green as her mother's.

"No."

"Oh. Please?"

"Geek . . ." in that mom-warning tone.

"God bless, then, Tom or whatever your name is." The girl wriggled her shoulders. That rustling again; it made Tom's skin crawl.

"Yes, God bless. God bless us all." Glee looked sad. "As we wait here on earth for Heaven to open its gates once more."

Tom made a decision.

"Um, you can just let me out here."

"But it's raining." The windshield was dotted with water.

"No, really. It's okay." Tom put his hand on the door handle, raised his voice. "Let me out."

The woman sighed. "All right." She slowed. "Come with us. We're just demoted, that's all. Please?"

"No, thanks."

Tom couldn't get out of the car fast enough.

It didn't take long for the red eyes of tail-lights to disappear.

Rain spit out of the sky. No traffic, nothing, dark. Soon he was shivering, rain trickling through thin spiked hair.

Later found him sitting on his backpack, shuddering with cold. He'd given up trying to look normal and had wrapped a T-shirt around his head.

No way of knowing the time.

Maybe he slept.

He came to, stiff and miserable. Light leaking into the sky. Not one single car had come by all night.

He wondered where Greeb was—probably half-way to New York. *Guardian angels.* Idiot. Kindness—Greeb's Holy Grail—was just another cover for self-interest. People were nice to get laid, or get money, or be liked because that led to getting laid or money.

Mom tries to be kind, the thought came. No. Her martyred attempts to get him to behave, so she didn't look like a bad mother, weren't kindness. He shut his heart against her tears, her furtive attempts to bribe him into loving her.

As for his father . . .

Lights down the road.

Tom pulled the T-shirt from his head and stood. He stuck his arm out, thumb rising high.

The car sped by.

Still, it had been a car. Light grew, revealing the shitty roadscape. Strip malls on either side, closed down. Empty farmers' fields. Trees. The woman had dropped him on the moon.

Cars went by. No-one stopped. Tom ate his three granola bars, wanted coffee so bad he thought he'd throw up. The monotony of the landscape was a nightmare, or waves of pain. Closed peeling strip malls. Fragmented forest. Abandoned fields.

New York—the fantasy of making out with a guy he'd never seen before, of not being the faggot who lost his shit in high school (yeah, that story had followed him to Boston, thanks to Gardner High's graduating class of 2012)—was enough to keep his hand unfolding like a machine with every passing car. His feet in their crappy sneakers hurt. It was intolerably boring. It got dark.

Rain began again, driving into his face. He wrapped the T-shirt around his head, kept walking. Of course no-one picked him up; it was some curse that warned people off, something wrong with him. That, and the world was fucked. No-one was *kind*. Kin. Kinship. *Someone always picks you up.*

When he'd accepted the bet, Tom had asked, *Do I have to believe in your kindness theory?*

Greeb's eerie green eyes had looked grave behind his glasses. *Why would you accept a bet if you don't believe in the terms?*

I just don't believe people pick you up out of kindness.

But he wanted to get out of friggin' Massachusetts. *Ascend.* This wasn't philosophical. He wanted a warm car ride off this fucking moon.

Rubber legs, god, was it never going to end? The shoulder crumbled into peaty brownness, but he kept on. One foot in front of the other.

Headlights, a roar behind him. He didn't bother turning around. Light grew and his shadow lengthened and danced. Then the squeal of brakes and it was a dragon's breath, close, hot, hot and huge and hard, lifting him up from behind and he was flying.

Tom hurt. Jerked around like a giant dog had him in its jaws. AC/DC blaring, smoke and sulphur, red and orange light. A dashboard, him slumped against metal. Burgundy velour seats, door handle missing.

"Jesus, I thought you was a goner there." Driver a giant, taking up half the cab. "I thought you was dead!" Tom tried to sit up; pain ripped through him and he screamed. "Broke your arm there, blood on your head. Jesus Mary I thought you was a goner!"

Camouflage hat, jacket, pants, the red cheeks and blonde eyelashes of a red-head; clenched his cigarette so hard that it looked like he'd bite it off.

"I'm taking you to hospital."

Tom managed to say, "Boston."

"Providence. I'm in the army. Yeah, just visiting family." The man threw his butt on the floor, lit another. "Girls won't look at you if you're in the army. Not a fucking glance. Wife dumped me. By *text*. While I was in *Afghanistan*. Fucking bitch. Know what I mean? Know what I mean? Bitches. You're not a faggot are you?"

The truck jolted; Tom bit back another scream.

"Don't worry, I got nothing against little faggots. My little brother's one. We got nothing in common but the green eyes and the wings." The man laughed. "Thought I'd hit a dog back there. I was just going to drive on but then I saw you in the headlights of an oncoming car. Also, I had a witness, didn't I? Had to pick you up! My name's Gormless, by the way."

Gormless? And that red hair . . . "Is your little brother named Greeb?"

"They'll fix you up good in Providence. Stop trying to move, don't be fucking stupid."

The pain then got so bad that Tom threw up. That was the last thing he remembered for a while.

Elbow broken; his funny bone. Concussion. The humiliating phone call to his mother to see if the medical insurance still covered him. Strange that his back wasn't injured where the truck hit him; he tried to tell them but no-one would listen. They put him under, wired his bones, stapled the skin like Bride of Frankenstein. Nausea that wouldn't go away, they shoved a needle of Gravol into his thigh.

They kept him a few days.

A doctor offered to take him back to Gardner. "If that's where you're going." High and pleasant voice.

"Sure," Tom said. No New York now. The doctor had goddamn green eyes, it was a pandemic around here. But Tom accepted the offer.

He limped out into the parking lot, sky spread overhead like a warning. He had a nice ass, the doctor. A pickup truck, much shinier than that of the crazed army man. Tom climbed inside; everything was harder with one arm.

"So that guy who brought you in, that was pretty nice of him."

"That guy? Nice? He hit me on the road."

"What?"

"I said," Tom enunciated, "he hit me. Only took me into the hospital because he thought someone witnessed the accident."

The doctor drove on in silence for a bit. "Mind if I smoke?"

This surprised Tom. "Go ahead."

The doctor lit up. "There was no evidence of that kind of trauma."

"What?" it was Tom's turn to say.

"I said, there was no evidence of that kind of trauma."

The doctor thought he was lying or crazy. "He hit my backpack, sent me flying," Tom almost yelled.

"Sure."

Silence.

"You live in Providence?" Tom asked.

"I wish. No. Go to Boston to party sometimes."

He flashed a glance and suddenly Tom saw it, soft-hard look in the guy's eyes.

"You?" the doctor said.

"What?"

"You party much?"

The doctor was looking right at him now, not at the road; shifting in his seat as he drove, spreading his legs. He was coming on to Tom, here, in this truck. Tom's heart beat faster. "Sometimes," he said. The doctor was bigger than he'd thought, his shoulders took up half the cab. He'd given Tom a ride for this, for sex of course. Not "kindness." *Wrong again, Greeb,* Tom thought. "Sometimes."

The doctor laughed, deep and loud, butching out or something; okay, Tom could deal.

"I thought you were a goner," the doctor said.

"On the operating table?"

"You like danger?"

Danger? Fear and excitement coiled in the pit of Tom's stomach. "I've had enough danger for one lifetime."

The man laughed again. He shifted his shoulders, scratching his back against the seat; a papery rustling filled the cab. Tom shrank back against the passenger door, cradling his aching arm. "You like boxing?"

"No." Maybe this guy was a psycho. He should've called his mom from the hospital; she'd come out to get him, Christ, even his old man would've sprung him.

"You know what I love? The way they fall into each other's arms at the end of the round."

"Sure."

"It's like when I cut someone open. It's intimate. Visceral, you know? You ever hunted? You ever killed anyone?"

"No."

"You use email?"

"Of course."

"Use email or texting rather than talk on a phone?"

"Sometimes." Was this a test?

"How about meeting someone? You ever choose to actually meet someone rather than being their Facebook fucking friend?"

"Of course."

"You know what's wrong with this world?"

"What?"

"Everyone's in full retreat!"

"Sure."

"Don't just say *sure*; are you even listening?"

This fucker was like his old man, wanting to expound and humiliate. "Back off, okay?" Tom yelled. "Back off!"

The man threw his cigarette onto the floor, lit another. "That's the spirit."

Get me home, Tom prayed. He hated home. Just get me home.

"We're engaged in a mass performance."

Greeb had said that. Hadn't Greeb said that? Tom stared out the windshield. "Mass performance of what?"

"What do you think?"

What had Greeb said? "Of self-interest."

"No!" the man exploded. "The performance is a mass retreat from the visceral! From physicality, from the incomprehensibility of physicality!"

The man was crazy.

"My wife broke up with me by text," he went on. "Didn't even phone me."

"Your . . . wife?" Tom faltered.

"While I was on my last tour of duty in Afghanistan. Fucking bitch."

A scream broke from Tom; he clutched at the door but the handle was torn off. "Let me out of here, just stop and let me out!"

"Okay, calm down now." The man slowed. Someone, a girl, stood by the highway, hoodie up. She was smoking, hip jutted, insolent. "My daughter," the man said to Tom.

It was that kid, the kid from the car. Green eyes, they all had green eyes and pointed teeth.

Tom flailed at the seatbelt one-handed.

The man parked by the girl and peeled himself from the pickup. Wings, like a giant dragonfly's, down his back.

"How's your mother?" he asked the girl.

"Good. As usual." The girl pouted. "She's on her way."

The man opened the passenger door for Tom. "You don't have to do this, you know. Just accept the ride."

"Fuck you." Tom stumbled from the truck.

The girl, Glee, stared. She spread her double set of gossamer wings, scattering light, rustling in the breeze. "You didn't get very far."

A noise came from the back of the truck. Tom turned to see Greeb, emerging tousled from under a tarp.

"Hi." Greeb smiled at Tom. "Want a ride?"

Tom tried to back away, tangled one foot behind the other and fell on his ass.

"That's my brother," the big man said, tender, tired, proud. "My baby brother. He's the best of us. He keeps an eye on the gates, and one day they will open to us again and we will ascend."

"Greeb." The girl jerked her head at Tom. "Are you an idiot? Why didn't you tell him about the terms?"

Greeb's smile died. "Of course I told him. But he doesn't believe in kindness."

"You can't agree to a bet if you don't believe in the terms," the girl said to Tom. "You're stuck."

"Get the fuck away," Tom whispered.

A humming came out of the sky. Something that looked like a beam of light pierced the greyness; it resolved itself into a woman, the older woman, his first ride. She landed softly in the back of the truck, folding her wings along her back. Greeb's face lit up, and he shrank until he was little a winged baby. The woman took him in her arms.

The vast winged man spoke. "You taking me back, baby?"

"Of course, Gorm." She shifted her eyes to Tom. "Hello, Tom."

"He's not coming," Gormless said.

"Dad scared the poor little shit," the girl explained.

The woman's green eyes were full of kindness. "It's not dad's fault. Tom's not ready."

All of them, even the rust-downed baby, shook their heads.

The man and girl got into the truck. It was an awkward fit with wings, but after some adjustments they folded the gossamer appendages along their backs and settled in. The man brought the truck around in a tight U-turn.

They drove away, toward the place where they hoped they'd find heaven.

Tom could see the woman's face as she sat swaying in the cargo bed—Greeb in her arms—her sad, kind green eyes on him. The truck getting smaller and smaller, shrinking on the endless highway. Gone.

No cars, wind moaning.

Peeling abandoned strip malls, empty fields. Alone and waiting.

Tom stared in the direction that the truck had gone. Tire tracks along the pavement, still visible, into the distance.

Something itched between his shoulder blades, something pushing under the skin.

Tom walked onto the road in his holey sneakers. He lined himself up, feet in the tire tracks. He bounced a little, feeling his toes, the spring in his feet. And Tom began to run.

You're A Winner!

MATT MOORE

Squeeze the pump again. Nothing.

The fuck?

Knocking.

Takes a second to tell it's coming from the station's convenience store. Somebody knocking on the window. Head's so goddamn—

Sorry, Lord.

So fucking fuzzy. Can't think straight.

Guy behind the counter's looking at me. A dark smudge against the yellow light inside. He's pointing at a poster in the window. Lights are so bright. Everything's got a blue-white glow. The poster's red letters waving like hot blacktop on a July day. I squint. Think it says:

PRAY INSIDE UP TO LORD

Heart thudding. Oh Lord, is this a sign? Telling me what to do after sending me to the middle of fucking nowhere. Ain't nothing out here but trees and lakes and towns smaller than the block I grew up on. But how's praying going to make it right? Mufi don't let debts go. Even if it's just two hundred bucks.

But back in rehab, Father Molina told us junkie losers you're always showing us the way if we pay attention. If we look for signs.

So it must be your will that's had me going more than a day without sleep to get me out here. Thy will be done, Lord.

Just wish I knew what the fuck it was.

All right, take a deep breath. Give my head a shake. Pull it the fuck together.

I look up again, focus this time, and read:

PRE-PAY INSIDE AFTER 10 PM

Fuck. So I *am* going inside. No pump and run. Barely had fifty bucks when Ortega lost his shit. After this, I got nothing. How am I going to keep running with no cash? Can do some stick-ups, but sooner or later they'd catch me. Then they wouldn't send me back to rehab but the joint. And Mufi's got people on the inside. After what happened with Ortego? I'd be dead for sure.

Oh, Lord have mercy. This is where it all goes down, ain't it?

Through the window, counter jockey shrugs, like he's saying, "What's it gonna be?"

If this is your will, Lord . . .

Thy will be done.

I head for the door. Legs are heavy, feet a million miles away. Ground's shifting back and forth. Pistol's huge against my stomach.

So I gotta ask, Lord: The counter jockey, he seen my mug shot in the paper this morning? Read that shit about "armed and dangerous"? Least he's the only one inside. And ain't seen another car for fifteen minutes. Out into the blackness, just an empty road. One way going back the way I came, the other going someplace else. A long line of streetlights light up the bottom edges of pine trees far as I can see.

Can't tell if the lights are swaying or I am.

A bell above the door tinkles. Light in here's so goddamn—

Sorry, sorry.

So fucking yellow. Tiny place. Two aisles. Ten feet end to end. Racks of chips and cookies. Motor oil. Deodorant and razors. Big cooler of drinks on one end. Coffee station next to the check out.

But there's also cameras behind the counter.

I tug my ball cap low.

Counter jockey's watching me. Greasy black hair, few days' stubble. Least he don't look the paper-reading type. Lord, why'd my photo gotta show up so quick? That your work, telling me to give it up? Or keep running? And shit, I didn't do nothing. Ortega went nuts when Mufi's people started hassling us. When 'Tega got hit, you made his gun land right at my feet. And put that rusted out car in my path when I'm hauling ass down Fuller Avenue. Some dipshit leaves it running outside a KFC in that neighbourhood? Gotta be you telling me to run. Least then I knew what you wanted.

So what's it going to be now, Lord?

Coffee smells like shit, but I grab an extra large cup and pour. Need the caffeine. Besides, the extra large's got two of those peel-off game pieces instead of just one. Who knows, right?

I take a sip and wait for the kick. One of the tabs looks a little loose. What the fuck. I pull it. Got to read it twice to make sure it says:

YOU'RE A WINNER! Shoot Clerk & Empty Register!

I drop the tab, hands trembling. My knees almost give out. The fuck is this? I ain't no killer, Lord. Doing stick-ups is one thing, but kill this man? Why you asking me to do this? If this is your will, thy will be done, but they got cameras. I won't make it too far. Then it's life in the joint for sure if Mufi's people don't get me first.

I put the coffee on the counter and drop to my knees, looking for the tab. Couldn't have said that.

Floor's covered with those things. Spilled coffee and crap from people's shoes ground into them. They all say "Sorry! Try Again!"

"Yo, man, you win something?" counter jockey asks.

I get up before he thinks I'm some psycho or something. Heart's a jackhammer. "No," I tell him, turning. "Just . . ."

Need a second to think.

Oh Lord, this is why you led me here. This man needs killing and I get the money to pay back Mufi.

Thy will be done, Lord, but the cameras.

"Um, okay," counter jockey says. He hits a few keys. "Coffee's $1.29. How much gas you gonna put in?"

I dig in my pockets. Need a second. Lord, just one more second to figure this shit out. Father Molina never said nothing about something like this. Said to trust you, talk to you, watch for signs—

"And you got 'nother chance on that cup, ya know," counter jockey says.

Oh Lord. What else you got to say? Hands shaking, I almost knock over the cup pulling the second tab. I blink a few times before I can read:

YOU'RE A WINNER! Cameras Are Broken!

"Anything?"

The world's spinning.

"Hey, man, you okay?" counter jockey asks. He's reaching slowly to me with this right hand, like he's worried about me. But his left is moving under the counter. For a silent alarm?

Or a gun?

Oh Lord, Thy will be done.

Chant for Summer Darkness in Northwest Climes

NEILE GRAHAM

The taste of blue, as in bursting berries,
as in the air's weight on our tongues,
raspberry red as a summer's day turns.

West over water, the light once plum once
salmon turns aqua turns midnight blue
hazed with stars I make you name.

We can't stop talking because we don't
ever want to say goodnight good sleep
farewell goodbye *God be wy you*. This is

the life of brambles, of hedges, of continental
divides. How to speak of this: the value
of naught, of not, of the naughty knotty

thought of you. I want to read everything
about you, pages about your breath, so
invisible, so risible, the difference between

a green girl and a green man, vines spilling
from both our mouths. This is what I imagine.
You always here as the nights grow

long and cold, talking always talking,
our words like berries, plump, alive,
a falling abundance we can waste we can

taste we embrace. Until it's dawn and past dawn.
Until morning sun tattoos us until the world
is everything ripe and full and is ours.

Charlemagne and Florent
RANYLT RICHILDIS

This is what happened to *les deux bretons* before I met them, back in the 70s when they were boys in Vannes. One was abandoned at nineteen months (no one knows why, or by whom), the other orphaned by a car wreck at age three. I should say he was orphaned *in* a car wreck, strapped to a safety seat in the car in question. The fact of the child safety seat indicates the degree of his late parents' love for him; baby seats were indulgences in 1971. He was brought to the same agency as the foundling, where someone had the kindness to put them together in the same bassinet. Or—it might just as easily be said—someone made the mistake of placing them together.

The fair boy was registered under the unlikely name of *Charlemagne Kermorgant*, the dark one attached to the much less remarkable *Florent Edig*. Florent remembers the occasion of their meeting, just as he remembers the car wreck that erased his alternate life. He sees, when he tries, a characterless room, a lurking nurse, a dreary olive drape, and a toddler with matted white hair crawling up to peer at his eyes. A scent, one part applesauce, one part diaper. Children's squeaks and squalls. A pain in his left leg and another on the right side of his head. A rather stunning absence, quickly filled.

Charlemagne was so named by at least one of his derelict parents. The name was inscribed on a note taped to his wrist. There was no family name, of course, so *Kermorgant* became his surname, as it became the surname of all the ciphers left on the steps of the eponymous hospice. An interim label, it stuck to him through to the age of majority and sticks to him still.

Being younger and very blond, and possessed of magnanimous blue eyes that flattered the standards of time and place, he might have found replacement parents soon enough. But *les deux bretons* were freakishly canny and made themselves loathsome during viewings with nose-picks and worse. Prospective adopters turned from him with regret and left him bent under Florent's arm. Wards of the state, they forged a family from their separate parts. They were each other's reassurance, even then.

They came of age together in their blue-and-white world in Vannes, sipped in sea air, and wet their heads each summer in the Gulf of Morbihan. They wrote themselves a history of first shaves and first tattoos, of afterschool lessons in Breton and savate, of footsteps salting cobbled streets as the sea breeze salted roofs, of Florent's vigilance, of Charlemagne's restlessness that sent him bouncing off the world's surfaces as they raced through streetlets that mapped their trail between school and foster home.

Yes, a foster home. Together. Well, eventually, once the state accepted that Charlemagne and Florent were easier to deal with as a set than as units. Such had been their design. On the surface, it was Charlemagne who seemed to be more willful when separate routines or separate towns were proposed as options. His will was a symptom of his dynamism, staff believed, and the trouble he caused was manifest. It involved piercing sounds and cracked objects and a taut, troublesome body not easily restrained. Florent was thought to be the agreeable one. His will was latent, rarely tapped. It was dangerously undisclosed. Charlemagne's will tested patience, it's true, but Florent's ended up shaping the world.

It did so three times, each time bureaucrats tried to separate them. The first severing occurred when Charlemagne was four and Florent five. You must understand that Charlemagne shimmered, his fair hair blossoming around his narrow face, while Florent's dark hair draped across his narrow own and obscured his odd irises—one brown, one hazel—that disarmed strangers. So it was that Charlemagne, through contrast, drew the most attention, and the inevitable finally happened one summer. A local couple merely laughed, charmed, at the blond boy's less than charming efforts to dissuade them. They signed several packs of paper and took him home.

They smoothed his hair and dressed him brightly, gave him a bedroom of his own and made him a nest of toys. They painted a romping zoo on the walls of his room and pointed out the smiling elephant, the jigging civet. There was an embryonic love for him in that house on Rue des Salines, and better meals, and bigger windows, and lusher hedges, and *Epoisses*, and the promise of classmates and cousins and, perhaps one day, a proper brother or sister.

Charlemagne saw his new walls through a sheen of tears. He coughed at the tender man and woman who tried to help him adapt. He slumped on the floor of his bedroom and did nothing but cry, said nothing but a name. "Flor!" he yelled at the nearest wall, unimpressed by the happy elephant. "Flor!" until his face was red. "Flor!" until he vomited—not much of a conqueror then. He snotted the hem of his shirt and let his stomach grow empty. He resisted all embraces, twisting like a screw whenever the woman drew him to her, and when the bedroom door was closed on him, he "Flor!"ed until he was hoarse. He "Flor!"ed in a northward direction even after his voice gave out, after his new parents began to reconsider their choice.

From the north Florent came. He disappeared from the agency seven hours after Charlemagne was removed and reappeared on Rue des Salines two days later. There were reports, after the fact, of a slight, odd-eyed child padding barefoot through the streets of Vannes, evading traffic and random malevolence as if girded by a sphere. He didn't drown in the long neck of the oily La Marie, or lose composure in hectic, honking Place Gambetta as he wandered all the way up Rue Ferdinand le Dressay and all the way down Avenue du Maréchal de Lattre de Tassigny. He wasn't tempted by Vannes' quaint and sunny quays and their nodding yachts. He must be a very sensible child, authorities surmised, and he must have had a franc or two to buy a snack, a cup of juice. He must have found a nook to shelter in when night fell—he must be very quick to have evaded seeking, well-meaning hands.

But no one solved the question of how Florent knew where to find his anointed brother, how he entered the second-floor bedroom of a locked house in the dead of night, to be found tucked against the other's side, his feet as clean as seashell. Kermorgant staff were shame-faced, police were relieved, and Charlemagne's futile new parents were traumatized. They returned him to the agency along with the runaway, unwilling to take responsibility for a broken child and his formidable shadow.

Charlemagne was hardly broken. Reunited with Florent, his voice returned with his appetite, and his will abated. Florent grew agreeable again, the most helpful, pliable boy in the hospice. He was tacit, but since his grades were triumphantly average, adults let him be. They accepted his dial tone of a personality, and they checked Charlemagne's energy more days than not, but neither boy earned a tick in their file as routine carried them forward. They were good. The one was simply too quiet, the other a bit kinetic.

It was commonplace for children to walk themselves to class in the 70s, particularly in seaside towns where orphanages weren't more than five quiet turns of the street from primary schools. *Les deux bretons* were clannish, ignoring the other Kermorgant boys and girls without rudeness. They curled through the streets alone most days, the one indifferent to everything but his friend, the other beating with curiosity. Even then— even at six—Charlemagne tested every wall with hands, feet, and shoulders, sensing the latent physical intelligence he'd someday use to somersault off buildings with showy kips and flyaways.

But that was a year or two down the line. Now was the age of alphabet and arithmetic, of learning how to spell first and last names no matter how elaborate, of evading larger boys who taunted one with *Charle-minime* and the other with *Fleur*. If the bullies were persistent, the classroom dull, the institutional life they lived completely without character, the whole was preferable to the alternative, which arrived soon enough—inevitable.

Lesson learned after the Rue des Salines incident, the bureaucrats worked on their timing. They orchestrated a double-drop on the same day once every file was in order. Florent, age seven, was shipped to a foster home in Caen, while six-year-old Charlemagne was brought, indignant, to the tip of Quiberon. Each was instructed to adapt to new circles. Neither was told where the other could be found.

Charlemagne's second home lacked the first one's heart. The man and woman who sheltered him on Quiberon understood the arrangement to be temporary and offish. There were two other foster children under this roof—both girls, neither of whom had much to do with the newcomer. A clinical atmosphere was contained in that gabled house with turquoise shutters and trim—a house like any other off Avenue du Presqu'île, taking part in a peninsula-long repetition of whitewashed squares behind stony fences. Everything seemed to point south, towards colourful Port Maria, which was iced with winter's frozen spray. Everything seemed to remark on the expansive seaside sky.

Charlemagne had nothing to say about any of it. He drew inward and sulked. His fosterers maintained routine. The husband left each morning to attend to his seafood restaurant, however void of tourists. The wife sorted the girls off to school. Charlemagne was left alone while he adjusted to the change—no chores, no school, no chaffing. He took advantage of his fosterers' philosophy and spent his days ignoring platefuls of sardines and sweetened *fromage blanc*, whispering a syllable. He waited, confident, and studied the maritime tchotchkes his foster mother cluttered about the maritime-blue dining room.

This time it took a week and a day for Florent to materialize, so great the distance between them and so hard the weather. His feet tinged red, his toes puckered, he wandered naked into the house one morning, locked onto the dining room where Charlemagne practiced inertia, and closed the gap.

The wife rolled him in a blanket and called the husband back from the restaurant while Florent dozed in a corner with his friend. Only next gardening season would she discover an assortment of clothes bundled under the hedge that separated her gabled house from that of the neighbour: a dark green winter coat, a pair of black trousers, brown lace-up boots, gloves, a knitted cap, a scarf, and several layers of shirts. Everything was out of fashion and threadbare, as if rescued from a charity bin, and everything was fit for a grown man. There were two francs and twenty centimes in the pocket of the trousers, a clipped fingernail, and nothing else.

Authorities tried to trace the passage of an odd-eyed, determined child from Caen to Quiberon, but their efforts were in vain. They asked the wrong questions. Had they inquired about an odd-eyed adult roving across Brittany, they might have heard reports of such a man hiking southwards along a wintery causeway, hunched against the latest gale. Around him the swells tried to climb the seawall, made violent by the pressure of a heavy sunless sky that digested every shade of grey. The sea itself refused, momentarily, to mirror the happy blues of the province; it boiled with lurid turquoise, threw up its foam, sent wind shrieking into ears, and guttled the icy snow that lanced it.

The weather was remarkable that week, and so was the man who defied it, not just because he chose to walk the Quiberon peninsula in February. He'd been noticeably down on his luck, his clothes too large for his frame yet too short at the wrists and ankles. He'd been noticeably shivering, his coat and pants sopped by flying snow and foam. He'd been heterochromic like Edig, and narrow-built like Edig, and dark-locked like Edig, and heedless of the faces peering at him through car windows. He'd been tattered but tireless as he pushed southward against the wind.

In less than a day les deux bretons were back at the hospice, victorious. The boys attached themselves to old walls, old beds, old chores. Florent, after harrowing authorities from Caen to Quiberon for the span of a week and a day, resumed his role as Most Cooperative Boy. Charlemagne resumed his energetic thrumming. The one was boring, the other endearing despite it all. They were good again.

It was not commonplace for children in Vannes to enlist in martial arts classes, much less wards of the state who earned no more than the basics. It was, however, not unusual for business people to donate goods or services to l'Hospice Kermorgant. The Christmas after the Avenue du Presqu'île incident, when Charlemagne was seven and Florent eight, a local savate club offered free lessons to the lucky child (and a companion of his choice) who selected a certain gift under the institutional tree. Charlemagne, too small to grapple larger boxes out of the fray, clamped his hand on a book-sized present that revealed a manual of basic fighting techniques and a voucher.

Now was the age of *fouettes* and *chasses bas*, of learning to make weapons of hands, feet, and canes, of bullies growing reluctant to approach Charlemagne Kermorgant and Florent Edig. They were not yet known as *les deux bretons*, who in their teens and twenties would take several national titles between them in three different martial arts (one shod, two barefoot), but they were in development. Their instructor was so taken with nimble Char and Flor, so optimistic about their aptitude and form, that free lessons continued in exchange for helping out at the club.

One last time the state tried to accommodate these wards beyond the institution. There was a brief attempt to locate fosterers who would house both boys, but boys of an age were thought to be troublesome and there were no takers. A code of silence was put into place—a need-to-know venture whose details were kept in the heads of two bureaucrats, no more. Charlemagne was assigned a home in Brest, Florent in Rennes, and once again—after signatures were collected and relocation dates confirmed—*les deux bretons* were scattered. It took moments to collect them from their classrooms and wrangle them into separate vans. At just seven and eight years old, and just months into their savate training, they were hardly indomitable.

Charlemagne found himself lost in the largest town he'd ever seen, bolted to a naval couple who lived near the port. The husband was rarely out of uniform, and the wife—unable to have children of her own—was intrusive. Charlemagne was their first foster and their attention was a spotlight he couldn't elude. He was their practice son while they waited for a baby to adopt, and practice they did: family meals and family games exhausted him and he acted out. He broke a cup for the sake of breaking it and sampled every hiding spot he could find in the couple's button-tight home on Rue Bel air. He refused to speak and made a drama of baths and meals. He wanted his savate instructor nearly as much as he wanted Flor. He had never felt so robbed.

Florent, lost in a city even larger than Brest, was some time in finding his friend. Time enough for spring to show itself. Time enough for incessant rain to darken the already dark street and thicken its hedges and wash winter salt from the sides of its homes. Time enough for Charlemagne to lose pounds he couldn't afford to lose, for the husband to lose patience and introduce boy to palm, for the wife to lose interest in the entire exercise. Time enough for Charlemagne, obsessed with all things east, to scent his way to the edge of land and call at the sea until he was dragged away.

No one saw Florent enter the house on Rue Bel air, though it happened in the middle of a Saturday, when husband and wife were home with their maddening charge. They were at lunch—and then they were asleep. They dreamt, in that sleep, of colossal iron walls and green-and-brown mountains, of planets that could crush a sun, of booms that strip reason from minds. They dreamt of particles too small to be measured—to be known—which combined into ribbons that were spotlessly bright yet crimson-dark in the very same moment in time. They dreamt of things indefinite, interactive, and unobservable. They dreamt of a dogged and ceaseless spinning, and woke unnerved.

When they woke, lifting heads from tabletop, their faces stained with *cotriade*, Charlemagne was camped under the highboy with a dark-haired child. The one was wary as he blinked at the adults at the table, the other nodding off. The one looked immensely satisfied, the other bedraggled, shoes disintegrating off trembling feet.

Authorities never minded the question of Charlemagne and Florent, at first. They had larger mysteries to solve. Ten days before, a sleeping sickness descended on Rennes. So chaotic the result, no one had time to follow up reports about an odd-eyed runaway who dodged his fosterers in a Picard Surgelés and wasn't spotted again until he turned up in Brest. If anyone connected the bolting of Edig from the foodshop and the first mass case of sleeping sickness—which occurred in the shop in question—such a connection never made it to the papers. Journalists were too busy tracing the sickness westward, marvelling how it contained itself, threadlike, to less than a square kilometre radius, how it veered away from roads and towns. That was just as well, after the smashed glass and broken limbs that collected in Rennes as drivers, builders, cooks, and bathers dropped off in media res with sometimes dire results.

Events were much gentler beyond the capital. Victims tended to be innkeepers, hikers, dalliers. Rural families fell asleep without warning, at all hours, to wake on sofas or kitchen floors, food missing from fridges and pantries. A few outdoor cafés reported collective naps that overturned cups, tables, and chairs, but these were remote operations nestled in the Armorique Regional National Park. One lucky photographer benefitted from the phenomenon when she managed to wake before the others and snap a lucrative shot: patrons sagging on chairs, waiters supine on the ground, trays scattered, *éclairs* and *kouigns* transformed into pillows.

The naval man and his wife were the last of the sleepers; the sickness waned at Brest. *Les deux bretons* were returned to Vannes and given old spots and old roles at the hospice. They returned to school and savate lessons, and they agreed to sign up for instruction in Breton to earn more credit with the adults who ruled them. Charlemagne was once more amenable to food and baths. Florent made himself indispensable. They were so good—and so quick to win trophies for their local club—that their savate instructor and his wife opened their home to both boys less than a year later, and there they remained.

In time, they grew into lithe young men with charming faces that belied their love of the ring. In time, as they qualified for tournaments in Paris, Lyon, and Toulouse, they became known as *les deux bretons*, a label of respect, of expectation. It was expected that Kermorgant would disarm opponents with a joyous, bloody grin—he'd bite his tongue to dye his teeth when bouts were close. It was expected he would let his hair hang in his face while Edig pulled his into a ball so he might cut the air with his cheekbones and bore into opponents with his eerie two-tone gaze. It was expected they would eventually settle in Paris, a city of many bouts and clubs, where the one would make a modest living in restaurant kitchens (his kineticism served him well), the other as a martial arts instructor of equally modest means. It was expected that gaining the age of majority would liberate them, and it did, and they are together still, terrifying enemies with their less terrifying trick. If they miss the sea air, they've chosen not to tell me.

Standard Deviant
HOLLY SCHOFIELD

Ashley crouched behind the Audi, watching her boyfriend through the plate glass window of the Denny's restaurant. The red and yellow neon sign above punctured the darkness. *Pancakes. Coffee.* And, visible in the window below: her sweet, sweet Brut. He was sprawled sideways in the booth, leaning back against the window, plaid Hurley cap tilted, a cup at his lips. Maddog slouched on the opposite bench, grinning fiercely, his dreadlocks huge. Some chick sat beside him, skinny with spiky black hair, leaning toward Brut; who the hell was that? Plates, piled with bunched paper napkins and cutlery, lay scattered in front of them.

Ashley was late for the party.

As usual.

She shifted her feet and her metal boot studs rasped on the wet pavement. The drizzle had almost stopped but she wrapped her ratty army jacket around her more tightly anyway. She should cross the street and join them in the restaurant—at least it'd be warmer. *Eggs over easy. And hash browns.*

The Audi's windshield burst into a painful kaleidoscope of violets, pinks, and reds. Just her luck to hide behind a car that had some kind of weird electrical problem.

"We need an ambassador." The voice seemed to be coming from the flashing windshield. It was matter-of-fact and friendly.

"Piss off," Ashley said. She squatted even lower behind the car in case the flaring lights caught Brut's eye. *Homefries. And bacon.*

"We have only minutes to keep the wormhole open," the voice said. Ashley flipped her blue hair off her eyes. The hair colour was called "dystopcyan" and cost her the entire haul from a purse-snatching down on Fifth Avenue yesterday, but she'd thought Brut might like the colour. He'd liked her zombie-snake tattoo last week, enough to nuzzle her throat where the tail curled around.

"We will recruit you to spread the word. Our spot-checks indicate America and several other countries are finally progressive enough to enroll into the *buzz-buzz-buzz*," the voice said, then chuckled. "That clearly did not translate. Let's use the vernacular: you guys can enroll into the Galactic Federation. Peace and prosperity await."

Huh. Maybe she shouldn't have popped that little white pill she'd found in Maddog's bathroom earlier tonight.

She edged around to the front bumper and stared at Brut through the window again, glad the darkness provided cover. Soon. She'd go to him, soon.

Just not quite yet.

"Get a life," she told the voice. She hoped Brut would take his feet off the seat when she approached the booth.

Her throat was dry. She swallowed and looked more closely at the car in spite of herself.

It was a newer model Audi, dark red in the streetlights. The windows were tight and black, except the windshield which shifted colours in patterns too rapidly to make sense. Clearly, the Red Bull chaser had also been a bad idea.

"Our analyses indicate you are within the range of standard deviation for your country, race, and age," the voice said, with warmth.

"Yeah, a standard deviant, that's me," Ashley muttered. *Not even an original deviant.*

The patterns shifted and emerged into an almost-shape, like a word on the tip of her tongue. If this was a crazy mugger or some kind of scam, it was different than any she'd seen before. And, in four years on the street, she'd seen it *all*.

It might make a good story to impress Brut with. Something to make her stand out among the other chicks. Something to make his eyes glint and the corner of his mouth twitch. Maybe he'd let her spend the night in his apartment again. Maddog's sofa was getting lame.

"What's in it for me?" She put a hand on her hip and pouted at the windshield like a Japanese porn star.

"Improving mankind and expanding world knowledge is not your mandate, I see," said the voice, with a slight edge.

Ashley grinned and flipped a finger at the car. *I can piss anybody off, given a few minutes.*

"Perhaps this will convince you?" The kaleidoscope shifted to blackness so immense, so deep that Ashley gasped. Her skull began a not-unpleasant throb and her eyes felt stretched with infinite possibilities. A high that took her higher than she'd ever been, even that time in Arizona with the peyote.

Rotating planets and whirling galaxies flashed in a cadence that matched her thudding heart and she was lost in the universe, spiraling among the stars.

Finally, her mind found a tiny corner and tugged on it until it opened like a window on her phone. She rubbed a toe on the gritty sidewalk and cleared her throat.

"Why me?" she asked. "I'm, like, nobody. And, like, the most unreliable witness you'll ever find." Just what the cops had told her the night they released her stepdad for the eighth time. Without bail. No one ever did internal exams on trailer park trash.

"A hard truth," the voice said, with an emotion she couldn't label. "However, you are the only one on this street, the wormhole is closing, you have little to lose, and, sadly but most importantly, this nexus will not be disrupted since . . . well, actually . . . no one will miss you."

She glanced at the restaurant window. Brut was holding out his coffee cup and smirking at the unamused waitress. The new chick was on Brut's side of the booth, cuddled against him.

She climbed onto the hood of the car, one boot stud screeching a long silver gouge through the paint. She admired it for a minute then clambered into the whirling space where the windshield should have been. Her last thought, before reeling away into the cosmos, was of the last time she'd seen her mom: high heels clacking, pacing the kitchen floor, cell phone clamped to her ear as she made a date. Her mom had been laughing shrilly at something the client had said when Ashley had slipped out the door.

Ashley dropped gracefully to the street as the closing wormhole deposited her a few centimetres above the pavement. She was lucky to have caught this same nexus in front of the Denny's, almost ten years to the day after she'd left. The Federation had wondrous technology but it was hard science, not magic and not perfect. The space/time juncture was only open for a moment; no time to see how Earth had changed in the past decade.

That shouldn't matter. *She* had changed.

She was ready to be ambassador to the USA. To deliver her message to the country, the continent, the world.

Finally, she was about to do something with her life besides screw it up.

She kept her eyes squeezed shut, waiting for the transit afterglow to recede. She smoothed her chestnut hair behind her ears and straightened the collar of her sleek, form-fitting jumpsuit. She had amused the Federation staff by refusing to give up her boots—their worn leather now in sharp contrast to her chic appearance. The staff had fixed her brain chemistry—no more addictions or depression—as well as adjusting a slight pronation in her left foot and clearing up her herpes. Her muscles were magnificently toned and her posture impeccable. She was trained in politics, in psychology, in negotiation, in persuasion; a hundred years of education crammed into a decade. She was primed to bring humankind, with all their foibles, into the future, into an era of affluence and unbridled happiness.

She stretched joyfully and clicked her metal heels together, like a futuristic Dorothy.

Then she opened her eyes.

The Audi was gone. Litter blew across the street. The Denny's, boarded up and graffitied, loomed at her in the predawn light. She walked toward the restaurant. Her foot hit something soft and she looked down. A rotting corpse lay in the gutter. She hurried past it and up the far curb. A crude newsletter tacked to an unlit lamppost caught her eye. The headline proclaimed: "World Economic Devastation Continues, Billions Starving."

Her message would go unheard.

The party was already over.

Kafka's Notebooks

JOCKO BENOIT

His old lover waits apprehensively
while the Nazi border officer
inspects one of Kafka's notebooks.
on the first page he reads an idea
for a story about a border guard
inspecting a notebook. He hands it to
his colleague. A single line of prose
snakes off the page and whips up
to his neck, burrowing towards
his brain. He shudders, acutely
aware he's become a cobra, although
no one notices any change.
Their scientists investigate the notebooks
to determine usefulness as weapons.
But the men soon succumb to paranoia
and one of them finds himself strapped
down while his friend tries to force
a notebook down his throat. The experiment
ends and rumour has it Hitler keeps
the books as bedtime reading.

They never turn up again, although
some say a secret society
scattered them to all parts of the globe
so they would do less harm. But
now and then an obnoxious executive,
red as a rage berry, takes off
his pants on a plane. A cop leaves out
a list of women he'd like to
cook and eat. At the bottom
of some beer mugs is a line from
the notebooks—a bottomless
nightmare koan turning a drunk
driver's keys into a pack
of wild dogs. And the punctilious
bureaucrat feels the knot at the back
of her hair tightening until
her face is taut and agonized
on the spear of her perfectly
straight spine while everyone else
eats a little more, unable to fill the vast
spaces between their certainties.

Soon comes the global surrender
to the surreal weather, and living in
high rise icebergs. Gravity affects
people differently, some flattening,
others feeling lighter than the breath
they leave behind on the ground.
Some try to find the books again
for some hint of closure
and when they do all there is
are lists of errands and gripes
between large blank spaces.
But these are proven forgeries
by an expert who later turns out
to not exist, although he has been
widely cited for decades,
which means everything science
has learned is off by several

centimetres or parsecs. We aren't
where we thought we were
standing. God actually lives
next door and pesters us
to borrow sugar and milk.

I am keeping a journal of all
the changes, but one day I learn
I am actually one of the lost notebooks.
I don't know what's inside me,
but it affects everyone differently.
I've seen many versions of
delight, terror, puzzlement,
knowing and disgust. I'll never
have an ISBN. Just when you think
of the genre I best fit, your hands
will suffer third-degree burns.
I am finished, Mein Herr.
You may pass me on to the next.

Giants

PETER WATTS

So many eons, slept away while the universe wound down around him. He's dead to human eyes. Even the machines barely see the chemistry ticking over in those cells: an ancient molecule of hydrogen sulphide, frozen in a hemoglobin embrace; an electron shuttled sluggishly down some metabolic pathway two weeks ago. Back on Earth there used to be life deep in the rocks, halfway to the mantle; empires rose and fell in the time it took those microbes to draw breath. Next to Hakim's, their lives blurred past in an eyeblink. (Next to all of ours. I was every bit as dead, just a week ago.)

I'm still not sure it's a good idea, bringing him back.

Flat lines shiver in their endless march along the x-axis: molecules starting to bump against each other, core temp edging up a fraction of a fraction. A lonely spark flickers in the hypothalamus; another wriggles across the prefrontal cortex (a passing thought, millennia past its best-before, released from amber). Millivolts trickle down some random path and an eyelid twitches.

The body shudders, tries to breathe but it's too soon: it's still anoxic in there, pure H_2S gumming up the works and shutting the machinery of life down to a whisper. The Chimp starts a nitrox flush; swarms of fireflies bloom across *Pulmonary* and *Vascular*. Hakim's cold empty husk fills with light from the inside out: red and yellow isotherms, pulsing arteries, a trillion reawakening neurons stippling across the translucent avatar in my head. A real breath this time. Another. His fingers twitch and stutter, tap a random tattoo against the floor of his sarcophagus.

The lid slides open. His eyes, too, a moment later: they roll unfocused in their sockets, suffused in a haze of resurrection dementia. He can't see me. He sees soft lights and vague shadows, hears the faint underwater echo of nearby machinery, but his mind is still stuck to the past and the present hasn't sunk in yet.

A tongue dry as leather flicks into view against his upper lip. A drinking tube emerges from its burrow and nudges Hakim's cheek. His takes it in his mouth and nurses, reflexive as a newborn.

I lean into what passes for his field of view: "Lazarus, come forth."

It anchors him. I see sudden focus resolving in those eyes, see the past welling up behind them. I see memories and hearsay loading in the wake of my voice. Confusion evaporates; something sharper takes its place. Hakim stares up at me from the grave, his eyes hard as obsidian.

"You asshole," he says. "I can't believe we haven't killed you yet."

I give him space. I retreat to the forest, wander endless twilit caverns while he learns to live again. Down here I can barely see my own hand in front of my face: grey fingers, faint sapphire accents. Photophores glimmer around me like dim constellations, each tiny star lit by the glow of a trillion microbes: photosynthesis instead of fusion. You can't get truly lost in *Eriophora*—the Chimp always knows where you are—but here in the dark, there's comfort to be had in the illusion.

Eventually, though, I have to stop stalling. I sample myriad feeds as I rise though the depths of the asteroid, find Hakim in the starboard bridge. I watch as he enters painstaking questions, processes answers, piles each new piece on top of the last in a rickety climb to insight. Lots of debris in this system, yes: more than enough material for a build. Call up the transponders and—what's this? No in-system scaffolding, no half-constructed jump gate, no asteroid mining or factory fleet. So why—?

System dynamics, now. Lagrange points. Nothing on this side, anyway, even though there are at least three planetary bodies in—whoa, those *orbits*—

Our orbit . . .

By the time I join him in the flesh he's motionless, staring into the tac tank. A bright dimensionless point floats in the centre of that display: *Eriophora*. The ice giant looms dark and massive to port, the red one—orders of magnitude larger—seethes in the distance behind. (If I stepped outside I'd see an incandescent barrier stretching across half the universe, with the barest hint of a curve on the horizon; tac reduces it to a cherry globe floating in an aquarium.) A million bits of detritus, from planets to pebbles, careen through the neighbourhood. We're not even relativistic and still the Chimp hasn't had time to tag them all.

None of those tags make sense anyway. We're aeons from the nearest earthly constellation; every alphabet, every astronomical convention has been exhausted by the stars we've passed in the meantime. Maybe the Chimp invented his own taxonomy while we were sleeping, some arcane gibberish of hex and ascii that makes sense to him and him alone. A hobby, perhaps, although he's supposed to be too stupid for anything like that.

I slept through most of that scenery. I've been awake for barely a hundred builds; *my* mythological reservoir is nowhere near exhausted. I have my own names for these monsters.

The cold giant is Thule. The hot one is Surtr.

Hakim ignores my arrival. He moves sliders back and forth: trajectories extrude from bodies in motion, predict the future according to Newton. Eventually all those threads converge and he rewinds time, reverses entropy, reassembles the shattered teacup and sets it running again. He does it three times as I watch. The result never changes.

He turns, his face bloodless. "We're going to hit. We're going to ram straight into the fucking thing."

I swallow and nod.

"That's how it starts," I tell him.

We're going to hit. We're *aiming* to hit, we're going to let the lesser monster devour us before the greater one devours it. We'll lower *Eriophora* by her own bootstraps, sink through roiling bands of hydrogen and helium and a thousand exotic hydrocarbons, down to whatever residual deep-space chill Thule's been hoarding since—who knows? Maybe almost as long as *we've* been in flight.

It won't last, of course. The planet's been warming ever since it started its long fall from the long dark. Its bones will survive the passage through the stellar envelope easily enough: five hours in and out, give or take. Its atmosphere won't be so lucky, though. Every step of the way Surtr's going to be stripping it down like a child licking an ice cream cone.

We'll make it through by balancing in the ever-shrinking sweet spot between a red-hot sky and the pressure cooker at Thule's core. The numbers say it'll work.

Hakim should know this already. He would have *awakened* knowing if not for that idiotic uprising of theirs. But they chose to blind themselves instead, burn out their links, cut themselves off from the very heart of the mission. So now I have to *explain* things. I have to *show* things. All that instantaneous insight we once shared, gone: one ancient fit of pique and I have to use *words*, scribble out *diagrams*, etch out painstaking codes and tokens while the clock runs down. I'd hoped that maybe, after all these red-shifted millennia, they might have reconsidered; but the look in Hakim's eyes leaves no doubt. As far as he's concerned it all happened yesterday.

I do my best. I keep the conversation strictly professional, focus on the story so far: a build, aborted. Chaos and inertia, imminent annihilation, the insane counterintuitive necessity of passing *through* a star instead of going *around* it. "What are we doing here?" Hakim asks once I've finished.

"It looked like a perfect spot." I gesture at the tank. "From a distance. Chimp even sent out the vons, but—" I shrug. "The closer we got, the worse it turned out to be."

He stares at me without speaking, so I add context: "Far as we can tell, something big came through a few hundred thousand years back, knocked everything haywire. None of the planetary masses are even on the ecliptic anymore. We can't find anything orbiting with an eccentricity of less than point six, there's a shitload of rogues zipping around in the halo—but by the time those numbers came back, we were already committed. So now we just buckle down through the heavy traffic, steal a gravity-assist, get back on the road."

He shakes his head. "What are we doing here?"

Oh, *that's* what he means. I tap an innerface, timelapse the red giant. It jerks in the tank like a fibrillating heart. "Turns out it's an irregular variable. One complication too many, right?" Not that we'll be able thread the needle any better than the Chimp can (although of course Hakim's going to try, in these few hours left to him). But the mission has parameters. The Chimp has his algorithms. Too many unexpected variables and he wakes up the meat. That's what we're here for, after all.

That's *all* we're here for.

One more time, Hakim asks: "What are *we* doing here?"

Oh.

"You're the numbers guy," I say after a moment. "One of 'em, anyway." Out of how many thousand, stored down in the crypt?

Doesn't matter. They probably all know about me by now.

"Guess it was just your rotation," I add.

He nods. "And you? You a *numbers guy* too, now?"

"We come back in pairs," I say softly. "You know that."

"So it just happened to be *your rotation* as well."

"Look—"

"Nothing to do with your *Chimp* wanting its own personal sock-puppet on hand to keep an eye on things."

"Fuck, Hakim, what do you want me to say?" I spread my hands. "That he might want someone on deck who won't try to pull the plug the first chance they get? You think that's *unreasonable*, given what happened?" But he doesn't even know what happened, not first-hand. Hakim wasn't up when the mutiny went down; someone obviously told him, down through the epochs. Christ knows how much of what he heard is truth, lies, legend.

A few million years go by and suddenly I'm the bogeyman.

We fall towards ice. Ice falls towards fire. Both spill through the link and spread across the back of my skull in glorious terrifying first-person. Orders of magnitude aren't empty abstractions in here: they're life-size, you feel them in your gut. Surtr may be small to a textbook—at seven million kilometres across, it's barely big enough to get into the giants' club—but that doesn't mean shit when you meet it face to face. That's not a star out there: that's the scorching edge of all creation, that's heat-death incarnate. Its breath stinks of leftover lithium from the worlds it's *already* devoured. And the dark blemish marching across its face isn't just a *planet*. It's a melting hellscape twice the size of Uranus, it's frozen methane and liquid hydrogen and a core hot and heavy enough to bake diamonds. Already it's coming apart before my eyes, any moons long since lost, the tattered remnants of a ring system shredding around it like a rotting halo. Storms boil across its face; aurorae flicker madly at both poles. A supercyclone pinwheels at the centre of the dark side, fed by turbulent streamers fleeing from light into shadow. Its stares back at me like the eye of a blind god.

Meanwhile, Hakim pushes balls around inside an aquarium.

He's been at it for hours: a bright blue marble here, a sullen red basketball over there, threads of tinsel looping through time and trajectory like the webbing of some crazed spacefaring spider. Maybe pull our centre of mass to starboard, start gentle then ramp up to max? Break some rocks on the way, suffer some structural damage but nothing the drones won't be able to patch up in time for the next build.

No?

Maybe cut smooth and fast into full reverse. *Eri*'s not built for it but if we keep the vectors dead along the centreline, no turn no torque just a straight linear one-eighty back out the way we came—

But no.

If only we hadn't already fallen so far down the well. If only we hadn't slowed down to open the trunk, all these N-bodies wouldn't have been able to get such a grip on us. But now we're only fast, not fast enough; we're big but still too small.

Now, the only way out is through.

Hakim's not an idiot. He knows the rules as well as I do. He keeps trying, though. He'd rather rewrite the laws of physics than trust himself to the enemy. We'll be deaf and blind in there, after all; the convulsions of Thule's disintegrating atmosphere will fog our sight at short range, the roar of Surtr's magnetic field will deafen us in the long. There'll be no way of telling where we are, nothing but the Chimp's math to tell us where we should be.

Hakim doesn't see the world like I do. He doesn't like having to take things on faith.

Now he's getting desperate, blasting chunks off his toy asteroid in an attempt to reduce its momentum. He hasn't yet considered how that might impact our radiation shielding once we get back up to speed. He's still stuck on whether we can scavenge enough in-system debris to patch the holes on our way out.

"It won't work," I tell him, though I'm wandering deep in the catacombs half a kilometre from his location. (I'm not spying because he knows I'm watching. Of course he knows.)

"Won't it now."

"Not enough mass along the escape trajectory, even if the vons *could* grab it all and get it back in time."

"We don't know how much mass is out there. Haven't plotted it all yet."

He's being deliberately obtuse, but I go along with it; at least we're talking. "Come on. You don't need to plot every piece of gravel to get a mass distribution. It won't work. Check with the Chimp if you don't believe me. He'll tell you."

"It just *has* told me," he says.

I stop walking. I force myself to take a slow breath.

"I'm *linked*, Hakim. Not possessed. It's just an innerface."

"It's a corpus callosum."

"I'm just as autonomous as you are."

"Define *I*."

"I don't—"

"Minds are holograms. Split one in half, you get two. Stitch two together, you get one. Maybe you were human back before your *upgrade*. Right now you've got about as much standalone soul as my parietal lobe."

I look back along the vaulted corridor (I suppose the cathedral architecture might just be coincidence), where the dead sleep stacked on all sides.

They're much better company like this.

"If that's true," I ask them all, "then how did *you* ever get free?"

Hakim doesn't speak for a moment.

"The day you figure that out," he says, "is the day we lose the war."

It's not a war. It's a fucking tantrum. They tried to derail the mission and the Chimp stopped them. Simple as that, and perfectly predictable. That's why the engineers made the Chimp so minimalist in the first place, why the mission isn't run by some transcendent AI with an eight-dimensional IQ: so that things will *stay* predictable. If my fellow meat sacks couldn't see it coming, they're more stupid than the thing they're fighting.

Hakim knows that on some level, of course. He just refuses to believe it: that he and his buddies got outsmarted by something with half his synapse count. *The Chimp.* The idiot savant, the artificial stupidity. The number-cruncher explicitly designed to be so dim that even with half the lifespan of a universe to play around in, it could never develop its own agenda.

They just can't believe it beat them in a fair fight.

That's why they need me. I let them tell each other that it *cheated*. No way that glorified finger-counter would've won if I hadn't betrayed my own kind.

This is the nature of my betrayal; I stepped in to save their lives. Not that their lives were really in danger, of course, no matter what they say. It was just a strategy. That was predictable too.

I'm sure the Chimp would have turned the air back on before things went too far.

Thule's graduated from world to wall while I wasn't looking: a dark churning expanse of thunderheads and planet-shredding tornadoes. There's no sign of Surtr lurking behind, not so much as a faint glow on the horizon. We huddle in the shadow of the lesser giant and it's almost as though the greater one has simply gone away.

We're technically in the atmosphere now, a mountain wallowing high above the clouds with its nose to the stars. You could draw a line from the hot hydrogen slush of Thule's core through the cold small singularity of our own, straight out through the gaping conical maw at our bow. Hakim does just that, in the tac tank. Maybe it makes him feel a little more in control.

Eriophora sticks out her tongue.

You can only see it in X-ray or Hawking, maybe the slightest nimbus of gamma radiation if you tune the sensors just right. A tiny bridge opens at the back of *Eri*'s mouth: a hole in spacetime reaching back to the hole in our heart. Our centre of mass *smears* a little off-centre, seeks some elastic equilibrium between those points. The Chimp nudges the far point farther and our centre follows in its wake. The asteroid tugs upward, falling after itself; Thule pulls us back. We hang balanced in the sky while the wormhole's tip edges past the crust, past that abraded mouth of blue-sanded basalt, out past the forward sensor hoop.

We've never stretched ourselves so thin before. Usually there's no need; with lightyears and epochs to play in, even the slowest fall brings us up to speed in plenty of time. We can't go past twenty percent lightspeed anyway, not without getting cooked by the blueshift. Usually *Eri* keeps her tongue in her mouth.

Not this time. This time we're just another one of Hakim's holiday ornaments, dangling from a thread in a hurricane. According to the Chimp, that thread should hold. There are error bars, though, and not a lot of empirical observation to hang them on. The database on singularities nested inside asteroids nested inside incinerating ice giants is pretty heavy on the handwaving.

And that's just the problem *within* the problem. Atmospheric docking with a world falling at two hundred kilometres a second is downright trivial next to predicting Thule's course inside the star: the drag inflicted by a millionth of a red-hot gram per cubic centimetre, stellar winds and thermohaline mixing, the deep magnetic torque of fossil helium. It's tough enough figuring out what "inside" even *means* when the gradient from vacuum to degenerate matter blurs across three million kilometres. Depending on your definition we might already be in the damn thing.

Hakim turns to me as the Chimp lowers us toward the storm. "Maybe we should wake them up."

"Who?"

"Sunday. Ishmael. All of them."

"You know how many thousands of us are stacked up down there?" *I* know. Hakim might guess but this traitor knows right down to the last soul, without checking.

Not that any of them would pat me on the back for that.

"What for?" I ask.

He shrugs. "It's all theory. You know that. We could all be dead in a day."

"You want to bring them back so they can be awake when they die?"

"So they can—I don't know. Write a poem. Grow a sculpture. Shit, one or two of them might even be willing to make their peace with *you* before the end."

"Say we wake them up and we're *not* all dead in day. You've just pushed our life support three orders of mag past spec."

He rolls his eyes. "Then we put everyone back down again. So it spikes the CO_2. Nothing the forest won't be able to clear in a few centuries."

I can barely hear the tremor in his voice.

He's scared. That's what this is. He's scared, and he doesn't want to die alone. And I don't count.

I suppose it's a start.

"Come on. At the very least it'll be a hell of a solstice party."

"Ask the Chimp," I suggest.

His face goes hard. I keep mine blank.

I'm pretty sure he wasn't serious anyway.

The depths of the troposphere. The heart of the storm. Cliffs of water and ammonia billow across our path: airborne oceans shattered down to droplets, to crystals. They crash into our mountain at the speed of sound, freeze solid or cascade into space depending on the mood. Lightning flashes everywhere, stamps my brain stem with half-glimpsed afterimages: demon faces, and great clawed hands with too many fingers.

Somehow the deck stays solid beneath my feet, unmoved even by the death throes of a world. I can't entirely suppress my own incredulity; even anchored by two million tonnes of basalt and a black hole, it seems impossible that we're not being tossed around like a mote in a wind tunnel.

I squash the feed and the carnage vanishes, leaving nothing behind but bots and bulkheads and a ribbon of transparent quartz looking down onto the factory floor. I kill some time watching the assembly lines boot up in there, watching maintenance drones gestate in the vacuum past the viewport. Even best-case there's going to be damage. Cameras blinded by needles of supersonic ice or sheets of boiling acid. The whiskers of long-range antennae, drooping in the heat. Depending on the breaks it could take an army to repair the damage after we complete our passage. I take some comfort from the sight of the Chimp's troops assembling themselves.

For an instant I think I hear a faint shriek down some far-off corridor: a breach, a decompression? No alarms, though. Probably just one of the roaches skidding around a bend in the corridor, looking for a recharge.

I'm not imagining the beeping in my head, though: Hakim, calling down from the bridge. "You need to be up here," he says when I open the channel.

"I'm on the other side of the—"

"*Please*," he says, and forks me a live feed: one of the bow clusters, pointing at the sky.

A feature has emerged from the featureless overcast: a bright dimple on the dark sky, like a finger poking down through the roof of the world. It's invisible in visible light, hidden by torrents of ammonia and hydrocarbon hurricanes: but it shimmers in infrared like a rippling ember.

I have no idea what it is.

I draw an imaginary line through the ends of the wormhole. "It's in line with our displacement vector."

"No *shit* it's in line. I think the wormhole's—provoking it, somehow."

It's radiating at over two thousand Kelvin.

"So we're inside the star," I say, and hope Hakim takes it as good news. If nothing else, it means we're on schedule.

We've got so little to go on. We don't know how far we are from the ceiling: it keeps ablating away above us. We don't know how close we are to the core: it keeps swelling beneath the easing weight of all this shedding atmosphere. All we know is that temperature rises overhead and we descend; pressure rises from beneath and we climb. We're specks in the belly of some fish in empty mid-ocean, surface and seabed equally hypothetical. None of our reference points are any more fixed than we are. The Chimp presents estimates based on gravity and inertia, but even those are little more than guesses thanks to wormhole corruption of the local spacetime. We're stretched across the probability wave, waiting for the box to open so the universe can observe whether we're dead or alive.

Hakim eyes me from across the tank, his face flickering in the light of a hundred cam feeds. "Something's wrong. We should be through by now."

He's been saying that for the past hour.

"There's bound to be variability," I remind him. "The model—"

"The *model*." He manages a short, bitter laugh. "Based on all those zettabytes we collected the *other* times we hitched a ride through a red giant. The model's *shit*. One hiccup in the magnetic field and we could be going *down* instead of *out*."

"We're still here."

"That's exactly the problem."

"It's still dark." The atmosphere's still thick enough to keep Surtr's blinding interior at bay.

"Always darkest before the dawn," Hakim says grimly, and points to that brightening smudge of infrared overhead.

The Chimp can't explain it, for all the fresh realtime data he stuffs into his equations. All we know is that whatever it is, it hasn't budged from our displacement vector and it's getting hotter. Or maybe closer. It's hard to tell; our senses are hazy that far out, and we're not about to stick our heads above the clouds for a better view.

Whatever it is, the Chimp doesn't think it's worth worrying about. He says we're almost through.

The storm no longer freezes on impact. It spits and hisses, turns instantly to steam. Incessant lightning strobes the sky, stop-animates towering jigsaw monsters of methane and acetylene.

God's mind might look like this, if He were an epileptic.

We get in the way sometimes, block some deific synapse in mid-discharge: a million volts spike the hull and a patch of basalt turns to slag, or *Eri* goes blind in another eye. I've lost count of the cameras and antennae and radar dishes we've already lost. I just add it to the tally when another facet flares and goes dark at the edge of the collage.

Hakim doesn't. "Play that again," he tells the Chimp. "That feed. Just before it fratzed."

The last moments of the latest casualty: *Eri's* cratered skin, outcroppings of half-buried machinery. Lightning flickers in from Stage Left, stabs a radiator fin halfway to our lumpy horizon. A flash. A banal and overfamiliar phrase:

No Signal.

"Again," Hakim says. "The strike in the middle distance. Freeze on that."

Three bolts, caught in the act—and Hakim's onto something, I see now. There's something different about them, something less—random—than the fractal bifurcations of more distant lightning. Different colour, too—more of a bluish edge—and smaller. The bolts in the distance are massive. These things arcing across the crust don't look much thicker than my own arm.

They converge towards some bright mass just barely out of camera range.

"Static discharge of some kind," I suggest.

"Yeah? What *kind*, exactly?"

I can't see anything similar in the current mosaic, but the bridge bulkheads only hold so many windows and our surface cams still number in the thousands. Even my link can't handle that many feeds at once. "Chimp: any other phenomena like that on the surface?"

"Yes," says the Chimp, and high-grades the display:

Bright meshes swarming over stone and steel. Formations of ball lightning, *walking* on jagged stilts of electricity. Some kind of flat flickering plasma, sliding along *Eri*'s crust like a stingray.

"*Shittttt*..." Hakim hisses. "Where did *they* come from?"

Our compound eye loses another facet.

"They're targeting the sensors." Hakim's face is ashen.

"They?" Could just be electricity arcing to alloy.

"They're blinding us. Oh Jesus fuck being trapped inside a star isn't bad enough there's gotta be *hostile aliens* in the bargain."

My eyes flicker to the ceiling pickup. "Chimp, what *are* those things?"

"I don't know. They could be something like Saint Elmo's Fire, or a buoyant plasma. I can't rule out some sort of maser effect either, but I'm not detecting any significant microwave emissions."

Another camera goes down. "Lightning bugs," Hakim says, and emits a hysterical giggle.

"Are they alive?" I wonder.

"Not organically," the Chimp tells me. "I don't know if they'd meet definitions based on entropy restriction."

No conventional morphology there. Those aren't legs exactly, they're— transient voltage arcs of some kind. And body shape—if *body* even applies—seems to be optional and fluid. Auroras bunch up into sparking balls; balls sprout loops or limbs or just blow away at Mach 2, vanishing into the storm.

I call up a tactical composite. Huh: clustered distribution. A flock gathered at the skeletal remains of a long-dead thruster nozzle; another flickering across an evagineering hutch halfway down the starboard lateral line. A whole party in *Eri*'s crater-mouth, swarming around our invisible bootstrap like water circling a drain.

"Holes," Hakim says softly. "Depressions. Hatches."

But something's caught my eye that doesn't involve any of those things, something unfolding overhead while our other eyes are fixed on the ground—

"They're trying to get in. That's what they're doing."

A sudden bright smudge in the sky. Then a tear; a hole; the dilating pupil of some great demonic eye. Dim bloody light floods down across the battered landscape as a cyclone opens over our heads, wreathed in an inflammation of lightning.

Surtr's finger stretches down from Hades, visible at last to naked eyes.

"Holy *shit . . .*" Hakim whispers.

It's an incandescent tornado, a pillar of fire. It's outside reaching in, and if anything short of magic can explain its existence it's not known to me or the Chimp or the accumulated wisdom of all the astrophysicists nesting in our archives. It reaches down and touches our wormhole, just *so.* It *bulges,* as if inflamed by an embedded splinter; the swollen tip wobbles absurdly for a moment, then bursts—

—and fire gushes down from the heavens in a liquid cascade. The things beneath scatter fast as forked lightning can carry them; here in the bridge, the view sparks and dies. From a dozen other viewpoints I see tongues of soft red plasma splashing across *Eriophora*'s crust.

Some rough alarm whispers *fuck fuck fuck fuck* at my side while *Eri* feeds me intelligence: something happening back at that lateral hutch. All those cams are down but there's a pressure surge at the outer hatch and a rhythmic hissing sound crackles in along the intercom.

Hakim's vanished from the bridge. I hear the soft whine of his roach receding at full throttle. I duck out into the corridor, grab my own roach from its socket, follow. There's really no question where he's headed; I'd know that even if the Chimp hadn't already laid out the map in my head.

Way back along our starboard flank, something's knocking on the door.

He's in the prep compartment by the time I catch up, scrambling into an EVA suit like some panicky insect trying to climb back into its cocoon. "Outer hatch is breached," he tells me, forgetting.

Just metres away. Past racks and suit alcoves, just the other side of that massive biosteel drawbridge, something's looking for a way in. It could find one, too; I can see heat shimmering off the hatch. I can hear the pop and crackle of arcing electricity coming through from the other side, the faint howl of distant hurricanes.

"No weapons." Hakim fumbles with his gauntlets. "Mission to the end of time and *they don't even give us weapons.*" Which is not entirely true. They certainly gave us the means to *build* weapons. I don't know if Hakim ever availed himself of that option but I remember his buddies, not so far from this very spot. I remember them pointing their weapons at me.

"What are we doing here?" I gesture at the hatch; is it my imagination, or has it brightened a little in the centre?

He shakes his head, his breathing fast and shallow. "I was gonna—you know, the welding torches. The lasers. Thought we could stand them off."

All stored on the other side.

He's suited up to the neck. His helmet hangs on its hook within easy reach: a grab and a twist and he'll be self-contained again. For a while.

Something pounds hard on the hatch. "Oh shit," Hakim says weakly.

I keep my voice level. "What's the plan?"

He takes a breath, steadies himself. "We, um—we retreat. Out past the nearest dropgate." The Chimp takes the hint and throws an overlay across my inner map; back into the corridor and fifteen metres forward. "Anything breaches, the gates come down." He nods at an alcove. "Grab a suit, just in—"

"And when they breach the dropgates?" I wonder. The biosteel's definitely glowing, there in the centre.

"The *next* set goes down. Jesus, you know the drill."

"That's your plan? Give up *Eri* in stages?"

"*Small* stages." He nods and swallows. "Buy time. Figure out their weak spot." He grabs his helmet and turns towards the corridor.

I lay a restraining hand on his shoulder. "How do we do that, exactly?"

He shrugs it off. "Wing it for fucksake! Get Chimp to customize some drones to go in and, and *ground* them or something." He heads for the door.

This time the hand I lay on him is more than a suggestion. This time it clamps down, spins him around, pushes him against the bulkhead. His helmet bounces across the deck. His clumsy gloved hands come up to fend me off but there's no strength in them. His eyes do a mad little jig in his face.

"You're not thinking this through," I say, very calmly.

"*There's no* time *to think it through!* They might not even *get* past the gates, maybe they're not even *trying*, I mean—" His eyes brighten with faint and ridiculous hope. "Maybe it's not even an attack, I bet it's not, you know, they're just—they're *dying*. It's the end of the world and their home's on fire and they're just looking for a place to hide, they're not looking for a way *in* they're looking for a way *out*—"

"What makes you think that inside's any less lethal to them than outside is to us?"

"They don't have to be *smart!*" he cries out. "They just have to be *scared!*"

Fingers of faint electricity flicker and crackle around the edges of the hatch: heat lightning, maybe. Or maybe something more *prehensile*.

I keep Hakim pinned. "What if they *are* smart? What if they're not just burrowing on instinct? What if *they're* the ones with the plan, hmm?"

He spreads his hands. "What else can we do?"

"We don't give them the chance to breach. We get out of here *now*."

"Get—"

"Ditch the ice giant. Take our chances in the star."

He stops struggling and stares, waiting for the punchline. "You're insane," he whispers when I fail to deliver.

"Why? Chimp says we're almost through anyway."

"He said that *half an hour ago*! And we were an hour past predicted exit even *then*!"

"Chimp?" I say, not for the AI's benefit but for Hakim's.

"Right here."

"Say we max the wormhole. Throw out as much mass as we can, shortest path out of the envelope."

"Tidal stress tears *Eriophora* into two debris clouds of roughly equal mass, each one centred on—"

"Amend that. Say we optimize distance and displacement to maximize velocity *without* losing structural integrity."

I can tell by the wait that there are going to be serious confidence limits attached to the answer. "*Eriophora* is directly exposed to the stellar envelope for 1300 corsecs," he says at last. "Give or take 450."

At 2300 Kelvin. Basalt melts at 1724.

But the Chimp hasn't finished. "We would also risk significant structural damage due to the migration of secondary centres-of-mass beyond *Eriophora's* hardlined displacement channels."

"Do we make it?"

"I don't know."

Hakim throws up his hands. "Why the hell not? It's what you *do*!"

"My models can't account for the plasma invagination overhead or the electrical events on the hull," the Chimp tells him. "Therefore they're missing at least one important variable. You can't trust my predictions."

Down at the end of the compartment, the hatch glows red as the sky. Electricity sizzles and pops and *grabs*.

"Do it," Hakim says suddenly.

"I need consensus," the Chimp replies.

Of course. The Chimp takes his lead from us meat sacks when he gets lost; but looking to us for wisdom, he wouldn't know whose to follow if we disagreed.

Hakim waits, manic, his eyes flicking between me and the hatch. "Well?" he says after a moment.

It all comes down to me. I could cancel him out.

"What are you waiting for? *It was your fucking idea!*"

I feel an urge to lean close and whisper in his ear. *Not just Chimp's sock puppet* now, *am I, motherfucker?* I resist it. "Sure," I say instead. "Give it a shot."

Wheels begin to turn. *Eriophora* trembles and groans, torqued by vectors she was never designed for. Unfamiliar sensations tickle my backbrain, move forward, root in my gut: the impossible, indescribable sense of *down* being in two places at once. One of those places is safe and familiar, beneath my feet, beneath decks and forests and bedrock at the very heart of the ship; but the other's getting stronger, and it's *moving. . . .*

I hear the scream of distant metal. I hear the clatter of loose objects crashing into walls. *Eriophora* lurches, staggers to port, turns ponderously on some axis spread across too many sickening dimensions. There's something moving behind the wall, deep in the rocks; I can't see it but I feel its pull, hear the cracking of new fault lines splitting ancient stone. A dozen crimson icons bloom like tumors in my brain, *Subsystem Failure* and *Critical Coolant* and *Primary Channel Interrupt*. A half-empty squeezebulb, discarded decades or centuries or millennia ago, wobbles half-levitating into view around the corner. It falls sideways and slides along the bulkhead, caught up in the tide-monster's wake.

I'm standing on the deck at forty-five degrees. I think I'm going to be sick.

The *down* beneath my feet is less than a whisper. I give silent thanks for superconducting ceramics, piezoelectric trusses, all reinforcements brute and magical that keep this little worldlet from crumbling to dust while the Chimp plays havoc with the laws of physics. I offer a diffuse and desperate prayer that they're up to the task. Then I'm falling forward, upward, *out*: Hakim and I smack into the forward bulkhead as a rubber band, stretched to its limit, snaps free and hurls us forward.

Surtr roars in triumph as we emerge, snatches at this tiny unexpected prize shaken free of the larger one. Jagged spiders leap away and vanish into blinding fog. Wireframe swirls of magnetic force twist in the heat, spun off from the dynamo way down in the giant's helium heart—or maybe that's just the Chimp, feeding me models and imaginings. I'm pretty sure it's not real; our eyes and ears and fingertips have all been licked away, our windows all gone dark. Skin and bones will be next to go: warm basalt, softening down to plastic. Maybe it's happening already. No way to tell any more. Nothing to do but fall out as the air flattens and shimmers in the rising heat.

I'm saving your life, Hakim. You better fucking appreciate it.

Yeats was wrong. The centre held after all.

Now we are only half-blind, and wholly ballistic. A few eyes remain smouldering on the hull, pitted with cataracts; most are gone entirely. Charred stumps spark fitfully where sensors used to be. *Eri*'s centre of mass has snapped back into itself and is sleeping off the hangover down in the basement. We coast on pure inertia, as passive as any other rock.

But we are through, and we are alive, and we have ten thousand years to lick our wounds.

It won't take anywhere near that long, of course. The Chimp has already deployed his army; they burned their way out through the slagged doorways of a dozen service tunnels, laden with newly-refined metals dug from the heart of the mountain. Now they clamber across the surface like great metal insects, swapping good parts for bad and cauterizing our wounds with bright light. Every now and then another dead window flickers back to life; the universe returns to us in bits and pieces. Surtr simmers in our wake, still vast but receding, barely hot enough to boil water this far out.

I prefer the view ahead: deep comforting darkness, swirls of stars, glittering constellations we'll never see again and can't be bothered to name. Just passing through.

Hakim should be down in the crypt by now, getting ready to turn in. Instead I find him back in the starboard bridge, watching fingers of blue-white lightning leap across the hull. It's a short clip and it always ends the same way, but he seems to find value in repeat viewings.

He turns at my approach. "Sanduloviciu plasma."

"What?"

"Electrons on the outside, positive ions on the inside. Self-organizing membranes. Live ball lightning. Although I don't know what they'd use as a rep code. Some kind of quantum spin liquid, maybe." He shrugs. "The guys who discovered these things didn't have much to say about heredity."

He's talking about primitive experiments with gas and electricity, back in some prehistoric lab from the days before we launched (I know: Chimp fed me the archive file the moment Hakim accessed it). "*We're* the guys who discovered them," I point out; the things that clawed at our doorstep were lightyears beyond anything those cavemen ever put together.

"No we didn't."

I wait.

"*They* discovered *us*," he tells me.

I feel a half-smile pulling at the corner of my mouth.

"I keep thinking about the odds," Hakim says. "A system that looks so right from a distance and turns out to be so wrong after we've committed to the flyby. All that mass and all those potential trajectories, and somehow the only way out is through the goddamn star. Oh, and there's one convenient ice giant that just *happens* to be going our way. Any idea what those odds are?"

"Astronomical." I keep a straight face.

He shakes his head. "Infinitesimal."

"I've been thinking the same thing," I admit.

Hakim gives me a sharp glance. "Have you now."

"The way the whole system seemed primed to draw us into the star. The way that thing reached down to grab us once we were inside. Your *lightning bugs*: I don't think they were native to the planet at all, not if they were plasma-based."

"You think they were from the star."

I shrug.

"Star aliens," Hakim says.

"Or drones of some kind. Either way, you're right; this system didn't just happen. It was a sampling transect. A trapline."

"Which makes us what, exactly? Specimens? Pets? Hunting trophies?"

"Almost. Maybe. Who knows?"

"Maybe *buddies*, hmm?"

I glance up at the sudden edge in his voice.

"Maybe just *allies*," he muses. "In adversity. Because it's all for one against the common enemy, right?"

"That's generally good strategy." It felt good, too, not being the bad guy for a change. Being the guy who actually pulled asses *out* of the fire.

I'll settle for *allies*.

"Because I can see a couple of other coincidences, if I squint." He's not squinting, though. He's staring straight through me. "Like the way the Chimp happened to pair me up with the one person on the whole roster I'd just as soon chuck out an airlock."

"That's hardly a coincidence," I snort. "It'd be next to impossible to find someone who *didn't*—"

Oh.

The accusation hangs in the air like static electricity. Hakim waits for my defense.

"You think the Chimp used this situation to—"

"Used," he says, "or *invented*."

"That's insane. You saw it with your own eyes, you can *still* see—"

"I saw models in a tank. I saw pixels on bulkheads. I never threw on a suit to go see for myself. You'd have to be suicidal, right?"

He's actually smiling.

"They tried to break in," I remind him.

"Oh, I know *something* was pounding on the door. I'm just not sold on the idea that it was built by aliens."

"You think this whole thing was some kind of trick?" I shake my head in disbelief. "We'll have surface access in a couple of weeks. Hell, just cut a hole into Fab right now, crawl out through one of the service tunnels. See for yourself."

"See what? A star off the stern?" He shrugs. "Red giants are common as dirt. Doesn't mean the specs on this system were anywhere near as restrictive as Chimp says. Doesn't mean we had to go *through*, doesn't even mean we did. For all I know the Chimp had its bots strafing the hull with lasers and blowtorches for the past hundred years, slagging things down to look nice and convincing just in case I *did* pop out for a look-see." Hakim shakes his head. "All I know is, it's only had one meat sack in its corner since the mutiny, and he's not much good if no one will talk to him. But how can you keep hating someone after he's saved your life?"

It astonishes me, the degree to which people torture reason. Just to protect their precious preconceptions.

"The weird thing," Hakim adds, almost to himself, "is that it worked."

It takes a moment for that to sink in.

"Because I don't think you were in on it," he explains. "I don't think you had a clue. How could you? You're not even a whole person, you're just a—a glorified subroutine. And subroutines don't question their inputs. A thought pops into your head, you just assume it's yours. You believe everything that miserable piece of hardware tells you, because you don't have a choice. Maybe you never did.

"How can I hate you for that?" he asks.

I don't answer, so he does: "I can't. Not anymore. I can only—"

"Shut the fuck up," I say, and turn my back.

He leaves me then, leaves me surrounded by all these pixels and pictures he refuses to accept. He heads back to the crypt to join his friends. The sleeping dead. The weak links. Every last one of them would scuttle the mission, given half a chance.

If it was up to me none of them would ever wake up again. But Chimp reminds me of the obvious: a mission built for aeons, the impossibility of anticipating even a fraction of the obstacles we're bound to encounter. The need for *flexibility*, for the wet sloppy intelligence that long-dead engineers excluded from his architecture in the name of mission stability. Billions of years ahead of us, perhaps, and only a few thousand meat sacks to deal with the unexpected. There may not be enough of us as it is.

And yet, with all that vaunted human intellect, Hakim can't see the obvious. None of them can. I'm not even human to those humans. A subroutine, he says. A lobe in something else's brain. But I don't need his fucking pity. He'd realize that if he thought about it for more than a split-second, if he was willing to examine that mountain of unexamined assumptions he calls a worldview.

He won't, though. He refuses to look into the mirror long enough to see what's looking back. He can't even tell the difference between brain and brawn. The Chimp drives the ship; the Chimp builds the jump gates; the Chimp runs life support. We try to take the reins of our own destiny and it's the Chimp who hammers us down.

So the Chimp is in control. The Chimp is always in control; and when minds merge across this high-bandwidth link in my head, surely it will be the mech that absorbs the meat.

It astonishes me that he can't see the fallacy. He knows the Chimp's synapse count as well as I do, but he'd rather fall back on prejudice than run the numbers.

I'm not the Chimp's subroutine at all.

The Chimp is mine.

Death and the Girl from Pi Delta Zeta
HELEN MARSHALL

Carissa first sees Death at the Pan-Hellenic Graffiti mixer where he is circled by the guys from Sigma Rho. They can't seem to help crowding him even though they clearly don't want to be there. She has gone with several of the Sig-Rho boys. All of them have. But she has never gone with anyone like Death before.

Death is wearing a black track jacket, with a black t-shirt on beneath and faded black jeans. Carissa, like all the other girls, is wearing a white cotton tank top with the letters Pi Delta Zeta embroidered in dark pink. She is also carrying a marker. The boys from Sig-Rho have already begun to make use of the marker to write things around her breasts and stomach and neck, things like "Sig-Rho 4Evr" and "Love your body" and "Kevin likes it with mittens on."

The guy with the black t-shirt and black jeans doesn't call himself Death though. This is what he says.

"Hi," says Death. "My name is David."

"Hi," says Carissa. She wants to say more but Logan Frees has grabbed her in a big, meaty, underarm embrace so that he can write "Occupy my crotch" on the small of her back, except he is drunk so it comes out as "Occupy my crouch," which doesn't make any sense.

It is only later that Marelaine points him out to her.

"There," says Marelaine. "On the couch. That's Death."

"Oh," says Carissa. "He said his name was David. How do you know that's really Death?"

"Death is like a movie star: he can't just tell you his real name. He has to go incognito. But you can tell anyway." Marelaine punctuates this with a sniff. Marelaine is the former Miss Texas Polestar. Her talents include trick-shooting, world change through bake sales, and getting what she wants. She has mastered the sniff. She has also mastered the ponytail flip, the high-gloss lipstick pout, and the cross-body cleavage thrust. Only Sydney, from the third floor, has a better cross-body cleavage thrust.

Carissa is concentrating on the pitch and execution of Marelaine's sniff. She misses what she is saying.

"What?" asks Carissa.

"You know, when that Phi Lamb girl died last term. Staci. Or Traci. Or Christy. Whatever. He was there. When you've seen him once, you always recognize him. He's Death."

"I think he's kind of cute," says Carissa.

"If you like that type," says Marelaine. This time her sniff is deadly.

Death's face is smooth and white as marble. His eyes are the colour of pigeon feathers. His smile has many teeth to it and some of them are baby teeth, which are less frightening, and some of them are shark's teeth, which are more frightening.

This is what Death looks like, except Death looks nothing like this at all.

His hair is cowlicked, brown with flecks of gold at the temples. His chin has a stylishly faint shadow of stubble. His cheeks curve into dimples when he smiles, which he does often, and it is not frightening at all.

Marelaine is watching as Carissa approaches Death, and Carissa knows that Marelaine is watching. She wonders if she should attempt the three-ounce vodka flounce or try for something more subtle. She has an apple-flavoured cooler beading droplets of water in one hand. She taps Death on the shoulder with the other.

"Have we met?" asks Carissa.

"Not the way you mean," says Death. He is smiling at her with that dimpled smile. "I don't come out to these things very much."

"Why is that?" asks Carissa.

"People make me nervous," Death answers. "I'm only here for work." He laughs at this, and his laughter is not what she expects it to be. It is cool and soft. It has the texture of velvet. It is intelligent laughter, and Carissa feels charmed by it, by its simplicity, its brevity, the way it sounds nothing like church gates yawning, the way it doesn't smack of eternity. She decides she likes talking to someone as famous as Death.

"That's a pity," says Carissa, and her fingers brush her white cotton top, pulling it tighter around her breasts. "Would you like to give it a go?" She hands him the marker.

"What do you want me to write?"

"Write me a magic word," says Carissa.

Death's writing is easy and graceful. There are many loops to it. He chooses a place somewhere near her left shoulder blade, and when he bends over to do it Carissa can feel the warmth of him, even though his skin is so white it is bloodless. He writes, "Abracadabra" first, and then "Open up" and then "I know you're in there" and signs it with a D.

Carissa smiles at him.

Later they play Spin the Bottle and every time Death sends the vodka twenty-sixer whirling it points at Carissa. Carissa wonders if she should try the closed-mouth kiss, the single-lip kiss, or the tongue-flick kiss. She knows she is best at the tongue-flick kiss, or at least that is what she has been told by the Sig-Rho boys. She tries the tongue-flick kiss but finds, unexpectedly, that she has transitioned first into a bottom-lip nibble and next into the deeper and more complex one-inch tongue glide.

At the end, Carissa smiles at Death, and Death smiles back at Carissa.

"Don't eat the lemon squares," he whispers with a wink. And then he carefully writes his number on the hem of her tank top.

Carissa thinks Marelaine would be proud of her for this, but then, reconsidering, thinks she probably wouldn't be after all. Soon she stops thinking about Marelaine, and instead thinks about the feel of Death's teeth, both the smoothed, tiny pearls and the sharp, jagged ones.

Carissa waits a week after Sydney's funeral before she gets up the nerve to call.

Death takes Carissa to a fancy restaurant, somewhere where they serve French food and French wine and all the entrees have French names she can't pronounce. Death has a certain celebrity status, and they are shown to the table immediately.

At one point one of the other diners comes to their table. Carissa is eating the *poulet à la Provençale* which is delicious, and Death is most of the way through his *filet de boeuf sauce au poivre*.

"It's you, isn't it?" The man is sweating. Damp patches have bloomed at his armpits.

"Yes," says Death.

"I bet you don't remember, but you were there when my wife died." The man pauses. "I just wanted to say thank you. Thank you so much. She was in such pain." He plucks at his moustache nervously. "Could I get an autograph?"

Death is gracious. He signs the napkin in large, looping letters.

"Thank you," the man says. "Thank you for taking such good care of her."

Death smiles.

Afterwards, Death is walking Carissa back to the house, and they laugh about it. "Does that really happen all the time?"

"All the time," Death says, and he slips his arm around her.

Carissa wonders what Death's Johnson will look like. Does Death have a Johnson? Will he put it inside her, and what will happen when he does? Does Death have a mother? Does he call her on Sundays and on her birthday, or is he too busy with being famous and being Death to remember the people who were there before he was Death?

As it turns out Death does have a Johnson after all.

He is a gentle lover unlike the many lovers Carissa has had in the past, most of whom taste of stale beer; most of whom smell like old socks. But Death is sweet and attentive and polite.

He brings her flowers first. These flowers are not ironic. They are not lilies. They are not roses with petals dyed to black velvet. They are not grave myrtle, cut-finger, vervain, deadnettle or sorcerer's violets. They are not death camus or Flower-of-Death. Death hates irony.

Instead, Death brings her a bouquet of yellow and deep orange celandines, which he says are named after the Greek word for *swallow*, and will bring her pleasant dreams.

Marelaine and the other Pi Delta Zeta girls are jealous of the flowers, and they slip into Carissa's room when she has gone to class and cut away some of the blossoms for themselves. In the morning at the breakfast table they talk in hushed whispers about their dreams.

They dream of Death, but the Death they dream of is the death of sorority girls: killers with long, hooked knives and fraying ski masks; they dream of sizzling in superhot tanning beds; they dream endless shower scenes in which they discover their names written in fogged mirrors and their blood on the white, porcelain tiling.

But when Carissa breathes in the blossoms, she dreams about

Knick-knack, the shepherd mutt she got when she was eight. Knick-knack who waited patiently for her to come home for Christmas break before he collapsed that first evening home on her bedroom carpet unable to move his legs, waiting noiseless, not a whimper, until she woke up and held him. Carissa dreams that Knick-knack is a puppy, and she holds his velveteen muzzle close to her cheek while his tail ricochets back and forth like a live wire. She dreams about him nuzzling her under the blankets with his cold, wet nose.

Their wedding is the September following graduation, and it is a surprise to everyone.

"You're so young," her mother coos.

"Will he be able to support you?" her father demands.

Carissa sends out invitations to all the girls from Pi Delta Zeta: You are cordially invited to witness the union of Carissa and Death. They have not included last names because Death does not have a last name. All the girls send their RSVPs immediately. Marelaine is her maid of honour.

It is a celebrity wedding. Carissa wears a beautiful wedding dress with a chapel train and the bridesmaids wear taffeta. Death wears black.

Carissa and Death have decided on a simple double-lip graze-and-peck kiss for the ceremony because Carissa's parents are both religious. Even though it is not entirely proper she ends up halfway into a tongue glide anyway, but she remembers where she is and what she is doing. When they pull away from each other, they are both a bit embarrassed, but nevertheless they smile as if they have both gotten away with something.

Later, as they are standing in the receiving line, Death introduces his brother, Dennis. Death has never mentioned that he has a brother, and so there is some initial awkwardness, but Carissa is a Pi Delta Zeta and so she is good at recovering. She takes his hand, and it is warm and slightly damp. There are fine golden hairs on his fingers, and he has long eyelashes. He looks the way that Death sometimes looks when he is not being Death.

"I'm so pleased to meet you, Dennis," Carissa says. "Death talks about you all the time." Carissa wonders why he doesn't.

Dennis smiles, and he has the same dimples that Death has. He holds her hand for too long. She lets go first.

"Welcome to the family," he says.

Later, after the cake has been cut, Marelaine pulls Carissa aside.

"Who's he?" she asks. She is pointing at Dennis, who is trying to teach her mother how to foxtrot.

"That's Dennis," Carissa says. "Death's brother."

"Oh," says Marelaine. "He's quite a looker, isn't he? I mean, he's not Death. But."

In a year, she receives an invitation that says "You are cordially invited to the union of Marelaine and Dennis." She wonders if she should RSVP.

They live happily ever after.

When Death dies it is very sudden.

Neither of them planned for this, and so Carissa is caught off-guard when she hears the news. She thought they would have more time. She thought she would die first, and Death would be there for it, to help her through.

At the funeral Carissa wears black. Death is also wearing black. Death is lying in a coffin, and makeup has been applied to his skin to give it a deep, bronze tan that makes him into a stranger.

Carissa secretly hopes that Death will attend the funeral, and she is disappointed when he does not. She wants to see him one last time.

Marelaine hosts the post-funeral reception. At first Carissa thinks she has gotten fat, but then Carissa realizes she has gotten pregnant. Dennis is there as well. He pats her hand, and he fetches her cocktail shrimp, which Carissa doesn't even like.

"How are you holding up?" Dennis asks. Dennis smiles, and his cheeks are still dimpled.

"Don't ask her that," says Marelaine. "How do you think she's holding up? Just look at her."

Carissa finds herself thinking that Death must have been so mindlessly bored if this was what he did all day at work.

Carissa is lonely.

She tries Ouija boards, but she can never get anyone on the other line.

Sometimes Dennis comes over.

At first he is purely solicitous. He brings over frozen lasagnas that Marelaine has prepared meticulously. He brings over casseroles. He brings over pies. And then he collects the baking pans, and the casserole dishes, and the pie plates, only so that he and Marelaine can fill them all over again.

After the first month Carissa wonders if she is pregnant, but then she realizes she is only getting fat.

One time when Dennis comes over, his hand accidentally grazes against her ass as he washes a two-quart dish that had previously contained a tuna casserole.

"Oops," he says, smiling. His hands are dripping water and soap onto the kitchen floor. Carissa doesn't say anything.

The next time he comes over, he brings a bottle of cabernet sauvignon along with a black cherry pie that Marelaine just baked this morning. She has crisscrossed the top with strips of dough with scalloped edges the way that pies always look when they are on television.

"How are you getting on today?" Dennis asks, and his voice sounds to Carissa like a famous person's voice. It is smooth and cool and easy to listen to, but it is not Death's voice.

"I'm fine," she says, and she takes a sip of her wine. It tastes better than the pie. "I'm fine," she says again.

They finish the bottle of wine quickly. Carissa suggests that they play Ouija because there are two of them, and Dennis agrees. Carissa has lost the pointer so they use an ace of hearts instead, and it circles and circles and circles but it only ever stops on the picture of the crescent moon. Dennis suggests that they play Spin the Bottle, and Carissa feels like it's only polite so she agrees.

The bottle spins and spins and spins, but there are only the two of them so no matter where it ends up pointing, she still has to kiss Dennis. His teeth are entirely smooth.

Carissa wakes in the middle of the night, and Dennis is still beside her. The sheets are all askew and somehow she has ended up on the wrong side of the bed. From this side, the bedroom seems strange, like it could be another place. Like she could be another person sleeping in it.

Dennis is beautiful. She cannot tell whether his hair is blond or grey in the moonlight, and so she decides that it must be both at the same time. She decides she likes to look at him while he is sleeping.

She takes the marker from the bedside table and she writes on Dennis' perfect, moon-white skin.

"Abracadabra," she writes.

"Open up," she writes.

"I know you're in there."

"Did he tell you he was going to die?" asks Carissa.

"I never asked him," Dennis answers. "We didn't talk that much. He was Death."

Carissa is quiet for a while.

"Do you want to run away with me?" Carissa asks.

"Yes," says Dennis.

Dennis decides that they must tell Marelaine in person. Carissa wonders if she is nervous, but she decides that, in the end, she isn't. But when Dennis opens the door, Death is sitting at the table with Marelaine.

"Darling," says Dennis.

"I knew it," says Marelaine. "And with *her* too. I knew it would be with *her*."

"No," says Dennis. "It's not like that. We're in love."

"We're not in love," says Carissa. "I don't love you."

They both look at her.

"I knew it," says Marelaine once more, and she rushes out of the room. Dennis follows after her. Carissa wonders if she is supposed to go as well, but decides that she probably shouldn't. Sometimes it seems as if real life is exactly like sorority life.

"Why didn't you ever come to see me?" asks Carissa.

"That's not how it works," Death says at last. "I'm Death. I couldn't be David forever."

"I've missed you," says Carissa.

Death says nothing. He is still handsome, although Carissa can see the glint of a few threads of silver near his temples. He looks older. He looks tired. She wonders what she must look like to him.

"What are you doing here?" Carissa asks at last.

"Triple homicide," says Death.

BANG goes Marelaine's gun somewhere upstairs. And BANG again. There is a sound as bodies hit the floor.

"Oh," says Carissa. She considers this. "Oh."

They sit together in silence, and, for the first time since the funeral, Carissa feels happy again. She decides that Death does not look that old. He looks good. Death is supposed to have some grey to him. It makes him look distinguished.

"That was only two gunshots," she says.

"I know," Death says. After a moment, he says, "It was arsenic in the pies. You know. Marelaine always was such a bitch." He pauses, and pours a glass of wine for her. "I think we'll both have to wait for a bit."

"It's good to see you," Carissa says.

"I've been waiting for such a long time," says Death. "I've brought you flowers." He removes a single, yellow celandine blossom from his jacket pocket. Carissa smiles. She takes it from him gently, afraid to crush the petals. Their fingers touch, and his hand is warm, familiar.

"Where are we going?" she asks.

"You'll see," Death says. "Don't worry, darling. I'll take you there."

She breathes in the scent.

When she dreams it is of Death, and she is happy.

The Perfect Library

DAVID CLINK

For Carolyn Clink
After Patrick O'Leary's "The Perfect City"

Imagine, if you will, a perfect library
where the reading room is lit by the soft
pulsing lights of fireflies & the wood that furnishes it
is from exquisite trees felled by mountain men
with bulging biceps.
Where you can find the fold-out book of universes
& newspapers including *The Barsoom Evening Post*,
The Fanciful Times of London, *The Atlantis Monthly*.
Where you can find dictionaries of made up words,
the histories and alternate histories
of things that never happened,
the book of extinctions & lost civilizations,
the book of the living, the book of the dead,
the book of the living dead.
Where the reference desk is staffed by ancient librarians
with leathery wings who can tell you about the Big Bang
& everything since because they were there.
A perfect library where the books read other books
& join book clubs, arguing what they're about,
& when they're done they shelve themselves.

Where you can find books smaller than a fingernail
& larger than a bus.
Where the listening room has pillow headphones
handed out by flapper girls sporting steampunk goggles
so you can hear the music mountains make,
the pent up frustration of dormant volcanoes,
the budding awareness of spring moss growing
on the sides of trees, the stirring of the planets.
The perfect library where documentaries are available
in a screening room with reclining bucket seats
& fresh-popped buttered popcorn & drinks are served
by male models wearing gladiator & toreador costumes.
Where the photocopiers never run out of toner,
paper, or patience & never break down.
Where the carpets are cleaned by pilot fish
taking a break from *Shark Week*. Where bathrooms
are hands free & faeries use the pressed leaves
from gilded books to fan your hands dry.
Where the map room has an infinite number of maps
& old sea serpents using walkers gingerly slip
from the canvasses to lead library tours.
Where the archives & special collections contain books
that have turned to dust & patrons are asked
to wear white gloves & to refrain from sneezing.
Where people in the quiet room can hear the building settle.
I have not mentioned the mermaid swing,
the petting zoo of extinct species, the corridors
where classic lines float through the air like balloon help,
the *2,000 Years of Cement* exhibit,
the crystal conveyor belt made from the wishes of children
that appears out of mid-air, bringing the books you want,
the dungeon of dead technologies,
the wall of human existence,
the glass tube ride through the sunken city.
This *is* the library you dream about, the perfect library,
& I can see you want to go there,
you want to knock on its heavy oak doors & say, *Let me in!*
& if you finally find yourself there

you will discover the perfect place,
past the reading room of exquisite wood & fireflies,
past the guided tour, the swing, the dungeon,
past the gladiators & toreadors & flapper girls
to the place where you have a view on the garden,
the natural light finding its way in,
& there, in a glass case, you will find
the first library card you were issued,
the first book you signed out as a child,
& you are there with your parents again,
the place where you could barely see over the counter
& you are glad you finally have a chance to thank them
for taking you to your first library,
the perfect library,
& you realize, this is where you have been,
all along.

Honourable Mentions

Ashby, Madeline. "By The Time We Get to Arizona," *Hieroglyph: Stories and Visions for a Better Future*

Carre, Brenda. "Embrace of the Planets," *The Magazine of Fantasy & Science Fiction*

Church, Suzanne. "Mod Me Down," *Elements*

Dellamonica, A.M. "The Ugly Woman of Castello di Putti," Tor.com

Dellamonica, A.M. "Snow Angels," *Fractured: Tales of the Canadian Post-Apocalypse*

Deonarine, Phedra. "The Princess and the River Queen," What Wonderful Things.net, Issue 5

Chomichuk, G.M.B. "Manitou-Wapow," *Fractured: Tales of the Canadian Post-Apocalypse*

Clitheroe, Heather. "Cuts Both Ways," *Lightspeed Magazine*, Issue 49

Czerneda, Julie. "A Taste for Murder," *Solaris 3*

Deshane, Evelyn. "Baby Eyes," *The Grotesquerie: Women in Horror Fiction*

El-Mohtar, Amal. "Truth About Owls," *Kaleidoscope: Diverse Young Adult Science Fiction and Fantasy Stories*

Files, Gemma. "Furious Angels," *We Will All Go Down Together*

Files, Gemma. "The Harrow," *The Children of Old Leech*

Files, Gemma. "Helpless," *We Will All Go Down Together*

Files, Gemma. "History's Crust," *We Will All Go Down Together*

Files, Gemma. "Strange Weight," *We Will All Go Down Together*

Files, Gemma. "This Is Not for You," *Nightmare Magazine*

Fuller, David Jón. "A Deeper Echo," *Long Hidden: Speculative Fiction from the Margins of History*

Ginther, Chadwick. "Runt of the Litter," *On Spec*, Spring 2014

Goldberg, Kim. "Escape from Cyberia," *Dark Mountain*, Issue #5

Graham, Neile. "The Alchemy," *Goblin Fruit*, Winter 2014/2015

Graham, Neile. "Cairn By Dark By Cairn," *Apex Magazine* #62

Graham, Neile. "On the Exarnations of the Gods," *Apex Magazine* #65

Hannett, Lisa L. "A Girl of Feather and Music," *Postscripts* 32/33

Heartfield, Kate. "Bonsaiships of Venus," *Lackington's*, Issue 4

Heartfield, Kate. "Cattail Heart," *Daily Science Fiction*, August 2014

Hoffmann, Ada. "Memo from Neverland," *Kaleidotrope*, Winter Issue

Hoffmann, Ada. "The Self-Rescuing Princess," *Lakeside Circus*, Year One, Issue 2

Hoffmann, Ada. "Turning to Stone," *Stone Telling*, Issue #10

Humphrey, Claire. "The Witch of Tarup," *Long Hidden: Speculative Fiction from the Margins of History*

Iveniuk, Robert William. "Diyu," *Long Hidden: Speculative Fiction from the Margins of History*

Johnson, Matthew. "Beyond the Fields You Know," *Irregular Verbs and Other Stories*

Johnson, Matthew. "Rules of Engagement," *Asimov's*

Johnson, Matthew. "The Wise Foolish Son," *Irregular Verbs and Other Stories*

Kelly, Michael. "Bait," *Jamais Vu #1*

Kelly, Michael. "This Red Night," *Weird Fiction Review #4*

King, Barry. "A Cruel Intemperate Sea," *The Sea*

King, Barry. "Something in Our Minds Will Always Stay," *Unlikely Story*

Kuriata, Chris. "Hanging Ropes," *Blank Fiction*, Issue #4

Laycraft, Adria. "Fire Born, Water Made," *Orson Scott Card's InterGalactic Medicine Show*

Libling, Michael. "Draft 31," *The Magazine of Fantasy & Science Fiction*

Marshall, Helen. "A Brief History of Science Fiction," *Gifts for the One Who Comes After*

Marshall, Helen. "In the Year of Omens," *Fearful Symmetries*

Marshall, Helen. "Supply Limited, Act Now!" *Gifts for the One Who Comes After*

MacLeod, Catherine. "The Attic," *Fearful Symmetries*

Mehrotra, Rati. "Hatyasin," *Abyss & Apex*, Issue 52

Moreno-Garcia, Silvia. "To See Pedro Infante," *Love & Other Poisons*

Nickle, David. "The Nothing Book of the Dead," *Knife Fight and Other Struggles*

Page, Morgan M. "City Noise," *Fractured: Tales of the Canadian Post-Apocalypse*

Parrish, Rhonda. "The Grotesque," *Bête Noire*

Rogers, Ian. "Possession is Nine-Tenths of the Law," CZPeBook

Saad, Michael. "The Tal of Kal Trison," *Youth Imagination Magazine*

Shafiq, Tahmeed. "The Djinn Who Sought to Kill the Sun," *Lightspeed Magazine*, Issue 51

Steinfeld, J.J. "Futility," *The Impressment Gang*, Issue 1:1

Strantzas, Simon. "Emotional Dues," *Burnt Black Suns*

Strantzas, Simon. "On Ice," *Burnt Black Suns*

Strantzas, Simon. "One Last Bloom," *Burnt Black Suns*

Timermanis, Jason. "Appetite," *Carter V. Cooper Short Fiction Anthology*

Watts Peter. "Collateral," *Neil Clarke's Upgraded*

Watts Peter. "The Colonel," Tor.com

Watts Peter. "Hotshot," *Reach for Infinity*

Wise, A.C. "Dream of the Fisherman's Wife," *Shimmer #21*

Wise, A.C. "Matthew, Waiting," *Fractured: Tales of the Canadian Post-Apocalypse*

Yuan-Innes, Melissa. "Sharp Teeth," *Ricepaper Magazine*

Zelenyj, Alexander. "Maria, Here Come The Death Angels!" *Songs for the Lost*

Copyright Acknowledgements

"Bamboozled" by Kelley Armstrong. Copyright © 2014 Kelley Armstrong. First published in *Dead Man's Hand: An Anthology of the Weird West*, Titan Books, 2014. Reprinted by permission of the author.

"Introduction: Don't Be Alarmed" by Margaret Atwood. Copyright © 2015 Margaret Atwood.

"Witch I" and "Witch II" by Courtney Bates-Hardy. Copyright © 2014 Courtney Bates-Hardy. First published in *Room Magazine*, Geek Girls Issue, 37.3, Fall 2014. Reprinted by permission of the author.

"The Smut Story" by Greg Bechtel. Copyright © 2014 Greg Bechtel. First published in *Boundary Problems*, Freehand Books, 2014. Reprinted by permission by Freehand Books. The epigraph for "The Smut Story (III)" is quoted from "Being One's Own Pornographer," by Candas Jane Dorsey, copyright ©1996, as published in ParaDoxa, volume 2, issue 2. Used by permission of the author.

"Kafka's Notebooks" by Jocko Benoit. Copyright © 2014 Jocko Benoit. First published in *The Pedestal Magazine*, #74, 2014. Reprinted by permission of the author.

"The Full Lazenby" by Jeremy Butler. Copyright © 2014 Jeremy Butler. First published in *Unidentified Funny Objects 3*, UFO Publishing, 2014. Reprinted by permission of the author.

"Wendigo Nights" by Siobhan Carroll. Copyright © 2014 Siobhan Carroll. First published in *Fearful Symmetries*, ChiZine Publications, 2014. Reprinted by permission of the author.

"A Spell for Rebuilding Your Lover Out of Snow" by Peter Chiykowski. Copyright © 2014 Peter Chiykowski. First published in *Strange Horizons*, February 2014. Reprinted by permission of the author.

"Túshūguǎn" by Eric Choi. Copyright © 2014 Eric Choi. First published in *Ricepaper*, Fall 2014. Reprinted by permission of the author.

"Jelly and the D-Machine" by Suzanne Church. Copyright © 2014 Suzanne Church. First published in *Elements*, Edge Science Fiction & Fantasy Publishing, 2014. Reprinted by permission of the author.

"The Perfect Library" by David Clink. Copyright © 2014 David Clink. First published in *If the World Were to Stop Spinning*, Piquant Press, 2014. Reprinted by permission of the author.

"The Colour of Paradox" by A.M. Dellamonica. Copyright © 2014 A.M. Dellamonica. First published in *Tor.com*, 2014. Reprinted by permission of the author.

"The Man Who Sold the Moon" by Cory Doctorow. Copyright © 2014 Cory Doctorow. First published in *Hieroglyph: Stories and Visions for a Better Future*, William Morrow , 2014. Reprinted by permission of the author.

About the Editors

Sandra Kasturi is a Bram Stoker Award-winning editor as well as a writer, book reviewer, and award-winning poet. She is the co-publisher of the four-time World Fantasy Award-nominated and British Fantasy Award-winning press, ChiZine Publications. Her work has appeared in various venues, including *ON SPEC*, *Prairie Fire*, *Shadows & Tall Trees*, several *Tesseracts* anthologies, *Evolve*, *Evolve 2*, both *Chilling Tales* volumes, *A Verdant Green*, *Star*Line*, *Abyss & Apex*, *Taddle Creek*, *80! Memories & Reflections on Ursula K. Le Guin*, *They Have to Take You In*, and *Stamps, Vamps and Tramps*. She won the Arc Poetry Prize, and was longlisted for the Gwendolyn MacEwen Poetry Prize and the Poetry Society UK's International Poetry Prize. Sandra's two poetry collections were released by Tightrope Books: *The Animal Bridegroom* (with an introduction by Neil Gaiman) and *Come Late to the Love of Birds*. She is working on her next book, *Snake Handling for Beginners*, and reading for *Imaginarium 5*.

Jerome Stueart is a writer of science fiction, fantasy and memoir. He is a Fulbright fellow to Canada, and a graduate of the Lambda Literary Workshop for Emerging LGBT Voices, a fellow of the Milton Center for Writers of the Christian Imagination, and Clarion Writers Workshop, San Diego. His work has appeared in *Fantasy*, *Strange Horizons*, *Geist*, *Queers Destroy Science Fiction* (from *Lightspeed*), *On Spec*, *Joyland*, *Geez*, *Queerwolf*, *Evolve*, as well as three of the *Tesseracts* anthology series, and was the co-editor of *Tesseracts 18: Wrestling with Gods*. Jerome was runner up to the Fountain Award given by the Speculative Literature Foundation and has written and (sometimes) produced five radio series for CBC North, one of which, *Leaving America*, was heard round the world on Radio Canada International. His sketches of his train trip across Canada can be found in *Geist* this year. In Whitehorse, Yukon, he started *RocketFuel*, an afterschool program for teens who want to write science fiction and fantasy, and a *Writing Faith* memoir/fiction writing workshop for adults, both of which ran successfully for several years. Jerome's first novel, *One Nation Under Gods*, will be published by ChiZine Publications, late 2016. His collection of stories, *The Angels of Our Better Beasts* follows in 2017. He lived in Whitehorse for nearly ten years, became a Canadian citizen, and then moved to Ohio. He is currently teaching for the University of Dayton.

LICENCE EXPIRED: THE UNAUTHORIZED JAMES BOND

EDITED BY MADELINE ASHBY AND DAVID NICKLE

In Paris, James Bond meets his match over appetizers and cocktails—with an aperitif of industrial espionage and chilly sadism. Off the coast of Australia, he learns about a whole new level of betrayal under the scorching light of a ball of thunder. In Siberia, he dreams of endless carnage while his fate is decided by one of his most cunning enemies and perhaps the greatest of his many loves.

And in Canada—where Ian Fleming's work has entered public domain—James Bond finds freedom.

Licence Expired: The Unauthorized James Bond lives in this shadow space of copyright law: a collection of nineteen new, exciting, transformative James Bond stories by a diverse crew of 21st-century authors. Collected herein are new stories about Secret Agent 007, as the late Ian Fleming imagined and described him: a psychically wounded veteran of the Second World War and soldier of the Cold War, who treated his accumulated injuries with sex, alcohol, nicotine, and adrenaline. He was a good lover . . . but a terrible prospect.

AVAILABLE NOW
ISBN 978-1-77148-374-2
eISBN 978-1-77148-375-9

CHIZINEPUB.COM